British Mystery Multipack Vol. 12

British Mystery Multipack Vol. 12:
The G. K. Chesterton Collection

By

G. K. Chesterton

Enhanced Media
2016

British Mystery Multipack Volume 12 - The G. K. Chesterton Collection: 24 Father Brown mysteries, The Man Who Was Thursday and *The Man Who Knew Too Much.*

The Blue Cross, The Secret Garden, The Queer Feet, The Flying Stars, The Invisible Man, The Honour of Israel Gow, The Wrong Shape, The Sins of Prince Saradine, The Hammer of God, The Eye of Apollo, The Sign of the Broken Sword and *The Three Tools of Death* first published in *The Innocence of Father Brown* by G. K. Chesterton in 1911.

The Absence of Mr. Glass, The Paradise of Thieves, The Duel of Dr Hirsch, The Man in the Passage, The Mistake of the Machine, The Head of Caesar, The Purple Wig, The Perishing of the Pendragons, The God of the Gongs, The Salad of Colonel Cray, The Strange Crime of John Boulnois and *The Fairy Tale of Father Brown* first published in *The Wisdom of Father Brown* by G. K. Chesterton in 1914.

The Man Who Was Thursday by G. K. Chesterton. First published in 1908.

The Man Who Knew Too Much by G. K. Chesterton. First published in 1922.

British Mystery Multipack Volume 12 published 2016 by Enhanced Media.

Enhanced Media Publishing
Los Angeles, CA.

First Printing: 2016.

ISBN-13: 978-1532946851

ISBN-10: 1532946856

Contents

The Innocence of Father Brown by G. K. Chesterton

The Blue Cross

Between the silver ribbon of morning and the green glittering ribbon of sea, the boat touched Harwich and let loose a swarm of folk like flies, among whom the man we must follow was by no means conspicuous—nor wished to be. There was nothing notable about him, except a slight contrast between the holiday gaiety of his clothes and the official gravity of his face. His clothes included a slight, pale grey jacket, a white waistcoat, and a silver straw hat with a grey-blue ribbon. His lean face was dark by contrast, and ended in a curt black beard that looked Spanish and suggested an Elizabethan ruff. He was smoking a cigarette with the seriousness of an idler. There was nothing about him to indicate the fact that the grey jacket covered a loaded revolver, that the white waistcoat covered a police card, or that the straw hat covered one of the most powerful intellects in Europe. For this was Valentin himself, the head of the Paris police and the most famous investigator of the world; and he was coming from Brussels to London to make the greatest arrest of the century.

Flambeau was in England. The police of three countries had tracked the great criminal at last from Ghent to Brussels, from Brussels to the Hook of Holland; and it was conjectured that he would take some advantage of the unfamiliarity and confusion of the Eucharistic Congress, then taking place in London. Probably he would travel as some minor clerk or secretary connected with it; but, of course, Valentin could not be certain; nobody could be certain about Flambeau.

It is many years now since this colossus of crime suddenly ceased keeping the world in a turmoil; and when he ceased, as they said after the death of Roland, there was a great quiet upon the earth. But in his best days (I mean, of course, his worst) Flambeau was a figure as statuesque and international as the Kaiser. Almost every morning the daily paper announced that he had escaped the consequences of one extraordinary crime by committing another. He was a Gascon of gigantic stature and bodily daring; and the wildest tales were told of his outbursts of athletic humour; how he turned the *juge d'instruction* upside down and stood him on his head, "to clear his mind"; how he ran down the Rue de Rivoli with a policeman under each arm. It is due to him to say that his fantastic physical strength was generally employed in such bloodless though undignified scenes; his real crimes were chiefly those of ingenious and wholesale robbery. But each of his thefts was almost a new sin, and would make a story by itself. It was he who ran the great Tyrolean Dairy Company in London, with no dairies, no cows, no carts, no milk, but with some thousand subscribers. These he served by the simple operation of moving the little milk cans outside people's doors to the doors of his own customers. It was he who had kept up an unaccountable and close correspondence with a young lady whose whole letter-bag was intercepted, by the extraordinary trick of photographing his messages infinitesimally small upon the slides of a microscope. A sweeping simplicity, however, marked many of his experiments. It is said that he once repainted all the numbers in a street in the dead of night merely to divert one traveller into a trap. It is quite certain that he invented a portable pillar-box, which he put up at corners in quiet suburbs on the chance of strangers dropping postal orders into it. Lastly, he was known to be a startling acrobat; despite his huge figure, he could leap like a grasshopper and melt into the tree-tops like a monkey. Hence the great Valentin, when he set out to find Flambeau, was perfectly aware that his adventures would not end when he had found him.

But how was he to find him? On this the great Valentin's ideas were still in process of settlement.

There was one thing which Flambeau, with all his dexterity of disguise, could not cover, and that was his singular height. If Valentin's quick eye had caught a tall apple-woman, a tall grenadier, or even a tolerably tall duchess, he might have arrested them on the spot. But all along his train there was nobody that could be a disguised Flambeau, any more than a cat could be a disguised giraffe. About the people on the boat he had already satisfied himself; and the people picked up at Harwich or on the journey limited themselves with certainty to six. There was a short railway official travelling up to the terminus, three fairly short market gardeners picked up two stations afterwards, one very short widow lady going up from a small Essex town, and a very short Roman Catholic priest going up from a small Essex village. When it came to the last case, Valentin gave it up and almost laughed. The little priest was so much the essence of those Eastern flats; he had a face as round and dull as a Norfolk dumpling; he had eyes as empty as the North Sea; he had several brown paper parcels, which he was quite incapable of collecting. The Eucharistic Congress had doubtless sucked out of their local stagnation many such creatures, blind and helpless, like moles disinterred. Valentin was a sceptic in the severe style of France, and could have no love for priests. But he could have pity for them, and this one might have provoked pity in anybody. He had a large, shabby umbrella, which constantly fell on the floor. He did not seem to know which was the right end of his return ticket. He explained with a moon-calf simplicity to everybody in the carriage that he had to be careful, because he had something made of real silver "with blue stones" in one of his brown-paper parcels. His quaint blending of Essex flatness with saintly simplicity continuously amused the Frenchman till the priest arrived (somehow) at Tottenham with all his parcels, and came back for his umbrella. When he did the last, Valentin even had the good nature to warn him not to take care of the silver by telling everybody about it. But to whomever he talked, Valentin kept his eye open for someone else; he looked out steadily for anyone, rich or poor, male or female, who was well up to six feet; for Flambeau was four inches above it.

He alighted at Liverpool Street, however, quite conscientiously secure that he had not missed the criminal so far. He then went to Scotland Yard to regularise his position and arrange for help in case of need; he then lit another cigarette and went for a long stroll in the streets of London. As he was walking in the streets and squares beyond Victoria, he paused suddenly and stood. It was a quaint, quiet square, very typical of London, full of an accidental stillness. The tall, flat houses round looked at once prosperous and uninhabited; the square of shrubbery in the centre looked as deserted as a green Pacific islet. One of the four sides was much higher than the rest, like a dais; and the line of this side was broken by one of London's admirable accidents—a restaurant that looked as if it had strayed from Soho. It was an unreasonably attractive object, with dwarf plants in pots and long, striped blinds of lemon yellow and white. It stood specially high above the street, and in the usual patchwork way of London, a flight of steps from the street ran up to meet the front door almost as a fire-escape might run up to a first-floor window. Valentin stood and smoked in front of the yellow-white blinds and considered them long.

The most incredible thing about miracles is that they happen. A few clouds in heaven do come together into the staring shape of one human eye. A tree does stand up in the landscape of a doubtful journey in the exact and elaborate shape of a note of interrogation. I have seen both these things myself within the last few days. Nelson does die in the instant of victory; and a man named Williams does quite accidentally murder a man named Williamson; it sounds like a sort of infanticide. In short, there is in life an element of elfin coincidence which people reckoning on the prosaic may perpetually miss. As it has been well expressed in the paradox of Poe, wisdom should reckon on the unforeseen.

Aristide Valentin was unfathomably French; and the French intelligence is intelligence specially and solely. He was not "a thinking machine"; for that is a brainless phrase of modern fatalism and materialism. A machine only is a machine because it cannot think. But he was a thinking man, and a plain man at the same time. All his wonderful successes, that looked like conjuring, had been gained by plodding logic, by clear and commonplace French thought. The French electrify the world not by starting any paradox, they electrify it by carrying out a truism. They carry a truism so far—as in the French Revolution. But exactly because Valentin understood reason, he understood the limits of reason. Only a man who knows nothing of motors talks of motoring without petrol; only a man who knows nothing of reason talks of reasoning without strong, undisputed first principles. Here he had no strong first principles. Flambeau had been missed at Harwich; and if he was in London at all, he might be anything from a tall tramp on Wimbledon Common to a tall toast-master at the Hotel Metropole. In such a naked state of nescience, Valentin had a view and a method of his own.

In such cases he reckoned on the unforeseen. In such cases, when he could not follow the train of the reasonable, he coldly and carefully followed the train of the unreasonable. Instead of going to the right places—banks, police stations, rendezvous—he systematically went to the wrong places; knocked at every empty house, turned down every cul de sac, went up every lane blocked with rubbish, went round every crescent that led him uselessly out of the way. He defended this crazy course quite logically. He said that if one had a clue this was the worst way; but if one had no clue at all it was the best, because there was just the chance that any oddity that caught the eye of the pursuer might be the same that had caught the eye of the pursued. Somewhere a man must begin, and it had better be just where another man might stop. Something about that flight of steps up to the shop, something about the quietude and quaintness of the restaurant, roused all the detective's rare romantic fancy and made him resolve to strike at random. He went up the steps, and sitting down at a table by the window, asked for a cup of black coffee.

It was half-way through the morning, and he had not breakfasted; the slight litter of other breakfasts stood about on the table to remind him of his hunger; and adding a poached egg to his order, he proceeded musingly to shake some white sugar into his coffee, thinking all the time about Flambeau. He remembered how Flambeau had escaped, once by a pair of nail scissors, and once by a house on fire; once by having to pay for an unstamped letter, and once by getting people to look through a telescope at a comet that might destroy the world. He thought his detective brain as good as the criminal's, which was true. But he fully realised the disadvantage. "The criminal is the creative artist; the detective only the critic," he said with a sour smile, and lifted his coffee cup to his lips slowly, and put it down very quickly. He had put salt in it.

He looked at the vessel from which the silvery powder had come; it was certainly a sugar-basin; as unmistakably meant for sugar as a champagne-bottle for champagne. He wondered why they should keep salt in it. He looked to see if there were any more orthodox vessels. Yes; there were two salt-cellars quite full. Perhaps there was some speciality in the condiment in the salt-cellars. He tasted it; it was sugar. Then he looked round at the restaurant with a refreshed air of interest, to see if there were any other traces of that singular artistic taste which puts the sugar in the salt-cellars and the salt in the sugar-basin. Except for an odd splash of some dark fluid on one of the white-papered walls, the whole place appeared neat, cheerful and ordinary. He rang the bell for the waiter.

When that official hurried up, fuzzy-haired and somewhat blear-eyed at that early hour, the detective (who was not without an appreciation of the simpler forms of humour) asked him to taste the sugar and see if it was up to the high reputation of the hotel. The result was that the waiter yawned suddenly and woke up.

"Do you play this delicate joke on your customers every morning?" inquired Valentin. "Does changing the salt and sugar never pall on you as a jest?"

The waiter, when this irony grew clearer, stammeringly assured him that the establishment had certainly no such intention; it must be a most curious mistake. He picked up the sugar-basin and looked at it; he picked up the salt-cellar and looked at that, his face growing more and more bewildered. At last he abruptly excused himself, and hurrying away, returned in a few seconds with the proprietor. The proprietor also examined the sugar-basin and then the salt-cellar; the proprietor also looked bewildered.

Suddenly the waiter seemed to grow inarticulate with a rush of words.

"I zink," he stuttered eagerly, "I zink it is those two clergy-men."

"What two clergymen?"

"The two clergymen," said the waiter, "that threw soup at the wall."

"Threw soup at the wall?" repeated Valentin, feeling sure this must be some singular Italian metaphor.

"Yes, yes," said the attendant excitedly, and pointed at the dark splash on the white paper; "threw it over there on the wall."

Valentin looked his query at the proprietor, who came to his rescue with fuller reports.

"Yes, sir," he said, "it's quite true, though I don't suppose it has anything to do with the sugar and salt. Two clergymen came in and drank soup here very early, as soon as the shutters were taken down. They were both very quiet, respectable people; one of them paid the bill and went out; the other, who seemed a slower coach altogether, was some minutes longer getting his things together. But he went at last. Only, the instant before he stepped into the street he deliberately picked up his cup, which he had only half emptied, and threw the soup slap on the wall. I was in the back room myself, and so was the waiter; so I could only rush out in time to find the wall splashed and the shop empty. It don't do any particular damage, but it was confounded cheek; and I tried to catch the men in the street. They were too far off though; I only noticed they went round the next corner into Carstairs Street."

The detective was on his feet, hat settled and stick in hand. He had already decided that in the universal darkness of his mind he could only follow the first odd finger that pointed; and this finger was odd enough. Paying his bill and clashing the glass doors behind him, he was soon swinging round into the other street.

It was fortunate that even in such fevered moments his eye was cool and quick. Something in a shop-front went by him like a mere flash; yet he went back to look at it. The shop was a popular greengrocer and fruiterer's, an array of goods set out in the open air and plainly ticketed with their names and prices. In the two most prominent compartments were two heaps, of oranges and of nuts respectively. On the heap of nuts lay a scrap of cardboard, on which was written in bold, blue chalk, "Best tangerine oranges, two a penny." On the oranges was the equally clear and exact description, "Finest Brazil nuts, 4d. a lb." M. Valentin looked at these two placards and fancied he had met this highly subtle form of humour before, and that somewhat recently. He drew the attention of the red-faced fruiterer, who was looking rather sullenly up and down the street, to this inaccuracy in his advertisements. The fruiterer said nothing, but sharply put each card into its proper place. The detective, leaning elegantly on his walking-cane, continued to scrutinise the shop. At last he said, "Pray excuse my apparent irrelevance, my good sir, but I should like to ask you a question in experimental psychology and the association of ideas."

The red-faced shopman regarded him with an eye of menace; but he continued gaily, swinging his cane, "Why," he pursued, "why are two tickets wrongly placed in a greengrocer's shop like a shovel hat that has come to London for a holiday? Or, in case I do not make myself clear, what is the mystical association which connects the idea of nuts marked as oranges with the idea of two clergymen, one tall and the other short?"

The eyes of the tradesman stood out of his head like a snail's; he really seemed for an instant likely to fling himself upon the stranger. At last he stammered angrily: "I don't know what you 'ave to do with it, but if you're one of their friends, you can tell 'em from me that I'll knock their silly 'eads off, parsons or no parsons, if they upset my apples again."

"Indeed?" asked the detective, with great sympathy. "Did they upset your apples?"

"One of 'em did," said the heated shopman; "rolled 'em all over the street. I'd 'ave caught the fool but for havin' to pick 'em up."

"Which way did these parsons go?" asked Valentin.

"Up that second road on the left-hand side, and then across the square," said the other promptly.

"Thanks," replied Valentin, and vanished like a fairy. On the other side of the second square he found a policeman, and said: "This is urgent, constable; have you seen two clergymen in shovel hats?"

The policeman began to chuckle heavily. "I 'ave, sir; and if you arst me, one of 'em was drunk. He stood in the middle of the road that bewildered that—"

"Which way did they go?" snapped Valentin.

"They took one of them yellow buses over there," answered the man; "them that go to Hampstead."

Valentin produced his official card and said very rapidly: "Call up two of your men to come with me in pursuit," and crossed the road with such contagious energy that the ponderous policeman was moved to almost agile obedience. In a minute and a half the French detective was joined on the opposite pavement by an inspector and a man in plain clothes.

"Well, sir," began the former, with smiling importance, "and what may—?"

Valentin pointed suddenly with his cane. "I'll tell you on the top of that omnibus," he said, and was darting and dodging across the tangle of the traffic. When all three sank panting on the top seats of the yellow vehicle, the inspector said: "We could go four times as quick in a taxi."

"Quite true," replied their leader placidly, "if we only had an idea of where we were going."

"Well, where are you going?" asked the other, staring.

Valentin smoked frowningly for a few seconds; then, removing his cigarette, he said: "If you know what a man's doing, get in front of him; but if you want to guess what he's doing, keep behind him. Stray when he strays; stop when he stops; travel as slowly as he. Then you may see what he saw and may act as he acted. All we can do is to keep our eyes skinned for a queer thing."

"What sort of queer thing do you mean?" asked the inspector.

"Any sort of queer thing," answered Valentin, and relapsed into obstinate silence.

The yellow omnibus crawled up the northern roads for what seemed like hours on end; the great detective would not explain further, and perhaps his assistants felt a silent and growing doubt of his errand. Perhaps, also, they felt a silent and growing desire for lunch, for the hours crept long past the normal luncheon hour, and the long roads of the North London suburbs seemed to shoot out into length after length like an infernal telescope. It was one of those journeys on which a man perpetually feels that now at last he must have come to the end of the universe, and then finds he has only come to the beginning of Tufnell Park. London died away in draggled taverns and dreary scrubs, and then was unaccountably born again in blazing high streets and blatant hotels. It was like passing through thirteen separate vulgar cities all just touching each other. But though the winter twilight was already threatening the road ahead of them, the Parisian detective still sat silent and watchful, eyeing the frontage of the streets that slid by on either side. By the time they had left Camden Town behind, the policemen were nearly asleep; at least, they gave something like a jump as Valentin leapt erect, struck a hand on each man's shoulder, and shouted to the driver to stop.

They tumbled down the steps into the road without realising why they had been dislodged; when they looked round for enlightenment they found Valentin triumphantly pointing his finger towards a window on the left side of the road. It was a large window, forming part of the long facade of a gilt and palatial public-house; it was the part reserved for respectable dining, and labelled "Restaurant." This window, like all the rest along the frontage of the hotel, was of frosted and figured glass; but in the middle of it was a big, black smash, like a star in the ice.

"Our cue at last," cried Valentin, waving his stick; "the place with the broken window."

"What window? What cue?" asked his principal assistant. "Why, what proof is there that this has anything to do with them?"

Valentin almost broke his bamboo stick with rage.

"Proof!" he cried. "Good God! the man is looking for proof! Why, of course, the chances are twenty to one that it has nothing to do with them. But what else can we do? Don't you see we must either follow one wild possibility or else go home to bed?" He banged his way into the restaurant, followed by his companions, and they were soon seated at a late luncheon at a little table, and looked at the star of smashed glass from the inside. Not that it was very informative to them even then.

"Got your window broken, I see," said Valentin to the waiter as he paid the bill.

"Yes, sir," answered the attendant, bending busily over the change, to which Valentin silently added an enormous tip. The waiter straightened himself with mild but unmistakable animation.

"Ah, yes, sir," he said. "Very odd thing, that, sir."

"Indeed?" Tell us about it," said the detective with careless curiosity.

"Well, two gents in black came in," said the waiter; "two of those foreign parsons that are running about. They had a cheap and quiet little lunch, and one of them paid for it and went out. The other was just going out to join him when I looked at my change again and found he'd paid me more than three times too much. 'Here,' I says to the chap who was nearly out of the door, 'you've paid too much.' 'Oh,' he says, very cool, 'have we?' 'Yes,' I says, and picks up the bill to show him. Well, that was a knock-out."

"What do you mean?" asked his interlocutor.

"Well, I'd have sworn on seven Bibles that I'd put 4s. on that bill. But now I saw I'd put 14s., as plain as paint."

"Well?" cried Valentin, moving slowly, but with burning eyes, "and then?"

"The parson at the door he says all serene, 'Sorry to confuse your accounts, but it'll pay for the window.' 'What window?' I says. 'The one I'm going to break,' he says, and smashed that blessed pane with his umbrella."

All three inquirers made an exclamation; and the inspector said under his breath, "Are we after escaped lunatics?" The waiter went on with some relish for the ridiculous story:

"I was so knocked silly for a second, I couldn't do anything. The man marched out of the place and joined his friend just round the corner. Then they went so quick up Bullock Street that I couldn't catch them, though I ran round the bars to do it."

"Bullock Street," said the detective, and shot up that thoroughfare as quickly as the strange couple he pursued.

Their journey now took them through bare brick ways like tunnels; streets with few lights and even with few windows; streets that seemed built out of the blank backs of everything and everywhere. Dusk was deepening, and it was not easy even for the London policemen to guess in what exact direction they were treading. The inspector, however, was pretty certain that they would eventually strike some part of Hampstead Heath. Abruptly one bulging gas-lit window broke the blue twilight like a bull's-eye lantern; and Valentin stopped an instant before a little garish sweetstuff shop. After an instant's hesitation he went in; he stood amid the gaudy colours of the confectionery with entire gravity and bought thirteen chocolate cigars with a certain care. He was clearly preparing an opening; but he did not need one.

An angular, elderly young woman in the shop had regarded his elegant appearance with a merely automatic inquiry; but when she saw the door behind him blocked with the blue uniform of the inspector, her eyes seemed to wake up.

"Oh," she said, "if you've come about that parcel, I've sent it off already."

"Parcel?" repeated Valentin; and it was his turn to look inquiring.

"I mean the parcel the gentleman left—the clergyman gentleman."

"For goodness' sake," said Valentin, leaning forward with his first real confession of eagerness, "for Heaven's sake tell us what happened exactly."

"Well," said the woman a little doubtfully, "the clergymen came in about half an hour ago and bought some peppermints and talked a bit, and then went off towards the Heath. But a second after, one of them runs back into the shop and says, 'Have I left a parcel!' Well, I looked everywhere and couldn't see one; so he says, 'Never mind; but if it should turn up, please post it to this address,' and he left me the address and a shilling for my trouble. And sure enough, though I thought I'd looked everywhere, I found he'd left a brown paper parcel, so I posted it to the place he said. I can't remember the address now; it was somewhere in Westminster. But as the thing seemed so important, I thought perhaps the police had come about it."

"So they have," said Valentin shortly. "Is Hampstead Heath near here?"

"Straight on for fifteen minutes," said the woman, "and you'll come right out on the open." Valentin sprang out of the shop and began to run. The other detectives followed him at a reluctant trot.

The street they threaded was so narrow and shut in by shadows that when they came out unexpectedly into the void common and vast sky they were startled to find the evening still so light and clear. A perfect dome of peacock-green sank into gold amid the blackening trees and the dark violet distances. The glowing green tint was just deep enough to pick out in points of crystal one or two stars. All that was left of the daylight lay in a golden glitter across the edge of Hampstead and that popular hollow which is called the Vale of Health. The holiday makers who roam this region had not wholly dispersed; a few couples sat shapelessly on benches; and here and there a distant girl still shrieked in one of the swings. The glory of heaven deepened and darkened around the sublime vulgarity of man; and standing on the slope and looking across the valley, Valentin beheld the thing which he sought.

Among the black and breaking groups in that distance was one especially black which did not break—a group of two figures clerically clad. Though they seemed as small as insects, Valentin could see that one of them was much smaller than the other. Though the other had a student's stoop and an inconspicuous manner, he could see that the man was well over six feet high. He shut his teeth and went forward, whirling his stick impatiently. By the time he had substantially diminished the distance and magnified the two black figures as in a vast microscope, he had perceived something else; something which startled him, and yet which he had somehow expected. Whoever was the tall priest, there could be no doubt about the identity of the short one. It was his friend of the Harwich train, the stumpy little cure of Essex whom he had warned about his brown paper parcels.

Now, so far as this went, everything fitted in finally and rationally enough. Valentin had learned by his inquiries that morning that a Father Brown from Essex was bringing up a silver cross with sapphires, a relic of considerable value, to show some of the foreign priests at the congress. This undoubtedly was the "silver with blue stones"; and Father Brown undoubtedly was the little greenhorn in the train. Now there was nothing wonderful about the fact that what Valentin had found out Flambeau had also found out; Flambeau found out everything. Also there was nothing wonderful in the fact that when Flambeau heard of a sapphire cross he should try to steal it; that was the most natural thing in all natural history. And most certainly there was nothing wonderful about the fact that Flambeau should have it all his own way with such a silly sheep as the man with the umbrella and the parcels. He was the sort of man whom anybody could lead on a string to the North Pole; it was not surprising that an actor like Flambeau, dressed as another priest, could lead him to Hampstead Heath. So far the crime seemed clear enough; and while the detective pitied the priest for his helplessness, he almost despised Flambeau for condescending to so gullible a victim. But when Valentin thought of all that had happened in between, of all that had led him to his triumph, he racked his brains for the smallest rhyme or reason in it. What had the stealing of a blue-and-silver cross from a priest from Essex to do with chucking soup at wall paper? What had it to do with calling nuts oranges, or with paying for windows first and breaking them afterwards? He had come to the end of his chase; yet somehow he had missed the middle of it. When he failed (which was seldom), he had usually grasped the clue, but nevertheless missed the criminal. Here he had grasped the criminal, but still he could not grasp the clue.

The two figures that they followed were crawling like black flies across the huge green contour of a hill. They were evidently sunk in conversation, and perhaps did not notice where they were going; but they were certainly going to the wilder and more silent heights of the Heath. As their pursuers gained on them, the latter had to use the undignified attitudes of the deer-stalker, to crouch behind clumps of trees and even to crawl prostrate in deep grass. By these ungainly ingenuities the hunters even came close enough to the quarry to hear the murmur of the discussion, but no word could be distinguished except the word "reason" recurring frequently in a high and almost childish voice. Once over an abrupt dip of land and a dense tangle of thickets, the detectives actually lost the two figures they were following. They did not find the trail again for an agonising ten minutes, and then it led round the brow of a great dome of hill overlooking an amphitheatre of rich and desolate sunset scenery. Under a tree in this commanding yet neglected spot was an old ramshackle wooden seat. On this seat sat the two priests still in serious speech together. The gorgeous green and gold still clung to the darkening horizon; but the dome above was turning slowly from peacock-green to peacock-blue, and the stars detached themselves more and more like solid jewels. Mutely motioning to his followers, Valentin contrived to creep up behind the big branching tree, and, standing there in deathly silence, heard the words of the strange priests for the first time.

After he had listened for a minute and a half, he was gripped by a devilish doubt. Perhaps he had dragged the two English policemen to the wastes of a nocturnal heath on an errand no saner than seeking figs on its thistles. For the two priests were talking exactly like priests, piously, with learning and leisure, about the most aerial enigmas of theology. The little Essex priest spoke the more simply, with his round face turned to the strengthening stars; the other talked with his head bowed, as if he were not even worthy to look at them. But no more innocently clerical conversation could have been heard in any white Italian cloister or black Spanish cathedral.

The first he heard was the tail of one of Father Brown's sentences, which ended: "... what they really meant in the Middle Ages by the heavens being incorruptible."

The taller priest nodded his bowed head and said:

"Ah, yes, these modern infidels appeal to their reason; but who can look at those millions of worlds and not feel that there may well be wonderful universes above us where reason is utterly unreasonable?"

"No," said the other priest; "reason is always reasonable, even in the last limbo, in the lost borderland of things. I know that people charge the Church with lowering reason, but it is just the other way. Alone on earth, the Church makes reason really supreme. Alone on earth, the Church affirms that God himself is bound by reason."

The other priest raised his austere face to the spangled sky and said:

"Yet who knows if in that infinite universe—?"

"Only infinite physically," said the little priest, turning sharply in his seat, "not infinite in the sense of escaping from the laws of truth."

Valentin behind his tree was tearing his fingernails with silent fury. He seemed almost to hear the sniggers of the English detectives whom he had brought so far on a fantastic guess only to listen to the metaphysical gossip of two mild old parsons. In his impatience he lost the equally elaborate answer of the tall cleric, and when he listened again it was again Father Brown who was speaking:

"Reason and justice grip the remotest and the loneliest star. Look at those stars. Don't they look as if they were single diamonds and sapphires? Well, you can imagine any mad botany or geology you please. Think of forests of adamant with leaves of brilliants. Think the moon is a blue moon, a single elephantine sapphire. But don't fancy that all that frantic astronomy would make the smallest difference to the reason and justice of conduct. On plains of opal, under cliffs cut out of pearl, you would still find a notice-board, 'Thou shalt not steal.'"

Valentin was just in the act of rising from his rigid and crouching attitude and creeping away as softly as might be, felled by the one great folly of his life. But something in the very silence of the tall priest made him stop until the latter spoke. When at last he did speak, he said simply, his head bowed and his hands on his knees:

"Well, I think that other worlds may perhaps rise higher than our reason. The mystery of heaven is unfathomable, and I for one can only bow my head."

Then, with brow yet bent and without changing by the faintest shade his attitude or voice, he added:

"Just hand over that sapphire cross of yours, will you? We're all alone here, and I could pull you to pieces like a straw doll."

The utterly unaltered voice and attitude added a strange violence to that shocking change of speech. But the guarder of the relic only seemed to turn his head by the smallest section of the compass. He seemed still to have a somewhat foolish face turned to the stars. Perhaps he had not understood. Or, perhaps, he had understood and sat rigid with terror.

"Yes," said the tall priest, in the same low voice and in the same still posture, "yes, I am Flambeau."

Then, after a pause, he said:

"Come, will you give me that cross?"

"No," said the other, and the monosyllable had an odd sound.

Flambeau suddenly flung off all his pontifical pretensions. The great robber leaned back in his seat and laughed low but long.

"No," he cried, "you won't give it me, you proud prelate. You won't give it me, you little celibate simpleton. Shall I tell you why you won't give it me? Because I've got it already in my own breast-pocket."

The small man from Essex turned what seemed to be a dazed face in the dusk, and said, with the timid eagerness of "The Private Secretary":

"Are—are you sure?"

Flambeau yelled with delight.

"Really, you're as good as a three-act farce," he cried. "Yes, you turnip, I am quite sure. I had the sense to make a duplicate of the right parcel, and now, my friend, you've got the duplicate and I've got the jewels. An old dodge, Father Brown—a very old dodge."

"Yes," said Father Brown, and passed his hand through his hair with the same strange vagueness of manner. "Yes, I've heard of it before."

The colossus of crime leaned over to the little rustic priest with a sort of sudden interest.

"You have heard of it?" he asked. "Where have you heard of it?"

"Well, I mustn't tell you his name, of course," said the little man simply. "He was a penitent, you know. He had lived prosperously for about twenty years entirely on duplicate brown paper parcels. And so, you see, when I began to suspect you, I thought of this poor chap's way of doing it at once."

"Began to suspect me?" repeated the outlaw with increased intensity. "Did you really have the gumption to suspect me just because I brought you up to this bare part of the heath?"

"No, no," said Brown with an air of apology. "You see, I suspected you when we first met. It's that little bulge up the sleeve where you people have the spiked bracelet."

"How in Tartarus," cried Flambeau, "did you ever hear of the spiked bracelet?"

"Oh, one's little flock, you know!" said Father Brown, arching his eyebrows rather blankly. "When I was a curate in Hartlepool, there were three of them with spiked bracelets. So, as I suspected you from the first, don't you see, I made sure that the cross should go safe, anyhow. I'm afraid I watched you, you know. So at last I saw you change the parcels. Then, don't you see, I changed them back again. And then I left the right one behind."

"Left it behind?" repeated Flambeau, and for the first time there was another note in his voice beside his triumph.

"Well, it was like this," said the little priest, speaking in the same unaffected way. "I went back to that sweet-shop and asked if I'd left a parcel, and gave them a particular address if it turned up. Well, I knew I hadn't; but when I went away again I did. So, instead of running after me with that valuable parcel, they have sent it flying to a friend of mine in Westminster." Then he added rather sadly: "I learnt that, too, from a poor fellow in Hartlepool. He used to do it with handbags he stole at railway stations, but he's in a monastery now. Oh, one gets to know, you know," he added, rubbing his head again with the same sort of desperate apology. "We can't help being priests. People come and tell us these things."

Flambeau tore a brown-paper parcel out of his inner pocket and rent it in pieces. There was nothing but paper and sticks of lead inside it. He sprang to his feet with a gigantic gesture, and cried:

"I don't believe you. I don't believe a bumpkin like you could manage all that. I believe you've still got the stuff on you, and if you don't give it up—why, we're all alone, and I'll take it by force!"

"No," said Father Brown simply, and stood up also, "you won't take it by force. First, because I really haven't still got it. And, second, because we are not alone."

Flambeau stopped in his stride forward.

"Behind that tree," said Father Brown, pointing, "are two strong policemen and the greatest detective alive. How did they come here, do you ask? Why, I brought them, of course! How did I do it? Why, I'll tell you if you like! Lord bless you, we have to know twenty such things when we work among the criminal classes! Well, I wasn't sure you were a thief, and it would never do to make a scandal against one of our own clergy. So I just tested you to see if anything would make you show yourself. A man generally makes a small scene if he finds salt in his coffee; if he doesn't, he has some reason for keeping quiet. I changed the salt and sugar, and you kept quiet. A man generally objects if his bill is three times too big. If he pays it, he has some motive for passing unnoticed. I altered your bill, and you paid it."

The world seemed waiting for Flambeau to leap like a tiger. But he was held back as by a spell; he was stunned with the utmost curiosity.

"Well," went on Father Brown, with lumbering lucidity, "as you wouldn't leave any tracks for the police, of course somebody had to. At every place we went to, I took care to do something that would get us talked about for the rest of the day. I didn't do much harm—a splashed wall, spilt apples, a broken window; but I saved the cross, as the cross will always be saved. It is at Westminster by now. I rather wonder you didn't stop it with the Donkey's Whistle."

"With the what?" asked Flambeau.

"I'm glad you've never heard of it," said the priest, making a face. "It's a foul thing. I'm sure you're too good a man for a Whistler. I couldn't have countered it even with the Spots myself; I'm not strong enough in the legs."

"What on earth are you talking about?" asked the other.

"Well, I did think you'd know the Spots," said Father Brown, agreeably surprised. "Oh, you can't have gone so very wrong yet!"

"How in blazes do you know all these horrors?" cried Flambeau.

The shadow of a smile crossed the round, simple face of his clerical opponent.

"Oh, by being a celibate simpleton, I suppose," he said. "Has it never struck you that a man who does next to nothing but hear men's real sins is not likely to be wholly unaware of human evil? But, as a matter of fact, another part of my trade, too, made me sure you weren't a priest."

"What?" asked the thief, almost gaping.

"You attacked reason," said Father Brown. "It's bad theology."

And even as he turned away to collect his property, the three policemen came out from under the twilight trees. Flambeau was an artist and a sportsman. He stepped back and swept Valentin a great bow.

"Do not bow to me, mon ami," said Valentin with silver clearness. "Let us both bow to our master."

And they both stood an instant uncovered while the little Essex priest blinked about for his umbrella.

The Secret Garden

Aristide Valentin, Chief of the Paris Police, was late for his dinner, and some of his guests began to arrive before him. These were, however, reassured by his confidential servant, Ivan, the old man with a scar, and a face almost as grey as his moustaches, who always sat at a table in the entrance hall—a hall hung with weapons. Valentin's house was perhaps as peculiar and celebrated as its master. It was an old house, with high walls and tall poplars almost overhanging the Seine; but the oddity—and perhaps the police value—of its architecture was this: that there was no ultimate exit at all except through this front door, which was guarded by Ivan and the armoury. The garden was large and elaborate, and there were many exits from the house into the garden. But there was no exit from the garden into the world outside; all round it ran a tall, smooth, unscalable wall with special spikes at the top; no bad garden, perhaps, for a man to reflect in whom some hundred criminals had sworn to kill.

As Ivan explained to the guests, their host had telephoned that he was detained for ten minutes. He was, in truth, making some last arrangements about executions and such ugly things; and though these duties were rootedly repulsive to him, he always performed them with precision. Ruthless in the pursuit of criminals, he was very mild about their punishment. Since he had been supreme over French—and largely over European—policial methods, his great influence had been honourably used for the mitigation of sentences and the purification of prisons. He was one of the great humanitarian French freethinkers; and the only thing wrong with them is that they make mercy even colder than justice.

When Valentin arrived he was already dressed in black clothes and the red rosette—an elegant figure, his dark beard already streaked with grey. He went straight through his house to his study, which opened on the grounds behind. The garden door of it was open, and after he had carefully locked his box in its official place, he stood for a few seconds at the open door looking out upon the garden. A sharp moon was fighting with the flying rags and tatters of a storm, and Valentin regarded it with a wistfulness unusual in such scientific natures as his. Perhaps such scientific natures have some psychic prevision of the most tremendous problem of their lives. From any such occult mood, at least, he quickly recovered, for he knew he was late, and that his guests had already begun to arrive. A glance at his drawing-room when he entered it was enough to make certain that his principal guest was not there, at any rate. He saw all the other pillars of the little party; he saw Lord Galloway, the English Ambassador—a choleric old man with a russet face like an apple, wearing the blue ribbon of the Garter. He saw Lady Galloway, slim and threadlike, with silver hair and a face sensitive and superior. He saw her daughter, Lady Margaret Graham, a pale and pretty girl with an elfish face and copper-coloured hair. He saw the Duchess of Mont St. Michel, black-eyed and opulent, and with her her two daughters, black-eyed and opulent also. He saw Dr. Simon, a typical French scientist, with glasses, a pointed brown beard, and a forehead barred with those parallel wrinkles which are the penalty of superciliousness, since they come through constantly elevating the eyebrows. He saw Father Brown, of Cobhole, in Essex, whom he had recently met in England. He saw—perhaps with more interest than any of these—a tall man in uniform, who had bowed to the Galloways without receiving any very hearty acknowledgment, and who now advanced alone to pay his respects to his host. This was Commandant O'Brien, of the French Foreign Legion. He was a slim yet somewhat swaggering figure, clean-shaven, dark-haired, and blue-eyed, and, as seemed natural in an officer of that famous regiment of victorious failures and successful suicides, he had an air at once dashing and melancholy. He was by birth an Irish gentleman, and in boyhood had known the Galloways—especially Margaret Graham. He had left his country after some crash of debts, and now expressed his complete freedom from British etiquette by swinging about in uniform, sabre and spurs. When he bowed to the Ambassador's family, Lord and Lady Galloway bent stiffly, and Lady Margaret looked away.

But for whatever old causes such people might be interested in each other, their distinguished host was not specially interested in them. No one of them at least was in his eyes the guest of the evening. Valentin was expecting, for special reasons, a man of world-wide fame, whose friendship he had secured during some of his great detective tours and triumphs in the United States. He was expecting Julius K. Brayne, that multi-millionaire whose colossal and even crushing endowments of small religions have occasioned so much easy sport and easier solemnity for the American and English papers. Nobody could quite make out whether Mr. Brayne was an atheist or a Mormon or a Christian Scientist; but he was ready to pour money into any intellectual vessel, so long as it was an untried vessel. One of his hobbies was to wait for the American Shakespeare—a hobby more patient than angling. He admired Walt Whitman, but thought that Luke P. Tanner, of Paris, Pa., was more "progressive" than Whitman any day. He liked anything that he thought "progressive." He thought Valentin "progressive," thereby doing him a grave injustice.

The solid appearance of Julius K. Brayne in the room was as decisive as a dinner bell. He had this great quality, which very few of us can claim, that his presence was as big as his absence. He was a huge fellow, as fat as he was tall, clad in complete evening black, without so much relief as a watch-chain or a ring. His hair was white and well brushed back like a German's; his face was red, fierce and cherubic, with one dark tuft under the lower lip that threw up that otherwise infantile visage with an effect theatrical and even Mephistophelean. Not long, however, did that salon merely stare at the celebrated American; his lateness had already become a domestic problem, and he was sent with all speed into the dining-room with Lady Galloway on his arm.

Except on one point the Galloways were genial and casual enough. So long as Lady Margaret did not take the arm of that adventurer O'Brien, her father was quite satisfied; and she had not done so, she had decorously gone in with Dr. Simon. Nevertheless, old Lord Galloway was restless and almost rude. He was diplomatic enough during dinner, but when, over the cigars, three of the younger men—Simon the doctor, Brown the priest, and the detrimental O'Brien, the exile in a foreign uniform—all melted away to mix with the ladies or smoke in the conservatory, then the

English diplomatist grew very undiplomatic indeed. He was stung every sixty seconds with the thought that the scamp O'Brien might be signalling to Margaret somehow; he did not attempt to imagine how. He was left over the coffee with Brayne, the hoary Yankee who believed in all religions, and Valentin, the grizzled Frenchman who believed in none. They could argue with each other, but neither could appeal to him. After a time this "progressive" logomachy had reached a crisis of tedium; Lord Galloway got up also and sought the drawing-room. He lost his way in long passages for some six or eight minutes: till he heard the high-pitched, didactic voice of the doctor, and then the dull voice of the priest, followed by general laughter. They also, he thought with a curse, were probably arguing about "science and religion." But the instant he opened the salon door he saw only one thing—he saw what was not there. He saw that Commandant O'Brien was absent, and that Lady Margaret was absent too.

Rising impatiently from the drawing-room, as he had from the dining-room, he stamped along the passage once more. His notion of protecting his daughter from the Irish-Algerian n'er-do-well had become something central and even mad in his mind. As he went towards the back of the house, where was Valentin's study, he was surprised to meet his daughter, who swept past with a white, scornful face, which was a second enigma. If she had been with O'Brien, where was O'Brien! If she had not been with O'Brien, where had she been? With a sort of senile and passionate suspicion he groped his way to the dark back parts of the mansion, and eventually found a servants' entrance that opened on to the garden. The moon with her scimitar had now ripped up and rolled away all the storm-wrack. The argent light lit up all four corners of the garden. A tall figure in blue was striding across the lawn towards the study door; a glint of moonlit silver on his facings picked him out as Commandant O'Brien.

He vanished through the French windows into the house, leaving Lord Galloway in an indescribable temper, at once virulent and vague. The blue-and-silver garden, like a scene in a theatre, seemed to taunt him with all that tyrannic tenderness against which his worldly authority was at war. The length and grace of the Irishman's stride enraged him as if he were a rival instead of a father; the moonlight maddened him. He was trapped as if by magic into a garden of troubadours, a Watteau fairyland; and, willing to shake off such amorous imbecilities by speech, he stepped briskly after his enemy. As he did so he tripped over some tree or stone in the grass; looked down at it first with irritation and then a second time with curiosity. The next instant the moon and the tall poplars looked at an unusual sight—an elderly English diplomatist running hard and crying or bellowing as he ran.

His hoarse shouts brought a pale face to the study door, the beaming glasses and worried brow of Dr. Simon, who heard the nobleman's first clear words. Lord Galloway was crying: "A corpse in the grass—a blood-stained corpse." O'Brien at last had gone utterly out of his mind.

"We must tell Valentin at once," said the doctor, when the other had brokenly described all that he had dared to examine. "It is fortunate that he is here;" and even as he spoke the great detective entered the study, attracted by the cry. It was almost amusing to note his typical transformation; he had come with the common concern of a host and a gentleman, fearing that some guest or servant was ill. When he was told the gory fact, he turned with all his gravity instantly bright and businesslike; for this, however abrupt and awful, was his business.

"Strange, gentlemen," he said as they hurried out into the garden, "that I should have hunted mysteries all over the earth, and now one comes and settles in my own back-yard. But where is the place?" They crossed the lawn less easily, as a slight mist had begun to rise from the river; but under the guidance of the shaken Galloway they found the body sunken in deep grass—the body of a very tall and broad-shouldered man. He lay face downwards, so they could only see that his big shoulders were clad in black cloth, and that his big head was bald, except for a wisp or two of brown hair that clung to his skull like wet seaweed. A scarlet serpent of blood crawled from under his fallen face.

"At least," said Simon, with a deep and singular intonation, "he is none of our party."

"Examine him, doctor," cried Valentin rather sharply. "He may not be dead."

The doctor bent down. "He is not quite cold, but I am afraid he is dead enough," he answered. "Just help me to lift him up."

They lifted him carefully an inch from the ground, and all doubts as to his being really dead were settled at once and frightfully. The head fell away. It had been entirely sundered from the body; whoever had cut his throat had managed to sever the neck as well. Even Valentin was slightly shocked. "He must have been as strong as a gorilla," he muttered.

Not without a shiver, though he was used to anatomical abortions, Dr. Simon lifted the head. It was slightly slashed about the neck and jaw, but the face was substantially unhurt. It was a ponderous, yellow face, at once sunken and swollen, with a hawk-like nose and heavy lids—a face of a wicked Roman emperor, with, perhaps, a distant touch of a Chinese emperor. All present seemed to look at it with the coldest eye of ignorance. Nothing else could be noted about the man except that, as they had lifted his body, they had seen underneath it the white gleam of a shirt-front defaced with a red gleam of blood. As Dr. Simon said, the man had never been of their party. But he might very well have been trying to join it, for he had come dressed for such an occasion.

Valentin went down on his hands and knees and examined with his closest professional attention the grass and ground for some twenty yards round the body, in which he was assisted less skillfully by the doctor, and quite vaguely by the English lord. Nothing rewarded their grovellings except a few twigs, snapped or chopped into very small lengths, which Valentin lifted for an instant's examination and then tossed away.

"Twigs," he said gravely; "twigs, and a total stranger with his head cut off; that is all there is on this lawn."

There was an almost creepy stillness, and then the unnerved Galloway called out sharply:

"Who's that! Who's that over there by the garden wall!"

A small figure with a foolishly large head drew waveringly near them in the moonlit haze; looked for an instant like a goblin, but turned out to be the harmless little priest whom they had left in the drawing-room.

"I say," he said meekly, "there are no gates to this garden, do you know."

Valentin's black brows had come together somewhat crossly, as they did on principle at the sight of the cassock. But he was far too just a man to deny the relevance of the remark. "You are right," he said. "Before we find out how he came to be killed, we may have to find out how he came to be here. Now listen to me, gentlemen. If it can be done without prejudice to my position and duty, we shall all agree that certain distinguished names might well be kept out of this. There are ladies, gentlemen, and there is a foreign ambassador. If we must mark it down as a crime, then it must be followed up as a crime. But till then I can use my own discretion. I am the head of the police; I am so public that I can afford to be private. Please Heaven, I will clear everyone of my own guests before I call in my men to look for anybody else. Gentlemen, upon your honour, you will none of you leave the house till tomorrow at noon; there are bedrooms for all. Simon, I think you know where to find my man, Ivan, in the front hall; he is a confidential man. Tell him to leave another servant on guard and come to me at once. Lord Galloway, you are certainly the best person to tell the ladies what has happened, and prevent a panic. They also must stay. Father Brown and I will remain with the body."

When this spirit of the captain spoke in Valentin he was obeyed like a bugle. Dr. Simon went through to the armoury and routed out Ivan, the public detective's private detective. Galloway went to the drawing-room and told the terrible news tactfully enough, so that by the time the company assembled there the ladies were already startled and already soothed. Meanwhile the good priest and the good atheist stood at the head and foot of the dead man motionless in the moonlight, like symbolic statues of their two philosophies of death.

Ivan, the confidential man with the scar and the moustaches, came out of the house like a cannon ball, and came racing across the lawn to Valentin like a dog to his master. His livid face was quite lively with the glow of this domestic detective story, and it was with almost unpleasant eagerness that he asked his master's permission to examine the remains.

"Yes; look, if you like, Ivan," said Valentin, "but don't be long. We must go in and thrash this out in the house."

Ivan lifted the head, and then almost let it drop.

"Why," he gasped, "it's—no, it isn't; it can't be. Do you know this man, sir?"

"No," said Valentin indifferently; "we had better go inside."

Between them they carried the corpse to a sofa in the study, and then all made their way to the drawing-room.

The detective sat down at a desk quietly, and even without hesitation; but his eye was the iron eye of a judge at assize. He made a few rapid notes upon paper in front of him, and then said shortly: "Is everybody here?"

"Not Mr. Brayne," said the Duchess of Mont St. Michel, looking round.

"No," said Lord Galloway in a hoarse, harsh voice. "And not Mr. Neil O'Brien, I fancy. I saw that gentleman walking in the garden when the corpse was still warm."

"Ivan," said the detective, "go and fetch Commandant O'Brien and Mr. Brayne. Mr. Brayne, I know, is finishing a cigar in the dining-room; Commandant O'Brien, I think, is walking up and down the conservatory. I am not sure."

The faithful attendant flashed from the room, and before anyone could stir or speak Valentin went on with the same soldierly swiftness of exposition.

"Everyone here knows that a dead man has been found in the garden, his head cut clean from his body. Dr. Simon, you have examined it. Do you think that to cut a man's throat like that would need great force? Or, perhaps, only a very sharp knife?"

"I should say that it could not be done with a knife at all," said the pale doctor.

"Have you any thought," resumed Valentin, "of a tool with which it could be done?"

"Speaking within modern probabilities, I really haven't," said the doctor, arching his painful brows. "It's not easy to hack a neck through even clumsily, and this was a very clean cut. It could be done with a battle-axe or an old headsman's axe, or an old two-handed sword."

"But, good heavens!" cried the Duchess, almost in hysterics, "there aren't any two-handed swords and battle-axes round here."

Valentin was still busy with the paper in front of him. "Tell me," he said, still writing rapidly, "could it have been done with a long French cavalry sabre?"

A low knocking came at the door, which, for some unreasonable reason, curdled everyone's blood like the knocking in Macbeth. Amid that frozen silence Dr. Simon managed to say: "A sabre—yes, I suppose it could."

"Thank you," said Valentin. "Come in, Ivan."

The confidential Ivan opened the door and ushered in Commandant Neil O'Brien, whom he had found at last pacing the garden again.

The Irish officer stood up disordered and defiant on the threshold. "What do you want with me?" he cried.

"Please sit down," said Valentin in pleasant, level tones. "Why, you aren't wearing your sword. Where is it?"

"I left it on the library table," said O'Brien, his brogue deepening in his disturbed mood. "It was a nuisance, it was getting—"

"Ivan," said Valentin, "please go and get the Commandant's sword from the library." Then, as the servant vanished, "Lord Galloway says he saw you leaving the garden just before he found the corpse. What were you doing in the garden?"

The Commandant flung himself recklessly into a chair. "Oh," he cried in pure Irish, "admirin' the moon. Communing with Nature, me bhoy."

A heavy silence sank and endured, and at the end of it came again that trivial and terrible knocking. Ivan reappeared, carrying an empty steel scabbard. "This is all I can find," he said.

"Put it on the table," said Valentin, without looking up.

There was an inhuman silence in the room, like that sea of inhuman silence round the dock of the condemned murderer. The Duchess's weak exclamations had long ago died away. Lord Galloway's swollen hatred was satisfied and even sobered. The voice that came was quite unexpected.

"I think I can tell you," cried Lady Margaret, in that clear, quivering voice with which a courageous woman speaks publicly. "I can tell you what Mr. O'Brien was doing in the garden, since he is bound to silence. He was asking me to marry him. I refused; I said in my family circumstances I could give him nothing but my respect. He was a little angry at that; he did not seem to think much of my respect. I wonder," she added, with rather a wan smile, "if he will care at all for it now. For I offer it him now. I will swear anywhere that he never did a thing like this."

Lord Galloway had edged up to his daughter, and was intimidating her in what he imagined to be an undertone. "Hold your tongue, Maggie," he said in a thunderous whisper. "Why should you shield the fellow? Where's his sword? Where's his confounded cavalry—"

He stopped because of the singular stare with which his daughter was regarding him, a look that was indeed a lurid magnet for the whole group.

"You old fool!" she said in a low voice without pretence of piety, "what do you suppose you are trying to prove? I tell you this man was innocent while with me. But if he wasn't innocent, he was still with me. If he murdered a man in the garden, who was it who must have seen—who must at least have known? Do you hate Neil so much as to put your own daughter—"

Lady Galloway screamed. Everyone else sat tingling at the touch of those satanic tragedies that have been between lovers before now. They saw the proud, white face of the Scotch aristocrat and her lover, the Irish adventurer, like old portraits in a dark house. The long silence was full of formless historical memories of murdered husbands and poisonous paramours.

In the centre of this morbid silence an innocent voice said: "Was it a very long cigar?"

The change of thought was so sharp that they had to look round to see who had spoken.

"I mean," said little Father Brown, from the corner of the room, "I mean that cigar Mr. Brayne is finishing. It seems nearly as long as a walking-stick."

Despite the irrelevance there was assent as well as irritation in Valentin's face as he lifted his head.

"Quite right," he remarked sharply. "Ivan, go and see about Mr. Brayne again, and bring him here at once."

The instant the factotum had closed the door, Valentin addressed the girl with an entirely new earnestness.

"Lady Margaret," he said, "we all feel, I am sure, both gratitude and admiration for your act in rising above your lower dignity and explaining the Commandant's conduct. But there is a hiatus still. Lord Galloway, I understand, met you passing from the study to the drawing-room, and it was only some minutes afterwards that he found the garden and the Commandant still walking there."

"You have to remember," replied Margaret, with a faint irony in her voice, "that I had just refused him, so we should scarcely have come back arm in arm. He is a gentleman, anyhow; and he loitered behind—and so got charged with murder."

"In those few moments," said Valentin gravely, "he might really—"

The knock came again, and Ivan put in his scarred face.

"Beg pardon, sir," he said, "but Mr. Brayne has left the house."

"Left!" cried Valentin, and rose for the first time to his feet.

"Gone. Scooted. Evaporated," replied Ivan in humorous French. "His hat and coat are gone, too, and I'll tell you something to cap it all. I ran outside the house to find any traces of him, and I found one, and a big trace, too."

"What do you mean?" asked Valentin.

"I'll show you," said his servant, and reappeared with a flashing naked cavalry sabre, streaked with blood about the point and edge. Everyone in the room eyed it as if it were a thunderbolt; but the experienced Ivan went on quite quietly:

"I found this," he said, "flung among the bushes fifty yards up the road to Paris. In other words, I found it just where your respectable Mr. Brayne threw it when he ran away."

There was again a silence, but of a new sort. Valentin took the sabre, examined it, reflected with unaffected concentration of thought, and then turned a respectful face to O'Brien. "Commandant," he said, "we trust you will always produce this weapon if it is wanted for police examination. Meanwhile," he added, slapping the steel back in the ringing scabbard, "let me return you your sword."

At the military symbolism of the action the audience could hardly refrain from applause.

For Neil O'Brien, indeed, that gesture was the turning-point of existence. By the time he was wandering in the mysterious garden again in the colours of the morning the tragic futility of his ordinary mien had fallen from him; he was a man with many reasons for happiness. Lord Galloway was a gentleman, and had offered him an apology. Lady Margaret was something better than a lady, a woman at least, and had perhaps given him something better than an apology, as they drifted among the old flowerbeds before breakfast. The whole company was more lighthearted and humane, for though the riddle of the death remained, the load of suspicion was lifted off them all, and sent flying off to Paris with the strange millionaire—a man they hardly knew. The devil was cast out of the house—he had cast himself out.

Still, the riddle remained; and when O'Brien threw himself on a garden seat beside Dr. Simon, that keenly scientific person at once resumed it. He did not get much talk out of O'Brien, whose thoughts were on pleasanter things.

"I can't say it interests me much," said the Irishman frankly, "especially as it seems pretty plain now. Apparently Brayne hated this stranger for some reason; lured him into the garden, and killed him with my sword. Then he fled to the city, tossing the sword away as he went. By the way, Ivan tells me the dead man had a Yankee dollar in his pocket. So he was a countryman of Brayne's, and that seems to clinch it. I don't see any difficulties about the business."

"There are five colossal difficulties," said the doctor quietly; "like high walls within walls. Don't mistake me. I don't doubt that Brayne did it; his flight, I fancy, proves that. But as to how he did it. First difficulty: Why should a man kill another man with a great hulking sabre, when he can almost kill him with a pocket knife and put it back in his pocket? Second difficulty: Why was there no noise or outcry? Does a man commonly see another come up waving a scimitar and offer no remarks? Third difficulty: A servant watched the front door all the evening; and a rat cannot get into Valentin's garden anywhere. How did the dead man get into the garden? Fourth difficulty: Given the same conditions, how did Brayne get out of the garden?"

"And the fifth," said Neil, with eyes fixed on the English priest who was coming slowly up the path.

"Is a trifle, I suppose," said the doctor, "but I think an odd one. When I first saw how the head had been slashed, I supposed the assassin had struck more than once. But on examination I found many cuts across the truncated section; in other words, they were struck after the head was off. Did Brayne hate his foe so fiendishly that he stood sabring his body in the moonlight?"

"Horrible!" said O'Brien, and shuddered.

The little priest, Brown, had arrived while they were talking, and had waited, with characteristic shyness, till they had finished. Then he said awkwardly:

"I say, I'm sorry to interrupt. But I was sent to tell you the news!"

"News?" repeated Simon, and stared at him rather painfully through his glasses.

"Yes, I'm sorry," said Father Brown mildly. "There's been another murder, you know."

Both men on the seat sprang up, leaving it rocking.

"And, what's stranger still," continued the priest, with his dull eye on the rhododendrons, "it's the same disgusting sort; it's another beheading. They found the second head actually bleeding into the river, a few yards along Brayne's road to Paris; so they suppose that he—"

"Great Heaven!" cried O'Brien. "Is Brayne a monomaniac?"

"There are American vendettas," said the priest impassively. Then he added: "They want you to come to the library and see it."

Commandant O'Brien followed the others towards the inquest, feeling decidedly sick. As a soldier, he loathed all this secretive carnage; where were these extravagant amputations going to stop? First one head was hacked off, and then another; in this case (he told himself bitterly) it was not true that two heads were better than one. As he crossed the study he almost staggered at a shocking coincidence. Upon Valentin's table lay the coloured picture of yet a third bleeding head; and it was the head of Valentin himself. A second glance showed him it was only a Nationalist paper, called The Guillotine, which every week showed one of its political opponents with rolling eyes and writhing features just after execution; for Valentin was an anti-clerical of some note. But O'Brien was an Irishman, with a kind of chastity even in his sins; and his gorge rose against that great brutality of the intellect which belongs only to France. He felt Paris as a whole, from the grotesques on the Gothic churches to the gross caricatures in the newspapers. He remembered the gigantic jests of the Revolution. He saw the whole city as one ugly energy, from the sanguinary sketch lying on Valentin's table up to where, above a mountain and forest of gargoyles, the great devil grins on Notre Dame.

The library was long, low, and dark; what light entered it shot from under low blinds and had still some of the ruddy tinge of morning. Valentin and his servant Ivan were waiting for them at the upper end of a long, slightly-sloping desk, on which lay the mortal remains, looking enormous in the twilight. The big black figure and yellow face of the man found in the garden confronted them essentially unchanged. The second head, which had been fished from among the river reeds that morning, lay streaming and dripping beside it; Valentin's men were still seeking to recover the rest of this second corpse, which was supposed to be afloat. Father Brown, who did not seem to share O'Brien's sensibilities in the least, went up to the second head and examined it with his blinking care. It was little more than a mop of wet white hair, fringed with silver fire in the red and level morning light; the face, which seemed of an ugly, empurpled and perhaps criminal type, had been much battered against trees or stones as it tossed in the water.

"Good morning, Commandant O'Brien," said Valentin, with quiet cordiality. "You have heard of Brayne's last experiment in butchery, I suppose?"

Father Brown was still bending over the head with white hair, and he said, without looking up:

"I suppose it is quite certain that Brayne cut off this head, too."

"Well, it seems common sense," said Valentin, with his hands in his pockets. "Killed in the same way as the other. Found within a few yards of the other. And sliced by the same weapon which we know he carried away."

"Yes, yes; I know," replied Father Brown submissively. "Yet, you know, I doubt whether Brayne could have cut off this head."

"Why not?" inquired Dr. Simon, with a rational stare.

"Well, doctor," said the priest, looking up blinking, "can a man cut off his own head? I don't know."

O'Brien felt an insane universe crashing about his ears; but the doctor sprang forward with impetuous practicality and pushed back the wet white hair.

"Oh, there's no doubt it's Brayne," said the priest quietly. "He had exactly that chip in the left ear."

The detective, who had been regarding the priest with steady and glittering eyes, opened his clenched mouth and said sharply: "You seem to know a lot about him, Father Brown."

"I do," said the little man simply. "I've been about with him for some weeks. He was thinking of joining our church."

The star of the fanatic sprang into Valentin's eyes; he strode towards the priest with clenched hands. "And, perhaps," he cried, with a blasting sneer, "perhaps he was also thinking of leaving all his money to your church."

"Perhaps he was," said Brown stolidly; "it is possible."

"In that case," cried Valentin, with a dreadful smile, "you may indeed know a great deal about him. About his life and about his—"

Commandant O'Brien laid a hand on Valentin's arm. "Drop that slanderous rubbish, Valentin," he said, "or there may be more swords yet."

But Valentin (under the steady, humble gaze of the priest) had already recovered himself. "Well," he said shortly, "people's private opinions can wait. You gentlemen are still bound by your promise to stay; you must enforce it on yourselves—and on each other. Ivan here will tell you anything more you want to know; I must get to business and write to the authorities. We can't keep this quiet any longer. I shall be writing in my study if there is any more news."

"Is there any more news, Ivan?" asked Dr. Simon, as the chief of police strode out of the room.

"Only one more thing, I think, sir," said Ivan, wrinkling up his grey old face, "but that's important, too, in its way. There's that old buffer you found on the lawn," and he pointed without pretence of reverence at the big black body with the yellow head. "We've found out who he is, anyhow."

"Indeed!" cried the astonished doctor, "and who is he?"

"His name was Arnold Becker," said the under-detective, "though he went by many aliases. He was a wandering sort of scamp, and is known to have been in America; so that was where Brayne got his knife into him. We didn't have much to do with him ourselves, for he worked mostly in Germany. We've communicated, of course, with the German police. But, oddly enough, there was a twin brother of his, named Louis Becker, whom we had a great deal to do with. In fact, we found it necessary to guillotine him only yesterday. Well, it's a rum thing, gentlemen, but when I saw that fellow flat on the lawn I had the greatest jump of my life. If I hadn't seen Louis Becker guillotined with my own eyes, I'd have sworn it was Louis Becker lying there in the grass. Then, of course, I remembered his twin brother in Germany, and following up the clue—"

The explanatory Ivan stopped, for the excellent reason that nobody was listening to him. The Commandant and the doctor were both staring at Father Brown, who had sprung stiffly to his feet, and was holding his temples tight like a man in sudden and violent pain.

"Stop, stop, stop!" he cried; "stop talking a minute, for I see half. Will God give me strength? Will my brain make the one jump and see all? Heaven help me! I used to be fairly good at thinking. I could paraphrase any page in Aquinas once. Will my head split—or will it see? I see half—I only see half."

He buried his head in his hands, and stood in a sort of rigid torture of thought or prayer, while the other three could only go on staring at this last prodigy of their wild twelve hours.

When Father Brown's hands fell they showed a face quite fresh and serious, like a child's. He heaved a huge sigh, and said: "Let us get this said and done with as quickly as possible. Look here, this will be the quickest way to convince you all of the truth." He turned to the doctor. "Dr. Simon," he said, "you have a strong headpiece, and I heard you this morning asking the five hardest questions about this business. Well, if you will ask them again, I will answer them."

Simon's pince-nez dropped from his nose in his doubt and wonder, but he answered at once. "Well, the first question, you know, is why a man should kill another with a clumsy sabre at all when a man can kill with a bodkin?"

"A man cannot behead with a bodkin," said Brown calmly, "and for this murder beheading was absolutely necessary."

"Why?" asked O'Brien, with interest.

"And the next question?" asked Father Brown.

"Well, why didn't the man cry out or anything?" asked the doctor; "sabres in gardens are certainly unusual."

"Twigs," said the priest gloomily, and turned to the window which looked on the scene of death. "No one saw the point of the twigs. Why should they lie on that lawn (look at it) so far from any tree? They were not snapped off; they were chopped off. The murderer occupied his enemy with some tricks with the sabre, showing how he could cut a branch in mid-air, or what-not. Then, while his enemy bent down to see the result, a silent slash, and the head fell."

"Well," said the doctor slowly, "that seems plausible enough. But my next two questions will stump anyone."

The priest still stood looking critically out of the window and waited.

"You know how all the garden was sealed up like an air-tight chamber," went on the doctor. "Well, how did the strange man get into the garden?"

Without turning round, the little priest answered: "There never was any strange man in the garden."

There was a silence, and then a sudden cackle of almost childish laughter relieved the strain. The absurdity of Brown's remark moved Ivan to open taunts.

"Oh!" he cried; "then we didn't lug a great fat corpse on to a sofa last night? He hadn't got into the garden, I suppose?"

"Got into the garden?" repeated Brown reflectively. "No, not entirely."

"Hang it all," cried Simon, "a man gets into a garden, or he doesn't."

"Not necessarily," said the priest, with a faint smile. "What is the nest question, doctor?"

"I fancy you're ill," exclaimed Dr. Simon sharply; "but I'll ask the next question if you like. How did Brayne get out of the garden?"

"He didn't get out of the garden," said the priest, still looking out of the window.

"Didn't get out of the garden?" exploded Simon.

"Not completely," said Father Brown.

Simon shook his fists in a frenzy of French logic. "A man gets out of a garden, or he doesn't," he cried.

"Not always," said Father Brown.

Dr. Simon sprang to his feet impatiently. "I have no time to spare on such senseless talk," he cried angrily. "If you can't understand a man being on one side of a wall or the other, I won't trouble you further."

"Doctor," said the cleric very gently, "we have always got on very pleasantly together. If only for the sake of old friendship, stop and tell me your fifth question."

The impatient Simon sank into a chair by the door and said briefly: "The head and shoulders were cut about in a queer way. It seemed to be done after death."

"Yes," said the motionless priest, "it was done so as to make you assume exactly the one simple falsehood that you did assume. It was done to make you take for granted that the head belonged to the body."

The borderland of the brain, where all the monsters are made, moved horribly in the Gaelic O'Brien. He felt the chaotic presence of all the horse-men and fish-women that man's unnatural fancy has begotten. A voice older than his first fathers seemed saying in his ear: "Keep out of the monstrous garden where grows the tree with double fruit. Avoid the evil garden where died the man with two heads." Yet, while these shameful symbolic shapes passed across the ancient mirror of his Irish soul, his Frenchified intellect was quite alert, and was watching the odd priest as closely and incredulously as all the rest.

Father Brown had turned round at last, and stood against the window, with his face in dense shadow; but even in that shadow they could see it was pale as ashes. Nevertheless, he spoke quite sensibly, as if there were no Gaelic souls on earth.

"Gentlemen," he said, "you did not find the strange body of Becker in the garden. You did not find any strange body in the garden. In face of Dr. Simon's rationalism, I still affirm that Becker was only partly present. Look here!" (pointing to the black bulk of the mysterious corpse) "you never saw that man in your lives. Did you ever see this man?"

He rapidly rolled away the bald, yellow head of the unknown, and put in its place the white-maned head beside it. And there, complete, unified, unmistakable, lay Julius K. Brayne.

"The murderer," went on Brown quietly, "hacked off his enemy's head and flung the sword far over the wall. But he was too clever to fling the sword only. He flung the head over the wall also. Then he had only to clap on another head to the corpse, and (as he insisted on a private inquest) you all imagined a totally new man."

"Clap on another head!" said O'Brien staring. "What other head? Heads don't grow on garden bushes, do they?"

"No," said Father Brown huskily, and looking at his boots; "there is only one place where they grow. They grow in the basket of the guillotine, beside which the chief of police, Aristide Valentin, was standing not an hour before the murder. Oh, my friends, hear me a minute more before you tear me in pieces. Valentin is an honest man, if being mad for an arguable cause is honesty. But did you never see in that cold, grey eye of his that he is mad! He would do anything, anything, to break what he calls the superstition of the Cross. He has fought for it and starved for it, and now he has murdered for it. Brayne's crazy millions had hitherto been scattered among so many sects that they did little to alter the balance of things. But Valentin heard a whisper that Brayne, like so many scatter-brained sceptics, was drifting to us; and that was quite a different thing. Brayne would pour supplies into the impoverished and pugnacious Church of France; he would support six Nationalist newspapers like The Guillotine. The battle was already balanced on a point, and the fanatic took flame at the risk. He resolved to destroy the millionaire, and he did it as one would expect the greatest of detectives to commit his only crime. He abstracted the severed head of Becker on some criminological excuse, and took it home in his official box.

He had that last argument with Brayne, that Lord Galloway did not hear the end of; that failing, he led him out into the sealed garden, talked about swordsmanship, used twigs and a sabre for illustration, and—"

Ivan of the Scar sprang up. "You lunatic," he yelled; "you'll go to my master now, if I take you by—"

"Why, I was going there," said Brown heavily; "I must ask him to confess, and all that."

Driving the unhappy Brown before them like a hostage or sacrifice, they rushed together into the sudden stillness of Valentin's study.

The great detective sat at his desk apparently too occupied to hear their turbulent entrance. They paused a moment, and then something in the look of that upright and elegant back made the doctor run forward suddenly. A touch and a glance showed him that there was a small box of pills at Valentin's elbow, and that Valentin was dead in his chair; and on the blind face of the suicide was more than the pride of Cato.

The Queer Feet

If you meet a member of that select club, "The Twelve True Fishermen," entering the Vernon Hotel for the annual club dinner, you will observe, as he takes off his overcoat, that his evening coat is green and not black. If (supposing that you have the star-defying audacity to address such a being) you ask him why, he will probably answer that he does it to avoid being mistaken for a waiter. You will then retire crushed. But you will leave behind you a mystery as yet unsolved and a tale worth telling.

If (to pursue the same vein of improbable conjecture) you were to meet a mild, hard-working little priest, named Father Brown, and were to ask him what he thought was the most singular luck of his life, he would probably reply that upon the whole his best stroke was at the Vernon Hotel, where he had averted a crime and, perhaps, saved a soul, merely by listening to a few footsteps in a passage. He is perhaps a little proud of this wild and wonderful guess of his, and it is possible that he might refer to it. But since it is immeasurably unlikely that you will ever rise high enough in the social world to find "The Twelve True Fishermen," or that you will ever sink low enough among slums and criminals to find Father Brown, I fear you will never hear the story at all unless you hear it from me.

The Vernon Hotel at which The Twelve True Fishermen held their annual dinners was an institution such as can only exist in an oligarchical society which has almost gone mad on good manners. It was that topsy-turvy product—an "exclusive" commercial enterprise. That is, it was a thing which paid not by attracting people, but actually by turning people away. In the heart of a plutocracy tradesmen become cunning enough to be more fastidious than their customers. They positively create difficulties so that their wealthy and weary clients may spend money and diplomacy in overcoming them. If there were a fashionable hotel in London which no man could enter who was under six foot, society would meekly make up parties of six-foot men to dine in it. If there were an expensive restaurant which by a mere caprice of its proprietor was only open on Thursday afternoon, it would be crowded on Thursday afternoon. The Vernon Hotel stood, as if by accident, in the corner of a square in Belgravia. It was a small hotel; and a very inconvenient one. But its very inconveniences were considered as walls protecting a particular class. One inconvenience, in particular, was held to be of vital importance: the fact that practically only twenty-four people could dine in the place at once. The only big dinner table was the celebrated terrace table, which stood open to the air on a sort of veranda overlooking one of the most exquisite old gardens in London. Thus it happened that even the twenty-four seats at this table could only be enjoyed in warm weather; and this making the enjoyment yet more difficult made it yet more desired. The existing owner of the hotel was a Jew named Lever; and he made nearly a million out of it, by making it difficult to get into. Of course he combined with this limitation in the scope of his enterprise the most careful polish in its performance. The wines and cooking were really as good as any in Europe, and the demeanour of the attendants exactly mirrored the fixed mood of the English upper class. The proprietor knew all his waiters like the fingers on his hand; there were only fifteen of them all told. It was much easier to become a Member of Parliament than to become a waiter in that hotel. Each waiter was trained in terrible silence and smoothness, as if he were a gentleman's servant. And, indeed, there was generally at least one waiter to every gentleman who dined.

The club of The Twelve True Fishermen would not have consented to dine anywhere but in such a place, for it insisted on a luxurious privacy; and would have been quite upset by the mere thought that any other club was even dining in the same building. On the occasion of their annual dinner the Fishermen were in the habit of exposing all their treasures, as if they were in a private house, especially the celebrated set of fish knives and forks which were, as it were, the insignia of the society, each being exquisitely wrought in silver in the form of a fish, and each loaded at the hilt with one large pearl. These were always laid out for the fish course, and the fish course was always the most magnificent in that magnificent repast. The society had a vast number of ceremonies and observances, but it had no history and no object; that was where it was so very aristocratic. You did not have to be anything in order to be one of the Twelve Fishers; unless you were already a certain sort of person, you never even heard of them. It had been in existence twelve years. Its president was Mr. Audley. Its vice-president was the Duke of Chester.

If I have in any degree conveyed the atmosphere of this appalling hotel, the reader may feel a natural wonder as to how I came to know anything about it, and may even speculate as to how so ordinary a person as my friend Father Brown came to find himself in that golden galley. As far as that is concerned, my story is simple, or even vulgar. There is in the world a very aged rioter and demagogue who breaks into the most refined retreats with the dreadful information that all men are brothers, and wherever this leveller went on his pale horse it was Father Brown's trade to follow. One of the waiters, an Italian, had been struck down with a paralytic stroke that afternoon; and his Jewish employer, marvelling mildly at such superstitions, had consented to send for the nearest Popish priest. With what the waiter confessed to

Father Brown we are not concerned, for the excellent reason that that cleric kept it to himself; but apparently it involved him in writing out a note or statement for the conveying of some message or the righting of some wrong. Father Brown, therefore, with a meek impudence which he would have shown equally in Buckingham Palace, asked to be provided with a room and writing materials. Mr. Lever was torn in two. He was a kind man, and had also that bad imitation of kindness, the dislike of any difficulty or scene. At the same time the presence of one unusual stranger in his hotel that evening was like a speck of dirt on something just cleaned. There was never any borderland or anteroom in the Vernon Hotel, no people waiting in the hall, no customers coming in on chance. There were fifteen waiters. There were twelve guests. It would be as startling to find a new guest in the hotel that night as to find a new brother taking breakfast or tea in one's own family. Moreover, the priest's appearance was second-rate and his clothes muddy; a mere glimpse of him afar off might precipitate a crisis in the club. Mr. Lever at last hit on a plan to cover, since he might not obliterate, the disgrace. When you enter (as you never will) the Vernon Hotel, you pass down a short passage decorated with a few dingy but important pictures, and come to the main vestibule and lounge which opens on your right into passages leading to the public rooms, and on your left to a similar passage pointing to the kitchens and offices of the hotel. Immediately on your left hand is the corner of a glass office, which abuts upon the lounge—a house within a house, so to speak, like the old hotel bar which probably once occupied its place.

In this office sat the representative of the proprietor (nobody in this place ever appeared in person if he could help it), and just beyond the office, on the way to the servants' quarters, was the gentlemen's cloak room, the last boundary of the gentlemen's domain. But between the office and the cloak room was a small private room without other outlet, sometimes used by the proprietor for delicate and important matters, such as lending a duke a thousand pounds or declining to lend him sixpence. It is a mark of the magnificent tolerance of Mr. Lever that he permitted this holy place to be for about half an hour profaned by a mere priest, scribbling away on a piece of paper. The story which Father Brown was writing down was very likely a much better story than this one, only it will never be known. I can merely state that it was very nearly as long, and that the last two or three paragraphs of it were the least exciting and absorbing.

For it was by the time that he had reached these that the priest began a little to allow his thoughts to wander and his animal senses, which were commonly keen, to awaken. The time of darkness and dinner was drawing on; his own forgotten little room was without a light, and perhaps the gathering gloom, as occasionally happens, sharpened the sense of sound. As Father Brown wrote the last and least essential part of his document, he caught himself writing to the rhythm of a recurrent noise outside, just as one sometimes thinks to the tune of a railway train. When he became conscious of the thing he found what it was: only the ordinary patter of feet passing the door, which in an hotel was no very unlikely matter. Nevertheless, he stared at the darkened ceiling, and listened to the sound. After he had listened for a few seconds dreamily, he got to his feet and listened intently, with his head a little on one side. Then he sat down again and buried his brow in his hands, now not merely listening, but listening and thinking also.

The footsteps outside at any given moment were such as one might hear in any hotel; and yet, taken as a whole, there was something very strange about them. There were no other footsteps. It was always a very silent house, for the few familiar guests went at once to their own apartments, and the well-trained waiters were told to be almost invisible until they were wanted. One could not conceive any place where there was less reason to apprehend anything irregular. But these footsteps were so odd that one could not decide to call them regular or irregular. Father Brown followed them with his finger on the edge of the table, like a man trying to learn a tune on the piano.

First, there came a long rush of rapid little steps, such as a light man might make in winning a walking race. At a certain point they stopped and changed to a sort of slow, swinging stamp, numbering not a quarter of the steps, but occupying about the same time. The moment the last echoing stamp had died away would come again the run or ripple of light, hurrying feet, and then again the thud of the heavier walking. It was certainly the same pair of boots, partly because (as has been said) there were no other boots about, and partly because they had a small but unmistakable creak in them. Father Brown had the kind of head that cannot help asking questions; and on this apparently trivial question his head almost split. He had seen men run in order to jump. He had seen men run in order to slide. But why on earth should a man run in order to walk? Or, again, why should he walk in order to run? Yet no other description would cover the antics of this invisible pair of legs. The man was either walking very fast down one-half of the corridor in order to walk very slow down the other half; or he was walking very slow at one end to have the rapture of walking fast at the other. Neither suggestion seemed to make much sense. His brain was growing darker and darker, like his room.

Yet, as he began to think steadily, the very blackness of his cell seemed to make his thoughts more vivid; he began to see as in a kind of vision the fantastic feet capering along the corridor in unnatural or symbolic attitudes. Was it a heathen religious dance? Or some entirely new kind of scientific exercise? Father Brown began to ask himself with more exactness what the steps suggested. Taking the slow step first: it certainly was not the step of the proprietor. Men of his type walk with a rapid waddle, or they sit still. It could not be any servant or messenger waiting for directions. It did not sound like it. The poorer orders (in an oligarchy) sometimes lurch about when they are slightly drunk, but generally, and especially in such gorgeous scenes, they stand or sit in constrained attitudes. No; that heavy yet springy step, with a kind of careless emphasis, not specially noisy, yet not caring what noise it made, belonged to only one of the animals of this earth. It was a gentleman of western Europe, and probably one who had never worked for his living.

Just as he came to this solid certainty, the step changed to the quicker one, and ran past the door as feverishly as a rat. The listener remarked that though this step was much swifter it was also much more noiseless, almost as if the man were walking on tiptoe. Yet it was not associated in his mind with secrecy, but with something else—something that he could not remember. He was maddened by one of those half-memories that make a man feel half-witted. Surely he had heard that strange, swift walking somewhere. Suddenly he sprang to his feet with a new idea in his head, and walked to the door. His room had no direct outlet on the passage, but let on one side into the glass office, and on the other into the cloak room beyond. He tried the door into the office, and found it locked. Then he looked at the window, now a square pane full of purple cloud cleft by livid sunset, and for an instant he smelt evil as a dog smells rats.

The rational part of him (whether the wiser or not) regained its supremacy. He remembered that the proprietor had told him that he should lock the door, and would come later to release him. He told himself that twenty things he had not thought of might explain the eccentric sounds outside; he reminded himself that there was just enough light left to finish his own proper work. Bringing his paper to the window so as to catch the last stormy evening light, he resolutely plunged once more into the almost completed record. He had written for about twenty minutes, bending closer and closer to his paper in the lessening light; then suddenly he sat upright. He had heard the strange feet once more.

This time they had a third oddity. Previously the unknown man had walked, with levity indeed and lightning quickness, but he had walked. This time he ran. One could hear the swift, soft, bounding steps coming along the corridor, like the pads of a fleeing and leaping panther. Whoever was coming was a very strong, active man, in still yet tearing excitement. Yet, when the sound had swept up to the office like a sort of whispering whirlwind, it suddenly changed again to the old slow, swaggering stamp.

Father Brown flung down his paper, and, knowing the office door to be locked, went at once into the cloak room on the other side. The attendant of this place was temporarily absent, probably because the only guests were at dinner and his office was a sinecure. After groping through a grey forest of overcoats, he found that the dim cloak room opened on the lighted corridor in the form of a sort of counter or half-door, like most of the counters across which we have all handed umbrellas and received tickets. There was a light immediately above the semicircular arch of this opening. It threw little illumination on Father Brown himself, who seemed a mere dark outline against the dim sunset window behind him. But it threw an almost theatrical light on the man who stood outside the cloak room in the corridor.

He was an elegant man in very plain evening dress; tall, but with an air of not taking up much room; one felt that he could have slid along like a shadow where many smaller men would have been obvious and obstructive. His face, now flung back in the lamplight, was swarthy and vivacious, the face of a foreigner. His figure was good, his manners good humoured and confident; a critic could only say that his black coat was a shade below his figure and manners, and even bulged and bagged in an odd way. The moment he caught sight of Brown's black silhouette against the sunset, he tossed down a scrap of paper with a number and called out with amiable authority: "I want my hat and coat, please; I find I have to go away at once."

Father Brown took the paper without a word, and obediently went to look for the coat; it was not the first menial work he had done in his life. He brought it and laid it on the counter; meanwhile, the strange gentleman who had been feeling in his waistcoat pocket, said laughing: "I haven't got any silver; you can keep this." And he threw down half a sovereign, and caught up his coat.

Father Brown's figure remained quite dark and still; but in that instant he had lost his head. His head was always most valuable when he had lost it. In such moments he put two and two together and made four million. Often the Catholic Church (which is wedded to common sense) did not approve of it. Often he did not approve of it himself. But it was real inspiration—important at rare crises—when whosoever shall lose his head the same shall save it.

"I think, sir," he said civilly, "that you have some silver in your pocket."

The tall gentleman stared. "Hang it," he cried, "if I choose to give you gold, why should you complain?"

"Because silver is sometimes more valuable than gold," said the priest mildly; "that is, in large quantities."

The stranger looked at him curiously. Then he looked still more curiously up the passage towards the main entrance. Then he looked back at Brown again, and then he looked very carefully at the window beyond Brown's head, still coloured with the after-glow of the storm. Then he seemed to make up his mind. He put one hand on the counter, vaulted over as easily as an acrobat and towered above the priest, putting one tremendous hand upon his collar.

"Stand still," he said, in a hacking whisper. "I don't want to threaten you, but—"

"I do want to threaten you," said Father Brown, in a voice like a rolling drum, "I want to threaten you with the worm that dieth not, and the fire that is not quenched."

"You're a rum sort of cloak-room clerk," said the other.

"I am a priest, Monsieur Flambeau," said Brown, "and I am ready to hear your confession."

The other stood gasping for a few moments, and then staggered back into a chair.

The first two courses of the dinner of The Twelve True Fishermen had proceeded with placid success. I do not possess a copy of the menu; and if I did it would not convey anything to anybody. It was written in a sort of super-French employed by cooks, but quite unintelligible to Frenchmen. There was a tradition in the club that the hors d'oeuvres should be various and manifold to the point of madness. They were taken seriously because they were avowedly useless extras, like the whole dinner and the whole club. There was also a tradition that the soup course should be light and unpretending—a sort of simple and austere vigil for the feast of fish that was to come. The talk was that strange, slight talk which governs the British Empire, which governs it in secret, and yet would scarcely enlighten an ordinary Englishman even if he could overhear it. Cabinet ministers on both sides were alluded to by their Christian names with a sort of bored benignity. The Radical Chancellor of the Exchequer, whom the whole Tory party was supposed to be cursing for his extortions, was praised for his minor poetry, or his saddle in the hunting field. The Tory leader, whom all Liberals were supposed to hate as a tyrant, was discussed and, on the whole, praised—as a Liberal. It seemed somehow that politicians were very important. And yet, anything seemed important about them except their politics. Mr. Audley, the chairman, was an amiable, elderly man who still wore Gladstone collars; he was a kind of symbol of all that phantasmal and yet fixed society. He had never done anything—not even anything wrong. He was not fast; he was not even particularly rich. He was simply in the thing; and there was an end of it. No party could ignore him, and if he had wished to be in the Cabinet he certainly would have been put there. The Duke of Chester, the vice-president, was a young and rising politician. That is to say, he was a pleasant youth, with flat, fair hair and a freckled face, with moderate intelligence and enormous estates. In public his appearances were always successful and his principle was simple enough. When he thought of a joke he made it, and was called brilliant. When he could not think of a joke he said that this was no time for trifling, and was called able. In private, in a club of his own class, he was simply quite pleasantly frank and silly, like a schoolboy. Mr. Audley, never having been in politics, treated them a little more seriously. Sometimes he even embarrassed the company by phrases suggesting that there was some difference between a Liberal and a Conservative. He himself was a Conservative, even in private life. He had a roll of grey hair over the back of his collar, like certain old-fashioned statesmen, and seen from behind he looked like the man the empire wants. Seen from the front he looked like a mild, self-indulgent bachelor, with rooms in the Albany—which he was.

As has been remarked, there were twenty-four seats at the terrace table, and only twelve members of the club. Thus they could occupy the terrace in the most luxurious style of all, being ranged along the inner side of the table, with no one opposite, commanding an uninterrupted view of the garden, the colours of which were still vivid, though evening was closing in somewhat luridly for the time of year. The chairman sat in the centre of the line, and the vice-president at the right-hand end of it. When the twelve guests first trooped into their seats it was the custom (for some unknown reason) for all the fifteen waiters to stand lining the wall like troops presenting arms to the king, while the fat proprietor stood and bowed to the club with radiant surprise, as if he had never heard of them before. But before the first chink of knife and fork this army of retainers had vanished, only the one or two required to collect and distribute the plates darting about in deathly silence. Mr. Lever, the proprietor, of course had disappeared in convulsions of courtesy long before. It would be exaggerative, indeed irreverent, to say that he ever positively appeared again. But when the important course, the fish course, was being brought on, there was—how shall I put it?—a vivid shadow, a projection of his personality, which told that he was hovering near. The sacred fish course consisted (to the eyes of the vulgar) in a sort of monstrous pudding, about the size and shape of a wedding cake, in which some considerable number of interesting fishes had finally lost the shapes which God had given to them. The Twelve True Fishermen took up their celebrated fish knives and fish forks, and approached it as gravely as if every inch of the pudding cost as much as the silver fork it was eaten with. So it did, for all I know. This course was dealt with in eager and devouring silence; and it was only when his plate was nearly empty that the young duke made the ritual remark: "They can't do this anywhere but here."

"Nowhere," said Mr. Audley, in a deep bass voice, turning to the speaker and nodding his venerable head a number of times. "Nowhere, assuredly, except here. It was represented to me that at the Cafe Anglais—"

Here he was interrupted and even agitated for a moment by the removal of his plate, but he recaptured the valuable thread of his thoughts. "It was represented to me that the same could be done at the Cafe Anglais. Nothing like it, sir," he said, shaking his head ruthlessly, like a hanging judge. "Nothing like it."

"Overrated place," said a certain Colonel Pound, speaking (by the look of him) for the first time for some months.

"Oh, I don't know," said the Duke of Chester, who was an optimist, "it's jolly good for some things. You can't beat it at—"

A waiter came swiftly along the room, and then stopped dead. His stoppage was as silent as his tread; but all those vague and kindly gentlemen were so used to the utter smoothness of the unseen machinery which surrounded and supported their lives, that a waiter doing anything unexpected was a start and a jar. They felt as you and I would feel if the inanimate world disobeyed—if a chair ran away from us.

The waiter stood staring a few seconds, while there deepened on every face at table a strange shame which is wholly the product of our time. It is the combination of modern humanitarianism with the horrible modern abyss between the souls of the rich and poor. A genuine historic aristocrat would have thrown things at the waiter, beginning with empty bottles, and very probably ending with money. A genuine democrat would have asked him, with comrade-like clearness of speech, what the devil he was doing. But these modern plutocrats could not bear a poor man near to them, either as a slave or as a friend. That something had gone wrong with the servants was merely a dull, hot embarrassment. They did not want to be brutal, and they dreaded the need to be benevolent. They wanted the thing, whatever it was, to be over. It was over. The waiter, after standing for some seconds rigid, like a cataleptic, turned round and ran madly out of the room.

When he reappeared in the room, or rather in the doorway, it was in company with another waiter, with whom he whispered and gesticulated with southern fierceness. Then the first waiter went away, leaving the second waiter, and reappeared with a third waiter. By the time a fourth waiter had joined this hurried synod, Mr. Audley felt it necessary to break the silence in the interests of Tact. He used a very loud cough, instead of a presidential hammer, and said: "Splendid work young Moocher's doing in Burmah. Now, no other nation in the world could have—"

A fifth waiter had sped towards him like an arrow, and was whispering in his ear: "So sorry. Important! Might the proprietor speak to you?"

The chairman turned in disorder, and with a dazed stare saw Mr. Lever coming towards them with his lumbering quickness. The gait of the good proprietor was indeed his usual gait, but his face was by no means usual. Generally it was a genial copper-brown; now it was a sickly yellow.

"You will pardon me, Mr. Audley," he said, with asthmatic breathlessness. "I have great apprehensions. Your fish-plates, they are cleared away with the knife and fork on them!"

"Well, I hope so," said the chairman, with some warmth.

"You see him?" panted the excited hotel keeper; "you see the waiter who took them away? You know him?"

"Know the waiter?" answered Mr. Audley indignantly. "Certainly not!"

Mr. Lever opened his hands with a gesture of agony. "I never send him," he said. "I know not when or why he come. I send my waiter to take away the plates, and he find them already away."

Mr. Audley still looked rather too bewildered to be really the man the empire wants; none of the company could say anything except the man of wood—Colonel Pound—who seemed galvanised into an unnatural life. He rose rigidly from his chair, leaving all the rest sitting, screwed his eyeglass into his eye, and spoke in a raucous undertone as if he had half-forgotten how to speak. "Do you mean," he said, "that somebody has stolen our silver fish service?"

The proprietor repeated the open-handed gesture with even greater helplessness and in a flash all the men at the table were on their feet.

"Are all your waiters here?" demanded the colonel, in his low, harsh accent.

"Yes; they're all here. I noticed it myself," cried the young duke, pushing his boyish face into the inmost ring. "Always count 'em as I come in; they look so queer standing up against the wall."

"But surely one cannot exactly remember," began Mr. Audley, with heavy hesitation.

"I remember exactly, I tell you," cried the duke excitedly. "There never have been more than fifteen waiters at this place, and there were no more than fifteen tonight, I'll swear; no more and no less."

The proprietor turned upon him, quaking in a kind of palsy of surprise. "You say—you say," he stammered, "that you see all my fifteen waiters?"

"As usual," assented the duke. "What is the matter with that!"

"Nothing," said Lever, with a deepening accent, "only you did not. For one of zem is dead upstairs."

There was a shocking stillness for an instant in that room. It may be (so supernatural is the word death) that each of those idle men looked for a second at his soul, and saw it as a small dried pea. One of them—the duke, I think—even said with the idiotic kindness of wealth: "Is there anything we can do?"

"He has had a priest," said the Jew, not untouched.

Then, as to the clang of doom, they awoke to their own position. For a few weird seconds they had really felt as if the fifteenth waiter might be the ghost of the dead man upstairs. They had been dumb under that oppression, for ghosts were to them an embarrassment, like beggars. But the remembrance of the silver broke the spell of the miraculous; broke it abruptly and with a brutal reaction. The colonel flung over his chair and strode to the door. "If there was a fifteenth man here, friends," he said, "that fifteenth fellow was a thief. Down at once to the front and back doors and secure everything; then we'll talk. The twenty-four pearls of the club are worth recovering."

Mr. Audley seemed at first to hesitate about whether it was gentlemanly to be in such a hurry about anything; but, seeing the duke dash down the stairs with youthful energy, he followed with a more mature motion.

At the same instant a sixth waiter ran into the room, and declared that he had found the pile of fish plates on a sideboard, with no trace of the silver.

The crowd of diners and attendants that tumbled helter-skelter down the passages divided into two groups. Most of the Fishermen followed the proprietor to the front room to demand news of any exit. Colonel Pound, with the chairman, the vice-president, and one or two others darted down the corridor leading to the servants' quarters, as the more likely line of escape. As they did so they passed the dim alcove or cavern of the cloak room, and saw a short, black-coated figure, presumably an attendant, standing a little way back in the shadow of it.

"Hallo, there!" called out the duke. "Have you seen anyone pass?"

The short figure did not answer the question directly, but merely said: "Perhaps I have got what you are looking for, gentlemen."

They paused, wavering and wondering, while he quietly went to the back of the cloak room, and came back with both hands full of shining silver, which he laid out on the counter as calmly as a salesman. It took the form of a dozen quaintly shaped forks and knives.

"You—you—" began the colonel, quite thrown off his balance at last. Then he peered into the dim little room and saw two things: first, that the short, black-clad man was dressed like a clergyman; and, second, that the window of the room behind him was burst, as if someone had passed violently through. "Valuable things to deposit in a cloak room, aren't they?" remarked the clergyman, with cheerful composure.

"Did—did you steal those things?" stammered Mr. Audley, with staring eyes.

"If I did," said the cleric pleasantly, "at least I am bringing them back again."

"But you didn't," said Colonel Pound, still staring at the broken window.

"To make a clean breast of it, I didn't," said the other, with some humour. And he seated himself quite gravely on a stool. "But you know who did," said the, colonel.

"I don't know his real name," said the priest placidly, "but I know something of his fighting weight, and a great deal about his spiritual difficulties. I formed the physical estimate when he was trying to throttle me, and the moral estimate when he repented."

"Oh, I say—repented!" cried young Chester, with a sort of crow of laughter.

Father Brown got to his feet, putting his hands behind him. "Odd, isn't it," he said, "that a thief and a vagabond should repent, when so many who are rich and secure remain hard and frivolous, and without fruit for God or man? But there, if you will excuse me, you trespass a little upon my province. If you doubt the penitence as a practical fact, there are your knives and forks. You are The Twelve True Fishers, and there are all your silver fish. But He has made me a fisher of men."

"Did you catch this man?" asked the colonel, frowning.

Father Brown looked him full in his frowning face. "Yes," he said, "I caught him, with an unseen hook and an invisible line which is long enough to let him wander to the ends of the world, and still to bring him back with a twitch upon the thread."

There was a long silence. All the other men present drifted away to carry the recovered silver to their comrades, or to consult the proprietor about the queer condition of affairs. But the grim-faced colonel still sat sideways on the counter, swinging his long, lank legs and biting his dark moustache.

At last he said quietly to the priest: "He must have been a clever fellow, but I think I know a cleverer."

"He was a clever fellow," answered the other, "but I am not quite sure of what other you mean."

"I mean you," said the colonel, with a short laugh. "I don't want to get the fellow jailed; make yourself easy about that. But I'd give a good many silver forks to know exactly how you fell into this affair, and how you got the stuff out of him. I reckon you're the most up-to-date devil of the present company."

Father Brown seemed rather to like the saturnine candour of the soldier. "Well," he said, smiling, "I mustn't tell you anything of the man's identity, or his own story, of course; but there's no particular reason why I shouldn't tell you of the mere outside facts which I found out for myself."

He hopped over the barrier with unexpected activity, and sat beside Colonel Pound, kicking his short legs like a little boy on a gate. He began to tell the story as easily as if he were telling it to an old friend by a Christmas fire.

"You see, colonel," he said, "I was shut up in that small room there doing some writing, when I heard a pair of feet in this passage doing a dance that was as queer as the dance of death. First came quick, funny little steps, like a man walking on tiptoe for a wager; then came slow, careless, creaking steps, as of a big man walking about with a cigar. But they were both made by the same feet, I swear, and they came in rotation; first the run and then the walk, and then the run again. I wondered at first idly and then wildly why a man should act these two parts at once. One walk I knew; it was just like yours, colonel. It was the walk of a well-fed gentleman waiting for something, who strolls about rather because he is physically alert than because he is mentally impatient. I knew that I knew the other walk, too, but I could not remember what it was. What wild creature had I met on my travels that tore along on tiptoe in that extraordinary style? Then I heard a clink of plates somewhere; and the answer stood up as plain as St. Peter's. It was the walk of a waiter—that walk with the body slanted forward, the eyes looking down, the ball of the toe spurning away the ground, the coat tails and napkin flying. Then I thought for a minute and a half more. And I believe I saw the manner of the crime, as clearly as if I were going to commit it."

Colonel Pound looked at him keenly, but the speaker's mild grey eyes were fixed upon the ceiling with almost empty wistfulness.

"A crime," he said slowly, "is like any other work of art. Don't look surprised; crimes are by no means the only works of art that come from an infernal workshop. But every work of art, divine or diabolic, has one indispensable mark—I mean, that the centre of it is simple, however much the fulfilment may be complicated. Thus, in Hamlet, let us say, the grotesqueness of the grave-digger, the flowers of the mad girl, the fantastic finery of Osric, the pallor of the ghost and the grin of the skull are all oddities in a sort of tangled wreath round one plain tragic figure of a man in black. Well, this also," he said, getting slowly down from his seat with a smile, "this also is the plain tragedy of a man in black. Yes," he went on, seeing the colonel look up in some wonder, "the whole of this tale turns on a black coat. In this, as in Hamlet, there are the rococo excrescences—yourselves, let us say. There is the dead waiter, who was there when he could not be there. There is the invisible hand that swept your table clear of silver and melted into air. But every clever crime is founded ultimately on some one quite simple fact—some fact that is not itself mysterious. The mystification comes in covering it up, in leading men's thoughts away from it. This large and subtle and (in the ordinary course) most profitable crime, was built on the plain fact that a gentleman's evening dress is the same as a waiter's. All the rest was acting, and thundering good acting, too."

"Still," said the colonel, getting up and frowning at his boots, "I am not sure that I understand."

"Colonel," said Father Brown, "I tell you that this archangel of impudence who stole your forks walked up and down this passage twenty times in the blaze of all the lamps, in the glare of all the eyes. He did not go and hide in dim corners where suspicion might have searched for him. He kept constantly on the move in the lighted corridors, and everywhere that he went he seemed to be there by right. Don't ask me what he was like; you have seen him yourself six or seven times tonight. You were waiting with all the other grand people in the reception room at the end of the passage there, with the terrace just beyond. Whenever he came among you gentlemen, he came in the lightning style of a waiter, with bent head, flapping napkin and flying feet. He shot out on to the terrace, did something to the table cloth, and shot back again towards the office and the waiters' quarters. By the time he had come under the eye of the office clerk and the waiters he had become another man in every inch of his body, in every instinctive gesture. He strolled among the servants with the absent-minded insolence which they have all seen in their patrons. It was no new thing to them that a swell from the dinner party should pace all parts of the house like an animal at the Zoo; they know that nothing marks the Smart Set more than a habit of walking where one chooses. When he was magnificently weary of walking down that particular passage he would wheel round and pace back past the office; in the shadow of the arch just beyond he was altered as by a blast of magic, and went hurrying forward again among the Twelve Fishermen, an obsequious attendant. Why should the gentlemen look at a chance waiter? Why should the waiters suspect a first-rate walking gentleman? Once or twice he played the coolest tricks. In the proprietor's private quarters he called out breezily for a syphon of soda water, saying he was thirsty. He said genially that he would carry it himself, and he did; he carried it quickly and correctly through the thick of you, a waiter with an obvious errand. Of course, it could not have been kept up long, but it only had to be kept up till the end of the fish course.

"His worst moment was when the waiters stood in a row; but even then he contrived to lean against the wall just round the corner in such a way that for that important instant the waiters thought him a gentleman, while the gentlemen thought him a waiter. The rest went like winking. If any waiter caught him away from the table, that waiter caught a languid aristocrat. He had only to time himself two minutes before the fish was cleared, become a swift servant, and clear it himself. He put the plates down on a sideboard, stuffed the silver in his breast pocket, giving it a bulgy look, and ran like a hare (I heard him coming) till he came to the cloak room. There he had only to be a plutocrat again—a plutocrat called away suddenly on business. He had only to give his ticket to the cloak-room attendant, and go out again elegantly as he had come in. Only—only I happened to be the cloak-room attendant."

"What did you do to him?" cried the colonel, with unusual intensity. "What did he tell you?"

"I beg your pardon," said the priest immovably, "that is where the story ends."

"And the interesting story begins," muttered Pound. "I think I understand his professional trick. But I don't seem to have got hold of yours."

"I must be going," said Father Brown.

They walked together along the passage to the entrance hall, where they saw the fresh, freckled face of the Duke of Chester, who was bounding buoyantly along towards them.

"Come along, Pound," he cried breathlessly. "I've been looking for you everywhere. The dinner's going again in spanking style, and old Audley has got to make a speech in honour of the forks being saved. We want to start some new ceremony, don't you know, to commemorate the occasion. I say, you really got the goods back, what do you suggest?"

"Why," said the colonel, eyeing him with a certain sardonic approval, "I should suggest that henceforward we wear green coats, instead of black. One never knows what mistakes may arise when one looks so like a waiter."

"Oh, hang it all!" said the young man, "a gentleman never looks like a waiter."

"Nor a waiter like a gentleman, I suppose," said Colonel Pound, with the same lowering laughter on his face. "Reverend sir, your friend must have been very smart to act the gentleman."

Father Brown buttoned up his commonplace overcoat to the neck, for the night was stormy, and took his commonplace umbrella from the stand.

"Yes," he said; "it must be very hard work to be a gentleman; but, do you know, I have sometimes thought that it may be almost as laborious to be a waiter."

And saying "Good evening," he pushed open the heavy doors of that palace of pleasures. The golden gates closed behind him, and he went at a brisk walk through the damp, dark streets in search of a penny omnibus.

The Flying Stars

"The most beautiful crime I ever committed," Flambeau would say in his highly moral old age, "was also, by a singular coincidence, my last. It was committed at

Christmas. As an artist I had always attempted to provide crimes suitable to the special season or landscapes in which I found myself, choosing this or that terrace or garden for a catastrophe, as if for a statuary group. Thus squires should be swindled in long rooms panelled with oak; while Jews, on the other hand, should rather find themselves unexpectedly penniless among the lights and screens of the Cafe Riche. Thus, in England, if I wished to relieve a dean of his riches (which is not so easy as you might suppose), I wished to frame him, if I make myself clear, in the green lawns and grey towers of some cathedral town. Similarly, in France, when I had got money out of a rich and wicked peasant (which is almost impossible), it gratified me to get his indignant head relieved against a grey line of clipped poplars, and those solemn plains of Gaul over which broods the mighty spirit of Millet.

"Well, my last crime was a Christmas crime, a cheery, cosy, English middle-class crime; a crime of Charles Dickens. I did it in a good old middle-class house near Putney, a house with a crescent of carriage drive, a house with a stable by the side of it, a house with the name on the two outer gates, a house with a monkey tree. Enough, you know the species. I really think my imitation of Dickens's style was dexterous and literary. It seems almost a pity I repented the same evening."

Flambeau would then proceed to tell the story from the inside; and even from the inside it was odd. Seen from the outside it was perfectly incomprehensible, and it is from the outside that the stranger must study it. From this standpoint the drama may be said to have begun when the front doors of the house with the stable opened on the garden with the monkey tree, and a young girl came out with bread to feed the birds on the afternoon of Boxing Day. She had a pretty face, with brave brown eyes; but her figure was beyond conjecture, for she was so wrapped up in brown furs that it was hard to say which was hair and which was fur. But for the attractive face she might have been a small toddling bear.

The winter afternoon was reddening towards evening, and already a ruby light was rolled over the bloomless beds, filling them, as it were, with the ghosts of the dead roses. On one side of the house stood the stable, on the other an alley or cloister of laurels led to the larger garden behind. The young lady, having scattered bread for the birds (for the fourth or fifth time that day, because the dog ate it), passed unobtrusively down the lane of laurels and into a glimmering plantation of evergreens behind. Here she gave an exclamation of wonder, real or ritual, and looking up at the high garden wall above her, beheld it fantastically bestridden by a somewhat fantastic figure.

"Oh, don't jump, Mr. Crook," she called out in some alarm; "it's much too high."

The individual riding the party wall like an aerial horse was a tall, angular young man, with dark hair sticking up like a hair brush, intelligent and even distinguished lineaments, but a sallow and almost alien complexion. This showed the more plainly because he wore an aggressive red tie, the only part of his costume of which he seemed to take any care. Perhaps it was a symbol. He took no notice of the girl's alarmed adjuration, but leapt like a grasshopper to the ground beside her, where he might very well have broken his legs.

"I think I was meant to be a burglar," he said placidly, "and I have no doubt I should have been if I hadn't happened to be born in that nice house next door. I can't see any harm in it, anyhow."

"How can you say such things!" she remonstrated.

"Well," said the young man, "if you're born on the wrong side of the wall, I can't see that it's wrong to climb over it."

"I never know what you will say or do next," she said.

"I don't often know myself," replied Mr. Crook; "but then I am on the right side of the wall now."

"And which is the right side of the wall?" asked the young lady, smiling.

"Whichever side you are on," said the young man named Crook.

As they went together through the laurels towards the front garden a motor horn sounded thrice, coming nearer and nearer, and a car of splendid speed, great elegance, and a pale green colour swept up to the front doors like a bird and stood throbbing.

"Hullo, hullo!" said the young man with the red tie, "here's somebody born on the right side, anyhow. I didn't know, Miss Adams, that your Santa Claus was so modern as this."

"Oh, that's my godfather, Sir Leopold Fischer. He always comes on Boxing Day."

Then, after an innocent pause, which unconsciously betrayed some lack of enthusiasm, Ruby Adams added:

"He is very kind."

John Crook, journalist, had heard of that eminent City magnate; and it was not his fault if the City magnate had not heard of him; for in certain articles in The Clarion or The New Age Sir Leopold had been dealt with austerely. But he said nothing and grimly watched the unloading of the motor-car, which was rather a long process. A large, neat chauffeur in green got out from the front, and a small, neat manservant in grey got out from the back, and between them they deposited Sir Leopold on the doorstep and began to unpack him, like some very carefully protected parcel. Rugs enough to stock a bazaar, furs of all the beasts of the forest, and scarves of all the colours of the rainbow were unwrapped one by one, till they revealed something resembling the human form; the form of a friendly, but foreign-looking old gentleman, with a grey goat-like beard and a beaming smile, who rubbed his big fur gloves together.

Long before this revelation was complete the two big doors of the porch had opened in the middle, and Colonel Adams (father of the furry young lady) had come out himself to invite his eminent guest inside. He was a tall, sunburnt, and very silent man, who wore a red smoking-cap like a fez, making him look like one of the English Sirdars or Pashas in Egypt. With him was his brother-in-law, lately come from Canada, a big and rather boisterous young gentleman-farmer, with a yellow beard, by name James Blount. With him also was the more insignificant figure of the priest from the neighbouring Roman Church; for the colonel's late wife had been a Catholic, and the children, as is common in such cases, had been trained to follow her. Everything seemed undistinguished about the priest, even down to his name, which was Brown; yet the colonel had always found something companionable about him, and frequently asked him to such family gatherings.

In the large entrance hall of the house there was ample room even for Sir Leopold and the removal of his wraps. Porch and vestibule, indeed, were unduly large in proportion to the house, and formed, as it were, a big room with the front door at one end, and the bottom of the staircase at the other. In front of the large hall fire, over which hung the colonel's sword, the process was completed and the company, including the saturnine Crook, presented to Sir Leopold Fischer. That venerable financier, however, still seemed struggling with portions of his well-lined attire, and at length produced from a very interior tail-coat pocket, a black oval case which he radiantly explained to be his Christmas present for his god-daughter. With an unaffected vain-glory that had something disarming about it he held out the case before them all; it flew open at a touch and half-blinded them. It was just as if a crystal fountain had spurted in their eyes. In a nest of orange velvet lay like three eggs, three white and vivid diamonds that seemed to set the very air on fire all round them. Fischer stood beaming benevolently and drinking deep of the astonishment and ecstasy of the girl, the grim admiration and gruff thanks of the colonel, the wonder of the whole group.

"I'll put 'em back now, my dear," said Fischer, returning the case to the tails of his coat. "I had to be careful of 'em coming down. They're the three great African diamonds called 'The Flying Stars,' because they've been stolen so often. All the big criminals are on the track; but even the rough men about in the streets and hotels could hardly have kept their hands off them. I might have lost them on the road here. It was quite possible."

"Quite natural, I should say," growled the man in the red tie. "I shouldn't blame 'em if they had taken 'em. When they ask for bread, and you don't even give them a stone, I think they might take the stone for themselves."

"I won't have you talking like that," cried the girl, who was in a curious glow. "You've only talked like that since you became a horrid what's-his-name. You know what I mean. What do you call a man who wants to embrace the chimney-sweep?"

"A saint," said Father Brown.

"I think," said Sir Leopold, with a supercilious smile, "that Ruby means a Socialist."

"A radical does not mean a man who lives on radishes," remarked Crook, with some impatience; "and a Conservative does not mean a man who preserves jam. Neither, I assure you, does a Socialist mean a man who desires a social evening with the chimney-sweep. A Socialist means a man who wants all the chimneys swept and all the chimney-sweeps paid for it."

"But who won't allow you," put in the priest in a low voice, "to own your own soot."

Crook looked at him with an eye of interest and even respect. "Does one want to own soot?" he asked.

"One might," answered Brown, with speculation in his eye. "I've heard that gardeners use it. And I once made six children happy at Christmas when the conjuror didn't come, entirely with soot—applied externally."

"Oh, splendid," cried Ruby. "Oh, I wish you'd do it to this company."

The boisterous Canadian, Mr. Blount, was lifting his loud voice in applause, and the astonished financier his (in some considerable deprecation), when a knock sounded at the double front doors. The priest opened them, and they showed again the front garden of evergreens, monkey-tree and all, now gathering gloom against a gorgeous violet sunset. The scene thus framed was so coloured and quaint, like a back scene in a play, that they forgot a moment the insignificant figure standing in the door. He was dusty-looking and in a frayed coat, evidently a common messenger. "Any of you gentlemen Mr. Blount?" he asked, and held forward a letter doubtfully. Mr. Blount started, and stopped in his shout of assent. Ripping up the envelope with evident astonishment he read it; his face clouded a little, and then cleared, and he turned to his brother-in-law and host.

"I'm sick at being such a nuisance, colonel," he said, with the cheery colonial conventions; "but would it upset you if an old acquaintance called on me here to-night on business? In point of fact it's Florian, that famous French acrobat and comic actor; I knew him years ago out West (he was a French-Canadian by birth), and he seems to have business for me, though I hardly guess what."

"Of course, of course," replied the colonel carelessly—"My dear chap, any friend of yours. No doubt he will prove an acquisition."

"He'll black his face, if that's what you mean," cried Blount, laughing. "I don't doubt he'd black everyone else's eyes. I don't care; I'm not refined. I like the jolly old pantomime where a man sits on his top hat."

"Not on mine, please," said Sir Leopold Fischer, with dignity.

"Well, well," observed Crook, airily, "don't let's quarrel. There are lower jokes than sitting on a top hat."

Dislike of the red-tied youth, born of his predatory opinions and evident intimacy with the pretty godchild, led Fischer to say, in his most sarcastic, magisterial manner: "No doubt you have found something much lower than sitting on a top hat. What is it, pray?"

"Letting a top hat sit on you, for instance," said the Socialist.

"Now, now, now," cried the Canadian farmer with his barbarian benevolence, "don't let's spoil a jolly evening. What I say is, let's do something for the company tonight. Not blacking faces or sitting on hats, if you don't like those—but something of the sort. Why couldn't we have a proper old English pantomime—clown, columbine, and so on. I saw one when I left England at twelve years old, and it's blazed in my brain like a bonfire ever since. I came back to the old country only last year, and I find the thing's extinct. Nothing but a lot of snivelling fairy plays. I want a hot poker and a policeman made into sausages, and they give me princesses moralising by moonlight, Blue Birds, or something. Blue Beard's more in my line, and him I like best when he turned into the pantaloon."

"I'm all for making a policeman into sausages," said John Crook. "It's a better definition of Socialism than some recently given. But surely the get-up would be too big a business."

"Not a scrap," cried Blount, quite carried away. "A harlequinade's the quickest thing we can do, for two reasons. First, one can gag to any degree; and, second, all the objects are household things—tables and towel-horses and washing baskets, and things like that."

"That's true," admitted Crook, nodding eagerly and walking about. "But I'm afraid I can't have my policeman's uniform? Haven't killed a policeman lately."

Blount frowned thoughtfully a space, and then smote his thigh. "Yes, we can!" he cried. "I've got Florian's address here, and he knows every costumier in London. I'll phone him to bring a police dress when he comes." And he went bounding away to the telephone.

"Oh, it's glorious, godfather," cried Ruby, almost dancing. "I'll be columbine and you shall be pantaloon."

The millionaire held himself stiff with a sort of heathen solemnity. "I think, my dear," he said, "you must get someone else for pantaloon."

"I will be pantaloon, if you like," said Colonel Adams, taking his cigar out of his mouth, and speaking for the first and last time.

"You ought to have a statue," cried the Canadian, as he came back, radiant, from the telephone. "There, we are all fitted. Mr. Crook shall be clown; he's a journalist and knows all the oldest jokes. I can be harlequin, that only wants long legs and jumping about. My friend Florian 'phones he's bringing the police costume; he's changing on the way. We can act it in this very hall, the audience sitting on those broad stairs opposite, one row above another. These front doors can be the back scene, either open or shut. Shut, you see an English interior. Open, a moonlit garden. It all goes by magic." And snatching a chance piece of billiard chalk from his pocket, he ran it across the hall floor, half-way between the front door and the staircase, to mark the line of the footlights.

How even such a banquet of bosh was got ready in the time remained a riddle. But they went at it with that mixture of recklessness and industry that lives when youth is in a house; and youth was in that house that night, though not all may have isolated the two faces and hearts from which it flamed. As always happens, the invention grew wilder and wilder through the very tameness of the bourgeois conventions from which it had to create. The columbine looked charming in an outstanding skirt that strangely resembled the large lamp-shade in the drawing-room. The clown and pantaloon made themselves white with flour from the cook, and red with rouge from some other domestic, who remained (like all true Christian benefactors) anonymous. The harlequin, already clad in silver paper out of cigar boxes, was, with difficulty, prevented from smashing the old Victorian lustre chandeliers, that he might cover himself with resplendent crystals. In fact he would certainly have done so, had not Ruby unearthed some old pantomime paste jewels she had worn at a fancy dress party as the Queen of Diamonds. Indeed, her uncle, James Blount, was getting almost out of hand in his excitement; he was like a schoolboy. He put a paper donkey's head unexpectedly on Father Brown, who bore it patiently, and even found some private manner of moving his ears. He even essayed to put the paper donkey's tail to the coat-tails of Sir Leopold Fischer. This, however, was frowned down. "Uncle is too absurd," cried Ruby to Crook, round whose shoulders she had seriously placed a string of sausages. "Why is he so wild?"

"He is harlequin to your columbine," said Crook. "I am only the clown who makes the old jokes."

"I wish you were the harlequin," she said, and left the string of sausages swinging.

Father Brown, though he knew every detail done behind the scenes, and had even evoked applause by his transformation of a pillow into a pantomime baby, went round to the front and sat among the audience with all the solemn expectation of a child at his first matinee. The spectators were few, relations, one or two local friends, and the servants; Sir Leopold sat in the front seat, his full and still fur-collared figure largely obscuring the view of the little cleric behind him; but it has never been settled by artistic authorities whether the cleric lost much. The panto-mime was utterly chaotic, yet not contemptible; there ran through it a rage of improvisation which came chiefly from Crook the clown. Commonly he was a clev-er man, and he was inspired tonight with a wild omniscience, a folly wiser than the world, that which comes to a young man who has seen for an instant a particular expression on a particular face. He was supposed to be the clown, but he was really almost everything else, the author (so far as there was an author), the prompter, the scene-painter, the scene-shifter, and, above all, the orchestra. At abrupt intervals in the outrageous performance he would hurl himself in full costume at the piano and bang out some popular music equally absurd and appropriate.

The climax of this, as of all else, was the moment when the two front doors at the back of the scene flew open, showing the lovely moonlit garden, but showing more prominently the famous professional guest; the great Florian, dressed up as a policeman. The clown at the piano played the constabulary chorus in the "Pirates of Penzance," but it was drowned in the deafening applause, for every gesture of the great comic actor was an admirable though restrained version of the carriage and manner of the police. The harlequin leapt upon him and hit him over the helmet; the pianist playing "Where did you get that hat?" he faced about in admirably simulated astonishment, and then the leaping harlequin hit him again (the pianist suggesting a few bars of "Then we had another one"). Then the harlequin rushed right into the arms of the policeman and fell on top of him, amid a roar of applause. Then it was that the strange actor gave that celebrated imitation of a dead man, of which the fame still lingers round Putney. It was almost impossible to believe that a living person could appear so limp.

The athletic harlequin swung him about like a sack or twisted or tossed him like an Indian club; all the time to the most maddeningly ludicrous tunes from the piano. When the harlequin heaved the comic constable heavily off the floor the clown played "I arise from dreams of thee." When he shuffled him across his back, "With my bundle on my shoulder," and when the harlequin finally let fall the po-liceman with a most convincing thud, the lunatic at the instrument struck into a jingling measure with some words which are still believed to have been, "I sent a letter to my love and on the way I dropped it."

At about this limit of mental anarchy Father Brown's view was obscured alto-gether; for the City magnate in front of him rose to his full height and thrust his hands savagely into all his pockets. Then he sat down nervously, still fumbling, and then stood up again. For an instant it seemed seriously likely that he would stride across the footlights; then he turned a glare at the clown playing the piano; and then he burst in silence out of the room.

The priest had only watched for a few more minutes the absurd but not inelegant dance of the amateur harlequin over his splendidly unconscious foe. With real though rude art, the harlequin danced slowly backwards out of the door into the garden, which was full of moonlight and stillness. The vamped dress of silver paper and paste, which had been too glaring in the footlights, looked more and more magical and silvery as it danced away under a brilliant moon. The audience was closing in with a cataract of applause, when Brown felt his arm abruptly touched, and he was asked in a whisper to come into the colonel's study.

He followed his summoner with increasing doubt, which was not dispelled by a solemn comicality in the scene of the study. There sat Colonel Adams, still unaffectedly dressed as a pantaloon, with the knobbed whalebone nodding above his brow, but with his poor old eyes sad enough to have sobered a Saturnalia. Sir Leopold Fischer was leaning against the mantelpiece and heaving with all the importance of panic.

"This is a very painful matter, Father Brown," said Adams. "The truth is, those diamonds we all saw this afternoon seem to have vanished from my friend's tailcoat pocket. And as you—"

"As I," supplemented Father Brown, with a broad grin, "was sitting just behind him—"

"Nothing of the sort shall be suggested," said Colonel Adams, with a firm look at Fischer, which rather implied that some such thing had been suggested. "I only ask you to give me the assistance that any gentleman might give."

"Which is turning out his pockets," said Father Brown, and proceeded to do so, displaying seven and sixpence, a return ticket, a small silver crucifix, a small breviary, and a stick of chocolate.

The colonel looked at him long, and then said, "Do you know, I should like to see the inside of your head more than the inside of your pockets. My daughter is one of your people, I know; well, she has lately—" and he stopped.

"She has lately," cried out old Fischer, "opened her father's house to a cutthroat Socialist, who says openly he would steal anything from a richer man. This is the end of it. Here is the richer man—and none the richer."

"If you want the inside of my head you can have it," said Brown rather wearily. "What it's worth you can say afterwards. But the first thing I find in that disused pocket is this: that men who mean to steal diamonds don't talk Socialism. They are more likely," he added demurely, "to denounce it."

Both the others shifted sharply and the priest went on:

"You see, we know these people, more or less. That Socialist would no more steal a diamond than a Pyramid. We ought to look at once to the one man we don't know. The fellow acting the policeman—Florian. Where is he exactly at this minute, I wonder."

The pantaloon sprang erect and strode out of the room. An interlude ensued, during which the millionaire stared at the priest, and the priest at his breviary; then the pantaloon returned and said, with staccato gravity, "The policeman is still lying on the stage. The curtain has gone up and down six times; he is still lying there."

Father Brown dropped his book and stood staring with a look of blank mental ruin. Very slowly a light began to creep in his grey eyes, and then he made the scarcely obvious answer.

"Please forgive me, colonel, but when did your wife die?"

"Wife!" replied the staring soldier, "she died this year two months. Her brother James arrived just a week too late to see her."

The little priest bounded like a rabbit shot. "Come on!" he cried in quite unusual excitement. "Come on! We've got to go and look at that policeman!"

They rushed on to the now curtained stage, breaking rudely past the columbine and clown (who seemed whispering quite contentedly), and Father Brown bent over the prostrate comic policeman.

"Chloroform," he said as he rose; "I only guessed it just now."

There was a startled stillness, and then the colonel said slowly, "Please say seriously what all this means."

Father Brown suddenly shouted with laughter, then stopped, and only struggled with it for instants during the rest of his speech. "Gentlemen," he gasped, "there's not much time to talk. I must run after the criminal. But this great French actor who played the policeman—this clever corpse the harlequin waltzed with and dandled and threw about—he was—" His voice again failed him, and he turned his back to run.

"He was?" called Fischer inquiringly.

"A real policeman," said Father Brown, and ran away into the dark.

There were hollows and bowers at the extreme end of that leafy garden, in which the laurels and other immortal shrubs showed against sapphire sky and silver moon, even in that midwinter, warm colours as of the south. The green gaiety of the waving laurels, the rich purple indigo of the night, the moon like a monstrous crystal, make an almost irresponsible romantic picture; and among the top branches of the garden trees a strange figure is climbing, who looks not so much romantic as impossible. He sparkles from head to heel, as if clad in ten million moons; the real moon catches him at every movement and sets a new inch of him on fire. But he swings, flashing and successful, from the short tree in this garden to the tall, rambling tree in the other, and only stops there because a shade has slid under the smaller tree and has unmistakably called up to him.

"Well, Flambeau," says the voice, "you really look like a Flying Star; but that always means a Falling Star at last."

The silver, sparkling figure above seems to lean forward in the laurels and, confident of escape, listens to the little figure below.

"You never did anything better, Flambeau. It was clever to come from Canada (with a Paris ticket, I suppose) just a week after Mrs. Adams died, when no one was in a mood to ask questions. It was cleverer to have marked down the Flying Stars and the very day of Fischer's coming. But there's no cleverness, but mere genius, in what followed. Stealing the stones, I suppose, was nothing to you. You could have done it by sleight of hand in a hundred other ways besides that pretence of putting a paper donkey's tail to Fischer's coat. But in the rest you eclipsed yourself."

The silvery figure among the green leaves seems to linger as if hypnotised, though his escape is easy behind him; he is staring at the man below.

"Oh, yes," says the man below, "I know all about it. I know you not only forced the pantomime, but put it to a double use. You were going to steal the stones quietly; news came by an accomplice that you were already suspected, and a capable police officer was coming to rout you up that very night. A common thief would have been thankful for the warning and fled; but you are a poet. You already had the clever notion of hiding the jewels in a blaze of false stage jewellery. Now, you saw that if the dress were a harlequin's the appearance of a policeman would be quite in keeping. The worthy officer started from Putney police station to find you, and walked into the queerest trap ever set in this world. When the front door opened he walked straight on to the stage of a Christmas pantomime, where he could be kicked, clubbed, stunned and drugged by the dancing harlequin, amid roars of laughter from all the most respectable people in Putney. Oh, you will never do anything better. And now, by the way, you might give me back those diamonds."

The green branch on which the glittering figure swung, rustled as if in astonishment; but the voice went on:

"I want you to give them back, Flambeau, and I want you to give up this life. There is still youth and honour and humour in you; don't fancy they will last in that trade. Men may keep a sort of level of good, but no man has ever been able to keep on one level of evil. That road goes down and down. The kind man drinks and turns cruel; the frank man kills and lies about it. Many a man I've known started like you to be an honest outlaw, a merry robber of the rich, and ended stamped into slime. Maurice Blum started out as an anarchist of principle, a father of the poor; he ended a greasy spy and tale-bearer that both sides used and despised. Harry Burke started his free money movement sincerely enough; now he's sponging on a half-starved sister for endless brandies and sodas. Lord Amber went into wild society in a sort of chivalry; now he's paying blackmail to the lowest vultures in London. Captain Barillon was the great gentleman-apache before your time; he died in a madhouse, screaming with fear of the "narks" and receivers that had betrayed him and hunted him down. I know the woods look very free behind you, Flambeau; I know that in a flash you could melt into them like a monkey. But some day you will be an old grey monkey, Flambeau. You will sit up in your free forest cold at heart and close to death, and the tree-tops will be very bare."

Everything continued still, as if the small man below held the other in the tree in some long invisible leash; and he went on:

"Your downward steps have begun. You used to boast of doing nothing mean, but you are doing something mean tonight. You are leaving suspicion on an honest boy with a good deal against him already; you are separating him from the woman he loves and who loves him. But you will do meaner things than that before you die."

Three flashing diamonds fell from the tree to the turf. The small man stooped to pick them up, and when he looked up again the green cage of the tree was emptied of its silver bird.

The restoration of the gems (accidentally picked up by Father Brown, of all people) ended the evening in uproarious triumph; and Sir Leopold, in his height of good humour, even told the priest that though he himself had broader views, he could respect those whose creed required them to be cloistered and ignorant of this world.

The Invisible Man

In the cool blue twilight of two steep streets in Camden Town, the shop at the corner, a confectioner's, glowed like the butt of a cigar. One should rather say, perhaps, like the butt of a firework, for the light was of many colours and some complexity, broken up by many mirrors and dancing on many gilt and gaily-coloured cakes and sweetmeats. Against this one fiery glass were glued the noses of many gutter-snipes, for the chocolates were all wrapped in those red and gold and green metallic colours which are almost better than chocolate itself; and the huge white wedding-cake in the window was somehow at once remote and satisfying, just as if the whole North Pole were good to eat. Such rainbow provocations could naturally collect the youth of the neighbourhood up to the ages of ten or twelve. But this corner was also attractive to youth at a later stage; and a young man, not less than twenty-four, was staring into the same shop window. To him, also, the shop was of fiery charm, but this attraction was not wholly to be explained by chocolates; which, however, he was far from despising.

He was a tall, burly, red-haired young man, with a resolute face but a listless manner. He carried under his arm a flat, grey portfolio of black-and-white sketches, which he had sold with more or less success to publishers ever since his uncle (who was an admiral) had disinherited him for Socialism, because of a lecture which he had delivered against that economic theory. His name was John Turnbull Angus.

Entering at last, he walked through the confectioner's shop to the back room, which was a sort of pastry-cook restaurant, merely raising his hat to the young lady who was serving there. She was a dark, elegant, alert girl in black, with a high colour and very quick, dark eyes; and after the ordinary interval she followed him into the inner room to take his order.

His order was evidently a usual one. "I want, please," he said with precision, "one halfpenny bun and a small cup of black coffee." An instant before the girl could turn away he added, "Also, I want you to marry me."

The young lady of the shop stiffened suddenly and said, "Those are jokes I don't allow."

The red-haired young man lifted grey eyes of an unexpected gravity.

"Really and truly," he said, "it's as serious—as serious as the halfpenny bun. It is expensive, like the bun; one pays for it. It is indigestible, like the bun. It hurts."

The dark young lady had never taken her dark eyes off him, but seemed to be studying him with almost tragic exactitude. At the end of her scrutiny she had something like the shadow of a smile, and she sat down in a chair.

"Don't you think," observed Angus, absently, "that it's rather cruel to eat these halfpenny buns? They might grow up into penny buns. I shall give up these brutal sports when we are married."

The dark young lady rose from her chair and walked to the window, evidently in a state of strong but not unsympathetic cogitation. When at last she swung round again with an air of resolution she was bewildered to observe that the young man was carefully laying out on the table various objects from the shop-window. They included a pyramid of highly coloured sweets, several plates of sandwiches, and the two decanters containing that mysterious port and sherry which are peculiar to pastry-cooks. In the middle of this neat arrangement he had carefully let down the enormous load of white sugared cake which had been the huge ornament of the window.

"What on earth are you doing?" she asked.

"Duty, my dear Laura," he began.

"Oh, for the Lord's sake, stop a minute," she cried, "and don't talk to me in that way. I mean, what is all that?"

"A ceremonial meal, Miss Hope."

"And what is that?" she asked impatiently, pointing to the mountain of sugar.

"The wedding-cake, Mrs. Angus," he said.

The girl marched to that article, removed it with some clatter, and put it back in the shop window; she then returned, and, putting her elegant elbows on the table, regarded the young man not unfavourably but with considerable exasperation.

"You don't give me any time to think," she said.

"I'm not such a fool," he answered; "that's my Christian humility."

She was still looking at him; but she had grown considerably graver behind the smile.

"Mr. Angus," she said steadily, "before there is a minute more of this nonsense I must tell you something about myself as shortly as I can."

"Delighted," replied Angus gravely. "You might tell me something about myself, too, while you are about it."

"Oh, do hold your tongue and listen," she said. "It's nothing that I'm ashamed of, and it isn't even anything that I'm specially sorry about. But what would you say if there were something that is no business of mine and yet is my nightmare?"

"In that case," said the man seriously, "I should suggest that you bring back the cake."

"Well, you must listen to the story first," said Laura, persistently. "To begin with, I must tell you that my father owned the inn called the 'Red Fish' at Ludbury, and I used to serve people in the bar."

"I have often wondered," he said, "why there was a kind of a Christian air about this one confectioner's shop."

"Ludbury is a sleepy, grassy little hole in the Eastern Counties, and the only kind of people who ever came to the 'Red Fish' were occasional commercial travellers, and for the rest, the most awful people you can see, only you've never seen them. I mean little, loungy men, who had just enough to live on and had nothing to do but lean about in bar-rooms and bet on horses, in bad clothes that were just too good for them. Even these wretched young rotters were not very common at our house; but there were two of them that were a lot too common—common in every sort of way. They both lived on money of their own, and were wearisomely idle and over-dressed. But yet I was a bit sorry for them, because I half believe they slunk into our little empty bar because each of them had a slight deformity; the sort of thing that some yokels laugh at. It wasn't exactly a deformity either; it was more an oddity. One of them was a surprisingly small man, something like a dwarf, or at least like a jockey. He was not at all jockeyish to look at, though; he had a round black head and a well-trimmed black beard, bright eyes like a bird's; he jingled money in his pockets; he jangled a great gold watch chain; and he never turned up except dressed just too much like a gentleman to be one. He was no fool though, though a futile idler; he was curiously clever at all kinds of things that couldn't be the slightest use; a sort of impromptu conjuring; making fifteen matches set fire to each other like a regular firework; or cutting a banana or some such thing into a dancing doll. His name was Isidore Smythe; and I can see him still, with his little dark face, just coming up to the counter, making a jumping kangaroo out of five cigars.

"The other fellow was more silent and more ordinary; but somehow he alarmed me much more than poor little Smythe. He was very tall and slight, and light-haired; his nose had a high bridge, and he might almost have been handsome in a spectral sort of way; but he had one of the most appalling squints I have ever seen or heard of. When he looked straight at you, you didn't know where you were yourself, let alone what he was looking at. I fancy this sort of disfigurement embittered the poor chap a little; for while Smythe was ready to show off his monkey tricks anywhere, James Welkin (that was the squinting man's name) never did anything except soak in our bar parlour, and go for great walks by himself in the flat, grey country all round. All the same, I think Smythe, too, was a little sensitive about being so small, though he carried it off more smartly. And so it was that I was really puzzled, as well as startled, and very sorry, when they both offered to marry me in the same week.

"Well, I did what I've since thought was perhaps a silly thing. But, after all, these freaks were my friends in a way; and I had a horror of their thinking I refused them for the real reason, which was that they were so impossibly ugly. So I made up some gas of another sort, about never meaning to marry anyone who hadn't carved his way in the world. I said it was a point of principle with me not to live on money that was just inherited like theirs. Two days after I had talked in this well-meaning sort of way, the whole trouble began. The first thing I heard was that both of them had gone off to seek their fortunes, as if they were in some silly fairy tale.

"Well, I've never seen either of them from that day to this. But I've had two letters from the little man called Smythe, and really they were rather exciting."

"Ever heard of the other man?" asked Angus.

"No, he never wrote," said the girl, after an instant's hesitation. "Smythe's first letter was simply to say that he had started out walking with Welkin to London; but Welkin was such a good walker that the little man dropped out of it, and took a rest by the roadside. He happened to be picked up by some travelling show, and, partly because he was nearly a dwarf, and partly because he was really a clever little wretch, he got on quite well in the show business, and was soon sent up to the Aquarium, to do some tricks that I forget. That was his first letter. His second was much more of a startler, and I only got it last week."

The man called Angus emptied his coffee-cup and regarded her with mild and patient eyes. Her own mouth took a slight twist of laughter as she resumed, "I suppose you've seen on the hoardings all about this 'Smythe's Silent Service'? Or you must be the only person that hasn't. Oh, I don't know much about it, it's some clockwork invention for doing all the housework by machinery. You know the sort of thing: 'Press a Button—A Butler who Never Drinks.' 'Turn a Handle—Ten Housemaids who Never Flirt.' You must have seen the advertisements. Well, whatever these machines are, they are making pots of money; and they are making it all for that little imp whom I knew down in Ludbury. I can't help feeling pleased the poor little chap has fallen on his feet; but the plain fact is, I'm in terror of his turning up any minute and telling me he's carved his way in the world—as he certainly has."

"And the other man?" repeated Angus with a sort of obstinate quietude.

Laura Hope got to her feet suddenly. "My friend," she said, "I think you are a witch. Yes, you are quite right. I have not seen a line of the other man's writing; and I have no more notion than the dead of what or where he is. But it is of him that I am frightened. It is he who is all about my path. It is he who has half driven me mad. Indeed, I think he has driven me mad; for I have felt him where he could not have been, and I have heard his voice when he could not have spoken."

"Well, my dear," said the young man, cheerfully, "if he were Satan himself, he is done for now you have told somebody. One goes mad all alone, old girl. But when was it you fancied you felt and heard our squinting friend?"

"I heard James Welkin laugh as plainly as I hear you speak," said the girl, steadily. "There was nobody there, for I stood just outside the shop at the corner, and could see down both streets at once. I had forgotten how he laughed, though his laugh was as odd as his squint. I had not thought of him for nearly a year. But it's a solemn truth that a few seconds later the first letter came from his rival."

"Did you ever make the spectre speak or squeak, or anything?" asked Angus, with some interest.

Laura suddenly shuddered, and then said, with an unshaken voice, "Yes. Just when I had finished reading the second letter from Isidore Smythe announcing his success. Just then, I heard Welkin say, 'He shan't have you, though.' It was quite plain, as if he were in the room. It is awful, I think I must be mad."

"If you really were mad," said the young man, "you would think you must be sane. But certainly there seems to me to be something a little rum about this unseen gentleman. Two heads are better than one—I spare you allusions to any other organs and really, if you would allow me, as a sturdy, practical man, to bring back the wedding-cake out of the window—"

Even as he spoke, there was a sort of steely shriek in the street outside, and a small motor, driven at devilish speed, shot up to the door of the shop and stuck there. In the same flash of time a small man in a shiny top hat stood stamping in the outer room.

Angus, who had hitherto maintained hilarious ease from motives of mental hygiene, revealed the strain of his soul by striding abruptly out of the inner room and confronting the new-comer. A glance at him was quite sufficient to confirm the savage guesswork of a man in love. This very dapper but dwarfish figure, with the spike of black beard carried insolently forward, the clever unrestful eyes, the neat but very nervous fingers, could be none other than the man just described to him: Isidore Smythe, who made dolls out of banana skins and match-boxes; Isidore Smythe, who made millions out of undrinking butlers and unflirting housemaids of metal. For a moment the two men, instinctively understanding each other's air of possession, looked at each other with that curious cold generosity which is the soul of rivalry.

Mr. Smythe, however, made no allusion to the ultimate ground of their antagonism, but said simply and explosively, "Has Miss Hope seen that thing on the window?"

"On the window?" repeated the staring Angus.

"There's no time to explain other things," said the small millionaire shortly. "There's some tomfoolery going on here that has to be investigated."

He pointed his polished walking-stick at the window, recently depleted by the bridal preparations of Mr. Angus; and that gentleman was astonished to see along the front of the glass a long strip of paper pasted, which had certainly not been on the window when he looked through it some time before. Following the energetic Smythe outside into the street, he found that some yard and a half of stamp paper had been carefully gummed along the glass outside, and on this was written in straggly characters, "If you marry Smythe, he will die."

"Laura," said Angus, putting his big red head into the shop, "you're not mad."

"It's the writing of that fellow Welkin," said Smythe gruffly. "I haven't seen him for years, but he's always bothering me. Five times in the last fortnight he's had threatening letters left at my flat, and I can't even find out who leaves them, let alone if it is Welkin himself. The porter of the flats swears that no suspicious characters have been seen, and here he has pasted up a sort of dado on a public shop window, while the people in the shop—"

"Quite so," said Angus modestly, "while the people in the shop were having tea. Well, sir, I can assure you I appreciate your common sense in dealing so directly with the matter. We can talk about other things afterwards. The fellow cannot be very far off yet, for I swear there was no paper there when I went last to the window, ten or fifteen minutes ago. On the other hand, he's too far off to be chased, as we don't even know the direction. If you'll take my advice, Mr. Smythe, you'll put this at once in the hands of some energetic inquiry man, private rather than public. I know an extremely clever fellow, who has set up in business five minutes from here in your car. His name's Flambeau, and though his youth was a bit stormy, he's a strictly honest man now, and his brains are worth money. He lives in Lucknow Mansions, Hampstead."

"That is odd," said the little man, arching his black eyebrows. "I live, myself, in Himylaya Mansions, round the corner. Perhaps you might care to come with me; I can go to my rooms and sort out these queer Welkin documents, while you run round and get your friend the detective."

"You are very good," said Angus politely. "Well, the sooner we act the better."

Both men, with a queer kind of impromptu fairness, took the same sort of formal farewell of the lady, and both jumped into the brisk little car. As Smythe took the handles and they turned the great corner of the street, Angus was amused to see a gigantesque poster of "Smythe's Silent Service," with a picture of a huge headless iron doll, carrying a saucepan with the legend, "A Cook Who is Never Cross."

"I use them in my own flat," said the little black-bearded man, laughing, "partly for advertisements, and partly for real convenience. Honestly, and all above board, those big clockwork dolls of mine do bring your coals or claret or a timetable quicker than any live servants I've ever known, if you know which knob to press. But I'll never deny, between ourselves, that such servants have their disadvantages, too."

"Indeed?" said Angus; "is there something they can't do?"

"Yes," replied Smythe coolly; "they can't tell me who left those threatening letters at my flat."

The man's motor was small and swift like himself; in fact, like his domestic service, it was of his own invention. If he was an advertising quack, he was one who believed in his own wares. The sense of something tiny and flying was accentuated as they swept up long white curves of road in the dead but open daylight of evening. Soon the white curves came sharper and dizzier; they were upon ascending spirals, as they say in the modern religions. For, indeed, they were cresting a corner of London which is almost as precipitous as Edinburgh, if not quite so picturesque. Terrace rose above terrace, and the special tower of flats they sought, rose above them all to almost Egyptian height, gilt by the level sunset. The change, as they turned the corner and entered the crescent known as Himylaya Mansions, was as abrupt as the opening of a window; for they found that pile of flats sitting above London as above a green sea of slate. Opposite to the mansions, on the other side of the gravel crescent, was a bushy enclosure more like a steep hedge or dyke than a garden, and some way below that ran a strip of artificial water, a sort of canal, like the moat of that embowered fortress. As the car swept round the crescent it passed, at one corner, the stray stall of a man selling chestnuts; and right away at the other end of the curve, Angus could see a dim blue policeman walking slowly. These were the only human shapes in that high suburban solitude; but he had an irrational sense that they expressed the speechless poetry of London. He felt as if they were figures in a story.

The little car shot up to the right house like a bullet, and shot out its owner like a bomb shell. He was immediately inquiring of a tall commissionaire in shining braid, and a short porter in shirt sleeves, whether anybody or anything had been seeking his apartments. He was assured that nobody and nothing had passed these officials since his last inquiries; whereupon he and the slightly bewildered Angus were shot up in the lift like a rocket, till they reached the top floor.

"Just come in for a minute," said the breathless Smythe. "I want to show you those Welkin letters. Then you might run round the corner and fetch your friend." He pressed a button concealed in the wall, and the door opened of itself.

It opened on a long, commodious ante-room, of which the only arresting features, ordinarily speaking, were the rows of tall half-human mechanical figures that stood up on both sides like tailors' dummies. Like tailors' dummies they were headless; and like tailors' dummies they had a handsome unnecessary humpiness in the shoulders, and a pigeon-breasted protuberance of chest; but barring this, they were not much more like a human figure than any automatic machine at a station that is about the human height. They had two great hooks like arms, for carrying trays; and they were painted pea-green, or vermilion, or black for convenience of distinction; in every other way they were only automatic machines and nobody would have looked twice at them. On this occasion, at least, nobody did. For between the two rows of these domestic dummies lay something more interesting than most of the mechanics of the world. It was a white, tattered scrap of paper scrawled with red ink; and the agile inventor had snatched it up almost as soon as the door flew open. He handed it to Angus without a word. The red ink on it actually was not dry, and the message ran, "If you have been to see her today, I shall kill you."

There was a short silence, and then Isidore Smythe said quietly, "Would you like a little whiskey? I rather feel as if I should."

"Thank you; I should like a little Flambeau," said Angus, gloomily. "This business seems to me to be getting rather grave. I'm going round at once to fetch him."

"Right you are," said the other, with admirable cheerfulness. "Bring him round here as quick as you can."

But as Angus closed the front door behind him he saw Smythe push back a button, and one of the clockwork images glided from its place and slid along a groove in the floor carrying a tray with syphon and decanter. There did seem something a trifle weird about leaving the little man alone among those dead servants, who were coming to life as the door closed.

Six steps down from Smythe's landing the man in shirt sleeves was doing something with a pail. Angus stopped to extract a promise, fortified with a prospective bribe, that he would remain in that place until the return with the detective, and would keep count of any kind of stranger coming up those stairs. Dashing down to the front hall he then laid similar charges of vigilance on the commissionaire at the front door, from whom he learned the simplifying circumstances that there was no back door. Not content with this, he captured the floating policeman and induced him to stand opposite the entrance and watch it; and finally paused an instant for a pennyworth of chestnuts, and an inquiry as to the probable length of the merchant's stay in the neighbourhood.

The chestnut seller, turning up the collar of his coat, told him he should probably be moving shortly, as he thought it was going to snow. Indeed, the evening was growing grey and bitter, but Angus, with all his eloquence, proceeded to nail the chestnut man to his post.

"Keep yourself warm on your own chestnuts," he said earnestly. "Eat up your whole stock; I'll make it worth your while. I'll give you a sovereign if you'll wait here till I come back, and then tell me whether any man, woman, or child has gone into that house where the commissionaire is standing."

He then walked away smartly, with a last look at the besieged tower.

"I've made a ring round that room, anyhow," he said. "They can't all four of them be Mr. Welkin's accomplices."

Lucknow Mansions were, so to speak, on a lower platform of that hill of houses, of which Himylaya Mansions might be called the peak. Mr. Flambeau's semi-official flat was on the ground floor, and presented in every way a marked contrast to the American machinery and cold hotel-like luxury of the flat of the Silent Service. Flambeau, who was a friend of Angus, received him in a rococo artistic den behind his office, of which the ornaments were sabres, harquebuses, Eastern curiosities, flasks of Italian wine, savage cooking-pots, a plumy Persian cat, and a small dusty-looking Roman Catholic priest, who looked particularly out of place.

"This is my friend Father Brown," said Flambeau. "I've often wanted you to meet him. Splendid weather, this; a little cold for Southerners like me."

"Yes, I think it will keep clear," said Angus, sitting down on a violet-striped Eastern ottoman.

"No," said the priest quietly, "it has begun to snow."

And, indeed, as he spoke, the first few flakes, foreseen by the man of chestnuts, began to drift across the darkening windowpane.

"Well," said Angus heavily. "I'm afraid I've come on business, and rather jumpy business at that. The fact is, Flambeau, within a stone's throw of your house is a fellow who badly wants your help; he's perpetually being haunted and threatened by an invisible enemy—a scoundrel whom nobody has even seen." As Angus proceeded to tell the whole tale of Smythe and Welkin, beginning with Laura's story, and going on with his own, the supernatural laugh at the corner of two empty streets, the strange distinct words spoken in an empty room, Flambeau grew more and more vividly concerned, and the little priest seemed to be left out of it, like a piece of furniture. When it came to the scribbled stamp-paper pasted on the window, Flambeau rose, seeming to fill the room with his huge shoulders.

"If you don't mind," he said, "I think you had better tell me the rest on the nearest road to this man's house. It strikes me, somehow, that there is no time to be lost."

"Delighted," said Angus, rising also, "though he's safe enough for the present, for I've set four men to watch the only hole to his burrow."

They turned out into the street, the small priest trundling after them with the docility of a small dog. He merely said, in a cheerful way, like one making conversation, "How quick the snow gets thick on the ground."

As they threaded the steep side streets already powdered with silver, Angus finished his story; and by the time they reached the crescent with the towering flats, he had leisure to turn his attention to the four sentinels. The chestnut seller, both before and after receiving a sovereign, swore stubbornly that he had watched the door and seen no visitor enter. The policeman was even more emphatic. He said he had had experience of crooks of all kinds, in top hats and in rags; he wasn't so green as to expect suspicious characters to look suspicious; he looked out for anybody, and, so help him, there had been nobody. And when all three men gathered round the gilded commissionaire, who still stood smiling astride of the porch, the verdict was more final still.

"I've got a right to ask any man, duke or dustman, what he wants in these flats," said the genial and gold-laced giant, "and I'll swear there's been nobody to ask since this gentleman went away."

The unimportant Father Brown, who stood back, looking modestly at the pavement, here ventured to say meekly, "Has nobody been up and down stairs, then, since the snow began to fall? It began while we were all round at Flambeau's."

"Nobody's been in here, sir, you can take it from me," said the official, with beaming authority.

"Then I wonder what that is?" said the priest, and stared at the ground blankly like a fish.

The others all looked down also; and Flambeau used a fierce exclamation and a French gesture. For it was unquestionably true that down the middle of the entrance guarded by the man in gold lace, actually between the arrogant, stretched legs of that colossus, ran a stringy pattern of grey footprints stamped upon the white snow.

"God!" cried Angus involuntarily, "the Invisible Man!"

Without another word he turned and dashed up the stairs, with Flambeau following; but Father Brown still stood looking about him in the snow-clad street as if he had lost interest in his query.

Flambeau was plainly in a mood to break down the door with his big shoulders; but the Scotchman, with more reason, if less intuition, fumbled about on the frame of the door till he found the invisible button; and the door swung slowly open.

It showed substantially the same serried interior; the hall had grown darker, though it was still struck here and there with the last crimson shafts of sunset, and one or two of the headless machines had been moved from their places for this or that purpose, and stood here and there about the twilit place. The green and red of their coats were all darkened in the dusk; and their likeness to human shapes slightly increased by their very shapelessness. But in the middle of them all, exactly where the paper with the red ink had lain, there lay something that looked like red ink spilt out of its bottle. But it was not red ink.

With a French combination of reason and violence Flambeau simply said "Murder!" and, plunging into the flat, had explored, every corner and cupboard of it in five minutes. But if he expected to find a corpse he found none. Isidore Smythe was not in the place, either dead or alive. After the most tearing search the two men met each other in the outer hall, with streaming faces and staring eyes. "My friend," said Flambeau, talking French in his excitement, "not only is your murderer invisible, but he makes invisible also the murdered man."

Angus looked round at the dim room full of dummies, and in some Celtic corner of his Scotch soul a shudder started. One of the life-size dolls stood immediately overshadowing the blood stain, summoned, perhaps, by the slain man an instant before he fell. One of the high-shouldered hooks that served the thing for arms, was a little lifted, and Angus had suddenly the horrid fancy that poor Smythe's own iron child had struck him down. Matter had rebelled, and these machines had killed their master. But even so, what had they done with him?

"Eaten him?" said the nightmare at his ear; and he sickened for an instant at the idea of rent, human remains absorbed and crushed into all that acephalous clockwork.

He recovered his mental health by an emphatic effort, and said to Flambeau, "Well, there it is. The poor fellow has evaporated like a cloud and left a red streak on the floor. The tale does not belong to this world."

"There is only one thing to be done," said Flambeau, "whether it belongs to this world or the other. I must go down and talk to my friend."

They descended, passing the man with the pail, who again asseverated that he had let no intruder pass, down to the commissionaire and the hovering chestnut man, who rigidly reasserted their own watchfulness. But when Angus looked round for his fourth confirmation he could not see it, and called out with some nervousness, "Where is the policeman?"

"I beg your pardon," said Father Brown; "that is my fault. I just sent him down the road to investigate something—that I just thought worth investigating."

"Well, we want him back pretty soon," said Angus abruptly, "for the wretched man upstairs has not only been murdered, but wiped out."

"How?" asked the priest.

"Father," said Flambeau, after a pause, "upon my soul I believe it is more in your department than mine. No friend or foe has entered the house, but Smythe is gone, as if stolen by the fairies. If that is not supernatural, I—"

As he spoke they were all checked by an unusual sight; the big blue policeman came round the corner of the crescent, running. He came straight up to Brown.

"You're right, sir," he panted, "they've just found poor Mr. Smythe's body in the canal down below."

Angus put his hand wildly to his head. "Did he run down and drown himself?" he asked.

"He never came down, I'll swear," said the constable, "and he wasn't drowned either, for he died of a great stab over the heart."

"And yet you saw no one enter?" said Flambeau in a grave voice.

"Let us walk down the road a little," said the priest.

As they reached the other end of the crescent he observed abruptly, "Stupid of me! I forgot to ask the policeman something. I wonder if they found a light brown sack."

"Why a light brown sack?" asked Angus, astonished.

"Because if it was any other coloured sack, the case must begin over again," said Father Brown; "but if it was a light brown sack, why, the case is finished."

"I am pleased to hear it," said Angus with hearty irony. "It hasn't begun, so far as I am concerned."

"You must tell us all about it," said Flambeau with a strange heavy simplicity, like a child.

Unconsciously they were walking with quickening steps down the long sweep of road on the other side of the high crescent, Father Brown leading briskly, though in silence. At last he said with an almost touching vagueness, "Well, I'm afraid you'll think it so prosy. We always begin at the abstract end of things, and you can't begin this story anywhere else.

"Have you ever noticed this—that people never answer what you say? They answer what you mean—or what they think you mean. Suppose one lady says to another in a country house, 'Is anybody staying with you?' the lady doesn't answer 'Yes; the butler, the three footmen, the parlourmaid, and so on,' though the parlourmaid may be in the room, or the butler behind her chair. She says 'There is nobody staying with us,' meaning nobody of the sort you mean. But suppose a doctor inquiring into an epidemic asks, 'Who is staying in the house?' then the lady will remember the butler, the parlourmaid, and the rest. All language is used like that; you never get a question answered literally, even when you get it answered truly. When those four quite honest men said that no man had gone into the Mansions, they did not really mean that no man had gone into them. They meant no man whom they could suspect of being your man. A man did go into the house, and did come out of it, but they never noticed him."

"An invisible man?" inquired Angus, raising his red eyebrows. "A mentally invisible man," said Father Brown.

A minute or two after he resumed in the same unassuming voice, like a man thinking his way. "Of course you can't think of such a man, until you do think of him. That's where his cleverness comes in. But I came to think of him through two or three little things in the tale Mr. Angus told us. First, there was the fact that this Welkin went for long walks. And then there was the vast lot of stamp paper on the window. And then, most of all, there were the two things the young lady said—things that couldn't be true. Don't get annoyed," he added hastily, noting a sudden movement of the Scotchman's head; "she thought they were true. A person can't be quite alone in a street a second before she receives a letter. She can't be quite alone in a street when she starts reading a letter just received. There must be somebody pretty near her; he must be mentally invisible."

"Why must there be somebody near her?" asked Angus.

"Because," said Father Brown, "barring carrier-pigeons, somebody must have brought her the letter."

"Do you really mean to say," asked Flambeau, with energy, "that Welkin carried his rival's letters to his lady?"

"Yes," said the priest. "Welkin carried his rival's letters to his lady. You see, he had to."

"Oh, I can't stand much more of this," exploded Flambeau. "Who is this fellow? What does he look like? What is the usual get-up of a mentally invisible man?"

"He is dressed rather handsomely in red, blue and gold," replied the priest promptly with precision, "and in this striking, and even showy, costume he entered Himylaya Mansions under eight human eyes; he killed Smythe in cold blood, and came down into the street again carrying the dead body in his arms—"

"Reverend sir," cried Angus, standing still, "are you raving mad, or am I?"

"You are not mad," said Brown, "only a little unobservant. You have not noticed such a man as this, for example."

He took three quick strides forward, and put his hand on the shoulder of an ordinary passing postman who had bustled by them unnoticed under the shade of the trees.

"Nobody ever notices postmen somehow," he said thoughtfully; "yet they have passions like other men, and even carry large bags where a small corpse can be stowed quite easily."

The postman, instead of turning naturally, had ducked and tumbled against the garden fence. He was a lean fair-bearded man of very ordinary appearance, but as he turned an alarmed face over his shoulder, all three men were fixed with an almost fiendish squint.

Flambeau went back to his sabres, purple rugs and Persian cat, having many things to attend to. John Turnbull Angus went back to the lady at the shop, with whom that imprudent young man contrives to be extremely comfortable. But Father Brown walked those snow-covered hills under the stars for many hours with a murderer, and what they said to each other will never be known.

The Honour of Israel Gow

A stormy evening of olive and silver was closing in, as Father Brown, wrapped in a grey Scotch plaid, came to the end of a grey Scotch valley and beheld the strange castle of Glengyle. It stopped one end of the glen or hollow like a blind alley; and it looked like the end of the world. Rising in steep roofs and spires of seagreen slate in the manner of the old French-Scotch chateaux, it reminded an Englishman of the sinister steeple-hats of witches in fairy tales; and the pine woods that rocked round the green turrets looked, by comparison, as black as numberless flocks of ravens. This note of a dreamy, almost a sleepy devilry, was no mere fancy from the landscape. For there did rest on the place one of those clouds of pride and madness and mysterious sorrow which lie more heavily on the noble houses of Scotland than on any other of the children of men. For Scotland has a double dose of the poison called heredity; the sense of blood in the aristocrat, and the sense of doom in the Calvinist.

The priest had snatched a day from his business at Glasgow to meet his friend Flambeau, the amateur detective, who was at Glengyle Castle with another more formal officer investigating the life and death of the late Earl of Glengyle. That mysterious person was the last representative of a race whose valour, insanity, and violent cunning had made them terrible even among the sinister nobility of their nation in the sixteenth century. None were deeper in that labyrinthine ambition, in chamber within chamber of that palace of lies that was built up around Mary Queen of Scots.

The rhyme in the country-side attested the motive and the result of their machinations candidly:

As green sap to the simmer trees
Is red gold to the Ogilvies.

For many centuries there had never been a decent lord in Glengyle Castle; and with the Victorian era one would have thought that all eccentricities were exhausted. The last Glengyle, however, satisfied his tribal tradition by doing the only thing that was left for him to do; he disappeared. I do not mean that he went abroad; by all accounts he was still in the castle, if he was anywhere. But though his name was in the church register and the big red Peerage, nobody ever saw him under the sun.

If anyone saw him it was a solitary man-servant, something between a groom and a gardener. He was so deaf that the more business-like assumed him to be dumb; while the more penetrating declared him to be half-witted. A gaunt, red-haired labourer, with a dogged jaw and chin, but quite blank blue eyes, he went by the name of Israel Gow, and was the one silent servant on that deserted estate. But the energy with which he dug potatoes, and the regularity with which he disappeared into the kitchen gave people an impression that he was providing for the meals of a superior, and that the strange earl was still concealed in the castle. If society needed any further proof that he was there, the servant persistently asserted that he was not at home. One morning the provost and the minister (for the Glengyles were Presbyterian) were summoned to the castle. There they found that the gardener, groom and cook had added to his many professions that of an undertaker, and had nailed up his noble master in a coffin. With how much or how little further inquiry this odd fact was passed, did not as yet very plainly appear; for the thing had never been legally investigated till Flambeau had gone north two or three days before. By then the body of Lord Glengyle (if it was the body) had lain for some time in the little churchyard on the hill.

As Father Brown passed through the dim garden and came under the shadow of the chateau, the clouds were thick and the whole air damp and thundery. Against the last stripe of the green-gold sunset he saw a black human silhouette; a man in a chimney-pot hat, with a big spade over his shoulder. The combination was queerly suggestive of a sexton; but when Brown remembered the deaf servant who dug potatoes, he thought it natural enough. He knew something of the Scotch peasant; he knew the respectability which might well feel it necessary to wear "blacks" for an official inquiry; he knew also the economy that would not lose an hour's digging for that. Even the man's start and suspicious stare as the priest went by were consonant enough with the vigilance and jealousy of such a type.

The great door was opened by Flambeau himself, who had with him a lean man with iron-grey hair and papers in his hand: Inspector Craven from Scotland Yard. The entrance hall was mostly stripped and empty; but the pale, sneering faces of one or two of the wicked Ogilvies looked down out of black periwigs and blackening canvas.

Following them into an inner room, Father Brown found that the allies had been seated at a long oak table, of which their end was covered with scribbled papers, flanked with whisky and cigars. Through the whole of its remaining length it was occupied by detached objects arranged at intervals; objects about as inexplicable as any objects could be. One looked like a small heap of glittering broken glass. Another looked like a high heap of brown dust. A third appeared to be a plain stick of wood.

"You seem to have a sort of geological museum here," he said, as he sat down, jerking his head briefly in the direction of the brown dust and the crystalline fragments.

"Not a geological museum," replied Flambeau; "say a psychological museum."

"Oh, for the Lord's sake," cried the police detective laughing, "don't let's begin with such long words."

"Don't you know what psychology means?" asked Flambeau with friendly surprise. "Psychology means being off your chump."

"Still I hardly follow," replied the official.

"Well," said Flambeau, with decision, "I mean that we've only found out one thing about Lord Glengyle. He was a maniac."

The black silhouette of Gow with his top hat and spade passed the window, dimly outlined against the darkening sky. Father Brown stared passively at it and answered:

"I can understand there must have been something odd about the man, or he wouldn't have buried himself alive—nor been in such a hurry to bury himself dead. But what makes you think it was lunacy?"

"Well," said Flambeau, "you just listen to the list of things Mr. Craven has found in the house."

"We must get a candle," said Craven, suddenly. "A storm is getting up, and it's too dark to read."

"Have you found any candles," asked Brown smiling, "among your oddities?"

Flambeau raised a grave face, and fixed his dark eyes on his friend.

"That is curious, too," he said. "Twenty-five candles, and not a trace of a candlestick."

In the rapidly darkening room and rapidly rising wind, Brown went along the table to where a bundle of wax candles lay among the other scrappy exhibits. As he did so he bent accidentally over the heap of red-brown dust; and a sharp sneeze cracked the silence.

"Hullo!" he said, "snuff!"

He took one of the candles, lit it carefully, came back and stuck it in the neck of the whisky bottle. The unrestful night air, blowing through the crazy window, waved the long flame like a banner. And on every side of the castle they could hear the miles and miles of black pine wood seething like a black sea around a rock.

"I will read the inventory," began Craven gravely, picking up one of the papers, "the inventory of what we found loose and unexplained in the castle. You are to understand that the place generally was dismantled and neglected; but one or two rooms had plainly been inhabited in a simple but not squalid style by somebody; somebody who was not the servant Gow. The list is as follows:

"First item. A very considerable hoard of precious stones, nearly all diamonds, and all of them loose, without any setting whatever. Of course, it is natural that the Ogilvies should have family jewels; but those are exactly the jewels that are almost always set in particular articles of ornament. The Ogilvies would seem to have kept theirs loose in their pockets, like coppers.

"Second item. Heaps and heaps of loose snuff, not kept in a horn, or even a pouch, but lying in heaps on the mantelpieces, on the sideboard, on the piano, anywhere. It looks as if the old gentleman would not take the trouble to look in a pocket or lift a lid.

"Third item. Here and there about the house curious little heaps of minute pieces of metal, some like steel springs and some in the form of microscopic wheels. As if they had gutted some mechanical toy.

"Fourth item. The wax candles, which have to be stuck in bottle necks because there is nothing else to stick them in. Now I wish you to note how very much queerer all this is than anything we anticipated. For the central riddle we are prepared; we have all seen at a glance that there was something wrong about the last earl. We have come here to find out whether he really lived here, whether he really died here, whether that red-haired scarecrow who did his burying had anything to do with his dying. But suppose the worst in all this, the most lurid or melodramatic solution you like. Suppose the servant really killed the master, or suppose the master isn't really dead, or suppose the master is dressed up as the servant, or suppose the servant is buried for the master; invent what Wilkie Collins' tragedy you like, and you still have not explained a candle without a candlestick, or why an elderly gentleman of good family should habitually spill snuff on the piano. The core of the tale we could imagine; it is the fringes that are mysterious. By no stretch of fancy can the human mind connect together snuff and diamonds and wax and loose clockwork."

"I think I see the connection," said the priest. "This Glengyle was mad against the French Revolution. He was an enthusiast for the ancien regime, and was trying to re-enact literally the family life of the last Bourbons. He had snuff because it was the eighteenth century luxury; wax candles, because they were the eighteenth century lighting; the mechanical bits of iron represent the locksmith hobby of Louis XVI; the diamonds are for the Diamond Necklace of Marie Antoinette."

Both the other men were staring at him with round eyes. "What a perfectly extraordinary notion!" cried Flambeau. "Do you really think that is the truth?"

"I am perfectly sure it isn't," answered Father Brown, "only you said that nobody could connect snuff and diamonds and clockwork and candles. I give you that connection off-hand. The real truth, I am very sure, lies deeper."

He paused a moment and listened to the wailing of the wind in the turrets. Then he said, "The late Earl of Glengyle was a thief. He lived a second and darker life as a desperate housebreaker. He did not have any candlesticks because he only used these candles cut short in the little lantern he carried. The snuff he employed as the fiercest French criminals have used pepper: to fling it suddenly in dense masses in the face of a captor or pursuer. But the final proof is in the curious coincidence of the diamonds and the small steel wheels. Surely that makes everything plain to you? Diamonds and small steel wheels are the only two instruments with which you can cut out a pane of glass."

The bough of a broken pine tree lashed heavily in the blast against the windowpane behind them, as if in parody of a burglar, but they did not turn round. Their eyes were fastened on Father Brown.

"Diamonds and small wheels," repeated Craven ruminating. "Is that all that makes you think it the true explanation?"

"I don't think it the true explanation," replied the priest placidly; "but you said that nobody could connect the four things. The true tale, of course, is something much more humdrum. Glengyle had found, or thought he had found, precious stones on his estate. Somebody had bamboozled him with those loose brilliants, saying they were found in the castle caverns. The little wheels are some diamond-cutting affair. He had to do the thing very roughly and in a small way, with the help of a few shepherds or rude fellows on these hills. Snuff is the one great luxury of such Scotch shepherds; it's the one thing with which you can bribe them. They didn't have candlesticks because they didn't want them; they held the candles in their hands when they explored the caves."

"Is that all?" asked Flambeau after a long pause. "Have we got to the dull truth at last?"

"Oh, no," said Father Brown.

As the wind died in the most distant pine woods with a long hoot as of mockery Father Brown, with an utterly impassive face, went on:

"I only suggested that because you said one could not plausibly connect snuff with clockwork or candles with bright stones. Ten false philosophies will fit the universe; ten false theories will fit Glengyle Castle. But we want the real explanation of the castle and the universe. But are there no other exhibits?"

Craven laughed, and Flambeau rose smiling to his feet and strolled down the long table.

"Items five, six, seven, etc.," he said, "and certainly more varied than instructive. A curious collection, not of lead pencils, but of the lead out of lead pencils. A senseless stick of bamboo, with the top rather splintered. It might be the instrument of the crime. Only, there isn't any crime. The only other things are a few old missals and little Catholic pictures, which the Ogilvies kept, I suppose, from the Middle Ages—their family pride being stronger than their Puritanism. We only put them in the museum because they seem curiously cut about and defaced."

The heady tempest without drove a dreadful wrack of clouds across Glengyle and threw the long room into darkness as Father Brown picked up the little illuminated pages to examine them. He spoke before the drift of darkness had passed; but it was the voice of an utterly new man.

"Mr. Craven," said he, talking like a man ten years younger, "you have got a legal warrant, haven't you, to go up and examine that grave? The sooner we do it the better, and get to the bottom of this horrible affair. If I were you I should start now."

"Now," repeated the astonished detective, "and why now?"

"Because this is serious," answered Brown; "this is not spilt snuff or loose pebbles, that might be there for a hundred reasons. There is only one reason I know of for this being done; and the reason goes down to the roots of the world. These religious pictures are not just dirtied or torn or scrawled over, which might be done in idleness or bigotry, by children or by Protestants. These have been treated very carefully—and very queerly. In every place where the great ornamental name of God comes in the old illuminations it has been elaborately taken out. The only other thing that has been removed is the halo round the head of the Child Jesus. Therefore, I say, let us get our warrant and our spade and our hatchet, and go up and break open that coffin."

"What do you mean?" demanded the London officer.

"I mean," answered the little priest, and his voice seemed to rise slightly in the roar of the gale. "I mean that the great devil of the universe may be sitting on the top tower of this castle at this moment, as big as a hundred elephants, and roaring like the Apocalypse. There is black magic somewhere at the bottom of this."

"Black magic," repeated Flambeau in a low voice, for he was too enlightened a man not to know of such things; "but what can these other things mean?"

"Oh, something damnable, I suppose," replied Brown impatiently. "How should I know? How can I guess all their mazes down below? Perhaps you can make a torture out of snuff and bamboo. Perhaps lunatics lust after wax and steel filings. Perhaps there is a maddening drug made of lead pencils! Our shortest cut to the mystery is up the hill to the grave."

His comrades hardly knew that they had obeyed and followed him till a blast of the night wind nearly flung them on their faces in the garden. Nevertheless they had obeyed him like automata; for Craven found a hatchet in his hand, and the warrant in his pocket; Flambeau was carrying the heavy spade of the strange gardener; Father Brown was carrying the little gilt book from which had been torn the name of God.

The path up the hill to the churchyard was crooked but short; only under that stress of wind it seemed laborious and long. Far as the eye could see, farther and farther as they mounted the slope, were seas beyond seas of pines, now all aslope one way under the wind. And that universal gesture seemed as vain as it was vast, as vain as if that wind were whistling about some unpeopled and purposeless planet. Through all that infinite growth of grey-blue forests sang, shrill and high, that ancient sorrow that is in the heart of all heathen things. One could fancy that the voices from the under world of unfathomable foliage were cries of the lost and wandering pagan gods: gods who had gone roaming in that irrational forest, and who will never find their way back to heaven.

"You see," said Father Brown in low but easy tone, "Scotch people before Scotland existed were a curious lot. In fact, they're a curious lot still. But in the prehistoric times I fancy they really worshipped demons. That," he added genially, "is why they jumped at the Puritan theology."

"My friend," said Flambeau, turning in a kind of fury, "what does all that snuff mean?"

"My friend," replied Brown, with equal seriousness, "there is one mark of all genuine religions: materialism. Now, devil-worship is a perfectly genuine religion."

They had come up on the grassy scalp of the hill, one of the few bald spots that stood clear of the crashing and roaring pine forest. A mean enclosure, partly timber and partly wire, rattled in the tempest to tell them the border of the graveyard. But by the time Inspector Craven had come to the corner of the grave, and Flambeau had planted his spade point downwards and leaned on it, they were both almost as shaken as the shaky wood and wire. At the foot of the grave grew great tall thistles, grey and silver in their decay. Once or twice, when a ball of thistledown broke under the breeze and flew past him, Craven jumped slightly as if it had been an arrow.

Flambeau drove the blade of his spade through the whistling grass into the wet clay below. Then he seemed to stop and lean on it as on a staff.

"Go on," said the priest very gently. "We are only trying to find the truth. What are you afraid of?"

"I am afraid of finding it," said Flambeau.

The London detective spoke suddenly in a high crowing voice that was meant to be conversational and cheery. "I wonder why he really did hide himself like that. Something nasty, I suppose; was he a leper?"

"Something worse than that," said Flambeau.

"And what do you imagine," asked the other, "would be worse than a leper?"

"I don't imagine it," said Flambeau.

He dug for some dreadful minutes in silence, and then said in a choked voice, "I'm afraid of his not being the right shape."

"Nor was that piece of paper, you know," said Father Brown quietly, "and we survived even that piece of paper."

Flambeau dug on with a blind energy. But the tempest had shouldered away the choking grey clouds that clung to the hills like smoke and revealed grey fields of faint starlight before he cleared the shape of a rude timber coffin, and somehow tipped it up upon the turf. Craven stepped forward with his axe; a thistle-top touched him, and he flinched. Then he took a firmer stride, and hacked and wrenched with an energy like Flambeau's till the lid was torn off, and all that was there lay glimmering in the grey starlight.

"Bones," said Craven; and then he added, "but it is a man," as if that were something unexpected.

"Is he," asked Flambeau in a voice that went oddly up and down, "is he all right?"

"Seems so," said the officer huskily, bending over the obscure and decaying skeleton in the box. "Wait a minute."

A vast heave went over Flambeau's huge figure. "And now I come to think of it," he cried, "why in the name of madness shouldn't he be all right? What is it gets hold of a man on these cursed cold mountains? I think it's the black, brainless repetition; all these forests, and over all an ancient horror of unconsciousness. It's like the dream of an atheist. Pine-trees and more pine-trees and millions more pine-trees—"

"God!" cried the man by the coffin, "but he hasn't got a head."

While the others stood rigid the priest, for the first time, showed a leap of startled concern.

"No head!" he repeated. "No head?" as if he had almost expected some other deficiency.

Half-witted visions of a headless baby born to Glengyle, of a headless youth hiding himself in the castle, of a headless man pacing those ancient halls or that gorgeous garden, passed in panorama through their minds. But even in that stiffened instant the tale took no root in them and seemed to have no reason in it. They stood listening to the loud woods and the shrieking sky quite foolishly, like exhausted animals. Thought seemed to be something enormous that had suddenly slipped out of their grasp.

"There are three headless men," said Father Brown, "standing round this open grave."

The pale detective from London opened his mouth to speak, and left it open like a yokel, while a long scream of wind tore the sky; then he looked at the axe in his hands as if it did not belong to him, and dropped it.

"Father," said Flambeau in that infantile and heavy voice he used very seldom, "what are we to do?"

His friend's reply came with the pent promptitude of a gun going off.

"Sleep!" cried Father Brown. "Sleep. We have come to the end of the ways. Do you know what sleep is? Do you know that every man who sleeps believes in God? It is a sacrament; for it is an act of faith and it is a food. And we need a sacrament, if only a natural one. Something has fallen on us that falls very seldom on men; perhaps the worst thing that can fall on them."

Craven's parted lips came together to say, "What do you mean?"

The priest had turned his face to the castle as he answered: "We have found the truth; and the truth makes no sense."

He went down the path in front of them with a plunging and reckless step very rare with him, and when they reached the castle again he threw himself upon sleep with the simplicity of a dog.

Despite his mystic praise of slumber, Father Brown was up earlier than anyone else except the silent gardener; and was found smoking a big pipe and watching that expert at his speechless labours in the kitchen garden. Towards daybreak the rocking storm had ended in roaring rains, and the day came with a curious freshness. The gardener seemed even to have been conversing, but at sight of the detectives he planted his spade sullenly in a bed and, saying something about his breakfast, shifted along the lines of cabbages and shut himself in the kitchen. "He's a valuable man, that," said Father Brown. "He does the potatoes amazingly. Still," he added, with a dispassionate charity, "he has his faults; which of us hasn't? He doesn't dig this bank quite regularly. There, for instance," and he stamped suddenly on one spot. "I'm really very doubtful about that potato."

"And why?" asked Craven, amused with the little man's hobby.

"I'm doubtful about it," said the other, "because old Gow was doubtful about it himself. He put his spade in methodically in every place but just this. There must be a mighty fine potato just here."

Flambeau pulled up the spade and impetuously drove it into the place. He turned up, under a load of soil, something that did not look like a potato, but rather like a monstrous, over-domed mushroom. But it struck the spade with a cold click; it rolled over like a ball, and grinned up at them.

"The Earl of Glengyle," said Brown sadly, and looked down heavily at the skull.

Then, after a momentary meditation, he plucked the spade from Flambeau, and, saying "We must hide it again," clamped the skull down in the earth. Then he leaned his little body and huge head on the great handle of the spade, that stood up stiffly in the earth, and his eyes were empty and his forehead full of wrinkles. "If one could only conceive," he muttered, "the meaning of this last monstrosity." And leaning on the large spade handle, he buried his brows in his hands, as men do in church.

All the corners of the sky were brightening into blue and silver; the birds were chattering in the tiny garden trees; so loud it seemed as if the trees themselves were talking. But the three men were silent enough.

"Well, I give it all up," said Flambeau at last boisterously. "My brain and this world don't fit each other; and there's an end of it. Snuff, spoilt Prayer Books, and the insides of musical boxes—what—"

Brown threw up his bothered brow and rapped on the spade handle with an intolerance quite unusual with him. "Oh, tut, tut, tut, tut!" he cried. "All that is as plain as a pikestaff. I understood the snuff and clockwork, and so on, when I first opened my eyes this morning. And since then I've had it out with old Gow, the gardener, who is neither so deaf nor so stupid as he pretends. There's nothing amiss about the loose items. I was wrong about the torn mass-book, too; there's no harm in that. But it's this last business. Desecrating graves and stealing dead men's heads—surely there's harm in that? Surely there's black magic still in that? That doesn't fit in to the quite simple story of the snuff and the candles." And, striding about again, he smoked moodily.

"My friend," said Flambeau, with a grim humour, "you must be careful with me and remember I was once a criminal. The great advantage of that estate was that I always made up the story myself, and acted it as quick as I chose. This detective business of waiting about is too much for my French impatience. All my life, for good or evil, I have done things at the instant; I always fought duels the next morning; I always paid bills on the nail; I never even put off a visit to the dentist—"

Father Brown's pipe fell out of his mouth and broke into three pieces on the gravel path. He stood rolling his eyes, the exact picture of an idiot. "Lord, what a turnip I am!" he kept saying. "Lord, what a turnip!" Then, in a somewhat groggy kind of way, he began to laugh.

"The dentist!" he repeated. "Six hours in the spiritual abyss, and all because I never thought of the dentist! Such a simple, such a beautiful and peaceful thought! Friends, we have passed a night in hell; but now the sun is risen, the birds are singing, and the radiant form of the dentist consoles the world."

"I will get some sense out of this," cried Flambeau, striding forward, "if I use the tortures of the Inquisition."

Father Brown repressed what appeared to be a momentary disposition to dance on the now sunlit lawn and cried quite piteously, like a child, "Oh, let me be silly a little. You don't know how unhappy I have been. And now I know that there has been no deep sin in this business at all. Only a little lunacy, perhaps—and who minds that?"

He spun round once more, then faced them with gravity.

"This is not a story of crime," he said; "rather it is the story of a strange and crooked honesty. We are dealing with the one man on earth, perhaps, who has taken no more than his due. It is a study in the savage living logic that has been the religion of this race.

"That old local rhyme about the house of Glengyle—

As green sap to the simmer trees
Is red gold to the Ogilvies—

was literal as well as metaphorical. It did not merely mean that the Glengyles sought for wealth; it was also true that they literally gathered gold; they had a huge collection of ornaments and utensils in that metal. They were, in fact, misers whose mania took that turn. In the light of that fact, run through all the things we found in the castle. Diamonds without their gold rings; candles without their gold candlesticks; snuff without the gold snuff-boxes; pencil-leads without the gold pencilcases; a walking stick without its gold top; clockwork without the gold clocks—or rather watches. And, mad as it sounds, because the halos and the name of God in the old missals were of real gold; these also were taken away."

The garden seemed to brighten, the grass to grow gayer in the strengthening sun, as the crazy truth was told. Flambeau lit a cigarette as his friend went on.

"Were taken away," continued Father Brown; "were taken away—but not stolen. Thieves would never have left this mystery. Thieves would have taken the gold snuff-boxes, snuff and all; the gold pencil-cases, lead and all. We have to deal with a man with a peculiar conscience, but certainly a conscience. I found that mad moralist this morning in the kitchen garden yonder, and I heard the whole story.

"The late Archibald Ogilvie was the nearest approach to a good man ever born at Glengyle. But his bitter virtue took the turn of the misanthrope; he moped over the dishonesty of his ancestors, from which, somehow, he generalised a dishonesty of all men. More especially he distrusted philanthropy or free-giving; and he swore if he could find one man who took his exact rights he should have all the gold of Glengyle. Having delivered this defiance to humanity he shut himself up, without the smallest expectation of its being answered. One day, however, a deaf and seemingly senseless lad from a distant village brought him a belated telegram; and Glengyle, in his acrid pleasantry, gave him a new farthing. At least he thought he had done so, but when he turned over his change he found the new farthing still there and a sovereign gone. The accident offered him vistas of sneering speculation. Either way, the boy would show the greasy greed of the species. Either he would vanish, a thief stealing a coin; or he would sneak back with it virtuously, a snob seeking a reward. In the middle of that night Lord Glengyle was knocked up out of his bed—for he lived alone—and forced to open the door to the deaf idiot. The idiot brought with him, not the sovereign, but exactly nineteen shillings and eleven-pence three-farthings in change.

"Then the wild exactitude of this action took hold of the mad lord's brain like fire. He swore he was Diogenes, that had long sought an honest man, and at last had found one. He made a new will, which I have seen. He took the literal youth into his huge, neglected house, and trained him up as his solitary servant and—after an odd manner—his heir. And whatever that queer creature understands, he understood absolutely his lord's two fixed ideas: first, that the letter of right is everything; and second, that he himself was to have the gold of Glengyle. So far, that is all; and that is simple. He has stripped the house of gold, and taken not a grain that was not gold; not so much as a grain of snuff. He lifted the gold leaf off an old illumination, fully satisfied that he left the rest unspoilt. All that I understood; but I could not understand this skull business. I was really uneasy about that human head buried among the potatoes. It distressed me—till Flambeau said the word.

"It will be all right. He will put the skull back in the grave, when he has taken the gold out of the tooth."

And, indeed, when Flambeau crossed the hill that morning, he saw that strange being, the just miser, digging at the desecrated grave, the plaid round his throat thrashing out in the mountain wind; the sober top hat on his head.

The Wrong Shape

Certain of the great roads going north out of London continue far into the country a sort of attenuated and interrupted spectre of a street, with great gaps in the building, but preserving the line. Here will be a group of shops, followed by a fenced field or paddock, and then a famous public-house, and then perhaps a market garden or a nursery garden, and then one large private house, and then another field and another inn, and so on. If anyone walks along one of these roads he will pass a house which will probably catch his eye, though he may not be able to explain its attraction. It is a long, low house, running parallel with the road, painted mostly white and pale green, with a veranda and sun-blinds, and porches capped with those quaint sort of cupolas like wooden umbrellas that one sees in some old-fashioned houses. In fact, it is an old-fashioned house, very English and very suburban in the good old wealthy Clapham sense. And yet the house has a look of having been built chiefly for the hot weather. Looking at its white paint and sun-blinds one thinks vaguely of pugarees and even of palm trees. I cannot trace the feeling to its root; perhaps the place was built by an Anglo-Indian.

Anyone passing this house, I say, would be namelessly fascinated by it; would feel that it was a place about which some story was to be told. And he would have been right, as you shall shortly hear. For this is the story—the story of the strange things that did really happen in it in the Whitsuntide of the year 18—:

Anyone passing the house on the Thursday before Whit-Sunday at about half-past four p.m. would have seen the front door open, and Father Brown, of the small church of St. Mungo, come out smoking a large pipe in company with a very tall

French friend of his called Flambeau, who was smoking a very small cigarette. These persons may or may not be of interest to the reader, but the truth is that they were not the only interesting things that were displayed when the front door of the white-and-green house was opened. There are further peculiarities about this house, which must be described to start with, not only that the reader may understand this tragic tale, but also that he may realise what it was that the opening of the door revealed.

The whole house was built upon the plan of a T, but a T with a very long cross piece and a very short tail piece. The long cross piece was the frontage that ran along in face of the street, with the front door in the middle; it was two stories high, and contained nearly all the important rooms. The short tail piece, which ran out at the back immediately opposite the front door, was one story high, and consisted only of two long rooms, the one leading into the other. The first of these two rooms was the study in which the celebrated Mr. Quinton wrote his wild Oriental poems and romances. The farther room was a glass conservatory full of tropical blossoms of quite unique and almost monstrous beauty, and on such afternoons as these glowing with gorgeous sunlight. Thus when the hall door was open, many a passer-by literally stopped to stare and gasp; for he looked down a perspective of rich apartments to something really like a transformation scene in a fairy play: purple clouds and golden suns and crimson stars that were at once scorchingly vivid and yet transparent and far away.

Leonard Quinton, the poet, had himself most carefully arranged this effect; and it is doubtful whether he so perfectly expressed his personality in any of his poems. For he was a man who drank and bathed in colours, who indulged his lust for colour somewhat to the neglect of form—even of good form. This it was that had turned his genius so wholly to eastern art and imagery; to those bewildering carpets or blinding embroideries in which all the colours seem fallen into a fortunate chaos, having nothing to typify or to teach. He had attempted, not perhaps with complete artistic success, but with acknowledged imagination and invention, to compose epics and love stories reflecting the riot of violent and even cruel colour; tales of tropical heavens of burning gold or blood-red copper; of eastern heroes who rode with twelve-turbaned mitres upon elephants painted purple or peacock green; of gigantic jewels that a hundred negroes could not carry, but which burned with ancient and strange-hued fires.

In short (to put the matter from the more common point of view), he dealt much in eastern heavens, rather worse than most western hells; in eastern monarchs, whom we might possibly call maniacs; and in eastern jewels which a Bond Street jeweller (if the hundred staggering negroes brought them into his shop) might possibly not regard as genuine. Quinton was a genius, if a morbid one; and even his morbidity appeared more in his life than in his work. In temperament he was weak and waspish, and his health had suffered heavily from oriental experiments with opium. His wife—a handsome, hard-working, and, indeed, over-worked woman objected to the opium, but objected much more to a live Indian hermit in white and yellow robes, whom her husband insisted on entertaining for months together, a Virgil to guide his spirit through the heavens and the hells of the east.

It was out of this artistic household that Father Brown and his friend stepped on to the door-step; and to judge from their faces, they stepped out of it with much relief. Flambeau had known Quinton in wild student days in Paris, and they had renewed the acquaintance for a week-end; but apart from Flambeau's more responsible developments of late, he did not get on well with the poet now. Choking oneself with opium and writing little erotic verses on vellum was not his notion of how a gentleman should go to the devil. As the two paused on the door-step, before taking a turn in the garden, the front garden gate was thrown open with violence, and a young man with a billycock hat on the back of his head tumbled up the steps in his eagerness. He was a dissipated-looking youth with a gorgeous red necktie all awry, as if he had slept in it, and he kept fidgeting and lashing about with one of those little jointed canes.

"I say," he said breathlessly, "I want to see old Quinton. I must see him. Has he gone?"

"Mr. Quinton is in, I believe," said Father Brown, cleaning his pipe, "but I do not know if you can see him. The doctor is with him at present."

The young man, who seemed not to be perfectly sober, stumbled into the hall; and at the same moment the doctor came out of Quinton's study, shutting the door and beginning to put on his gloves.

"See Mr. Quinton?" said the doctor coolly. "No, I'm afraid you can't. In fact, you mustn't on any account. Nobody must see him; I've just given him his sleeping draught."

"No, but look here, old chap," said the youth in the red tie, trying affectionately to capture the doctor by the lapels of his coat. "Look here. I'm simply sewn up, I tell you. I—"

"It's no good, Mr. Atkinson," said the doctor, forcing him to fall back; "when you can alter the effects of a drug I'll alter my decision," and, settling on his hat, he stepped out into the sunlight with the other two. He was a bull-necked, good-tempered little man with a small moustache, inexpressibly ordinary, yet giving an impression of capacity.

The young man in the billycock, who did not seem to be gifted with any tact in dealing with people beyond the general idea of clutching hold of their coats, stood outside the door, as dazed as if he had been thrown out bodily, and silently watched the other three walk away together through the garden.

"That was a sound, spanking lie I told just now," remarked the medical man, laughing. "In point of fact, poor Quinton doesn't have his sleeping draught for nearly half an hour. But I'm not going to have him bothered with that little beast, who only wants to borrow money that he wouldn't pay back if he could. He's a dirty little scamp, though he is Mrs. Quinton's brother, and she's as fine a woman as ever walked."

"Yes," said Father Brown. "She's a good woman."

"So I propose to hang about the garden till the creature has cleared off," went on the doctor, "and then I'll go in to Quinton with the medicine. Atkinson can't get in, because I locked the door."

"In that case, Dr. Harris," said Flambeau, "we might as well walk round at the back by the end of the conservatory. There's no entrance to it that way, but it's worth seeing, even from the outside."

"Yes, and I might get a squint at my patient," laughed the doctor, "for he prefers to lie on an ottoman right at the end of the conservatory amid all those blood-red poinsettias; it would give me the creeps. But what are you doing?"

Father Brown had stopped for a moment, and picked up out of the long grass, where it had almost been wholly hidden, a queer, crooked Oriental knife, inlaid exquisitely in coloured stones and metals.

"What is this?" asked Father Brown, regarding it with some disfavour.

"Oh, Quinton's, I suppose," said Dr. Harris carelessly; "he has all sorts of Chinese knickknacks about the place. Or perhaps it belongs to that mild Hindoo of his whom he keeps on a string."

"What Hindoo?" asked Father Brown, still staring at the dagger in his hand.

"Oh, some Indian conjuror," said the doctor lightly; "a fraud, of course."

"You don't believe in magic?" asked Father Brown, without looking up.

"O crickey! magic!" said the doctor.

"It's very beautiful," said the priest in a low, dreaming voice; "the colours are very beautiful. But it's the wrong shape."

"What for?" asked Flambeau, staring.

"For anything. It's the wrong shape in the abstract. Don't you ever feel that about Eastern art? The colours are intoxicatingly lovely; but the shapes are mean and bad—deliberately mean and bad. I have seen wicked things in a Turkey carpet."

"Mon Dieu!" cried Flambeau, laughing.

"They are letters and symbols in a language I don't know; but I know they stand for evil words," went on the priest, his voice growing lower and lower. "The lines go wrong on purpose—like serpents doubling to escape."

"What the devil are you talking about?" said the doctor with a loud laugh.

Flambeau spoke quietly to him in answer. "The Father sometimes gets this mystic's cloud on him," he said; "but I give you fair warning that I have never known him to have it except when there was some evil quite near."

"Oh, rats!" said the scientist.

"Why, look at it," cried Father Brown, holding out the crooked knife at arm's length, as if it were some glittering snake. "Don't you see it is the wrong shape? Don't you see that it has no hearty and plain purpose? It does not point like a spear. It does not sweep like a scythe. It does not look like a weapon. It looks like an instrument of torture."

"Well, as you don't seem to like it," said the jolly Harris, "it had better be taken back to its owner. Haven't we come to the end of this confounded conservatory yet? This house is the wrong shape, if you like."

"You don't understand," said Father Brown, shaking his head. "The shape of this house is quaint—it is even laughable. But there is nothing wrong about it."

As they spoke they came round the curve of glass that ended the conservatory, an uninterrupted curve, for there was neither door nor window by which to enter at that end. The glass, however, was clear, and the sun still bright, though beginning to set; and they could see not only the flamboyant blossoms inside, but the frail figure of the poet in a brown velvet coat lying languidly on the sofa, having, apparently, fallen half asleep over a book. He was a pale, slight man, with loose, chestnut hair and a fringe of beard that was the paradox of his face, for the beard made him look less manly. These traits were well known to all three of them; but even had it not been so, it may be doubted whether they would have looked at Quinton just then. Their eyes were riveted on another object.

Exactly in their path, immediately outside the round end of the glass building, was standing a tall man, whose drapery fell to his feet in faultless white, and whose bare, brown skull, face, and neck gleamed in the setting sun like splendid bronze. He was looking through the glass at the sleeper, and he was more motionless than a mountain.

"Who is that?" cried Father Brown, stepping back with a hissing intake of his breath.

"Oh, it is only that Hindoo humbug," growled Harris; "but I don't know what the deuce he's doing here."

"It looks like hypnotism," said Flambeau, biting his black moustache.

"Why are you unmedical fellows always talking bosh about hypnotism?" cried the doctor. "It looks a deal more like burglary."

"Well, we will speak to it, at any rate," said Flambeau, who was always for action. One long stride took him to the place where the Indian stood. Bowing from his great height, which overtopped even the Oriental's, he said with placid impudence:

"Good evening, sir. Do you want anything?"

Quite slowly, like a great ship turning into a harbour, the great yellow face turned, and looked at last over its white shoulder. They were startled to see that its yellow eyelids were quite sealed, as in sleep. "Thank you," said the face in excellent English. "I want nothing." Then, half opening the lids, so as to show a slit of opalescent eyeball, he repeated, "I want nothing." Then he opened his eyes wide with a startling stare, said, "I want nothing," and went rustling away into the rapidly darkening garden.

"The Christian is more modest," muttered Father Brown; "he wants something."

"What on earth was he doing?" asked Flambeau, knitting his black brows and lowering his voice.

"I should like to talk to you later," said Father Brown.

The sunlight was still a reality, but it was the red light of evening, and the bulk of the garden trees and bushes grew blacker and blacker against it. They turned round the end of the conservatory, and walked in silence down the other side to get round to the front door. As they went they seemed to wake something, as one startles a bird, in the deeper corner between the study and the main building; and again they saw the white-robed fakir slide out of the shadow, and slip round towards the front door. To their surprise, however, he had not been alone. They found themselves abruptly pulled up and forced to banish their bewilderment by the appearance of Mrs. Quinton, with her heavy golden hair and square pale face, advancing on them out of the twilight. She looked a little stern, but was entirely courteous.

"Good evening, Dr. Harris," was all she said.

"Good evening, Mrs. Quinton," said the little doctor heartily. "I am just going to give your husband his sleeping draught."

"Yes," she said in a clear voice. "I think it is quite time." And she smiled at them, and went sweeping into the house.

"That woman's over-driven," said Father Brown; "that's the kind of woman that does her duty for twenty years, and then does something dreadful."

The little doctor looked at him for the first time with an eye of interest. "Did you ever study medicine?" he asked.

"You have to know something of the mind as well as the body," answered the priest; "we have to know something of the body as well as the mind."

"Well," said the doctor, "I think I'll go and give Quinton his stuff."

They had turned the corner of the front facade, and were approaching the front doorway. As they turned into it they saw the man in the white robe for the third time. He came so straight towards the front door that it seemed quite incredible that he had not just come out of the study opposite to it. Yet they knew that the study door was locked.

Father Brown and Flambeau, however, kept this weird contradiction to themselves, and Dr. Harris was not a man to waste his thoughts on the impossible. He permitted the omnipresent Asiatic to make his exit, and then stepped briskly into the hall. There he found a figure which he had already forgotten. The inane Atkinson was still hanging about, humming and poking things with his knobby cane. The doctor's face had a spasm of disgust and decision, and he whispered rapidly to his companion: "I must lock the door again, or this rat will get in. But I shall be out again in two minutes."

He rapidly unlocked the door and locked it again behind him, just balking a blundering charge from the young man in the billycock. The young man threw himself impatiently on a hall chair. Flambeau looked at a Persian illumination on the wall; Father Brown, who seemed in a sort of daze, dully eyed the door. In about four minutes the door was opened again. Atkinson was quicker this time. He sprang forward, held the door open for an instant, and called out: "Oh, I say, Quinton, I want—"

From the other end of the study came the clear voice of Quinton, in something between a yawn and a yell of weary laughter.

"Oh, I know what you want. Take it, and leave me in peace. I'm writing a song about peacocks."

Before the door closed half a sovereign came flying through the aperture; and Atkinson, stumbling forward, caught it with singular dexterity.

"So that's settled," said the doctor, and, locking the door savagely, he led the way out into the garden.

"Poor Leonard can get a little peace now," he added to Father Brown; "he's locked in all by himself for an hour or two."

"Yes," answered the priest; "and his voice sounded jolly enough when we left him." Then he looked gravely round the garden, and saw the loose figure of Atkinson standing and jingling the half-sovereign in his pocket, and beyond, in the purple twilight, the figure of the Indian sitting bolt upright upon a bank of grass with his face turned towards the setting sun. Then he said abruptly: "Where is Mrs. Quinton!"

"She has gone up to her room," said the doctor. "That is her shadow on the blind."

Father Brown looked up, and frowningly scrutinised a dark outline at the gas-lit window.

"Yes," he said, "that is her shadow," and he walked a yard or two and threw himself upon a garden seat.

Flambeau sat down beside him; but the doctor was one of those energetic people who live naturally on their legs. He walked away, smoking, into the twilight, and the two friends were left together.

"My father," said Flambeau in French, "what is the matter with you?"

Father Brown was silent and motionless for half a minute, then he said: "Superstition is irreligious, but there is something in the air of this place. I think it's that Indian—at least, partly."

He sank into silence, and watched the distant outline of the Indian, who still sat rigid as if in prayer. At first sight he seemed motionless, but as Father Brown watched him he saw that the man swayed ever so slightly with a rhythmic movement, just as the dark tree-tops swayed ever so slightly in the wind that was creeping up the dim garden paths and shuffling the fallen leaves a little.

The landscape was growing rapidly dark, as if for a storm, but they could still see all the figures in their various places. Atkinson was leaning against a tree with a listless face; Quinton's wife was still at her window; the doctor had gone strolling round the end of the conservatory; they could see his cigar like a will-o'-the-wisp; and the fakir still sat rigid and yet rocking, while the trees above him began to rock and almost to roar. Storm was certainly coming.

"When that Indian spoke to us," went on Brown in a conversational undertone, "I had a sort of vision, a vision of him and all his universe. Yet he only said the same thing three times. When first he said 'I want nothing,' it meant only that he was impenetrable, that Asia does not give itself away. Then he said again, 'I want nothing,' and I knew that he meant that he was sufficient to himself, like a cosmos, that he needed no God, neither admitted any sins. And when he said the third time, 'I want nothing,' he said it with blazing eyes. And I knew that he meant literally what he said; that nothing was his desire and his home; that he was weary for nothing as for wine; that annihilation, the mere destruction of everything or anything—"

Two drops of rain fell; and for some reason Flambeau started and looked up, as if they had stung him. And the same instant the doctor down by the end of the conservatory began running towards them, calling out something as he ran.

As he came among them like a bombshell the restless Atkinson happened to be taking a turn nearer to the house front; and the doctor clutched him by the collar in a convulsive grip. "Foul play!" he cried; "what have you been doing to him, you dog?"

The priest had sprung erect, and had the voice of steel of a soldier in command.

"No fighting," he cried coolly; "we are enough to hold anyone we want to. What is the matter, doctor?"

"Things are not right with Quinton," said the doctor, quite white. "I could just see him through the glass, and I don't like the way he's lying. It's not as I left him, anyhow."

"Let us go in to him," said Father Brown shortly. "You can leave Mr. Atkinson alone. I have had him in sight since we heard Quinton's voice."

"I will stop here and watch him," said Flambeau hurriedly. "You go in and see."

The doctor and the priest flew to the study door, unlocked it, and fell into the room. In doing so they nearly fell over the large mahogany table in the centre at which the poet usually wrote; for the place was lit only by a small fire kept for the invalid. In the middle of this table lay a single sheet of paper, evidently left there on purpose. The doctor snatched it up, glanced at it, handed it to Father Brown, and crying, "Good God, look at that!" plunged toward the glass room beyond, where the terrible tropic flowers still seemed to keep a crimson memory of the sunset.

Father Brown read the words three times before he put down the paper. The words were: "I die by my own hand; yet I die murdered!" They were in the quite inimitable, not to say illegible, handwriting of Leonard Quinton.

Then Father Brown, still keeping the paper in his hand, strode towards the conservatory, only to meet his medical friend coming back with a face of assurance and collapse. "He's done it," said Harris.

They went together through the gorgeous unnatural beauty of cactus and azalea and found Leonard Quinton, poet and romancer, with his head hanging downward off his ottoman and his red curls sweeping the ground. Into his left side was thrust the queer dagger that they had picked up in the garden, and his limp hand still rested on the hilt.

Outside the storm had come at one stride, like the night in Coleridge, and garden and glass roof were darkened with driving rain. Father Brown seemed to be studying the paper more than the corpse; he held it close to his eyes; and seemed trying to read it in the twilight. Then he held it up against the faint light, and, as he did so, lightning stared at them for an instant so white that the paper looked black against it.

Darkness full of thunder followed, and after the thunder Father Brown's voice said out of the dark: "Doctor, this paper is the wrong shape."

"What do you mean?" asked Doctor Harris, with a frowning stare.

"It isn't square," answered Brown. "It has a sort of edge snipped off at the corner. What does it mean?"

"How the deuce should I know?" growled the doctor. "Shall we move this poor chap, do you think? He's quite dead."

"No," answered the priest; "we must leave him as he lies and send for the police." But he was still scrutinising the paper.

As they went back through the study he stopped by the table and picked up a small pair of nail scissors. "Ah," he said, with a sort of relief, "this is what he did it with. But yet—" And he knitted his brows.

"Oh, stop fooling with that scrap of paper," said the doctor emphatically. "It was a fad of his. He had hundreds of them. He cut all his paper like that," as he pointed to a stack of sermon paper still unused on another and smaller table. Father Brown went up to it and held up a sheet. It was the same irregular shape.

"Quite so," he said. "And here I see the corners that were snipped off." And to the indignation of his colleague he began to count them.

"That's all right," he said, with an apologetic smile. "Twenty-three sheets cut and twenty-two corners cut off them. And as I see you are impatient we will rejoin the others."

"Who is to tell his wife?" asked Dr. Harris. "Will you go and tell her now, while I send a servant for the police?"

"As you will," said Father Brown indifferently. And he went out to the hall door.

Here also he found a drama, though of a more grotesque sort. It showed nothing less than his big friend Flambeau in an attitude to which he had long been unaccustomed, while upon the pathway at the bottom of the steps was sprawling with his boots in the air the amiable Atkinson, his billycock hat and walking cane sent flying in opposite directions along the path. Atkinson had at length wearied of Flambeau's almost paternal custody, and had endeavoured to knock him down, which was by no means a smooth game to play with the Roi des Apaches, even after that monarch's abdication.

Flambeau was about to leap upon his enemy and secure him once more, when the priest patted him easily on the shoulder.

"Make it up with Mr. Atkinson, my friend," he said. "Beg a mutual pardon and say 'Good night.' We need not detain him any longer." Then, as Atkinson rose somewhat doubtfully and gathered his hat and stick and went towards the garden gate, Father Brown said in a more serious voice: "Where is that Indian?"

They all three (for the doctor had joined them) turned involuntarily towards the dim grassy bank amid the tossing trees purple with twilight, where they had last seen the brown man swaying in his strange prayers. The Indian was gone.

"Confound him," cried the doctor, stamping furiously. "Now I know that it was that nigger that did it."

"I thought you didn't believe in magic," said Father Brown quietly.

"No more I did," said the doctor, rolling his eyes. "I only know that I loathed that yellow devil when I thought he was a sham wizard. And I shall loathe him more if I come to think he was a real one."

"Well, his having escaped is nothing," said Flambeau. "For we could have proved nothing and done nothing against him. One hardly goes to the parish constable with a story of suicide imposed by witchcraft or auto-suggestion."

Meanwhile Father Brown had made his way into the house, and now went to break the news to the wife of the dead man.

When he came out again he looked a little pale and tragic, but what passed between them in that interview was never known, even when all was known.

Flambeau, who was talking quietly with the doctor, was surprised to see his friend reappear so soon at his elbow; but Brown took no notice, and merely drew the doctor apart. "You have sent for the police, haven't you?" he asked.

"Yes," answered Harris. "They ought to be here in ten minutes."

"Will you do me a favour?" said the priest quietly. "The truth is, I make a collection of these curious stories, which often contain, as in the case of our Hindoo friend, elements which can hardly be put into a police report. Now, I want you to write out a report of this case for my private use. Yours is a clever trade," he said, looking the doctor gravely and steadily in the face. "I sometimes think that you know some details of this matter which you have not thought fit to mention. Mine is a confidential trade like yours, and I will treat anything you write for me in strict confidence. But write the whole."

The doctor, who had been listening thoughtfully with his head a little on one side, looked the priest in the face for an instant, and said: "All right," and went into the study, closing the door behind him.

"Flambeau," said Father Brown, "there is a long seat there under the veranda, where we can smoke out of the rain. You are my only friend in the world, and I want to talk to you. Or, perhaps, be silent with you."

They established themselves comfortably in the veranda seat; Father Brown, against his common habit, accepted a good cigar and smoked it steadily in silence, while the rain shrieked and rattled on the roof of the veranda.

"My friend," he said at length, "this is a very queer case. A very queer case."

"I should think it was," said Flambeau, with something like a shudder.

"You call it queer, and I call it queer," said the other, "and yet we mean quite opposite things. The modern mind always mixes up two different ideas: mystery in the sense of what is marvellous, and mystery in the sense of what is complicated. That is half its difficulty about miracles. A miracle is startling; but it is simple. It is simple because it is a miracle. It is power coming directly from God (or the devil) instead of indirectly through nature or human wills. Now, you mean that this business is marvellous because it is miraculous, because it is witchcraft worked by a wicked Indian. Understand, I do not say that it was not spiritual or diabolic. Heaven and hell only know by what surrounding influences strange sins come into the lives of men. But for the present my point is this: If it was pure magic, as you think, then it is marvellous; but it is not mysterious—that is, it is not complicated. The quality of a miracle is mysterious, but its manner is simple. Now, the manner of this business has been the reverse of simple."

The storm that had slackened for a little seemed to be swelling again, and there came heavy movements as of faint thunder. Father Brown let fall the ash of his cigar and went on:

"There has been in this incident," he said, "a twisted, ugly, complex quality that does not belong to the straight bolts either of heaven or hell. As one knows the crooked track of a snail, I know the crooked track of a man."

The white lightning opened its enormous eye in one wink, the sky shut up again, and the priest went on:

"Of all these crooked things, the crookedest was the shape of that piece of paper. It was crookeder than the dagger that killed him."

"You mean the paper on which Quinton confessed his suicide," said Flambeau.

"I mean the paper on which Quinton wrote, 'I die by my own hand,'" answered Father Brown. "The shape of that paper, my friend, was the wrong shape; the wrong shape, if ever I have seen it in this wicked world."

"It only had a corner snipped off," said Flambeau, "and I understand that all Quinton's paper was cut that way."

"It was a very odd way," said the other, "and a very bad way, to my taste and fancy. Look here, Flambeau, this Quinton—God receive his soul!—was perhaps a bit of a cur in some ways, but he really was an artist, with the pencil as well as the pen. His handwriting, though hard to read, was bold and beautiful. I can't prove what I say; I can't prove anything. But I tell you with the full force of conviction that he could never have cut that mean little piece off a sheet of paper. If he had wanted to cut down paper for some purpose of fitting in, or binding up, or what not, he would have made quite a different slash with the scissors. Do you remember the shape? It was a mean shape. It was a wrong shape. Like this. Don't you remember?"

And he waved his burning cigar before him in the darkness, making irregular squares so rapidly that Flambeau really seemed to see them as fiery hieroglyphics upon the darkness—hieroglyphics such as his friend had spoken of, which are undecipherable, yet can have no good meaning.

"But," said Flambeau, as the priest put his cigar in his mouth again and leaned back, staring at the roof, "suppose somebody else did use the scissors. Why should somebody else, cutting pieces off his sermon paper, make Quinton commit suicide?"

Father Brown was still leaning back and staring at the roof, but he took his cigar out of his mouth and said: "Quinton never did commit suicide."

Flambeau stared at him. "Why, confound it all," he cried, "then why did he confess to suicide?"

The priest leant forward again, settled his elbows on his knees, looked at the ground, and said, in a low, distinct voice: "He never did confess to suicide."

Flambeau laid his cigar down. "You mean," he said, "that the writing was forged?"

"No," said Father Brown. "Quinton wrote it all right."

"Well, there you are," said the aggravated Flambeau; "Quinton wrote, 'I die by my own hand,' with his own hand on a plain piece of paper."

"Of the wrong shape," said the priest calmly.

"Oh, the shape be damned!" cried Flambeau. "What has the shape to do with it?"

"There were twenty-three snipped papers," resumed Brown unmoved, "and only twenty-two pieces snipped off. Therefore one of the pieces had been destroyed, probably that from the written paper. Does that suggest anything to you?"

A light dawned on Flambeau's face, and he said: "There was something else written by Quinton, some other words. 'They will tell you I die by my own hand,' or 'Do not believe that—'"

"Hotter, as the children say," said his friend. "But the piece was hardly half an inch across; there was no room for one word, let alone five. Can you think of anything hardly bigger than a comma which the man with hell in his heart had to tear away as a testimony against him?"

"I can think of nothing," said Flambeau at last.

"What about quotation marks?" said the priest, and flung his cigar far into the darkness like a shooting star.

All words had left the other man's mouth, and Father Brown said, like one going back to fundamentals:

"Leonard Quinton was a romancer, and was writing an Oriental romance about wizardry and hypnotism. He—"

At this moment the door opened briskly behind them, and the doctor came out with his hat on. He put a long envelope into the priest's hands.

"That's the document you wanted," he said, "and I must be getting home. Good night."

"Good night," said Father Brown, as the doctor walked briskly to the gate. He had left the front door open, so that a shaft of gaslight fell upon them. In the light of this Brown opened the envelope and read the following words:

DEAR FATHER BROWN,—Vicisti Galilee. Otherwise, damn your eyes, which are very penetrating ones. Can it be possible that there is something in all that stuff of yours after all?

I am a man who has ever since boyhood believed in Nature and in all natural functions and instincts, whether men called them moral or immoral. Long before I became a doctor, when I was a schoolboy keeping mice and spiders, I believed that to be a good animal is the best thing in the world. But just now I am shaken; I have believed in Nature; but it seems as if Nature could betray a man. Can there be anything in your bosh? I am really getting morbid.

I loved Quinton's wife. What was there wrong in that? Nature told me to, and it's love that makes the world go round. I also thought quite sincerely that she would be happier with a clean animal like me than with that tormenting little lunatic. What was there wrong in that? I was only facing facts, like a man of science. She would have been happier.

According to my own creed I was quite free to kill Quinton, which was the best thing for everybody, even himself. But as a healthy animal I had no notion of killing myself. I resolved, therefore, that I would never do it until I saw a chance that would leave me scot free. I saw that chance this morning.

I have been three times, all told, into Quinton's study today. The first time I went in he would talk about nothing but the weird tale, called "The Cure of a Saint," which he was writing, which was all about how some Indian hermit made an English colonel kill himself by thinking about him. He showed me the last sheets, and even read me the last paragraph, which was something like this:

"The conqueror of the Punjab, a mere yellow skeleton, but still gigantic, managed to lift himself on his elbow and gasp in his nephew's ear: 'I die by my own hand, yet I die murdered!'"

It so happened by one chance out of a hundred, that those last words were written at the top of a new sheet of paper. I left the room, and went out into the garden intoxicated with a frightful opportunity.

We walked round the house; and two more things happened in my favour. You suspected an Indian, and you found a dagger which the Indian might most probably use. Taking the opportunity to stuff it in my pocket I went back to Quinton's study, locked the door, and gave him his sleeping draught. He was against answering Atkinson at all, but I urged him to call out and quiet the fellow, because I wanted a clear proof that Quinton was alive when I left the room for the second time. Quinton lay down in the conservatory, and I came through the study. I am a quick man with my hands, and in a minute and a half I had done what I wanted to do. I had emptied all the first part of Quinton's romance into the fireplace, where it burnt to ashes. Then I saw that the quotation marks wouldn't do, so I snipped them off, and to make it seem likelier, snipped the whole quire to match. Then I came out with the knowledge that Quinton's confession of suicide lay on the front table, while Quinton lay alive but asleep in the conservatory beyond.

The last act was a desperate one; you can guess it: I pretended to have seen Quinton dead and rushed to his room. I delayed you with the paper, and, being a quick man with my hands, killed Quinton while you were looking at his confession of suicide. He was half-asleep, being drugged, and I put his own hand on the knife and drove it into his body. The knife was of so queer a shape that no one but an operator could have calculated the angle that would reach his heart. I wonder if you noticed this.

When I had done it, the extraordinary thing happened. Nature deserted me. I felt ill. I felt just as if I had done something wrong. I think my brain is breaking up; I feel some sort of desperate pleasure in thinking I have told the thing to somebody; that I shall not have to be alone with it if I marry and have children. What is the matter with me?... Madness... or can one have remorse, just as if one were in Byron's poems! I cannot write any more.

James Erskine Harris.

Father Brown carefully folded up the letter, and put it in his breast pocket just as there came a loud peal at the gate bell, and the wet waterproofs of several policemen gleamed in the road outside.

The Sins of Prince Saradine

When Flambeau took his month's holiday from his office in Westminster he took it in a small sailing-boat, so small that it passed much of its time as a rowing-boat. He took it, moreover, in little rivers in the Eastern counties, rivers so small that the boat looked like a magic boat, sailing on land through meadows and corn-fields. The vessel was just comfortable for two people; there was room only for necessities, and Flambeau had stocked it with such things as his special philosophy considered necessary. They reduced themselves, apparently, to four essentials: tins of salmon, if he should want to eat; loaded revolvers, if he should want to fight; a bottle of brandy, presumably in case he should faint; and a priest, presumably in case he should die. With this light luggage he crawled down the little Norfolk rivers, intending to reach the Broads at last, but meanwhile delighting in the overhanging gardens and meadows, the mirrored mansions or villages, lingering to fish in the pools and corners, and in some sense hugging the shore.

Like a true philosopher, Flambeau had no aim in his holiday; but, like a true philosopher, he had an excuse. He had a sort of half purpose, which he took just so seriously that its success would crown the holiday, but just so lightly that its failure would not spoil it. Years ago, when he had been a king of thieves and the most fa-mous figure in Paris, he had often received wild communications of approval, denunciation, or even love; but one had, somehow, stuck in his memory. It consist-ed simply of a visiting-card, in an envelope with an English postmark. On the back of the card was written in French and in green ink: "If you ever retire and become respectable, come and see me. I want to meet you, for I have met all the other great men of my time. That trick of yours of getting one detective to arrest the other was the most splendid scene in French history." On the front of the card was engraved in the formal fashion, "Prince Saradine, Reed House, Reed Island, Norfolk."

He had not troubled much about the prince then, beyond ascertaining that he had been a brilliant and fashionable figure in southern Italy. In his youth, it was said, he had eloped with a married woman of high rank; the escapade was scarcely startling in his social world, but it had clung to men's minds because of an addition-al tragedy: the alleged suicide of the insulted husband, who appeared to have flung himself over a precipice in Sicily. The prince then lived in Vienna for a time, but his more recent years seemed to have been passed in perpetual and restless travel. But when Flambeau, like the prince himself, had left European celebrity and settled in England, it occurred to him that he might pay a surprise visit to this eminent exile in the Norfolk Broads. Whether he should find the place he had no idea; and, indeed, it was sufficiently small and forgotten. But, as things fell out, he found it much sooner than he expected.

They had moored their boat one night under a bank veiled in high grasses and short pollarded trees. Sleep, after heavy sculling, had come to them early, and by a corresponding accident they awoke before it was light. To speak more strictly, they awoke before it was daylight; for a large lemon moon was only just setting in the forest of high grass above their heads, and the sky was of a vivid violet-blue, noc-turnal but bright. Both men had simultaneously a reminiscence of childhood, of the elfin and adventurous time when tall weeds close over us like woods. Standing up thus against the large low moon, the daisies really seemed to be giant daisies, the dandelions to be giant dandelions. Somehow it reminded them of the dado of a nursery wall-paper. The drop of the river-bed sufficed to sink them under the roots of all shrubs and flowers and make them gaze upwards at the grass. "By Jove!" said Flambeau, "it's like being in fairyland."

Father Brown sat bolt upright in the boat and crossed himself. His movement was so abrupt that his friend asked him, with a mild stare, what was the matter.

"The people who wrote the mediaeval ballads," answered the priest, "knew more about fairies than you do. It isn't only nice things that happen in fairyland."

"Oh, bosh!" said Flambeau. "Only nice things could happen under such an innocent moon. I am for pushing on now and seeing what does really come. We may die and rot before we ever see again such a moon or such a mood."

"All right," said Father Brown. "I never said it was always wrong to enter fairyland. I only said it was always dangerous."

They pushed slowly up the brightening river; the glowing violet of the sky and the pale gold of the moon grew fainter and fainter, and faded into that vast colourless cosmos that precedes the colours of the dawn. When the first faint stripes of red and gold and grey split the horizon from end to end they were broken by the black bulk of a town or village which sat on the river just ahead of them. It was already an easy twilight, in which all things were visible, when they came under the hanging roofs and bridges of this riverside hamlet. The houses, with their long, low, stooping roofs, seemed to come down to drink at the river, like huge grey and red cattle. The broadening and whitening dawn had already turned to working daylight before they saw any living creature on the wharves and bridges of that silent town. Eventually they saw a very placid and prosperous man in his shirt sleeves, with a face as round as the recently sunken moon, and rays of red whisker around the low arc of it, who was leaning on a post above the sluggish tide. By an impulse not to be analysed, Flambeau rose to his full height in the swaying boat and shouted at the man to ask if he knew Reed Island or Reed House. The prosperous man's smile grew slightly more expansive, and he simply pointed up the river towards the next bend of it. Flambeau went ahead without further speech.

The boat took many such grassy corners and followed many such reedy and silent reaches of river; but before the search had become monotonous they had swung round a specially sharp angle and come into the silence of a sort of pool or lake, the sight of which instinctively arrested them. For in the middle of this wider piece of water, fringed on every side with rushes, lay a long, low islet, along which ran a long, low house or bungalow built of bamboo or some kind of tough tropic cane. The upstanding rods of bamboo which made the walls were pale yellow, the sloping rods that made the roof were of darker red or brown, otherwise the long house was a thing of repetition and monotony. The early morning breeze rustled the reeds round the island and sang in the strange ribbed house as in a giant pan-pipe.

"By George!" cried Flambeau; "here is the place, after all! Here is Reed Island, if ever there was one. Here is Reed House, if it is anywhere. I believe that fat man with whiskers was a fairy."

"Perhaps," remarked Father Brown impartially. "If he was, he was a bad fairy."

But even as he spoke the impetuous Flambeau had run his boat ashore in the rattling reeds, and they stood in the long, quaint islet beside the odd and silent house.

The house stood with its back, as it were, to the river and the only landing-stage; the main entrance was on the other side, and looked down the long island garden. The visitors approached it, therefore, by a small path running round nearly three sides of the house, close under the low eaves. Through three different windows on three different sides they looked in on the same long, well-lit room, panelled in light wood, with a large number of looking-glasses, and laid out as for an elegant lunch. The front door, when they came round to it at last, was flanked by two turquoise-blue flower pots. It was opened by a butler of the drearier type—long, lean, grey and listless—who murmured that Prince Saradine was from home at present, but was expected hourly; the house being kept ready for him and his guests. The exhibition of the card with the scrawl of green ink awoke a flicker of life in the parchment face of the depressed retainer, and it was with a certain shaky courtesy that he suggested that the strangers should remain. "His Highness may be here any minute," he said, "and would be distressed to have just missed any gentleman he had invited. We have orders always to keep a little cold lunch for him and his friends, and I am sure he would wish it to be offered."

Moved with curiosity to this minor adventure, Flambeau assented gracefully, and followed the old man, who ushered him ceremoniously into the long, lightly panelled room. There was nothing very notable about it, except the rather unusual alternation of many long, low windows with many long, low oblongs of looking-glass, which gave a singular air of lightness and unsubstantialness to the place. It was somehow like lunching out of doors. One or two pictures of a quiet kind hung in the corners, one a large grey photograph of a very young man in uniform, another a red chalk sketch of two long-haired boys. Asked by Flambeau whether the soldier-ly person was the prince, the butler answered shortly in the negative; it was the prince's younger brother, Captain Stephen Saradine, he said. And with that the old man seemed to dry up suddenly and lose all taste for conversation.

After lunch had tailed off with exquisite coffee and liqueurs, the guests were introduced to the garden, the library, and the housekeeper—a dark, handsome lady, of no little majesty, and rather like a plutonic Madonna. It appeared that she and the butler were the only survivors of the prince's original foreign menage the other servants now in the house being new and collected in Norfolk by the housekeeper. This latter lady went by the name of Mrs. Anthony, but she spoke with a slight Italian accent, and Flambeau did not doubt that Anthony was a Norfolk version of some more Latin name. Mr. Paul, the butler, also had a faintly foreign air, but he was in tongue and training English, as are many of the most polished men-servants of the cosmopolitan nobility.

Pretty and unique as it was, the place had about it a curious luminous sadness. Hours passed in it like days. The long, well-windowed rooms were full of daylight, but it seemed a dead daylight. And through all other incidental noises, the sound of talk, the clink of glasses, or the passing feet of servants, they could hear on all sides of the house the melancholy noise of the river.

"We have taken a wrong turning, and come to a wrong place," said Father Brown, looking out of the window at the grey-green sedges and the silver flood. "Never mind; one can sometimes do good by being the right person in the wrong place."

Father Brown, though commonly a silent, was an oddly sympathetic little man, and in those few but endless hours he unconsciously sank deeper into the secrets of Reed House than his professional friend. He had that knack of friendly silence which is so essential to gossip; and saying scarcely a word, he probably obtained from his new acquaintances all that in any case they would have told. The butler indeed was naturally uncommunicative. He betrayed a sullen and almost animal affection for his master; who, he said, had been very badly treated. The chief offender seemed to be his highness's brother, whose name alone would lengthen the old man's lantern jaws and pucker his parrot nose into a sneer. Captain Stephen was a ne'er-do-well, apparently, and had drained his benevolent brother of hundreds and thousands; forced him to fly from fashionable life and live quietly in this retreat. That was all Paul, the butler, would say, and Paul was obviously a partisan.

The Italian housekeeper was somewhat more communicative, being, as Brown fancied, somewhat less content. Her tone about her master was faintly acid; though not without a certain awe. Flambeau and his friend were standing in the room of the looking-glasses examining the red sketch of the two boys, when the housekeeper swept in swiftly on some domestic errand. It was a peculiarity of this glittering, glass-panelled place that anyone entering was reflected in four or five mirrors at once; and Father Brown, without turning round, stopped in the middle of a sentence of family criticism. But Flambeau, who had his face close up to the picture, was already saying in a loud voice, "The brothers Saradine, I suppose. They both look innocent enough. It would be hard to say which is the good brother and which the bad." Then, realising the lady's presence, he turned the conversation with some triviality, and strolled out into the garden. But Father Brown still gazed steadily at the red crayon sketch; and Mrs. Anthony still gazed steadily at Father Brown.

She had large and tragic brown eyes, and her olive face glowed darkly with a curious and painful wonder—as of one doubtful of a stranger's identity or purpose. Whether the little priest's coat and creed touched some southern memories of confession, or whether she fancied he knew more than he did, she said to him in a low voice as to a fellow plotter, "He is right enough in one way, your friend. He says it would be hard to pick out the good and bad brothers. Oh, it would be hard, it would be mighty hard, to pick out the good one."

"I don't understand you," said Father Brown, and began to move away.

The woman took a step nearer to him, with thunderous brows and a sort of savage stoop, like a bull lowering his horns.

"There isn't a good one," she hissed. "There was badness enough in the captain taking all that money, but I don't think there was much goodness in the prince giving it. The captain's not the only one with something against him."

A light dawned on the cleric's averted face, and his mouth formed silently the word "blackmail." Even as he did so the woman turned an abrupt white face over her shoulder and almost fell. The door had opened soundlessly and the pale Paul stood like a ghost in the doorway. By the weird trick of the reflecting walls, it seemed as if five Pauls had entered by five doors simultaneously.

"His Highness," he said, "has just arrived."

In the same flash the figure of a man had passed outside the first window, crossing the sunlit pane like a lighted stage. An instant later he passed at the second window and the many mirrors repainted in successive frames the same eagle profile and marching figure. He was erect and alert, but his hair was white and his complexion of an odd ivory yellow. He had that short, curved Roman nose which generally goes with long, lean cheeks and chin, but these were partly masked by moustache and imperial. The moustache was much darker than the beard, giving an effect slightly theatrical, and he was dressed up to the same dashing part, having a white top hat, an orchid in his coat, a yellow waistcoat and yellow gloves which he flapped and swung as he walked. When he came round to the front door they heard the stiff Paul open it, and heard the new arrival say cheerfully, "Well, you see I have come." The stiff Mr. Paul bowed and answered in his inaudible manner; for a few minutes their conversation could not be heard. Then the butler said, "Everything is at your disposal;" and the glove-flapping Prince Saradine came gaily into the room to greet them. They beheld once more that spectral scene—five princes entering a room with five doors.

The prince put the white hat and yellow gloves on the table and offered his hand quite cordially.

"Delighted to see you here, Mr. Flambeau," he said. "Knowing you very well by reputation, if that's not an indiscreet remark."

"Not at all," answered Flambeau, laughing. "I am not sensitive. Very few reputations are gained by unsullied virtue."

The prince flashed a sharp look at him to see if the retort had any personal point; then he laughed also and offered chairs to everyone, including himself.

"Pleasant little place, this, I think," he said with a detached air. "Not much to do, I fear; but the fishing is really good."

The priest, who was staring at him with the grave stare of a baby, was haunted by some fancy that escaped definition. He looked at the grey, carefully curled hair, yellow white visage, and slim, somewhat foppish figure. These were not unnatural, though perhaps a shade prononcé, like the outfit of a figure behind the footlights. The nameless interest lay in something else, in the very framework of the face; Brown was tormented with a half memory of having seen it somewhere before. The man looked like some old friend of his dressed up. Then he suddenly remembered the mirrors, and put his fancy down to some psychological effect of that multiplication of human masks.

Prince Saradine distributed his social attentions between his guests with great gaiety and tact. Finding the detective of a sporting turn and eager to employ his holiday, he guided Flambeau and Flambeau's boat down to the best fishing spot in the stream, and was back in his own canoe in twenty minutes to join Father Brown in the library and plunge equally politely into the priest's more philosophic pleasures. He seemed to know a great deal both about the fishing and the books, though of these not the most edifying; he spoke five or six languages, though chiefly the slang of each. He had evidently lived in varied cities and very motley societies, for some of his cheerfullest stories were about gambling hells and opium dens, Australian bushrangers or Italian brigands. Father Brown knew that the once-celebrated Saradine had spent his last few years in almost ceaseless travel, but he had not guessed that the travels were so disreputable or so amusing.

Indeed, with all his dignity of a man of the world, Prince Saradine radiated to such sensitive observers as the priest, a certain atmosphere of the restless and even the unreliable. His face was fastidious, but his eye was wild; he had little nervous tricks, like a man shaken by drink or drugs, and he neither had, nor professed to have, his hand on the helm of household affairs. All these were left to the two old servants, especially to the butler, who was plainly the central pillar of the house. Mr. Paul, indeed, was not so much a butler as a sort of steward or, even, chamberlain; he dined privately, but with almost as much pomp as his master; he was feared by all the servants; and he consulted with the prince decorously, but somewhat unbendingly—rather as if he were the prince's solicitor. The sombre housekeeper was a mere shadow in comparison; indeed, she seemed to efface herself and wait only on the butler, and Brown heard no more of those volcanic whispers which had half told him of the younger brother who blackmailed the elder. Whether the prince was really being thus bled by the absent captain, he could not be certain, but there was something insecure and secretive about Saradine that made the tale by no means incredible.

When they went once more into the long hall with the windows and the mirrors, yellow evening was dropping over the waters and the willowy banks; and a bittern sounded in the distance like an elf upon his dwarfish drum. The same singular sentiment of some sad and evil fairyland crossed the priest's mind again like a little grey cloud. "I wish Flambeau were back," he muttered.

"Do you believe in doom?" asked the restless Prince Saradine suddenly.

"No," answered his guest. "I believe in Doomsday."

The prince turned from the window and stared at him in a singular manner, his face in shadow against the sunset. "What do you mean?" he asked.

"I mean that we here are on the wrong side of the tapestry," answered Father Brown. "The things that happen here do not seem to mean anything; they mean something somewhere else. Somewhere else retribution will come on the real offender. Here it often seems to fall on the wrong person."

The prince made an inexplicable noise like an animal; in his shadowed face the eyes were shining queerly. A new and shrewd thought exploded silently in the other's mind. Was there another meaning in Saradine's blend of brilliancy and abruptness? Was the prince—Was he perfectly sane? He was repeating, "The wrong person—the wrong person," many more times than was natural in a social exclamation.

Then Father Brown awoke tardily to a second truth. In the mirrors before him he could see the silent door standing open, and the silent Mr. Paul standing in it, with his usual pallid impassiveness.

"I thought it better to announce at once," he said, with the same stiff respectfulness as of an old family lawyer, "a boat rowed by six men has come to the landing-stage, and there's a gentleman sitting in the stern."

"A boat!" repeated the prince; "a gentleman?" and he rose to his feet.

There was a startled silence punctuated only by the odd noise of the bird in the sedge; and then, before anyone could speak again, a new face and figure passed in profile round the three sunlit windows, as the prince had passed an hour or two before. But except for the accident that both outlines were aquiline, they had little in common. Instead of the new white topper of Saradine, was a black one of antiquated or foreign shape; under it was a young and very solemn face, clean shaven, blue about its resolute chin, and carrying a faint suggestion of the young Napoleon. The association was assisted by something old and odd about the whole get-up, as of a man who had never troubled to change the fashions of his fathers. He had a shabby blue frock coat, a red, soldierly looking waistcoat, and a kind of coarse white trousers common among the early Victorians, but strangely incongruous today. From all this old clothes-shop his olive face stood out strangely young and monstrously sincere.

"The deuce!" said Prince Saradine, and clapping on his white hat he went to the front door himself, flinging it open on the sunset garden.

By that time the new-comer and his followers were drawn up on the lawn like a small stage army. The six boatmen had pulled the boat well up on shore, and were guarding it almost menacingly, holding their oars erect like spears. They were swarthy men, and some of them wore earrings. But one of them stood forward beside the olive-faced young man in the red waistcoat, and carried a large black case of unfamiliar form.

"Your name," said the young man, "is Saradine?"

Saradine assented rather negligently.

The new-comer had dull, dog-like brown eyes, as different as possible from the restless and glittering grey eyes of the prince. But once again Father Brown was tortured with a sense of having seen somewhere a replica of the face; and once again he remembered the repetitions of the glass-panelled room, and put down the coincidence to that. "Confound this crystal palace!" he muttered. "One sees everything too many times. It's like a dream."

"If you are Prince Saradine," said the young man, "I may tell you that my name is Antonelli."

"Antonelli," repeated the prince languidly. "Somehow I remember the name."

"Permit me to present myself," said the young Italian.

With his left hand he politely took off his old-fashioned top-hat; with his right he caught Prince Saradine so ringing a crack across the face that the white top hat rolled down the steps and one of the blue flower-pots rocked upon its pedestal.

The prince, whatever he was, was evidently not a coward; he sprang at his enemy's throat and almost bore him backwards to the grass. But his enemy extricated himself with a singularly inappropriate air of hurried politeness.

"That is all right," he said, panting and in halting English. "I have insulted. I will give satisfaction. Marco, open the case."

The man beside him with the earrings and the big black case proceeded to unlock it. He took out of it two long Italian rapiers, with splendid steel hilts and blades, which he planted point downwards in the lawn. The strange young man standing facing the entrance with his yellow and vindictive face, the two swords standing up in the turf like two crosses in a cemetery, and the line of the ranked towers behind, gave it all an odd appearance of being some barbaric court of justice. But everything else was unchanged, so sudden had been the interruption. The sunset gold still glowed on the lawn, and the bittern still boomed as announcing some small but dreadful destiny.

"Prince Saradine," said the man called Antonelli, "when I was an infant in the cradle you killed my father and stole my mother; my father was the more fortunate. You did not kill him fairly, as I am going to kill you. You and my wicked mother took him driving to a lonely pass in Sicily, flung him down a cliff, and went on your way. I could imitate you if I chose, but imitating you is too vile. I have followed you all over the world, and you have always fled from me. But this is the end of the world—and of you. I have you now, and I give you the chance you never gave my father. Choose one of those swords."

Prince Saradine, with contracted brows, seemed to hesitate a moment, but his ears were still singing with the blow, and he sprang forward and snatched at one of the hilts. Father Brown had also sprung forward, striving to compose the dispute; but he soon found his personal presence made matters worse. Saradine was a French freemason and a fierce atheist, and a priest moved him by the law of contraries. And for the other man neither priest nor layman moved him at all. This young man with the Bonaparte face and the brown eyes was something far sterner than a puritan—a pagan. He was a simple slayer from the morning of the earth; a man of the stone age—a man of stone.

One hope remained, the summoning of the household; and Father Brown ran back into the house. He found, however, that all the under servants had been given a holiday ashore by the autocrat Paul, and that only the sombre Mrs. Anthony moved uneasily about the long rooms. But the moment she turned a ghastly face upon him, he resolved one of the riddles of the house of mirrors. The heavy brown eyes of Antonelli were the heavy brown eyes of Mrs. Anthony; and in a flash he saw half the story.

"Your son is outside," he said without wasting words; "either he or the prince will be killed. Where is Mr. Paul?"

"He is at the landing-stage," said the woman faintly. "He is—he is—signalling for help."

"Mrs. Anthony," said Father Brown seriously, "there is no time for nonsense. My friend has his boat down the river fishing. Your son's boat is guarded by your son's men. There is only this one canoe; what is Mr. Paul doing with it?"

"Santa Maria! I do not know," she said; and swooned all her length on the matted floor.

Father Brown lifted her to a sofa, flung a pot of water over her, shouted for help, and then rushed down to the landing-stage of the little island. But the canoe was already in mid-stream, and old Paul was pulling and pushing it up the river with an energy incredible at his years.

"I will save my master," he cried, his eyes blazing maniacally. "I will save him yet!"

Father Brown could do nothing but gaze after the boat as it struggled upstream and pray that the old man might waken the little town in time.

"A duel is bad enough," he muttered, rubbing up his rough dust-coloured hair, "but there's something wrong about this duel, even as a duel. I feel it in my bones. But what can it be?"

As he stood staring at the water, a wavering mirror of sunset, he heard from the other end of the island garden a small but unmistakable sound—the cold concussion of steel. He turned his head.

Away on the farthest cape or headland of the long islet, on a strip of turf beyond the last rank of roses, the duellists had already crossed swords. Evening above them was a dome of virgin gold, and, distant as they were, every detail was picked out. They had cast off their coats, but the yellow waistcoat and white hair of Saradine, the red waistcoat and white trousers of Antonelli, glittered in the level light like the colours of the dancing clockwork dolls. The two swords sparkled from point to pommel like two diamond pins. There was something frightful in the two figures appearing so little and so gay. They looked like two butterflies trying to pin each other to a cork.

Father Brown ran as hard as he could, his little legs going like a wheel. But when he came to the field of combat he found he was born too late and too early— too late to stop the strife, under the shadow of the grim Sicilians leaning on their oars, and too early to anticipate any disastrous issue of it. For the two men were singularly well matched, the prince using his skill with a sort of cynical confidence, the Sicilian using his with a murderous care. Few finer fencing matches can ever have been seen in crowded amphitheatres than that which tinkled and sparkled on that forgotten island in the reedy river. The dizzy fight was balanced so long that hope began to revive in the protesting priest; by all common probability Paul must soon come back with the police. It would be some comfort even if Flambeau came back from his fishing, for Flambeau, physically speaking, was worth four other men. But there was no sign of Flambeau, and, what was much queerer, no sign of Paul or the police. No other raft or stick was left to float on; in that lost island in that vast nameless pool, they were cut off as on a rock in the Pacific.

Almost as he had the thought the ringing of the rapiers quickened to a rattle, the prince's arms flew up, and the point shot out behind between his shoulder-blades. He went over with a great whirling movement, almost like one throwing the half of a boy's cart-wheel. The sword flew from his hand like a shooting star, and dived into the distant river. And he himself sank with so earth-shaking a subsidence that he broke a big rose-tree with his body and shook up into the sky a cloud of red earth—like the smoke of some heathen sacrifice. The Sicilian had made blood-offering to the ghost of his father.

The priest was instantly on his knees by the corpse; but only to make too sure that it was a corpse. As he was still trying some last hopeless tests he heard for the first time voices from farther up the river, and saw a police boat shoot up to the landing-stage, with constables and other important people, including the excited Paul. The little priest rose with a distinctly dubious grimace.

"Now, why on earth," he muttered, "why on earth couldn't he have come before?"

Some seven minutes later the island was occupied by an invasion of townsfolk and police, and the latter had put their hands on the victorious duellist, ritually reminding him that anything he said might be used against him.

"I shall not say anything," said the monomaniac, with a wonderful and peaceful face. "I shall never say anything more. I am very happy, and I only want to be hanged."

Then he shut his mouth as they led him away, and it is the strange but certain truth that he never opened it again in this world, except to say "Guilty" at his trial.

Father Brown had stared at the suddenly crowded garden, the arrest of the man of blood, the carrying away of the corpse after its examination by the doctor, rather as one watches the break-up of some ugly dream; he was motionless, like a man in a nightmare. He gave his name and address as a witness, but declined their offer of a boat to the shore, and remained alone in the island garden, gazing at the broken rose bush and the whole green theatre of that swift and inexplicable tragedy. The light died along the river; mist rose in the marshy banks; a few belated birds flitted fitfully across.

Stuck stubbornly in his sub-consciousness (which was an unusually lively one) was an unspeakable certainty that there was something still unexplained. This sense that had clung to him all day could not be fully explained by his fancy about "looking-glass land." Somehow he had not seen the real story, but some game or masque. And yet people do not get hanged or run through the body for the sake of a charade.

As he sat on the steps of the landing-stage ruminating he grew conscious of the tall, dark streak of a sail coming silently down the shining river, and sprang to his feet with such a backrush of feeling that he almost wept.

"Flambeau!" he cried, and shook his friend by both hands again and again, much to the astonishment of that sportsman, as he came on shore with his fishing tackle. "Flambeau," he said, "so you're not killed?"

"Killed!" repeated the angler in great astonishment. "And why should I be killed?"

"Oh, because nearly everybody else is," said his companion rather wildly. "Saradine got murdered, and Antonelli wants to be hanged, and his mother's fainted, and I, for one, don't know whether I'm in this world or the next. But, thank God, you're in the same one." And he took the bewildered Flambeau's arm.

As they turned from the landing-stage they came under the eaves of the low bamboo house, and looked in through one of the windows, as they had done on their first arrival. They beheld a lamp-lit interior well calculated to arrest their eyes. The table in the long dining-room had been laid for dinner when Saradine's destroyer had fallen like a stormbolt on the island. And the dinner was now in placid progress, for Mrs. Anthony sat somewhat sullenly at the foot of the table, while at the head of it was Mr. Paul, the major domo, eating and drinking of the best, his bleared, bluish eyes standing queerly out of his face, his gaunt countenance inscrutable, but by no means devoid of satisfaction.

With a gesture of powerful impatience, Flambeau rattled at the window, wrenched it open, and put an indignant head into the lamp-lit room.

"Well," he cried. "I can understand you may need some refreshment, but really to steal your master's dinner while he lies murdered in the garden—"

"I have stolen a great many things in a long and pleasant life," replied the strange old gentleman placidly; "this dinner is one of the few things I have not stolen. This dinner and this house and garden happen to belong to me."

A thought flashed across Flambeau's face. "You mean to say," he began, "that the will of Prince Saradine—"

"I am Prince Saradine," said the old man, munching a salted almond.

Father Brown, who was looking at the birds outside, jumped as if he were shot, and put in at the window a pale face like a turnip.

"You are what?" he repeated in a shrill voice.

"Paul, Prince Saradine, A vos ordres," said the venerable person politely, lifting a glass of sherry. "I live here very quietly, being a domestic kind of fellow; and for the sake of modesty I am called Mr. Paul, to distinguish me from my unfortunate brother Mr. Stephen. He died, I hear, recently—in the garden. Of course, it is not my fault if enemies pursue him to this place. It is owing to the regrettable irregularity of his life. He was not a domestic character."

He relapsed into silence, and continued to gaze at the opposite wall just above the bowed and sombre head of the woman. They saw plainly the family likeness that had haunted them in the dead man. Then his old shoulders began to heave and shake a little, as if he were choking, but his face did not alter.

"My God!" cried Flambeau after a pause, "he's laughing!"

"Come away," said Father Brown, who was quite white. "Come away from this house of hell. Let us get into an honest boat again."

Night had sunk on rushes and river by the time they had pushed off from the island, and they went down-stream in the dark, warming themselves with two big cigars that glowed like crimson ships' lanterns. Father Brown took his cigar out of his mouth and said:

"I suppose you can guess the whole story now? After all, it's a primitive story. A man had two enemies. He was a wise man. And so he discovered that two enemies are better than one."

"I do not follow that," answered Flambeau.

"Oh, it's really simple," rejoined his friend. "Simple, though anything but innocent. Both the Saradines were scamps, but the prince, the elder, was the sort of scamp that gets to the top, and the younger, the captain, was the sort that sinks to the bottom. This squalid officer fell from beggar to blackmailer, and one ugly day he got his hold upon his brother, the prince. Obviously it was for no light matter, for

Prince Paul Saradine was frankly 'fast,' and had no reputation to lose as to the mere sins of society. In plain fact, it was a hanging matter, and Stephen literally had a rope round his brother's neck. He had somehow discovered the truth about the Sicilian affair, and could prove that Paul murdered old Antonelli in the mountains. The captain raked in the hush money heavily for ten years, until even the prince's splendid fortune began to look a little foolish.

"But Prince Saradine bore another burden besides his blood-sucking brother. He knew that the son of Antonelli, a mere child at the time of the murder, had been trained in savage Sicilian loyalty, and lived only to avenge his father, not with the gibbet (for he lacked Stephen's legal proof), but with the old weapons of vendetta. The boy had practised arms with a deadly perfection, and about the time that he was old enough to use them Prince Saradine began, as the society papers said, to travel. The fact is that he began to flee for his life, passing from place to place like a hunted criminal; but with one relentless man upon his trail. That was Prince Paul's position, and by no means a pretty one. The more money he spent on eluding Antonelli the less he had to silence Stephen. The more he gave to silence Stephen the less chance there was of finally escaping Antonelli. Then it was that he showed himself a great man—a genius like Napoleon.

"Instead of resisting his two antagonists, he surrendered suddenly to both of them. He gave way like a Japanese wrestler, and his foes fell prostrate before him. He gave up the race round the world, and he gave up his address to young Antonelli; then he gave up everything to his brother. He sent Stephen money enough for smart clothes and easy travel, with a letter saying roughly: 'This is all I have left. You have cleaned me out. I still have a little house in Norfolk, with servants and a cellar, and if you want more from me you must take that. Come and take possession if you like, and I will live there quietly as your friend or agent or anything.' He knew that the Sicilian had never seen the Saradine brothers save, perhaps, in pictures; he knew they were somewhat alike, both having grey, pointed beards. Then he shaved his own face and waited. The trap worked. The unhappy captain, in his new clothes, entered the house in triumph as a prince, and walked upon the Sicilian's sword.

"There was one hitch, and it is to the honour of human nature. Evil spirits like Saradine often blunder by never expecting the virtues of mankind. He took it for granted that the Italian's blow, when it came, would be dark, violent and nameless, like the blow it avenged; that the victim would be knifed at night, or shot from behind a hedge, and so die without speech. It was a bad minute for Prince Paul when Antonelli's chivalry proposed a formal duel, with all its possible explanations. It was then that I found him putting off in his boat with wild eyes. He was fleeing, bareheaded, in an open boat before Antonelli should learn who he was.

"But, however agitated, he was not hopeless. He knew the adventurer and he knew the fanatic. It was quite probable that Stephen, the adventurer, would hold his tongue, through his mere histrionic pleasure in playing a part, his lust for clinging to his new cosy quarters, his rascal's trust in luck, and his fine fencing. It was certain that Antonelli, the fanatic, would hold his tongue, and be hanged without telling tales of his family. Paul hung about on the river till he knew the fight was over.

Then he roused the town, brought the police, saw his two vanquished enemies taken away forever, and sat down smiling to his dinner."

"Laughing, God help us!" said Flambeau with a strong shudder. "Do they get such ideas from Satan?"

"He got that idea from you," answered the priest.

"God forbid!" ejaculated Flambeau. "From me! What do you mean!"

The priest pulled a visiting-card from his pocket and held it up in the faint glow of his cigar; it was scrawled with green ink.

"Don't you remember his original invitation to you?" he asked, "and the compliment to your criminal exploit? 'That trick of yours,' he says, 'of getting one detective to arrest the other'? He has just copied your trick. With an enemy on each side of him, he slipped swiftly out of the way and let them collide and kill each other."

Flambeau tore Prince Saradine's card from the priest's hands and rent it savagely in small pieces.

"There's the last of that old skull and crossbones," he said as he scattered the pieces upon the dark and disappearing waves of the stream; "but I should think it would poison the fishes."

The last gleam of white card and green ink was drowned and darkened; a faint and vibrant colour as of morning changed the sky, and the moon behind the grasses grew paler. They drifted in silence.

"Father," said Flambeau suddenly, "do you think it was all a dream?"

The priest shook his head, whether in dissent or agnosticism, but remained mute. A smell of hawthorn and of orchards came to them through the darkness, telling them that a wind was awake; the next moment it swayed their little boat and swelled their sail, and carried them onward down the winding river to happier places and the homes of harmless men.

The Hammer of God

The little village of Bohun Beacon was perched on a hill so steep that the tall spire of its church seemed only like the peak of a small mountain. At the foot of the church stood a smithy, generally red with fires and always littered with hammers and scraps of iron; opposite to this, over a rude cross of cobbled paths, was "The Blue Boar," the only inn of the place. It was upon this crossway, in the lifting of a leaden and silver daybreak, that two brothers met in the street and spoke; though one was beginning the day and the other finishing it. The Rev. and Hon. Wilfred Bohun was very devout, and was making his way to some austere exercises of prayer or contemplation at dawn. Colonel the Hon. Norman Bohun, his elder brother, was by no means devout, and was sitting in evening dress on the bench outside "The Blue Boar," drinking what the philosophic observer was free to regard either as his last glass on Tuesday or his first on Wednesday. The colonel was not particular.

The Bohuns were one of the very few aristocratic families really dating from the Middle Ages, and their pennon had actually seen Palestine. But it is a great mistake to suppose that such houses stand high in chivalric tradition. Few except the poor preserve traditions. Aristocrats live not in traditions but in fashions. The Bohuns had been Mohocks under Queen Anne and Mashers under Queen Victoria. But like more than one of the really ancient houses, they had rotted in the last two centuries into mere drunkards and dandy degenerates, till there had even come a whisper of insanity. Certainly there was something hardly human about the colonel's wolfish pursuit of pleasure, and his chronic resolution not to go home till morning had a touch of the hideous clarity of insomnia. He was a tall, fine animal, elderly, but with hair still startlingly yellow. He would have looked merely blonde and leonine, but his blue eyes were sunk so deep in his face that they looked black. They were a little too close together. He had very long yellow moustaches; on each side of them a fold or furrow from nostril to jaw, so that a sneer seemed cut into his face. Over his evening clothes he wore a curious pale yellow coat that looked more like a very light dressing gown than an overcoat, and on the back of his head was stuck an extraordinary broad-brimmed hat of a bright green colour, evidently some oriental curiosity caught up at random. He was proud of appearing in such incongruous attires—proud of the fact that he always made them look congruous.

His brother the curate had also the yellow hair and the elegance, but he was buttoned up to the chin in black, and his face was clean-shaven, cultivated, and a little nervous. He seemed to live for nothing but his religion; but there were some who said (notably the blacksmith, who was a Presbyterian) that it was a love of Gothic architecture rather than of God, and that his haunting of the church like a ghost was only another and purer turn of the almost morbid thirst for beauty which sent his brother raging after women and wine. This charge was doubtful, while the man's practical piety was indubitable. Indeed, the charge was mostly an ignorant misunderstanding of the love of solitude and secret prayer, and was founded on his being often found kneeling, not before the altar, but in peculiar places, in the crypts or gallery, or even in the belfry. He was at the moment about to enter the church through the yard of the smithy, but stopped and frowned a little as he saw his brother's cavernous eyes staring in the same direction. On the hypothesis that the colonel was interested in the church he did not waste any speculations. There only remained the blacksmith's shop, and though the blacksmith was a Puritan and none of his people, Wilfred Bohun had heard some scandals about a beautiful and rather celebrated wife. He flung a suspicious look across the shed, and the colonel stood up laughing to speak to him.

"Good morning, Wilfred," he said. "Like a good landlord I am watching sleeplessly over my people. I am going to call on the blacksmith."

Wilfred looked at the ground, and said: "The blacksmith is out. He is over at Greenford."

"I know," answered the other with silent laughter; "that is why I am calling on him."

"Norman," said the cleric, with his eye on a pebble in the road, "are you ever afraid of thunderbolts?"

"What do you mean?" asked the colonel. "Is your hobby meteorology?"

"I mean," said Wilfred, without looking up, "do you ever think that God might strike you in the street?"

"I beg your pardon," said the colonel; "I see your hobby is folk-lore."

"I know your hobby is blasphemy," retorted the religious man, stung in the one live place of his nature. "But if you do not fear God, you have good reason to fear man."

The elder raised his eyebrows politely. "Fear man?" he said.

"Barnes the blacksmith is the biggest and strongest man for forty miles round," said the clergyman sternly. "I know you are no coward or weakling, but he could throw you over the wall."

This struck home, being true, and the lowering line by mouth and nostril darkened and deepened. For a moment he stood with the heavy sneer on his face. But in an instant Colonel Bohun had recovered his own cruel good humour and laughed, showing two dog-like front teeth under his yellow moustache. "In that case, my dear Wilfred," he said quite carelessly, "it was wise for the last of the Bohuns to come out partially in armour."

And he took off the queer round hat covered with green, showing that it was lined within with steel. Wilfred recognised it indeed as a light Japanese or Chinese helmet torn down from a trophy that hung in the old family hall.

"It was the first hat to hand," explained his brother airily; "always the nearest hat—and the nearest woman."

"The blacksmith is away at Greenford," said Wilfred quietly; "the time of his return is unsettled."

And with that he turned and went into the church with bowed head, crossing himself like one who wishes to be quit of an unclean spirit. He was anxious to forget such grossness in the cool twilight of his tall Gothic cloisters; but on that morning it was fated that his still round of religious exercises should be everywhere arrested by small shocks. As he entered the church, hitherto always empty at that hour, a kneeling figure rose hastily to its feet and came towards the full daylight of the doorway. When the curate saw it he stood still with surprise. For the early worshipper was none other than the village idiot, a nephew of the blacksmith, one who neither would nor could care for the church or for anything else. He was always called "Mad Joe," and seemed to have no other name; he was a dark, strong, slouching lad, with a heavy white face, dark straight hair, and a mouth always open. As he passed the priest, his moon-calf countenance gave no hint of what he had been doing or thinking of. He had never been known to pray before. What sort of prayers was he saying now? Extraordinary prayers surely.

Wilfred Bohun stood rooted to the spot long enough to see the idiot go out into the sunshine, and even to see his dissolute brother hail him with a sort of avuncular jocularity. The last thing he saw was the colonel throwing pennies at the open mouth of Joe, with the serious appearance of trying to hit it.

This ugly sunlit picture of the stupidity and cruelty of the earth sent the ascetic finally to his prayers for purification and new thoughts. He went up to a pew in the gallery, which brought him under a coloured window which he loved and always quieted his spirit; a blue window with an angel carrying lilies. There he began to think less about the half-wit, with his livid face and mouth like a fish. He began to think less of his evil brother, pacing like a lean lion in his horrible hunger. He sank deeper and deeper into those cold and sweet colours of silver blossoms and sapphire sky.

In this place half an hour afterwards he was found by Gibbs, the village cobbler, who had been sent for him in some haste. He got to his feet with promptitude, for he knew that no small matter would have brought Gibbs into such a place at all. The cobbler was, as in many villages, an atheist, and his appearance in church was a shade more extraordinary than Mad Joe's. It was a morning of theological enigmas.

"What is it?" asked Wilfred Bohun rather stiffly, but putting out a trembling hand for his hat.

The atheist spoke in a tone that, coming from him, was quite startlingly respectful, and even, as it were, huskily sympathetic.

"You must excuse me, sir," he said in a hoarse whisper, "but we didn't think it right not to let you know at once. I'm afraid a rather dreadful thing has happened, sir. I'm afraid your brother——"

Wilfred clenched his frail hands. "What devilry has he done now?" he cried in voluntary passion.

"Why, sir," said the cobbler, coughing, "I'm afraid he's done nothing, and won't do anything. I'm afraid he's done for. You had really better come down, sir."

The curate followed the cobbler down a short winding stair which brought them out at an entrance rather higher than the street. Bohun saw the tragedy in one glance, flat underneath him like a plan. In the yard of the smithy were standing five or six men mostly in black, one in an inspector's uniform. They included the doctor, the Presbyterian minister, and the priest from the Roman Catholic chapel, to which the blacksmith's wife belonged. The latter was speaking to her, indeed, very rapidly, in an undertone, as she, a magnificent woman with red-gold hair, was sobbing blindly on a bench. Between these two groups, and just clear of the main heap of hammers, lay a man in evening dress, spread-eagled and flat on his face. From the height above Wilfred could have sworn to every item of his costume and appearance, down to the Bohun rings upon his fingers; but the skull was only a hideous splash, like a star of blackness and blood.

Wilfred Bohun gave but one glance, and ran down the steps into the yard. The doctor, who was the family physician, saluted him, but he scarcely took any notice. He could only stammer out: "My brother is dead. What does it mean? What is this horrible mystery?" There was an unhappy silence; and then the cobbler, the most outspoken man present, answered: "Plenty of horror, sir," he said; "but not much mystery."

"What do you mean?" asked Wilfred, with a white face.

"It's plain enough," answered Gibbs. "There is only one man for forty miles round that could have struck such a blow as that, and he's the man that had most reason to."

"We must not prejudge anything," put in the doctor, a tall, black-bearded man, rather nervously; "but it is competent for me to corroborate what Mr. Gibbs says about the nature of the blow, sir; it is an incredible blow. Mr. Gibbs says that only

104

one man in this district could have done it. I should have said myself that nobody could have done it."

A shudder of superstition went through the slight figure of the curate. "I can hardly understand," he said.

"Mr. Bohun," said the doctor in a low voice, "metaphors literally fail me. It is inadequate to say that the skull was smashed to bits like an eggshell. Fragments of bone were driven into the body and the ground like bullets into a mud wall. It was the hand of a giant."

He was silent a moment, looking grimly through his glasses; then he added: "The thing has one advantage—that it clears most people of suspicion at one stroke. If you or I or any normally made man in the country were accused of this crime, we should be acquitted as an infant would be acquitted of stealing the Nelson column."

"That's what I say," repeated the cobbler obstinately; "there's only one man that could have done it, and he's the man that would have done it. Where's Simeon Barnes, the blacksmith?"

"He's over at Greenford," faltered the curate.

"More likely over in France," muttered the cobbler.

"No; he is in neither of those places," said a small and colourless voice, which came from the little Roman priest who had joined the group. "As a matter of fact, he is coming up the road at this moment."

The little priest was not an interesting man to look at, having stubbly brown hair and a round and stolid face. But if he had been as splendid as Apollo no one would have looked at him at that moment. Everyone turned round and peered at the pathway which wound across the plain below, along which was indeed walking, at his own huge stride and with a hammer on his shoulder, Simeon the smith. He was a bony and gigantic man, with deep, dark, sinister eyes and a dark chin beard. He was walking and talking quietly with two other men; and though he was never specially cheerful, he seemed quite at his ease.

"My God!" cried the atheistic cobbler, "and there's the hammer he did it with."

"No," said the inspector, a sensible-looking man with a sandy moustache, speaking for the first time. "There's the hammer he did it with over there by the church wall. We have left it and the body exactly as they are."

All glanced round and the short priest went across and looked down in silence at the tool where it lay. It was one of the smallest and the lightest of the hammers, and would not have caught the eye among the rest; but on the iron edge of it were blood and yellow hair.

After a silence the short priest spoke without looking up, and there was a new note in his dull voice. "Mr. Gibbs was hardly right," he said, "in saying that there is no mystery. There is at least the mystery of why so big a man should attempt so big a blow with so little a hammer."

"Oh, never mind that," cried Gibbs, in a fever. "What are we to do with Simeon Barnes?"

"Leave him alone," said the priest quietly. "He is coming here of himself. I know those two men with him. They are very good fellows from Greenford, and they have come over about the Presbyterian chapel."

Even as he spoke the tall smith swung round the corner of the church, and strode into his own yard. Then he stood there quite still, and the hammer fell from his hand. The inspector, who had preserved impenetrable propriety, immediately went up to him.

"I won't ask you, Mr. Barnes," he said, "whether you know anything about what has happened here. You are not bound to say. I hope you don't know, and that you will be able to prove it. But I must go through the form of arresting you in the King's name for the murder of Colonel Norman Bohun."

"You are not bound to say anything," said the cobbler in officious excitement. "They've got to prove everything. They haven't proved yet that it is Colonel Bohun, with the head all smashed up like that."

"That won't wash," said the doctor aside to the priest. "That's out of the detective stories. I was the colonel's medical man, and I knew his body better than he did. He had very fine hands, but quite peculiar ones. The second and third fingers were the same length. Oh, that's the colonel right enough."

As he glanced at the brained corpse upon the ground the iron eyes of the motionless blacksmith followed them and rested there also.

"Is Colonel Bohun dead?" said the smith quite calmly. "Then he's damned."

"Don't say anything! Oh, don't say anything," cried the atheist cobbler, dancing about in an ecstasy of admiration of the English legal system. For no man is such a legalist as the good Secularist.

The blacksmith turned on him over his shoulder the august face of a fanatic.

"It's well for you infidels to dodge like foxes because the world's law favours you," he said; "but God guards His own in His pocket, as you shall see this day."

Then he pointed to the colonel and said: "When did this dog die in his sins?"

"Moderate your language," said the doctor.

"Moderate the Bible's language, and I'll moderate mine. When did he die?"

"I saw him alive at six o'clock this morning," stammered Wilfred Bohun.

"God is good," said the smith. "Mr. Inspector, I have not the slightest objection to being arrested. It is you who may object to arresting me. I don't mind leaving the court without a stain on my character. You do mind perhaps leaving the court with a bad set-back in your career."

The solid inspector for the first time looked at the blacksmith with a lively eye; as did everybody else, except the short, strange priest, who was still looking down at the little hammer that had dealt the dreadful blow.

"There are two men standing outside this shop," went on the blacksmith with ponderous lucidity, "good tradesmen in Greenford whom you all know, who will swear that they saw me from before midnight till daybreak and long after in the committee room of our Revival Mission, which sits all night, we save souls so fast. In Greenford itself twenty people could swear to me for all that time. If I were a heathen, Mr. Inspector, I would let you walk on to your downfall. But as a Christian man I feel bound to give you your chance, and ask you whether you will hear my alibi now or in court."

The inspector seemed for the first time disturbed, and said, "Of course I should be glad to clear you altogether now."

The smith walked out of his yard with the same long and easy stride, and returned to his two friends from Greenford, who were indeed friends of nearly everyone present. Each of them said a few words which no one ever thought of disbelieving. When they had spoken, the innocence of Simeon stood up as solid as the great church above them.

One of those silences struck the group which are more strange and insufferable than any speech. Madly, in order to make conversation, the curate said to the Catholic priest:

"You seem very much interested in that hammer, Father Brown."

"Yes, I am," said Father Brown; "why is it such a small hammer?"

The doctor swung round on him.

"By George, that's true," he cried; "who would use a little hammer with ten larger hammers lying about?"

Then he lowered his voice in the curate's ear and said: "Only the kind of person that can't lift a large hammer. It is not a question of force or courage between the sexes. It's a question of lifting power in the shoulders. A bold woman could commit ten murders with a light hammer and never turn a hair. She could not kill a beetle with a heavy one."

Wilfred Bohun was staring at him with a sort of hypnotised horror, while Father Brown listened with his head a little on one side, really interested and attentive. The doctor went on with more hissing emphasis:

"Why do these idiots always assume that the only person who hates the wife's lover is the wife's husband? Nine times out of ten the person who most hates the wife's lover is the wife. Who knows what insolence or treachery he had shown her—look there!"

He made a momentary gesture towards the red-haired woman on the bench. She had lifted her head at last and the tears were drying on her splendid face. But the eyes were fixed on the corpse with an electric glare that had in it something of idiocy.

The Rev. Wilfred Bohun made a limp gesture as if waving away all desire to know; but Father Brown, dusting off his sleeve some ashes blown from the furnace, spoke in his indifferent way.

"You are like so many doctors," he said; "your mental science is really suggestive. It is your physical science that is utterly impossible. I agree that the woman wants to kill the co-respondent much more than the petitioner does. And I agree that a woman will always pick up a small hammer instead of a big one. But the difficulty is one of physical impossibility. No woman ever born could have smashed a man's skull out flat like that." Then he added reflectively, after a pause: "These people haven't grasped the whole of it. The man was actually wearing an iron helmet, and the blow scattered it like broken glass. Look at that woman. Look at her arms."

Silence held them all up again, and then the doctor said rather sulkily: "Well, I may be wrong; there are objections to everything. But I stick to the main point. No man but an idiot would pick up that little hammer if he could use a big hammer."

With that the lean and quivering hands of Wilfred Bohun went up to his head and seemed to clutch his scanty yellow hair. After an instant they dropped, and he cried: "That was the word I wanted; you have said the word."

Then he continued, mastering his discomposure: "The words you said were, 'No man but an idiot would pick up the small hammer.'"

"Yes," said the doctor. "Well?"

"Well," said the curate, "no man but an idiot did." The rest stared at him with eyes arrested and riveted, and he went on in a febrile and feminine agitation.

"I am a priest," he cried unsteadily, "and a priest should be no shedder of blood. I—I mean that he should bring no one to the gallows. And I thank God that I see the criminal clearly now—because he is a criminal who cannot be brought to the gallows."

"You will not denounce him?" inquired the doctor.

"He would not be hanged if I did denounce him," answered Wilfred with a wild but curiously happy smile. "When I went into the church this morning I found a madman praying there—that poor Joe, who has been wrong all his life. God knows what he prayed; but with such strange folk it is not incredible to suppose that their prayers are all upside down. Very likely a lunatic would pray before killing a man. When I last saw poor Joe he was with my brother. My brother was mocking him."

"By Jove!" cried the doctor, "this is talking at last. But how do you explain—"

The Rev. Wilfred was almost trembling with the excitement of his own glimpse of the truth. "Don't you see; don't you see," he cried feverishly; "that is the only theory that covers both the queer things, that answers both the riddles. The two riddles are the little hammer and the big blow. The smith might have struck the big blow, but would not have chosen the little hammer. His wife would have chosen the little hammer, but she could not have struck the big blow. But the madman might have done both. As for the little hammer—why, he was mad and might have picked up anything. And for the big blow, have you never heard, doctor, that a maniac in his paroxysm may have the strength of ten men?"

The doctor drew a deep breath and then said, "By golly, I believe you've got it."

Father Brown had fixed his eyes on the speaker so long and steadily as to prove that his large grey, ox-like eyes were not quite so insignificant as the rest of his face. When silence had fallen he said with marked respect: "Mr. Bohun, yours is the only theory yet propounded which holds water every way and is essentially un-assailable. I think, therefore, that you deserve to be told, on my positive knowledge, that it is not the true one." And with that the old little man walked away and stared again at the hammer.

"That fellow seems to know more than he ought to," whispered the doctor peevishly to Wilfred. "Those popish priests are deucedly sly."

"No, no," said Bohun, with a sort of wild fatigue. "It was the lunatic. It was the lunatic."

The group of the two clerics and the doctor had fallen away from the more of-ficial group containing the inspector and the man he had arrested. Now, however, that their own party had broken up, they heard voices from the others. The priest looked up quietly and then looked down again as he heard the blacksmith say in a loud voice:

"I hope I've convinced you, Mr. Inspector. I'm a strong man, as you say, but I couldn't have flung my hammer bang here from Greenford. My hammer hasn't got wings that it should come flying half a mile over hedges and fields."

The inspector laughed amicably and said: "No, I think you can be considered out of it, though it's one of the rummiest coincidences I ever saw. I can only ask you to give us all the assistance you can in finding a man as big and strong as yourself. By George! you might be useful, if only to hold him! I suppose you yourself have no guess at the man?"

"I may have a guess," said the pale smith, "but it is not at a man." Then, seeing the scared eyes turn towards his wife on the bench, he put his huge hand on her shoulder and said: "Nor a woman either."

"What do you mean?" asked the inspector jocularly. "You don't think cows use hammers, do you?"

"I think no thing of flesh held that hammer," said the blacksmith in a stifled voice; "mortally speaking, I think the man died alone."

Wilfred made a sudden forward movement and peered at him with burning eyes.

"Do you mean to say, Barnes," came the sharp voice of the cobbler, "that the hammer jumped up of itself and knocked the man down?"

"Oh, you gentlemen may stare and snigger," cried Simeon; "you clergymen who tell us on Sunday in what a stillness the Lord smote Sennacherib. I believe that One who walks invisible in every house defended the honour of mine, and laid the defiler dead before the door of it. I believe the force in that blow was just the force there is in earthquakes, and no force less."

Wilfred said, with a voice utterly undescribable: "I told Norman myself to beware of the thunderbolt."

"That agent is outside my jurisdiction," said the inspector with a slight smile.

"You are not outside His," answered the smith; "see you to it," and, turning his broad back, he went into the house.

The shaken Wilfred was led away by Father Brown, who had an easy and friendly way with him. "Let us get out of this horrid place, Mr. Bohun," he said. "May I look inside your church? I hear it's one of the oldest in England. We take some interest, you know," he added with a comical grimace, "in old English churches."

Wilfred Bohun did not smile, for humour was never his strong point. But he nodded rather eagerly, being only too ready to explain the Gothic splendours to someone more likely to be sympathetic than the Presbyterian blacksmith or the atheist cobbler.

"By all means," he said; "let us go in at this side." And he led the way into the high side entrance at the top of the flight of steps. Father Brown was mounting the first step to follow him when he felt a hand on his shoulder, and turned to behold the dark, thin figure of the doctor, his face darker yet with suspicion.

"Sir," said the physician harshly, "you appear to know some secrets in this black business. May I ask if you are going to keep them to yourself?"

"Why, doctor," answered the priest, smiling quite pleasantly, "there is one very good reason why a man of my trade should keep things to himself when he is not sure of them, and that is that it is so constantly his duty to keep them to himself when he is sure of them. But if you think I have been discourteously reticent with you or anyone, I will go to the extreme limit of my custom. I will give you two very large hints."

"Well, sir?" said the doctor gloomily.

"First," said Father Brown quietly, "the thing is quite in your own province. It is a matter of physical science. The blacksmith is mistaken, not perhaps in saying that the blow was divine, but certainly in saying that it came by a miracle. It was no miracle, doctor, except in so far as man is himself a miracle, with his strange and wicked and yet half-heroic heart. The force that smashed that skull was a force well known to scientists—one of the most frequently debated of the laws of nature."

The doctor, who was looking at him with frowning intentness, only said: "And the other hint?"

"The other hint is this," said the priest. "Do you remember the blacksmith, though he believes in miracles, talking scornfully of the impossible fairy tale that his hammer had wings and flew half a mile across country?"

"Yes," said the doctor, "I remember that."

"Well," added Father Brown, with a broad smile, "that fairy tale was the nearest thing to the real truth that has been said today." And with that he turned his back and stumped up the steps after the curate.

The Reverend Wilfred, who had been waiting for him, pale and impatient, as if this little delay were the last straw for his nerves, led him immediately to his favourite corner of the church, that part of the gallery closest to the carved roof and lit by the wonderful window with the angel. The little Latin priest explored and admired everything exhaustively, talking cheerfully but in a low voice all the time. When in the course of his investigation he found the side exit and the winding stair down which Wilfred had rushed to find his brother dead, Father Brown ran not down but up, with the agility of a monkey, and his clear voice came from an outer platform above.

"Come up here, Mr. Bohun," he called. "The air will do you good."

Bohun followed him, and came out on a kind of stone gallery or balcony outside the building, from which one could see the illimitable plain in which their small hill stood, wooded away to the purple horizon and dotted with villages and farms. Clear and square, but quite small beneath them, was the blacksmith's yard, where the inspector still stood taking notes and the corpse still lay like a smashed fly.

"Might be the map of the world, mightn't it?" said Father Brown.

"Yes," said Bohun very gravely, and nodded his head.

Immediately beneath and about them the lines of the Gothic building plunged outwards into the void with a sickening swiftness akin to suicide. There is that element of Titan energy in the architecture of the Middle Ages that, from whatever aspect it be seen, it always seems to be rushing away, like the strong back of some maddened horse. This church was hewn out of ancient and silent stone, bearded with old fungoids and stained with the nests of birds. And yet, when they saw it from below, it sprang like a fountain at the stars; and when they saw it, as now, from above, it poured like a cataract into a voiceless pit. For these two men on the tower were left alone with the most terrible aspect of Gothic; the monstrous fore-shortening and disproportion, the dizzy perspectives, the glimpses of great things small and small things great; a topsy-turvydom of stone in the mid-air. Details of stone, enormous by their proximity, were relieved against a pattern of fields and farms, pygmy in their distance. A carved bird or beast at a corner seemed like some vast walking or flying dragon wasting the pastures and villages below. The whole atmosphere was dizzy and dangerous, as if men were upheld in air amid the gyrating wings of colossal genii; and the whole of that old church, as tall and rich as a cathedral, seemed to sit upon the sunlit country like a cloudburst.

"I think there is something rather dangerous about standing on these high places even to pray," said Father Brown. "Heights were made to be looked at, not to be looked from."

"Do you mean that one may fall over," asked Wilfred.

"I mean that one's soul may fall if one's body doesn't," said the other priest.

"I scarcely understand you," remarked Bohun indistinctly.

"Look at that blacksmith, for instance," went on Father Brown calmly; "a good man, but not a Christian—hard, imperious, unforgiving. Well, his Scotch religion was made up by men who prayed on hills and high crags, and learnt to look down on the world more than to look up at heaven. Humility is the mother of giants. One sees great things from the valley; only small things from the peak."

"But he—he didn't do it," said Bohun tremulously.

"No," said the other in an odd voice; "we know he didn't do it."

After a moment he resumed, looking tranquilly out over the plain with his pale grey eyes. "I knew a man," he said, "who began by worshipping with others before the altar, but who grew fond of high and lonely places to pray from, corners or niches in the belfry or the spire. And once in one of those dizzy places, where the whole world seemed to turn under him like a wheel, his brain turned also, and he fancied he was God. So that, though he was a good man, he committed a great crime."

Wilfred's face was turned away, but his bony hands turned blue and white as they tightened on the parapet of stone.

"He thought it was given to him to judge the world and strike down the sinner. He would never have had such a thought if he had been kneeling with other men upon a floor. But he saw all men walking about like insects. He saw one especially strutting just below him, insolent and evident by a bright green hat—a poisonous insect."

Rooks cawed round the corners of the belfry; but there was no other sound till Father Brown went on.

"This also tempted him, that he had in his hand one of the most awful engines of nature; I mean gravitation, that mad and quickening rush by which all earth's creatures fly back to her heart when released. See, the inspector is strutting just below us in the smithy. If I were to toss a pebble over this parapet it would be something like a bullet by the time it struck him. If I were to drop a hammer—even a small hammer—"

Wilfred Bohun threw one leg over the parapet, and Father Brown had him in a minute by the collar.

"Not by that door," he said quite gently; "that door leads to hell."

Bohun staggered back against the wall, and stared at him with frightful eyes.

"How do you know all this?" he cried. "Are you a devil?"

"I am a man," answered Father Brown gravely; "and therefore have all devils in my heart. Listen to me," he said after a short pause. "I know what you did—at least, I can guess the great part of it. When you left your brother you were racked with no unrighteous rage, to the extent even that you snatched up a small hammer, half inclined to kill him with his foulness on his mouth. Recoiling, you thrust it under your buttoned coat instead, and rushed into the church. You pray wildly in many places, under the angel window, upon the platform above, and a higher platform still, from which you could see the colonel's Eastern hat like the back of a green beetle crawling about. Then something snapped in your soul, and you let God's thunderbolt fall."

Wilfred put a weak hand to his head, and asked in a low voice: "How did you know that his hat looked like a green beetle?"

"Oh, that," said the other with the shadow of a smile, "that was common sense. But hear me further. I say I know all this; but no one else shall know it. The next step is for you; I shall take no more steps; I will seal this with the seal of confession. If you ask me why, there are many reasons, and only one that concerns you. I leave things to you because you have not yet gone very far wrong, as assassins go. You did not help to fix the crime on the smith when it was easy; or on his wife, when that was easy. You tried to fix it on the imbecile because you knew that he could not suffer. That was one of the gleams that it is my business to find in assassins. And now come down into the village, and go your own way as free as the wind; for I have said my last word."

They went down the winding stairs in utter silence, and came out into the sunlight by the smithy. Wilfred Bohun carefully unlatched the wooden gate of the yard, and going up to the inspector, said: "I wish to give myself up; I have killed my brother."

The Eye of Apollo

That singular smoky sparkle, at once a confusion and a transparency, which is the strange secret of the Thames, was changing more and more from its grey to its glittering extreme as the sun climbed to the zenith over Westminster, and two men crossed Westminster Bridge. One man was very tall and the other very short; they might even have been fantastically compared to the arrogant clock-tower of Parliament and the humbler humped shoulders of the Abbey, for the short man was in clerical dress. The official description of the tall man was M. Hercule Flambeau, private detective, and he was going to his new offices in a new pile of flats facing the Abbey entrance. The official description of the short man was the Reverend J. Brown, attached to St. Francis Xavier's Church, Camberwell, and he was coming from a Camberwell deathbed to see the new offices of his friend.

The building was American in its sky-scraping altitude, and American also in the oiled elaboration of its machinery of telephones and lifts. But it was barely finished and still understaffed; only three tenants had moved in; the office just above Flambeau was occupied, as also was the office just below him; the two floors above that and the three floors below were entirely bare. But the first glance at the new tower of flats caught something much more arresting. Save for a few relics of scaffolding, the one glaring object was erected outside the office just above Flambeau's. It was an enormous gilt effigy of the human eye, surrounded with rays of gold, and taking up as much room as two or three of the office windows.

"What on earth is that?" asked Father Brown, and stood still. "Oh, a new religion," said Flambeau, laughing; "one of those new religions that forgive your sins by saying you never had any. Rather like Christian Science, I should think. The fact is that a fellow calling himself Kalon (I don't know what his name is, except that it can't be that) has taken the flat just above me. I have two lady typewriters underneath me, and this enthusiastic old humbug on top. He calls himself the New Priest of Apollo, and he worships the sun."

"Let him look out," said Father Brown. "The sun was the cruellest of all the gods. But what does that monstrous eye mean?"

"As I understand it, it is a theory of theirs," answered Flambeau, "that a man can endure anything if his mind is quite steady. Their two great symbols are the sun and the open eye; for they say that if a man were really healthy he could stare at the sun."

"If a man were really healthy," said Father Brown, "he would not bother to stare at it."

"Well, that's all I can tell you about the new religion," went on Flambeau carelessly. "It claims, of course, that it can cure all physical diseases."

"Can it cure the one spiritual disease?" asked Father Brown, with a serious curiosity.

"And what is the one spiritual disease?" asked Flambeau, smiling.

"Oh, thinking one is quite well," said his friend.

Flambeau was more interested in the quiet little office below him than in the flamboyant temple above. He was a lucid Southerner, incapable of conceiving himself as anything but a Catholic or an atheist; and new religions of a bright and pallid sort were not much in his line. But humanity was always in his line, especially when it was good-looking; moreover, the ladies downstairs were characters in their way. The office was kept by two sisters, both slight and dark, one of them tall and striking. She had a dark, eager and aquiline profile, and was one of those women whom one always thinks of in profile, as of the clean-cut edge of some weapon. She seemed to cleave her way through life. She had eyes of startling brilliancy, but it was the brilliancy of steel rather than of diamonds; and her straight, slim figure was a shade too stiff for its grace. Her younger sister was like her shortened shadow, a little greyer, paler, and more insignificant. They both wore a business-like black, with little masculine cuffs and collars. There are thousands of such curt, strenuous ladies in the offices of London, but the interest of these lay rather in their real than their apparent position.

For Pauline Stacey, the elder, was actually the heiress of a crest and half a county, as well as great wealth; she had been brought up in castles and gardens, before a frigid fierceness (peculiar to the modern woman) had driven her to what she considered a harsher and a higher existence. She had not, indeed, surrendered her money; in that there would have been a romantic or monkish abandon quite alien to her masterful utilitarianism. She held her wealth, she would say, for use upon practical social objects. Part of it she had put into her business, the nucleus of a model typewriting emporium; part of it was distributed in various leagues and causes for the advancement of such work among women. How far Joan, her sister and partner, shared this slightly prosaic idealism no one could be very sure. But she followed her leader with a dog-like affection which was somehow more attractive, with its touch of tragedy, than the hard, high spirits of the elder. For Pauline Stacey had nothing to say to tragedy; she was understood to deny its existence.

Her rigid rapidity and cold impatience had amused Flambeau very much on the first occasion of his entering the flats. He had lingered outside the lift in the entrance hall waiting for the lift-boy, who generally conducts strangers to the various floors. But this bright-eyed falcon of a girl had openly refused to endure such official delay. She said sharply that she knew all about the lift, and was not dependent on boys—or men either. Though her flat was only three floors above, she managed in the few seconds of ascent to give Flambeau a great many of her fundamental views in an off-hand manner; they were to the general effect that she was a modern working woman and loved modern working machinery. Her bright black eyes blazed with abstract anger against those who rebuke mechanic science and ask for the return of romance. Everyone, she said, ought to be able to manage machines, just as she could manage the lift. She seemed almost to resent the fact of Flambeau opening the lift-door for her; and that gentleman went up to his own apartments smiling with somewhat mingled feelings at the memory of such spit-fire self-dependence.

She certainly had a temper, of a snappy, practical sort; the gestures of her thin, elegant hands were abrupt or even destructive.

Once Flambeau entered her office on some typewriting business, and found she had just flung a pair of spectacles belonging to her sister into the middle of the floor and stamped on them. She was already in the rapids of an ethical tirade about the "sickly medical notions" and the morbid admission of weakness implied in such an apparatus. She dared her sister to bring such artificial, unhealthy rubbish into the place again. She asked if she was expected to wear wooden legs or false hair or glass eyes; and as she spoke her eyes sparkled like the terrible crystal.

Flambeau, quite bewildered with this fanaticism, could not refrain from asking Miss Pauline (with direct French logic) why a pair of spectacles was a more morbid sign of weakness than a lift, and why, if science might help us in the one effort, it might not help us in the other.

"That is so different," said Pauline Stacey, loftily. "Batteries and motors and all those things are marks of the force of man—yes, Mr. Flambeau, and the force of woman, too! We shall take our turn at these great engines that devour distance and defy time. That is high and splendid—that is really science. But these nasty props and plasters the doctors sell—why, they are just badges of poltroonery. Doctors stick on legs and arms as if we were born cripples and sick slaves. But I was free-born, Mr. Flambeau! People only think they need these things because they have been trained in fear instead of being trained in power and courage, just as the silly nurses tell children not to stare at the sun, and so they can't do it without blinking. But why among the stars should there be one star I may not see? The sun is not my master, and I will open my eyes and stare at him whenever I choose."

"Your eyes," said Flambeau, with a foreign bow, "will dazzle the sun." He took pleasure in complimenting this strange stiff beauty, partly because it threw her a little off her balance. But as he went upstairs to his floor he drew a deep breath and whistled, saying to himself: "So she has got into the hands of that conjurer upstairs with his golden eye." For, little as he knew or cared about the new religion of Kalon, he had heard of his special notion about sun-gazing.

He soon discovered that the spiritual bond between the floors above and below him was close and increasing. The man who called himself Kalon was a magnificent creature, worthy, in a physical sense, to be the pontiff of Apollo. He was nearly as tall even as Flambeau, and very much better looking, with a golden beard, strong blue eyes, and a mane flung back like a lion's. In structure he was the blonde beast of Nietzsche, but all this animal beauty was heightened, brightened and softened by genuine intellect and spirituality. If he looked like one of the great Saxon kings, he looked like one of the kings that were also saints. And this despite the cockney incongruity of his surroundings; the fact that he had an office half-way up a building in Victoria Street; that the clerk (a commonplace youth in cuffs and collars) sat in the outer room, between him and the corridor; that his name was on a brass plate, and the gilt emblem of his creed hung above his street, like the advertisement of an oculist. All this vulgarity could not take away from the man called Kalon the vivid oppression and inspiration that came from his soul and body. When all was said, a man in the presence of this quack did feel in the presence of a great man. Even in the loose jacket-suit of linen that he wore as a workshop dress in his office he was a fascinating and formidable figure; and when robed in the white vestments and crowned with the golden circlet, in which he daily saluted the sun, he really looked so splendid that the laughter of the street people sometimes died suddenly on their lips. For three times in the day the new sun-worshipper went out on his little balcony, in the face of all Westminster, to say some litany to his shining lord: once at daybreak, once at sunset, and once at the shock of noon. And it was while the shock of noon still shook faintly from the towers of Parliament and parish church that Father Brown, the friend of Flambeau, first looked up and saw the white priest of Apollo.

Flambeau had seen quite enough of these daily salutations of Phoebus, and plunged into the porch of the tall building without even looking for his clerical friend to follow. But Father Brown, whether from a professional interest in ritual or a strong individual interest in tomfoolery, stopped and stared up at the balcony of the sun-worshipper, just as he might have stopped and stared up at a Punch and Judy. Kalon the Prophet was already erect, with argent garments and uplifted hands, and the sound of his strangely penetrating voice could be heard all the way down the busy street uttering his solar litany. He was already in the middle of it; his eyes were fixed upon the flaming disc. It is doubtful if he saw anything or anyone on this earth; it is substantially certain that he did not see a stunted, round-faced priest who, in the crowd below, looked up at him with blinking eyes. That was perhaps the most startling difference between even these two far divided men. Father Brown could not look at anything without blinking; but the priest of Apollo could look on the blaze at noon without a quiver of the eyelid.

"O sun," cried the prophet, "O star that art too great to be allowed among the stars! O fountain that flowest quietly in that secret spot that is called space. White Father of all white unwearied things, white flames and white flowers and white peaks. Father, who art more innocent than all thy most innocent and quiet children; primal purity, into the peace of which—"

A rush and crash like the reversed rush of a rocket was cloven with a strident and incessant yelling. Five people rushed into the gate of the mansions as three people rushed out, and for an instant they all deafened each other. The sense of some utterly abrupt horror seemed for a moment to fill half the street with bad news—bad news that was all the worse because no one knew what it was. Two figures remained still after the crash of commotion: the fair priest of Apollo on the balcony above, and the ugly priest of Christ below him.

At last the tall figure and titanic energy of Flambeau appeared in the doorway of the mansions and dominated the little mob. Talking at the top of his voice like a fog-horn, he told somebody or anybody to go for a surgeon; and as he turned back into the dark and thronged entrance his friend Father Brown dipped in insignificantly after him. Even as he ducked and dived through the crowd he could still hear the magnificent melody and monotony of the solar priest still calling on the happy god who is the friend of fountains and flowers.

Father Brown found Flambeau and some six other people standing round the enclosed space into which the lift commonly descended. But the lift had not descended. Something else had descended; something that ought to have come by a lift.

For the last four minutes Flambeau had looked down on it; had seen the brained and bleeding figure of that beautiful woman who denied the existence of tragedy. He had never had the slightest doubt that it was Pauline Stacey; and, though he had sent for a doctor, he had not the slightest doubt that she was dead.

He could not remember for certain whether he had liked her or disliked her; there was so much both to like and dislike. But she had been a person to him, and the unbearable pathos of details and habit stabbed him with all the small daggers of bereavement. He remembered her pretty face and priggish speeches with a sudden secret vividness which is all the bitterness of death. In an instant like a bolt from the blue, like a thunderbolt from nowhere, that beautiful and defiant body had been dashed down the open well of the lift to death at the bottom. Was it suicide? With so insolent an optimist it seemed impossible. Was it murder? But who was there in those hardly inhabited flats to murder anybody? In a rush of raucous words, which he meant to be strong and suddenly found weak, he asked where was that fellow Kalon. A voice, habitually heavy, quiet and full, assured him that Kalon for the last fifteen minutes had been away up on his balcony worshipping his god. When Flambeau heard the voice, and felt the hand of Father Brown, he turned his swarthy face and said abruptly:

"Then, if he has been up there all the time, who can have done it?"

"Perhaps," said the other, "we might go upstairs and find out. We have half an hour before the police will move."

Leaving the body of the slain heiress in charge of the surgeons, Flambeau dashed up the stairs to the typewriting office, found it utterly empty, and then dashed up to his own. Having entered that, he abruptly returned with a new and white face to his friend.

"Her sister," he said, with an unpleasant seriousness, "her sister seems to have gone out for a walk."

Father Brown nodded. "Or, she may have gone up to the office of that sun man," he said. "If I were you I should just verify that, and then let us all talk it over in your office. No," he added suddenly, as if remembering something, "shall I ever get over that stupidity of mine? Of course, in their office downstairs."

Flambeau stared; but he followed the little father downstairs to the empty flat of the Staceys, where that impenetrable pastor took a large red-leather chair in the very entrance, from which he could see the stairs and landings, and waited. He did not wait very long. In about four minutes three figures descended the stairs, alike only in their solemnity. The first was Joan Stacey, the sister of the dead woman—evidently she had been upstairs in the temporary temple of Apollo; the second was the priest of Apollo himself, his litany finished, sweeping down the empty stairs in utter magnificence—something in his white robes, beard and parted hair had the look of Dore's Christ leaving the Pretorium; the third was Flambeau, black browed and somewhat bewildered.

Miss Joan Stacey, dark, with a drawn face and hair prematurely touched with grey, walked straight to her own desk and set out her papers with a practical flap. The mere action rallied everyone else to sanity. If Miss Joan Stacey was a criminal, she was a cool one. Father Brown regarded her for some time with an odd little smile, and then, without taking his eyes off her, addressed himself to somebody else.

"Prophet," he said, presumably addressing Kalon, "I wish you would tell me a lot about your religion."

"I shall be proud to do it," said Kalon, inclining his still crowned head, "but I am not sure that I understand."

"Why, it's like this," said Father Brown, in his frankly doubtful way: "We are taught that if a man has really bad first principles, that must be partly his fault. But, for all that, we can make some difference between a man who insults his quite clear conscience and a man with a conscience more or less clouded with sophistries. Now, do you really think that murder is wrong at all?"

"Is this an accusation?" asked Kalon very quietly.

"No," answered Brown, equally gently, "it is the speech for the defence."

In the long and startled stillness of the room the prophet of Apollo slowly rose; and really it was like the rising of the sun. He filled that room with his light and life in such a manner that a man felt he could as easily have filled Salisbury Plain. His robed form seemed to hang the whole room with classic draperies; his epic gesture seemed to extend it into grander perspectives, till the little black figure of the modern cleric seemed to be a fault and an intrusion, a round, black blot upon some splendour of Hellas.

"We meet at last, Caiaphas," said the prophet. "Your church and mine are the only realities on this earth. I adore the sun, and you the darkening of the sun; you are the priest of the dying and I of the living God. Your present work of suspicion and slander is worthy of your coat and creed. All your church is but a black police; you are only spies and detectives seeking to tear from men confessions of guilt, whether by treachery or torture. You would convict men of crime, I would convict them of innocence. You would convince them of sin, I would convince them of virtue.

"Reader of the books of evil, one more word before I blow away your baseless nightmares for ever. Not even faintly could you understand how little I care whether you can convict me or no. The things you call disgrace and horrible hanging are to me no more than an ogre in a child's toy-book to a man once grown up. You said you were offering the speech for the defence. I care so little for the cloudland of this life that I will offer you the speech for the prosecution. There is but one thing that can be said against me in this matter, and I will say it myself. The woman that is dead was my love and my bride; not after such manner as your tin chapels call lawful, but by a law purer and sterner than you will ever understand. She and I walked another world from yours, and trod palaces of crystal while you were plodding through tunnels and corridors of brick. Well, I know that policemen, theological and otherwise, always fancy that where there has been love there must soon be hatred; so there you have the first point made for the prosecution. But the second point is stronger; I do not grudge it you. Not only is it true that Pauline loved me, but it is also true that this very morning, before she died, she wrote at that table a will leaving me and my new church half a million. Come, where are the handcuffs? Do you suppose I care what foolish things you do with me? Penal servitude will only be like waiting for her at a wayside station. The gallows will only be going to her in a headlong car."

He spoke with the brain-shaking authority of an orator, and Flambeau and Joan Stacey stared at him in amazed admiration. Father Brown's face seemed to express nothing but extreme distress; he looked at the ground with one wrinkle of pain across his forehead. The prophet of the sun leaned easily against the mantelpiece and resumed:

"In a few words I have put before you the whole case against me—the only possible case against me. In fewer words still I will blow it to pieces, so that not a trace of it remains. As to whether I have committed this crime, the truth is in one sentence: I could not have committed this crime. Pauline Stacey fell from this floor to the ground at five minutes past twelve. A hundred people will go into the witness-box and say that I was standing out upon the balcony of my own rooms above from just before the stroke of noon to a quarter-past—the usual period of my public prayers. My clerk (a respectable youth from Clapham, with no sort of connection with me) will swear that he sat in my outer office all the morning, and that no communication passed through. He will swear that I arrived a full ten minutes before the hour, fifteen minutes before any whisper of the accident, and that I did not leave the office or the balcony all that time. No one ever had so complete an alibi; I could subpoena half Westminster. I think you had better put the handcuffs away again. The case is at an end.

"But last of all, that no breath of this idiotic suspicion remain in the air, I will tell you all you want to know. I believe I do know how my unhappy friend came by her death. You can, if you choose, blame me for it, or my faith and philosophy at least; but you certainly cannot lock me up. It is well known to all students of the higher truths that certain adepts and illuminati have in history attained the power of levitation—that is, of being self-sustained upon the empty air. It is but a part of that general conquest of matter which is the main element in our occult wisdom. Poor Pauline was of an impulsive and ambitious temper. I think, to tell the truth, she thought herself somewhat deeper in the mysteries than she was; and she has often said to me, as we went down in the lift together, that if one's will were strong enough, one could float down as harmlessly as a feather. I solemnly believe that in some ecstasy of noble thoughts she attempted the miracle. Her will, or faith, must have failed her at the crucial instant, and the lower law of matter had its horrible revenge. There is the whole story, gentlemen, very sad and, as you think, very presumptuous and wicked, but certainly not criminal or in any way connected with me. In the short-hand of the police-courts, you had better call it suicide. I shall always call it heroic failure for the advance of science and the slow scaling of heaven."

It was the first time Flambeau had ever seen Father Brown vanquished. He still sat looking at the ground, with a painful and corrugated brow, as if in shame. It was impossible to avoid the feeling which the prophet's winged words had fanned, that here was a sullen, professional suspecter of men overwhelmed by a prouder and purer spirit of natural liberty and health. At last he said, blinking as if in bodily distress: "Well, if that is so, sir, you need do no more than take the testamentary paper you spoke of and go. I wonder where the poor lady left it."

"It will be over there on her desk by the door, I think," said Kalon, with that massive innocence of manner that seemed to acquit him wholly. "She told me specially she would write it this morning, and I actually saw her writing as I went up in the lift to my own room."

"Was her door open then?" asked the priest, with his eye on the corner of the matting.

"Yes," said Kalon calmly.

"Ah! it has been open ever since," said the other, and resumed his silent study of the mat.

"There is a paper over here," said the grim Miss Joan, in a somewhat singular voice. She had passed over to her sister's desk by the doorway, and was holding a sheet of blue foolscap in her hand. There was a sour smile on her face that seemed unfit for such a scene or occasion, and Flambeau looked at her with a darkening brow.

Kalon the prophet stood away from the paper with that loyal unconsciousness that had carried him through. But Flambeau took it out of the lady's hand, and read it with the utmost amazement. It did, indeed, begin in the formal manner of a will, but after the words "I give and bequeath all of which I die possessed" the writing abruptly stopped with a set of scratches, and there was no trace of the name of any legatee. Flambeau, in wonder, handed this truncated testament to his clerical friend, who glanced at it and silently gave it to the priest of the sun.

An instant afterwards that pontiff, in his splendid sweeping draperies, had crossed the room in two great strides, and was towering over Joan Stacey, his blue eyes standing from his head.

"What monkey tricks have you been playing here?" he cried. "That's not all Pauline wrote."

They were startled to hear him speak in quite a new voice, with a Yankee shrillness in it; all his grandeur and good English had fallen from him like a cloak.

"That is the only thing on her desk," said Joan, and confronted him steadily with the same smile of evil favour.

Of a sudden the man broke out into blasphemies and cataracts of incredulous words. There was something shocking about the dropping of his mask; it was like a man's real face falling off.

"See here!" he cried in broad American, when he was breathless with cursing, "I may be an adventurer, but I guess you're a murderess. Yes, gentlemen, here's your death explained, and without any levitation. The poor girl is writing a will in my favour; her cursed sister comes in, struggles for the pen, drags her to the well, and throws her down before she can finish it. Sakes! I reckon we want the handcuffs after all."

"As you have truly remarked," replied Joan, with ugly calm, "your clerk is a very respectable young man, who knows the nature of an oath; and he will swear in any court that I was up in your office arranging some typewriting work for five minutes before and five minutes after my sister fell. Mr. Flambeau will tell you that he found me there."

There was a silence.

"Why, then," cried Flambeau, "Pauline was alone when she fell, and it was suicide!"

"She was alone when she fell," said Father Brown, "but it was not suicide."

"Then how did she die?" asked Flambeau impatiently.

"She was murdered."

"But she was alone," objected the detective.

"She was murdered when she was all alone," answered the priest.

All the rest stared at him, but he remained sitting in the same old dejected attitude, with a wrinkle in his round forehead and an appearance of impersonal shame and sorrow; his voice was colourless and sad.

"What I want to know," cried Kalon, with an oath, "is when the police are coming for this bloody and wicked sister. She's killed her flesh and blood; she's robbed me of half a million that was just as sacredly mine as—"

"Come, come, prophet," interrupted Flambeau, with a kind of sneer; "remember that all this world is a cloudland."

The hierophant of the sun-god made an effort to climb back on his pedestal. "It is not the mere money," he cried, "though that would equip the cause throughout the world. It is also my beloved one's wishes. To Pauline all this was holy. In Pauline's eyes—"

Father Brown suddenly sprang erect, so that his chair fell over flat behind him. He was deathly pale, yet he seemed fired with a hope; his eyes shone.

"That's it!" he cried in a clear voice. "That's the way to begin. In Pauline's eyes—"

The tall prophet retreated before the tiny priest in an almost mad disorder. "What do you mean? How dare you?" he cried repeatedly.

"In Pauline's eyes," repeated the priest, his own shining more and more. "Go on—in God's name, go on. The foulest crime the fiends ever prompted feels lighter after confession; and I implore you to confess. Go on, go on—in Pauline's eyes—"

"Let me go, you devil!" thundered Kalon, struggling like a giant in bonds. "Who are you, you cursed spy, to weave your spiders' webs round me, and peep and peer? Let me go."

"Shall I stop him?" asked Flambeau, bounding towards the exit, for Kalon had already thrown the door wide open.

"No; let him pass," said Father Brown, with a strange deep sigh that seemed to come from the depths of the universe. "Let Cain pass by, for he belongs to God."

There was a long-drawn silence in the room when he had left it, which was to Flambeau's fierce wits one long agony of interrogation. Miss Joan Stacey very coolly tidied up the papers on her desk.

"Father," said Flambeau at last, "it is my duty, not my curiosity only—it is my duty to find out, if I can, who committed the crime."

"Which crime?" asked Father Brown.

"The one we are dealing with, of course," replied his impatient friend.

"We are dealing with two crimes," said Brown, "crimes of very different weight—and by very different criminals."

Miss Joan Stacey, having collected and put away her papers, proceeded to lock up her drawer. Father Brown went on, noticing her as little as she noticed him.

"The two crimes," he observed, "were committed against the same weakness of the same person, in a struggle for her money. The author of the larger crime found himself thwarted by the smaller crime; the author of the smaller crime got the money."

"Oh, don't go on like a lecturer," groaned Flambeau; "put it in a few words."

"I can put it in one word," answered his friend.

Miss Joan Stacey skewered her business-like black hat on to her head with a business-like black frown before a little mirror, and, as the conversation proceeded, took her handbag and umbrella in an unhurried style, and left the room.

"The truth is one word, and a short one," said Father Brown. "Pauline Stacey was blind."

"Blind!" repeated Flambeau, and rose slowly to his whole huge stature.

"She was subject to it by blood," Brown proceeded. "Her sister would have started eyeglasses if Pauline would have let her; but it was her special philosophy or fad that one must not encourage such diseases by yielding to them. She would not admit the cloud; or she tried to dispel it by will. So her eyes got worse and worse with straining; but the worst strain was to come. It came with this precious prophet, or whatever he calls himself, who taught her to stare at the hot sun with the naked eye. It was called accepting Apollo. Oh, if these new pagans would only be old pagans, they would be a little wiser! The old pagans knew that mere naked Nature-worship must have a cruel side. They knew that the eye of Apollo can blast and blind."

There was a pause, and the priest went on in a gentle and even broken voice. "Whether or no that devil deliberately made her blind, there is no doubt that he deliberately killed her through her blindness. The very simplicity of the crime is sickening. You know he and she went up and down in those lifts without official help; you know also how smoothly and silently the lifts slide. Kalon brought the lift to the girl's landing, and saw her, through the open door, writing in her slow, sightless way the will she had promised him. He called out to her cheerily that he had the lift ready for her, and she was to come out when she was ready. Then he pressed a button and shot soundlessly up to his own floor, walked through his own office, out on to his own balcony, and was safely praying before the crowded street when the poor girl, having finished her work, ran gaily out to where lover and lift were to receive her, and stepped—"

"Don't!" cried Flambeau.

"He ought to have got half a million by pressing that button," continued the little father, in the colourless voice in which he talked of such horrors. "But that went smash. It went smash because there happened to be another person who also wanted the money, and who also knew the secret about poor Pauline's sight. There was one thing about that will that I think nobody noticed: although it was unfinished and without signature, the other Miss Stacey and some servant of hers had already signed it as witnesses. Joan had signed first, saying Pauline could finish it later, with a typical feminine contempt for legal forms. Therefore, Joan wanted her sister to sign the will without real witnesses. Why? I thought of the blindness, and felt sure she had wanted Pauline to sign in solitude because she had wanted her not to sign at all.

"People like the Staceys always use fountain pens; but this was specially natural to Pauline. By habit and her strong will and memory she could still write almost as well as if she saw; but she could not tell when her pen needed dipping. Therefore, her fountain pens were carefully filled by her sister—all except this fountain pen. This was carefully not filled by her sister; the remains of the ink held out for a few lines and then failed altogether. And the prophet lost five hundred thousand pounds and committed one of the most brutal and brilliant murders in human history for nothing."

Flambeau went to the open door and heard the official police ascending the stairs. He turned and said: "You must have followed everything devilish close to have traced the crime to Kalon in ten minutes."

Father Brown gave a sort of start.

"Oh! to him," he said. "No; I had to follow rather close to find out about Miss Joan and the fountain pen. But I knew Kalon was the criminal before I came into the front door."

"You must be joking!" cried Flambeau.

"I'm quite serious," answered the priest. "I tell you I knew he had done it, even before I knew what he had done."

"But why?"

"These pagan stoics," said Brown reflectively, "always fail by their strength. There came a crash and a scream down the street, and the priest of Apollo did not start or look round. I did not know what it was. But I knew that he was expecting it."

The Sign of the Broken Sword

The thousand arms of the forest were grey, and its million fingers silver. In a sky of dark green-blue-like slate the stars were bleak and brilliant like splintered ice. All that thickly wooded and sparsely tenanted countryside was stiff with a bitter and brittle frost. The black hollows between the trunks of the trees looked like bottomless, black caverns of that Scandinavian hell, a hell of incalculable cold. Even the square stone tower of the church looked northern to the point of heathenry, as if it were some barbaric tower among the sea rocks of Iceland. It was a queer night for anyone to explore a churchyard. But, on the other hand, perhaps it was worth exploring.

It rose abruptly out of the ashen wastes of forest in a sort of hump or shoulder of green turf that looked grey in the starlight. Most of the graves were on a slant, and the path leading up to the church was as steep as a staircase. On the top of the hill, in the one flat and prominent place, was the monument for which the place was famous. It contrasted strangely with the featureless graves all round, for it was the work of one of the greatest sculptors of modern Europe; and yet his fame was at once forgotten in the fame of the man whose image he had made. It showed, by touches of the small silver pencil of starlight, the massive metal figure of a soldier recumbent, the strong hands sealed in an everlasting worship, the great head pillowed upon a gun. The venerable face was bearded, or rather whiskered, in the old, heavy Colonel Newcome fashion. The uniform, though suggested with the few strokes of simplicity, was that of modern war. By his right side lay a sword, of which the tip was broken off; on the left side lay a Bible. On glowing summer afternoons wagonettes came full of Americans and cultured suburbans to see the sepulchre; but even then they felt the vast forest land with its one dumpy dome of churchyard and church as a place oddly dumb and neglected. In this freezing darkness of mid-winter one would think he might be left alone with the stars.

Nevertheless, in the stillness of those stiff woods a wooden gate creaked, and two dim figures dressed in black climbed up the little path to the tomb.

So faint was that frigid starlight that nothing could have been traced about them except that while they both wore black, one man was enormously big, and the other (perhaps by contrast) almost startlingly small. They went up to the great graven tomb of the historic warrior, and stood for a few minutes staring at it. There was no human, perhaps no living, thing for a wide circle; and a morbid fancy might well have wondered if they were human themselves. In any case, the beginning of their conversation might have seemed strange. After the first silence the small man said to the other:

"Where does a wise man hide a pebble?"

And the tall man answered in a low voice: "On the beach."

The small man nodded, and after a short silence said: "Where does a wise man hide a leaf?"

And the other answered: "In the forest."

There was another stillness, and then the tall man resumed: "Do you mean that when a wise man has to hide a real diamond he has been known to hide it among sham ones?"

"No, no," said the little man with a laugh, "we will let bygones be bygones."

He stamped his cold feet for a second or two, and then said: "I'm not thinking of that at all, but of something else; something rather peculiar. Just strike a match, will you?"

The big man fumbled in his pocket, and soon a scratch and a flare painted gold the whole flat side of the monument. On it was cut in black letters the well-known words which so many Americans had reverently read: "Sacred to the Memory of General Sir Arthur St. Clare, Hero and Martyr, who Always Vanquished his Enemies and Always Spared Them, and Was Treacherously Slain by Them At Last. May God in Whom he Trusted both Reward and Revenge him."

The match burnt the big man's fingers, blackened, and dropped. He was about to strike another, but his small companion stopped him. "That's all right, Flambeau, old man; I saw what I wanted. Or, rather, I didn't see what I didn't want. And now we must walk a mile and a half along the road to the next inn, and I will try to tell you all about it. For Heaven knows a man should have a fire and ale when he dares tell such a story."

They descended the precipitous path, they relatched the rusty gate, and set off at a stamping, ringing walk down the frozen forest road. They had gone a full quarter of a mile before the smaller man spoke again. He said: "Yes; the wise man hides a pebble on the beach. But what does he do if there is no beach? Do you know anything of that great St. Clare trouble?"

"I know nothing about English generals, Father Brown," answered the large man, laughing, "though a little about English policemen. I only know that you have dragged me a precious long dance to all the shrines of this fellow, whoever he is. One would think he got buried in six different places. I've seen a memorial to General St. Clare in Westminster Abbey. I've seen a ramping equestrian statue of General St. Clare on the Embankment. I've seen a medallion of St. Clare in the street he was born in, and another in the street he lived in; and now you drag me after dark to his coffin in the village churchyard. I am beginning to be a bit tired of his magnificent personality, especially as I don't in the least know who he was. What are you hunting for in all these crypts and effigies?"

"I am only looking for one word," said Father Brown. "A word that isn't there."

"Well," asked Flambeau; "are you going to tell me anything about it?"

"I must divide it into two parts," remarked the priest. "First there is what everybody knows; and then there is what I know. Now, what everybody knows is short and plain enough. It is also entirely wrong."

"Right you are," said the big man called Flambeau cheerfully. "Let's begin at the wrong end. Let's begin with what everybody knows, which isn't true."

"If not wholly untrue, it is at least very inadequate," continued Brown; "for in point of fact, all that the public knows amounts precisely to this: The public knows that Arthur St. Clare was a great and successful English general. It knows that after splendid yet careful campaigns both in India and Africa he was in command against Brazil when the great Brazilian patriot Olivier issued his ultimatum. It knows that on that occasion St. Clare with a very small force attacked Olivier with a very large one, and was captured after heroic resistance. And it knows that after his capture, and to the abhorrence of the civilised world, St. Clare was hanged on the nearest tree. He was found swinging there after the Brazilians had retired, with his broken sword hung round his neck."

"And that popular story is untrue?" suggested Flambeau.

"No," said his friend quietly, "that story is quite true, so far as it goes."

"Well, I think it goes far enough!" said Flambeau; "but if the popular story is true, what is the mystery?"

They had passed many hundreds of grey and ghostly trees before the little priest answered. Then he bit his finger reflectively and said: "Why, the mystery is a mystery of psychology. Or, rather, it is a mystery of two psychologies. In that Brazilian business two of the most famous men of modern history acted flat against their characters. Mind you, Olivier and St. Clare were both heroes—the old thing, and no mistake; it was like the fight between Hector and Achilles. Now, what would you say to an affair in which Achilles was timid and Hector was treacherous?"

"Go on," said the large man impatiently as the other bit his finger again.

"Sir Arthur St. Clare was a soldier of the old religious type—the type that saved us during the Mutiny," continued Brown. "He was always more for duty than for dash; and with all his personal courage was decidedly a prudent commander, particularly indignant at any needless waste of soldiers. Yet in this last battle he attempted something that a baby could see was absurd. One need not be a strategist to see it was as wild as wind; just as one need not be a strategist to keep out of the way of a motor-bus. Well, that is the first mystery; what had become of the English general's head? The second riddle is, what had become of the Brazilian general's heart? President Olivier might be called a visionary or a nuisance; but even his enemies admitted that he was magnanimous to the point of knight errantry. Almost every other prisoner he had ever captured had been set free or even loaded with benefits. Men who had really wronged him came away touched by his simplicity and sweetness. Why the deuce should he diabolically revenge himself only once in his life; and that for the one particular blow that could not have hurt him? Well, there you have it. One of the wisest men in the world acted like an idiot for no reason. One of the best men in the world acted like a fiend for no reason. That's the long and the short of it; and I leave it to you, my boy."

"No, you don't," said the other with a snort. "I leave it to you; and you jolly well tell me all about it."

"Well," resumed Father Brown, "it's not fair to say that the public impression is just what I've said, without adding that two things have happened since. I can't say they threw a new light; for nobody can make sense of them. But they threw a new kind of darkness; they threw the darkness in new directions. The first was this. The family physician of the St. Clares quarrelled with that family, and began publishing a violent series of articles, in which he said that the late general was a religious maniac; but as far as the tale went, this seemed to mean little more than a religious man.

"Anyhow, the story fizzled out. Everyone knew, of course, that St. Clare had some of the eccentricities of puritan piety. The second incident was much more arresting. In the luckless and unsupported regiment which made that rash attempt at the Black River there was a certain Captain Keith, who was at that time engaged to St. Clare's daughter, and who afterwards married her. He was one of those who were captured by Olivier, and, like all the rest except the general, appears to have been bounteously treated and promptly set free. Some twenty years afterwards this man, then Lieutenant-Colonel Keith, published a sort of autobiography called 'A British Officer in Burmah and Brazil.' In the place where the reader looks eagerly for some account of the mystery of St. Clare's disaster may be found the following words: 'Everywhere else in this book I have narrated things exactly as they occurred, holding as I do the old-fashioned opinion that the glory of England is old enough to take care of itself. The exception I shall make is in this matter of the defeat by the Black River; and my reasons, though private, are honourable and compelling. I will, however, add this in justice to the memories of two distinguished men. General St. Clare has been accused of incapacity on this occasion; I can at least testify that this action, properly understood, was one of the most brilliant and sagacious of his life. President Olivier by similar report is charged with savage injustice. I think it due to the honour of an enemy to say that he acted on this occasion with even more than his characteristic good feeling. To put the matter popularly, I can assure my countrymen that St. Clare was by no means such a fool nor Olivier such a brute as he looked. This is all I have to say; nor shall any earthly consideration induce me to add a word to it.'"

A large frozen moon like a lustrous snowball began to show through the tangle of twigs in front of them, and by its light the narrator had been able to refresh his memory of Captain Keith's text from a scrap of printed paper. As he folded it up and put it back in his pocket Flambeau threw up his hand with a French gesture.

"Wait a bit, wait a bit," he cried excitedly. "I believe I can guess it at the first go."

He strode on, breathing hard, his black head and bull neck forward, like a man winning a walking race. The little priest, amused and interested, had some trouble in trotting beside him. Just before them the trees fell back a little to left and right, and the road swept downwards across a clear, moonlit valley, till it dived again like a rabbit into the wall of another wood. The entrance to the farther forest looked small and round, like the black hole of a remote railway tunnel. But it was within some hundred yards, and gaped like a cavern before Flambeau spoke again.

"I've got it," he cried at last, slapping his thigh with his great hand. "Four minutes' thinking, and I can tell your whole story myself."

"All right," assented his friend. "You tell it."

Flambeau lifted his head, but lowered his voice. "General Sir Arthur St. Clare," he said, "came of a family in which madness was hereditary; and his whole aim was to keep this from his daughter, and even, if possible, from his future son-in-law. Rightly or wrongly, he thought the final collapse was close, and resolved on suicide. Yet ordinary suicide would blazon the very idea he dreaded. As the campaign approached the clouds came thicker on his brain; and at last in a mad moment he sacrificed his public duty to his private. He rushed rashly into battle, hoping to fall by the first shot. When he found that he had only attained capture and discredit, the sealed bomb in his brain burst, and he broke his own sword and hanged himself."

He stared firmly at the grey facade of forest in front of him, with the one black gap in it, like the mouth of the grave, into which their path plunged. Perhaps something menacing in the road thus suddenly swallowed reinforced his vivid vision of the tragedy, for he shuddered.

"A horrid story," he said.

"A horrid story," repeated the priest with bent head. "But not the real story."

Then he threw back his head with a sort of despair and cried: "Oh, I wish it had been."

The tall Flambeau faced round and stared at him.

"Yours is a clean story," cried Father Brown, deeply moved. "A sweet, pure, honest story, as open and white as that moon. Madness and despair are innocent enough. There are worse things, Flambeau."

Flambeau looked up wildly at the moon thus invoked; and from where he stood one black tree-bough curved across it exactly like a devil's horn.

"Father—father," cried Flambeau with the French gesture and stepping yet more rapidly forward, "do you mean it was worse than that?"

"Worse than that," said Paul like a grave echo. And they plunged into the black cloister of the woodland, which ran by them in a dim tapestry of trunks, like one of the dark corridors in a dream.

They were soon in the most secret entrails of the wood, and felt close about them foliage that they could not see, when the priest said again:

"Where does a wise man hide a leaf? In the forest. But what does he do if there is no forest?"

"Well, well," cried Flambeau irritably, "what does he do?"

"He grows a forest to hide it in," said the priest in an obscure voice. "A fearful sin."

"Look here," cried his friend impatiently, for the dark wood and the dark saying got a little on his nerves; "will you tell me this story or not? What other evidence is there to go on?"

"There are three more bits of evidence," said the other, "that I have dug up in holes and corners; and I will give them in logical rather than chronological order. First of all, of course, our authority for the issue and event of the battle is in Olivier's own dispatches, which are lucid enough. He was entrenched with two or three regiments on the heights that swept down to the Black River, on the other side of which was lower and more marshy ground. Beyond this again was gently rising country, on which was the first English outpost, supported by others which lay, however, considerably in its rear. The British forces as a whole were greatly superior in numbers; but this particular regiment was just far enough from its base to make Olivier consider the project of crossing the river to cut it off. By sunset, however, he had decided to retain his own position, which was a specially strong one. At daybreak next morning he was thunderstruck to see that this stray handful of English, entirely unsupported from their rear, had flung themselves across the river, half by a bridge to the right, and the other half by a ford higher up, and were massed upon the marshy bank below him.

"That they should attempt an attack with such numbers against such a position was incredible enough; but Olivier noticed something yet more extraordinary. For instead of attempting to seize more solid ground, this mad regiment, having put the river in its rear by one wild charge, did nothing more, but stuck there in the mire like flies in treacle. Needless to say, the Brazilians blew great gaps in them with artillery, which they could only return with spirited but lessening rifle fire. Yet they never broke; and Olivier's curt account ends with a strong tribute of admiration for the mystic valour of these imbeciles. 'Our line then advanced finally,' writes Olivier, 'and drove them into the river; we captured General St. Clare himself and several other officers. The colonel and the major had both fallen in the battle. I cannot resist saying that few finer sights can have been seen in history than the last stand of this extraordinary regiment; wounded officers picking up the rifles of dead soldiers, and the general himself facing us on horseback bareheaded and with a broken sword.' On what happened to the general afterwards Olivier is as silent as Captain Keith."

"Well," grunted Flambeau, "get on to the next bit of evidence."

"The next evidence," said Father Brown, "took some time to find, but it will not take long to tell. I found at last in an almshouse down in the Lincolnshire Fens an old soldier who not only was wounded at the Black River, but had actually knelt beside the colonel of the regiment when he died. This latter was a certain Colonel Clancy, a big bull of an Irishman; and it would seem that he died almost as much of rage as of bullets. He, at any rate, was not responsible for that ridiculous raid; it must have been imposed on him by the general. His last edifying words, according to my informant, were these: 'And there goes the damned old donkey with the end of his sword knocked off. I wish it was his head.' You will remark that everyone seems to have noticed this detail about the broken sword blade, though most people regard it somewhat more reverently than did the late Colonel Clancy. And now for the third fragment."

Their path through the woodland began to go upward, and the speaker paused a little for breath before he went on. Then he continued in the same business-like tone:

"Only a month or two ago a certain Brazilian official died in England, having quarrelled with Olivier and left his country. He was a well-known figure both here and on the Continent, a Spaniard named Espado; I knew him myself, a yellow-faced old dandy, with a hooked nose. For various private reasons I had permission to see the documents he had left; he was a Catholic, of course, and I had been with him towards the end. There was nothing of his that lit up any corner of the black St. Clare business, except five or six common exercise books filled with the diary of some English soldier. I can only suppose that it was found by the Brazilians on one of those that fell. Anyhow, it stopped abruptly the night before the battle.

"But the account of that last day in the poor fellow's life was certainly worth reading. I have it on me; but it's too dark to read it here, and I will give you a resume. The first part of that entry is full of jokes, evidently flung about among the men, about somebody called the Vulture. It does not seem as if this person, whoever he was, was one of themselves, nor even an Englishman; neither is he exactly spoken of as one of the enemy. It sounds rather as if he were some local go-between and non-combatant; perhaps a guide or a journalist. He has been closeted with old Colonel Clancy; but is more often seen talking to the major. Indeed, the major is somewhat prominent in this soldier's narrative; a lean, dark-haired man, apparently, of the name of Murray—a north of Ireland man and a Puritan. There are continual jests about the contrast between this Ulsterman's austerity and the conviviality of Colonel Clancy. There is also some joke about the Vulture wearing bright-coloured clothes.

"But all these levities are scattered by what may well be called the note of a bugle. Behind the English camp and almost parallel to the river ran one of the few great roads of that district. Westward the road curved round towards the river, which it crossed by the bridge before mentioned. To the east the road swept backwards into the wilds, and some two miles along it was the next English outpost. From this direction there came along the road that evening a glitter and clatter of light cavalry, in which even the simple diarist could recognise with astonishment the general with his staff. He rode the great white horse which you have seen so often in illustrated papers and Academy pictures; and you may be sure that the salute they gave him was not merely ceremonial. He, at least, wasted no time on ceremony, but, springing from the saddle immediately, mixed with the group of officers, and fell into emphatic though confidential speech. What struck our friend the diarist most was his special disposition to discuss matters with Major Murray; but, indeed, such a selection, so long as it was not marked, was in no way unnatural. The two men were made for sympathy; they were men who 'read their Bibles'; they were both the old Evangelical type of officer. However this may be, it is certain that when the general mounted again he was still talking earnestly to Murray; and that as he walked his horse slowly down the road towards the river, the tall Ulsterman still walked by his bridle rein in earnest debate. The soldiers watched the two until they vanished behind a clump of trees where the road turned towards the river. The colonel had gone back to his tent, and the men to their pickets; the man with the diary lingered for another four minutes, and saw a marvellous sight.

"The great white horse which had marched slowly down the road, as it had marched in so many processions, flew back, galloping up the road towards them as if it were mad to win a race. At first they thought it had run away with the man on its back; but they soon saw that the general, a fine rider, was himself urging it to full speed. Horse and man swept up to them like a whirlwind; and then, reining up the reeling charger, the general turned on them a face like flame, and called for the colonel like the trumpet that wakes the dead.

"I conceive that all the earthquake events of that catastrophe tumbled on top of each other rather like lumber in the minds of men such as our friend with the diary. With the dazed excitement of a dream, they found themselves falling—literally falling—into their ranks, and learned that an attack was to be led at once across the river. The general and the major, it was said, had found out something at the bridge, and there was only just time to strike for life. The major had gone back at once to call up the reserve along the road behind; it was doubtful if even with that prompt appeal help could reach them in time. But they must pass the stream that night, and seize the heights by morning. It is with the very stir and throb of that romantic nocturnal march that the diary suddenly ends."

Father Brown had mounted ahead; for the woodland path grew smaller, steeper, and more twisted, till they felt as if they were ascending a winding staircase. The priest's voice came from above out of the darkness.

"There was one other little and enormous thing. When the general urged them to their chivalric charge he half drew his sword from the scabbard; and then, as if ashamed of such melodrama, thrust it back again. The sword again, you see."

A half-light broke through the network of boughs above them, flinging the ghost of a net about their feet; for they were mounting again to the faint luminosity of the naked night. Flambeau felt truth all round him as an atmosphere, but not as an idea. He answered with bewildered brain: "Well, what's the matter with the sword? Officers generally have swords, don't they?"

"They are not often mentioned in modern war," said the other dispassionately; "but in this affair one falls over the blessed sword everywhere."

"Well, what is there in that?" growled Flambeau; "it was a twopence coloured sort of incident; the old man's blade breaking in his last battle. Anyone might bet the papers would get hold of it, as they have. On all these tombs and things it's shown broken at the point. I hope you haven't dragged me through this Polar expedition merely because two men with an eye for a picture saw St. Clare's broken sword."

"No," cried Father Brown, with a sharp voice like a pistol shot; "but who saw his unbroken sword?"

"What do you mean?" cried the other, and stood still under the stars. They had come abruptly out of the grey gates of the wood.

"I say, who saw his unbroken sword?" repeated Father Brown obstinately. "Not the writer of the diary, anyhow; the general sheathed it in time."

Flambeau looked about him in the moonlight, as a man struck blind might look in the sun; and his friend went on, for the first time with eagerness:

"Flambeau," he cried, "I cannot prove it, even after hunting through the tombs. But I am sure of it. Let me add just one more tiny fact that tips the whole thing over. The colonel, by a strange chance, was one of the first struck by a bullet. He was struck long before the troops came to close quarters. But he saw St. Clare's sword broken. Why was it broken? How was it broken? My friend, it was broken before the battle."

"Oh!" said his friend, with a sort of forlorn jocularity; "and pray where is the other piece?"

"I can tell you," said the priest promptly. "In the northeast corner of the cemetery of the Protestant Cathedral at Belfast."

"Indeed?" inquired the other. "Have you looked for it?"

"I couldn't," replied Brown, with frank regret. "There's a great marble monument on top of it; a monument to the heroic Major Murray, who fell fighting gloriously at the famous Battle of the Black River."

Flambeau seemed suddenly galvanised into existence. "You mean," he cried hoarsely, "that General St. Clare hated Murray, and murdered him on the field of battle because—"

"You are still full of good and pure thoughts," said the other. "It was worse than that."

"Well," said the large man, "my stock of evil imagination is used up."

The priest seemed really doubtful where to begin, and at last he said again:

"Where would a wise man hide a leaf? In the forest."

The other did not answer.

"If there were no forest, he would make a forest. And if he wished to hide a dead leaf, he would make a dead forest."

There was still no reply, and the priest added still more mildly and quietly:

"And if a man had to hide a dead body, he would make a field of dead bodies to hide it in."

Flambeau began to stamp forward with an intolerance of delay in time or space; but Father Brown went on as if he were continuing the last sentence:

"Sir Arthur St. Clare, as I have already said, was a man who read his Bible. That was what was the matter with him. When will people understand that it is useless for a man to read his Bible unless he also reads everybody else's Bible? A printer reads a Bible for misprints. A Mormon reads his Bible, and finds polygamy; a Christian Scientist reads his, and finds we have no arms and legs. St. Clare was an old Anglo-Indian Protestant soldier. Now, just think what that might mean; and, for Heaven's sake, don't cant about it. It might mean a man physically formidable living under a tropic sun in an Oriental society, and soaking himself without sense or guidance in an Oriental Book. Of course, he read the Old Testament rather than the New. Of course, he found in the Old Testament anything that he wanted—lust, tyranny, treason. Oh, I dare say he was honest, as you call it. But what is the good of a man being honest in his worship of dishonesty?

"In each of the hot and secret countries to which the man went he kept a harem, he tortured witnesses, he amassed shameful gold; but certainly he would have said with steady eyes that he did it to the glory of the Lord. My own theology is sufficiently expressed by asking which Lord? Anyhow, there is this about such evil, that it opens door after door in hell, and always into smaller and smaller chambers. This is the real case against crime, that a man does not become wilder and wilder, but only meaner and meaner. St. Clare was soon suffocated by difficulties of bribery and blackmail; and needed more and more cash. And by the time of the Battle of the Black River he had fallen from world to world to that place which Dante makes the lowest floor of the universe."

"What do you mean?" asked his friend again.

"I mean that," retorted the cleric, and suddenly pointed at a puddle sealed with ice that shone in the moon. "Do you remember whom Dante put in the last circle of ice?"

"The traitors," said Flambeau, and shuddered. As he looked around at the inhuman landscape of trees, with taunting and almost obscene outlines, he could almost fancy he was Dante, and the priest with the rivulet of a voice was, indeed, a Virgil leading him through a land of eternal sins.

The voice went on: "Olivier, as you know, was quixotic, and would not permit a secret service and spies. The thing, however, was done, like many other things, behind his back. It was managed by my old friend Espado; he was the bright-clad fop, whose hook nose got him called the Vulture. Posing as a sort of philanthropist at the front, he felt his way through the English Army, and at last got his fingers on its one corrupt man—please God!—and that man at the top. St. Clare was in foul need of money, and mountains of it. The discredited family doctor was threatening those extraordinary exposures that afterwards began and were broken off; tales of monstrous and prehistoric things in Park Lane; things done by an English Evangelist that smelt like human sacrifice and hordes of slaves. Money was wanted, too, for his daughter's dowry; for to him the fame of wealth was as sweet as wealth itself. He snapped the last thread, whispered the word to Brazil, and wealth poured in from the enemies of England. But another man had talked to Espado the Vulture as well as he. Somehow the dark, grim young major from Ulster had guessed the hideous truth; and when they walked slowly together down that road towards the bridge Murray was telling the general that he must resign instantly, or be court-martialled and shot. The general temporised with him till they came to the fringe of tropic trees by the bridge; and there by the singing river and the sunlit palms (for I can see the picture) the general drew his sabre and plunged it through the body of the major."

The wintry road curved over a ridge in cutting frost, with cruel black shapes of bush and thicket; but Flambeau fancied that he saw beyond it faintly the edge of an aureole that was not starlight and moonlight, but some fire such as is made by men. He watched it as the tale drew to its close.

"St. Clare was a hell-hound, but he was a hound of breed. Never, I'll swear, was he so lucid and so strong as when poor Murray lay a cold lump at his feet. Never in all his triumphs, as Captain Keith said truly, was the great man so great as he was in this last world-despised defeat. He looked coolly at his weapon to wipe off the blood; he saw the point he had planted between his victim's shoulders had broken off in the body. He saw quite calmly, as through a club windowpane, all that must follow. He saw that men must find the unaccountable corpse; must extract the unaccountable sword-point; must notice the unaccountable broken sword—or absence of sword. He had killed, but not silenced. But his imperious intellect rose against the facer; there was one way yet. He could make the corpse less unaccountable. He could create a hill of corpses to cover this one. In twenty minutes eight hundred English soldiers were marching down to their death."

The warmer glow behind the black winter wood grew richer and brighter, and Flambeau strode on to reach it. Father Brown also quickened his stride; but he seemed merely absorbed in his tale.

"Such was the valour of that English thousand, and such the genius of their commander, that if they had at once attacked the hill, even their mad march might have met some luck. But the evil mind that played with them like pawns had other aims and reasons. They must remain in the marshes by the bridge at least till British corpses should be a common sight there. Then for the last grand scene; the silver-haired soldier-saint would give up his shattered sword to save further slaughter. Oh, it was well organised for an impromptu. But I think (I cannot prove), I think that it was while they stuck there in the bloody mire that someone doubted—and someone guessed."

He was mute a moment, and then said: "There is a voice from nowhere that tells me the man who guessed was the lover... the man to wed the old man's child."

"But what about Olivier and the hanging?" asked Flambeau.

"Olivier, partly from chivalry, partly from policy, seldom encumbered his march with captives," explained the narrator. "He released everybody in most cases. He released everybody in this case."

"Everybody but the general," said the tall man.

"Everybody," said the priest.

Flambeau knit his black brows. "I don't grasp it all yet," he said.

"There is another picture, Flambeau," said Brown in his more mystical undertone. "I can't prove it; but I can do more—I can see it. There is a camp breaking up on the bare, torrid hills at morning, and Brazilian uniforms massed in blocks and columns to march. There is the red shirt and long black beard of Olivier, which blows as he stands, his broad-brimmed hat in his hand. He is saying farewell to the great enemy he is setting free—the simple, snow-headed English veteran, who thanks him in the name of his men. The English remnant stand behind at attention; beside them are stores and vehicles for the retreat. The drums roll; the Brazilians are moving; the English are still like statues. So they abide till the last hum and flash of the enemy have faded from the tropic horizon. Then they alter their postures all at once, like dead men coming to life; they turn their fifty faces upon the general—faces not to be forgotten."

Flambeau gave a great jump. "Ah," he cried, "you don't mean—"

"Yes," said Father Brown in a deep, moving voice. "It was an English hand that put the rope round St. Clare's neck; I believe the hand that put the ring on his daughter's finger. They were English hands that dragged him up to the tree of shame; the hands of men that had adored him and followed him to victory. And they were English souls (God pardon and endure us all!) who stared at him swinging in that foreign sun on the green gallows of palm, and prayed in their hatred that he might drop off it into hell."

As the two topped the ridge there burst on them the strong scarlet light of a red-curtained English inn. It stood sideways in the road, as if standing aside in the amplitude of hospitality. Its three doors stood open with invitation; and even where they stood they could hear the hum and laughter of humanity happy for a night.

"I need not tell you more," said Father Brown. "They tried him in the wilderness and destroyed him; and then, for the honour of England and of his daughter, they took an oath to seal up for ever the story of the traitor's purse and the assassin's sword blade. Perhaps—Heaven help them—they tried to forget it. Let us try to forget it, anyhow; here is our inn."

"With all my heart," said Flambeau, and was just striding into the bright, noisy bar when he stepped back and almost fell on the road.

"Look there, in the devil's name!" he cried, and pointed rigidly at the square wooden sign that overhung the road. It showed dimly the crude shape of a sabre hilt and a shortened blade; and was inscribed in false archaic lettering, "The Sign of the Broken Sword."

"Were you not prepared?" asked Father Brown gently. "He is the god of this country; half the inns and parks and streets are named after him and his story."

"I thought we had done with the leper," cried Flambeau, and spat on the road.

"You will never have done with him in England," said the priest, looking down, "while brass is strong and stone abides. His marble statues will erect the souls of proud, innocent boys for centuries, his village tomb will smell of loyalty as of lilies. Millions who never knew him shall love him like a father—this man whom the last few that knew him dealt with like dung. He shall be a saint; and the truth shall never be told of him, because I have made up my mind at last. There is so much good and evil in breaking secrets, that I put my conduct to a test. All these newspapers will perish; the anti-Brazil boom is already over; Olivier is already honoured everywhere. But I told myself that if anywhere, by name, in metal or marble that will endure like the pyramids, Colonel Clancy, or Captain Keith, or President Olivier, or any innocent man was wrongly blamed, then I would speak. If it were only that St. Clare was wrongly praised, I would be silent. And I will."

They plunged into the red-curtained tavern, which was not only cosy, but even luxurious inside. On a table stood a silver model of the tomb of St. Clare, the silver head bowed, the silver sword broken. On the walls were coloured photographs of the same scene, and of the system of wagonettes that took tourists to see it. They sat down on the comfortable padded benches.

"Come, it's cold," cried Father Brown; "let's have some wine or beer."

"Or brandy," said Flambeau.

The Three Tools of Death

Both by calling and conviction Father Brown knew better than most of us, that every man is dignified when he is dead. But even he felt a pang of incongruity when he was knocked up at daybreak and told that Sir Aaron Armstrong had been murdered. There was something absurd and unseemly about secret violence in connection with so entirely entertaining and popular a figure. For Sir Aaron Armstrong was entertaining to the point of being comic; and popular in such a manner as to be almost legendary. It was like hearing that Sunny Jim had hanged himself; or that Mr. Pickwick had died in Hanwell. For though Sir Aaron was a philanthropist, and thus dealt with the darker side of our society, he prided himself on dealing with it in the brightest possible style. His political and social speeches were cataracts of anecdotes and "loud laughter"; his bodily health was of a bursting sort; his ethics were all optimism; and he dealt with the Drink problem (his favourite topic) with that immortal or even monotonous gaiety which is so often a mark of the prosperous total abstainer.

The established story of his conversion was familiar on the more puritanic platforms and pulpits, how he had been, when only a boy, drawn away from Scotch theology to Scotch whisky, and how he had risen out of both and become (as he modestly put it) what he was. Yet his wide white beard, cherubic face, and sparkling spectacles, at the numberless dinners and congresses where they appeared, made it hard to believe, somehow, that he had ever been anything so morbid as either a dram-drinker or a Calvinist. He was, one felt, the most seriously merry of all the sons of men.

He had lived on the rural skirt of Hampstead in a handsome house, high but not broad, a modern and prosaic tower. The narrowest of its narrow sides overhung the steep green bank of a railway, and was shaken by passing trains. Sir Aaron Armstrong, as he boisterously explained, had no nerves. But if the train had often given a shock to the house, that morning the tables were turned, and it was the house that gave a shock to the train.

The engine slowed down and stopped just beyond that point where an angle of the house impinged upon the sharp slope of turf. The arrest of most mechanical things must be slow; but the living cause of this had been very rapid. A man clad completely in black, even (it was remembered) to the dreadful detail of black gloves, appeared on the ridge above the engine, and waved his black hands like some sable windmill. This in itself would hardly have stopped even a lingering train. But there came out of him a cry which was talked of afterwards as something utterly unnatural and new. It was one of those shouts that are horridly distinct even when we cannot hear what is shouted. The word in this case was "Murder!"

But the engine-driver swears he would have pulled up just the same if he had heard only the dreadful and definite accent and not the word.

The train once arrested, the most superficial stare could take in many features of the tragedy. The man in black on the green bank was Sir Aaron Armstrong's man-servant Magnus. The baronet in his optimism had often laughed at the black gloves of this dismal attendant; but no one was likely to laugh at him just now.

So soon as an inquirer or two had stepped off the line and across the smoky hedge, they saw, rolled down almost to the bottom of the bank, the body of an old man in a yellow dressing-gown with a very vivid scarlet lining. A scrap of rope seemed caught about his leg, entangled presumably in a struggle. There was a smear or so of blood, though very little; but the body was bent or broken into a posture impossible to any living thing. It was Sir Aaron Armstrong. A few more bewildered moments brought out a big fair-bearded man, whom some travellers could salute as the dead man's secretary, Patrick Royce, once well known in Bohemian society and even famous in the Bohemian arts. In a manner more vague, but even more convincing, he echoed the agony of the servant. By the time the third figure of that household, Alice Armstrong, daughter of the dead man, had come already tottering and waving into the garden, the engine-driver had put a stop to his stoppage. The whistle had blown and the train had panted on to get help from the next station.

Father Brown had been thus rapidly summoned at the request of Patrick Royce, the big ex-Bohemian secretary. Royce was an Irishman by birth; and that casual kind of Catholic that never remembers his religion until he is really in a hole. But Royce's request might have been less promptly complied with if one of the official detectives had not been a friend and admirer of the unofficial Flambeau; and it was impossible to be a friend of Flambeau without hearing numberless stories about Father Brown. Hence, while the young detective (whose name was Merton) led the little priest across the fields to the railway, their talk was more confidential than could be expected between two total strangers.

"As far as I can see," said Mr. Merton candidly, "there is no sense to be made of it at all. There is nobody one can suspect. Magnus is a solemn old fool; far too much of a fool to be an assassin. Royce has been the baronet's best friend for years; and his daughter undoubtedly adored him. Besides, it's all too absurd. Who would kill such a cheery old chap as Armstrong? Who could dip his hands in the gore of an after-dinner speaker? It would be like killing Father Christmas."

"Yes, it was a cheery house," assented Father Brown. "It was a cheery house while he was alive. Do you think it will be cheery now he is dead?"

Merton started a little and regarded his companion with an enlivened eye. "Now he is dead?" he repeated.

"Yes," continued the priest stolidly, "he was cheerful. But did he communicate his cheerfulness? Frankly, was anyone else in the house cheerful but he?"

A window in Merton's mind let in that strange light of surprise in which we see for the first time things we have known all along. He had often been to the Armstrongs', on little police jobs of the philanthropist; and, now he came to think of it, it was in itself a depressing house. The rooms were very high and very cold; the decoration mean and provincial; the draughty corridors were lit by electricity that was bleaker than moonlight. And though the old man's scarlet face and silver beard had blazed like a bonfire in each room or passage in turn, it did not leave any warmth behind it. Doubtless this spectral discomfort in the place was partly due to the very vitality and exuberance of its owner; he needed no stoves or lamps, he would say, but carried his own warmth with him. But when Merton recalled the other inmates, he was compelled to confess that they also were as shadows of their lord. The moody man-servant, with his monstrous black gloves, was almost a nightmare; Royce, the secretary, was solid enough, a big bull of a man, in tweeds, with a short beard; but the straw-coloured beard was startlingly salted with grey like the tweeds, and the broad forehead was barred with premature wrinkles. He was good-natured enough also, but it was a sad sort of good-nature, almost a heart-broken sort—he had the general air of being some sort of failure in life. As for Armstrong's daughter, it was almost incredible that she was his daughter; she was so pallid in colour and sensitive in outline. She was graceful, but there was a quiver in the very shape of her that was like the lines of an aspen. Merton had sometimes wondered if she had learnt to quail at the crash of the passing trains.

"You see," said Father Brown, blinking modestly, "I'm not sure that the Armstrong cheerfulness is so very cheerful—for other people. You say that nobody could kill such a happy old man, but I'm not sure; ne nos inducas in tentationem. If ever I murdered somebody," he added quite simply, "I dare say it might be an Optimist."

"Why?" cried Merton amused. "Do you think people dislike cheerfulness?"

"People like frequent laughter," answered Father Brown, "but I don't think they like a permanent smile. Cheerfulness without humour is a very trying thing."

They walked some way in silence along the windy grassy bank by the rail, and just as they came under the far-flung shadow of the tall Armstrong house, Father Brown said suddenly, like a man throwing away a troublesome thought rather than offering it seriously: "Of course, drink is neither good nor bad in itself. But I can't help sometimes feeling that men like Armstrong want an occasional glass of wine to sadden them."

Merton's official superior, a grizzled and capable detective named Gilder, was standing on the green bank waiting for the coroner, talking to Patrick Royce, whose big shoulders and bristly beard and hair towered above him. This was the more noticeable because Royce walked always with a sort of powerful stoop, and seemed to be going about his small clerical and domestic duties in a heavy and humbled style, like a buffalo drawing a go-cart.

He raised his head with unusual pleasure at the sight of the priest, and took him a few paces apart. Meanwhile Merton was addressing the older detective respectfully indeed, but not without a certain boyish impatience.

"Well, Mr. Gilder, have you got much farther with the mystery?"

"There is no mystery," replied Gilder, as he looked under dreamy eyelids at the rooks.

"Well, there is for me, at any rate," said Merton, smiling.

"It is simple enough, my boy," observed the senior investigator, stroking his grey, pointed beard. "Three minutes after you'd gone for Mr. Royce's parson the whole thing came out. You know that pasty-faced servant in the black gloves who stopped the train?"

"I should know him anywhere. Somehow he rather gave me the creeps."

"Well," drawled Gilder, "when the train had gone on again, that man had gone too. Rather a cool criminal, don't you think, to escape by the very train that went off for the police?"

"You're pretty sure, I suppose," remarked the young man, "that he really did kill his master?"

"Yes, my son, I'm pretty sure," replied Gilder drily, "for the trifling reason that he has gone off with twenty thousand pounds in papers that were in his master's desk. No, the only thing worth calling a difficulty is how he killed him. The skull seems broken as with some big weapon, but there's no weapon at all lying about, and the murderer would have found it awkward to carry it away, unless the weapon was too small to be noticed."

"Perhaps the weapon was too big to be noticed," said the priest, with an odd little giggle.

Gilder looked round at this wild remark, and rather sternly asked Brown what he meant.

"Silly way of putting it, I know," said Father Brown apologetically. "Sounds like a fairy tale. But poor Armstrong was killed with a giant's club, a great green club, too big to be seen, and which we call the earth. He was broken against this green bank we are standing on."

"How do you mean?" asked the detective quickly.

Father Brown turned his moon face up to the narrow facade of the house and blinked hopelessly up. Following his eyes, they saw that right at the top of this otherwise blind back quarter of the building, an attic window stood open.

"Don't you see," he explained, pointing a little awkwardly like a child, "he was thrown down from there?"

Gilder frowningly scrutinised the window, and then said: "Well, it is certainly possible. But I don't see why you are so sure about it."

Brown opened his grey eyes wide. "Why," he said, "there's a bit of rope round the dead man's leg. Don't you see that other bit of rope up there caught at the corner of the window?"

At that height the thing looked like the faintest particle of dust or hair, but the shrewd old investigator was satisfied. "You're quite right, sir," he said to Father Brown; "that is certainly one to you."

Almost as he spoke a special train with one carriage took the curve of the line on their left, and, stopping, disgorged another group of policemen, in whose midst was the hangdog visage of Magnus, the absconded servant.

"By Jove! they've got him," cried Gilder, and stepped forward with quite a new alertness.

"Have you got the money!" he cried to the first policeman.

The man looked him in the face with a rather curious expression and said: "No." Then he added: "At least, not here."

"Which is the inspector, please?" asked the man called Magnus.

When he spoke everyone instantly understood how this voice had stopped a train. He was a dull-looking man with flat black hair, a colourless face, and a faint suggestion of the East in the level slits in his eyes and mouth. His blood and name, indeed, had remained dubious, ever since Sir Aaron had "rescued" him from a waitership in a London restaurant, and (as some said) from more infamous things. But his voice was as vivid as his face was dead. Whether through exactitude in a foreign language, or in deference to his master (who had been somewhat deaf), Magnus's tones had a peculiarly ringing and piercing quality, and the whole group quite jumped when he spoke.

"I always knew this would happen," he said aloud with brazen blandness. "My poor old master made game of me for wearing black; but I always said I should be ready for his funeral."

And he made a momentary movement with his two dark-gloved hands.

"Sergeant," said Inspector Gilder, eyeing the black hands with wrath, "aren't you putting the bracelets on this fellow; he looks pretty dangerous."

"Well, sir," said the sergeant, with the same odd look of wonder, "I don't know that we can."

"What do you mean?" asked the other sharply. "Haven't you arrested him?"

A faint scorn widened the slit-like mouth, and the whistle of an approaching train seemed oddly to echo the mockery.

"We arrested him," replied the sergeant gravely, "just as he was coming out of the police station at Highgate, where he had deposited all his master's money in the care of Inspector Robinson."

Gilder looked at the man-servant in utter amazement. "Why on earth did you do that?" he asked of Magnus.

"To keep it safe from the criminal, of course," replied that person placidly.

"Surely," said Gilder, "Sir Aaron's money might have been safely left with Sir Aaron's family."

The tail of his sentence was drowned in the roar of the train as it went rocking and clanking; but through all the hell of noises to which that unhappy house was periodically subject, they could hear the syllables of Magnus's answer, in all their bell-like distinctness: "I have no reason to feel confidence in Sir Aaron's family."

All the motionless men had the ghostly sensation of the presence of some new person; and Merton was scarcely surprised when he looked up and saw the pale face of Armstrong's daughter over Father Brown's shoulder. She was still young and beautiful in a silvery style, but her hair was of so dusty and hueless a brown that in some shadows it seemed to have turned totally grey.

"Be careful what you say," said Royce gruffly, "you'll frighten Miss Armstrong."

"I hope so," said the man with the clear voice.

As the woman winced and everyone else wondered, he went on: "I am somewhat used to Miss Armstrong's tremors. I have seen her trembling off and on for years. And some said she was shaking with cold and some she was shaking with fear, but I know she was shaking with hate and wicked anger—fiends that have had their feast this morning. She would have been away by now with her lover and all the money but for me. Ever since my poor old master prevented her from marrying that tipsy blackguard—"

"Stop," said Gilder very sternly. "We have nothing to do with your family fancies or suspicions. Unless you have some practical evidence, your mere opinions—"

"Oh! I'll give you practical evidence," cut in Magnus, in his hacking accent. "You'll have to subpoena me, Mr. Inspector, and I shall have to tell the truth. And the truth is this: An instant after the old man was pitched bleeding out of the window, I ran into the attic, and found his daughter swooning on the floor with a red dagger still in her hand. Allow me to hand that also to the proper authorities." He took from his tail-pocket a long horn-hilted knife with a red smear on it, and handed it politely to the sergeant. Then he stood back again, and his slits of eyes almost faded from his face in one fat Chinese sneer.

Merton felt an almost bodily sickness at the sight of him; and he muttered to Gilder: "Surely you would take Miss Armstrong's word against his?"

Father Brown suddenly lifted a face so absurdly fresh that it looked somehow as if he had just washed it. "Yes," he said, radiating innocence, "but is Miss Armstrong's word against his?"

The girl uttered a startled, singular little cry; everyone looked at her. Her figure was rigid as if paralysed; only her face within its frame of faint brown hair was alive with an appalling surprise. She stood like one of a sudden lassooed and throttled.

"This man," said Mr. Gilder gravely, "actually says that you were found grasping a knife, insensible, after the murder."

"He says the truth," answered Alice.

The next fact of which they were conscious was that Patrick Royce strode with his great stooping head into their ring and uttered the singular words: "Well, if I've got to go, I'll have a bit of pleasure first."

His huge shoulder heaved and he sent an iron fist smash into Magnus's bland Mongolian visage, laying him on the lawn as flat as a starfish. Two or three of the police instantly put their hands on Royce; but to the rest it seemed as if all reason had broken up and the universe were turning into a brainless harlequinade.

"None of that, Mr. Royce," Gilder had called out authoritatively. "I shall arrest you for assault."

"No, you won't," answered the secretary in a voice like an iron gong, "you will arrest me for murder."

Gilder threw an alarmed glance at the man knocked down; but since that outraged person was already sitting up and wiping a little blood off a substantially uninjured face, he only said shortly: "What do you mean?"

"It is quite true, as this fellow says," explained Royce, "that Miss Armstrong fainted with a knife in her hand. But she had not snatched the knife to attack her father, but to defend him."

"To defend him," repeated Gilder gravely. "Against whom?"

"Against me," answered the secretary.

Alice looked at him with a complex and baffling face; then she said in a low voice: "After it all, I am still glad you are brave."

"Come upstairs," said Patrick Royce heavily, "and I will show you the whole cursed thing."

The attic, which was the secretary's private place (and rather a small cell for so large a hermit), had indeed all the vestiges of a violent drama. Near the centre of the floor lay a large revolver as if flung away; nearer to the left was rolled a whisky bottle, open but not quite empty. The cloth of the little table lay dragged and trampled, and a length of cord, like that found on the corpse, was cast wildly across the windowsill. Two vases were smashed on the mantelpiece and one on the carpet.

"I was drunk," said Royce; and this simplicity in the prematurely battered man somehow had the pathos of the first sin of a baby.

"You all know about me," he continued huskily; "everybody knows how my story began, and it may as well end like that too. I was called a clever man once, and might have been a happy one; Armstrong saved the remains of a brain and body from the taverns, and was always kind to me in his own way, poor fellow! Only he wouldn't let me marry Alice here; and it will always be said that he was right enough. Well, you can form your own conclusions, and you won't want me to go into details. That is my whisky bottle half emptied in the corner; that is my revolver quite emptied on the carpet. It was the rope from my box that was found on the corpse, and it was from my window the corpse was thrown. You need not set detectives to grub up my tragedy; it is a common enough weed in this world. I give myself to the gallows; and, by God, that is enough!"

At a sufficiently delicate sign, the police gathered round the large man to lead him away; but their unobtrusiveness was somewhat staggered by the remarkable appearance of Father Brown, who was on his hands and knees on the carpet in the doorway, as if engaged in some kind of undignified prayers. Being a person utterly insensible to the social figure he cut, he remained in this posture, but turned a bright round face up at the company, presenting the appearance of a quadruped with a very comic human head.

"I say," he said good-naturedly, "this really won't do at all, you know. At the beginning you said we'd found no weapon. But now we're finding too many; there's the knife to stab, and the rope to strangle, and the pistol to shoot; and after all he broke his neck by falling out of a window! It won't do. It's not economical." And he shook his head at the ground as a horse does grazing.

Inspector Gilder had opened his mouth with serious intentions, but before he could speak the grotesque figure on the floor had gone on quite volubly.

"And now three quite impossible things. First, these holes in the carpet, where the six bullets have gone in. Why on earth should anybody fire at the carpet? A drunken man lets fly at his enemy's head, the thing that's grinning at him. He doesn't pick a quarrel with his feet, or lay siege to his slippers. And then there's the rope"—and having done with the carpet the speaker lifted his hands and put them in his pocket, but continued unaffectedly on his knees—"in what conceivable intoxication would anybody try to put a rope round a man's neck and finally put it round his leg? Royce, anyhow, was not so drunk as that, or he would be sleeping like a log by now. And, plainest of all, the whisky bottle. You suggest a dipsomaniac fought for the whisky bottle, and then having won, rolled it away in a corner, spilling one half and leaving the other. That is the very last thing a dipsomaniac would do."

He scrambled awkwardly to his feet, and said to the self-accused murderer in tones of limpid penitence: "I'm awfully sorry, my dear sir, but your tale is really rubbish."

"Sir," said Alice Armstrong in a low tone to the priest, "can I speak to you alone for a moment?"

This request forced the communicative cleric out of the gangway, and before he could speak in the next room, the girl was talking with strange incisiveness.

"You are a clever man," she said, "and you are trying to save Patrick, I know. But it's no use. The core of all this is black, and the more things you find out the more there will be against the miserable man I love."

"Why?" asked Brown, looking at her steadily.

"Because," she answered equally steadily, "I saw him commit the crime myself."

"Ah!" said the unmoved Brown, "and what did he do?"

"I was in this room next to them," she explained; "both doors were closed, but I suddenly heard a voice, such as I had never heard on earth, roaring 'Hell, hell, hell,' again and again, and then the two doors shook with the first explosion of the revolver. Thrice again the thing banged before I got the two doors open and found the room full of smoke; but the pistol was smoking in my poor, mad Patrick's hand; and I saw him fire the last murderous volley with my own eyes. Then he leapt on my father, who was clinging in terror to the window-sill, and, grappling, tried to strangle him with the rope, which he threw over his head, but which slipped over his struggling shoulders to his feet. Then it tightened round one leg and Patrick dragged him along like a maniac. I snatched a knife from the mat, and, rushing between them, managed to cut the rope before I fainted."

"I see," said Father Brown, with the same wooden civility. "Thank you."

As the girl collapsed under her memories, the priest passed stiffly into the next room, where he found Gilder and Merton alone with Patrick Royce, who sat in a chair, handcuffed. There he said to the Inspector submissively:

"Might I say a word to the prisoner in your presence; and might he take off those funny cuffs for a minute?"

"He is a very powerful man," said Merton in an undertone. "Why do you want them taken off?"

"Why, I thought," replied the priest humbly, "that perhaps I might have the very great honour of shaking hands with him."

Both detectives stared, and Father Brown added: "Won't you tell them about it, sir?"

The man on the chair shook his tousled head, and the priest turned impatiently.

"Then I will," he said. "Private lives are more important than public reputations. I am going to save the living, and let the dead bury their dead."

He went to the fatal window, and blinked out of it as he went on talking.

"I told you that in this case there were too many weapons and only one death. I tell you now that they were not weapons, and were not used to cause death. All those grisly tools, the noose, the bloody knife, the exploding pistol, were instruments of a curious mercy. They were not used to kill Sir Aaron, but to save him."

"To save him!" repeated Gilder. "And from what?"

"From himself," said Father Brown. "He was a suicidal maniac."

"What?" cried Merton in an incredulous tone. "And the Religion of Cheerfulness—"

"It is a cruel religion," said the priest, looking out of the window. "Why couldn't they let him weep a little, like his fathers before him? His plans stiffened, his views grew cold; behind that merry mask was the empty mind of the atheist. At last, to keep up his hilarious public level, he fell back on that dram-drinking he had abandoned long ago. But there is this horror about alcoholism in a sincere teetotaler: that he pictures and expects that psychological inferno from which he has warned others. It leapt upon poor Armstrong prematurely, and by this morning he was in such a case that he sat here and cried he was in hell, in so crazy a voice that his daughter did not know it. He was mad for death, and with the monkey tricks of the mad he had scattered round him death in many shapes—a running noose and his friend's revolver and a knife. Royce entered accidentally and acted in a flash. He flung the knife on the mat behind him, snatched up the revolver, and having no time to unload it, emptied it shot after shot all over the floor. The suicide saw a fourth shape of death, and made a dash for the window. The rescuer did the only thing he could—ran after him with the rope and tried to tie him hand and foot. Then it was that the unlucky girl ran in, and misunderstanding the struggle, strove to slash her father free. At first she only slashed poor Royce's knuckles, from which has come all the little blood in this affair. But, of course, you noticed that he left blood, but no wound, on that servant's face? Only before the poor woman swooned, she did hack her father loose, so that he went crashing through that window into eternity."

There was a long stillness slowly broken by the metallic noises of Gilder unlocking the handcuffs of Patrick Royce, to whom he said: "I think I should have told the truth, sir. You and the young lady are worth more than Armstrong's obituary notices."

"Confound Armstrong's notices," cried Royce roughly. "Don't you see it was because she mustn't know?"

"Mustn't know what?" asked Merton.

"Why, that she killed her father, you fool!" roared the other. "He'd have been alive now but for her. It might craze her to know that."

"No, I don't think it would," remarked Father Brown, as he picked up his hat. "I rather think I should tell her. Even the most murderous blunders don't poison life like sins; anyhow, I think you may both be the happier now. I've got to go back to the Deaf School."

As he went out on to the gusty grass an acquaintance from Highgate stopped him and said:

"The Coroner has arrived. The inquiry is just going to begin."

"I've got to get back to the Deaf School," said Father Brown. "I'm sorry I can't stop for the inquiry."

The Absence of Mr Glass

THE consulting-rooms of Dr Orion Hood, the eminent criminologist and specialist in certain moral disorders, lay along the sea-front at Scarborough, in a series of very large and well-lighted french windows, which showed the North Sea like one endless outer wall of blue-green marble. In such a place the sea had something of the monotony of a blue-green dado: for the chambers themselves were ruled throughout by a terrible tidiness not unlike the terrible tidiness of the sea. It must not be supposed that Dr Hood's apartments excluded luxury, or even poetry. These things were there, in their place; but one felt that they were never allowed out of their place. Luxury was there: there stood upon a special table eight or ten boxes of the best cigars; but they were built upon a plan so that the strongest were always nearest the wall and the mildest nearest the window. A tantalus containing three kinds of spirit, all of a liqueur excellence, stood always on this table of luxury; but the fanciful have asserted that the whisky, brandy, and rum seemed always to stand at the same level. Poetry was there: the left-hand corner of the room was lined with as complete a set of English classics as the right hand could show of English and foreign physiologists. But if one took a volume of Chaucer or Shelley from that rank, its absence irritated the mind like a gap in a man's front teeth. One could not say the books were never read; probably they were, but there was a sense of their being chained to their places, like the Bibles in the old churches. Dr Hood treated his private book-shelf as if it were a public library. And if this strict scientific intangibility steeped even the shelves laden with lyrics and ballads and the tables laden with drink and tobacco, it goes without saying that yet more of such heathen holiness protected the other shelves that held the specialist's library, and the other tables that sustained the frail and even fairylike instruments of chemistry or mechanics.

Dr Hood paced the length of his string of apartments, bounded—as the boys' geographies say—on the east by the North Sea and on the west by the serried ranks of his sociological and criminologist library. He was clad in an artist's velvet, but with none of an artist's negligence; his hair was heavily shot with grey, but growing thick and healthy; his face was lean, but sanguine and expectant. Everything about him and his room indicated something at once rigid and restless, like that great northern sea by which (on pure principles of hygiene) he had built his home.

Fate, being in a funny mood, pushed the door open and introduced into those long, strict, sea-flanked apartments one who was perhaps the most startling opposite of them and their master. In answer to a curt but civil summons, the door opened inwards and there shambled into the room a shapeless little figure, which seemed to find its own hat and umbrella as unmanageable as a mass of luggage. The umbrella was a black and prosaic bundle long past repair; the hat was a broad-curved black hat, clerical but not common in England; the man was the very embodiment of all that is homely and helpless.

The doctor regarded the new-comer with a restrained astonishment, not unlike that he would have shown if some huge but obviously harmless sea-beast had crawled into his room. The new-comer regarded the doctor with that beaming but breathless geniality which characterizes a corpulent charwoman who has just managed to stuff herself into an omnibus. It is a rich confusion of social self-congratulation and bodily disarray. His hat tumbled to the carpet, his heavy umbrella slipped between his knees with a thud; he reached after the one and ducked after the other, but with an unimpaired smile on his round face spoke simultaneously as follows:

"My name is Brown. Pray excuse me. I've come about that business of the MacNabs. I have heard, you often help people out of such troubles. Pray excuse me if I am wrong."

By this time he had sprawlingly recovered the hat, and made an odd little bobbing bow over it, as if setting everything quite right.

"I hardly understand you," replied the scientist, with a cold intensity of manner. "I fear you have mistaken the chambers. I am Dr Hood, and my work is almost entirely literary and educational. It is true that I have sometimes been consulted by the police in cases of peculiar difficulty and importance, but—"

"Oh, this is of the greatest importance," broke in the little man called Brown. "Why, her mother won't let them get engaged." And he leaned back in his chair in radiant rationality.

The brows of Dr Hood were drawn down darkly, but the eyes under them were bright with something that might be anger or might be amusement. "And still," he said, "I do not quite understand."

"You see, they want to get married," said the man with the clerical hat. "Maggie MacNab and young Todhunter want to get married. Now, what can be more important than that?"

The great Orion Hood's scientific triumphs had deprived him of many things—some said of his health, others of his God; but they had not wholly despoiled him of his sense of the absurd. At the last plea of the ingenuous priest a chuckle broke out of him from inside, and he threw himself into an arm-chair in an ironical attitude of the consulting physician.

"Mr Brown," he said gravely, "it is quite fourteen and a half years since I was personally asked to test a personal problem: then it was the case of an attempt to poison the French President at a Lord Mayor's Banquet. It is now, I understand, a question of whether some friend of yours called Maggie is a suitable fiancee for some friend of hers called Todhunter. Well, Mr Brown, I am a sportsman. I will take it on. I will give the MacNab family my best advice, as good as I gave the French Republic and the King of England—no, better: fourteen years better. I have nothing else to do this afternoon. Tell me your story."

The little clergyman called Brown thanked him with unquestionable warmth, but still with a queer kind of simplicity. It was rather as if he were thanking a stranger in a smoking-room for some trouble in passing the matches, than as if he were (as he was) practically thanking the Curator of Kew Gardens for coming with him into a field to find a four-leaved clover. With scarcely a semi-colon after his hearty thanks, the little man began his recital:

"I told you my name was Brown; well, that's the fact, and I'm the priest of the little Catholic Church I dare say you've seen beyond those straggly streets, where the town ends towards the north. In the last and straggliest of those streets which runs along the sea like a sea-wall there is a very honest but rather sharp-tempered member of my flock, a widow called MacNab. She has one daughter, and she lets lodgings, and between her and the daughter, and between her and the lodgers—well, I dare say there is a great deal to be said on both sides. At present she has only one lodger, the young man called Todhunter; but he has given more trouble than all the rest, for he wants to marry the young woman of the house."

"And the young woman of the house," asked Dr Hood, with huge and silent amusement, "what does she want?"

"Why, she wants to marry him," cried Father Brown, sitting up eagerly. "That is just the awful complication."

"It is indeed a hideous enigma," said Dr Hood.

"This young James Todhunter," continued the cleric, "is a very decent man so far as I know; but then nobody knows very much. He is a bright, brownish little fellow, agile like a monkey, clean-shaven like an actor, and obliging like a born courtier. He seems to have quite a pocketful of money, but nobody knows what his trade is. Mrs MacNab, therefore (being of a pessimistic turn), is quite sure it is something dreadful, and probably connected with dynamite. The dynamite must be of a shy and noiseless sort, for the poor fellow only shuts himself up for several hours of the day and studies something behind a locked door. He declares his privacy is temporary and justified, and promises to explain before the wedding. That is all that anyone knows for certain, but Mrs MacNab will tell you a great deal more than even she is certain of. You know how the tales grow like grass on such a patch of ignorance as that. There are tales of two voices heard talking in the room; though, when the door is opened, Todhunter is always found alone. There are tales of a mysterious tall man in a silk hat, who once came out of the sea-mists and apparently out of the sea, stepping softly across the sandy fields and through the small back garden at twilight, till he was heard talking to the lodger at his open window. The colloquy seemed to end in a quarrel. Todhunter dashed down his window with violence, and the man in the high hat melted into the sea-fog again. This story is told by the family with the fiercest mystification; but I really think Mrs MacNab prefers her own original tale: that the Other Man (or whatever it is) crawls out every night from the big box in the corner, which is kept locked all day. You see, therefore, how this sealed door of Todhunter's is treated as the gate of all the fancies and monstrosities of the 'Thousand and One Nights'. And yet there is the little fellow in his respectable black jacket, as punctual and innocent as a parlour clock. He pays his rent to the tick; he is practically a teetotaller; he is tirelessly kind with the younger children, and can keep them amused for a day on end; and, last and most urgent of all, he has made himself equally popular with the eldest daughter, who is ready to go to church with him tomorrow."

A man warmly concerned with any large theories has always a relish for applying them to any triviality. The great specialist having condescended to the priest's simplicity, condescended expansively. He settled himself with comfort in his arm-chair and began to talk in the tone of a somewhat absent-minded lecturer:

"Even in a minute instance, it is best to look first to the main tendencies of Nature. A particular flower may not be dead in early winter, but the flowers are dying; a particular pebble may never be wetted with the tide, but the tide is coming in. To the scientific eye all human history is a series of collective movements, destructions or migrations, like the massacre of flies in winter or the return of birds in spring. Now the root fact in all history is Race. Race produces religion; Race produces legal and ethical wars. There is no stronger case than that of the wild, unworldly and perishing stock which we commonly call the Celts, of whom your friends the MacNabs are specimens. Small, swarthy, and of this dreamy and drifting blood, they accept easily the superstitious explanation of any incidents, just as they still accept (you will excuse me for saying) that superstitious explanation of all incidents which you and your Church represent. It is not remarkable that such people, with the sea moaning behind them and the Church (excuse me again) droning in front of them, should put fantastic features into what are probably plain events. You, with your small parochial responsibilities, see only this particular Mrs MacNab, terrified with this particular tale of two voices and a tall man out of the sea. But the man with the scientific imagination sees, as it were, the whole clans of MacNab scattered over the whole world, in its ultimate average as uniform as a tribe of birds. He sees thousands of Mrs MacNabs, in thousands of houses, dropping their little drop of morbidity in the tea-cups of their friends; he sees—"

Before the scientist could conclude his sentence, another and more impatient summons sounded from without; someone with swishing skirts was marshalled hurriedly down the corridor, and the door opened on a young girl, decently dressed but disordered and red-hot with haste. She had sea-blown blonde hair, and would have been entirely beautiful if her cheek-bones had not been, in the Scotch manner, a little high in relief as well as in colour. Her apology was almost as abrupt as a command.

"I'm sorry to interrupt you, sir," she said, "but I had to follow Father Brown at once; it's nothing less than life or death."

Father Brown began to get to his feet in some disorder. "Why, what has happened, Maggie?" he said.

"James has been murdered, for all I can make out," answered the girl, still breathing hard from her rush. "That man Glass has been with him again; I heard them talking through the door quite plain. Two separate voices: for James speaks low, with a burr, and the other voice was high and quavery."

"That man Glass?" repeated the priest in some perplexity.

"I know his name is Glass," answered the girl, in great impatience. "I heard it through the door. They were quarrelling—about money, I think—for I heard James say again and again, 'That's right, Mr Glass,' or 'No, Mr Glass,' and then, 'Two or three, Mr Glass.' But we're talking too much; you must come at once, and there may be time yet."

"But time for what?" asked Dr Hood, who had been studying the young lady with marked interest. "What is there about Mr Glass and his money troubles that should impel such urgency?"

"I tried to break down the door and couldn't," answered the girl shortly, "Then I ran to the back-yard, and managed to climb on to the window-sill that looks into the room. It was all dim, and seemed to be empty, but I swear I saw James lying huddled up in a corner, as if he were drugged or strangled."

"This is very serious," said Father Brown, gathering his errant hat and umbrella and standing up; "in point of fact I was just putting your case before this gentleman, and his view—"

"Has been largely altered," said the scientist gravely. "I do not think this young lady is so Celtic as I had supposed. As I have nothing else to do, I will put on my hat and stroll down town with you."

In a few minutes all three were approaching the dreary tail of the MacNabs' street: the girl with the stern and breathless stride of the mountaineer, the criminologist with a lounging grace (which was not without a certain leopard-like swiftness), and the priest at an energetic trot entirely devoid of distinction. The aspect of this edge of the town was not entirely without justification for the doctor's hints about desolate moods and environments. The scattered houses stood farther and farther apart in a broken string along the seashore; the afternoon was closing with a premature and partly lurid twilight; the sea was of an inky purple and murmuring ominously. In the scrappy back garden of the MacNabs which ran down towards the sand, two black, barren-looking trees stood up like demon hands held up in astonishment, and as Mrs MacNab ran down the street to meet them with lean hands similarly spread, and her fierce face in shadow, she was a little like a demon herself. The doctor and the priest made scant reply to her shrill reiterations of her daughter's story, with more disturbing details of her own, to the divided vows of vengeance against Mr Glass for murdering, and against Mr Todhunter for being murdered, or against the latter for having dared to want to marry her daughter, and for not having lived to do it. They passed through the narrow passage in the front of the house until they came to the lodger's door at the back, and there Dr Hood, with the trick of an old detective, put his shoulder sharply to the panel and burst in the door.

It opened on a scene of silent catastrophe. No one seeing it, even for a flash, could doubt that the room had been the theatre of some thrilling collision between two, or perhaps more, persons. Playing-cards lay littered across the table or fluttered about the floor as if a game had been interrupted. Two wine glasses stood ready for wine on a side-table, but a third lay smashed in a star of crystal upon the carpet. A few feet from it lay what looked like a long knife or short sword, straight, but with an ornamental and pictured handle, its dull blade just caught a grey glint from the dreary window behind, which showed the black trees against the leaden level of the sea. Towards the opposite corner of the room was rolled a gentleman's silk top hat, as if it had just been knocked off his head; so much so, indeed, that one almost looked to see it still rolling. And in the corner behind it, thrown like a sack of potatoes, but corded like a railway trunk, lay Mr James Todhunter, with a scarf across his mouth, and six or seven ropes knotted round his elbows and ankles. His brown eyes were alive and shifted alertly.

Dr Orion Hood paused for one instant on the doormat and drank in the whole scene of voiceless violence. Then he stepped swiftly across the carpet, picked up the tall silk hat, and gravely put it upon the head of the yet pinioned Todhunter. It was so much too large for him that it almost slipped down on to his shoulders.

"Mr Glass's hat," said the doctor, returning with it and peering into the inside with a pocket lens. "How to explain the absence of Mr Glass and the presence of Mr Glass's hat? For Mr Glass is not a careless man with his clothes. That hat is of a stylish shape and systematically brushed and burnished, though not very new. An old dandy, I should think."

"But, good heavens!" called out Miss MacNab, "aren't you going to untie the man first?"

"I say 'old' with intention, though not with certainty" continued the expositor; "my reason for it might seem a little far-fetched. The hair of human beings falls out in very varying degrees, but almost always falls out slightly, and with the lens I should see the tiny hairs in a hat recently worn. It has none, which leads me to guess that Mr Glass is bald. Now when this is taken with the high-pitched and querulous voice which Miss MacNab described so vividly (patience, my dear lady, patience), when we take the hairless head together with the tone common in senile anger, I should think we may deduce some advance in years. Nevertheless, he was probably vigorous, and he was almost certainly tall. I might rely in some degree on the story of his previous appearance at the window, as a tall man in a silk hat, but I think I have more exact indication. This wineglass has been smashed all over the place, but one of its splinters lies on the high bracket beside the mantelpiece. No such fragment could have fallen there if the vessel had been smashed in the hand of a comparatively short man like Mr Todhunter."

"By the way," said Father Brown, "might it not be as well to untie Mr Todhunter?"

"Our lesson from the drinking-vessels does not end here," proceeded the specialist. "I may say at once that it is possible that the man Glass was bald or nervous through dissipation rather than age. Mr Todhunter, as has been remarked, is a quiet thrifty gentleman, essentially an abstainer. These cards and wine-cups are no part of his normal habit; they have been produced for a particular companion. But, as it happens, we may go farther. Mr Todhunter may or may not possess this wine-service, but there is no appearance of his possessing any wine. What, then, were these vessels to contain? I would at once suggest some brandy or whisky, perhaps of a luxurious sort, from a flask in the pocket of Mr Glass. We have thus something like a picture of the man, or at least of the type: tall, elderly, fashionable, but somewhat frayed, certainly fond of play and strong waters, perhaps rather too fond of them. Mr Glass is a gentleman not unknown on the fringes of society."

"Look here," cried the young woman, "if you don't let me pass to untie him I'll run outside and scream for the police."

"I should not advise you, Miss MacNab," said Dr Hood gravely, "to be in any hurry to fetch the police. Father Brown, I seriously ask you to compose your flock, for their sakes, not for mine. Well, we have seen something of the figure and quality of Mr Glass; what are the chief facts known of Mr Todhunter? They are substantially three: that he is economical, that he is more or less wealthy, and that he has a secret. Now, surely it is obvious that there are the three chief marks of the kind of man who is blackmailed. And surely it is equally obvious that the faded finery, the profligate habits, and the shrill irritation of Mr Glass are the unmistakable marks of the kind of man who blackmails him. We have the two typical figures of a tragedy of hush money: on the one hand, the respectable man with a mystery; on the other, the West-end vulture with a scent for a mystery. These two men have met here to-day and have quarrelled, using blows and a bare weapon."

"Are you going to take those ropes off?" asked the girl stubbornly.

Dr Hood replaced the silk hat carefully on the side table, and went across to the captive. He studied him intently, even moving him a little and half-turning him round by the shoulders, but he only answered:

"No; I think these ropes will do very well till your friends the police bring the handcuffs."

Father Brown, who had been looking dully at the carpet, lifted his round face and said: "What do you mean?"

The man of science had picked up the peculiar dagger-sword from the carpet and was examining it intently as he answered:

"Because you find Mr Todhunter tied up," he said, "you all jump to the conclusion that Mr Glass had tied him up; and then, I suppose, escaped. There are four objections to this: First, why should a gentleman so dressy as our friend Glass leave his hat behind him, if he left of his own free will? Second," he continued, moving towards the window, "this is the only exit, and it is locked on the inside. Third, this blade here has a tiny touch of blood at the point, but there is no wound on Mr Todhunter. Mr Glass took that wound away with him, dead or alive. Add to all this primary probability. It is much more likely that the blackmailed person would try to kill his incubus, rather than that the blackmailer would try to kill the goose that lays his golden egg. There, I think, we have a pretty complete story."

"But the ropes?" inquired the priest, whose eyes had remained open with a rather vacant admiration.

"Ah, the ropes," said the expert with a singular intonation. "Miss MacNab very much wanted to know why I did not set Mr Todhunter free from his ropes. Well, I will tell her. I did not do it because Mr Todhunter can set himself free from them at any minute he chooses."

"What?" cried the audience on quite different notes of astonishment.

"I have looked at all the knots on Mr Todhunter," reiterated Hood quietly. "I happen to know something about knots; they are quite a branch of criminal science. Every one of those knots he has made himself and could loosen himself; not one of them would have been made by an enemy really trying to pinion him. The whole of this affair of the ropes is a clever fake, to make us think him the victim of the struggle instead of the wretched Glass, whose corpse may be hidden in the garden or stuffed up the chimney."

There was a rather depressed silence; the room was darkening, the sea-blighted boughs of the garden trees looked leaner and blacker than ever, yet they seemed to have come nearer to the window. One could almost fancy they were sea-monsters like krakens or cuttlefish, writhing polypi who had crawled up from the sea to see the end of this tragedy, even as he, the villain and victim of it, the terrible man in the tall hat, had once crawled up from the sea. For the whole air was dense with the morbidity of blackmail, which is the most morbid of human things, because it is a crime concealing a crime; a black plaster on a blacker wound.

The face of the little Catholic priest, which was commonly complacent and even comic, had suddenly become knotted with a curious frown. It was not the blank curiosity of his first innocence. It was rather that creative curiosity which comes when a man has the beginnings of an idea. "Say it again, please," he said in a simple, bothered manner; "do you mean that Todhunter can tie himself up all alone and untie himself all alone?"

"That is what I mean," said the doctor.

"Jerusalem!" ejaculated Brown suddenly, "I wonder if it could possibly be that!"

He scuttled across the room rather like a rabbit, and peered with quite a new impulsiveness into the partially-covered face of the captive. Then he turned his own rather fatuous face to the company. "Yes, that's it!" he cried in a certain excitement. "Can't you see it in the man's face? Why, look at his eyes!"

Both the Professor and the girl followed the direction of his glance. And though the broad black scarf completely masked the lower half of Todhunter's visage, they did grow conscious of something struggling and intense about the upper part of it.

"His eyes do look queer," cried the young woman, strongly moved. "You brutes; I believe it's hurting him!"

"Not that, I think," said Dr Hood; "the eyes have certainly a singular expression. But I should interpret those transverse wrinkles as expressing rather such slight psychological abnormality—"

"Oh, bosh!" cried Father Brown: "can't you see he's laughing?"

"Laughing!" repeated the doctor, with a start; "but what on earth can he be laughing at?"

"Well," replied the Reverend Brown apologetically, "not to put too fine a point on it, I think he is laughing at you. And indeed, I'm a little inclined to laugh at myself, now I know about it."

"Now you know about what?" asked Hood, in some exasperation.

"Now I know," replied the priest, "the profession of Mr Todhunter."

He shuffled about the room, looking at one object after another with what seemed to be a vacant stare, and then invariably bursting into an equally vacant laugh, a highly irritating process for those who had to watch it. He laughed very much over the hat, still more uproariously over the broken glass, but the blood on the sword point sent him into mortal convulsions of amusement. Then he turned to the fuming specialist.

"Dr Hood," he cried enthusiastically, "you are a great poet! You have called an uncreated being out of the void. How much more godlike that is than if you had only ferreted out the mere facts! Indeed, the mere facts are rather commonplace and comic by comparison."

"I have no notion what you are talking about," said Dr Hood rather haughtily; "my facts are all inevitable, though necessarily incomplete. A place may be permitted to intuition, perhaps (or poetry if you prefer the term), but only because the corresponding details cannot as yet be ascertained. In the absence of Mr Glass—"

"That's it, that's it," said the little priest, nodding quite eagerly, "that's the first idea to get fixed; the absence of Mr Glass. He is so extremely absent. I suppose," he added reflectively, "that there was never anybody so absent as Mr Glass."

"Do you mean he is absent from the town?" demanded the doctor.

"I mean he is absent from everywhere," answered Father Brown; "he is absent from the Nature of Things, so to speak."

"Do you seriously mean," said the specialist with a smile, "that there is no such person?"

The priest made a sign of assent. "It does seem a pity," he said.

Orion Hood broke into a contemptuous laugh. "Well," he said, "before we go on to the hundred and one other evidences, let us take the first proof we found; the first fact we fell over when we fell into this room. If there is no Mr Glass, whose hat is this?"

"It is Mr Todhunter's," replied Father Brown.

"But it doesn't fit him," cried Hood impatiently. "He couldn't possibly wear it!"

Father Brown shook his head with ineffable mildness. "I never said he could wear it," he answered. "I said it was his hat. Or, if you insist on a shade of difference, a hat that is his."

"And what is the shade of difference?" asked the criminologist with a slight sneer.

"My good sir," cried the mild little man, with his first movement akin to impatience, "if you will walk down the street to the nearest hatter's shop, you will see that there is, in common speech, a difference between a man's hat and the hats that are his."

"But a hatter," protested Hood, "can get money out of his stock of new hats. What could Todhunter get out of this one old hat?"

"Rabbits," replied Father Brown promptly.

"What?" cried Dr Hood.

"Rabbits, ribbons, sweetmeats, goldfish, rolls of coloured paper," said the reverend gentleman with rapidity. "Didn't you see it all when you found out the faked ropes? It's just the same with the sword. Mr Todhunter hasn't got a scratch on him, as you say; but he's got a scratch in him, if you follow me."

"Do you mean inside Mr Todhunter's clothes?" inquired Mrs MacNab sternly.

"I do not mean inside Mr Todhunter's clothes," said Father Brown. "I mean inside Mr Todhunter."

"Well, what in the name of Bedlam do you mean?"

"Mr Todhunter," explained Father Brown placidly, "is learning to be a professional conjurer, as well as juggler, ventriloquist, and expert in the rope trick. The conjuring explains the hat. It is without traces of hair, not because it is worn by the prematurely bald Mr Glass, but because it has never been worn by anybody. The juggling explains the three glasses, which Todhunter was teaching himself to throw up and catch in rotation. But, being only at the stage of practice, he smashed one glass against the ceiling. And the juggling also explains the sword, which it was Mr Todhunter's professional pride and duty to swallow. But, again, being at the stage of practice, he very slightly grazed the inside of his throat with the weapon. Hence he has a wound inside him, which I am sure (from the expression on his face) is not a serious one. He was also practising the trick of a release from ropes, like the Davenport Brothers, and he was just about to free himself when we all burst into the room. The cards, of course, are for card tricks, and they are scattered on the floor because he had just been practising one of those dodges of sending them flying through the air. He merely kept his trade secret, because he had to keep his tricks secret, like any other conjurer. But the mere fact of an idler in a top hat having once looked in at his back window, and been driven away by him with great indignation, was enough to set us all on a wrong track of romance, and make us imagine his whole life overshadowed by the silk-hatted spectre of Mr Glass."

"But what about the two voices?" asked Maggie, staring.

"Have you never heard a ventriloquist?" asked Father Brown. "Don't you know they speak first in their natural voice, and then answer themselves in just that shrill, squeaky, unnatural voice that you heard?"

There was a long silence, and Dr Hood regarded the little man who had spoken with a dark and attentive smile. "You are certainly a very ingenious person," he said; "it could not have been done better in a book. But there is just one part of Mr Glass you have not succeeded in explaining away, and that is his name. Miss MacNab distinctly heard him so addressed by Mr Todhunter."

The Rev. Mr Brown broke into a rather childish giggle. "Well, that," he said, "that's the silliest part of the whole silly story. When our juggling friend here threw up the three glasses in turn, he counted them aloud as he caught them, and also commented aloud when he failed to catch them. What he really said was: 'One, two and three—missed a glass one, two—missed a glass.' And so on."

There was a second of stillness in the room, and then everyone with one accord burst out laughing. As they did so the figure in the corner complacently uncoiled all the ropes and let them fall with a flourish. Then, advancing into the middle of the room with a bow, he produced from his pocket a big bill printed in blue and red, which announced that ZALADIN, the World's Greatest Conjurer, Contortionist, Ventriloquist and Human Kangaroo would be ready with an entirely new series of Tricks at the Empire Pavilion, Scarborough, on Monday next at eight o'clock precisely.

The Paradise of Thieves

THE great Muscari, most original of the young Tuscan poets, walked swiftly into his favourite restaurant, which overlooked the Mediterranean, was covered by an awning and fenced by little lemon and orange trees. Waiters in white aprons were already laying out on white tables the insignia of an early and elegant lunch; and this seemed to increase a satisfaction that already touched the top of swagger. Muscari had an eagle nose like Dante; his hair and neckerchief were dark and flowing; he carried a black cloak, and might almost have carried a black mask, so much did he bear with him a sort of Venetian melodrama. He acted as if a troubadour had still a definite social office, like a bishop. He went as near as his century permitted to walking the world literally like Don Juan, with rapier and guitar.

For he never travelled without a case of swords, with which he had fought many brilliant duels, or without a corresponding case for his mandolin, with which he had actually serenaded Miss Ethel Harrogate, the highly conventional daughter of a Yorkshire banker on a holiday. Yet he was neither a charlatan nor a child; but a hot, logical Latin who liked a certain thing and was it. His poetry was as straightforward as anyone else's prose. He desired fame or wine or the beauty of women with a torrid directness inconceivable among the cloudy ideals or cloudy compromises of the north; to vaguer races his intensity smelt of danger or even crime. Like fire or the sea, he was too simple to be trusted.

The banker and his beautiful English daughter were staying at the hotel attached to Muscari's restaurant; that was why it was his favourite restaurant. A glance flashed around the room told him at once, however, that the English party had not descended. The restaurant was glittering, but still comparatively empty. Two priests were talking at a table in a corner, but Muscari (an ardent Catholic) took no more notice of them than of a couple of crows. But from a yet farther seat, partly concealed behind a dwarf tree golden with oranges, there rose and advanced towards the poet a person whose costume was the most aggressively opposite to his own.

This figure was clad in tweeds of a piebald check, with a pink tie, a sharp collar and protuberant yellow boots. He contrived, in the true tradition of 'Arry at Margate, to look at once startling and commonplace. But as the Cockney apparition drew nearer, Muscari was astounded to observe that the head was distinctly different from the body. It was an Italian head: fuzzy, swarthy and very vivacious, that rose abruptly out of the standing collar like cardboard and the comic pink tie. In fact it was a head he knew. He recognized it, above all the dire erection of English holiday array, as the face of an old but forgotten friend name Ezza. This youth had been a prodigy at college, and European fame was promised him when he was barely fifteen; but when he appeared in the world he failed, first publicly as a dramatist and a demagogue, and then privately for years on end as an actor, a traveller, a commission agent or a journalist. Muscari had known him last behind the footlights; he was but too well attuned to the excitements of that profession, and it was believed that some moral calamity had swallowed him up.

"Ezza!" cried the poet, rising and shaking hands in a pleasant astonishment. "Well, I've seen you in many costumes in the green room; but I never expected to see you dressed up as an Englishman."

"This," answered Ezza gravely, "is not the costume of an Englishman, but of the Italian of the future."

"In that case," remarked Muscari, "I confess I prefer the Italian of the past."

"That is your old mistake, Muscari," said the man in tweeds, shaking his head; "and the mistake of Italy. In the sixteenth century we Tuscans made the morning: we had the newest steel, the newest carving, the newest chemistry. Why should we not now have the newest factories, the newest motors, the newest finance—the newest clothes?"

"Because they are not worth having," answered Muscari. "You cannot make Italians really progressive; they are too intelligent. Men who see the short cut to good living will never go by the new elaborate roads."

"Well, to me Marconi, or D'Annunzio, is the star of Italy" said the other. "That is why I have become a Futurist—and a courier."

"A courier!" cried Muscari, laughing. "Is that the last of your list of trades? And whom are you conducting?"

"Oh, a man of the name of Harrogate, and his family, I believe."

"Not the banker in this hotel?" inquired the poet, with some eagerness.

"That's the man," answered the courier.

"Does it pay well?" asked the troubadour innocently.

"It will pay me," said Ezza, with a very enigmatic smile. "But I am a rather curious sort of courier." Then, as if changing the subject, he said abruptly: "He has a daughter—and a son."

"The daughter is divine," affirmed Muscari, "the father and son are, I suppose, human. But granted his harmless qualities doesn't that banker strike you as a splendid instance of my argument? Harrogate has millions in his safes, and I have—the hole in my pocket. But you daren't say—you can't say—that he's cleverer than I, or bolder than I, or even more energetic. He's not clever, he's got eyes like blue buttons; he's not energetic, he moves from chair to chair like a paralytic. He's a conscientious, kindly old blockhead; but he's got money simply because he collects money, as a boy collects stamps. You're too strong-minded for business, Ezza. You won't get on. To be clever enough to get all that money, one must be stupid enough to want it."

"I'm stupid enough for that," said Ezza gloomily. "But I should suggest a suspension of your critique of the banker, for here he comes."

Mr Harrogate, the great financier, did indeed enter the room, but nobody looked at him. He was a massive elderly man with a boiled blue eye and faded grey-sandy moustaches; but for his heavy stoop he might have been a colonel. He carried several unopened letters in his hand. His son Frank was a really fine lad, curly-haired, sun-burnt and strenuous; but nobody looked at him either. All eyes, as usual, were riveted, for the moment at least, upon Ethel Harrogate, whose golden Greek head and colour of the dawn seemed set purposely above that sapphire sea, like a goddess's. The poet Muscari drew a deep breath as if he were drinking something, as indeed he was. He was drinking the Classic; which his fathers made. Ezza studied her with a gaze equally intense and far more baffling.

Miss Harrogate was specially radiant and ready for conversation on this occasion; and her family had fallen into the easier Continental habit, allowing the stranger Muscari and even the courier Ezza to share their table and their talk. In Ethel Harrogate conventionality crowned itself with a perfection and splendour of its own. Proud of her father's prosperity, fond of fashionable pleasures, a fond daughter but an arrant flirt, she was all these things with a sort of golden good-nature that made her very pride pleasing and her worldly respectability a fresh and hearty thing.

They were in an eddy of excitement about some alleged peril in the mountain path they were to attempt that week. The danger was not from rock and avalanche, but from something yet more romantic. Ethel had been earnestly assured that brigands, the true cut-throats of the modern legend, still haunted that ridge and held that pass of the Apennines.

"They say," she cried, with the awful relish of a schoolgirl, "that all that country isn't ruled by the King of Italy, but by the King of Thieves. Who is the King of Thieves?"

"A great man," replied Muscari, "worthy to rank with your own Robin Hood, signorina. Montano, the King of Thieves, was first heard of in the mountains some ten years ago, when people said brigands were extinct. But his wild authority spread with the swiftness of a silent revolution. Men found his fierce proclamations nailed in every mountain village; his sentinels, gun in hand, in every mountain ravine. Six times the Italian Government tried to dislodge him, and was defeated in six pitched battles as if by Napoleon."

"Now that sort of thing," observed the banker weightily, "would never be allowed in England; perhaps, after all, we had better choose another route. But the courier thought it perfectly safe."

"It is perfectly safe," said the courier contemptuously. "I have been over it twenty times. There may have been some old jailbird called a King in the time of our grandmothers; but he belongs to history if not to fable. Brigandage is utterly stamped out."

"It can never be utterly stamped out," Muscari answered; "because armed revolt is a recreation natural to southerners. Our peasants are like their mountains, rich in grace and green gaiety, but with the fires beneath. There is a point of human despair where the northern poor take to drink—and our own poor take to daggers."

"A poet is privileged," replied Ezza, with a sneer. "If Signor Muscari were English he would still be looking for highwaymen in Wandsworth. Believe me, there is no more danger of being captured in Italy than of being scalped in Boston."

"Then you propose to attempt it?" asked Mr Harrogate, frowning.

"Oh, it sounds rather dreadful," cried the girl, turning her glorious eyes on Muscari. "Do you really think the pass is dangerous?"

Muscari threw back his black mane. "I know it is dangerous:" he said. "I am crossing it tomorrow."

The young Harrogate was left behind for a moment emptying a glass of white wine and lighting a cigarette, as the beauty retired with the banker, the courier and the poet, distributing peals of silvery satire. At about the same instant the two priests in the corner rose; the taller, a white-haired Italian, taking his leave. The shorter priest turned and walked towards the banker's son, and the latter was astonished to realize that though a Roman priest the man was an Englishman. He vaguely remembered meeting him at the social crushes of some of his Catholic friends. But the man spoke before his memories could collect themselves.

"Mr Frank Harrogate, I think," he said. "I have had an introduction, but I do not mean to presume on it. The odd thing I have to say will come far better from a stranger. Mr Harrogate, I say one word and go: take care of your sister in her great sorrow."

Even for Frank's truly fraternal indifference the radiance and derision of his sister still seemed to sparkle and ring; he could hear her laughter still from the garden of the hotel, and he stared at his sombre adviser in puzzledom.

"Do you mean the brigands?" he asked; and then, remembering a vague fear of his own, "or can you be thinking of Muscari?"

"One is never thinking of the real sorrow," said the strange priest. "One can only be kind when it comes."

And he passed promptly from the room, leaving the other almost with his mouth open.

A day or two afterwards a coach containing the company was really crawling and staggering up the spurs of the menacing mountain range. Between Ezza's cheery denial of the danger and Muscari's boisterous defiance of it, the financial family were firm in their original purpose; and Muscari made his mountain journey coincide with theirs. A more surprising feature was the appearance at the coast-town station of the little priest of the restaurant; he alleged merely that business led him also to cross the mountains of the midland. But young Harrogate could not but connect his presence with the mystical fears and warnings of yesterday.

The coach was a kind of commodious wagonette, invented by the modernist talent of the courier, who dominated the expedition with his scientific activity and breezy wit. The theory of danger from thieves was banished from thought and speech; though so far conceded in formal act that some slight protection was employed. The courier and the young banker carried loaded revolvers, and Muscari (with much boyish gratification) buckled on a kind of cutlass under his black cloak.

He had planted his person at a flying leap next to the lovely Englishwoman; on the other side of her sat the priest, whose name was Brown and who was fortunately a silent individual; the courier and the father and son were on the banc behind. Muscari was in towering spirits, seriously believing in the peril, and his talk to Ethel might well have made her think him a maniac. But there was something in the crazy and gorgeous ascent, amid crags like peaks loaded with woods like orchards, that dragged her spirit up alone with his into purple preposterous heavens with wheeling suns. The white road climbed like a white cat; it spanned sunless chasms like a tight-rope; it was flung round far-off headlands like a lasso.

And yet, however high they went, the desert still blossomed like the rose. The fields were burnished in sun and wind with the colour of kingfisher and parrot and humming-bird, the hues of a hundred flowering flowers. There are no lovelier meadows and woodlands than the English, no nobler crests or chasms than those of Snowdon and Glencoe. But Ethel Harrogate had never before seen the southern parks tilted on the splintered northern peaks; the gorge of Glencoe laden with the fruits of Kent. There was nothing here of that chill and desolation that in Britain one associates with high and wild scenery. It was rather like a mosaic palace, rent with earthquakes; or like a Dutch tulip garden blown to the stars with dynamite.

"It's like Kew Gardens on Beachy Head," said Ethel.

"It is our secret," answered he, "the secret of the volcano; that is also the secret of the revolution—that a thing can be violent and yet fruitful."

"You are rather violent yourself," and she smiled at him.

"And yet rather fruitless," he admitted; "if I die tonight I die unmarried and a fool."

"It is not my fault if you have come," she said after a difficult silence.

"It is never your fault," answered Muscari; "it was not your fault that Troy fell."

As they spoke they came under overwhelming cliffs that spread almost like wings above a corner of peculiar peril. Shocked by the big shadow on the narrow ledge, the horses stirred doubtfully. The driver leapt to the earth to hold their heads, and they became ungovernable. One horse reared up to his full height—the titanic and terrifying height of a horse when he becomes a biped. It was just enough to alter the equilibrium; the whole coach heeled over like a ship and crashed through the fringe of bushes over the cliff. Muscari threw an arm round Ethel, who clung to him, and shouted aloud. It was for such moments that he lived.

At the moment when the gorgeous mountain walls went round the poet's head like a purple windmill a thing happened which was superficially even more startling. The elderly and lethargic banker sprang erect in the coach and leapt over the precipice before the tilted vehicle could take him there. In the first flash it looked as wild as suicide; but in the second it was as sensible as a safe investment. The Yorkshireman had evidently more promptitude, as well as more sagacity, than Muscari had given him credit for; for he landed in a lap of land which might have been specially padded with turf and clover to receive him. As it happened, indeed, the whole company were equally lucky, if less dignified in their form of ejection. Immediately under this abrupt turn of the road was a grassy and flowery hollow like a sunken meadow; a sort of green velvet pocket in the long, green, trailing garments of the hills. Into this they were all tipped or tumbled with little damage, save that their smallest baggage and even the contents of their pockets were scattered in the grass around them. The wrecked coach still hung above, entangled in the tough hedge, and the horses plunged painfully down the slope. The first to sit up was the little priest, who scratched his head with a face of foolish wonder. Frank Harrogate heard him say to himself: "Now why on earth have we fallen just here?"

He blinked at the litter around him, and recovered his own very clumsy umbrella. Beyond it lay the broad sombrero fallen from the head of Muscari, and beside it a sealed business letter which, after a glance at the address, he returned to the elder Harrogate. On the other side of him the grass partly hid Miss Ethel's sunshade, and just beyond it lay a curious little glass bottle hardly two inches long. The priest picked it up; in a quick, unobtrusive manner he uncorked and sniffed it, and his heavy face turned the colour of clay.

"Heaven deliver us!" he muttered; "it can't be hers! Has her sorrow come on her already?" He slipped it into his own waistcoat pocket. "I think I'm justified," he said, "till I know a little more."

He gazed painfully at the girl, at that moment being raised out of the flowers by Muscari, who was saying: "We have fallen into heaven; it is a sign. Mortals climb up and they fall down; but it is only gods and goddesses who can fall upwards."

And indeed she rose out of the sea of colours so beautiful and happy a vision that the priest felt his suspicion shaken and shifted. "After all," he thought, "perhaps the poison isn't hers; perhaps it's one of Muscari's melodramatic tricks."

Muscari set the lady lightly on her feet, made her an absurdly theatrical bow, and then, drawing his cutlass, hacked hard at the taut reins of the horses, so that they scrambled to their feet and stood in the grass trembling. When he had done so, a most remarkable thing occurred. A very quiet man, very poorly dressed and extremely sunburnt, came out of the bushes and took hold of the horses' heads. He had a queer-shaped knife, very broad and crooked, buckled on his belt; there was nothing else remarkable about him, except his sudden and silent appearance. The poet asked him who he was, and he did not answer.

Looking around him at the confused and startled group in the hollow, Muscari then perceived that another tanned and tattered man, with a short gun under his arm, was looking at them from the ledge just below, leaning his elbows on the edge of the turf. Then he looked up at the road from which they had fallen and saw, looking down on them, the muzzles of four other carbines and four other brown faces with bright but quite motionless eyes.

"The brigands!" cried Muscari, with a kind of monstrous gaiety. "This was a trap. Ezza, if you will oblige me by shooting the coachman first, we can cut our way out yet. There are only six of them."

"The coachman," said Ezza, who was standing grimly with his hands in his pockets, "happens to be a servant of Mr Harrogate's."

"Then shoot him all the more," cried the poet impatiently; "he was bribed to upset his master. Then put the lady in the middle, and we will break the line up there—with a rush."

And, wading in wild grass and flowers, he advanced fearlessly on the four carbines; but finding that no one followed except young Harrogate, he turned, brandishing his cutlass to wave the others on. He beheld the courier still standing slightly astride in the centre of the grassy ring, his hands in his pockets; and his lean, ironical Italian face seemed to grow longer and longer in the evening light.

"You thought, Muscari, I was the failure among our schoolfellows," he said, "and you thought you were the success. But I have succeeded more than you and fill a bigger place in history. I have been acting epics while you have been writing them."

"Come on, I tell you!" thundered Muscari from above. "Will you stand there talking nonsense about yourself with a woman to save and three strong men to help you? What do you call yourself?"

"I call myself Montano," cried the strange courier in a voice equally loud and full. "I am the King of Thieves, and I welcome you all to my summer palace."

And even as he spoke five more silent men with weapons ready came out of the bushes, and looked towards him for their orders. One of them held a large paper in his hand.

"This pretty little nest where we are all picnicking," went on the courier-brigand, with the same easy yet sinister smile, "is, together with some caves underneath it, known by the name of the Paradise of Thieves. It is my principal stronghold on these hills; for (as you have doubtless noticed) the eyrie is invisible both from the road above and from the valley below. It is something better than impregnable; it is unnoticeable. Here I mostly live, and here I shall certainly die, if the gendarmes ever track me here. I am not the kind of criminal that 'reserves his defence,' but the better kind that reserves his last bullet."

All were staring at him thunderstruck and still, except Father Brown, who heaved a huge sigh as of relief and fingered the little phial in his pocket. "Thank God!" he muttered; "that's much more probable. The poison belongs to this robber-chief, of course. He carries it so that he may never be captured, like Cato."

The King of Thieves was, however, continuing his address with the same kind of dangerous politeness. "It only remains for me," he said, "to explain to my guests the social conditions upon which I have the pleasure of entertaining them. I need not expound the quaint old ritual of ransom, which it is incumbent upon me to keep up; and even this only applies to a part of the company. The Reverend Father Brown and the celebrated Signor Muscari I shall release tomorrow at dawn and escort to my outposts. Poets and priests, if you will pardon my simplicity of speech, never have any money. And so (since it is impossible to get anything out of them), let us, seize the opportunity to show our admiration for classic literature and our reverence for Holy Church."

He paused with an unpleasing smile; and Father Brown blinked repeatedly at him, and seemed suddenly to be listening with great attention. The brigand captain took the large paper from the attendant brigand and, glancing over it, continued: "My other intentions are clearly set forth in this public document, which I will hand round in a moment; and which after that will be posted on a tree by every village in the valley, and every cross-road in the hills. I will not weary you with the verbalism, since you will be able to check it; the substance of my proclamation is this: I announce first that I have captured the English millionaire, the colossus of finance, Mr Samuel Harrogate. I next announce that I have found on his person notes and bonds for two thousand pounds, which he has given up to me. Now since it would be really immoral to announce such a thing to a credulous public if it had not occurred, I suggest it should occur without further delay. I suggest that Mr Harrogate senior should now give me the two thousand pounds in his pocket."

160

The banker looked at him under lowering brows, red-faced and sulky, but seemingly cowed. That leap from the failing carriage seemed to have used up his last virility. He had held back in a hang-dog style when his son and Muscari had made a bold movement to break out of the brigand trap. And now his red and trembling hand went reluctantly to his breast-pocket, and passed a bundle of papers and envelopes to the brigand.

"Excellent!" cried that outlaw gaily; "so far we are all cosy. I resume the points of my proclamation, so soon to be published to all Italy. The third item is that of ransom. I am asking from the friends of the Harrogate family a ransom of three thousand pounds, which I am sure is almost insulting to that family in its moderate estimate of their importance. Who would not pay triple this sum for another day's association with such a domestic circle? I will not conceal from you that the document ends with certain legal phrases about the unpleasant things that may happen if the money is not paid; but meanwhile, ladies and gentlemen, let me assure you that I am comfortably off here for accommodation, wine and cigars, and bid you for the present a sportsman-like welcome to the luxuries of the Paradise of Thieves."

All the time that he had been speaking, the dubious-looking men with carbines and dirty slouch hats had been gathering silently in such preponderating numbers that even Muscari was compelled to recognize his sally with the sword as hopeless. He glanced around him; but the girl had already gone over to soothe and comfort her father, for her natural affection for his person was as strong or stronger than her somewhat snobbish pride in his success. Muscari, with the illogicality of a lover, admired this filial devotion, and yet was irritated by it. He slapped his sword back in the scabbard and went and flung himself somewhat sulkily on one of the green banks. The priest sat down within a yard or two, and Muscari turned his aquiline nose on him in an instantaneous irritation.

"Well," said the poet tartly, "do people still think me too romantic? Are there, I wonder, any brigands left in the mountains?"

"There may be," said Father Brown agnostically.

"What do you mean?" asked the other sharply.

"I mean I am puzzled," replied the priest. "I am puzzled about Ezza or Montano, or whatever his name is. He seems to me much more inexplicable as a brigand even than he was as a courier."

"But in what way?" persisted his companion. "Santa Maria! I should have thought the brigand was plain enough."

"I find three curious difficulties," said the priest in a quiet voice. "I should like to have your opinion on them. First of all I must tell you I was lunching in that restaurant at the seaside. As four of you left the room, you and Miss Harrogate went ahead, talking and laughing; the banker and the courier came behind, speaking sparely and rather low. But I could not help hearing Ezza say these words—'Well, let her have a little fun; you know the blow may smash her any minute.' Mr Harrogate answered nothing; so the words must have had some meaning. On the impulse of the moment I warned her brother that she might be in peril; I said nothing of its nature, for I did not know. But if it meant this capture in the hills, the thing is nonsense. Why should the brigand-courier warn his patron, even by a hint, when it was his whole purpose to lure him into the mountain-mousetrap? It could not have meant that. But if not, what is this disaster, known both to courier and banker, which hangs over Miss Harrogate's head?"

"Disaster to Miss Harrogate!" ejaculated the poet, sitting up with some ferocity. "Explain yourself; go on."

"All my riddles, however, revolve round our bandit chief," resumed the priest reflectively. "And here is the second of them. Why did he put so prominently in his demand for ransom the fact that he had taken two thousand pounds from his victim on the spot? It had no faintest tendency to evoke the ransom. Quite the other way, in fact. Harrogate's friends would be far likelier to fear for his fate if they thought the thieves were poor and desperate. Yet the spoliation on the spot was emphasized and even put first in the demand. Why should Ezza Montano want so specially to tell all Europe that he had picked the pocket before he levied the blackmail?"

"I cannot imagine," said Muscari, rubbing up his black hair for once with an unaffected gesture. "You may think you enlighten me, but you are leading me deeper in the dark. What may be the third objection to the King of the Thieves?" "The third objection," said Father Brown, still in meditation, "is this bank we are sitting on. Why does our brigand-courier call this his chief fortress and the Paradise of Thieves? It is certainly a soft spot to fall on and a sweet spot to look at. It is also quite true, as he says, that it is invisible from valley and peak, and is therefore a hiding-place. But it is not a fortress. It never could be a fortress. I think it would be the worst fortress in the world. For it is actually commanded from above by the common high-road across the mountains—the very place where the police would most probably pass. Why, five shabby short guns held us helpless here about half an hour ago. The quarter of a company of any kind of soldiers could have blown us over the precipice. Whatever is the meaning of this odd little nook of grass and flowers, it is not an entrenched position. It is something else; it has some other strange sort of importance; some value that I do not understand. It is more like an accidental theatre or a natural green-room; it is like the scene for some romantic comedy; it is like...."

As the little priest's words lengthened and lost themselves in a dull and dreamy sincerity, Muscari, whose animal senses were alert and impatient, heard a new noise in the mountains. Even for him the sound was as yet very small and faint; but he could have sworn the evening breeze bore with it something like the pulsation of horses' hoofs and a distant hallooing.

At the same moment, and long before the vibration had touched the less-experienced English ears, Montano the brigand ran up the bank above them and stood in the broken hedge, steadying himself against a tree and peering down the road. He was a strange figure as he stood there, for he had assumed a flapped fantastic hat and swinging baldric and cutlass in his capacity of bandit king, but the bright prosaic tweed of the courier showed through in patches all over him.

The next moment he turned his olive, sneering face and made a movement with his hand. The brigands scattered at the signal, not in confusion, but in what was evidently a kind of guerrilla discipline. Instead of occupying the road along the ridge, they sprinkled themselves along the side of it behind the trees and the hedge, as if watching unseen for an enemy. The noise beyond grew stronger, beginning to shake the mountain road, and a voice could be clearly heard calling out orders. The brigands swayed and huddled, cursing and whispering, and the evening air was full of little metallic noises as they cocked their pistols, or loosened their knives, or trailed their scabbards over the stones. Then the noises from both quarters seemed to meet on the road above; branches broke, horses neighed, men cried out.

"A rescue!" cried Muscari, springing to his feet and waving his hat; "the gendarmes are on them! Now for freedom and a blow for it! Now to be rebels against robbers! Come, don't let us leave everything to the police; that is so dreadfully modern. Fall on the rear of these ruffians. The gendarmes are rescuing us; come, friends, let us rescue the gendarmes!"

And throwing his hat over the trees, he drew his cutlass once more and began to escalade the slope up to the road. Frank Harrogate jumped up and ran across to help him, revolver in hand, but was astounded to hear himself imperatively recalled by the raucous voice of his father, who seemed to be in great agitation.

"I won't have it," said the banker in a choking voice; "I command you not to interfere."

"But, father," said Frank very warmly, "an Italian gentleman has led the way. You wouldn't have it said that the English hung back."

"It is useless," said the older man, who was trembling violently, "it is useless. We must submit to our lot."

Father Brown looked at the banker; then he put his hand instinctively as if on his heart, but really on the little bottle of poison; and a great light came into his face like the light of the revelation of death.

Muscari meanwhile, without waiting for support, had crested the bank up to the road, and struck the brigand king heavily on the shoulder, causing him to stagger and swing round. Montano also had his cutlass unsheathed, and Muscari, without further speech, sent a slash at his head which he was compelled to catch and parry. But even as the two short blades crossed and clashed the King of Thieves deliberately dropped his point and laughed.

"What's the good, old man?" he said in spirited Italian slang; "this damned farce will soon be over."

"What do you mean, you shuffler?" panted the fire-eating poet. "Is your courage a sham as well as your honesty?"

"Everything about me is a sham," responded the ex-courier in complete good humour. "I am an actor; and if I ever had a private character, I have forgotten it. I am no more a genuine brigand than I am a genuine courier. I am only a bundle of masks, and you can't fight a duel with that." And he laughed with boyish pleasure and fell into his old straddling attitude, with his back to the skirmish up the road.

Darkness was deepening under the mountain walls, and it was not easy to discern much of the progress of the struggle, save that tall men were pushing their horses' muzzles through a clinging crowd of brigands, who seemed more inclined to harass and hustle the invaders than to kill them. It was more like a town crowd preventing the passage of the police than anything the poet had ever pictured as the last stand of doomed and outlawed men of blood. Just as he was rolling his eyes in bewilderment he felt a touch on his elbow, and found the odd little priest standing there like a small Noah with a large hat, and requesting the favour of a word or two.

"Signor Muscari," said the cleric, "in this queer crisis personalities may be pardoned. I may tell you without offence of a way in which you will do more good than by helping the gendarmes, who are bound to break through in any case. You will permit me the impertinent intimacy, but do you care about that girl? Care enough to marry her and make her a good husband, I mean?"

"Yes," said the poet quite simply.

"Does she care about you?"

"I think so," was the equally grave reply.

"Then go over there and offer yourself," said the priest: "offer her everything you can; offer her heaven and earth if you've got them. The time is short."

"Why?" asked the astonished man of letters.

"Because," said Father Brown, "her Doom is coming up the road."

"Nothing is coming up the road," argued Muscari, "except the rescue."

"Well, you go over there," said his adviser, "and be ready to rescue her from the rescue."

Almost as he spoke the hedges were broken all along the ridge by a rush of the escaping brigands. They dived into bushes and thick grass like defeated men pursued; and the great cocked hats of the mounted gendarmerie were seen passing along above the broken hedge. Another order was given; there was a noise of dismounting, and a tall officer with cocked hat, a grey imperial, and a paper in his hand appeared in the gap that was the gate of the Paradise of Thieves. There was a momentary silence, broken in an extraordinary way by the banker, who cried out in a hoarse and strangled voice: "Robbed! I've been robbed!"

"Why, that was hours ago," cried his son in astonishment: "when you were robbed of two thousand pounds."

"Not of two thousand pounds," said the financier, with an abrupt and terrible composure, "only of a small bottle."

The policeman with the grey imperial was striding across the green hollow. Encountering the King of the Thieves in his path, he clapped him on the shoulder with something between a caress and a buffet and gave him a push that sent him staggering away. "You'll get into trouble, too," he said, "if you play these tricks."

Again to Muscari's artistic eye it seemed scarcely like the capture of a great outlaw at bay. Passing on, the policeman halted before the Harrogate group and said: "Samuel Harrogate, I arrest you in the name of the law for embezzlement of the funds of the Hull and Huddersfield Bank."

The great banker nodded with an odd air of business assent, seemed to reflect a moment, and before they could interpose took a half turn and a step that brought him to the edge of the outer mountain wall. Then, flinging up his hands, he leapt exactly as he leapt out of the coach. But this time he did not fall into a little meadow just beneath; he fell a thousand feet below, to become a wreck of bones in the valley.

The anger of the Italian policeman, which he expressed volubly to Father Brown, was largely mixed with admiration. "It was like him to escape us at last," he said. "He was a great brigand if you like. This last trick of his I believe to be absolutely unprecedented. He fled with the company's money to Italy, and actually got himself captured by sham brigands in his own pay, so as to explain both the disappearance of the money and the disappearance of himself. That demand for ransom was really taken seriously by most of the police. But for years he's been doing things as good as that, quite as good as that. He will be a serious loss to his family."

Muscari was leading away the unhappy daughter, who held hard to him, as she did for many a year after. But even in that tragic wreck he could not help having a smile and a hand of half-mocking friendship for the indefensible Ezza Montano. "And where are you going next?" he asked him over his shoulder.

"Birmingham," answered the actor, puffing a cigarette. "Didn't I tell you I was a Futurist? I really do believe in those things if I believe in anything. Change, bustle and new things every morning. I am going to Manchester, Liverpool, Leeds, Hull, Huddersfield, Glasgow, Chicago—in short, to enlightened, energetic, civilized society!"

"In short," said Muscari, "to the real Paradise of Thieves."

The Duel of Dr Hirsch

M. MAURICE BRUN and M. Armand Armagnac were crossing the sunlit Champs Elysee with a kind of vivacious respectability. They were both short, brisk and bold. They both had black beards that did not seem to belong to their faces, after the strange French fashion which makes real hair look like artificial. M. Brun had a dark wedge of beard apparently affixed under his lower lip. M. Armagnac, by way of a change, had two beards; one sticking out from each corner of his emphatic chin. They were both young. They were both atheists, with a depressing fixity of outlook but great mobility of exposition. They were both pupils of the great Dr Hirsch, scientist, publicist and moralist.

M. Brun had become prominent by his proposal that the common expression "Adieu" should be obliterated from all the French classics, and a slight fine imposed for its use in private life. "Then," he said, "the very name of your imagined God will have echoed for the last time in the ear of man." M. Armagnac specialized rather in a resistance to militarism, and wished the chorus of the Marseillaise altered from "Aux armes, citoyens" to "Aux greves, citoyens". But his antimilitarism was of a peculiar and Gallic sort. An eminent and very wealthy English Quaker, who had come to see him to arrange for the disarmament of the whole planet, was rather distressed by Armagnac's proposal that (by way of beginning) the soldiers should shoot their officers.

And indeed it was in this regard that the two men differed most from their leader and father in philosophy. Dr Hirsch, though born in France and covered with the most triumphant favours of French education, was temperamentally of another type—mild, dreamy, humane; and, despite his sceptical system, not devoid of transcendentalism. He was, in short, more like a German than a Frenchman; and much as they admired him, something in the subconsciousness of these Gauls was irritated at his pleading for peace in so peaceful a manner. To their party throughout Europe, however, Paul Hirsch was a saint of science. His large and daring cosmic theories advertised his austere life and innocent, if somewhat frigid, morality; he held something of the position of Darwin doubled with the position of Tolstoy. But he was neither an anarchist nor an antipatriot; his views on disarmament were moderate and evolutionary—the Republican Government put considerable confidence in him as to various chemical improvements. He had lately even discovered a noiseless explosive, the secret of which the Government was carefully guarding.

His house stood in a handsome street near the Elysee—a street which in that strong summer seemed almost as full of foliage as the park itself; a row of chestnuts shattered the sunshine, interrupted only in one place where a large cafe ran out into the street. Almost opposite to this were the white and green blinds of the great scientist's house, an iron balcony, also painted green, running along in front of the first-floor windows. Beneath this was the entrance into a kind of court, gay with shrubs and tiles, into which the two Frenchmen passed in animated talk.

The door was opened to them by the doctor's old servant, Simon, who might very well have passed for a doctor himself, having a strict suit of black, spectacles, grey hair, and a confidential manner. In fact, he was a far more presentable man of science than his master, Dr Hirsch, who was a forked radish of a fellow, with just enough bulb of a head to make his body insignificant. With all the gravity of a great physician handling a prescription, Simon handed a letter to M. Armagnac. That gentleman ripped it up with a racial impatience, and rapidly read the following:

I cannot come down to speak to you. There is a man in this house whom I refuse to meet. He is a Chauvinist officer, Dubosc. He is sitting on the stairs. He has been kicking the furniture about in all the other rooms; I have locked myself in my study, opposite that cafe. If you love me, go over to the cafe and wait at one of the tables outside. I will try to send him over to you. I want you to answer him and deal with him. I cannot meet him myself. I cannot: I will not.

There is going to be another Dreyfus case.

P. HIRSCH

M. Armagnac looked at M. Brun. M. Brun borrowed the letter, read it, and looked at M. Armagnac. Then both betook themselves briskly to one of the little tables under the chestnuts opposite, where they procured two tall glasses of horrible green absinthe, which they could drink apparently in any weather and at any time. Otherwise the cafe seemed empty, except for one soldier drinking coffee at one table, and at another a large man drinking a small syrup and a priest drinking nothing.

Maurice Brun cleared his throat and said: "Of course we must help the master in every way, but—"

There was an abrupt silence, and Armagnac said: "He may have excellent reasons for not meeting the man himself, but—"

Before either could complete a sentence, it was evident that the invader had been expelled from the house opposite. The shrubs under the archway swayed and burst apart, as that unwelcome guest was shot out of them like a cannon-ball.

166

He was a sturdy figure in a small and tilted Tyrolean felt hat, a figure that had indeed something generally Tyrolean about it. The man's shoulders were big and broad, but his legs were neat and active in knee-breeches and knitted stockings. His face was brown like a nut; he had very bright and restless brown eyes; his dark hair was brushed back stiffly in front and cropped close behind, outlining a square and powerful skull; and he had a huge black moustache like the horns of a bison. Such a substantial head is generally based on a bull neck; but this was hidden by a big coloured scarf, swathed round up the man's ears and falling in front inside his jacket like a sort of fancy waistcoat. It was a scarf of strong dead colours, dark red and old gold and purple, probably of Oriental fabrication. Altogether the man had something a shade barbaric about him; more like a Hungarian squire than an ordinary French officer. His French, however, was obviously that of a native; and his French patriotism was so impulsive as to be slightly absurd. His first act when he burst out of the archway was to call in a clarion voice down the street: "Are there any Frenchmen here?" as if he were calling for Christians in Mecca.

Armagnac and Brun instantly stood up; but they were too late. Men were already running from the street corners; there was a small but ever-clustering crowd. With the prompt French instinct for the politics of the street, the man with the black moustache had already run across to a corner of the cafe, sprung on one of the tables, and seizing a branch of chestnut to steady himself, shouted as Camille Desmoulins once shouted when he scattered the oak-leaves among the populace.

"Frenchmen!" he volleyed; "I cannot speak! God help me, that is why I am speaking! The fellows in their filthy parliaments who learn to speak also learn to be silent—silent as that spy cowering in the house opposite! Silent as he is when I beat on his bedroom door! Silent as he is now, though he hears my voice across this street and shakes where he sits! Oh, they can be silent eloquently—the politicians! But the time has come when we that cannot speak must speak. You are betrayed to the Prussians. Betrayed at this moment. Betrayed by that man. I am Jules Dubosc, Colonel of Artillery, Belfort. We caught a German spy in the Vosges yesterday, and a paper was found on him—a paper I hold in my hand. Oh, they tried to hush it up; but I took it direct to the man who wrote it—the man in that house! It is in his hand. It is signed with his initials. It is a direction for finding the secret of this new Noiseless Powder. Hirsch invented it; Hirsch wrote this note about it. This note is in German, and was found in a German's pocket. 'Tell the man the formula for powder is in grey envelope in first drawer to the left of Secretary's desk, War Office, in red ink. He must be careful. P.H.'"

He rattled short sentences like a quick-firing gun, but he was plainly the sort of man who is either mad or right. The mass of the crowd was Nationalist, and already in threatening uproar; and a minority of equally angry Intellectuals, led by Armagnac and Brun, only made the majority more militant.

"If this is a military secret," shouted Brun, "why do you yell about it in the street?"

"I will tell you why I do!" roared Dubosc above the roaring crowd. "I went to this man in straight and civil style. If he had any explanation it could have been given in complete confidence. He refuses to explain. He refers me to two strangers in a cafe as to two flunkeys. He has thrown me out of the house, but I am going back into it, with the people of Paris behind me!"

A shout seemed to shake the very facade of mansions and two stones flew, one breaking a window above the balcony. The indignant Colonel plunged once more under the archway and was heard crying and thundering inside. Every instant the human sea grew wider and wider; it surged up against the rails and steps of the traitor's house; it was already certain that the place would be burst into like the Bastille, when the broken french window opened and Dr Hirsch came out on the balcony. For an instant the fury half turned to laughter; for he was an absurd figure in such a scene. His long bare neck and sloping shoulders were the shape of a champagne bottle, but that was the only festive thing about him. His coat hung on him as on a peg; he wore his carrot-coloured hair long and weedy; his cheeks and chin were fully fringed with one of those irritating beards that begin far from the mouth. He was very pale, and he wore blue spectacles.

Livid as he was, he spoke with a sort of prim decision, so that the mob fell silent in the middle of his third sentence.

"...only two things to say to you now. The first is to my foes, the second to my friends. To my foes I say: It is true I will not meet M. Dubosc, though he is storming outside this very room. It is true I have asked two other men to confront him for me. And I will tell you why! Because I will not and must not see him—because it would be against all rules of dignity and honour to see him. Before I am triumphantly cleared before a court, there is another arbitration this gentleman owes me as a gentleman, and in referring him to my seconds I am strictly—"

Armagnac and Brun were waving their hats wildly, and even the Doctor's enemies roared applause at this unexpected defiance. Once more a few sentences were inaudible, but they could hear him say: "To my friends—I myself should always prefer weapons purely intellectual, and to these an evolved humanity will certainly confine itself. But our own most precious truth is the fundamental force of matter and heredity. My books are successful; my theories are unrefuted; but I suffer in politics from a prejudice almost physical in the French. I cannot speak like Clemenceau and Deroulede, for their words are like echoes of their pistols. The French ask for a duellist as the English ask for a sportsman. Well, I give my proofs: I will pay this barbaric bribe, and then go back to reason for the rest of my life."

Two men were instantly found in the crowd itself to offer their services to Colonel Dubosc, who came out presently, satisfied. One was the common soldier with the coffee, who said simply: "I will act for you, sir. I am the Duc de Valognes." The other was the big man, whom his friend the priest sought at first to dissuade; and then walked away alone.

In the early evening a light dinner was spread at the back of the Cafe Charlemagne. Though unroofed by any glass or gilt plaster, the guests were nearly all under a delicate and irregular roof of leaves; for the ornamental trees stood so thick around and among the tables as to give something of the dimness and the dazzle of a small orchard. At one of the central tables a very stumpy little priest sat in complete solitude, and applied himself to a pile of whitebait with the gravest sort of enjoyment. His daily living being very plain, he had a peculiar taste for sudden and isolated luxuries; he was an abstemious epicure. He did not lift his eyes from his plate, round which red pepper, lemons, brown bread and butter, etc., were rigidly ranked, until a tall shadow fell across the table, and his friend Flambeau sat down opposite. Flambeau was gloomy.

"I'm afraid I must chuck this business," said he heavily. "I'm all on the side of the French soldiers like Dubosc, and I'm all against the French atheists like Hirsch; but it seems to me in this case we've made a mistake. The Duke and I thought it as well to investigate the charge, and I must say I'm glad we did."

"Is the paper a forgery, then?" asked the priest

"That's just the odd thing," replied Flambeau. "It's exactly like Hirsch's writing, and nobody can point out any mistake in it. But it wasn't written by Hirsch. If he's a French patriot he didn't write it, because it gives information to Germany. And if he's a German spy he didn't write it, well—because it doesn't give information to Germany."

"You mean the information is wrong?" asked Father Brown.

"Wrong," replied the other, "and wrong exactly where Dr Hirsch would have been right—about the hiding-place of his own secret formula in his own official department. By favour of Hirsch and the authorities, the Duke and I have actually been allowed to inspect the secret drawer at the War Office where the Hirsch formula is kept. We are the only people who have ever known it, except the inventor himself and the Minister for War; but the Minister permitted it to save Hirsch from fighting. After that we really can't support Dubosc if his revelation is a mare's nest."

"And it is?" asked Father Brown.

"It is," said his friend gloomily. "It is a clumsy forgery by somebody who knew nothing of the real hiding-place. It says the paper is in the cupboard on the right of the Secretary's desk. As a fact the cupboard with the secret drawer is some way to the left of the desk. It says the grey envelope contains a long document written in red ink. It isn't written in red ink, but in ordinary black ink. It's manifestly absurd to say that Hirsch can have made a mistake about a paper that nobody knew of but himself; or can have tried to help a foreign thief by telling him to fumble in the wrong drawer. I think we must chuck it up and apologize to old Carrots."

Father Brown seemed to cogitate; he lifted a little whitebait on his fork. "You are sure the grey envelope was in the left cupboard?" he asked.

"Positive," replied Flambeau. "The grey envelope—it was a white envelope really—was—"

Father Brown put down the small silver fish and the fork and stared across at his companion. "What?" he asked, in an altered voice.

"Well, what?" repeated Flambeau, eating heartily.

"It was not grey," said the priest. "Flambeau, you frighten me."

"What the deuce are you frightened of?"

"I'm frightened of a white envelope," said the other seriously, "If it had only just been grey! Hang it all, it might as well have been grey. But if it was white, the whole business is black. The Doctor has been dabbling in some of the old brimstone after all."

"But I tell you he couldn't have written such a note!" cried Flambeau. "The note is utterly wrong about the facts. And innocent or guilty, Dr Hirsch knew all about the facts."

"The man who wrote that note knew all about the facts," said his clerical companion soberly. "He could never have got 'em so wrong without knowing about 'em. You have to know an awful lot to be wrong on every subject—like the devil."

"Do you mean—?"

"I mean a man telling lies on chance would have told some of the truth," said his friend firmly. "Suppose someone sent you to find a house with a green door and a blue blind, with a front garden but no back garden, with a dog but no cat, and where they drank coffee but not tea. You would say if you found no such house that it was all made up. But I say no. I say if you found a house where the door was blue and the blind green, where there was a back garden and no front garden, where cats were common and dogs instantly shot, where tea was drunk in quarts and coffee forbidden—then you would know you had found the house. The man must have known that particular house to be so accurately inaccurate."

"But what could it mean?" demanded the diner opposite.

"I can't conceive," said Brown; "I don't understand this Hirsch affair at all. As long as it was only the left drawer instead of the right, and red ink instead of black, I thought it must be the chance blunders of a forger, as you say. But three is a mystical number; it finishes things. It finishes this. That the direction about the drawer, the colour of ink, the colour of envelope, should none of them be right by accident, that can't be a coincidence. It wasn't."

"What was it, then? Treason?" asked Flambeau, resuming his dinner.

"I don't know that either," answered Brown, with a face of blank bewilderment. "The only thing I can think of.... Well, I never understood that Dreyfus case. I can always grasp moral evidence easier than the other sorts. I go by a man's eyes and voice, don't you know, and whether his family seems happy, and by what subjects he chooses—and avoids. Well, I was puzzled in the Dreyfus case. Not by the horrible things imputed both ways; I know (though it's not modern to say so) that human nature in the highest places is still capable of being Cenci or Borgia. No—, what puzzled me was the sincerity of both parties. I don't mean the political parties; the rank and file are always roughly honest, and often duped. I mean the persons of the play. I mean the conspirators, if they were conspirators. I mean the traitor, if he was a traitor. I mean the men who must have known the truth. Now Dreyfus went on like a man who knew he was a wronged man. And yet the French statesmen and soldiers went on as if they knew he wasn't a wronged man but simply a wrong 'un. I don't mean they behaved well; I mean they behaved as if they were sure. I can't describe these things; I know what I mean."

"I wish I did," said his friend. "And what has it to do with old Hirsch?"

"Suppose a person in a position of trust," went on the priest, "began to give the enemy information because it was false information. Suppose he even thought he was saving his country by misleading the foreigner. Suppose this brought him into spy circles, and little loans were made to him, and little ties tied on to him. Suppose he kept up his contradictory position in a confused way by never telling the foreign spies the truth, but letting it more and more be guessed. The better part of him (what was left of it) would still say: 'I have not helped the enemy; I said it was the left drawer.' The meaner part of him would already be saying: 'But they may have the sense to see that means the right.' I think it is psychologically possible—in an enlightened age, you know."

"It may be psychologically possible," answered Flambeau, "and it certainly would explain Dreyfus being certain he was wronged and his judges being sure he was guilty. But it won't wash historically, because Dreyfus's document (if it was his document) was literally correct."

"I wasn't thinking of Dreyfus," said Father Brown.

Silence had sunk around them with the emptying of the tables; it was already late, though the sunlight still clung to everything, as if accidentally entangled in the trees. In the stillness Flambeau shifted his seat sharply—making an isolated and echoing noise—and threw his elbow over the angle of it. "Well," he said, rather harshly, "if Hirsch is not better than a timid treason-monger..."

"You mustn't be too hard on them," said Father Brown gently. "It's not entirely their fault; but they have no instincts. I mean those things that make a woman refuse to dance with a man or a man to touch an investment. They've been taught that it's all a matter of degree."

"Anyhow," cried Flambeau impatiently, "he's not a patch on my principal; and I shall go through with it. Old Dubosc may be a bit mad, but he's a sort of patriot after all."

Father Brown continued to consume whitebait.

Something in the stolid way he did so caused Flambeau's fierce black eyes to ramble over his companion afresh. "What's the matter with you?" Flambeau demanded. "Dubosc's all right in that way. You don't doubt him?"

"My friend," said the small priest, laying down his knife and fork in a kind of cold despair, "I doubt everything. Everything, I mean, that has happened today. I doubt the whole story, though it has been acted before my face. I doubt every sight that my eyes have seen since morning. There is something in this business quite different from the ordinary police mystery where one man is more or less lying and the other man more or less telling the truth. Here both men.... Well! I've told you the only theory I can think of that could satisfy anybody. It doesn't satisfy me."

"Nor me either," replied Flambeau frowning, while the other went on eating fish with an air of entire resignation. "If all you can suggest is that notion of a message conveyed by contraries, I call it uncommonly clever, but...well, what would you call it?"

"I should call it thin," said the priest promptly. "I should call it uncommonly thin. But that's the queer thing about the whole business. The lie is like a school-boy's. There are only three versions, Dubosc's and Hirsch's and that fancy of mine. Either that note was written by a French officer to ruin a French official; or it was written by the French official to help German officers; or it was written by the French official to mislead German officers. Very well. You'd expect a secret paper passing between such people, officials or officers, to look quite different from that. You'd expect, probably a cipher, certainly abbreviations; most certainly scientific and strictly professional terms. But this thing's elaborately simple, like a penny dreadful: 'In the purple grotto you will find the golden casket.' It looks as if... as if it were meant to be seen through at once."

Almost before they could take it in a short figure in French uniform had walked up to their table like the wind, and sat down with a sort of thump.

"I have extraordinary news," said the Duc de Valognes. "I have just come from this Colonel of ours. He is packing up to leave the country, and he asks us to make his excuses sur le terrain."

"What?" cried Flambeau, with an incredulity quite frightful—"apologize?"

"Yes," said the Duke gruffly; "then and there—before everybody—when the swords are drawn. And you and I have to do it while he is leaving the country."

"But what can this mean?" cried Flambeau. "He can't be afraid of that little Hirsch! Confound it!" he cried, in a kind of rational rage; "nobody could be afraid of Hirsch!"

"I believe it's some plot!" snapped Valognes—"some plot of the Jews and Freemasons. It's meant to work up glory for Hirsch..."

The face of Father Brown was commonplace, but curiously contented; it could shine with ignorance as well as with knowledge. But there was always one flash when the foolish mask fell, and the wise mask fitted itself in its place; and Flambeau, who knew his friend, knew that his friend had suddenly understood. Brown said nothing, but finished his plate of fish.

"Where did you last see our precious Colonel?" asked Flambeau, irritably.

"He's round at the Hotel Saint Louis by the Elysee, where we drove with him. He's packing up, I tell you."

"Will he be there still, do you think?" asked Flambeau, frowning at the table.

"I don't think he can get away yet," replied the Duke; "he's packing to go a long journey..."

"No," said Father Brown, quite simply, but suddenly standing up, "for a very short journey. For one of the shortest, in fact. But we may still be in time to catch him if we go there in a motor-cab."

Nothing more could be got out of him until the cab swept round the corner by the Hotel Saint Louis, where they got out, and he led the party up a side lane already in deep shadow with the growing dusk. Once, when the Duke impatiently asked whether Hirsch was guilty of treason or not, he answered rather absently: "No; only of ambition—like Caesar." Then he somewhat inconsequently added: "He lives a very lonely life; he has had to do everything for himself."

"Well, if he's ambitious, he ought to be satisfied now," said Flambeau rather bitterly. "All Paris will cheer him now our cursed Colonel has turned tail."

"Don't talk so loud," said Father Brown, lowering his voice, "your cursed Colonel is just in front."

The other two started and shrank farther back into the shadow of the wall, for the sturdy figure of their runaway principal could indeed be seen shuffling along in the twilight in front, a bag in each hand. He looked much the same as when they first saw him, except that he had changed his picturesque mountaineering knickers for a conventional pair of trousers. It was clear he was already escaping from the hotel.

The lane down which they followed him was one of those that seem to be at the back of things, and look like the wrong side of the stage scenery. A colourless, continuous wall ran down one flank of it, interrupted at intervals by dull-hued and dirt-stained doors, all shut fast and featureless save for the chalk scribbles of some passing gamin. The tops of trees, mostly rather depressing evergreens, showed at intervals over the top of the wall, and beyond them in the grey and purple gloaming could be seen the back of some long terrace of tall Parisian houses, really comparatively close, but somehow looking as inaccessible as a range of marble mountains. On the other side of the lane ran the high gilt railings of a gloomy park.

Flambeau was looking round him in rather a weird way. "Do you know," he said, "there is something about this place that—"

"Hullo!" called out the Duke sharply; "that fellow's disappeared. Vanished, like a blasted fairy!"

"He has a key," explained their clerical friend. "He's only gone into one of these garden doors," and as he spoke they heard one of the dull wooden doors close again with a click in front of them.

Flambeau strode up to the door thus shut almost in his face, and stood in front of it for a moment, biting his black moustache in a fury of curiosity. Then he threw up his long arms and swung himself aloft like a monkey and stood on the top of the wall, his enormous figure dark against the purple sky, like the dark tree-tops.

The Duke looked at the priest. "Dubosc's escape is more elaborate than we thought," he said; "but I suppose he is escaping from France."

"He is escaping from everywhere," answered Father Brown.

Valognes's eyes brightened, but his voice sank. "Do you mean suicide?" he asked.

"You will not find his body," replied the other.

A kind of cry came from Flambeau on the wall above. "My God," he exclaimed in French, "I know what this place is now! Why, it's the back of the street where old Hirsch lives. I thought I could recognize the back of a house as well as the back of a man."

"And Dubosc's gone in there!" cried the Duke, smiting his hip. "Why, they'll meet after all!" And with sudden Gallic vivacity he hopped up on the wall beside Flambeau and sat there positively kicking his legs with excitement. The priest alone remained below, leaning against the wall, with his back to the whole theatre of events, and looking wistfully across to the park palings and the twinkling, twilit trees.

The Duke, however stimulated, had the instincts of an aristocrat, and desired rather to stare at the house than to spy on it; but Flambeau, who had the instincts of a burglar (and a detective), had already swung himself from the wall into the fork of a straggling tree from which he could crawl quite close to the only illuminated window in the back of the high dark house. A red blind had been pulled down over the light, but pulled crookedly, so that it gaped on one side, and by risking his neck along a branch that looked as treacherous as a twig, Flambeau could just see Colonel Dubosc walking about in a brilliantly-lighted and luxurious bedroom. But close as Flambeau was to the house, he heard the words of his colleagues by the wall, and repeated them in a low voice.

"Yes, they will meet now after all!"

"They will never meet," said Father Brown. "Hirsch was right when he said that in such an affair the principals must not meet. Have you read a queer psychological story by Henry James, of two persons who so perpetually missed meeting each other by accident that they began to feel quite frightened of each other, and to think it was fate? This is something of the kind, but more curious."

"There are people in Paris who will cure them of such morbid fancies," said Valognes vindictively. "They will jolly well have to meet if we capture them and force them to fight."

"They will not meet on the Day of Judgement," said the priest. "If God Almighty held the truncheon of the lists, if St Michael blew the trumpet for the swords to cross—even then, if one of them stood ready, the other would not come."

"Oh, what does all this mysticism mean?" cried the Duc de Valognes, impatiently; "why on earth shouldn't they meet like other people?"

"They are the opposite of each other," said Father Brown, with a queer kind of smile. "They contradict each other. They cancel out, so to speak."

He continued to gaze at the darkening trees opposite, but Valognes turned his head sharply at a suppressed exclamation from Flambeau. That investigator, peering into the lighted room, had just seen the Colonel, after a pace or two, proceed to take his coat off. Flambeau's first thought was that this really looked like a fight; but he soon dropped the thought for another. The solidity and squareness of Dubosc's chest and shoulders was all a powerful piece of padding and came off with his coat. In his shirt and trousers he was a comparatively slim gentleman, who walked across the bedroom to the bathroom with no more pugnacious purpose than that of washing himself. He bent over a basin, dried his dripping hands and face on a towel, and turned again so that the strong light fell on his face. His brown complexion had gone, his big black moustache had gone; he—was clean-shaven and very pale. Nothing remained of the Colonel but his bright, hawk-like, brown eyes. Under the wall Father Brown was going on in heavy meditation, as if to himself.

"It is all just like what I was saying to Flambeau. These opposites won't do. They don't work. They don't fight. If it's white instead of black, and solid instead of liquid, and so on all along the line—then there's something wrong, Monsieur, there's something wrong. One of these men is fair and the other dark, one stout and the other slim, one strong and the other weak. One has a moustache and no beard, so you can't see his mouth; the other has a beard and no moustache, so you can't see his chin. One has hair cropped to his skull, but a scarf to hide his neck; the other has low shirt-collars, but long hair to bide his skull. It's all too neat and correct, Monsieur, and there's something wrong. Things made so opposite are things that cannot quarrel. Wherever the one sticks out the other sinks in. Like a face and a mask, like a lock and a key..."

Flambeau was peering into the house with a visage as white as a sheet. The occupant of the room was standing with his back to him, but in front of a looking-

174

glass, and had already fitted round his face a sort of framework of rank red hair, hanging disordered from the head and clinging round the jaws and chin while leaving the mocking mouth uncovered. Seen thus in the glass the white face looked like the face of Judas laughing horribly and surrounded by capering flames of hell. For a spasm Flambeau saw the fierce, red-brown eyes dancing, then they were covered with a pair of blue spectacles. Slipping on a loose black coat, the figure vanished towards the front of the house. A few moments later a roar of popular applause from the street beyond announced that Dr Hirsch had once more appeared upon the balcony.

The Man in the Passage

TWO men appeared simultaneously at the two ends of a sort of passage running along the side of the Apollo Theatre in the Adelphi. The evening daylight in the streets was large and luminous, opalescent and empty. The passage was comparatively long and dark, so each man could see the other as a mere black silhouette at the other end. Nevertheless, each man knew the other, even in that inky outline; for they were both men of striking appearance and they hated each other.

The covered passage opened at one end on one of the steep streets of the Adelphi, and at the other on a terrace overlooking the sunset-coloured river. One side of the passage was a blank wall, for the building it supported was an old unsuccessful theatre restaurant, now shut up. The other side of the passage contained two doors, one at each end. Neither was what was commonly called the stage door; they were a sort of special and private stage doors used by very special performers, and in this case by the star actor and actress in the Shakespearean performance of the day. Persons of that eminence often like to have such private exits and entrances, for meeting friends or avoiding them.

The two men in question were certainly two such friends, men who evidently knew the doors and counted on their opening, for each approached the door at the upper end with equal coolness and confidence. Not, however, with equal speed; but the man who walked fast was the man from the other end of the tunnel, so they both arrived before the secret stage door almost at the same instant. They saluted each other with civility, and waited a moment before one of them, the sharper walker who seemed to have the shorter patience, knocked at the door.

In this and everything else each man was opposite and neither could be called inferior. As private persons both were handsome, capable and popular. As public persons, both were in the first public rank. But everything about them, from their glory to their good looks, was of a diverse and incomparable kind. Sir Wilson Seymour was the kind of man whose importance is known to everybody who knows. The more you mixed with the innermost ring in every polity or profession, the more often you met Sir Wilson Seymour. He was the one intelligent man on twenty unintelligent committees—on every sort of subject, from the reform of the Royal Academy to the project of bimetallism for Greater Britain. In the Arts especially he was omnipotent. He was so unique that nobody could quite decide whether he was a great aristocrat who had taken up Art, or a great artist whom the aristocrats had taken up. But you could not meet him for five minutes without realizing that you had really been ruled by him all your life.

His appearance was "distinguished" in exactly the same sense; it was at once conventional and unique. Fashion could have found no fault with his high silk hat—, yet it was unlike anyone else's hat—a little higher, perhaps, and adding something to his natural height. His tall, slender figure had a slight stoop yet it looked the reverse of feeble. His hair was silver-grey, but he did not look old; it was worn longer than the common yet he did not look effeminate; it was curly but it did not look curled. His carefully pointed beard made him look more manly and militant than otherwise, as it does in those old admirals of Velazquez with whose dark portraits his house was hung. His grey gloves were a shade bluer, his silver-knobbed cane a shade longer than scores of such gloves and canes flapped and flourished about the theatres and the restaurants.

The other man was not so tall, yet would have struck nobody as short, but merely as strong and handsome. His hair also was curly, but fair and cropped close to a strong, massive head—the sort of head you break a door with, as Chaucer said of the Miller's. His military moustache and the carriage of his shoulders showed him a soldier, but he had a pair of those peculiar frank and piercing blue eyes which are more common in sailors. His face was somewhat square, his jaw was square, his shoulders were square, even his jacket was square. Indeed, in the wild school of caricature then current, Mr Max Beerbohm had represented him as a proposition in the fourth book of Euclid.

For he also was a public man, though with quite another sort of success. You did not have to be in the best society to have heard of Captain Cutler, of the siege of Hong-Kong, and the great march across China. You could not get away from hearing of him wherever you were; his portrait was on every other postcard; his maps and battles in every other illustrated paper; songs in his honour in every other music-hall turn or on every other barrel-organ. His fame, though probably more temporary, was ten times more wide, popular and spontaneous than the other man's. In thousands of English homes he appeared enormous above England, like Nelson. Yet he had infinitely less power in England than Sir Wilson Seymour.

The door was opened to them by an aged servant or "dresser", whose broken-down face and figure and black shabby coat and trousers contrasted queerly with the glittering interior of the great actress's dressing-room. It was fitted and filled with looking-glasses at every angle of refraction, so that they looked like the hundred facets of one huge diamond—if one could get inside a diamond. The other features of luxury, a few flowers, a few coloured cushions, a few scraps of stage costume, were multiplied by all the mirrors into the madness of the Arabian Nights, and danced and changed places perpetually as the shuffling attendant shifted a mirror outwards or shot one back against the wall.

They both spoke to the dingy dresser by name, calling him Parkinson, and asking for the lady as Miss Aurora Rome. Parkinson said she was in the other room, but he would go and tell her. A shade crossed the brow of both visitors; for the other room was the private room of the great actor with whom Miss Aurora was performing, and she was of the kind that does not inflame admiration without inflaming jealousy. In about half a minute, however, the inner door opened, and she entered as she always did, even in private life, so that the very silence seemed to be a roar of applause, and one well-deserved. She was clad in a somewhat strange garb of peacock green and peacock blue satins, that gleamed like blue and green metals, such as delight children and aesthetes, and her heavy, hot brown hair framed one of those magic faces which are dangerous to all men, but especially to boys and to men growing grey. In company with her male colleague, the great American actor, Isidore Bruno, she was producing a particularly poetical and fantastic interpretation of Midsummer Night's Dream: in which the artistic prominence was given to Oberon and Titania, or in other words to Bruno and herself. Set in dreamy and exquisite scenery, and moving in mystical dances, the green costume, like burnished beetle-wings, expressed all the elusive individuality of an elfin queen. But when personally confronted in what was still broad daylight, a man looked only at the woman's face.

She greeted both men with the beaming and baffling smile which kept so many males at the same just dangerous distance from her. She accepted some flowers from Cutler, which were as tropical and expensive as his victories; and another sort of present from Sir Wilson Seymour, offered later on and more nonchalantly by that gentleman. For it was against his breeding to show eagerness, and against his conventional unconventionality to give anything so obvious as flowers. He had picked up a trifle, he said, which was rather a curiosity, it was an ancient Greek dagger of the Mycenaean Epoch, and might well have been worn in the time of Theseus and Hippolyta. It was made of brass like all the Heroic weapons, but, oddly enough, sharp enough to prick anyone still. He had really been attracted to it by the leaf-like shape; it was as perfect as a Greek vase. If it was of any interest to Miss Rome or could come in anywhere in the play, he hoped she would—

The inner door burst open and a big figure appeared, who was more of a contrast to the explanatory Seymour than even Captain Cutler. Nearly six-foot-six, and of more than theatrical thews and muscles, Isidore Bruno, in the gorgeous leopard skin and golden-brown garments of Oberon, looked like a barbaric god. He leaned on a sort of hunting-spear, which across a theatre looked a slight, silvery wand, but which in the small and comparatively crowded room looked as plain as a pike-staff—and as menacing. His vivid black eyes rolled volcanically, his bronzed face, handsome as it was, showed at that moment a combination of high cheekbones with set white teeth, which recalled certain American conjectures about his origin in the Southern plantations.

"Aurora," he began, in that deep voice like a drum of passion that had moved so many audiences, "will you—"

He stopped indecisively because a sixth figure had suddenly presented itself just inside the doorway—a figure so incongruous in the scene as to be almost comic. It was a very short man in the black uniform of the Roman secular clergy, and looking (especially in such a presence as Bruno's and Aurora's) rather like the wooden Noah out of an ark. He did not, however, seem conscious of any contrast, but said with dull civility: "I believe Miss Rome sent for me."

A shrewd observer might have remarked that the emotional temperature rather rose at so unemotional an interruption. The detachment of a professional celibate seemed to reveal to the others that they stood round the woman as a ring of amorous rivals; just as a stranger coming in with frost on his coat will reveal that a room is like a furnace. The presence of the one man who did not care about her increased Miss Rome's sense that everybody else was in love with her, and each in a somewhat dangerous way: the actor with all the appetite of a savage and a spoilt child; the soldier with all the simple selfishness of a man of will rather than mind; Sir Wilson with that daily hardening concentration with which old Hedonists take to a hobby; nay, even the abject Parkinson, who had known her before her triumphs, and who followed her about the room with eyes or feet, with the dumb fascination of a dog.

A shrewd person might also have noted a yet odder thing. The man like a black wooden Noah (who was not wholly without shrewdness) noted it with a considerable but contained amusement. It was evident that the great Aurora, though by no means indifferent to the admiration of the other sex, wanted at this moment to get rid of all the men who admired her and be left alone with the man who did not— did not admire her in that sense at least; for the little priest did admire and even enjoy the firm feminine diplomacy with which she set about her task. There was, perhaps, only one thing that Aurora Rome was clever about, and that was one half of humanity—the other half. The little priest watched, like a Napoleonic campaign, the swift precision of her policy for expelling all while banishing none. Bruno, the big actor, was so babyish that it was easy to send him off in brute sulks, banging the door. Cutler, the British officer, was pachydermatous to ideas, but punctilious about behaviour. He would ignore all hints, but he would die rather than ignore a definite commission from a lady. As to old Seymour, he had to be treated differently; he had to be left to the last. The only way to move him was to appeal to him in confidence as an old friend, to let him into the secret of the clearance. The priest did really admire Miss Rome as she achieved all these three objects in one selected action.

She went across to Captain Cutler and said in her sweetest manner: "I shall value all these flowers, because they must be your favourite flowers. But they won't be complete, you know, without my favourite flower. Do go over to that shop round the corner and get me some lilies-of-the-valley, and then it will be quite lovely."

The first object of her diplomacy, the exit of the enraged Bruno, was at once achieved. He had already handed his spear in a lordly style, like a sceptre, to the piteous Parkinson, and was about to assume one of the cushioned seats like a throne. But at this open appeal to his rival there glowed in his opal eyeballs all the sensitive insolence of the slave; he knotted his enormous brown fists for an instant, and then, dashing open the door, disappeared into his own apartments beyond. But meanwhile Miss Rome's experiment in mobilizing the British Army had not succeeded so simply as seemed probable. Cutler had indeed risen stiffly and suddenly, and walked towards the door, hatless, as if at a word of command. But perhaps there was something ostentatiously elegant about the languid figure of Seymour leaning against one of the looking-glasses that brought him up short at the entrance, turning his head this way and that like a bewildered bulldog.

"I must show this stupid man where to go," said Aurora in a whisper to Seymour, and ran out to the threshold to speed the parting guest.

Seymour seemed to be listening, elegant and unconscious as was his posture, and he seemed relieved when he heard the lady call out some last instructions to the Captain, and then turn sharply and run laughing down the passage towards the other end, the end on the terrace above the Thames. Yet a second or two after Seymour's brow darkened again. A man in his position has so many rivals, and he remembered that at the other end of the passage was the corresponding entrance to Bruno's private room. He did not lose his dignity; he said some civil words to Father Brown about the revival of Byzantine architecture in the Westminster Cathedral, and then, quite naturally, strolled out himself into the upper end of the passage. Father Brown and Parkinson were left alone, and they were neither of them men with a taste for superfluous conversation. The dresser went round the room, pulling out looking-glasses and pushing them in again, his dingy dark coat and trousers looking all the more dismal since he was still holding the festive fairy spear of King Oberon. Every time he pulled out the frame of a new glass, a new black figure of Father Brown appeared; the absurd glass chamber was full of Father Browns, upside down in the air like angels, turning somersaults like acrobats, turning their backs to everybody like very rude persons.

Father Brown seemed quite unconscious of this cloud of witnesses, but followed Parkinson with an idly attentive eye till he took himself and his absurd spear into the farther room of Bruno. Then he abandoned himself to such abstract meditations as always amused him—calculating the angles of the mirrors, the angles of each refraction, the angle at which each must fit into the wall...when he heard a strong but strangled cry.

He sprang to his feet and stood rigidly listening. At the same instant Sir Wilson Seymour burst back into the room, white as ivory. "Who's that man in the passage?" he cried. "Where's that dagger of mine?"

Before Father Brown could turn in his heavy boots Seymour was plunging about the room looking for the weapon. And before he could possibly find that weapon or any other, a brisk running of feet broke upon the pavement outside, and the square face of Cutler was thrust into the same doorway. He was still grotesquely grasping a bunch of lilies-of-the-valley. "What's this?" he cried. "What's that creature down the passage? Is this some of your tricks?"

"My tricks!" hissed his pale rival, and made a stride towards him.

In the instant of time in which all this happened Father Brown stepped out into the top of the passage, looked down it, and at once walked briskly towards what he saw.

At this the other two men dropped their quarrel and darted after him, Cutler calling out: "What are you doing? Who are you?"

"My name is Brown," said the priest sadly, as he bent over something and straightened himself again. "Miss Rome sent for me, and I came as quickly as I could. I have come too late."

The three men looked down, and in one of them at least the life died in that late light of afternoon. It ran along the passage like a path of gold, and in the midst of it Aurora Rome lay lustrous in her robes of green and gold, with her dead face turned upwards. Her dress was torn away as in a struggle, leaving the right shoulder bare, but the wound from which the blood was welling was on the other side. The brass dagger lay flat and gleaming a yard or so away.

There was a blank stillness for a measurable time, so that they could hear far off a flower-girl's laugh outside Charing Cross, and someone whistling furiously for a taxicab in one of the streets off the Strand. Then the Captain, with a movement so sudden that it might have been passion or play-acting, took Sir Wilson Seymour by the throat.

Seymour looked at him steadily without either fight or fear. "You need not kill me," he said in a voice quite cold; "I shall do that on my own account."

The Captain's hand hesitated and dropped; and the other added with the same icy candour: "If I find I haven't the nerve to do it with that dagger I can do it in a month with drink."

"Drink isn't good enough for me," replied Cutler, "but I'll have blood for this before I die. Not yours—but I think I know whose."

And before the others could appreciate his intention he snatched up the dagger, sprang at the other door at the lower end of the passage, burst it open, bolt and all, and confronted Bruno in his dressing-room. As he did so, old Parkinson tottered in his wavering way out of the door and caught sight of the corpse lying in the passage. He moved shakily towards it; looked at it weakly with a working face; then moved shakily back into the dressing-room again, and sat down suddenly on one of the richly cushioned chairs. Father Brown instantly ran across to him, taking no notice of Cutler and the colossal actor, though the room already rang with their blows and they began to struggle for the dagger. Seymour, who retained some practical sense, was whistling for the police at the end of the passage.

When the police arrived it was to tear the two men from an almost ape-like grapple; and, after a few formal inquiries, to arrest Isidore Bruno upon a charge of murder, brought against him by his furious opponent. The idea that the great national hero of the hour had arrested a wrongdoer with his own hand doubtless had its weight with the police, who are not without elements of the journalist. They treated Cutler with a certain solemn attention, and pointed out that he had got a slight slash on the hand. Even as Cutler bore him back across tilted chair and table, Bruno had twisted the dagger out of his grasp and disabled him just below the wrist. The injury was really slight, but till he was removed from the room the half-savage prisoner stared at the running blood with a steady smile.

"Looks a cannibal sort of chap, don't he?" said the constable confidentially to Cutler.

Cutler made no answer, but said sharply a moment after: "We must attend to the...the death..." and his voice escaped from articulation.

"The two deaths," came in the voice of the priest from the farther side of the room. "This poor fellow was gone when I got across to him." And he stood looking down at old Parkinson, who sat in a black huddle on the gorgeous chair. He also had paid his tribute, not without eloquence, to the woman who had died.

The silence was first broken by Cutler, who seemed not untouched by a rough tenderness. "I wish I was him," he said huskily. "I remember he used to watch her wherever she walked more than—anybody. She was his air, and he's dried up. He's just dead."

"We are all dead," said Seymour in a strange voice, looking down the road.

They took leave of Father Brown at the corner of the road, with some random apologies for any rudeness they might have shown. Both their faces were tragic, but also cryptic.

The mind of the little priest was always a rabbit-warren of wild thoughts that jumped too quickly for him to catch them. Like the white tail of a rabbit he had the vanishing thought that he was certain of their grief, but not so certain of their innocence.

"We had better all be going," said Seymour heavily; "we have done all we can to help."

"Will you understand my motives," asked Father Brown quietly, "if I say you have done all you can to hurt?"

They both started as if guiltily, and Cutler said sharply: "To hurt whom?"

"To hurt yourselves," answered the priest. "I would not add to your troubles if it weren't common justice to warn you. You've done nearly everything you could do to hang yourselves, if this actor should be acquitted. They'll be sure to subpoena me; I shall be bound to say that after the cry was heard each of you rushed into the room in a wild state and began quarrelling about a dagger. As far as my words on oath can go, you might either of you have done it. You hurt yourselves with that; and then Captain Cutler must have hurt himself with the dagger."

"Hurt myself!" exclaimed the Captain, with contempt. "A silly little scratch."

"Which drew blood," replied the priest, nodding. "We know there's blood on the brass now. And so we shall never know whether there was blood on it before."

There was a silence; and then Seymour said, with an emphasis quite alien to his daily accent: "But I saw a man in the passage."

"I know you did," answered the cleric Brown with a face of wood, "so did Captain Cutler. That's what seems so improbable."

Before either could make sufficient sense of it even to answer, Father Brown had politely excused himself and gone stumping up the road with his stumpy old umbrella.

As modern newspapers are conducted, the most honest and most important news is the police news. If it be true that in the twentieth century more space is given to murder than to politics, it is for the excellent reason that murder is a more serious subject. But even this would hardly explain the enormous omnipresence and widely distributed detail of "The Bruno Case," or "The Passage Mystery," in the Press of London and the provinces. So vast was the excitement that for some weeks the Press really told the truth; and the reports of examination and cross-examination, if interminable, even if intolerable are at least reliable. The true reason, of course, was the coincidence of persons. The victim was a popular actress; the accused was a popular actor; and the accused had been caught red-handed, as it were, by the most popular soldier of the patriotic season. In those extraordinary circumstances the Press was paralysed into probity and accuracy; and the rest of this somewhat singular business can practically be recorded from reports of Bruno's trial.

The trial was presided over by Mr Justice Monkhouse, one of those who are jeered at as humorous judges, but who are generally much more serious than the serious judges, for their levity comes from a living impatience of professional solemnity; while the serious judge is really filled with frivolity, because he is filled with vanity. All the chief actors being of a worldly importance, the barristers were well balanced; the prosecutor for the Crown was Sir Walter Cowdray, a heavy, but weighty advocate of the sort that knows how to seem English and trustworthy, and how to be rhetorical with reluctance. The prisoner was defended by Mr Patrick Butler, K.C., who was mistaken for a mere flaneur by those who misunderstood the Irish character—and those who had not been examined by him. The medical evidence involved no contradictions, the doctor, whom Seymour had summoned on the spot, agreeing with the eminent surgeon who had later examined the body. Aurora Rome had been stabbed with some sharp instrument such as a knife or dagger; some instrument, at least, of which the blade was short. The wound was just over the heart, and she had died instantly. When the doctor first saw her she could hardly have been dead for twenty minutes. Therefore when Father Brown found her she could hardly have been dead for three.

Some official detective evidence followed, chiefly concerned with the presence or absence of any proof of a struggle; the only suggestion of this was the tearing of the dress at the shoulder, and this did not seem to fit in particularly well with the direction and finality of the blow. When these details had been supplied, though not explained, the first of the important witnesses was called.

Sir Wilson Seymour gave evidence as he did everything else that he did at all—not only well, but perfectly. Though himself much more of a public man than the judge, he conveyed exactly the fine shade of self-effacement before the King's justice; and though everyone looked at him as they would at the Prime Minister or the Archbishop of Canterbury, they could have said nothing of his part in it but that it was that of a private gentleman, with an accent on the noun. He was also refreshingly lucid, as he was on the committees. He had been calling on Miss Rome at the theatre; he had met Captain Cutler there; they had been joined for a short time by the accused, who had then returned to his own dressing-room; they had then been joined by a Roman Catholic priest, who asked for the deceased lady and said his name was Brown. Miss Rome had then gone just outside the theatre to the entrance of the passage, in order to point out to Captain Cutler a flower-shop at which he was to buy her some more flowers; and the witness had remained in the room, exchanging a few words with the priest. He had then distinctly heard the deceased, having sent the Captain on his errand, turn round laughing and run down the passage towards its other end, where was the prisoner's dressing-room. In idle curiosity as to the rapid movement of his friends, he had strolled out to the head of the passage himself and looked down it towards the prisoner's door. Did he see anything in the passage? Yes; he saw something in the passage.

Sir Walter Cowdray allowed an impressive interval, during which the witness looked down, and for all his usual composure seemed to have more than his usual pallor. Then the barrister said in a lower voice, which seemed at once sympathetic and creepy: "Did you see it distinctly?"

Sir Wilson Seymour, however moved, had his excellent brains in full working-order. "Very distinctly as regards its outline, but quite indistinctly, indeed not at all, as regards the details inside the outline. The passage is of such length that anyone in the middle of it appears quite black against the light at the other end." The witness lowered his steady eyes once more and added: "I had noticed the fact before, when Captain Cutler first entered it." There was another silence, and the judge leaned forward and made a note.

"Well," said Sir Walter patiently, "what was the outline like? Was it, for instance, like the figure of the murdered woman?"

"Not in the least," answered Seymour quietly.

"What did it look like to you?"

"It looked to me," replied the witness, "like a tall man."

Everyone in court kept his eyes riveted on his pen, or his umbrella-handle, or his book, or his boots or whatever he happened to be looking at. They seemed to be holding their eyes away from the prisoner by main force; but they felt his figure in the dock, and they felt it as gigantic. Tall as Bruno was to the eye, he seemed to swell taller and taller when an eyes had been torn away from him.

Cowdray was resuming his seat with his solemn face, smoothing his black silk robes, and white silk whiskers. Sir Wilson was leaving the witness-box, after a few final particulars to which there were many other witnesses, when the counsel for the defence sprang up and stopped him.

"I shall only detain you a moment," said Mr Butler, who was a rustic-looking person with red eyebrows and an expression of partial slumber. "Will you tell his lordship how you knew it was a man?"

A faint, refined smile seemed to pass over Seymour's features. "I'm afraid it is the vulgar test of trousers," he said. "When I saw daylight between the long legs I was sure it was a man, after all."

Butler's sleepy eyes opened as suddenly as some silent explosion. "After all!" he repeated slowly. "So you did think at first it was a woman?"

Seymour looked troubled for the first time. "It is hardly a point of fact," he said, "but if his lordship would like me to answer for my impression, of course I shall do so. There was something about the thing that was not exactly a woman and yet was not quite a man; somehow the curves were different. And it had something that looked like long hair."

"Thank you," said Mr Butler, K.C., and sat down suddenly, as if he had got what he wanted.

Captain Cutler was a far less plausible and composed witness than Sir Wilson, but his account of the opening incidents was solidly the same. He described the return of Bruno to his dressing-room, the dispatching of himself to buy a bunch of lilies-of-the-valley, his return to the upper end of the passage, the thing he saw in the passage, his suspicion of Seymour, and his struggle with Bruno. But he could give little artistic assistance about the black figure that he and Seymour had seen. Asked about its outline, he said he was no art critic—with a somewhat too obvious sneer at Seymour. Asked if it was a man or a woman, he said it looked more like a beast—with a too obvious snarl at the prisoner. But the man was plainly shaken with sorrow and sincere anger, and Cowdray quickly excused him from confirming facts that were already fairly clear.

The defending counsel also was again brief in his cross-examination; although (as was his custom) even in being brief, he seemed to take a long time about it. "You used a rather remarkable expression," he said, looking at Cutler sleepily. "What do you mean by saying that it looked more like a beast than a man or a woman?"

Cutler seemed seriously agitated. "Perhaps I oughtn't to have said that," he said; "but when the brute has huge humped shoulders like a chimpanzee, and bristles sticking out of its head like a pig—"

Mr Butler cut short his curious impatience in the middle. "Never mind whether its hair was like a pig's," he said, "was it like a woman's?"

"A woman's!" cried the soldier. "Great Scott, no!"

"The last witness said it was," commented the counsel, with unscrupulous swiftness. "And did the figure have any of those serpentine and semi-feminine curves to which eloquent allusion has been made? No? No feminine curves? The figure, if I understand you, was rather heavy and square than otherwise?"

"He may have been bending forward," said Cutler, in a hoarse and rather faint voice.

"Or again, he may not," said Mr Butler, and sat down suddenly for the second time.

The third, witness called by Sir Walter Cowdray was the little Catholic clergyman, so little, compared with the others, that his head seemed hardly to come above the box, so that it was like cross-examining a child. But unfortunately Sir Walter had somehow got it into his head (mostly by some ramifications of his family's religion) that Father Brown was on the side of the prisoner, because the prisoner was wicked and foreign and even partly black. Therefore he took Father Brown up sharply whenever that proud pontiff tried to explain anything; and told him to answer yes or no, and tell the plain facts without any jesuitry. When Father Brown began, in his simplicity, to say who he thought the man in the passage was, the barrister told him that he did not want his theories.

"A black shape was seen in the passage. And you say you saw the black shape. Well, what shape was it?"

Father Brown blinked as under rebuke; but he had long known the literal nature of obedience. "The shape," he said, "was short and thick, but had two sharp, black projections curved upwards on each side of the head or top, rather like horns, and—"

"Oh! the devil with horns, no doubt," ejaculated Cowdray, sitting down in triumphant jocularity. "It was the devil come to eat Protestants."

"No," said the priest dispassionately; "I know who it was."

Those in court had been wrought up to an irrational, but real sense of some monstrosity. They had forgotten the figure in the dock and thought only of the figure in the passage. And the figure in the passage, described by three capable and respectable men who had all seen it, was a shifting nightmare: one called it a woman, and the other a beast, and the other a devil....

The judge was looking at Father Brown with level and piercing eyes. "You are a most extraordinary witness," he said; "but there is something about you that makes me think you are trying to tell the truth. Well, who was the man you saw in the passage?"

"He was myself," said Father Brown.

Butler, K.C., sprang to his feet in an extraordinary stillness, and said quite calmly: "Your lordship will allow me to cross-examine?" And then, without stopping, he shot at Brown the apparently disconnected question: "You have heard about this dagger; you know the experts say the crime was committed with a short blade?"

"A short blade," assented Brown, nodding solemnly like an owl, "but a very long hilt."

Before the audience could quite dismiss the idea that the priest had really seen himself doing murder with a short dagger with a long hilt (which seemed somehow to make it more horrible), he had himself hurried on to explain.

"I mean daggers aren't the only things with short blades. Spears have short blades. And spears catch at the end of the steel just like daggers, if they're that sort of fancy spear they had in theatres; like the spear poor old Parkinson killed his wife with, just when she'd sent for me to settle their family troubles—and I came just too late, God forgive me! But he died penitent—he just died of being penitent. He couldn't bear what he'd done."

The general impression in court was that the little priest, who was gobbling away, had literally gone mad in the box. But the judge still looked at him with bright and steady eyes of interest; and the counsel for the defence went on with his questions unperturbed.

"If Parkinson did it with that pantomime spear," said Butler, "he must have thrust from four yards away. How do you account for signs of struggle, like the dress dragged off the shoulder?" He had slipped into treating his mere witness as an expert; but no one noticed it now.

"The poor lady's dress was torn," said the witness, "because it was caught in a panel that slid to just behind her. She struggled to free herself, and as she did so Parkinson came out of the prisoner's room and lunged with the spear."

"A panel?" repeated the barrister in a curious voice.

"It was a looking-glass on the other side," explained Father Brown. "When I was in the dressing-room I noticed that some of them could probably be slid out into the passage."

There was another vast and unnatural silence, and this time it was the judge who spoke. "So you really mean that when you looked down that passage, the man you saw was yourself—in a mirror?"

"Yes, my lord; that was what I was trying to say," said Brown, "but they asked me for the shape; and our hats have corners just like horns, and so I—"

The judge leaned forward, his old eyes yet more brilliant, and said in specially distinct tones: "Do you really mean to say that when Sir Wilson Seymour saw that wild what-you-call-him with curves and a woman's hair and a man's trousers, what he saw was Sir Wilson Seymour?"

"Yes, my lord," said Father Brown.

"And you mean to say that when Captain Cutler saw that chimpanzee with humped shoulders and hog's bristles, he simply saw himself?"

"Yes, my lord."

The judge leaned back in his chair with a luxuriance in which it was hard to separate the cynicism and the admiration. "And can you tell us why," he asked, "you should know your own figure in a looking-glass, when two such distinguished men don't?"

Father Brown blinked even more painfully than before; then he stammered: "Really, my lord, I don't know unless it's because I don't look at it so often."

The Mistake of the Machine

FLAMBEAU and his friend the priest were sitting in the Temple Gardens about sunset; and their neighbourhood or some such accidental influence had turned their talk to matters of legal process. From the problem of the licence in cross-examination, their talk strayed to Roman and mediaeval torture, to the examining magistrate in France and the Third Degree in America.

"I've been reading," said Flambeau, "of this new psychometric method they talk about so much, especially in America. You know what I mean; they put a pulsometer on a man's wrist and judge by how his heart goes at the pronunciation of certain words. What do you think of it?"

"I think it very interesting," replied Father Brown; "it reminds me of that interesting idea in the Dark Ages that blood would flow from a corpse if the murderer touched it."

"Do you really mean," demanded his friend, "that you think the two methods equally valuable?"

"I think them equally valueless," replied Brown. "Blood flows, fast or slow, in dead folk or living, for so many more million reasons than we can ever know. Blood will have to flow very funnily; blood will have to flow up the Matterhorn, before I will take it as a sign that I am to shed it."

"The method," remarked the other, "has been guaranteed by some of the greatest American men of science."

"What sentimentalists men of science are!" exclaimed Father Brown, "and how much more sentimental must American men of science be! Who but a Yankee would think of proving anything from heart-throbs? Why, they must be as sentimental as a man who thinks a woman is in love with him if she blushes. That's a test from the circulation of the blood, discovered by the immortal Harvey; and a jolly rotten test, too."

"But surely," insisted Flambeau, "it might point pretty straight at something or other."

"There's a disadvantage in a stick pointing straight," answered the other. "What is it? Why, the other end of the stick always points the opposite way. It depends whether you get hold of the stick by the right end. I saw the thing done once and I've never believed in it since." And he proceeded to tell the story of his disillusionment.

It happened nearly twenty years before, when he was chaplain to his co-religionists in a prison in Chicago—where the Irish population displayed a capacity both for crime and penitence which kept him tolerably busy. The official second-in-command under the Governor was an ex-detective named Greywood Usher, a cadaverous, careful-spoken Yankee philosopher, occasionally varying a very rigid visage with an odd apologetic grimace. He liked Father Brown in a slightly patronizing way; and Father Brown liked him, though he heartily disliked his theories. His theories were extremely complicated and were held with extreme simplicity.

One evening he had sent for the priest, who, according to his custom, took a seat in silence at a table piled and littered with papers, and waited. The official selected from the papers a scrap of newspaper cutting, which he handed across to the cleric, who read it gravely. It appeared to be an extract from one of the pinkest of American Society papers, and ran as follows:

"Society's brightest widower is once more on the Freak Dinner stunt. All our exclusive citizens will recall the Perambulator Parade Dinner, in which Last-Trick Todd, at his palatial home at Pilgrim's Pond, caused so many of our prominent debutantes to look even younger than their years. Equally elegant and more miscellaneous and large-hearted in social outlook was Last-Trick's show the year previous, the popular Cannibal Crush Lunch, at which the confections handed round were sarcastically moulded in the forms of human arms and legs, and during which more than one of our gayest mental gymnasts was heard offering to eat his partner. The witticism which will inspire this evening is as yet in Mr Todd's pretty reticent intellect, or locked in the jewelled bosoms of our city's gayest leaders; but there is talk of a pretty parody of the simple manners and customs at the other end of Society's scale. This would be all the more telling, as hospitable Todd is entertaining in Lord Falconroy, the famous traveller, a true-blooded aristocrat fresh from England's oak-groves. Lord Falconroy's travels began before his ancient feudal title was resurrected, he was in the Republic in his youth, and fashion murmurs a sly reason for his return. Miss Etta Todd is one of our deep-souled New Yorkers, and comes into an income of nearly twelve hundred million dollars."

"Well," asked Usher, "does that interest you?"

"Why, words rather fail me," answered Father Brown. "I cannot think at this moment of anything in this world that would interest me less. And, unless the just anger of the Republic is at last going to electrocute journalists for writing like that, I don't quite see why it should interest you either."

"Ah!" said Mr Usher dryly, and handing across another scrap of newspaper. "Well, does that interest you?"

The paragraph was headed "Savage Murder of a Warder. Convict Escapes," and ran: "Just before dawn this morning a shout for help was heard in the Convict Settlement at Sequah in this State. The authorities, hurrying in the direction of the cry, found the corpse of the warder who patrols the top of the north wall of the prison, the steepest and most difficult exit, for which one man has always been found sufficient. The unfortunate officer had, however, been hurled from the high wall, his brains beaten out as with a club, and his gun was missing. Further inquiries showed that one of the cells was empty; it had been occupied by a rather sullen ruffian giving his name as Oscar Rian. He was only temporarily detained for some comparatively trivial assault; but he gave everyone the impression of a man with a black past and a dangerous future. Finally, when daylight had fully revealed the scene of murder, it was found that he had written on the wall above the body a fragmentary sentence, apparently with a finger dipped in blood: 'This was self-defence and he had the gun. I meant no harm to him or any man but one. I am keeping the bullet for Pilgrim's Pond—O.R.' A man must have used most fiendish treachery or most savage and amazing bodily daring to have stormed such a wall in spite of an armed man."

"Well, the literary style is somewhat improved," admitted the priest cheerfully, "but still I don't see what I can do for you. I should cut a poor figure, with my short legs, running about this State after an athletic assassin of that sort. I doubt whether anybody could find him. The convict settlement at Sequah is thirty miles from here; the country between is wild and tangled enough, and the country beyond, where he will surely have the sense to go, is a perfect no-man's land tumbling away to the prairies. He may be in any hole or up any tree."

"He isn't in any hole," said the governor; "he isn't up any tree."

"Why, how do you know?" asked Father Brown, blinking.

"Would you like to speak to him?" inquired Usher.

Father Brown opened his innocent eyes wide. "He is here?" he exclaimed. "Why, how did your men get hold of him?"

"I got hold of him myself," drawled the American, rising and lazily stretching his lanky legs before the fire. "I got hold of him with the crooked end of a walking-stick. Don't look so surprised. I really did. You know I sometimes take a turn in the country lanes outside this dismal place; well, I was walking early this evening up a steep lane with dark hedges and grey-looking ploughed fields on both sides; and a young moon was up and silvering the road. By the light of it I saw a man running across the field towards the road; running with his body bent and at a good mile-race trot. He appeared to be much exhausted; but when he came to the thick black hedge he went through it as if it were made of spiders' webs;—or rather (for I heard the strong branches breaking and snapping like bayonets) as if he himself were made of stone. In the instant in which he appeared up against the moon, crossing the road, I slung my hooked cane at his legs, tripping him and bringing him down. Then I blew my whistle long and loud, and our fellows came running up to secure him."

"It would have been rather awkward," remarked Brown, "if you had found he was a popular athlete practising a mile race."

"He was not," said Usher grimly. "We soon found out who he was; but I had guessed it with the first glint of the moon on him."

"You thought it was the runaway convict," observed the priest simply, "because you had read in the newspaper cutting that morning that a convict had run away."

"I had somewhat better grounds," replied the governor coolly. "I pass over the first as too simple to be emphasized—I mean that fashionable athletes do not run

188

across ploughed fields or scratch their eyes out in bramble hedges. Nor do they run all doubled up like a crouching dog. There were more decisive details to a fairly well-trained eye. The man was clad in coarse and ragged clothes, but they were something more than merely coarse and ragged. They were so ill-fitting as to be quite grotesque; even as he appeared in black outline against the moonrise, the coat-collar in which his head was buried made him look like a hunchback, and the long loose sleeves looked as if he had no hands. It at once occurred to me that he had somehow managed to change his convict clothes for some confederate's clothes which did not fit him. Second, there was a pretty stiff wind against which he was running; so that I must have seen the streaky look of blowing hair, if the hair had not been very short. Then I remembered that beyond these ploughed fields he was crossing lay Pilgrim's Pond, for which (you will remember) the convict was keeping his bullet; and I sent my walking-stick flying."

"A brilliant piece of rapid deduction," said Father Brown; "but had he got a gun?"

As Usher stopped abruptly in his walk the priest added apologetically: "I've been told a bullet is not half so useful without it."

"He had no gun," said the other gravely; "but that was doubtless due to some very natural mischance or change of plans. Probably the same policy that made him change the clothes made him drop the gun; he began to repent the coat he had left behind him in the blood of his victim."

"Well, that is possible enough," answered the priest.

"And it's hardly worth speculating on," said Usher, turning to some other papers, "for we know it's the man by this time."

His clerical friend asked faintly: "But how?" And Greywood Usher threw down the newspapers and took up the two press-cuttings again.

"Well, since you are so obstinate," he said, "let's begin at the beginning. You will notice that these two cuttings have only one thing in common, which is the mention of Pilgrim's Pond, the estate, as you know, of the millionaire Ireton Todd. You also know that he is a remarkable character; one of those that rose on stepping-stones—"

"Of our dead selves to higher things," assented his companion. "Yes; I know that. Petroleum, I think."

"Anyhow," said Usher, "Last-Trick Todd counts for a great deal in this rum affair."

He stretched himself once more before the fire and continued talking in his expansive, radiantly explanatory style.

"To begin with, on the face of it, there is no mystery here at all. It is not mysterious, it is not even odd, that a jailbird should take his gun to Pilgrim's Pond. Our people aren't like the English, who will forgive a man for being rich if he throws away money on hospitals or horses. Last-Trick Todd has made himself big by his own considerable abilities; and there's no doubt that many of those on whom he has shown his abilities would like to show theirs on him with a shot-gun. Todd might easily get dropped by some man he'd never even heard of; some labourer he'd locked out, or some clerk in a business he'd busted. Last-Trick is a man of mental endowments and a high public character; but in this country the relations of employers and employed are considerably strained.

"That's how the whole thing looks supposing this Rian made for Pilgrim's Pond to kill Todd. So it looked to me, till another little discovery woke up what I have of the detective in me. When I had my prisoner safe, I picked up my cane again and strolled down the two or three turns of country road that brought me to one of the side entrances of Todd's grounds, the one nearest to the pool or lake after which the place is named. It was some two hours ago, about seven by this time; the moonlight was more luminous, and I could see the long white streaks of it lying on the mysterious mere with its grey, greasy, half-liquid shores in which they say our fathers used to make witches walk until they sank. I'd forgotten the exact tale; but you know the place I mean; it lies north of Todd's house towards the wilderness, and has two queer wrinkled trees, so dismal that they look more like huge fungoids than decent foliage. As I stood peering at this misty pool, I fancied I saw the faint figure of a man moving from the house towards it, but it was all too dim and distant for one to be certain of the fact, and still less of the details. Besides, my attention was very sharply arrested by something much closer. I crouched behind the fence which ran not more than two hundred yards from one wing of the great mansion, and which was fortunately split in places, as if specially for the application of a cautious eye. A door had opened in the dark bulk of the left wing, and a figure appeared black against the illuminated interior—a muffled figure bending forward, evidently peering out into the night. It closed the door behind it, and I saw it was carrying a lantern, which threw a patch of imperfect light on the dress and figure of the wearer. It seemed to be the figure of a woman, wrapped up in a ragged cloak and evidently disguised to avoid notice; there was something very strange both about the rags and the furtiveness in a person coming out of those rooms lined with gold. She took cautiously the curved garden path which brought her within half a hundred yards of me—, then she stood up for an instant on the terrace of turf that looks towards the slimy lake, and holding her flaming lantern above her head she deliberately swung it three times to and fro as for a signal. As she swung it the second time a flicker of its light fell for a moment on her own face, a face that I knew. She was unnaturally pale, and her head was bundled in her borrowed plebeian shawl; but I am certain it was Etta Todd, the millionaire's daughter.

"She retraced her steps in equal secrecy and the door closed behind her again. I was about to climb the fence and follow, when I realized that the detective fever that had lured me into the adventure was rather undignified; and that in a more authoritative capacity I already held all the cards in my hand. I was just turning away when a new noise broke on the night. A window was thrown up in one of the upper floors, but just round the corner of the house so that I could not see it; and a voice of terrible distinctness was heard shouting across the dark garden to know where Lord Falconroy was, for he was missing from every room in the house. There was no mistaking that voice. I have heard it on many a political platform or meeting of directors; it was Ireton Todd himself. Some of the others seemed to have gone to the lower windows or on to the steps, and were calling up to him that Falconroy had gone for a stroll down to the Pilgrim's Pond an hour before, and could not be traced since. Then Todd cried 'Mighty Murder!' and shut down the window violently; and I could hear him plunging down the stairs inside. Repossessing myself of my former and wiser purpose, I whipped out of the way of the general search that must follow; and returned here not later than eight o'clock.

"I now ask you to recall that little Society paragraph which seemed to you so painfully lacking in interest. If the convict was not keeping the shot for Todd, as he evidently wasn't, it is most likely that he was keeping it for Lord Falconroy; and it looks as if he had delivered the goods. No more handy place to shoot a man than in the curious geological surroundings of that pool, where a body thrown down would sink through thick slime to a depth practically unknown. Let us suppose, then, that our friend with the cropped hair came to kill Falconroy and not Todd. But, as I have pointed out, there are many reasons why people in America might want to kill Todd. There is no reason why anybody in America should want to kill an English lord newly landed, except for the one reason mentioned in the pink paper—that the lord is paying his attentions to the millionaire's daughter. Our crop-haired friend, despite his ill-fitting clothes, must be an aspiring lover.

"I know the notion will seem to you jarring and even comic; but that's because you are English. It sounds to you like saying the Archbishop of Canterbury's daughter will be married in St George's, Hanover Square, to a crossing-sweeper on ticket-of-leave. You don't do justice to the climbing and aspiring power of our more remarkable citizens. You see a good-looking grey-haired man in evening-dress with a sort of authority about him, you know he is a pillar of the State, and you fancy he had a father. You are in error. You do not realize that a comparatively few years ago he may have been in a tenement or (quite likely) in a jail. You don't allow for our national buoyancy and uplift. Many of our most influential citizens have not only risen recently, but risen comparatively late in life. Todd's daughter was fully eighteen when her father first made his pile; so there isn't really anything impossible in her having a hanger-on in low life; or even in her hanging on to him, as I think she must be doing, to judge by the lantern business. If so, the hand that held the lantern may not be unconnected with the hand that held the gun. This case, sir, will make a noise."

"Well," said the priest patiently, "and what did you do next?"

"I reckon you'll be shocked," replied Greywood Usher, "as I know you don't cotton to the march of science in these matters. I am given a good deal of discretion here, and perhaps take a little more than I'm given; and I thought it was an excellent opportunity to test that Psychometric Machine I told you about. Now, in my opinion, that machine can't lie."

"No machine can lie," said Father Brown; "nor can it tell the truth."

"It did in this case, as I'll show you," went on Usher positively. "I sat the man in the ill-fitting clothes in a comfortable chair, and simply wrote words on a blackboard; and the machine simply recorded the variations of his pulse; and I simply observed his manner. The trick is to introduce some word connected with the supposed crime in a list of words connected with something quite different, yet a list in which it occurs quite naturally. Thus I wrote 'heron' and 'eagle' and 'owl', and when I wrote 'falcon' he was tremendously agitated; and when I began to make an 'r' at the end of the word, that machine just bounded. Who else in this republic has any reason to jump at the name of a newly-arrived Englishman like Falconroy except the man who's shot him? Isn't that better evidence than a lot of gabble from witnesses— if the evidence of a reliable machine?"

"You always forget," observed his companion, "that the reliable machine always has to be worked by an unreliable machine."

"Why, what do you mean?" asked the detective.

"I mean Man," said Father Brown, "the most unreliable machine I know of. I don't want to be rude; and I don't think you will consider Man to be an offensive or inaccurate description of yourself. You say you observed his manner; but how do you know you observed it right? You say the words have to come in a natural way; but how do you know that you did it naturally? How do you know, if you come to that, that he did not observe your manner? Who is to prove that you were not tremendously agitated? There was no machine tied on to your pulse."

"I tell you," cried the American in the utmost excitement, "I was as cool as a cucumber."

"Criminals also can be as cool as cucumbers," said Brown with a smile. "And almost as cool as you."

"Well, this one wasn't," said Usher, throwing the papers about. "Oh, you make me tired!"

"I'm sorry," said the other. "I only point out what seems a reasonable possibility. If you could tell by his manner when the word that might hang him had come, why shouldn't he tell from your manner that the word that might hang him was coming? I should ask for more than words myself before I hanged anybody."

Usher smote the table and rose in a sort of angry triumph.

"And that," he cried, "is just what I'm going to give you. I tried the machine first just in order to test the thing in other ways afterwards and the machine, sir, is right."

He paused a moment and resumed with less excitement. "I rather want to insist, if it comes to that, that so far I had very little to go on except the scientific experiment. There was really nothing against the man at all. His clothes were ill-fitting, as I've said, but they were rather better, if anything, than those of the submerged class to which he evidently belonged. Moreover, under all the stains of his plunging through ploughed fields or bursting through dusty hedges, the man was comparatively clean. This might mean, of course, that he had only just broken prison; but it reminded me more of the desperate decency of the comparatively respectable poor. His demeanour was, I am bound to confess, quite in accordance with theirs. He was silent and dignified as they are; he seemed to have a big, but buried, grievance, as they do. He professed total ignorance of the crime and the whole question; and showed nothing but a sullen impatience for something sensible that might come to take him out of his meaningless scrape. He asked me more than once if he could telephone for a lawyer who had helped him a long time ago in a trade dispute, and in every sense acted as you would expect an innocent man to act. There was nothing against him in the world except that little finger on the dial that pointed to the change of his pulse.

192

"Then, sir, the machine was on its trial; and the machine was right. By the time I came with him out of the private room into the vestibule where all sorts of other people were awaiting examination, I think he had already more or less made up his mind to clear things up by something like a confession. He turned to me and began to say in a low voice: 'Oh, I can't stick this any more. If you must know all about me—'

"At the same instant one of the poor women sitting on the long bench stood up, screaming aloud and pointing at him with her finger. I have never in my life heard anything more demoniacally distinct. Her lean finger seemed to pick him out as if it were a pea-shooter. Though the word was a mere howl, every syllable was as clear as a separate stroke on the clock.

"'Drugger Davis!' she shouted. 'They've got Drugger Davis!'

"Among the wretched women, mostly thieves and streetwalkers, twenty faces were turned, gaping with glee and hate. If I had never heard the words, I should have known by the very shock upon his features that the so-called Oscar Rian had heard his real name. But I'm not quite so ignorant, you may be surprised to hear. Drugger Davis was one of the most terrible and depraved criminals that ever baffled our police. It is certain he had done murder more than once long before his last exploit with the warder. But he was never entirely fixed for it, curiously enough because he did it in the same manner as those milder—or meaner—crimes for which he was fixed pretty often. He was a handsome, well-bred-looking brute, as he still is, to some extent; and he used mostly to go about with barmaids or shop-girls and do them out of their money. Very often, though, he went a good deal farther; and they were found drugged with cigarettes or chocolates and their whole property missing. Then came one case where the girl was found dead; but deliberation could not quite be proved, and, what was more practical still, the criminal could not be found. I heard a rumour of his having reappeared somewhere in the opposite character this time, lending money instead of borrowing it; but still to such poor widows as he might personally fascinate, but still with the same bad result for them. Well, there is your innocent man, and there is his innocent record. Even, since then, four criminals and three warders have identified him and confirmed the story. Now what have you got to say to my poor little machine after that? Hasn't the machine done for him? Or do you prefer to say that the woman and I have done for him?"

"As to what you've done for him," replied Father Brown, rising and shaking himself in a floppy way, "you've saved him from the electrical chair. I don't think they can kill Drugger Davis on that old vague story of the poison; and as for the convict who killed the warder, I suppose it's obvious that you haven't got him. Mr Davis is innocent of that crime, at any rate."

"What do you mean?" demanded the other. "Why should he be innocent of that crime?"

"Why, bless us all!" cried the small man in one of his rare moments of animation, "why, because he's guilty of the other crimes! I don't know what you people are made of. You seem to think that all sins are kept together in a bag. You talk as if a miser on Monday were always a spendthrift on Tuesday. You tell me this man you have here spent weeks and months wheedling needy women out of small sums of money; that he used a drug at the best, and a poison at the worst; that he turned up afterwards as the lowest kind of moneylender, and cheated most poor people in the same patient and pacific style. Let it be granted—let us admit, for the sake of argument, that he did all this. If that is so, I will tell you what he didn't do. He didn't storm a spiked wall against a man with a loaded gun. He didn't write on the wall with his own hand, to say he had done it. He didn't stop to state that his justification was self-defence. He didn't explain that he had no quarrel with the poor warder. He didn't name the house of the rich man to which he was going with the gun. He didn't write his own, initials in a man's blood. Saints alive! Can't you see the whole character is different, in good and evil? Why, you don't seem to be like I am a bit. One would think you'd never had any vices of your own."

The amazed American had already parted his lips in protest when the door of his private and official room was hammered and rattled in an unceremonious way to which he was totally unaccustomed.

The door flew open. The moment before Greywood Usher had been coming to the conclusion that Father Brown might possibly be mad. The moment after he began to think he was mad himself. There burst and fell into his private room a man in the filthiest rags, with a greasy squash hat still askew on his head, and a shabby green shade shoved up from one of his eyes, both of which were glaring like a tiger's The rest of his face was almost undiscoverable, being masked with a matted beard and whiskers through which the nose could barely thrust itself, and further buried in a squalid red scarf or handkerchief. Mr Usher prided himself on having seen most of the roughest specimens in the State, but he thought he had never seen such a baboon dressed as a scarecrow as this. But, above all, he had never in all his placid scientific existence heard a man like that speak to him first.

"See here, old man Usher," shouted the being in the red handkerchief, "I'm getting tired. Don't you try any of your hide-and-seek on me; I don't get fooled any. Leave go of my guests, and I'll let up on the fancy clockwork. Keep him here for a split instant and you'll feel pretty mean. I reckon I'm not a man with no pull."

The eminent Usher was regarding the bellowing monster with an amazement which had dried up all other sentiments. The mere shock to his eyes had rendered his ears, almost useless. At last he rang a bell with a hand of violence. While the bell was still strong and pealing, the voice of Father Brown fell soft but distinct.

"I have a suggestion to make," he said, "but it seems a little confusing. I don't know this gentleman—but—but I think I know him. Now, you know him—you know him quite well—but you don't know him—naturally. Sounds paradoxical, I know."

"I reckon the Cosmos is cracked," said Usher, and fell asprawl in his round office chair.

"Now, see here," vociferated the stranger, striking the table, but speaking in a voice that was all the more mysterious because it was comparatively mild and rational though still resounding. "I won't let you in. I want—"

"Who in hell are you?" yelled Usher, suddenly sitting up straight.

"I think the gentleman's name is Todd," said the priest.

Then he picked up the pink slip of newspaper.

"I fear you don't read the Society papers properly," he said, and began to read out in a monotonous voice, "'Or locked in the jewelled bosoms of our city's gayest leaders; but there is talk of a pretty parody of the manners and customs of the other end of Society's scale.' There's been a big Slum Dinner up at Pilgrim's Pond tonight; and a man, one of the guests, disappeared. Mr Ireton Todd is a good host, and has tracked him here, without even waiting to take off his fancy-dress."

"What man do you mean?"

"I mean the man with comically ill-fitting clothes you saw running across the ploughed field. Hadn't you better go and investigate him? He will be rather impatient to get back to his champagne, from which he ran away in such a hurry, when the convict with the gun hove in sight."

"Do you seriously mean—" began the official.

"Why, look here, Mr Usher," said Father Brown quietly, "you said the machine couldn't make a mistake; and in one sense it didn't. But the other machine did; the machine that worked it. You assumed that the man in rags jumped at the name of Lord Falconroy, because he was Lord Falconroy's murderer. He jumped at the name of Lord Falconroy because he is Lord Falconroy."

"Then why the blazes didn't he say so?" demanded the staring Usher.

"He felt his plight and recent panic were hardly patrician," replied the priest, "so he tried to keep the name back at first. But he was just going to tell it you, when"—and Father Brown looked down at his boots—"when a woman found another name for him."

"But you can't be so mad as to say," said Greywood Usher, very white, "that Lord Falconroy was Drugger Davis."

The priest looked at him very earnestly, but with a baffling and undecipherable face.

"I am not saying anything about it," he said. "I leave all the rest to you. Your pink paper says that the title was recently revived for him; but those papers are very unreliable. It says he was in the States in youth; but the whole story seems very strange. Davis and Falconroy are both pretty considerable cowards, but so are lots of other men. I would not hang a dog on my own opinion about this. But I think," he went on softly and reflectively, "I think you Americans are too modest. I think you idealize the English aristocracy—even in assuming it to be so aristocratic. You see a good-looking Englishman in evening-dress; you know he's in the House of Lords; and you fancy he has a father. You don't allow for our national buoyancy and uplift. Many of our most influential noblemen have not only risen recently, but—"

"Oh, stop it!" cried Greywood Usher, wringing one lean hand in impatience against a shade of irony in the other's face.

"Don't stay talking to this lunatic!" cried Todd brutally. "Take me to my friend."

Next morning Father Brown appeared with the same demure expression, carrying yet another piece of pink newspaper.

"I'm afraid you neglect the fashionable press rather," he said, "but this cutting may interest you."

Usher read the headlines, "Last-Trick's Strayed Revellers: Mirthful Incident near Pilgrim's Pond." The paragraph went on: "A laughable occurrence took place outside Wilkinson's Motor Garage last night. A policeman on duty had his attention drawn by larrikins to a man in prison dress who was stepping with considerable coolness into the steering-seat of a pretty high-toned Panhard; he was accompanied by a girl wrapped in a ragged shawl. On the police interfering, the young woman threw back the shawl, and all recognized Millionaire Todd's daughter, who had just come from the Slum Freak Dinner at the Pond, where all the choicest guests were in a similar deshabille. She and the gentleman who had donned prison uniform were going for the customary joy-ride."

Under the pink slip Mr Usher found a strip of a later paper, headed, "Astounding Escape of Millionaire's Daughter with Convict. She had Arranged Freak Dinner. Now Safe in—"

Mr Greenwood Usher lifted his eyes, but Father Brown was gone.

The Head of Caesar

THERE is somewhere in Brompton or Kensington an interminable avenue of tall houses, rich but largely empty, that looks like a terrace of tombs. The very steps up to the dark front doors seem as steep as the side of pyramids; one would hesitate to knock at the door, lest it should be opened by a mummy. But a yet more depressing feature in the grey facade is its telescopic length and changeless continuity. The pilgrim walking down it begins to think he will never come to a break or a corner; but there is one exception—a very small one, but hailed by the pilgrim almost with a shout. There is a sort of mews between two of the tall mansions, a mere slit like the crack of a door by comparison with the street, but just large enough to permit a pigmy ale-house or eating-house, still allowed by the rich to their stable-servants, to stand in the angle. There is something cheery in its very dinginess, and something free and elfin in its very insignificance. At the feet of those grey stone giants it looks like a lighted house of dwarfs.

Anyone passing the place during a certain autumn evening, itself almost fairy-like, might have seen a hand pull aside the red half-blind which (along with some large white lettering) half hid the interior from the street, and a face peer out not unlike a rather innocent goblin's. It was, in fact, the face of one with the harmless human name of Brown, formerly priest of Cobhole in Essex, and now working in London. His friend, Flambeau, a semi-official investigator, was sitting opposite him, making his last notes of a case he had cleared up in the neighbourhood. They were sitting at a small table, close up to the window, when the priest pulled the curtain back and looked out. He waited till a stranger in the street had passed the window, to let the curtain fall into its place again. Then his round eyes rolled to the large white lettering on the window above his head, and then strayed to the next table, at which sat only a navvy with beer and cheese, and a young girl with red hair and a glass of milk. Then (seeing his friend put away the pocket-book), he said softly:

"If you've got ten minutes, I wish you'd follow that man with the false nose."

Flambeau looked up in surprise; but the girl with the red hair also looked up, and with something that was stronger than astonishment. She was simply and even loosely dressed in light brown sacking stuff; but she was a lady, and even, on a second glance, a rather needlessly haughty one. "The man with the false nose!" repeated Flambeau. "Who's he?"

"I haven't a notion," answered Father Brown. "I want you to find out; I ask it as a favour. He went down there"—and he jerked his thumb over his shoulder in one of his undistinguished gestures—"and can't have passed three lamp-posts yet. I only want to know the direction."

Flambeau gazed at his friend for some time, with an expression between perplexity and amusement; and then, rising from the table; squeezed his huge form out of the little door of the dwarf tavern, and melted into the twilight.

Father Brown took a small book out of his pocket and began to read steadily; he betrayed no consciousness of the fact that the red-haired lady had left her own table and sat down opposite him. At last she leaned over and said in a low, strong voice: "Why do you say that? How do you know it's false?"

He lifted his rather heavy eyelids, which fluttered in considerable embarrassment. Then his dubious eye roamed again to the white lettering on the glass front of the public-house. The young woman's eyes followed his, and rested there also, but in pure puzzledom.

"No," said Father Brown, answering her thoughts. "It doesn't say 'Sela', like the thing in the Psalms; I read it like that myself when I was wool-gathering just now; it says 'Ales.'"

"Well?" inquired the staring young lady. "What does it matter what it says?"

His ruminating eye roved to the girl's light canvas sleeve, round the wrist of which ran a very slight thread of artistic pattern, just enough to distinguish it from a working-dress of a common woman and make it more like the working-dress of a lady art-student. He seemed to find much food for thought in this; but his reply was very slow and hesitant. "You see, madam," he said, "from outside the place looks— well, it is a perfectly decent place—but ladies like you don't—don't generally think so. They never go into such places from choice, except—"

"Well?" she repeated.

"Except an unfortunate few who don't go in to drink milk."

"You are a most singular person," said the young lady. "What is your object in all this?"

"Not to trouble you about it," he replied, very gently. "Only to arm myself with knowledge enough to help you, if ever you freely ask my help."

"But why should I need help?"

He continued his dreamy monologue. "You couldn't have come in to see protegees, humble friends, that sort of thing, or you'd have gone through into the parlour... and you couldn't have come in because you were ill, or you'd have spoken to the woman of the place, who's obviously respectable... besides, you don't look ill in that way, but only unhappy.... This street is the only original long lane that has no turning; and the houses on both sides are shut up.... I could only suppose that you'd seen somebody coming whom you didn't want to meet; and found the public-house was the only shelter in this wilderness of stone.... I don't think I went beyond the licence of a stranger in glancing at the only man who passed immediately after.... And as I thought he looked like the wrong sort... and you looked like the right sort.... I held myself ready to help if he annoyed you; that is all. As for my friend, he'll be back soon; and he certainly can't find out anything by stumping down a road like this.... I didn't think he could."

"Then why did you send him out?" she cried, leaning forward with yet warmer curiosity. She had the proud, impetuous face that goes with reddish colouring, and a Roman nose, as it did in Marie Antoinette.

He looked at her steadily for the first time, and said: "Because I hoped you would speak to me."

She looked back at him for some time with a heated face, in which there hung a red shadow of anger; then, despite her anxieties, humour broke out of her eyes and the corners of her mouth, and she answered almost grimly: "Well, if you're so keen on my conversation, perhaps you'll answer my question." After a pause she added: "I had the honour to ask you why you thought the man's nose was false."

"The wax always spots like that just a little in this weather," answered Father Brown with entire simplicity.

"But it's such a crooked nose," remonstrated the red-haired girl.

The priest smiled in his turn. "I don't say it's the sort of nose one would wear out of mere foppery," he admitted. "This man, I think, wears it because his real nose is so much nicer."

"But why?" she insisted.

"What is the nursery-rhyme?" observed Brown absent-mindedly. "There was a crooked man and he went a crooked mile.... That man, I fancy, has gone a very crooked road—by following his nose."

"Why, what's he done?" she demanded, rather shakily.

"I don't want to force your confidence by a hair," said Father Brown, very quietly. "But I think you could tell me more about that than I can tell you."

The girl sprang to her feet and stood quite quietly, but with clenched hands, like one about to stride away; then her hands loosened slowly, and she sat down again. "You are more of a mystery than all the others," she said desperately, "but I feel there might be a heart in your mystery."

"What we all dread most," said the priest in a low voice, "is a maze with no centre. That is why atheism is only a nightmare." "I will tell you everything," said the red-haired girl doggedly, "except why I am telling you; and that I don't know."

She picked at the darned table-cloth and went on: "You look as if you knew what isn't snobbery as well as what is; and when I say that ours is a good old family, you'll understand it is a necessary part of the story; indeed, my chief danger is in my brother's high-and-dry notions, noblesse oblige and all that. Well, my name is Christabel Carstairs; and my father was that Colonel Carstairs you've probably heard of, who made the famous Carstairs Collection of Roman coins. I could never describe my father to you; the nearest I can say is that he was very like a Roman coin himself. He was as handsome and as genuine and as valuable and as metallic and as out-of-date. He was prouder of his Collection than of his coat-of-arms—nobody could say more than that. His extraordinary character came out most in his will. He had two sons and one daughter. He quarrelled with one son, my brother Giles, and sent him to Australia on a small allowance. He then made a will leaving the Carstairs Collection, actually with a yet smaller allowance, to my brother Arthur. He meant it as a reward, as the highest honour he could offer, in acknowledgement of Arthur's loyalty and rectitude and the distinctions he had already gained in mathematics and economics at Cambridge. He left me practically all his pretty large fortune; and I am sure he meant it in contempt.

"Arthur, you may say, might well complain of this; but Arthur is my father over again. Though he had some differences with my father in early youth, no sooner had he taken over the Collection than he became like a pagan priest dedicated to a temple. He mixed up these Roman halfpence with the honour of the Carstairs family in the same stiff, idolatrous way as his father before him. He acted as if Roman money must be guarded by all the Roman virtues. He took no pleasures; he spent nothing on himself; he lived for the Collection. Often he would not trouble to dress for his simple meals; but pattered about among the corded brown-paper parcels (which no one else was allowed to touch) in an old brown dressing-gown. With its rope and tassel and his pale, thin, refined face, it made him look like an old ascetic monk. Every now and then, though, he would appear dressed like a decidedly fashionable gentleman; but that was only when he went up to the London sales or shops to make an addition to the Carstairs Collection.

"Now, if you've known any young people, you won't be shocked if I say that I got into rather a low frame of mind with all this; the frame of mind in which one begins to say that the Ancient Romans were all very well in their way. I'm not like my brother Arthur; I can't help enjoying enjoyment. I got a lot of romance and rubbish where I got my red hair, from the other side of the family. Poor Giles was the same; and I think the atmosphere of coins might count in excuse for him; though he really did wrong and nearly went to prison. But he didn't behave any worse than I did; as you shall hear.

"I come now to the silly part of the story. I think a man as clever as you can guess the sort of thing that would begin to relieve the monotony for an unruly girl of seventeen placed in such a position. But I am so rattled with more dreadful things that I can hardly read my own feeling; and don't know whether I despise it now as a flirtation or bear it as a broken heart. We lived then at a little seaside watering-place in South Wales, and a retired sea-captain living a few doors off had a son about five years older than myself, who had been a friend of Giles before he went to the Colonies. His name does not affect my tale; but I tell you it was Philip Hawker, because I am telling you everything. We used to go shrimping together, and said and thought we were in love with each other; at least he certainly said he was, and I certainly thought I was. If I tell you he had bronzed curly hair and a falconish sort of face, bronzed by the sea also, it's not for his sake, I assure you, but for the story; for it was the cause of a very curious coincidence.

"One summer afternoon, when I had promised to go shrimping along the sands with Philip, I was waiting rather impatiently in the front drawing-room, watching

Arthur handle some packets of coins he had just purchased and slowly shunt them, one or two at a time, into his own dark study and museum which was at the back of the house. As soon as I heard the heavy door close on him finally, I made a bolt for my shrimping-net and tam-o'-shanter and was just going to slip out, when I saw that my brother had left behind him one coin that lay gleaming on the long bench by the window. It was a bronze coin, and the colour, combined with the exact curve of the Roman nose and something in the very lift of the long, wiry neck, made the head of Caesar on it the almost precise portrait of Philip Hawker. Then I suddenly remembered Giles telling Philip of a coin that was like him, and Philip wishing he had it. Perhaps you can fancy the wild, foolish thoughts with which my head went round; I felt as if I had had a gift from the fairies. It seemed to me that if I could only run away with this, and give it to Philip like a wild sort of wedding-ring, it would be a bond between us for ever; I felt a thousand such things at once. Then there yawned under me, like the pit, the enormous, awful notion of what I was doing; above all, the unbearable thought, which was like touching hot iron, of what Arthur would think of it. A Carstairs a thief; and a thief of the Carstairs treasure! I believe my brother could see me burned like a witch for such a thing, But then, the very thought of such fanatical cruelty heightened my old hatred of his dingy old antiquarian fussiness and my longing for the youth and liberty that called to me from the sea. Outside was strong sunlight with a wind; and a yellow head of some broom or gorse in the garden rapped against the glass of the window. I thought of that living and growing gold calling to me from all the heaths of the world—and then of that dead, dull gold and bronze and brass of my brother's growing dustier and dustier as life went by. Nature and the Carstairs Collection had come to grips at last.

"Nature is older than the Carstairs Collection. As I ran down the streets to the sea, the coin clenched tight in my fist, I felt all the Roman Empire on my back as well as the Carstairs pedigree. It was not only the old lion argent that was roaring in my ear, but all the eagles of the Caesars seemed flapping and screaming in pursuit of me. And yet my heart rose higher and higher like a child's kite, until I came over the loose, dry sand-hills and to the flat, wet sands, where Philip stood already up to his ankles in the shallow shining water, some hundred yards out to sea. There was a great red sunset; and the long stretch of low water, hardly rising over the ankle for half a mile, was like a lake of ruby flame. It was not till I had torn off my shoes and stockings and waded to where he stood, which was well away from the dry land, that I turned and looked round. We were quite alone in a circle of sea-water and wet sand, and I gave him the head of Caesar.

"At the very instant I had a shock of fancy: that a man far away on the sand-hills was looking at me intently. I must have felt immediately after that it was a mere leap of unreasonable nerves; for the man was only a dark dot in the distance, and I could only just see that he was standing quite still and gazing, with his head a little on one side. There was no earthly logical evidence that he was looking at me; he might have been looking at a ship, or the sunset, or the sea-gulls, or at any of the people who still strayed here and there on the shore between us. Nevertheless, whatever my start sprang from was prophetic; for, as I gazed, he started walking briskly in a bee-line towards us across the wide wet sands. As he drew nearer and nearer I saw that he was dark and bearded, and that his eyes were marked with dark spectacles. He was dressed poorly but respectably in black, from the old black top hat on his head to the solid black boots on his feet. In spite of these he walked straight into the sea without a flash of hesitation, and came on at me with the steadiness of a travelling bullet.

"I can't tell you the sense of monstrosity and miracle I had when he thus silently burst the barrier between land and water. It was as if he had walked straight off a cliff and still marched steadily in mid-air. It was as if a house had flown up into the sky or a man's head had fallen off. He was only wetting his boots; but he seemed to be a demon disregarding a law of Nature. If he had hesitated an instant at the water's edge it would have been nothing. As it was, he seemed to look so much at me alone as not to notice the ocean. Philip was some yards away with his back to me, bending over his net. The stranger came on till he stood within two yards of me, the water washing half-way up to his knees. Then he said, with a clearly modulated and rather mincing articulation: 'Would it discommode you to contribute elsewhere a coin with a somewhat different superscription?'

"With one exception there was nothing definably abnormal about him. His tinted glasses were not really opaque, but of a blue kind common enough, nor were the eyes behind them shifty, but regarded me steadily. His dark beard was not really long or wild—, but he looked rather hairy, because the beard began very high up in his face, just under the cheek-bones. His complexion was neither sallow nor livid, but on the contrary rather clear and youthful; yet this gave a pink-and-white wax look which somehow (I don't know why) rather increased the horror. The only oddity one could fix was that his nose, which was otherwise of a good shape, was just slightly turned sideways at the tip; as if, when it was soft, it had been tapped on one side with a toy hammer. The thing was hardly a deformity; yet I cannot tell you what a living nightmare it was to me. As he stood there in the sunset-stained water he affected me as some hellish sea-monster just risen roaring out of a sea like blood. I don't know why a touch on the nose should affect my imagination so much. I think it seemed as if he could move his nose like a finger. And as if he had just that moment moved it.

"'Any little assistance,' he continued with the same queer, priggish accent, 'that may obviate the necessity of my communicating with the family.'

"Then it rushed over me that I was being blackmailed for the theft of the bronze piece; and all my merely superstitious fears and doubts were swallowed up in one overpowering, practical question. How could he have found out? I had stolen the thing suddenly and on impulse; I was certainly alone; for I always made sure of being unobserved when I slipped out to see Philip in this way. I had not, to all appearance, been followed in the street; and if I had, they could not 'X-ray' the coin in my closed hand. The man standing on the sand-hills could no more have seen what I gave Philip than shoot a fly in one eye, like the man in the fairy-tale.

"'Philip,' I cried helplessly, 'ask this man what he wants.'

"When Philip lifted his head at last from mending his net he looked rather red, as if sulky or ashamed; but it may have been only the exertion of stooping and the red evening light; I may have only had another of the morbid fancies that seemed to be dancing about me. He merely said gruffly to the man: 'You clear out of this.' And, motioning me to follow, set off wading shoreward without paying further attention to him. He stepped on to a stone breakwater that ran out from among the roots of the sand-hills, and so struck homeward, perhaps thinking our incubus would find it less easy to walk on such rough stones, green and slippery with seaweed, than we, who were young and used to it. But my persecutor walked as daintily as he talked; and he still followed me, picking his way and picking his phrases. I heard his delicate, detestable voice appealing to me over my shoulder, until at last, when we had crested the sand-hills, Philip's patience (which was by no means so conspicuous on most occasions) seemed to snap. He turned suddenly, saying, 'Go back. I can't talk to you now.' And as the man hovered and opened his mouth, Philip struck him a buffet on it that sent him flying from the top of the tallest sand-hill to the bottom. I saw him crawling out below, covered with sand.

"This stroke comforted me somehow, though it might well increase my peril; but Philip showed none of his usual elation at his own prowess. Though as affectionate as ever, he still seemed cast down; and before I could ask him anything fully, he parted with me at his own gate, with two remarks that struck me as strange. He said that, all things considered, I ought to put the coin back in the Collection; but that he himself would keep it 'for the present'. And then he added quite suddenly and irrelevantly: 'You know Giles is back from Australia?'"

The door of the tavern opened and the gigantic shadow of the investigator Flambeau fell across the table. Father Brown presented him to the lady in his own slight, persuasive style of speech, mentioning his knowledge and sympathy in such cases; and almost without knowing, the girl was soon reiterating her story to two listeners. But Flambeau, as he bowed and sat down, handed the priest a small slip of paper. Brown accepted it with some surprise and read on it: "Cab to Wagga Wagga, 379, Mafeking Avenue, Putney." The girl was going on with her story.

"I went up the steep street to my own house with my head in a whirl; it had not begun to clear when I came to the doorstep, on which I found a milk-can—and the man with the twisted nose. The milk-can told me the servants were all out; for, of course, Arthur, browsing about in his brown dressing-gown in a brown study, would not hear or answer a bell. Thus there was no one to help me in the house, except my brother, whose help must be my ruin. In desperation I thrust two shillings into the horrid thing's hand, and told him to call again in a few days, when I had thought it out. He went off sulking, but more sheepishly than I had expected—perhaps he had been shaken by his fall—and I watched the star of sand splashed on his back receding down the road with a horrid vindictive pleasure. He turned a corner some six houses down.

"Then I let myself in, made myself some tea, and tried to think it out. I sat at the drawing-room window looking on to the garden, which still glowed with the last full evening light. But I was too distracted and dreamy to look at the lawns and flower-pots and flower-beds with any concentration. So I took the shock the more sharply because I'd seen it so slowly.

"The man or monster I'd sent away was standing quite still in the middle of the garden. Oh, we've all read a lot about pale-faced phantoms in the dark; but this was more dreadful than anything of that kind could ever be. Because, though he cast a long evening shadow, he still stood in warm sunlight. And because his face was not pale, but had that waxen bloom still upon it that belongs to a barber's dummy. He stood quite still, with his face towards me; and I can't tell you how horrid he looked among the tulips and all those tall, gaudy, almost hothouse-looking flowers. It looked as if we'd stuck up a waxwork instead of a statue in the centre of our garden.

"Yet almost the instant he saw me move in the window he turned and ran out of the garden by the back gate, which stood open and by which he had undoubtedly entered. This renewed timidity on his part was so different from the impudence with which he had walked into the sea, that I felt vaguely comforted. I fancied, perhaps, that he feared confronting Arthur more than I knew. Anyhow, I settled down at last, and had a quiet dinner alone (for it was against the rules to disturb Arthur when he was rearranging the museum), and, my thoughts, a little released, fled to Philip and lost themselves, I suppose. Anyhow, I was looking blankly, but rather pleasantly than otherwise, at another window, uncurtained, but by this time black as a slate with the final night-fall. It seemed to me that something like a snail was on the outside of the window-pane. But when I stared harder, it was more like a man's thumb pressed on the pane; it had that curled look that a thumb has. With my fear and courage re-awakened together, I rushed at the window and then recoiled with a strangled scream that any man but Arthur must have heard.

"For it was not a thumb, any more than it was a snail. It was the tip of a crooked nose, crushed against the glass; it looked white with the pressure; and the staring face and eyes behind it were at first invisible and afterwards grey like a ghost. I slammed the shutters together somehow, rushed up to my room and locked myself in. But, even as I passed, I could swear I saw a second black window with something on it that was like a snail.

"It might be best to go to Arthur after all. If the thing was crawling close all around the house like a cat, it might have purposes worse even than blackmail. My brother might cast me out and curse me for ever, but he was a gentleman, and would defend me on the spot. After ten minutes' curious thinking, I went down, knocked on the door and then went in: to see the last and worst sight.

"My brother's chair was empty, and he was obviously out. But the man with the crooked nose was sitting waiting for his return, with his hat still insolently on his head, and actually reading one of my brother's books under my brother's lamp. His face was composed and occupied, but his nose-tip still had the air of being the most mobile part of his face, as if it had just turned from left to right like an elephant's proboscis. I had thought him poisonous enough while he was pursuing and watching me; but I think his unconsciousness of my presence was more frightful still.

"I think I screamed loud and long; but that doesn't matter. What I did next does matter: I gave him all the money I had, including a good deal in paper which, though it was mine, I dare say I had no right to touch. He went off at last, with hateful, tactful regrets all in long words; and I sat down, feeling ruined in every sense. And yet I was saved that very night by a pure accident. Arthur had gone off suddenly to London, as he so often did, for bargains; and returned, late but radiant, having nearly secured a treasure that was an added splendour even to the family Collection.

He was so resplendent that I was almost emboldened to confess the abstraction of the lesser gem—, but he bore down all other topics with his over-powering projects. Because the bargain might still misfire any moment, he insisted on my packing at once and going up with him to lodgings he had already taken in Fulham, to be near the curio-shop in question. Thus in spite of myself, I fled from my foe almost in the dead of night—but from Philip also.... My brother was often at the South Kensington Museum, and, in order to make some sort of secondary life for myself, I paid for a few lessons at the Art Schools. I was coming back from them this evening, when I saw the abomination of desolation walking alive down the long straight street and the rest is as this gentleman has said.

"I've got only one thing to say. I don't deserve to be helped; and I don't question or complain of my punishment; it is just, it ought to have happened. But I still question, with bursting brains, how it can have happened. Am I punished by miracle? or how can anyone but Philip and myself know I gave him a tiny coin in the middle of the sea?"

"It is an extraordinary problem," admitted Flambeau.

"Not so extraordinary as the answer," remarked Father Brown rather gloomily. "Miss Carstairs, will you be at home if we call at your Fulham place in an hour and a half hence?"

The girl looked at him, and then rose and put her gloves on. "Yes," she said, "I'll be there"; and almost instantly left the place.

That night the detective and the priest were still talking of the matter as they drew near the Fulham house, a tenement strangely mean even for a temporary residence of the Carstairs family.

"Of course the superficial, on reflection," said Flambeau, "would think first of this Australian brother who's been in trouble before, who's come back so suddenly and who's just the man to have shabby confederates. But I can't see how he can come into the thing by any process of thought, unless..."

"Well?" asked his companion patiently.

Flambeau lowered his voice. "Unless the girl's lover comes in, too, and he would be the blacker villain. The Australian chap did know that Hawker wanted the coin. But I can't see how on earth he could know that Hawker had got it, unless Hawker signalled to him or his representative across the shore."

"That is true," assented the priest, with respect.

"Have you noted another thing?" went on Flambeau eagerly, "this Hawker hears his love insulted, but doesn't strike till he's got to the soft sand-hills, where he can be victor in a mere sham-fight. If he'd struck amid rocks and sea, he might have hurt his ally."

"That is true again," said Father Brown, nodding.

"And now, take it from the start. It lies between few people, but at least three. You want one person for suicide; two people for murder; but at least three people for blackmail"

"Why?" asked the priest softly.

"Well, obviously," cried his friend, "there must be one to be exposed; one to threaten exposure; and one at least whom exposure would horrify."

After a long ruminant pause, the priest said: "You miss a logical step. Three persons are needed as ideas. Only two are needed as agents."

"What can you mean?" asked the other.

"Why shouldn't a blackmailer," asked Brown, in a low voice, "threaten his victim with himself? Suppose a wife became a rigid teetotaller in order to frighten her husband into concealing his pub-frequenting, and then wrote him blackmailing letters in another hand, threatening to tell his wife! Why shouldn't it work? Suppose a father forbade a son to gamble and then, following him in a good disguise, threatened the boy with his own sham paternal strictness! Suppose—but, here we are, my friend."

"My God!" cried Flambeau; "you don't mean—"

An active figure ran down the steps of the house and showed under the golden lamplight the unmistakable head that resembled the Roman coin. "Miss Carstairs," said Hawker without ceremony, "wouldn't go in till you came."

"Well," observed Brown confidently, "don't you think it's the best thing she can do to stop outside—with you to look after her? You see, I rather guess you have guessed it all yourself."

"Yes," said the young man, in an undertone, "I guessed on the sands and now I know; that was why I let him fall soft."

Taking a latchkey from the girl and the coin from Hawker, Flambeau let himself and his friend into the empty house and passed into the outer parlour. It was empty of all occupants but one. The man whom Father Brown had seen pass the tavern was standing against the wall as if at bay; unchanged, save that he had taken off his black coat and was wearing a brown dressing-gown.

"We have come," said Father Brown politely, "to give back this coin to its owner." And he handed it to the man with the nose.

Flambeau's eyes rolled. "Is this man a coin-collector?" he asked.

"This man is Mr Arthur Carstairs," said the priest positively, "and he is a coin-collector of a somewhat singular kind."

The man changed colour so horribly that the crooked nose stood out on his face like a separate and comic thing. He spoke, nevertheless, with a sort of despairing dignity. "You shall see, then," he said, "that I have not lost all the family qualities." And he turned suddenly and strode into an inner room, slamming the door.

"Stop him!" shouted Father Brown, bounding and half falling over a chair; and, after a wrench or two, Flambeau had the door open. But it was too late. In dead silence Flambeau strode across and telephoned for doctor and police.

An empty medicine bottle lay on the floor. Across the table the body of the man in the brown dressing-gown lay amid his burst and gaping brown-paper parcels; out of which poured and rolled, not Roman, but very modern English coins.

The priest held up the bronze head of Caesar. "This," he said, "was all that was left of the Carstairs Collection."

After a silence he went on, with more than common gentleness: "It was a cruel will his wicked father made, and you see he did resent it a little. He hated the Roman money he had, and grew fonder of the real money denied him. He not only sold the Collection bit by bit, but sank bit by bit to the basest ways of making money—even to blackmailing his own family in a disguise. He blackmailed his brother from Australia for his little forgotten crime (that is why he took the cab to Wagga Wagga in Putney), he blackmailed his sister for the theft he alone could have noticed. And that, by the way, is why she had that supernatural guess when he was away on the sand-dunes. Mere figure and gait, however distant, are more likely to remind us of somebody than a well-made-up face quite close."

There was another silence. "Well," growled the detective, "and so this great numismatist and coin-collector was nothing but a vulgar miser."

"Is there so great a difference?" asked Father Brown, in the same strange, indulgent tone. "What is there wrong about a miser that is not often as wrong about a collector? What is wrong, except... thou shalt not make to thyself any graven image; thou shalt not bow down to them nor serve them, for I...but we must go and see how the poor young people are getting on."

"I think," said Flambeau, "that in spite of everything, they are probably getting on very well."

The Purple Wig

MR EDWARD NUTT, the industrious editor of the Daily Reformer, sat at his desk, opening letters and marking proofs to the merry tune of a typewriter, worked by a vigorous young lady.

He was a stoutish, fair man, in his shirt-sleeves; his movements were resolute, his mouth firm and his tones final; but his round, rather babyish blue eyes had a bewildered and even wistful look that rather contradicted all this. Nor indeed was the expression altogether misleading. It might truly be said of him, as for many journalists in authority, that his most familiar emotion was one of continuous fear; fear of libel actions, fear of lost advertisements, fear of misprints, fear of the sack.

His life was a series of distracted compromises between the proprietor of the paper (and of him), who was a senile soap-boiler with three ineradicable mistakes in his mind, and the very able staff he had collected to run the paper; some of whom were brilliant and experienced men and (what was even worse) sincere enthusiasts for the political policy of the paper.

A letter from one of these lay immediately before him, and rapid and resolute as he was, he seemed almost to hesitate before opening it. He took up a strip of proof instead, ran down it with a blue eye, and a blue pencil, altered the word "adultery" to the word "impropriety," and the word "Jew" to the word "Alien," rang a bell and sent it flying upstairs.

Then, with a more thoughtful eye, he ripped open the letter from his more distinguished contributor, which bore a postmark of Devonshire, and read as follows:

DEAR NUTT,—As I see you're working Spooks and Dooks at the same time, what about an article on that rum business of the Eyres of Exmoor; or as the old women call it down here, the Devil's Ear of Eyre? The head of the family, you know, is the Duke of Exmoor; he is one of the few really stiff old Tory aristocrats left, a sound old crusted tyrant it is quite in our line to make trouble about. And I think I'm on the track of a story that will make trouble.

Of course I don't believe in the old legend about James I; and as for you, you don't believe in anything, not even in journalism. The legend, you'll probably remember, was about the blackest business in English history—the poisoning of Overbury by that witch's cat Frances Howard, and the quite mysterious terror which forced the King to pardon the murderers. There was a lot of alleged witchcraft mixed up with it; and the story goes that a man-servant listening at the keyhole heard the truth in a talk between the King and Carr; and the bodily ear with which he heard grew large and monstrous as by magic, so awful was the secret. And though he had to be loaded with lands and gold and made an ancestor of dukes, the elf-shaped ear is still recurrent in the family. Well, you don't believe in black magic; and if you did, you couldn't use it for copy. If a miracle happened in your office, you'd have to hush it up, now so many bishops are agnostics. But that is not the point. The point is that there really is something queer about Exmoor and his family; something quite natural, I dare say, but quite abnormal. And the Ear is in it somehow, I fancy; either a symbol or a delusion or disease or something. Another tradition says that Cavaliers just after James I began to wear their hair long only to cover the ear of the first Lord Exmoor. This also is no doubt fanciful.

The reason I point it out to you is this: It seems to me that we make a mistake in attacking aristocracy entirely for its champagne and diamonds. Most men rather admire the nobs for having a good time, but I think we surrender too much when we admit that aristocracy has made even the aristocrats happy. I suggest a series of articles pointing out how dreary, how inhuman, how downright diabolist, is the very smell and atmosphere of some of these great houses. There are plenty of instances; but you couldn't begin with a better one than the Ear of the Eyres. By the end of the week I think I can get you the truth about it.—Yours ever, FRANCIS FINN.

Mr Nutt reflected a moment, staring at his left boot; then he called out in a strong, loud and entirely lifeless voice, in which every syllable sounded alike: "Miss Barlow, take down a letter to Mr Finn, please."

DEAR FINN,—I think it would do; copy should reach us second post Saturday.—Yours, E. NUTT.

This elaborate epistle he articulated as if it were all one word; and Miss Barlow rattled it down as if it were all one word. Then he took up another strip of proof and a blue pencil, and altered the word "supernatural" to the word "marvellous", and the expression "shoot down" to the expression "repress".

In such happy, healthful activities did Mr Nutt disport himself, until the ensuing Saturday found him at the same desk, dictating to the same typist, and using the same blue pencil on the first instalment of Mr Finn's revelations. The opening was a sound piece of slashing invective about the evil secrets of princes, and despair in the high places of the earth. Though written violently, it was in excellent English; but the editor, as usual, had given to somebody else the task of breaking it up into sub-headings, which were of a spicier sort, as "Peeress and Poisons", and "The Eerie Ear", "The Eyres in their Eyrie", and so on through a hundred happy changes. Then followed the legend of the Ear, amplified from Finn's first letter, and then the substance of his later discoveries, as follows:

I know it is the practice of journalists to put the end of the story at the beginning and call it a headline. I know that journalism largely consists in saying "Lord Jones Dead" to people who never knew that Lord Jones was alive. Your present correspondent thinks that this, like many other journalistic customs, is bad journalism; and that the Daily Reformer has to set a better example in such things. He proposes to tell his story as it occurred, step by step. He will use the real names of the parties, who in most cases are ready to confirm his testimony. As for the headlines, the sensational proclamations—they will come at the end.

I was walking along a public path that threads through a private Devonshire orchard and seems to point towards Devonshire cider, when I came suddenly upon just such a place as the path suggested. It was a long, low inn, consisting really of a cottage and two barns; thatched all over with the thatch that looks like brown and grey hair grown before history. But outside the door was a sign which called it the Blue Dragon; and under the sign was one of those long rustic tables that used to stand outside most of the free English inns, before teetotallers and brewers between them destroyed freedom. And at this table sat three gentlemen, who might have lived a hundred years ago.

Now that I know them all better, there is no difficulty about disentangling the impressions; but just then they looked like three very solid ghosts. The dominant figure, both because he was bigger in all three dimensions, and because he sat centrally in the length of the table, facing me, was a tall, fat man dressed completely in black, with a rubicund, even apoplectic visage, but a rather bald and rather bothered brow. Looking at him again, more strictly, I could not exactly say what it was that gave me the sense of antiquity, except the antique cut of his white clerical necktie and the barred wrinkles across his brow.

It was even less easy to fix the impression in the case of the man at the right end of the table, who, to say truth, was as commonplace a person as could be seen anywhere, with a round, brown-haired head and a round snub nose, but also clad in clerical black, of a stricter cut. It was only when I saw his broad curved hat lying on the table beside him that I realized why I connected him with anything ancient. He was a Roman Catholic priest.

Perhaps the third man, at the other end of the table, had really more to do with it than the rest, though he was both slighter in physical presence and more inconsiderate in his dress. His lank limbs were clad, I might also say clutched, in very tight grey sleeves and pantaloons; he had a long, sallow, aquiline face which seemed somehow all the more saturnine because his lantern jaws were imprisoned in his collar and neck-cloth more in the style of the old stock; and his hair (which ought to have been dark brown) was of an odd dim, russet colour which, in conjunction with his yellow face, looked rather purple than red. The unobtrusive yet unusual colour was all the more notable because his hair was almost unnaturally healthy and curling, and he wore it full. But, after all analysis, I incline to think that what gave me my first old-fashioned impression was simply a set of tall, old-fashioned wine-glasses, one or two lemons and two churchwarden pipes. And also, perhaps, the old-world errand on which I had come.

Being a hardened reporter, and it being apparently a public inn, I did not need to summon much of my impudence to sit down at the long table and order some cider. The big man in black seemed very learned, especially about local antiquities; the small man in black, though he talked much less, surprised me with a yet wider culture. So we got on very well together; but the third man, the old gentleman in the tight pantaloons, seemed rather distant and haughty, until I slid into the subject of the Duke of Exmoor and his ancestry.

I thought the subject seemed to embarrass the other two a little; but it broke the spell of the third man's silence most successfully. Speaking with restraint and with the accent of a highly educated gentleman, and puffing at intervals at his long churchwarden pipe, he proceeded to tell me some of the most horrible stories I have ever heard in my life: how one of the Eyres in the former ages had hanged his own father; and another had his wife scourged at the cart tail through the village; and another had set fire to a church full of children, and so on.

Some of the tales, indeed, are not fit for public print—, such as the story of the Scarlet Nuns, the abominable story of the Spotted Dog, or the thing that was done in the quarry. And all this red roll of impieties came from his thin, genteel lips rather primly than otherwise, as he sat sipping the wine out of his tall, thin glass.

I could see that the big man opposite me was trying, if anything, to stop him; but he evidently held the old gentleman in considerable respect, and could not venture to do so at all abruptly. And the little priest at the other end of the-table, though free from any such air of embarrassment, looked steadily at the table, and seemed to listen to the recital with great pain—as well as he might.

"You don't seem," I said to the narrator, "to be very fond of the Exmoor pedigree."

He looked at me a moment, his lips still prim, but whitening and tightening; then he deliberately broke his long pipe and glass on the table and stood up, the very picture of a perfect gentleman with the framing temper of a fiend.

"These gentlemen," he said, "will tell you whether I have cause to like it. The curse of the Eyres of old has lain heavy on this country, and many have suffered from it. They know there are none who have suffered from it as I have." And with that he crushed a piece of the fallen glass under his heel, and strode away among the green twilight of the twinkling apple-trees.

"That is an extraordinary old gentleman," I said to the other two; "do you happen to know what the Exmoor family has done to him? Who is he?"

The big man in black was staring at me with the wild air of a baffled bull; he did not at first seem to take it in. Then he said at last, "Don't you know who he is?"

I reaffirmed my ignorance, and there was another silence; then the little priest said, still looking at the table, "That is the Duke of Exmoor."

Then, before I could collect my scattered senses, he added equally quietly, but with an air of regularizing things: "My friend here is Doctor Mull, the Duke's librarian. My name is Brown."

"But," I stammered, "if that is the Duke, why does he damn all the old dukes like that?"

"He seems really to believe," answered the priest called Brown, "that they have left a curse on him." Then he added, with some irrelevance, "That's why he wears a wig."

It was a few moments before his meaning dawned on me. "You don't mean that fable about the fantastic ear?" I demanded. "I've heard of it, of course, but surely it must be a superstitious yarn spun out of something much simpler. I've sometimes thought it was a wild version of one of those mutilation stories. They used to crop criminals' ears in the sixteenth century."

"I hardly think it was that," answered the little man thoughtfully, "but it is not outside ordinary science or natural law for a family to have some deformity frequently reappearing—such as one ear bigger than the other."

The big librarian had buried his big bald brow in his big red hands, like a man trying to think out his duty. "No," he groaned. "You do the man a wrong after all. Understand, I've no reason to defend him, or even keep faith with him. He has been a tyrant to me as to everybody else. Don't fancy because you see him sitting here that he isn't a great lord in the worst sense of the word. He would fetch a man a mile to ring a bell a yard off—if it would summon another man three miles to fetch a matchbox three yards off. He must have a footman to carry his walking-stick; a body servant to hold up his opera-glasses—"

"But not a valet to brush his clothes," cut in the priest, with a curious dryness, "for the valet would want to brush his wig, too."

The librarian turned to him and seemed to forget my presence; he was strongly moved and, I think, a little heated with wine. "I don't know how you know it, Father Brown," he said, "but you are right. He lets the whole world do everything for him—except dress him. And that he insists on doing in a literal solitude like a desert. Anybody is kicked out of the house without a character who is so much as found near his dressing-room door.

"He seems a pleasant old party," I remarked.

"No," replied Dr Mull quite simply; "and yet that is just what I mean by saying you are unjust to him after all. Gentlemen, the Duke does really feel the bitterness about the curse that he uttered just now. He does, with sincere shame and terror, hide under that purple wig something he thinks it would blast the sons of man to see. I know it is so; and I know it is not a mere natural disfigurement, like a criminal mutilation, or a hereditary disproportion in the features. I know it is worse than that; because a man told me who was present at a scene that no man could invent, where a stronger man than any of us tried to defy the secret, and was scared away from it."

I opened my mouth to speak, but Mull went on in oblivion of me, speaking out of the cavern of his hands. "I don't mind telling you, Father, because it's really more defending the poor Duke than giving him away. Didn't you ever hear of the time when he very nearly lost all the estates?"

The priest shook his head; and the librarian proceeded to tell the tale as he had heard it from his predecessor in the same post, who had been his patron and instructor, and whom he seemed to trust implicitly. Up to a certain point it was a common enough tale of the decline of a great family's fortunes—the tale of a family lawyer. His lawyer, however, had the sense to cheat honestly, if the expression explains itself. Instead of using funds he held in trust, he took advantage of the Duke's carelessness to put the family in a financial hole, in which it might be necessary for the Duke to let him hold them in reality.

The lawyer's name was Isaac Green, but the Duke always called him Elisha; presumably in reference to the fact that he was quite bald, though certainly not more than thirty. He had risen very rapidly, but from very dirty beginnings; being first a "nark" or informer, and then a money-lender: but as solicitor to the Eyres he had the sense, as I say, to keep technically straight until he was ready to deal the final blow. The blow fell at dinner; and the old librarian said he should never forget the very look of the lampshades and the decanters, as the little lawyer, with a steady smile, proposed to the great landlord that they should halve the estates between them. The sequel certainly could not be overlooked; for the Duke, in dead silence, smashed a decanter on the man's bald head as suddenly as I had seen him smash the glass that day in the orchard. It left a red triangular scar on the scalp, and the lawyer's eyes altered, but not his smile.

He rose tottering to his feet, and struck back as such men do strike. "I am glad of that," he said, "for now I can take the whole estate. The law will give it to me."

Exmoor, it seems, was white as ashes, but his eyes still blazed. "The law will give it you," he said; "but you will not take it.... Why not? Why? because it would mean the crack of doom for me, and if you take it I shall take off my wig.... Why, you pitiful plucked fowl, anyone can see your bare head. But no man shall see mine and live."

Well, you may say what you like and make it mean what you like. But Mull swears it is the solemn fact that the lawyer, after shaking his knotted fists in the air for an instant, simply ran from the room and never reappeared in the countryside; and since then Exmoor has been feared more for a warlock than even for a landlord and a magistrate.

Now Dr Mull told his story with rather wild theatrical gestures, and with a passion I think at least partisan. I was quite conscious of the possibility that the whole was the extravagance of an old braggart and gossip. But before I end this half of my discoveries, I think it due to Dr Mull to record that my two first inquiries have confirmed his story. I learned from an old apothecary in the village that there was a bald man in evening dress, giving the name of Green, who came to him one night to have a three-cornered cut on his forehead plastered. And I learnt from the legal records and old newspapers that there was a lawsuit threatened, and at least begun, by one Green against the Duke of Exmoor.

Mr Nutt, of the Daily Reformer, wrote some highly incongruous words across the top of the copy, made some highly mysterious marks down the side of it, and called to Miss Barlow in the same loud, monotonous voice: "Take down a letter to Mr Finn."

DEAR FINN,—Your copy will do, but I have had to headline it a bit; and our public would never stand a Romanist priest in the story—you must keep your eye on the suburbs. I've altered him to Mr Brown, a Spiritualist.

Yours,

E. NUTT.

A day or two afterward found the active and judicious editor examining, with blue eyes that seemed to grow rounder and rounder, the second instalment of Mr Finn's tale of mysteries in high life. It began with the words:

I have made an astounding discovery. I freely confess it is quite different from anything I expected to discover, and will give a much more practical shock to the public. I venture to say, without any vanity, that the words I now write will be read all over Europe, and certainly all over America and the Colonies. And yet I heard all I have to tell before I left this same little wooden table in this same little wood of apple-trees.

I owe it all to the small priest Brown; he is an extraordinary man. The big librarian had left the table, perhaps ashamed of his long tongue, perhaps anxious about the storm in which his mysterious master had vanished: anyway, he betook himself heavily in the Duke's tracks through the trees. Father Brown had picked up one of the lemons and was eyeing it with an odd pleasure.

"What a lovely colour a lemon is!" he said. "There's one thing I don't like about the Duke's wig—the colour."

"I don't think I understand," I answered.

"I dare say he's got good reason to cover his ears, like King Midas," went on the priest, with a cheerful simplicity which somehow seemed rather flippant under the circumstances. "I can quite understand that it's nicer to cover them with hair than with brass plates or leather flaps. But if he wants to use hair, why doesn't he make it look like hair? There never was hair of that colour in this world. It looks more like a sunset-cloud coming through the wood. Why doesn't he conceal the family curse better, if he's really so ashamed of it? Shall I tell you? It's because he isn't ashamed of it. He's proud of it"

"It's an ugly wig to be proud of—and an ugly story," I said.

"Consider," replied this curious little man, "how you yourself really feel about such things. I don't suggest you're either more snobbish or more morbid than the rest of us: but don't you feel in a vague way that a genuine old family curse is rather a fine thing to have? Would you be ashamed, wouldn't you be a little proud, if the heir of the Glamis horror called you his friend? or if Byron's family had confided, to you only, the evil adventures of their race? Don't be too hard on the aristocrats themselves if their heads are as weak as ours would be, and they are snobs about their own sorrows."

"By Jove!" I cried; "and that's true enough. My own mother's family had a banshee; and, now I come to think of it, it has comforted me in many a cold hour."

"And think," he went on, "of that stream of blood and poison that spurted from his thin lips the instant you so much as mentioned his ancestors. Why should he show every stranger over such a Chamber of Horrors unless he is proud of it? He doesn't conceal his wig, he doesn't conceal his blood, he doesn't conceal his family curse, he doesn't conceal the family crimes—but—"

212

The little man's voice changed so suddenly, he shut his hand so sharply, and his eyes so rapidly grew rounder and brighter like a waking owl's, that it had all the abruptness of a small explosion on the table.

"But," he ended, "he does really conceal his toilet."

It somehow completed the thrill of my fanciful nerves that at that instant the Duke appeared again silently among the glimmering trees, with his soft foot and sunset-hued hair, coming round the corner of the house in company with his librarian. Before he came within earshot, Father Brown had added quite composedly, "Why does he really hide the secret of what he does with the purple wig? Because it isn't the sort of secret we suppose."

The Duke came round the corner and resumed his seat at the head of the table with all his native dignity. The embarrassment of the librarian left him hovering on his hind legs, like a huge bear. The Duke addressed the priest with great seriousness. "Father Brown," he said, "Doctor Mull informs me that you have come here to make a request. I no longer profess an observance of the religion of my fathers; but for their sakes, and for the sake of the days when we met before, I am very willing to hear you. But I presume you would rather be heard in private."

Whatever I retain of the gentleman made me stand up. Whatever I have attained of the journalist made me stand still. Before this paralysis could pass, the priest had made a momentarily detaining motion. "If," he said, "your Grace will permit me my real petition, or if I retain any right to advise you, I would urge that as many people as possible should be present. All over this country I have found hundreds, even of my own faith and flock, whose imaginations are poisoned by the spell which I implore you to break. I wish we could have all Devonshire here to see you do it."

"To see me do what?" asked the Duke, arching his eyebrows.

"To see you take off your wig," said Father Brown.

The Duke's face did not move; but he looked at his petitioner with a glassy stare which was the most awful expression I have ever seen on a human face. I could see the librarian's great legs wavering under him like the shadows of stems in a pool; and I could not banish from my own brain the fancy that the trees all around us were filling softly in the silence with devils instead of birds.

"I spare you," said the Duke in a voice of inhuman pity. "I refuse. If I gave you the faintest hint of the load of horror I have to bear alone, you would lie shrieking at these feet of mine and begging to know no more. I will spare you the hint. You shall not spell the first letter of what is written on the altar of the Unknown God."

"I know the Unknown God," said the little priest, with an unconscious grandeur of certitude that stood up like a granite tower. "I know his name; it is Satan. The true God was made flesh and dwelt among us. And I say to you, wherever you find men ruled merely by mystery, it is the mystery of iniquity. If the devil tells you something is too fearful to look at, look at it. If he says something is too terrible to hear, hear it. If you think some truth unbearable, bear it. I entreat your Grace to end this nightmare now and here at this table."

"If I did," said the Duke in a low voice, "you and all you believe, and all by which alone you live, would be the first to shrivel and perish. You would have an instant to know the great Nothing before you died."

"The Cross of Christ be between me and harm," said Father Brown. "Take off your wig."

I was leaning over the table in ungovernable excitement; in listening to this extraordinary duel half a thought had come into my head. "Your Grace," I cried, "I call your bluff. Take off that wig or I will knock it off."

I suppose I can be prosecuted for assault, but I am very glad I did it. When he said, in the same voice of stone, "I refuse," I simply sprang on him. For three long instants he strained against me as if he had all hell to help him; but I forced his head until the hairy cap fell off it. I admit that, whilst wrestling, I shut my eyes as it fell.

I was awakened by a cry from Mull, who was also by this time at the Duke's side. His head and mine were both bending over the bald head of the wigless Duke. Then the silence was snapped by the librarian exclaiming: "What can it mean? Why, the man had nothing to hide. His ears are just like everybody else's."

"Yes," said Father Brown, "that is what he had to hide."

The priest walked straight up to him, but strangely enough did not even glance at his ears. He stared with an almost comical seriousness at his bald forehead, and pointed to a three-cornered cicatrice, long healed, but still discernible. "Mr Green, I think." he said politely, "and he did get the whole estate after all."

And now let me tell the readers of the Daily Reformer what I think the most remarkable thing in the whole affair. This transformation scene, which will seem to you as wild and purple as a Persian fairy-tale, has been (except for my technical assault) strictly legal and constitutional from its first beginnings. This man with the odd scar and the ordinary ears is not an impostor. Though (in one sense) he wears another man's wig and claims another man's ear, he has not stolen another man's coronet. He really is the one and only Duke of Exmoor. What happened was this. The old Duke really had a slight malformation of the ear, which really was more or less hereditary. He really was morbid about it; and it is likely enough that he did invoke it as a kind of curse in the violent scene (which undoubtedly happened) in which he struck Green with the decanter. But the contest ended very differently. Green pressed his claim and got the estates; the dispossessed nobleman shot himself and died without issue. After a decent interval the beautiful English Government revived the "extinct" peerage of Exmoor, and bestowed it, as is usual, on the most important person, the person who had got the property.

This man used the old feudal fables—properly, in his snobbish soul, really envied and admired them. So that thousands of poor English people trembled before a mysterious chieftain with an ancient destiny and a diadem of evil stars—when they are really trembling before a guttersnipe who was a pettifogger and a pawnbroker not twelve years ago. I think it very typical of the real case against our aristocracy as it is, and as it will be till God sends us braver men.

Mr Nutt put down the manuscript and called out with unusual sharpness: "Miss Barlow, please take down a letter to Mr Finn."

DEAR FINN,—You must be mad; we can't touch this. I wanted vampires and the bad old days and aristocracy hand-in-hand with superstition. They like that but you must know the Exmoors would never forgive this. And what would our people say then, I should like to know! Why, Sir Simon is one of Exmoor's greatest pals; and it would ruin that cousin of the Eyres that's standing for us at Bradford. Besides, old Soap-Suds was sick enough at not getting his peerage last year; he'd sack me by wire if I lost him it with such lunacy as this. And what about Duffey? He's doing us some rattling articles on "The Heel of the Norman." And how can he write about Normans if the man's only a solicitor? Do be reasonable.—Yours, E. NUTT.

As Miss Barlow rattled away cheerfully, he crumpled up the copy and tossed it into the waste-paper basket; but not before he had, automatically and by force of habit, altered the word "God" to the word "circumstances."

The Perishing of the Pendragons

FATHER BROWN was in no mood for adventures. He had lately fallen ill with over-work, and when he began to recover, his friend Flambeau had taken him on a cruise in a small yacht with Sir Cecil Fanshaw, a young Cornish squire and an enthusiast for Cornish coast scenery. But Brown was still rather weak; he was no very happy sailor; and though he was never of the sort that either grumbles or breaks down, his spirits did not rise above patience and civility. When the other two men praised the ragged violet sunset or the ragged volcanic crags, he agreed with them. When Flambeau pointed out a rock shaped like a dragon, he looked at it and thought it very like a dragon. When Fanshaw more excitedly indicated a rock that was like Merlin, he looked at it, and signified assent. When Flambeau asked whether this rocky gate of the twisted river was not the gate of Fairyland, he said "Yes." He heard the most important things and the most trivial with the same tasteless absorption. He heard that the coast was death to all but careful seamen; he also heard that the ship's cat was asleep. He heard that Fanshaw couldn't find his cigar-holder anywhere; he also heard the pilot deliver the oracle "Both eyes bright, she's all right; one eye winks, down she sinks." He heard Flambeau say to Fanshaw that no doubt this meant the pilot must keep both eyes open and be spry. And he heard Fanshaw say to Flambeau that, oddly enough, it didn't mean this: it meant that while they saw two of the coast lights, one near and the other distant, exactly side by side, they were in the right river-channel; but that if one light was hidden behind the other, they were going on the rocks. He heard Fanshaw add that his country was full of such quaint fables and idioms; it was the very home of romance; he even pitted this part of Cornwall against Devonshire, as a claimant to the laurels of Elizabethan seamanship. According to him there had been captains among these coves and islets compared with whom Drake was practically a landsman. He heard Flambeau laugh, and ask if, perhaps, the adventurous title of "Westward Ho!" only meant that all Devonshire men wished they were living in Cornwall. He heard Fanshaw say there was no need to be silly; that not only had Cornish captains been heroes, but that they were heroes still: that near that very spot there was an old admiral, now retired, who was scarred by thrilling voyages full of adventures; and who had in his youth found the last group of eight Pacific Islands that was added to the chart of the world. This Cecil Fanshaw was, in person, of the kind that commonly urges such crude but pleasing enthusiasms; a very young man, light-haired, high-coloured, with an eager profile; with a boyish bravado of spirits, but an almost girlish delicacy of tint and type. The big shoulders, black brows and black mousquetaire swagger of Flambeau were a great contrast.

All these trivialities Brown heard and saw; but heard them as a tired man hears a tune in the railway wheels, or saw them as a sick man sees the pattern of his wall-paper. No one can calculate the turns of mood in convalescence: but Father Brown's depression must have had a great deal to do with his mere unfamiliarity with the sea. For as the river mouth narrowed like the neck of a bottle, and the water grew calmer and the air warmer and more earthly, he seemed to wake up and take notice like a baby. They had reached that phase just after sunset when air and water both look bright, but earth and all its growing things look almost black by comparison. About this particular evening, however, there was something exceptional. It was one of those rare atmospheres in which a smoked-glass slide seems to have been slid away from between us and Nature; so that even dark colours on that day look more gorgeous than bright colours on cloudier days. The trampled earth of the river-banks and the peaty stain in the pools did not look drab but glowing umber, and the dark woods astir in the breeze did not look, as usual, dim blue with mere depth of dis-tance, but more like wind-tumbled masses of some vivid violet blossom. This magic clearness and intensity in the colours was further forced on Brown's slowly reviving senses by something romantic and even secret in the very form of the landscape.

The river was still well wide and deep enough for a pleasure boat so small as theirs; but the curves of the country-side suggested that it was closing in on either hand; the woods seemed to be making broken and flying attempts at bridge-building—as if the boat were passing from the romance of a valley to the romance of a hollow and so to the supreme romance of a tunnel. Beyond this mere look of things there was little for Brown's freshening fancy to feed on; he saw no human beings, except some gipsies trailing along the river bank, with faggots and osiers cut in the forest; and one sight no longer unconventional, but in such remote parts still uncommon: a dark-haired lady, bare-headed, and paddling her own canoe. If Father Brown ever attached any importance to either of these, he certainly forgot them at the next turn of the river which brought in sight a singular object.

The water seemed to widen and split, being cloven by the dark wedge of a fish-shaped and wooded islet. With the rate at which they went, the islet seemed to swim towards them like a ship; a ship with a very high prow—or, to speak more strictly, a very high funnel. For at the extreme point nearest them stood up an odd-looking building, unlike anything they could remember or connect with any pur-pose. It was not specially high, but it was too high for its breadth to be called anything but a tower. Yet it appeared to be built entirely of wood, and that in a most unequal and eccentric way. Some of the planks and beams were of good, seasoned oak; some of such wood cut raw and recent; some again of white pinewood, and a great deal more of the same sort of wood painted black with tar. These black beams were set crooked or crisscross at all kinds of angles, giving the whole a most patchy and puzzling appearance. There were one or two windows, which appeared to be coloured and leaded in an old-fashioned but more elaborate style. The travellers looked at it with that paradoxical feeling we have when something reminds us of something, and yet we are certain it is something very different.

Father Brown, even when he was mystified, was clever in analysing his own mystification. And he found himself reflecting that the oddity seemed to consist in a particular shape cut out in an incongruous material; as if one saw a top-hat made of tin, or a frock-coat cut out of tartan. He was sure he had seen timbers of different tints arranged like that somewhere, but never in such architectural proportions. The next moment a glimpse through the dark trees told him all he wanted to know and he laughed. Through a gap in the foliage there appeared for a moment one of those old wooden houses, faced with black beams, which are still to be found here and there in England, but which most of us see imitated in some show called "Old London" or "Shakespeare's England'. It was in view only long enough for the priest to see that, however old-fashioned, it was a comfortable and well-kept country-house, with flower-beds in front of it. It had none of the piebald and crazy look of the tower that seemed made out of its refuse.

"What on earth's this?" said Flambeau, who was still staring at the tower.

Fanshaw's eyes were shining, and he spoke triumphantly. "Aha! you've not seen a place quite like this before, I fancy; that's why I've brought you here, my friend. Now you shall see whether I exaggerate about the mariners of Cornwall. This place belongs to Old Pendragon, whom we call the Admiral; though he retired before getting the rank. The spirit of Raleigh and Hawkins is a memory with the Devon folk; it's a modern fact with the Pendragons. If Queen Elizabeth were to rise from the grave and come up this river in a gilded barge, she would be received by the Admiral in a house exactly such as she was accustomed to, in every corner and casement, in every panel on the wall or plate on the table. And she would find an English Captain still talking fiercely of fresh lands to be found in little ships, as much as if she had dined with Drake."

"She'd find a rum sort of thing in the garden," said Father Brown, "which would not please her Renaissance eye. That Elizabethan domestic architecture is charming in its way; but it's against the very nature of it to break out into turrets."

"And yet," answered Fanshaw, "that's the most romantic and Elizabethan part of the business. It was built by the Pendragons in the very days of the Spanish wars; and though it's needed patching and even rebuilding for another reason, it's always been rebuilt in the old way. The story goes that the lady of Sir Peter Pendragon built it in this place and to this height, because from the top you can just see the corner where vessels turn into the river mouth; and she wished to be the first to see her husband's ship, as he sailed home from the Spanish Main."

"For what other reason," asked Father Brown, "do you mean that it has been rebuilt?"

"Oh, there's a strange story about that, too," said the young squire with relish. "You are really in a land of strange stories. King Arthur was here and Merlin and the fairies before him. The story goes that Sir Peter Pendragon, who (I fear) had some of the faults of the pirates as well as the virtues of the sailor, was bringing home three Spanish gentlemen in honourable captivity, intending to escort them to Elizabeth's court. But he was a man of flaming and tigerish temper, and coming to high words with one of them, he caught him by the throat and flung him by accident or design, into the sea. A second Spaniard, who was the brother of the first, instantly drew his sword and flew at Pendragon, and after a short but furious combat in which both got three wounds in as many minutes, Pendragon drove his blade through the other's body and the second Spaniard was accounted for. As it happened the ship had already turned into the river mouth and was close to comparatively shallow water. The third Spaniard sprang over the side of the ship, struck out for the shore, and was soon near enough to it to stand up to his waist in water. And turning again to face the ship, and holding up both arms to Heaven—like a prophet calling plagues upon a wicked city—he called out to Pendragon in a piercing and terrible voice, that he at least was yet living, that he would go on living, that he would live for ever; and that generation after generation the house of Pendragon should never see him or his, but should know by very certain signs that he and his vengeance were alive. With that he dived under the wave, and was either drowned or swam so long under water that no hair of his head was seen afterwards."

"There's that girl in the canoe again," said Flambeau irrelevantly, for good-looking young women would call him off any topic. "She seems bothered by the queer tower just as we were."

Indeed, the black-haired young lady was letting her canoe float slowly and silently past the strange islet; and was looking intently up at the strange tower, with a strong glow of curiosity on her oval and olive face.

"Never mind girls," said Fanshaw impatiently, "there are plenty of them in the world, but not many things like the Pendragon Tower. As you may easily suppose, plenty of superstitions and scandals have followed in the track of the Spaniard's curse; and no doubt, as you would put it, any accident happening to this Cornish family would be connected with it by rural credulity. But it is perfectly true that this tower has been burnt down two or three times; and the family can't be called lucky, for more than two, I think, of the Admiral's near kin have perished by shipwreck; and one at least, to my own knowledge, on practically the same spot where Sir Peter threw the Spaniard overboard."

"What a pity!" exclaimed Flambeau. "She's going."

"When did your friend the Admiral tell you this family history?" asked Father Brown, as the girl in the canoe paddled off, without showing the least intention of extending her interest from the tower to the yacht, which Fanshaw had already caused to lie alongside the island.

"Many years ago," replied Fanshaw; "he hasn't been to sea for some time now, though he is as keen on it as ever. I believe there's a family compact or something. Well, here's the landing stage; let's come ashore and see the old boy."

They followed him on to the island, just under the tower, and Father Brown, whether from the mere touch of dry land, or the interest of something on the other bank of the river (which he stared at very hard for some seconds), seemed singularly improved in briskness. They entered a wooded avenue between two fences of thin greyish wood, such as often enclose parks or gardens, and over the top of which the dark trees tossed to and fro like black and purple plumes upon the hearse of a giant. The tower, as they left it behind, looked all the quainter, because such entrances are usually flanked by two towers; and this one looked lopsided. But for this, the avenue had the usual appearance of the entrance to a gentleman's grounds; and, being so curved that the house was now out of sight, somehow looked a much larger park than any plantation on such an island could really be. Father Brown was, perhaps, a little fanciful in his fatigue, but he almost thought the whole place must be growing larger, as things do in a nightmare. Anyhow, a mystical monotony was the only character of their march, until Fanshaw suddenly stopped, and pointed to something sticking out through the grey fence—something that looked at first rather like the imprisoned horn of some beast. Closer observation showed that it was a slightly curved blade of metal that shone faintly in the fading light.

Flambeau, who like all Frenchmen had been a soldier, bent over it and said in a startled voice: "Why, it's a sabre! I believe I know the sort, heavy and curved, but shorter than the cavalry; they used to have them in artillery and the—"

As he spoke the blade plucked itself out of the crack it had made and came down again with a more ponderous slash, splitting the fissiparous fence to the bottom with a rending noise. Then it was pulled out again, flashed above the fence some feet further along, and again split it halfway down with the first stroke; and after waggling a little to extricate itself (accompanied with curses in the darkness) split it down to the ground with a second. Then a kick of devilish energy sent the whole loosened square of thin wood flying into the pathway, and a great gap of dark coppice gaped in the paling.

Fanshaw peered into the dark opening and uttered an exclamation of astonishment. "My dear Admiral!" he exclaimed, "do you—er—do you generally cut out a new front door whenever you want to go for a walk?"

The voice in the gloom swore again, and then broke into a jolly laugh. "No," it said; "I've really got to cut down this fence somehow; it's spoiling all the plants, and no one else here can do it. But I'll only carve another bit off the front door, and then come out and welcome you."

And sure enough, he heaved up his weapon once more, and, hacking twice, brought down another and similar strip of fence, making the opening about fourteen feet wide in all. Then through this larger forest gateway he came out into the evening light, with a chip of grey wood sticking to his sword-blade.

He momentarily fulfilled all Fanshaw's fable of an old piratical Admiral; though the details seemed afterwards to decompose into accidents. For instance, he wore a broad-brimmed hat as protection against the sun; but the front flap of it was turned up straight to the sky, and the two corners pulled down lower than the ears, so that it stood across his forehead in a crescent like the old cocked hat worn by Nelson. He wore an ordinary dark-blue jacket, with nothing special about the buttons, but the combination of it with white linen trousers somehow had a sailorish look. He was tall and loose, and walked with a sort of swagger, which was not a sailor's roll, and yet somehow suggested it; and he held in his hand a short sabre which was like a navy cutlass, but about twice as big. Under the bridge of the hat his eagle face looked eager, all the more because it was not only clean-shaven, but without eyebrows. It seemed almost as if all the hair had come off his face from his thrusting it through a throng of elements. His eyes were prominent and piercing. His colour was curiously attractive, while partly tropical; it reminded one vaguely of a blood-orange. That is, that while it was ruddy and sanguine, there was a yellow in it that was in no way sickly, but seemed rather to glow like gold apples of the Hesperides—Father Brown thought he had never seen a figure so expressive of all the romances about the countries of the Sun.

When Fanshaw had presented his two friends to their host he fell again into a tone of rallying the latter about his wreckage of the fence and his apparent rage of profanity. The Admiral pooh-poohed it at first as a piece of necessary but annoying garden work; but at length the ring of real energy came back into his laughter, and he cried with a mixture of impatience and good humour:

"Well, perhaps I do go at it a bit rabidly, and feel a kind of pleasure in smashing anything. So would you if your only pleasure was in cruising about to find some new Cannibal Islands, and you had to stick on this muddy little rockery in a sort of rustic pond. When I remember how I've cut down a mile and a half of green poisonous jungle with an old cutlass half as sharp as this; and then remember I must stop here and chop this matchwood, because of some confounded old bargain scribbled in a family Bible, why, I—"

He swung up the heavy steel again; and this time sundered the wall of wood from top to bottom at one stroke.

"I feel like that," he said laughing, but furiously flinging the sword some yards down the path, "and now let's go up to the house; you must have some dinner."

The semicircle of lawn in front of the house was varied by three circular garden beds, one of red tulips, a second of yellow tulips, and the third of some white, waxen-looking blossoms that the visitors did not know and presumed to be exotic. A heavy, hairy and rather sullen-looking gardener was hanging up a heavy coil of garden hose. The corners of the expiring sunset which seemed to cling about the corners of the house gave glimpses here and there of the colours of remoter flowerbeds; and in a treeless space on one side of the house opening upon the river stood a tall brass tripod on which was tilted a big brass telescope. Just outside the steps of the porch stood a little painted green garden table, as if someone had just had tea there. The entrance was flanked with two of those half-featured lumps of stone with holes for eyes that are said to be South Sea idols; and on the brown oak beam across the doorway were some confused carvings that looked almost as barbaric.

As they passed indoors, the little cleric hopped suddenly on to the table, and standing on it peered unaffectedly through his spectacles at the mouldings in the oak. Admiral Pendragon looked very much astonished, though not particularly annoyed; while Fanshaw was so amused with what looked like a performing pigmy on his little stand, that he could not control his laughter. But Father Brown was not likely to notice either the laughter or the astonishment.

He was gazing at three carved symbols, which, though very worn and obscure, seemed still to convey some sense to him. The first seemed to be the outline of some tower or other building, crowned with what looked like curly-pointed ribbons.

The second was clearer: an old Elizabethan galley with decorative waves beneath it, but interrupted in the middle by a curious jagged rock, which was either a fault in the wood or some conventional representation of the water coming in. The third represented the upper half of a human figure, ending in an escalloped line like the waves; the face was rubbed and featureless, and both arms were held very stiffly up in the air.

"Well," muttered Father Brown, blinking, "here is the legend of the Spaniard plain enough. Here he is holding up his arms and cursing in the sea; and here are the two curses: the wrecked ship and the burning of Pendragon Tower."

Pendragon shook his head with a kind of venerable amusement. "And how many other things might it not be?" he said. "Don't you know that that sort of half-man, like a half-lion or half-stag, is quite common in heraldry? Might not that line through the ship be one of those parti-per-pale lines, indented, I think they call it? And though the third thing isn't so very heraldic, it would be more heraldic to suppose it a tower crowned with laurel than with fire; and it looks just as like it."

"But it seems rather odd," said Flambeau, "that it should exactly confirm the old legend."

"Ah," replied the sceptical traveller, "but you don't know how much of the old legend may have been made up from the old figures. Besides, it isn't the only old legend. Fanshaw, here, who is fond of such things, will tell you there are other versions of the tale, and much more horrible ones. One story credits my unfortunate ancestor with having had the Spaniard cut in two; and that will fit the pretty picture also. Another obligingly credits our family with the possession of a tower full of snakes and explains those little, wriggly things in that way. And a third theory supposes the crooked line on the ship to be a conventionalized thunderbolt; but that alone, if seriously examined, would show what a very little way these unhappy co-incidences really go."

"Why, how do you mean?" asked Fanshaw.

"It so happens," replied his host coolly, "that there was no thunder and lightning at all in the two or three shipwrecks I know of in our family."

"Oh!" said Father Brown, and jumped down from the little table.

There was another silence in which they heard the continuous murmur of the river; then Fanshaw said, in a doubtful and perhaps disappointed tone: "Then you don't think there is anything in the tales of the tower in flames?"

"There are the tales, of course," said the Admiral, shrugging his shoulders; "and some of them, I don't deny, on evidence as decent as one ever gets for such things. Someone saw a blaze hereabout, don't you know, as he walked home through a wood; someone keeping sheep on the uplands inland thought he saw a flame hovering over Pendragon Tower. Well, a damp dab of mud like this confounded island seems the last place where one would think of fires."

"What is that fire over there?" asked Father Brown with a gentle suddenness, pointing to the woods on the left river-bank. They were all thrown a little off their balance, and the more fanciful Fanshaw had even some difficulty in recovering his, as they saw a long, thin stream of blue smoke ascending silently into the end of the evening light.

Then Pendragon broke into a scornful laugh again. "Gipsies!" he said; "they've been camping about here for about a week. Gentlemen, you want your dinner," and he turned as if to enter the house.

But the antiquarian superstition in Fanshaw was still quivering, and he said hastily: "But, Admiral, what's that hissing noise quite near the island? It's very like fire."

"It's more like what it is," said the Admiral, laughing as he led the way; "it's only some canoe going by."

Almost as he spoke, the butler, a lean man in black, with very black hair and a very long, yellow face, appeared in the doorway and told him that dinner was served.

The dining-room was as nautical as the cabin of a ship; but its note was rather that of the modern than the Elizabethan captain. There were, indeed, three antiquated cutlasses in a trophy over the fireplace, and one brown sixteenth-century map with Tritons and little ships dotted about a curly sea. But such things were less prominent on the white panelling than some cases of quaint-coloured South American birds, very scientifically stuffed, fantastic shells from the Pacific, and several instruments so rude and queer in shape that savages might have used them either to kill their enemies or to cook them. But the alien colour culminated in the fact that, besides the butler, the Admiral's only servants were two negroes, somewhat quaintly clad in tight uniforms of yellow. The priest's instinctive trick of analysing his own impressions told him that the colour and the little neat coat-tails of these bipeds had suggested the word "Canary," and so by a mere pun connected them with southward travel. Towards the end of the dinner they took their yellow clothes and black faces out of the room, leaving only the black clothes and yellow face of the butler.

"I'm rather sorry you take this so lightly," said Fanshaw to the host; "for the truth is, I've brought these friends of mine with the idea of their helping you, as they know a good deal of these things. Don't you really believe in the family story at all?"

"I don't believe in anything," answered Pendragon very briskly, with a bright eye cocked at a red tropical bird. "I'm a man of science."

Rather to Flambeau's surprise, his clerical friend, who seemed to have entirely woken up, took up the digression and talked natural history with his host with a flow of words and much unexpected information, until the dessert and decanters were set down and the last of the servants vanished. Then he said, without altering his tone.

"Please don't think me impertinent, Admiral Pendragon. I don't ask for curiosity, but really for my guidance and your convenience. Have I made a bad shot if I guess you don't want these old things talked of before your butler?"

The Admiral lifted the hairless arches over his eyes and exclaimed: "Well, I don't know where you got it, but the truth is I can't stand the fellow, though I've no excuse for discharging a family servant. Fanshaw, with his fairy tales, would say my blood moved against men with that black, Spanish-looking hair."

Flambeau struck the table with his heavy fist. "By Jove!" he cried; "and so had that girl!"

"I hope it'll all end tonight," continued the Admiral, "when my nephew comes back safe from his ship. You looked surprised. You won't understand, I suppose, unless I tell you the story. You see, my father had two sons; I remained a bachelor, but my elder brother married, and had a son who became a sailor like all the rest of us, and will inherit the proper estate. Well, my father was a strange man; he somehow combined Fanshaw's superstition with a good deal of my scepticism—they were always fighting in him; and after my first voyages, he developed a notion which he thought somehow would settle finally whether the curse was truth or trash. If all the Pendragons sailed about anyhow, he thought there would be too much chance of natural catastrophes to prove anything. But if we went to sea one at a time in strict order of succession to the property, he thought it might show whether any connected fate followed the family as a family. It was a silly notion, I think, and I quarrelled with my father pretty heartily; for I was an ambitious man and was left to the last, coming, by succession, after my own nephew."

"And your father and brother," said the priest, very gently, "died at sea, I fear."

"Yes," groaned the Admiral; "by one of those brutal accidents on which are built all the lying mythologies of mankind, they were both shipwrecked. My father, coming up this coast out of the Atlantic, was washed up on these Cornish rocks. My brother's ship was sunk, no one knows where, on the voyage home from Tasmania. His body was never found. I tell you it was from perfectly natural mishap; lots of other people besides Pendragons were drowned; and both disasters are discussed in a normal way by navigators. But, of course, it set this forest of superstition on fire; and men saw the flaming tower everywhere. That's why I say it will be all right when Walter returns. The girl he's engaged to was coming today; but I was so afraid of some chance delay frightening her that I wired her not to come till she heard from me. But he's practically sure to be here some time tonight, and then it'll all end in smoke—tobacco smoke. We'll crack that old lie when we crack a bottle of this wine."

"Very good wine," said Father Brown, gravely lifting his glass, "but, as you see, a very bad wine-bibber. I most sincerely beg your pardon": for he had spilt a small spot of wine on the table-cloth. He drank and put down the glass with a composed face; but his hand had started at the exact moment when he became conscious of a face looking in through the garden window just behind the Admiral—the face of a woman, swarthy, with southern hair and eyes, and young, but like a mask of tragedy.

After a pause the priest spoke again in his mild manner. "Admiral," he said, "will you do me a favour? Let me, and my friends if they like, stop in that tower of yours just for tonight? Do you know that in my business you're an exorcist almost before anything else?"

Pendragon sprang to his feet and paced swiftly to and fro across the window, from which the face had instantly vanished. "I tell you there is nothing in it," he cried, with ringing violence. "There is one thing I know about this matter. You may call me an atheist. I am an atheist." Here he swung round and fixed Father Brown with a face of frightful concentration. "This business is perfectly natural. There is no curse in it at all."

Father Brown smiled. "In that case," he said, "there can't be any objection to my sleeping in your delightful summer-house."

"The idea is utterly ridiculous," replied the Admiral, beating a tattoo on the back of his chair.

"Please forgive me for everything," said Brown in his most sympathetic tone, "including spilling the wine. But it seems to me you are not quite so easy about the flaming tower as you try to be."

Admiral Pendragon sat down again as abruptly as he had risen; but he sat quite still, and when he spoke again it was in a lower voice. "You do it at your own peril," he said; "but wouldn't you be an atheist to keep sane in all this devilry?"

Some three hours afterwards Fanshaw, Flambeau and the priest were still dawdling about the garden in the dark; and it began to dawn on the other two that Father Brown had no intention of going to bed either in the tower or the house.

"I think the lawn wants weeding," said he dreamily. "If I could find a spud or something I'd do it myself."

They followed him, laughing and half remonstrating; but he replied with the utmost solemnity, explaining to them, in a maddening little sermon, that one can always find some small occupation that is helpful to others. He did not find a spud; but he found an old broom made of twigs, with which he began energetically to brush the fallen leaves off the grass.

"Always some little thing to be done," he said with idiotic cheerfulness; "as George Herbert says: 'Who sweeps an Admiral's garden in Cornwall as for Thy laws makes that and the action fine.' And now," he added, suddenly slinging the broom away, "Let's go and water the flowers."

With the same mixed emotions they watched him uncoil some considerable lengths of the large garden hose, saying with an air of wistful discrimination: "The red tulips before the yellow, I think. Look a bit dry, don't you think?"

He turned the little tap on the instrument, and the water shot out straight and solid as a long rod of steel.

"Look out, Samson," cried Flambeau; "why, you've cut off the tulip's head."

Father Brown stood ruefully contemplating the decapitated plant.

"Mine does seem to be a rather kill or cure sort of watering," he admitted, scratching his head. "I suppose it's a pity I didn't find the spud. You should have seen me with the spud! Talking of tools, you've got that swordstick, Flambeau, you always carry? That's right; and Sir Cecil could have that sword the Admiral threw away by the fence here. How grey everything looks!"

"The mist's rising from the river," said the staring Flambeau.

Almost as he spoke the huge figure of the hairy gardener appeared on a higher ridge of the trenched and terraced lawn, hailing them with a brandished rake and a horribly bellowing voice. "Put down that hose," he shouted; "put down that hose and go to your—"

"I am fearfully clumsy," replied the reverend gentleman weakly; "do you know, I upset some wine at dinner." He made a wavering half-turn of apology towards the gardener, with the hose still spouting in his hand. The gardener caught the cold crash of the water full in his face like the crash of a cannon-ball; staggered, slipped and went sprawling with his boots in the air.

"How very dreadful!" said Father Brown, looking round in a sort of wonder. "Why, I've hit a man!"

He stood with his head forward for a moment as if looking or listening; and then set off at a trot towards the tower, still trailing the hose behind him. The tower was quite close, but its outline was curiously dim.

"Your river mist," he said, "has a rum smell."

"By the Lord it has," cried Fanshaw, who was very white. "But you can't mean—"

"I mean," said Father Brown, "that one of the Admiral's scientific predictions is coming true tonight. This story is going to end in smoke."

As he spoke a most beautiful rose-red light seemed to burst into blossom like a gigantic rose; but accompanied with a crackling and rattling noise that was like the laughter of devils.

"My God! what is this?" cried Sir Cecil Fanshaw.

"The sign of the flaming tower," said Father Brown, and sent the driving water from his hose into the heart of the red patch.

"Lucky we hadn't gone to bed!" ejaculated Fanshaw. "I suppose it can't spread to the house."

"You may remember," said the priest quietly, "that the wooden fence that might have carried it was cut away."

Flambeau turned electrified eyes upon his friend, but Fanshaw only said rather absently: "Well, nobody can be killed, anyhow."

"This is rather a curious kind of tower," observed Father Brown, "when it takes to killing people, it always kills people who are somewhere else."

At the same instant the monstrous figure of the gardener with the streaming beard stood again on the green ridge against the sky, waving others to come on; but now waving not a rake but a cutlass. Behind him came the two negroes, also with the old crooked cutlasses out of the trophy. But in the blood-red glare, with their black faces and yellow figures, they looked like devils carrying instruments of torture. In the dim garden behind them a distant voice was heard calling out brief directions. When the priest heard the voice, a terrible change came over his countenance.

But he remained composed; and never took his eye off the patch of flame which had begun by spreading, but now seemed to shrink a little as it hissed under the torch of the long silver spear of water. He kept his finger along the nozzle of the pipe to ensure the aim, and attended to no other business, knowing only by the noise and that semi-conscious corner of the eye, the exciting incidents that began to tumble themselves about the island garden. He gave two brief directions to his friends. One was: "Knock these fellows down somehow and tie them up, whoever they are; there's rope down by those faggots. They want to take away my nice hose." The other was: "As soon as you get a chance, call out to that canoeing girl; she's over on the bank with the gipsies. Ask her if they could get some buckets across and fill them from the river." Then he closed his mouth and continued to water the new red flower as ruthlessly as he had watered the red tulip.

He never turned his head to look at the strange fight that followed between the foes and friends of the mysterious fire. He almost felt the island shake when Flambeau collided with the huge gardener; he merely imagined how it would whirl round them as they wrestled. He heard the crashing fall; and his friend's gasp of triumph as he dashed on to the first negro; and the cries of both the blacks as Flambeau and Fanshaw bound them. Flambeau's enormous strength more than redressed the odds in the fight, especially as the fourth man still hovered near the house, only a shadow and a voice. He heard also the water broken by the paddles of a canoe; the girl's voice giving orders, the voices of gipsies answering and coming nearer, the plumping and sucking noise of empty buckets plunged into a full stream; and finally the sound of many feet around the fire. But all this was less to him than the fact that the red rent, which had lately once more increased, had once more slightly diminished.

Then came a cry that very nearly made him turn his head. Flambeau and Fanshaw, now reinforced by some of the gipsies, had rushed after the mysterious man by the house; and he heard from the other end of the garden the Frenchman's cry of horror and astonishment. It was echoed by a howl not to be called human, as the being broke from their hold and ran along the garden. Three times at least it raced round the whole island, in a way that was as horrible as the chase of a lunatic, both in the cries of the pursued and the ropes carried by the pursuers; but was more horrible still, because it somehow suggested one of the chasing games of children in a garden. Then, finding them closing in on every side, the figure sprang upon one of the higher river banks and disappeared with a splash into the dark and driving river.

"You can do no more, I fear," said Brown in a voice cold with pain. "He has been washed down to the rocks by now, where he has sent so many others. He knew the use of a family legend."

"Oh, don't talk in these parables," cried Flambeau impatiently. "Can't you put it simply in words of one syllable?"

"Yes," answered Brown, with his eye on the hose. "'Both eyes bright, she's all right; one eye blinks, down she sinks.'"

The fire hissed and shrieked more and more, like a strangled thing, as it grew narrower and narrower under the flood from the pipe and buckets, but Father Brown still kept his eye on it as he went on speaking:

"I thought of asking this young lady, if it were morning yet, to look through that telescope at the river mouth and the river. She might have seen something to interest her: the sign of the ship, or Mr Walter Pendragon coming home, and perhaps even the sign of the half-man, for though he is certainly safe by now, he may very well have waded ashore. He has been within a shave of another shipwreck; and would never have escaped it, if the lady hadn't had the sense to suspect the old Admiral's telegram and come down to watch him. Don't let's talk about the old Admiral. Don't let's talk about anything. It's enough to say that whenever this tower, with its pitch and resin-wood, really caught fire, the spark on the horizon always looked like the twin light to the coast light-house."

"And that," said Flambeau, "is how the father and brother died. The wicked uncle of the legends very nearly got his estate after all."

Father Brown did not answer; indeed, he did not speak again, save for civilities, till they were all safe round a cigar-box in the cabin of the yacht. He saw that the frustrated fire was extinguished; and then refused to linger, though he actually heard young Pendragon, escorted by an enthusiastic crowd, come tramping up the river bank; and might (had he been moved by romantic curiosities) have received the combined thanks of the man from the ship and the girl from the canoe. But his fatigue had fallen on him once more, and he only started once, when Flambeau abruptly told him he had dropped cigar-ash on his trousers.

"That's no cigar-ash," he said rather wearily. "That's from the fire, but you don't think so because you're all smoking cigars. That's just the way I got my first faint suspicion about the chart."

"Do you mean Pendragon's chart of his Pacific Islands?" asked Fanshaw.

"You thought it was a chart of the Pacific Islands," answered Brown. "Put a feather with a fossil and a bit of coral and everyone will think it's a specimen. Put the same feather with a ribbon and an artificial flower and everyone will think it's for a lady's hat. Put the same feather with an ink-bottle, a book and a stack of writing-paper, and most men will swear they've seen a quill pen. So you saw that map among tropic birds and shells and thought it was a map of Pacific Islands. It was the map of this river."

"But how do you know?" asked Fanshaw.

"I saw the rock you thought was like a dragon, and the one like Merlin, and—"

"You seem to have noticed a lot as we came in," cried Fanshaw. "We thought you were rather abstracted."

"I was sea-sick," said Father Brown simply. "I felt simply horrible. But feeling horrible has nothing to do with not seeing things." And he closed his eyes.

"Do you think most men would have seen that?" asked Flambeau. He received no answer: Father Brown was asleep.

The God of the Gongs

IT was one of those chilly and empty afternoons in early winter, when the daylight is silver rather than gold and pewter rather than silver. If it was dreary in a hundred bleak offices and yawning drawing-rooms, it was drearier still along the edges of the flat Essex coast, where the monotony was the more inhuman for being broken at very long intervals by a lamp-post that looked less civilized than a tree, or a tree that looked more ugly than a lamp-post. A light fall of snow had half-melted into a few strips, also looking leaden rather than silver, when it had been fixed again by the seal of frost; no fresh snow had fallen, but a ribbon of the old snow ran along the very margin of the coast, so as to parallel the pale ribbon of the foam.

The line of the sea looked frozen in the very vividness of its violet-blue, like the vein of a frozen finger. For miles and miles, forward and back, there was no breathing soul, save two pedestrians, walking at a brisk pace, though one had much longer legs and took much longer strides than the other.

It did not seem a very appropriate place or time for a holiday, but Father Brown had few holidays, and had to take them when he could, and he always preferred, if possible, to take them in company with his old friend Flambeau, ex-criminal and ex-detective. The priest had had a fancy for visiting his old parish at Cobhole, and was going north-eastward along the coast.

After walking a mile or two farther, they found that the shore was beginning to be formally embanked, so as to form something like a parade; the ugly lamp-posts became less few and far between and more ornamental, though quite equally ugly. Half a mile farther on Father Brown was puzzled first by little labyrinths of flowerless flower-pots, covered with the low, flat, quiet-coloured plants that look less like a garden than a tessellated pavement, between weak curly paths studded with seats with curly backs. He faintly sniffed the atmosphere of a certain sort of seaside town that he did not specially care about, and, looking ahead along the parade by the sea, he saw something that put the matter beyond a doubt. In the grey distance the big bandstand of a watering-place stood up like a giant mushroom with six legs.

"I suppose," said Father Brown, turning up his coat-collar and drawing a woollen scarf rather closer round his neck, "that we are approaching a pleasure resort."

"I fear," answered Flambeau, "a pleasure resort to which few people just now have the pleasure of resorting. They try to revive these places in the winter, but it never succeeds except with Brighton and the old ones. This must be Seawood, I think—Lord Pooley's experiment; he had the Sicilian Singers down at Christmas, and there's talk about holding one of the great glove-fights here. But they'll have to chuck the rotten place into the sea; it's as dreary as a lost railway-carriage."

They had come under the big bandstand, and the priest was looking up at it with a curiosity that had something rather odd about it, his head a little on one side, like a bird's. It was the conventional, rather tawdry kind of erection for its purpose: a flattened dome or canopy, gilt here and there, and lifted on six slender pillars of painted wood, the whole being raised about five feet above the parade on a round wooden platform like a drum. But there was something fantastic about the snow combined with something artificial about the gold that haunted Flambeau as well as his friend with some association he could not capture, but which he knew was at once artistic and alien.

"I've got it," he said at last. "It's Japanese. It's like those fanciful Japanese prints, where the snow on the mountain looks like sugar, and the gilt on the pagodas is like gilt on gingerbread. It looks just like a little pagan temple."

"Yes," said Father Brown. "Let's have a look at the god." And with an agility hardly to be expected of him, he hopped up on to the raised platform.

"Oh, very well," said Flambeau, laughing; and the next instant his own towering figure was visible on that quaint elevation.

Slight as was the difference of height, it gave in those level wastes a sense of seeing yet farther and farther across land and sea. Inland the little wintry gardens faded into a confused grey copse; beyond that, in the distance, were long low barns of a lonely farmhouse, and beyond that nothing but the long East Anglian plains.

Seawards there was no sail or sign of life save a few seagulls: and even they looked like the last snowflakes, and seemed to float rather than fly.

Flambeau turned abruptly at an exclamation behind him. It seemed to come from lower down than might have been expected, and to be addressed to his heels rather than his head. He instantly held out his hand, but he could hardly help laughing at what he saw. For some reason or other the platform had given way under Father Brown, and the unfortunate little man had dropped through to the level of the parade. He was just tall enough, or short enough, for his head alone to stick out of the hole in the broken wood, looking like St John the Baptist's head on a charger. The face wore a disconcerted expression, as did, perhaps, that of St John the Baptist.

In a moment he began to laugh a little. "This wood must be rotten," said Flambeau. "Though it seems odd it should bear me, and you go through the weak place. Let me help you out."

But the little priest was looking rather curiously at the corners and edges of the wood alleged to be rotten, and there was a sort of trouble on his brow.

"Come along," cried Flambeau impatiently, still with his big brown hand extended. "Don't you want to get out?"

The priest was holding a splinter of the broken wood between his finger and thumb, and did not immediately reply. At last he said thoughtfully: "Want to get out? Why, no. I rather think I want to get in." And he dived into the darkness under the wooden floor so abruptly as to knock off his big curved clerical hat and leave it lying on the boards above, without any clerical head in it.

Flambeau looked once more inland and out to sea, and once more could see nothing but seas as wintry as the snow, and snows as level as the sea.

There came a scurrying noise behind him, and the little priest came scrambling out of the hole faster than he had fallen in. His face was no longer disconcerted, but rather resolute, and, perhaps only through the reflections of the snow, a trifle paler than usual.

"Well?" asked his tall friend. "Have you found the god of the temple?"

"No," answered Father Brown. "I have found what was sometimes more important. The Sacrifice."

"What the devil do you mean?" cried Flambeau, quite alarmed.

Father Brown did not answer. He was staring, with a knot in his forehead, at the landscape; and he suddenly pointed at it. "What's that house over there?" he asked.

Following his finger, Flambeau saw for the first time the corners of a building nearer than the farmhouse, but screened for the most part with a fringe of trees. It was not a large building, and stood well back from the shore—, but a glint of ornament on it suggested that it was part of the same watering-place scheme of decoration as the bandstand, the little gardens and the curly-backed iron seats.

Father Brown jumped off the bandstand, his friend following; and as they walked in the direction indicated the trees fell away to right and left, and they saw a small, rather flashy hotel, such as is common in resorts—the hotel of the Saloon Bar rather than the Bar Parlour. Almost the whole frontage was of gilt plaster and figured glass, and between that grey seascape and the grey, witch-like trees, its gimcrack quality had something spectral in its melancholy. They both felt vaguely that if any food or drink were offered at such a hostelry, it would be the paste-board ham and empty mug of the pantomime.

In this, however, they were not altogether confirmed. As they drew nearer and nearer to the place they saw in front of the buffet, which was apparently closed, one of the iron garden-seats with curly backs that had adorned the gardens, but much longer, running almost the whole length of the frontage. Presumably, it was placed so that visitors might sit there and look at the sea, but one hardly expected to find anyone doing it in such weather.

Nevertheless, just in front of the extreme end of the iron seat stood a small round restaurant table, and on this stood a small bottle of Chablis and a plate of almonds and raisins. Behind the table and on the seat sat a dark-haired young man, bareheaded, and gazing at the sea in a state of almost astonishing immobility.

But though he might have been a waxwork when they were within four yards of him, he jumped up like a jack-in-the-box when they came within three, and said in a deferential, though not undignified, manner: "Will you step inside, gentlemen? I have no staff at present, but I can get you anything simple myself."

"Much obliged," said Flambeau. "So you are the proprietor?"

"Yes," said the dark man, dropping back a little into his motionless manner. "My waiters are all Italians, you see, and I thought it only fair they should see their countryman beat the black, if he really can do it. You know the great fight between Malvoli and Nigger Ned is coming off after all?"

"I'm afraid we can't wait to trouble your hospitality seriously," said Father Brown. "But my friend would be glad of a glass of sherry, I'm sure, to keep out the cold and drink success to the Latin champion."

Flambeau did not understand the sherry, but he did not object to it in the least. He could only say amiably: "Oh, thank you very much."

"Sherry, sir—certainly," said their host, turning to his hostel. "Excuse me if I detain you a few minutes. As I told you, I have no staff—" And he went towards the black windows of his shuttered and unlighted inn.

"Oh, it doesn't really matter," began Flambeau, but the man turned to reassure him.

"I have the keys," he said. "I could find my way in the dark."

"I didn't mean—" began Father Brown.

He was interrupted by a bellowing human voice that came out of the bowels of the uninhabited hotel. It thundered some foreign name loudly but inaudibly, and the hotel proprietor moved more sharply towards it than he had done for Flambeau's sherry. As instant evidence proved, the proprietor had told, then and after, nothing but the literal truth. But both Flambeau and Father Brown have often confessed that, in all their (often outrageous) adventures, nothing had so chilled their blood as that voice of an ogre, sounding suddenly out of a silent and empty inn.

"My cook!" cried the proprietor hastily. "I had forgotten my cook. He will be starting presently. Sherry, sir?"

And, sure enough, there appeared in the doorway a big white bulk with white cap and white apron, as befits a cook, but with the needless emphasis of a black face. Flambeau had often heard that negroes made good cooks. But somehow something in the contrast of colour and caste increased his surprise that the hotel proprietor should answer the call of the cook, and not the cook the call of the proprietor. But he reflected that head cooks are proverbially arrogant; and, besides, the host had come back with the sherry, and that was the great thing.

"I rather wonder," said Father Brown, "that there are so few people about the beach, when this big fight is coming on after all. We only met one man for miles."

The hotel proprietor shrugged his shoulders. "They come from the other end of the town, you see—from the station, three miles from here. They are only interested in the sport, and will stop in hotels for the night only. After all, it is hardly weather for basking on the shore."

"Or on the seat," said Flambeau, and pointed to the little table.

"I have to keep a look-out," said the man with the motionless face. He was a quiet, well-featured fellow, rather sallow; his dark clothes had nothing distinctive about them, except that his black necktie was worn rather high, like a stock, and secured by a gold pin with some grotesque head to it. Nor was there anything notable in the face, except something that was probably a mere nervous trick—a habit of opening one eye more narrowly than the other, giving the impression that the other was larger, or was, perhaps, artificial.

The silence that ensued was broken by their host saying quietly: "Whereabouts did you meet the one man on your march?"

"Curiously enough," answered the priest, "close by here—just by that band-stand."

Flambeau, who had sat on the long iron seat to finish his sherry, put it down and rose to his feet, staring at his friend in amazement. He opened his mouth to speak, and then shut it again.

"Curious," said the dark-haired man thoughtfully. "What was he like?"

"It was rather dark when I saw him," began Father Brown, "but he was—"

As has been said, the hotel-keeper can be proved to have told the precise truth. His phrase that the cook was starting presently was fulfilled to the letter, for the cook came out, pulling his gloves on, even as they spoke.

But he was a very different figure from the confused mass of white and black that had appeared for an instant in the doorway. He was buttoned and buckled up to his bursting eyeballs in the most brilliant fashion. A tall black hat was tilted on his broad black head—a hat of the sort that the French wit has compared to eight mirrors. But somehow the black man was like the black hat. He also was black, and yet his glossy skin flung back the light at eight angles or more. It is needless to say that he wore white spats and a white slip inside his waistcoat. The red flower stood up in his buttonhole aggressively, as if it had suddenly grown there. And in the way he carried his cane in one hand and his cigar in the other there was a certain attitude— an attitude we must always remember when we talk of racial prejudices: something innocent and insolent—the cake walk.

"Sometimes," said Flambeau, looking after him, "I'm not surprised that they lynch them."

"I am never surprised," said Father Brown, "at any work of hell. But as I was saying," he resumed, as the negro, still ostentatiously pulling on his yellow gloves, betook himself briskly towards the watering-place, a queer music-hall figure against that grey and frosty scene—"as I was saying, I couldn't describe the man very minutely, but he had a flourish and old-fashioned whiskers and moustachios, dark or dyed, as in the pictures of foreign financiers, round his neck was wrapped a long purple scarf that thrashed out in the wind as he walked. It was fixed at the throat rather in the way that nurses fix children's comforters with a safety-pin. Only this," added the priest, gazing placidly out to sea, "was not a safety-pin."

The man sitting on the long iron bench was also gazing placidly out to sea. Now he was once more in repose. Flambeau felt quite certain that one of his eyes was naturally larger than the other. Both were now well opened, and he could almost fancy the left eye grew larger as he gazed.

"It was a very long gold pin, and had the carved head of a monkey or some such thing," continued the cleric; "and it was fixed in a rather odd way—he wore pince-nez and a broad black—"

The motionless man continued to gaze at the sea, and the eyes in his head might have belonged to two different men. Then he made a movement of blinding swiftness.

Father Brown had his back to him, and in that flash might have fallen dead on his face. Flambeau had no weapon, but his large brown hands were resting on the end of the long iron seat. His shoulders abruptly altered their shape, and he heaved the whole huge thing high over his head, like a headsman's axe about to fall. The mere height of the thing, as he held it vertical, looked like a long iron ladder by which he was inviting men to climb towards the stars. But the long shadow, in the level evening light, looked like a giant brandishing the Eiffel Tower. It was the shock of that shadow, before the shock of the iron crash, that made the stranger quail and dodge, and then dart into his inn, leaving the flat and shining dagger he had dropped exactly where it had fallen.

"We must get away from here instantly," cried Flambeau, flinging the huge seat away with furious indifference on the beach. He caught the little priest by the elbow and ran him down a grey perspective of barren back garden, at the end of which there was a closed back garden door. Flambeau bent over it an instant in violent silence, and then said: "The door is locked."

As he spoke a black feather from one of the ornamental firs fell, brushing the brim of his hat. It startled him more than the small and distant detonation that had come just before. Then came another distant detonation, and the door he was trying to open shook under the bullet buried in it. Flambeau's shoulders again filled out and altered suddenly. Three hinges and a lock burst at the same instant, and he went out into the empty path behind, carrying the great garden door with him, as Samson carried the gates of Gaza.

Then he flung the garden door over the garden wall, just as a third shot picked up a spurt of snow and dust behind his heel. Without ceremony he snatched up the little priest, slung him astraddle on his shoulders, and went racing towards Seawood as fast as his long legs could carry him. It was not until nearly two miles farther on that he set his small companion down. It had hardly been a dignified escape, in spite of the classic model of Anchises, but Father Brown's face only wore a broad grin.

"Well," said Flambeau, after an impatient silence, as they resumed their more conventional tramp through the streets on the edge of the town, where no outrage need be feared, "I don't know what all this means, but I take it I may trust my own eyes that you never met the man you have so accurately described."

"I did meet him in a way," Brown said, biting his finger rather nervously—"I did really. And it was too dark to see him properly, because it was under that band-stand affair. But I'm afraid I didn't describe him so very accurately after all, for his pince-nez was broken under him, and the long gold pin wasn't stuck through his purple scarf but through his heart."

"And I suppose," said the other in a lower voice, "that glass-eyed guy had something to do with it."

"I had hoped he had only a little," answered Brown in a rather troubled voice, "and I may have been wrong in what I did. I acted on impulse. But I fear this business has deep roots and dark."

They walked on through some streets in silence. The yellow lamps were beginning to be lit in the cold blue twilight, and they were evidently approaching the more central parts of the town. Highly coloured bills announcing the glove-fight between Nigger Ned and Malvoli were slapped about the walls.

"Well," said Flambeau, "I never murdered anyone, even in my criminal days, but I can almost sympathize with anyone doing it in such a dreary place. Of all God-forsaken dustbins of Nature, I think the most heart-breaking are places like that bandstand, that were meant to be festive and are forlorn. I can fancy a morbid man feeling he must kill his rival in the solitude and irony of such a scene. I remember once taking a tramp in your glorious Surrey hills, thinking of nothing but gorse and skylarks, when I came out on a vast circle of land, and over me lifted a vast, voiceless structure, tier above tier of seats, as huge as a Roman amphitheatre and as empty as a new letter-rack. A bird sailed in heaven over it. It was the Grand Stand at Epsom. And I felt that no one would ever be happy there again."

"It's odd you should mention Epsom," said the priest. "Do you remember what was called the Sutton Mystery, because two suspected men—ice-cream men, I think—happened to live at Sutton? They were eventually released. A man was found strangled, it was said, on the Downs round that part. As a fact, I know (from an Irish policeman who is a friend of mine) that he was found close up to the Epsom Grand Stand—in fact, only hidden by one of the lower doors being pushed back."

"That is queer," assented Flambeau. "But it rather confirms my view that such pleasure places look awfully lonely out of season, or the man wouldn't have been murdered there."

"I'm not so sure he—" began Brown, and stopped.

"Not so sure he was murdered?" queried his companion.

"Not so sure he was murdered out of the season," answered the little priest, with simplicity. "Don't you think there's something rather tricky about this solitude, Flambeau? Do you feel sure a wise murderer would always want the spot to be lonely? It's very, very seldom a man is quite alone. And, short of that, the more alone he is, the more certain he is to be seen. No; I think there must be some other—Why, here we are at the Pavilion or Palace, or whatever they call it."

They had emerged on a small square, brilliantly lighted, of which the principal building was gay with gilding, gaudy with posters, and flanked with two giant photographs of Malvoli and Nigger Ned.

"Hallo!" cried Flambeau in great surprise, as his clerical friend stumped straight up the broad steps. "I didn't know pugilism was your latest hobby. Are you going to see the fight?"

"I don't think there will be any fight," replied Father Brown.

They passed rapidly through ante-rooms and inner rooms; they passed through the hall of combat itself, raised, roped, and padded with innumerable seats and boxes, and still the cleric did not look round or pause till he came to a clerk at a desk outside a door marked "Committee". There he stopped and asked to see Lord Pooley.

The attendant observed that his lordship was very busy, as the fight was coming on soon, but Father Brown had a good-tempered tedium of reiteration for which the official mind is generally not prepared. In a few moments the rather baffled Flambeau found himself in the presence of a man who was still shouting directions to another man going out of the room. "Be careful, you know, about the ropes after the fourth—Well, and what do you want, I wonder!"

Lord Pooley was a gentleman, and, like most of the few remaining to our race, was worried—especially about money. He was half grey and half flaxen, and he had the eyes of fever and a high-bridged, frost-bitten nose.

"Only a word," said Father Brown. "I have come to prevent a man being killed."

Lord Pooley bounded off his chair as if a spring had flung him from it. "I'm damned if I'll stand any more of this!" he cried. "You and your committees and parsons and petitions! Weren't there parsons in the old days, when they fought without gloves? Now they're fighting with the regulation gloves, and there's not the rag of a possibility of either of the boxers being killed."

"I didn't mean either of the boxers," said the little priest.

"Well, well, well!" said the nobleman, with a touch of frosty humour. "Who's going to be killed? The referee?"

"I don't know who's going to be killed," replied Father Brown, with a reflective stare. "If I did I shouldn't have to spoil your pleasure. I could simply get him to escape. I never could see anything wrong about prize-fights. As it is, I must ask you to announce that the fight is off for the present."

"Anything else?" jeered the gentleman with feverish eyes. "And what do you say to the two thousand people who have come to see it?"

"I say there will be one thousand nine-hundred and ninety-nine of them left alive when they have seen it," said Father Brown.

Lord Pooley looked at Flambeau. "Is your friend mad?" he asked.

"Far from it," was the reply.

"And look here," resumed Pooley in his restless way, "it's worse than that. A whole pack of Italians have turned up to back Malvoli—swarthy, savage fellows of some country, anyhow. You know what these Mediterranean races are like. If I send out word that it's off we shall have Malvoli storming in here at the head of a whole Corsican clan."

"My lord, it is a matter of life and death," said the priest. "Ring your bell. Give your message. And see whether it is Malvoli who answers."

The nobleman struck the bell on the table with an odd air of new curiosity. He said to the clerk who appeared almost instantly in the doorway: "I have a serious announcement to make to the audience shortly. Meanwhile, would you kindly tell the two champions that the fight will have to be put off."

The clerk stared for some seconds as if at a demon and vanished.

"What authority have you for what you say?" asked Lord Pooley abruptly. "Whom did you consult?"

"I consulted a bandstand," said Father Brown, scratching his head. "But, no, I'm wrong; I consulted a book, too. I picked it up on a bookstall in London—very cheap, too."

He had taken out of his pocket a small, stout, leather-bound volume, and Flambeau, looking over his shoulder, could see that it was some book of old travels, and had a leaf turned down for reference.

"'The only form in which Voodoo—'" began Father Brown, reading aloud.

"In which what?" inquired his lordship.

"'In which Voodoo,'" repeated the reader, almost with relish, "'is widely organized outside Jamaica itself is in the form known as the Monkey, or the God of the Gongs, which is powerful in many parts of the two American continents, especially among half-breeds, many of whom look exactly like white men. It differs from most other forms of devil-worship and human sacrifice in the fact that the blood is not shed formally on the altar, but by a sort of assassination among the crowd. The gongs beat with a deafening din as the doors of the shrine open and the monkey-god is revealed; almost the whole congregation rivet ecstatic eyes on him. But after—'"

The door of the room was flung open, and the fashionable negro stood framed in it, his eyeballs rolling, his silk hat still insolently tilted on his head. "Huh!" he cried, showing his apish teeth. "What this? Huh! Huh! You steal a coloured gentleman's prize—prize his already—yo' think yo' jes' save that white 'Talian trash—"

"The matter is only deferred," said the nobleman quietly. "I will be with you to explain in a minute or two."

"Who you to—" shouted Nigger Ned, beginning to storm.

"My name is Pooley," replied the other, with a creditable coolness. "I am the organizing secretary, and I advise you just now to leave the room."

"Who this fellow?" demanded the dark champion, pointing to the priest disdainfully.

"My name is Brown," was the reply. "And I advise you just now to leave the country."

The prize-fighter stood glaring for a few seconds, and then, rather to the surprise of Flambeau and the others, strode out, sending the door to with a crash behind him.

"Well," asked Father Brown rubbing his dusty hair up, "what do you think of Leonardo da Vinci? A beautiful Italian head."

"Look here," said Lord Pooley, "I've taken a considerable responsibility, on your bare word. I think you ought to tell me more about this."

"You are quite right, my lord," answered Brown. "And it won't take long to tell." He put the little leather book in his overcoat pocket. "I think we know all that this can tell us, but you shall look at it to see if I'm right. That negro who has just swaggered out is one of the most dangerous men on earth, for he has the brains of a European, with the instincts of a cannibal. He has turned what was clean, common-sense butchery among his fellow-barbarians into a very modern and scientific secret society of assassins. He doesn't know I know it, nor, for the matter of that, that I can't prove it."

There was a silence, and the little man went on.

"But if I want to murder somebody, will it really be the best plan to make sure I'm alone with him?"

Lord Pooley's eyes recovered their frosty twinkle as he looked at the little clergyman. He only said: "If you want to murder somebody, I should advise it."

Father Brown shook his head, like a murderer of much riper experience. "So Flambeau said," he replied, with a sigh. "But consider. The more a man feels lonely the less he can be sure he is alone. It must mean empty spaces round him, and they are just what make him obvious. Have you never seen one ploughman from the heights, or one shepherd from the valleys? Have you never walked along a cliff, and seen one man walking along the sands? Didn't you know when he's killed a crab, and wouldn't you have known if it had been a creditor? No! No! No! For an intelligent murderer, such as you or I might be, it is an impossible plan to make sure that nobody is looking at you."

"But what other plan is there?"

"There is only one," said the priest. "To make sure that everybody is looking at something else. A man is throttled close by the big stand at Epsom. Anybody might have seen it done while the stand stood empty—any tramp under the hedges or motorist among the hills. But nobody would have seen it when the stand was crowded and the whole ring roaring, when the favourite was coming in first—or wasn't. The twisting of a neck-cloth, the thrusting of a body behind a door could be done in an instant—so long as it was that instant. It was the same, of course," he continued turning to Flambeau, "with that poor fellow under the bandstand. He was dropped through the hole (it wasn't an accidental hole) just at some very dramatic moment of the entertainment, when the bow of some great violinist or the voice of some great singer opened or came to its climax. And here, of course, when the knock-out blow came—it would not be the only one. That is the little trick Nigger Ned has adopted from his old God of Gongs."

"By the way, Malvoli—" Pooley began.

"Malvoli," said the priest, "has nothing to do with it. I dare say he has some Italians with him, but our amiable friends are not Italians. They are octoroons and African half-bloods of various shades, but I fear we English think all foreigners are much the same so long as they are dark and dirty. Also," he added, with a smile, "I fear the English decline to draw any fine distinction between the moral character produced by my religion and that which blooms out of Voodoo."

The blaze of the spring season had burst upon Seawood, littering its foreshore with famines and bathing-machines, with nomadic preachers and nigger minstrels, before the two friends saw it again, and long before the storm of pursuit after the strange secret society had died away. Almost on every hand the secret of their purpose perished with them. The man of the hotel was found drifting dead on the sea like so much seaweed; his right eye was closed in peace, but his left eye was wide open, and glistened like glass in the moon. Nigger Ned had been overtaken a mile or two away, and murdered three policemen with his closed left hand. The remaining officer was surprised—nay, pained—and the negro got away. But this was enough to set all the English papers in a flame, and for a month or two the main purpose of the British Empire was to prevent the buck nigger (who was so in both senses) escaping by any English port. Persons of a figure remotely reconcilable with his were subjected to quite extraordinary inquisitions, made to scrub their faces before going on board ship, as if each white complexion were made up like a mask, of greasepaint. Every negro in England was put under special regulations and made to report himself; the outgoing ships would no more have taken a nigger than a basilisk. For people had found out how fearful and vast and silent was the force of the savage secret society, and by the time Flambeau and Father Brown were leaning on the parade parapet in April, the Black Man meant in England almost what he once meant in Scotland.

"He must be still in England," observed Flambeau, "and horridly well hidden, too. They must have found him at the ports if he had only whitened his face."

"You see, he is really a clever man," said Father Brown apologetically. "And I'm sure he wouldn't whiten his face."

"Well, but what would he do?"

"I think," said Father Brown, "he would blacken his face."

Flambeau, leaning motionless on the parapet, laughed and said: "My dear fellow!"

Father Brown, also leaning motionless on the parapet, moved one finger for an instant into the direction of the soot-masked niggers singing on the sands.

The Salad of Colonel Cray

FATHER BROWN was walking home from Mass on a white weird morning when the mists were slowly lifting—one of those mornings when the very element of light appears as something mysterious and new. The scattered trees outlined themselves more and more out of the vapour, as if they were first drawn in grey chalk and then in charcoal. At yet more distant intervals appeared the houses upon the broken fringe of the suburb; their outlines became clearer and clearer until he recognized many in which he had chance acquaintances, and many more the names of whose owners he knew. But all the windows and doors were sealed; none of the people were of the sort that would be up at such a time, or still less on such an errand. But as he passed under the shadow of one handsome villa with verandas and wide ornate gardens, he heard a noise that made him almost involuntarily stop. It was the unmistakable noise of a pistol or carbine or some light firearm discharged; but it was not this that puzzled him most. The first full noise was immediately followed by a series of fainter noises—as he counted them, about six. He supposed it must be the echo; but the odd thing was that the echo was not in the least like the original sound. It was not like anything else that he could think of; the three things nearest to it seemed to be the noise made by siphons of soda-water, one of the many noises made by an animal, and the noise made by a person attempting to conceal laughter. None of which seemed to make much sense.

Father Brown was made of two men. There was a man of action, who was as modest as a primrose and as punctual as a clock; who went his small round of duties and never dreamed of altering it. There was also a man of reflection, who was much simpler but much stronger, who could not easily be stopped; whose thought was always (in the only intelligent sense of the words) free thought. He could not help, even unconsciously, asking himself all the questions that there were to be asked, and answering as many of them as he could; all that went on like his breathing or circulation. But he never consciously carried his actions outside the sphere of his own duty; and in this case the two attitudes were aptly tested. He was just about to resume his trudge in the twilight, telling himself it was no affair of his, but instinctively twisting and untwisting twenty theories about what the odd noises might mean. Then the grey sky-line brightened into silver, and in the broadening light he realized that he had been to the house which belonged to an Anglo-Indian Major named Putnam; and that the Major had a native cook from Malta who was of his communion. He also began to remember that pistol-shots are sometimes serious things; accompanied with consequences with which he was legitimately concerned. He turned back and went in at the garden gate, making for the front door.

Half-way down one side of the house stood out a projection like a very low shed; it was, as he afterwards discovered, a large dustbin. Round the corner of this came a figure, at first a mere shadow in the haze, apparently bending and peering about. Then, coming nearer, it solidified into a figure that was, indeed, rather unusually solid. Major Putnam was a bald-headed, bull-necked man, short and very broad, with one of those rather apoplectic faces that are produced by a prolonged attempt to combine the oriental climate with the occidental luxuries. But the face was a good-humoured one, and even now, though evidently puzzled and inquisitive, wore a kind of innocent grin. He had a large palm-leaf hat on the back of his head (suggesting a halo that was by no means appropriate to the face), but otherwise he was clad only in a very vivid suit of striped scarlet and yellow pyjamas; which, though glowing enough to behold, must have been, on a fresh morning, pretty chilly to wear. He had evidently come out of his house in a hurry, and the priest was not surprised when he called out without further ceremony: "Did you hear that noise?"

"Yes," answered Father Brown; "I thought I had better look in, in case anything was the matter."

The Major looked at him rather queerly with his good-humoured gooseberry eyes. "What do you think the noise was?" he asked.

"It sounded like a gun or something," replied the other, with some hesitation; "but it seemed to have a singular sort of echo."

The Major was still looking at him quietly, but with protruding eyes, when the front door was flung open, releasing a flood of gaslight on the face of the fading mist; and another figure in pyjamas sprang or tumbled out into the garden. The figure was much longer, leaner, and more athletic; the pyjamas, though equally tropical, were comparatively tasteful, being of white with a light lemon-yellow stripe. The man was haggard, but handsome, more sunburned than the other; he had an aquiline profile and rather deep-sunken eyes, and a slight air of oddity arising from the combination of coal-black hair with a much lighter moustache. All this Father Brown absorbed in detail more at leisure. For the moment he only saw one thing about the man; which was the revolver in his hand.

"Cray!" exclaimed the Major, staring at him; "did you fire that shot?"

"Yes, I did," retorted the black-haired gentleman hotly; "and so would you in my place. If you were chased everywhere by devils and nearly—"

The Major seemed to intervene rather hurriedly. "This is my friend Father Brown," he said. And then to Brown: "I don't know whether you've met Colonel Cray of the Royal Artillery."

"I have heard of him, of course," said the priest innocently. "Did you—did you hit anything?"

"I thought so," answered Cray with gravity.

"Did he—" asked Major Putnam in a lowered voice, "did he fall or cry out, or anything?"

Colonel Cray was regarding his host with a strange and steady stare. "I'll tell you exactly what he did," he said. "He sneezed."

Father Brown's hand went half-way to his head, with the gesture of a man remembering somebody's name. He knew now what it was that was neither soda-water nor the snorting of a dog.

"Well," ejaculated the staring Major, "I never heard before that a service revolver was a thing to be sneezed at."

"Nor I," said Father Brown faintly. "It's lucky you didn't turn your artillery on him or you might have given him quite a bad cold." Then, after a bewildered pause, he said: "Was it a burglar?"

"Let us go inside," said Major Putnam, rather sharply, and led the way into his house.

The interior exhibited a paradox often to be marked in such morning hours: that the rooms seemed brighter than the sky outside; even after the Major had turned out the one gaslight in the front hall. Father Brown was surprised to see the whole dining-table set out as for a festive meal, with napkins in their rings, and wine-glasses of some six unnecessary shapes set beside every plate. It was common enough, at that time of the morning, to find the remains of a banquet over-night; but to find it freshly spread so early was unusual.

While he stood wavering in the hall Major Putnam rushed past him and sent a raging eye over the whole oblong of the tablecloth. At last he spoke, spluttering: "All the silver gone!" he gasped. "Fish-knives and forks gone. Old cruet-stand gone. Even the old silver cream-jug gone. And now, Father Brown, I am ready to answer your question of whether it was a burglar."

"They're simply a blind," said Cray stubbornly. "I know better than you why people persecute this house; I know better than you why—"

The Major patted him on the shoulder with a gesture almost peculiar to the soothing of a sick child, and said: "It was a burglar. Obviously it was a burglar."

"A burglar with a bad cold," observed Father Brown, "that might assist you to trace him in the neighbourhood."

The Major shook his head in a sombre manner. "He must be far beyond trace now, I fear," he said.

Then, as the restless man with the revolver turned again towards the door in the garden, he added in a husky, confidential voice: "I doubt whether I should send for the police, for fear my friend here has been a little too free with his bullets, and got on the wrong side of the law. He's lived in very wild places; and, to be frank with you, I think he sometimes fancies things."

"I think you once told me," said Brown, "that he believes some Indian secret society is pursuing him."

Major Putnam nodded, but at the same time shrugged his shoulders. "I suppose we'd better follow him outside," he said. "I don't want any more—shall we say, sneezing?"

They passed out into the morning light, which was now even tinged with sunshine, and saw Colonel Cray's tall figure bent almost double, minutely examining the condition of gravel and grass. While the Major strolled unobtrusively towards him, the priest took an equally indolent turn, which took him round the next corner of the house to within a yard or two of the projecting dustbin.

He stood regarding this dismal object for some minute and a half—, then he stepped towards it, lifted the lid and put his head inside. Dust and other discolouring matter shook upwards as he did so; but Father Brown never observed his own appearance, whatever else he observed. He remained thus for a measurable period, as if engaged in some mysterious prayers. Then he came out again, with some ashes on his hair, and walked unconcernedly away.

By the time he came round to the garden door again he found a group there which seemed to roll away morbidities as the sunlight had already rolled away the mists. It was in no way rationally reassuring; it was simply broadly comic, like a cluster of Dickens's characters. Major Putnam had managed to slip inside and plunge into a proper shirt and trousers, with a crimson cummerbund, and a light square jacket over all; thus normally set off, his red festive face seemed bursting with a commonplace cordiality. He was indeed emphatic, but then he was talking to his cook—the swarthy son of Malta, whose lean, yellow and rather careworn face contrasted quaintly with his snow-white cap and costume. The cook might well be careworn, for cookery was the Major's hobby. He was one of those amateurs who always know more than the professional. The only other person he even admitted to be a judge of an omelette was his friend Cray—and as Brown remembered this, he turned to look for the other officer. In the new presence of daylight and people clothed and in their right mind, the sight of him was rather a shock. The taller and more elegant man was still in his night-garb, with tousled black hair, and now crawling about the garden on his hands and knees, still looking for traces of the burglar; and now and again, to all appearance, striking the ground with his hand in anger at not finding him. Seeing him thus quadrupedal in the grass, the priest raised his eyebrows rather sadly; and for the first time guessed that "fancies things" might be an euphemism.

The third item in the group of the cook and the epicure was also known to Father Brown; it was Audrey Watson, the Major's ward and housekeeper; and at this moment, to judge by her apron, tucked-up sleeves and resolute manner, much more the housekeeper than the ward.

"It serves you right," she was saying: "I always told you not to have that old-fashioned cruet-stand."

"I prefer it," said Putnam, placably. "I'm old-fashioned myself; and the things keep together."

"And vanish together, as you see," she retorted. "Well, if you are not going to bother about the burglar, I shouldn't bother about the lunch. It's Sunday, and we can't send for vinegar and all that in the town; and you Indian gentlemen can't enjoy what you call a dinner without a lot of hot things. I wish to goodness now you hadn't asked Cousin Oliver to take me to the musical service. It isn't over till half-past twelve, and the Colonel has to leave by then. I don't believe you men can manage alone."

"Oh yes, we can, my dear," said the Major, looking at her very amiably. "Marco has all the sauces, and we've often done ourselves well in very rough places, as you might know by now. And it's time you had a treat, Audrey; you mustn't be a housekeeper every hour of the day; and I know you want to hear the music."

"I want to go to church," she said, with rather severe eyes.

She was one of those handsome women who will always be handsome, because the beauty is not in an air or a tint, but in the very structure of the head and features. But though she was not yet middle-aged and her auburn hair was of a Titianesque fullness in form and colour, there was a look in her mouth and around her eyes which suggested that some sorrows wasted her, as winds waste at last the edges of a Greek temple. For indeed the little domestic difficulty of which she was now speaking so decisively was rather comic than tragic. Father Brown gathered, from the course of the conversation, that Cray, the other gourmet, had to leave before the usual lunch-time; but that Putnam, his host, not to be done out of a final feast with an old crony, had arranged for a special dejeuner to be set out and consumed in the course of the morning, while Audrey and other graver persons were at morning service. She was going there under the escort of a relative and old friend of hers, Dr Oliver Oman, who, though a scientific man of a somewhat bitter type, was enthusiastic for music, and would go even to church to get it. There was nothing in all this that could conceivably concern the tragedy in Miss Watson's face; and by a half conscious instinct, Father Brown turned again to the seeming lunatic grubbing about in the grass.

When he strolled across to him, the black, unbrushed head was lifted abruptly, as if in some surprise at his continued presence. And indeed, Father Brown, for reasons best known to himself, had lingered much longer than politeness required; or even, in the ordinary sense, permitted.

"Well!" cried Cray, with wild eyes. "I suppose you think I'm mad, like the rest?"

"I have considered the thesis," answered the little man, composedly. "And I incline to think you are not."

"What do you mean?" snapped Cray quite savagely.

"Real madmen," explained Father Brown, "always encourage their own morbidity. They never strive against it. But you are trying to find traces of the burglar; even when there aren't any. You are struggling against it. You want what no madman ever wants."

"And what is that?"

"You want to be proved wrong," said Brown.

During the last words Cray had sprung or staggered to his feet and was regarding the cleric with agitated eyes. "By hell, but that is a true word!" he cried. "They are all at me here that the fellow was only after the silver—as if I shouldn't be only too pleased to think so! She's been at me," and he tossed his tousled black head towards Audrey, but the other had no need of the direction, "she's been at me today about how cruel I was to shoot a poor harmless house-breaker, and how I have the devil in me against poor harmless natives. But I was a good-natured man once—as good-natured as Putnam."

After a pause he said: "Look here, I've never seen you before; but you shall judge of the whole story. Old Putnam and I were friends in the same mess; but, owing to some accidents on the Afghan border, I got my command much sooner than most men; only we were both invalided home for a bit. I was engaged to Audrey out there; and we all travelled back together. But on the journey back things happened. Curious things. The result of them was that Putnam wants it broken off, and even Audrey keeps it hanging on—and I know what they mean. I know what they think I am. So do you.

"Well, these are the facts. The last day we were in an Indian city I asked Putnam if I could get some Trichinopoli cigars, he directed me to a little place opposite his lodgings. I have since found he was quite right; but 'opposite' is a dangerous word when one decent house stands opposite five or six squalid ones; and I must have mistaken the door. It opened with difficulty, and then only on darkness; but as I turned back, the door behind me sank back and settled into its place with a noise as of innumerable bolts. There was nothing to do but to walk forward; which I did through passage after passage, pitch-dark. Then I came to a flight of steps, and then to a blind door, secured by a latch of elaborate Eastern ironwork, which I could only trace by touch, but which I loosened at last. I came out again upon gloom, which was half turned into a greenish twilight by a multitude of small but steady lamps below. They showed merely the feet or fringes of some huge and empty architec-

242

ture. Just in front of me was something that looked like a mountain. I confess I nearly fell on the great stone platform on which I had emerged, to realize that it was an idol. And worst of all, an idol with its back to me.

"It was hardly half human, I guessed; to judge by the small squat head, and still more by a thing like a tail or extra limb turned up behind and pointing, like a loathsome large finger, at some symbol graven in the centre of the vast stone back. I had begun, in the dim light, to guess at the hieroglyphic, not without horror, when a more horrible thing happened. A door opened silently in the temple wall behind me and a man came out, with a brown face and a black coat. He had a carved smile on his face, of copper flesh and ivory teeth; but I think the most hateful thing about him was that he was in European dress. I was prepared, I think, for shrouded priests or naked fakirs. But this seemed to say that the devilry was over all the earth. As indeed I found it to be.

"'If you had only seen the Monkey's Feet,' he said, smiling steadily, and without other preface, 'we should have been very gentle—you would only be tortured and die. If you had seen the Monkey's Face, still we should be very moderate, very tolerant—you would only be tortured and live. But as you have seen the Monkey's Tail, we must pronounce the worst sentence, which is—Go Free.'

"When he said the words I heard the elaborate iron latch with which I had struggled, automatically unlock itself: and then, far down the dark passages I had passed, I heard the heavy street-door shifting its own bolts backwards.

"'It is vain to ask for mercy; you must go free,' said the smiling man. 'Henceforth a hair shall slay you like a sword, and a breath shall bite you like an adder; weapons shall come against you out of nowhere; and you shall die many times.' And with that he was swallowed once more in the wall behind; and I went out into the street."

Cray paused; and Father Brown unaffectedly sat down on the lawn and began to pick daisies.

Then the soldier continued: "Putnam, of course, with his jolly common sense, pooh-poohed all my fears; and from that time dates his doubt of my mental balance. Well, I'll simply tell you, in the fewest words, the three things that have happened since; and you shall judge which of us is right.

"The first happened in an Indian village on the edge of the jungle, but hundreds of miles from the temple, or town, or type of tribes and customs where the curse had been put on me. I woke in black midnight, and lay thinking of nothing in particular, when I felt a faint tickling thing, like a thread or a hair, trailed across my throat. I shrank back out of its way, and could not help thinking of the words in the temple. But when I got up and sought lights and a mirror, the line across my neck was a line of blood.

"The second happened in a lodging in Port Said, later, on our journey home together. It was a jumble of tavern and curiosity-shop; and though there was nothing there remotely suggesting the cult of the Monkey, it is, of course, possible that some of its images or talismans were in such a place. Its curse was there, anyhow. I woke again in the dark with a sensation that could not be put in colder or more literal words than that a breath bit like an adder. Existence was an agony of extinction; I dashed my head against walls until I dashed it against a window; and fell rather than jumped into the garden below. Putnam, poor fellow, who had called the other thing a chance scratch, was bound to take seriously the fact of finding me half insensible on the grass at dawn. But I fear it was my mental state he took seriously; and not my story.

"The third happened in Malta. We were in a fortress there; and as it happened our bedrooms overlooked the open sea, which almost came up to our window-sills, save for a flat white outer wall as bare as the sea. I woke up again; but it was not dark. There was a full moon, as I walked to the window; I could have seen a bird on the bare battlement, or a sail on the horizon. What I did see was a sort of stick or branch circling, self-supported, in the empty sky. It flew straight in at my window and smashed the lamp beside the pillow I had just quitted. It was one of those queer-shaped war-clubs some Eastern tribes use. But it had come from no human hand."

Father Brown threw away a daisy-chain he was making, and rose with a wistful look. "Has Major Putnam," he asked, "got any Eastern curios, idols, weapons and so on, from which one might get a hint?"

"Plenty of those, though not much use, I fear," replied Cray; "but by all means come into his study."

As they entered they passed Miss Watson buttoning her gloves for church, and heard the voice of Putnam downstairs still giving a lecture on cookery to the cook. In the Major's study and den of curios they came suddenly on a third party, silk-hatted and dressed for the street, who was poring over an open book on the smoking-table—a book which he dropped rather guiltily, and turned.

Cray introduced him civilly enough, as Dr Oman, but he showed such disfavour in his very face that Brown guessed the two men, whether Audrey knew it or not, were rivals. Nor was the priest wholly unsympathetic with the prejudice. Dr Oman was a very well-dressed gentleman indeed; well-featured, though almost dark enough for an Asiatic. But Father Brown had to tell himself sharply that one should be in charity even with those who wax their pointed beards, who have small gloved hands, and who speak with perfectly modulated voices.

Cray seemed to find something specially irritating in the small prayer-book in Oman's dark-gloved hand. "I didn't know that was in your line," he said rather rudely.

Oman laughed mildly, but without offence. "This is more so, I know," he said, laying his hand on the big book he had dropped, "a dictionary of drugs and such things. But it's rather too large to take to church." Then he closed the larger book, and there seemed again the faintest touch of hurry and embarrassment.

"I suppose," said the priest, who seemed anxious to change the subject, "all these spears and things are from India?"

"From everywhere," answered the doctor. "Putnam is an old soldier, and has been in Mexico and Australia, and the Cannibal Islands for all I know."

"I hope it was not in the Cannibal Islands," said Brown, "that he learnt the art of cookery." And he ran his eyes over the stew-pots or other strange utensils on the wall.

At this moment the jolly subject of their conversation thrust his laughing, lobsterish face into the room. "Come along, Cray," he cried. "Your lunch is just coming in. And the bells are ringing for those who want to go to church."

Cray slipped upstairs to change; Dr Oman and Miss Watson betook themselves solemnly down the street, with a string of other churchgoers; but Father Brown noticed that the doctor twice looked back and scrutinized the house; and even came back to the corner of the street to look at it again.

The priest looked puzzled. "He can't have been at the dustbin," he muttered. "Not in those clothes. Or was he there earlier today?"

Father Brown, touching other people, was as sensitive as a barometer; but today he seemed about as sensitive as a rhinoceros. By no social law, rigid or implied, could he be supposed to linger round the lunch of the Anglo-Indian friends; but he lingered, covering his position with torrents of amusing but quite needless conversation. He was the more puzzling because he did not seem to want any lunch. As one after another of the most exquisitely balanced kedgerees of curries, accompanied with their appropriate vintages, were laid before the other two, he only repeated that it was one of his fast-days, and munched a piece of bread and sipped and then left untasted a tumbler of cold water. His talk, however, was exuberant.

"I'll tell you what I'll do for you," he cried—, "I'll mix you a salad! I can't eat it, but I'll mix it like an angel! You've got a lettuce there."

"Unfortunately it's the only thing we have got," answered the good-humoured Major. "You must remember that mustard, vinegar, oil and so on vanished with the cruet and the burglar."

"I know," replied Brown, rather vaguely. "That's what I've always been afraid would happen. That's why I always carry a cruet-stand about with me. I'm so fond of salads."

And to the amazement of the two men he took a pepper-pot out of his waistcoat pocket and put it on the table.

"I wonder why the burglar wanted mustard, too," he went on, taking a mustard-pot from another pocket. "A mustard plaster, I suppose. And vinegar"—and producing that condiment—"haven't I heard something about vinegar and brown paper? As for oil, which I think I put in my left—"

His garrulity was an instant arrested; for lifting his eyes, he saw what no one else saw—the black figure of Dr Oman standing on the sunlit lawn and looking steadily into the room. Before he could quite recover himself Cray had cloven in.

"You're an astounding card," he said, staring. "I shall come and hear your sermons, if they're as amusing as your manners." His voice changed a little, and he leaned back in his chair.

"Oh, there are sermons in a cruet-stand, too," said Father Brown, quite gravely. "Have you heard of faith like a grain of mustard-seed; or charity that anoints with oil? And as for vinegar, can any soldiers forget that solitary soldier, who, when the sun was darkened—"

Colonel Cray leaned forward a little and clutched the tablecloth.

Father Brown, who was making the salad, tipped two spoonfuls of the mustard into the tumbler of water beside him; stood up and said in a new, loud and sudden voice—"Drink that!"

At the same moment the motionless doctor in the garden came running, and bursting open a window cried: "Am I wanted? Has he been poisoned?"

"Pretty near," said Brown, with the shadow of a smile; for the emetic had very suddenly taken effect. And Cray lay in a deck-chair, gasping as for life, but alive.

Major Putnam had sprung up, his purple face mottled. "A crime!" he cried hoarsely. "I will go for the police!"

The priest could hear him dragging down his palm-leaf hat from the peg and tumbling out of the front door; he heard the garden gate slam. But he only stood looking at Cray; and after a silence said quietly:

"I shall not talk to you much; but I will tell you what you want to know. There is no curse on you. The Temple of the Monkey was either a coincidence or a part of the trick; the trick was the trick of a white man. There is only one weapon that will bring blood with that mere feathery touch: a razor held by a white man. There is one way of making a common room full of invisible, overpowering poison: turning on the gas—the crime of a white man. And there is only one kind of club that can be thrown out of a window, turn in mid-air and come back to the window next to it: the Australian boomerang. You'll see some of them in the Major's study."

With that he went outside and spoke for a moment to the doctor. The moment after, Audrey Watson came rushing into the house and fell on her knees beside Cray's chair. He could not hear what they said to each other; but their faces moved with amazement, not unhappiness. The doctor and the priest walked slowly towards the garden gate.

"I suppose the Major was in love with her, too," he said with a sigh; and when the other nodded, observed: "You were very generous, doctor. You did a fine thing. But what made you suspect?"

"A very small thing," said Oman; "but it kept me restless in church till I came back to see that all was well. That book on his table was a work on poisons; and was put down open at the place where it stated that a certain Indian poison, though deadly and difficult to trace, was particularly easily reversible by the use of the commonest emetics. I suppose he read that at the last moment—"

"And remembered that there were emetics in the cruet-stand," said Father Brown. "Exactly. He threw the cruet in the dustbin—where I found it, along with other silver—for the sake of a burglary blind. But if you look at that pepper-pot I put on the table, you'll see a small hole. That's where Cray's bullet struck, shaking up the pepper and making the criminal sneeze."

There was a silence. Then Dr Oman said grimly: "The Major is a long time looking for the police."

"Or the police in looking for the Major?" said the priest. "Well, good-bye."

The Strange Crime of John Boulnois

MR CALHOUN KIDD was a very young gentleman with a very old face, a face dried up with its own eagerness, framed in blue-black hair and a black butterfly tie. He was the emissary in England of the colossal American daily called the Western Sun—also humorously described as the "Rising Sunset". This was in allusion to a great journalistic declaration (attributed to Mr Kidd himself) that "he guessed the sun would rise in the west yet, if American citizens did a bit more hustling." Those, however, who mock American journalism from the standpoint of somewhat mellower traditions forget a certain paradox which partly redeems it. For while the journalism of the States permits a pantomimic vulgarity long past anything English, it also shows a real excitement about the most earnest mental problems, of which English papers are innocent, or rather incapable. The Sun was full of the most solemn matters treated in the most farcical way. William James figured there as well as "Weary Willie," and pragmatists alternated with pugilists in the long procession of its portraits.

Thus, when a very unobtrusive Oxford man named John Boulnois wrote in a very unreadable review called the Natural Philosophy Quarterly a series of articles on alleged weak points in Darwinian evolution, it fluttered no corner of the English papers; though Boulnois's theory (which was that of a comparatively stationary universe visited occasionally by convulsions of change) had some rather faddy fashionableness at Oxford, and got so far as to be named "Catastrophism". But many American papers seized on the challenge as a great event; and the Sun threw the shadow of Mr Boulnois quite gigantically across its pages. By the paradox already noted, articles of valuable intelligence and enthusiasm were presented with headlines apparently written by an illiterate maniac, headlines such as "Darwin Chews Dirt; Critic Boulnois says He Jumps the Shocks"—or "Keep Catastrophic, says Thinker Boulnois." And Mr Calhoun Kidd, of the Western Sun, was bidden to take his butterfly tie and lugubrious visage down to the little house outside Oxford where Thinker Boulnois lived in happy ignorance of such a title.

That fated philosopher had consented, in a somewhat dazed manner, to receive the interviewer, and had named the hour of nine that evening. The last of a summer sunset clung about Cumnor and the low wooded hills; the romantic Yankee was both doubtful of his road and inquisitive about his surroundings; and seeing the door of a genuine feudal old-country inn, The Champion Arms, standing open, he went in to make inquiries.

In the bar parlour he rang the bell, and had to wait some little time for a reply to it. The only other person present was a lean man with close red hair and loose, horsey-looking clothes, who was drinking very bad whisky, but smoking a very good cigar. The whisky, of course, was the choice brand of The Champion Arms;

the cigar he had probably brought with him from London. Nothing could be more different than his cynical negligence from the dapper dryness of the young American; but something in his pencil and open notebook, and perhaps in the expression of his alert blue eye, caused Kidd to guess, correctly, that he was a brother journalist.

"Could you do me the favour," asked Kidd, with the courtesy of his nation, "of directing me to the Grey Cottage, where Mr Boulnois lives, as I understand?"

"It's a few yards down the road," said the red-haired man, removing his cigar; "I shall be passing it myself in a minute, but I'm going on to Pendragon Park to try and see the fun."

"What is Pendragon Park?" asked Calhoun Kidd.

"Sir Claude Champion's place—haven't you come down for that, too?" asked the other pressman, looking up. "You're a journalist, aren't you?"

"I have come to see Mr Boulnois," said Kidd.

"I've come to see Mrs Boulnois," replied the other. "But I shan't catch her at home." And he laughed rather unpleasantly.

"Are you interested in Catastrophism?" asked the wondering Yankee.

"I'm interested in catastrophes; and there are going to be some," replied his companion gloomily. "Mine's a filthy trade, and I never pretend it isn't."

With that he spat on the floor; yet somehow in the very act and instant one could realize that the man had been brought up as a gentleman.

The American pressman considered him with more attention. His face was pale and dissipated, with the promise of formidable passions yet to be loosed; but it was a clever and sensitive face; his clothes were coarse and careless, but he had a good seal ring on one of his long, thin fingers. His name, which came out in the course of talk, was James Dalroy; he was the son of a bankrupt Irish landlord, and attached to a pink paper which he heartily despised, called Smart Society, in the capacity of reporter and of something painfully like a spy.

Smart Society, I regret to say, felt none of that interest in Boulnois on Darwin which was such a credit to the head and hearts of the Western Sun. Dalroy had come down, it seemed, to snuff up the scent of a scandal which might very well end in the Divorce Court, but which was at present hovering between Grey Cottage and Pendragon Park.

Sir Claude Champion was known to the readers of the Western Sun as well as Mr Boulnois. So were the Pope and the Derby Winner; but the idea of their intimate acquaintanceship would have struck Kidd as equally incongruous. He had heard of (and written about, nay, falsely pretended to know) Sir Claude Champion, as "one of the brightest and wealthiest of England's Upper Ten"; as the great sportsman who raced yachts round the world; as the great traveller who wrote books about the Himalayas, as the politician who swept constituencies with a startling sort of Tory Democracy, and as the great dabbler in art, music, literature, and, above all, acting. Sir Claude was really rather magnificent in other than American eyes. There was something of the Renascence Prince about his omnivorous culture and restless publicity—, he was not only a great amateur, but an ardent one. There was in him none of that antiquarian frivolity that we convey by the word "dilettante".

That faultless falcon profile with purple-black Italian eye, which had been snap-shotted so often both for Smart Society and the Western Sun, gave everyone the impression of a man eaten by ambition as by a fire, or even a disease. But though Kidd knew a great deal about Sir Claude—a great deal more, in fact, than there was to know—it would never have crossed his wildest dreams to connect so showy an aristocrat with the newly-unearthed founder of Catastrophism, or to guess that Sir Claude Champion and John Boulnois could be intimate friends. Such, according to Dalroy's account, was nevertheless the fact. The two had hunted in couples at school and college, and, though their social destinies had been very different (for Champion was a great landlord and almost a millionaire, while Boulnois was a poor scholar and, until just lately, an unknown one), they still kept in very close touch with each other. Indeed, Boulnois's cottage stood just outside the gates of Pendragon Park.

But whether the two men could be friends much longer was becoming a dark and ugly question. A year or two before, Boulnois had married a beautiful and not unsuccessful actress, to whom he was devoted in his own shy and ponderous style; and the proximity of the household to Champion's had given that flighty celebrity opportunities for behaving in a way that could not but cause painful and rather base excitement. Sir Claude had carried the arts of publicity to perfection; and he seemed to take a crazy pleasure in being equally ostentatious in an intrigue that could do him no sort of honour. Footmen from Pendragon were perpetually leaving bouquets for Mrs Boulnois; carriages and motor-cars were perpetually calling at the cottage for Mrs Boulnois; balls and masquerades perpetually filled the grounds in which the baronet paraded Mrs Boulnois, like the Queen of Love and Beauty at a tournament. That very evening, marked by Mr Kidd for the exposition of Catastrophism, had been marked by Sir Claude Champion for an open-air rendering of Romeo and Juliet, in which he was to play Romeo to a Juliet it was needless to name.

"I don't think it can go on without a smash," said the young man with red hair, getting up and shaking himself. "Old Boulnois may be squared—or he may be square. But if he's square he's thick—what you might call cubic. But I don't believe it's possible."

"He is a man of grand intellectual powers," said Calhoun Kidd in a deep voice.

"Yes," answered Dalroy; "but even a man of grand intellectual powers can't be such a blighted fool as all that. Must you be going on? I shall be following myself in a minute or two."

But Calhoun Kidd, having finished a milk and soda, betook himself smartly up the road towards the Grey Cottage, leaving his cynical informant to his whisky and tobacco. The last of the daylight had faded; the skies were of a dark, green-grey, like slate, studded here and there with a star, but lighter on the left side of the sky, with the promise of a rising moon.

The Grey Cottage, which stood entrenched, as it were, in a square of stiff, high thorn-hedges, was so close under the pines and palisades of the Park that Kidd at first mistook it for the Park Lodge. Finding the name on the narrow wooden gate, however, and seeing by his watch that the hour of the "Thinker's" appointment had just struck, he went in and knocked at the front door. Inside the garden hedge, he could see that the house, though unpretentious enough, was larger and more luxurious than it looked at first, and was quite a different kind of place from a porter's lodge. A dog-kennel and a beehive stood outside, like symbols of old English country-life; the moon was rising behind a plantation of prosperous pear trees, the dog that came out of the kennel was reverend-looking and reluctant to bark; and the plain, elderly man-servant who opened the door was brief but dignified.

"Mr Boulnois asked me to offer his apologies, sir," he said, "but he has been obliged to go out suddenly."

"But see here, I had an appointment," said the interviewer, with a rising voice. "Do you know where he went to?"

"To Pendragon Park, sir," said the servant, rather sombrely, and began to close the door.

Kidd started a little.

"Did he go with Mrs—with the rest of the party?" he asked rather vaguely.

"No, sir," said the man shortly; "he stayed behind, and then went out alone." And he shut the door, brutally, but with an air of duty not done.

The American, that curious compound of impudence and sensitiveness, was annoyed. He felt a strong desire to hustle them all along a bit and teach them business habits; the hoary old dog and the grizzled, heavy-faced old butler with his prehistoric shirt-front, and the drowsy old moon, and above all the scatter-brained old philosopher who couldn't keep an appointment.

"If that's the way he goes on he deserves to lose his wife's purest devotion," said Mr Calhoun Kidd. "But perhaps he's gone over to make a row. In that case I reckon a man from the Western Sun will be on the spot."

And turning the corner by the open lodge-gates, he set off, stumping up the long avenue of black pine-woods that pointed in abrupt perspective towards the inner gardens of Pendragon Park. The trees were as black and orderly as plumes upon a hearse; there were still a few stars. He was a man with more literary than direct natural associations; the word "Ravenswood" came into his head repeatedly. It was partly the raven colour of the pine-woods; but partly also an indescribable atmosphere almost described in Scott's great tragedy; the smell of something that died in the eighteenth century; the smell of dank gardens and broken urns, of wrongs that will never now be righted; of something that is none the less incurably sad because it is strangely unreal.

More than once, as he went up that strange, black road of tragic artifice, he stopped, startled, thinking he heard steps in front of him. He could see nothing in front but the twin sombre walls of pine and the wedge of starlit sky above them. At first he thought he must have fancied it or been mocked by a mere echo of his own tramp. But as he went on he was more and more inclined to conclude, with the remains of his reason, that there really were other feet upon the road. He thought hazily of ghosts; and was surprised how swiftly he could see the image of an appropriate and local ghost, one with a face as white as Pierrot's, but patched with black. The apex of the triangle of dark-blue sky was growing brighter and bluer, but he did not realize as yet that this was because he was coming nearer to the lights of the great house and garden. He only felt that the atmosphere was growing more intense, there was in the sadness more violence and secrecy—more—he hesitated for the word, and then said it with a jerk of laughter—Catastrophism.

More pines, more pathway slid past him, and then he stood rooted as by a blast of magic. It is vain to say that he felt as if he had got into a dream; but this time he felt quite certain that he had got into a book. For we human beings are used to inappropriate things; we are accustomed to the clatter of the incongruous; it is a tune to which we can go to sleep. If one appropriate thing happens, it wakes us up like the pang of a perfect chord. Something happened such as would have happened in such a place in a forgotten tale.

Over the black pine-wood came flying and flashing in the moon a naked sword—such a slender and sparkling rapier as may have fought many an unjust duel in that ancient park. It fell on the pathway far in front of him and lay there glistening like a large needle. He ran like a hare and bent to look at it. Seen at close quarters it had rather a showy look: the big red jewels in the hilt and guard were a little dubious. But there were other red drops upon the blade which were not dubious.

He looked round wildly in the direction from which the dazzling missile had come, and saw that at this point the sable facade of fir and pine was interrupted by a smaller road at right angles; which, when he turned it, brought him in full view of the long, lighted house, with a lake and fountains in front of it. Nevertheless, he did not look at this, having something more interesting to look at.

Above him, at the angle of the steep green bank of the terraced garden, was one of those small picturesque surprises common in the old landscape gardening; a kind of small round hill or dome of grass, like a giant mole-hill, ringed and crowned with three concentric fences of roses, and having a sundial in the highest point in the centre. Kidd could see the finger of the dial stand up dark against the sky like the dorsal fin of a shark and the vain moonlight clinging to that idle clock. But he saw something else clinging to it also, for one wild moment—the figure of a man.

Though he saw it there only for a moment, though it was outlandish and incredible in costume, being clad from neck to heel in tight crimson, with glints of gold, yet he knew in one flash of moonlight who it was. That white face flung up to heaven, clean-shaven and so unnaturally young, like Byron with a Roman nose, those black curls already grizzled—he had seen the thousand public portraits of Sir Claude Champion. The wild red figure reeled an instant against the sundial; the next it had rolled down the steep bank and lay at the American's feet, faintly moving one arm. A gaudy, unnatural gold ornament on the arm suddenly reminded Kidd of Romeo and Juliet; of course the tight crimson suit was part of the play. But there was a long red stain down the bank from which the man had rolled—that was no part of the play. He had been run through the body.

Mr Calhoun Kidd shouted and shouted again. Once more he seemed to hear phantasmal footsteps, and started to find another figure already near him. He knew the figure, and yet it terrified him. The dissipated youth who had called himself Dalroy had a horribly quiet way with him; if Boulnois failed to keep appointments that had been made, Dalroy had a sinister air of keeping appointments that hadn't. The moonlight discoloured everything, against Dalroy's red hair his wan face looked not so much white as pale green.

All this morbid impressionism must be Kidd's excuse for having cried out, brutally and beyond all reason: "Did you do this, you devil?"

James Dalroy smiled his unpleasing smile; but before he could speak, the fallen figure made another movement of the arm, waving vaguely towards the place where the sword fell; then came a moan, and then it managed to speak.

"Boulnois.... Boulnois, I say.... Boulnois did it... jealous of me...he was jealous, he was, he was..."

Kidd bent his head down to hear more, and just managed to catch the words: "Boulnois...with my own sword...he threw it..."

Again the failing hand waved towards the sword, and then fell rigid with a thud. In Kidd rose from its depth all that acrid humour that is the strange salt of the seriousness of his race.

"See here," he said sharply and with command, "you must fetch a doctor. This man's dead."

"And a priest, too, I suppose," said Dalroy in an undecipherable manner. "All these Champions are papists."

The American knelt down by the body, felt the heart, propped up the head and used some last efforts at restoration; but before the other journalist reappeared, followed by a doctor and a priest, he was already prepared to assert they were too late.

"Were you too late also?" asked the doctor, a solid prosperous-looking man, with conventional moustache and whiskers, but a lively eye, which darted over Kidd dubiously.

"In one sense," drawled the representative of the Sun. "I was too late to save the man, but I guess I was in time to hear something of importance. I heard the dead man denounce his assassin."

"And who was the assassin?" asked the doctor, drawing his eyebrows together.

"Boulnois," said Calhoun Kidd, and whistled softly.

The doctor stared at him gloomily with a reddening brow—, but he did not contradict. Then the priest, a shorter figure in the background, said mildly: "I understood that Mr Boulnois was not coming to Pendragon Park this evening."

"There again," said the Yankee grimly, "I may be in a position to give the old country a fact or two. Yes, sir, John Boulnois was going to stay in all this evening; he fixed up a real good appointment there with me. But John Boulnois changed his mind; John Boulnois left his home abruptly and all alone, and came over to this darned Park an hour or so ago. His butler told me so. I think we hold what the all-wise police call a clue—have you sent for them?"

"Yes," said the doctor, "but we haven't alarmed anyone else yet."

"Does Mrs Boulnois know?" asked James Dalroy, and again Kidd was conscious of an irrational desire to hit him on his curling mouth.

"I have not told her," said the doctor gruffly—, "but here come the police."

The little priest had stepped out into the main avenue, and now returned with the fallen sword, which looked ludicrously large and theatrical when attached to his dumpy figure, at once clerical and commonplace. "Just before the police come," he said apologetically, "has anyone got a light?"

The Yankee journalist took an electric torch from his pocket, and the priest held it close to the middle part of the blade, which he examined with blinking care. Then, without glancing at the point or pommel, he handed the long weapon to the doctor.

"I fear I'm no use here," he said, with a brief sigh. "I'll say good night to you, gentlemen." And he walked away up the dark avenue towards the house, his hands clasped behind him and his big head bent in cogitation.

The rest of the group made increased haste towards the lodge-gates, where an inspector and two constables could already be seen in consultation with the lodge-keeper. But the little priest only walked slower and slower in the dim cloister of pine, and at last stopped dead, on the steps of the house. It was his silent way of acknowledging an equally silent approach; for there came towards him a presence that might have satisfied even Calhoun Kidd's demands for a lovely and aristocratic ghost. It was a young woman in silvery satins of a Renascence design; she had golden hair in two long shining ropes, and a face so startlingly pale between them that she might have been chryselephantine—made, that is, like some old Greek statues, out of ivory and gold. But her eyes were very bright, and her voice, though low, was confident.

"Father Brown?" she said.

"Mrs Boulnois?" he replied gravely. Then he looked at her and immediately said: "I see you know about Sir Claude."

"How do you know I know?" she asked steadily.

He did not answer the question, but asked another: "Have you seen your husband?"

"My husband is at home," she said. "He has nothing to do with this."

Again he did not answer; and the woman drew nearer to him, with a curiously intense expression on her face.

"Shall I tell you something more?" she said, with a rather fearful smile. "I don't think he did it, and you don't either." Father Brown returned her gaze with a long, grave stare, and then nodded, yet more gravely.

"Father Brown," said the lady, "I am going to tell you all I know, but I want you to do me a favour first. Will you tell me why you haven't jumped to the conclusion of poor John's guilt, as all the rest have done? Don't mind what you say: I—I know about the gossip and the appearances that are against me."

Father Brown looked honestly embarrassed, and passed his hand across his forehead. "Two very little things," he said. "At least, one's very trivial and the other very vague. But such as they are, they don't fit in with Mr Boulnois being the murderer."

He turned his blank, round face up to the stars and continued absentmindedly: "To take the vague idea first. I attach a good deal of importance to vague ideas. All those things that 'aren't evidence' are what convince me. I think a moral impossibility the biggest of all impossibilities. I know your husband only slightly, but I think this crime of his, as generally conceived, something very like a moral impossibility. Please do not think I mean that Boulnois could not be so wicked. Anybody can be wicked—as wicked as he chooses. We can direct our moral wills; but we can't generally change our instinctive tastes and ways of doing things. Boulnois might commit a murder, but not this murder. He would not snatch Romeo's sword from its romantic scabbard; or slay his foe on the sundial as on a kind of altar; or leave his body among the roses, or fling the sword away among the pines. If Boulnois killed anyone he'd do it quietly and heavily, as he'd do any other doubtful thing—take a tenth glass of port, or read a loose Greek poet. No, the romantic setting is not like Boulnois. It's more like Champion."

"Ah!" she said, and looked at him with eyes like diamonds.

"And the trivial thing was this," said Brown. "There were finger-prints on that sword; finger-prints can be detected quite a time after they are made if they're on some polished surface like glass or steel. These were on a polished surface. They were half-way down the blade of the sword. Whose prints they were I have no earthly clue; but why should anybody hold a sword half-way down? It was a long sword, but length is an advantage in lunging at an enemy. At least, at most enemies. At all enemies except one."

"Except one," she repeated.

"There is only one enemy," said Father Brown, "whom it is easier to kill with a dagger than a sword."

"I know," said the woman. "Oneself."

There was a long silence, and then the priest said quietly but abruptly: "Am I right, then? Did Sir Claude kill himself?"

"Yes" she said, with a face like marble. "I saw him do it."

"He died," said Father Brown, "for love of you?"

An extraordinary expression flashed across her face, very different from pity, modesty, remorse, or anything her companion had expected: her voice became suddenly strong and full. "I don't believe," she said, "he ever cared about me a rap. He hated my husband."

"Why?" asked the other, and turned his round face from the sky to the lady.

"He hated my husband because...it is so strange I hardly know how to say it...because..."

"Yes?" said Brown patiently.

"Because my husband wouldn't hate him."

Father Brown only nodded, and seemed still to be listening; he differed from most detectives in fact and fiction in a small point—he never pretended not to understand when he understood perfectly well.

Mrs Boulnois drew near once more with the same contained glow of certainty. "My husband," she said, "is a great man. Sir Claude Champion was not a great man: he was a celebrated and successful man. My husband has never been celebrated or successful; and it is the solemn truth that he has never dreamed of being so. He no more expects to be famous for thinking than for smoking cigars. On all that side he has a sort of splendid stupidity. He has never grown up. He still liked Champion exactly as he liked him at school; he admired him as he would admire a conjuring trick done at the dinner-table. But he couldn't be got to conceive the notion of envying Champion. And Champion wanted to be envied. He went mad and killed himself for that."

254

"Yes," said Father Brown; "I think I begin to understand."

"Oh, don't you see?" she cried; "the whole picture is made for that—the place is planned for it. Champion put John in a little house at his very door, like a dependant—to make him feel a failure. He never felt it. He thinks no more about such things than—than an absent-minded lion. Champion would burst in on John's shabbiest hours or homeliest meals with some dazzling present or announcement or expedition that made it like the visit of Haroun Alraschid, and John would accept or refuse amiably with one eye off, so to speak, like one lazy schoolboy agreeing or disagreeing with another. After five years of it John had not turned a hair; and Sir Claude Champion was a monomaniac."

"And Haman began to tell them," said Father Brown, "of all the things wherein the king had honoured him; and he said: 'All these things profit me nothing while I see Mordecai the Jew sitting in the gate.'"

"The crisis came," Mrs Boulnois continued, "when I persuaded John to let me take down some of his speculations and send them to a magazine. They began to attract attention, especially in America, and one paper wanted to interview him. When Champion (who was interviewed nearly every day) heard of this late little crumb of success falling to his unconscious rival, the last link snapped that held back his devilish hatred. Then he began to lay that insane siege to my own love and honour which has been the talk of the shire. You will ask me why I allowed such atrocious attentions. I answer that I could not have declined them except by explaining to my husband, and there are some things the soul cannot do, as the body cannot fly. Nobody could have explained to my husband. Nobody could do it now. If you said to him in so many words, 'Champion is stealing your wife,' he would think the joke a little vulgar: that it could be anything but a joke—that notion could find no crack in his great skull to get in by. Well, John was to come and see us act this evening, but just as we were starting he said he wouldn't; he had got an interesting book and a cigar. I told this to Sir Claude, and it was his death-blow. The monomaniac suddenly saw despair. He stabbed himself, crying out like a devil that Boulnois was slaying him; he lies there in the garden dead of his own jealousy to produce jealousy, and John is sitting in the dining-room reading a book."

There was another silence, and then the little priest said: "There is only one weak point, Mrs Boulnois, in all your very vivid account. Your husband is not sitting in the dining-room reading a book. That American reporter told me he had been to your house, and your butler told him Mr Boulnois had gone to Pendragon Park after all."

Her bright eyes widened to an almost electric glare; and yet it seemed rather bewilderment than confusion or fear. "Why, what can you mean?" she cried. "All the servants were out of the house, seeing the theatricals. And we don't keep a butler, thank goodness!"

Father Brown started and spun half round like an absurd teetotum. "What, what?" he cried seeming galvanized into sudden life. "Look here—I say—can I make your husband hear if I go to the house?"

"Oh, the servants will be back by now," she said, wondering.

"Right, right!" rejoined the cleric energetically, and set off scuttling up the path towards the Park gates. He turned once to say: "Better get hold of that Yankee, or 'Crime of John Boulnois' will be all over the Republic in large letters."

"You don't understand," said Mrs Boulnois. "He wouldn't mind. I don't think he imagines that America really is a place."

When Father Brown reached the house with the beehive and the drowsy dog, a small and neat maid-servant showed him into the dining-room, where Boulnois sat reading by a shaded lamp, exactly as his wife described him. A decanter of port and a wineglass were at his elbow; and the instant the priest entered he noted the long ash stand out unbroken on his cigar.

"He has been here for half an hour at least," thought Father Brown. In fact, he had the air of sitting where he had sat when his dinner was cleared away.

"Don't get up, Mr Boulnois," said the priest in his pleasant, prosaic way. "I shan't interrupt you a moment. I fear I break in on some of your scientific studies."

"No," said Boulnois; "I was reading 'The Bloody Thumb.'" He said it with neither frown nor smile, and his visitor was conscious of a certain deep and virile indifference in the man which his wife had called greatness. He laid down a gory yellow "shocker" without even feeling its incongruity enough to comment on it humorously. John Boulnois was a big, slow-moving man with a massive head, partly grey and partly bald, and blunt, burly features. He was in shabby and very old-fashioned evening-dress, with a narrow triangular opening of shirt-front: he had assumed it that evening in his original purpose of going to see his wife act Juliet.

"I won't keep you long from 'The Bloody Thumb' or any other catastrophic affairs," said Father Brown, smiling. "I only came to ask you about the crime you committed this evening."

Boulnois looked at him steadily, but a red bar began to show across his broad brow; and he seemed like one discovering embarrassment for the first time.

"I know it was a strange crime," assented Brown in a low voice. "Stranger than murder perhaps—to you. The little sins are sometimes harder to confess than the big ones—but that's why it's so important to confess them. Your crime is committed by every fashionable hostess six times a week: and yet you find it sticks to your tongue like a nameless atrocity."

"It makes one feel," said the philosopher slowly, "such a damned fool."

"I know," assented the other, "but one often has to choose between feeling a damned fool and being one."

"I can't analyse myself well," went on Boulnois; "but sitting in that chair with that story I was as happy as a schoolboy on a half-holiday. It was security, eternity—I can't convey it... the cigars were within reach...the matches were within reach... the Thumb had four more appearances to...it was not only a peace, but a plenitude. Then that bell rang, and I thought for one long, mortal minute that I couldn't get out of that chair—literally, physically, muscularly couldn't. Then I did it like a man lifting the world, because I knew all the servants were out. I opened the front door, and there was a little man with his mouth open to speak and his notebook open to write in. I remembered the Yankee interviewer I had forgotten. His hair was parted in the middle, and I tell you that murder—"

"I understand," said Father Brown. "I've seen him."

"I didn't commit murder," continued the Catastrophist mildly, "but only perjury. I said I had gone across to Pendragon Park and shut the door in his face. That is my crime, Father Brown, and I don't know what penance you would inflict for it."

"I shan't inflict any penance," said the clerical gentleman, collecting his heavy hat and umbrella with an air of some amusement; "quite the contrary. I came here specially to let you off the little penance which would otherwise have followed your little offence."

"And what," asked Boulnois, smiling, "is the little penance I have so luckily been let off?"

"Being hanged," said Father Brown.

The Fairy Tale of Father Brown

THE picturesque city and state of Heiligwaldenstein was one of those toy kingdoms of which certain parts of the German Empire still consist. It had come under the Prussian hegemony quite late in history—hardly fifty years before the fine summer day when Flambeau and Father Brown found themselves sitting in its gardens and drinking its beer. There had been not a little of war and wild justice there within living memory, as soon will be shown. But in merely looking at it one could not dismiss that impression of childishness which is the most charming side of Germany—those little pantomime, paternal monarchies in which a king seems as domestic as a cook. The German soldiers by the innumerable sentry-boxes looked strangely like German toys, and the clean-cut battlements of the castle, gilded by the sunshine, looked the more like the gilt gingerbread. For it was brilliant weather. The sky was as Prussian a blue as Potsdam itself could require, but it was yet more like that lavish and glowing use of the colour which a child extracts from a shilling paint-box. Even the grey-ribbed trees looked young, for the pointed buds on them were still pink, and in a pattern against the strong blue looked like innumerable childish figures.

Despite his prosaic appearance and generally practical walk of life, Father Brown was not without a certain streak of romance in his composition, though he generally kept his daydreams to himself, as many children do. Amid the brisk, bright colours of such a day, and in the heraldic framework of such a town, he did feel rather as if he had entered a fairy tale. He took a childish pleasure, as a younger brother might, in the formidable sword-stick which Flambeau always flung as he walked, and which now stood upright beside his tall mug of Munich. Nay, in his sleepy irresponsibility, he even found himself eyeing the knobbed and clumsy head of his own shabby umbrella, with some faint memories of the ogre's club in a coloured toy-book. But he never composed anything in the form of fiction, unless it be the tale that follows:

"I wonder," he said, "whether one would have real adventures in a place like this, if one put oneself in the way? It's a splendid back-scene for them, but I always have a kind of feeling that they would fight you with pasteboard sabres more than real, horrible swords."

"You are mistaken," said his friend. "In this place they not only fight with swords, but kill without swords. And there's worse than that."

"Why, what do you mean?" asked Father Brown.

"Why," replied the other, "I should say this was the only place in Europe where a man was ever shot without firearms."

"Do you mean a bow and arrow?" asked Brown in some wonder.

"I mean a bullet in the brain," replied Flambeau. "Don't you know the story of the late Prince of this place? It was one of the great police mysteries about twenty years ago. You remember, of course, that this place was forcibly annexed at the time of Bismarck's very earliest schemes of consolidation—forcibly, that is, but not at all easily. The empire (or what wanted to be one) sent Prince Otto of Grossenmark to rule the place in the Imperial interests. We saw his portrait in the gallery there—a handsome old gentleman if he'd had any hair or eyebrows, and hadn't been wrinkled all over like a vulture; but he had things to harass him, as I'll explain in a minute. He was a soldier of distinguished skill and success, but he didn't have altogether an easy job with this little place. He was defeated in several battles by the celebrated Arnhold brothers—the three guerrilla patriots to whom Swinburne wrote a poem, you remember:

> Wolves with the hair of the ermine,
> Crows that are crowned and kings—
> These things be many as vermin,
> Yet Three shall abide these things.

Or something of that kind. Indeed, it is by no means certain that the occupation would ever have been successful had not one of the three brothers, Paul, despicably, but very decisively declined to abide these things any longer, and, by surrendering all the secrets of the insurrection, ensured its overthrow and his own ultimate promotion to the post of chamberlain to Prince Otto. After this, Ludwig, the one genuine hero among Mr Swinburne's heroes, was killed, sword in hand, in the capture of the city; and the third, Heinrich, who, though not a traitor, had always been tame and even timid compared with his active brothers, retired into something like a hermitage, became converted to a Christian quietism which was almost Quakerish, and never mixed with men except to give nearly all he had to the poor. They tell me that not long ago he could still be seen about the neighbourhood occasionally, a man in a black cloak, nearly blind, with very wild, white hair, but a face of astonishing softness."

"I know," said Father Brown. "I saw him once."

His friend looked at him in some surprise. "I didn't know you'd been here before," he said. "Perhaps you know as much about it as I do. Anyhow, that's the story of the Arnholds, and he was the last survivor of them. Yes, and of all the men who played parts in that drama."

"You mean that the Prince, too, died long before?"

"Died," repeated Flambeau, "and that's about as much as we can say. You must understand that towards the end of his life he began to have those tricks of the nerves not uncommon with tyrants. He multiplied the ordinary daily and nightly guard round his castle till there seemed to be more sentry-boxes than houses in the town, and doubtful characters were shot without mercy. He lived almost entirely in a little room that was in the very centre of the enormous labyrinth of all the other rooms, and even in this he erected another sort of central cabin or cupboard, lined with steel, like a safe or a battleship. Some say that under the floor of this again was a secret hole in the earth, no more than large enough to hold him, so that, in his anxiety to avoid the grave, he was willing to go into a place pretty much like it. But he went further yet. The populace had been supposed to be disarmed ever since the suppression of the revolt, but Otto now insisted, as governments very seldom insist, on an absolute and literal disarmament. It was carried out, with extraordinary thoroughness and severity, by very well-organized officials over a small and familiar area, and, so far as human strength and science can be absolutely certain of anything, Prince Otto was absolutely certain that nobody could introduce so much as a toy pistol into Heiligwaldenstein."

"Human science can never be quite certain of things like that," said Father Brown, still looking at the red budding of the branches over his head, "if only because of the difficulty about definition and connotation. What is a weapon? People have been murdered with the mildest domestic comforts; certainly with tea-kettles, probably with tea-cosies. On the other hand, if you showed an Ancient Briton a revolver, I doubt if he would know it was a weapon—until it was fired into him, of course. Perhaps somebody introduced a firearm so new that it didn't even look like a firearm. Perhaps it looked like a thimble or something. Was the bullet at all peculiar?"

"Not that I ever heard of," answered Flambeau; "but my information is fragmentary, and only comes from my old friend Grimm. He was a very able detective in the German service, and he tried to arrest me; I arrested him instead, and we had many interesting chats. He was in charge here of the inquiry about Prince Otto, but I forgot to ask him anything about the bullet. According to Grimm, what happened was this." He paused a moment to drain the greater part of his dark lager at a draught, and then resumed:

"On the evening in question, it seems, the Prince was expected to appear in one of the outer rooms, because he had to receive certain visitors whom he really wished to meet. They were geological experts sent to investigate the old question of the alleged supply of gold from the rocks round here, upon which (as it was said) the small city-state had so long maintained its credit and been able to negotiate with its neighbours even under the ceaseless bombardment of bigger armies. Hitherto it had never been found by the most exacting inquiry which could—"

"Which could be quite certain of discovering a toy pistol," said Father Brown with a smile. "But what about the brother who ratted? Hadn't he anything to tell the Prince?"

"He always asseverated that he did not know," replied Flambeau; "that this was the one secret his brothers had not told him. It is only right to say that it received some support from fragmentary words—spoken by the great Ludwig in the hour of death, when he looked at Heinrich but pointed at Paul, and said, 'You have not told him...' and was soon afterwards incapable of speech. Anyhow, the deputation of distinguished geologists and mineralogists from Paris and Berlin were there in the most magnificent and appropriate dress, for there are no men who like wearing their decorations so much as the men of science—as anybody knows who has ever been to a soiree of the Royal Society. It was a brilliant gathering, but very late, and gradually the Chamberlain—you saw his portrait, too: a man with black eyebrows, serious eyes, and a meaningless sort of smile underneath—the Chamberlain, I say, discovered there was everything there except the Prince himself. He searched all the outer salons; then, remembering the man's mad fits of fear, hurried to the inmost chamber. That also was empty, but the steel turret or cabin erected in the middle of it took some time to open. When it did open it was empty, too. He went and looked into the hole in the ground, which seemed deeper and somehow all the more like a grave—that is his account, of course. And even as he did so he heard a burst of cries and tumult in the long rooms and corridors without.

"First it was a distant din and thrill of something unthinkable on the horizon of the crowd, even beyond the castle. Next it was a wordless clamour startlingly close, and loud enough to be distinct if each word had not killed the other. Next came words of a terrible clearness, coming nearer, and next one man, rushing into the room and telling the news as briefly as such news is told.

"Otto, Prince of Heiligwaldenstein and Grossenmark, was lying in the dews of the darkening twilight in the woods beyond the castle, with his arms flung out and his face flung up to the moon. The blood still pulsed from his shattered temple and jaw, but it was the only part of him that moved like a living thing. He was clad in his full white and yellow uniform, as to receive his guests within, except that the sash or scarf had been unbound and lay rather crumpled by his side. Before he could be lifted he was dead. But, dead or alive, he was a riddle—he who had always hidden in the inmost chamber out there in the wet woods, unarmed and alone."

"Who found his body?" asked Father Brown.

"Some girl attached to the Court named Hedwig von something or other," replied his friend, "who had been out in the wood picking wild flowers."

"Had she picked any?" asked the priest, staring rather vacantly at the veil of the branches above him.

"Yes," replied Flambeau. "I particularly remember that the Chamberlain, or old Grimm or somebody, said how horrible it was, when they came up at her call, to see a girl holding spring flowers and bending over that—that bloody collapse. However, the main point is that before help arrived he was dead, and the news, of course, had to be carried back to the castle. The consternation it created was something beyond even that natural in a Court at the fall of a potentate. The foreign visitors, especially the mining experts, were in the wildest doubt and excitement, as well as many important Prussian officials, and it soon began to be clear that the scheme for finding the treasure bulked much bigger in the business than people had supposed. Experts and officials had been promised great prizes or international advantages, and some even said that the Prince's secret apartments and strong military protection were due less to fear of the populace than to the pursuit of some private investigation of—"

"Had the flowers got long stalks?" asked Father Brown.

Flambeau stared at him. "What an odd person you are!" he said. "That's exactly what old Grimm said. He said the ugliest part of it, he thought—uglier than the blood and bullet—was that the flowers were quite short, plucked close under the head."

"Of course," said the priest, "when a grown up girl is really picking flowers, she picks them with plenty of stalk. If she just pulled their heads off, as a child does, it looks as if—" And he hesitated.

"Well?" inquired the other.

"Well, it looks rather as if she had snatched them nervously, to make an excuse for being there after—well, after she was there."

"I know what you're driving at," said Flambeau rather gloomily. "But that and every other suspicion breaks down on the one point—the want of a weapon. He could have been killed, as you say, with lots of other things—even with his own military sash; but we have to explain not how he was killed, but how he was shot. And the fact is we can't. They had the girl most ruthlessly searched; for, to tell the truth, she was a little suspect, though the niece and ward of the wicked old Chamberlain, Paul Arnhold. But she was very romantic, and was suspected of sympathy with the old revolutionary enthusiasm in her family. All the same, however romantic you are, you can't imagine a big bullet into a man's jaw or brain without using a gun or pistol. And there was no pistol, though there were two pistol shots. I leave it to you, my friend."

"How do you know there were two shots?" asked the little priest.

"There was only one in his head," said his companion, "but there was another bullet-hole in the sash."

Father Brown's smooth brow became suddenly constricted. "Was the other bullet found?" he demanded.

Flambeau started a little. "I don't think I remember," he said.

"Hold on! Hold on! Hold on!" cried Brown, frowning more and more, with a quite unusual concentration of curiosity. "Don't think me rude. Let me think this out for a moment."

"All right," said Flambeau, laughing, and finished his beer. A slight breeze stirred the budding trees and blew up into the sky cloudlets of white and pink that seemed to make the sky bluer and the whole coloured scene more quaint. They might have been cherubs flying home to the casements of a sort of celestial nursery. The oldest tower of the castle, the Dragon Tower, stood up as grotesque as the ale-mug, but as homely. Only beyond the tower glimmered the wood in which the man had lain dead.

"What became of this Hedwig eventually?" asked the priest at last.

"She is married to General Schwartz," said Flambeau. "No doubt you've heard of his career, which was rather romantic. He had distinguished himself even, before his exploits at Sadowa and Gravelotte; in fact, he rose from the ranks, which is very unusual even in the smallest of the German..."

Father Brown sat up suddenly.

"Rose from the ranks!" he cried, and made a mouth as if to whistle. "Well, well, what a queer story! What a queer way of killing a man; but I suppose it was the only one possible. But to think of hate so patient—"

"What do you mean?" demanded the other. "In what way did they kill the man?"

"They killed him with the sash," said Brown carefully; and then, as Flambeau protested: "Yes, yes, I know about the bullet. Perhaps I ought to say he died of having a sash. I know it doesn't sound like having a disease."

"I suppose," said Flambeau, "that you've got some notion in your head, but it won't easily get the bullet out of his. As I explained before, he might easily have been strangled. But he was shot. By whom? By what?"

"He was shot by his own orders," said the priest.

"You mean he committed suicide?"

"I didn't say by his own wish," replied Father Brown. "I said by his own orders."

"Well, anyhow, what is your theory?"

Father Brown laughed. "I am only on my holiday," he said. "I haven't got any theories. Only this place reminds me of fairy stories, and, if you like, I'll tell you a story."

The little pink clouds, that looked rather like sweet-stuff, had floated up to crown the turrets of the gilt gingerbread castle, and the pink baby fingers of the budding trees seemed spreading and stretching to reach them; the blue sky began to take a bright violet of evening, when Father Brown suddenly spoke again:

"It was on a dismal night, with rain still dropping from the trees and dew already clustering, that Prince Otto of Grossenmark stepped hurriedly out of a side door of the castle and walked swiftly into the wood. One of the innumerable sentries saluted him, but he did not notice it. He had no wish to be specially noticed himself. He was glad when the great trees, grey and already greasy with rain, swallowed him up like a swamp. He had deliberately chosen the least frequented side of his palace, but even that was more frequented than he liked. But there was no particular chance of officious or diplomatic pursuit, for his exit had been a sudden impulse. All the full-dressed diplomatists he left behind were unimportant. He had realized suddenly that he could do without them.

"His great passion was not the much nobler dread of death, but the strange desire of gold. For this legend of the gold he had left Grossenmark and invaded Heiligwaldenstein. For this and only this he had bought the traitor and butchered the hero, for this he had long questioned and cross-questioned the false Chamberlain, until he had come to the conclusion that, touching his ignorance, the renegade really told the truth. For this he had, somewhat reluctantly, paid and promised money on the chance of gaining the larger amount; and for this he had stolen out of his palace like a thief in the rain, for he had thought of another way to get the desire of his eyes, and to get it cheap.

"Away at the upper end of a rambling mountain path to which he was making his way, among the pillared rocks along the ridge that hangs above the town, stood the hermitage, hardly more than a cavern fenced with thorn, in which the third of the great brethren had long hidden himself from the world. He, thought Prince Otto, could have no real reason for refusing to give up the gold. He had known its place for years, and made no effort to find it, even before his new ascetic creed had cut him off from property or pleasures. True, he had been an enemy, but he now professed a duty of having no enemies. Some concession to his cause, some appeal to his principles, would probably get the mere money secret out of him. Otto was no coward, in spite of his network of military precautions, and, in any case, his avarice was stronger than his fears. Nor was there much cause for fear. Since he was certain there were no private arms in the whole principality, he was a hundred times more certain there were none in the Quaker's little hermitage on the hill, where he lived on herbs, with two old rustic servants, and with no other voice of man for year after year. Prince Otto looked down with something of a grim smile at the bright, square labyrinths of the lamp-lit city below him. For as far as the eye could see there ran the rifles of his friends, and not one pinch of powder for his enemies. Rifles ranked so close even to that mountain path that a cry from him would bring the soldiers rushing up the hill, to say nothing of the fact that the wood and ridge were patrolled at regular intervals; rifles so far away, in the dim woods, dwarfed by distance, beyond the river, that an enemy could not slink into the town by any detour. And round the palace rifles at the west door and the east door, at the north door and the south, and all along the four facades linking them. He was safe.

"It was all the more clear when he had crested the ridge and found how naked was the nest of his old enemy. He found himself on a small platform of rock, broken abruptly by the three corners of precipice. Behind was the black cave, masked with green thorn, so low that it was hard to believe that a man could enter it. In front was the fall of the cliffs and the vast but cloudy vision of the valley. On the small rock platform stood an old bronze lectern or reading-stand, groaning under a great German Bible. The bronze or copper of it had grown green with the eating airs of that exalted place, and Otto had instantly the thought, 'Even if they had arms, they must be rusted by now.' Moonrise had already made a deathly dawn behind the crests and crags, and the rain had ceased.

"Behind the lectern, and looking across the valley, stood a very old man in a black robe that fell as straight as the cliffs around him, but whose white hair and weak voice seemed alike to waver in the wind. He was evidently reading some daily lesson as part of his religious exercises. 'They trust in their horses...'

"'Sir,' said the Prince of Heiligwaldenstein, with quite unusual courtesy, 'I should like only one word with you.'

"'...and in their chariots,' went on the old man weakly, 'but we will trust in the name of the Lord of Hosts....' His last words were inaudible, but he closed the book reverently and, being nearly blind, made a groping movement and gripped the reading-stand. Instantly his two servants slipped out of the low-browed cavern and supported him. They wore dull-black gowns like his own, but they had not the frosty silver on the hair, nor the frost-bitten refinement of the features. They were peasants, Croat or Magyar, with broad, blunt visages and blinking eyes. For the first time something troubled the Prince, but his courage and diplomatic sense stood firm.

"'I fear we have not met,' he said, 'since that awful cannonade in which your poor brother died.'

"'All my brothers died,' said the old man, still looking across the valley. Then, for one instant turning on Otto his drooping, delicate features, and the wintry hair that seemed to drip over his eyebrows like icicles, he added: 'You see, I am dead, too.'

"'I hope you'll understand,' said the Prince, controlling himself almost to a point of conciliation, 'that I do not come here to haunt you, as a mere ghost of those great quarrels. We will not talk about who was right or wrong in that, but at least there was one point on which we were never wrong, because you were always right. Whatever is to be said of the policy of your family, no one for one moment imagines that you were moved by the mere gold; you have proved yourself above the suspicion that...'

"The old man in the black gown had hitherto continued to gaze at him with watery blue eyes and a sort of weak wisdom in his face. But when the word 'gold' was said he held out his hand as if in arrest of something, and turned away his face to the mountains.

"'He has spoken of gold,' he said. 'He has spoken of things not lawful. Let him cease to speak.'

"Otto had the vice of his Prussian type and tradition, which is to regard success not as an incident but as a quality. He conceived himself and his like as perpetually conquering peoples who were perpetually being conquered. Consequently, he was ill acquainted with the emotion of surprise, and ill prepared for the next movement, which startled and stiffened him. He had opened his mouth to answer the hermit, when the mouth was stopped and the voice strangled by a strong, soft gag suddenly twisted round his head like a tourniquet. It was fully forty seconds before he even realized that the two Hungarian servants had done it, and that they had done it with his own military scarf.

"The old man went again weakly to his great brazen-supported Bible, turned over the leaves, with a patience that had something horrible about it, till he came to the Epistle of St James, and then began to read: 'The tongue is a little member, but—'

"Something in the very voice made the Prince turn suddenly and plunge down the mountain-path he had climbed. He was half-way towards the gardens of the palace before he even tried to tear the strangling scarf from his neck and jaws. He tried again and again, and it was impossible; the men who had knotted that gag knew the difference between what a man can do with his hands in front of him and what he can do with his hands behind his head. His legs were free to leap like an antelope on the mountains, his arms were free to use any gesture or wave any signal, but he could not speak. A dumb devil was in him.

"He had come close to the woods that walled in the castle before he had quite realized what his wordless state meant and was meant to mean. Once more he looked down grimly at the bright, square labyrinths of the lamp-lit city below him, and he smiled no more. He felt himself repeating the phrases of his former mood with a murderous irony. Far as the eye could see ran the rifles of his friends, every one of whom would shoot him dead if he could not answer the challenge. Rifles were so near that the wood and ridge could be patrolled at regular intervals; therefore it was useless to hide in the wood till morning. Rifles were ranked so far away that an enemy could not slink into the town by any detour; therefore it was vain to return to the city by any remote course. A cry from him would bring his soldiers rushing up the hill. But from him no cry would come.

"The moon had risen in strengthening silver, and the sky showed in stripes of bright, nocturnal blue between the black stripes of the pines about the castle. Flowers of some wide and feathery sort—for he had never noticed such things before—were at once luminous and discoloured by the moonshine, and seemed indescribably fantastic as they clustered, as if crawling about the roots of the trees. Perhaps his reason had been suddenly unseated by the unnatural captivity he carried with him, but in that wood he felt something unfathomably German—the fairy tale. He knew with half his mind that he was drawing near to the castle of an ogre—he had forgotten that he was the ogre. He remembered asking his mother if bears lived in the old park at home. He stooped to pick a flower, as if it were a charm against enchantment. The stalk was stronger than he expected, and broke with a slight snap. Carefully trying to place it in his scarf, he heard the halloo, 'Who goes there?' Then he remembered the scarf was not in its usual place.

"He tried to scream and was silent. The second challenge came; and then a shot that shrieked as it came and then was stilled suddenly by impact. Otto of Grossenmark lay very peacefully among the fairy trees, and would do no more harm either with gold or steel; only the silver pencil of the moon would pick out and trace here and there the intricate ornament of his uniform, or the old wrinkles on his brow. May God have mercy on his soul.

"The sentry who had fired, according to the strict orders of the garrison, naturally ran forward to find some trace of his quarry. He was a private named Schwartz, since not unknown in his profession, and what he found was a bald man in uniform, but with his face so bandaged by a kind of mask made of his own military scarf that nothing but open, dead eyes could be seen, glittering stonily in the moonlight. The bullet had gone through the gag into the jaw; that is why there was a shot-hole in the scarf, but only one shot. Naturally, if not correctly, young Schwartz tore off the mysterious silken mask and cast it on the grass; and then he saw whom he had slain.

"We cannot be certain of the next phase. But I incline to believe that there was a fairy tale, after all, in that little wood, horrible as was its occasion. Whether the young lady named Hedwig had any previous knowledge of the soldier she saved and eventually married, or whether she came accidentally upon the accident and their intimacy began that night, we shall probably never know. But we can know, I fancy, that this Hedwig was a heroine, and deserved to marry a man who became something of a hero. She did the bold and the wise thing. She persuaded the sentry to go back to his post, in which place there was nothing to connect him with the disaster; he was but one of the most loyal and orderly of fifty such sentries within call. She remained by the body and gave the alarm; and there was nothing to connect her with the disaster either, since she had not got, and could not have, any firearms.

"Well," said Father Brown rising cheerfully "I hope they're happy."

"Where are you going?" asked his friend.

"I'm going to have another look at that portrait of the Chamberlain, the Arnhold who betrayed his brethren," answered the priest. "I wonder what part—I wonder if a man is less a traitor when he is twice a traitor?"

And he ruminated long before the portrait of a white-haired man with black eyebrows and a pink, painted sort of smile that seemed to contradict the black warning in his eyes.

The Man Who Was Thursday by G. K. Chesterton

A Nightmare

DEDICATION

To Edmund Clerihew Bentley

A cloud was on the mind of men, and wailing went the weather,
Yea, a sick cloud upon the soul when we were boys together.
Science announced nonentity and art admired decay;
The world was old and ended: but you and I were gay;
Round us in antic order their crippled vices came—
Lust that had lost its laughter, fear that had lost its shame.
Like the white lock of Whistler, that lit our aimless gloom,
Men showed their own white feather as proudly as a plume.
Life was a fly that faded, and death a drone that stung;
The world was very old indeed when you and I were young.
They twisted even decent sin to shapes not to be named:
Men were ashamed of honour; but we were not ashamed.
Weak if we were and foolish, not thus we failed, not thus;
When that black Baal blocked the heavens he had no hymns from us
Children we were—our forts of sand were even as weak as we,
High as they went we piled them up to break that bitter sea.
Fools as we were in motley, all jangling and absurd,
When all church bells were silent our cap and bells were heard.

Not all unhelped we held the fort, our tiny flags unfurled;
Some giants laboured in that cloud to lift it from the world.
I find again the book we found, I feel the hour that flings
Far out of fish-shaped Paumanok some cry of cleaner things;
And the Green Carnation withered, as in forest fires that pass,
Roared in the wind of all the world ten million leaves of grass;
Or sane and sweet and sudden as a bird sings in the rain—
Truth out of Tusitala spoke and pleasure out of pain.
Yea, cool and clear and sudden as a bird sings in the grey,
Dunedin to Samoa spoke, and darkness unto day.
But we were young; we lived to see God break their bitter charms.
God and the good Republic come riding back in arms:
We have seen the City of Mansoul, even as it rocked, relieved—

Blessed are they who did not see, but being blind, believed.

This is a tale of those old fears, even of those emptied hells,
And none but you shall understand the true thing that it tells—
Of what colossal gods of shame could cow men and yet crash,
Of what huge devils hid the stars, yet fell at a pistol flash.
The doubts that were so plain to chase, so dreadful to withstand—
Oh, who shall understand but you; yea, who shall understand?
The doubts that drove us through the night as we two talked amain,
And day had broken on the streets e'er it broke upon the brain.
Between us, by the peace of God, such truth can now be told;
Yea, there is strength in striking root and good in growing old.
We have found common things at last and marriage and a creed,
And I may safely write it now, and you may safely read.

G. K. C.

CHAPTER I
THE TWO POETS OF SAFFRON PARK

THE suburb of Saffron Park lay on the sunset side of London, as red and ragged as a cloud of sunset. It was built of a bright brick throughout; its sky-line was
fantastic, and even its ground plan was wild. It had been the outburst of a specula-
tive builder, faintly tinged with art, who called its architecture sometimes
Elizabethan and sometimes Queen Anne, apparently under the impression that the
two sovereigns were identical. It was described with some justice as an artistic col-
ony, though it never in any definable way produced any art. But although its
pretensions to be an intellectual centre were a little vague, its pretensions to be a
pleasant place were quite indisputable. The stranger who looked for the first time at
the quaint red houses could only think how very oddly shaped the people must be
who could fit in to them.

Nor when he met the people was he disappointed in this respect. The place
was not only pleasant, but perfect, if once he could regard it not as a deception but
rather as a dream. Even if the people were not "artists," the whole was nevertheless
artistic. That young man with the long, auburn hair and the impudent face—that
young man was not really a poet; but surely he was a poem. That old gentleman
with the wild, white beard and the wild, white hat—that venerable humbug was not
really a philosopher; but at least he was the cause of philosophy in others. That scientific gentleman with the bald, egg-like head and the bare, bird-like neck had no
real right to the airs of science that he assumed. He had not discovered anything
new in biology; but what biological creature could he have discovered more singular than himself? Thus, and thus only, the whole place had properly to be regarded;
it had to be considered not so much as a workshop for artists, but as a frail but fin-

ished work of art. A man who stepped into its social atmosphere felt as if he had stepped into a written comedy.

More especially this attractive unreality fell upon it about nightfall, when the extravagant roofs were dark against the afterglow and the whole insane village seemed as separate as a drifting cloud. This again was more strongly true of the many nights of local festivity, when the little gardens were often illuminated, and the big Chinese lanterns glowed in the dwarfish trees like some fierce and monstrous fruit. And this was strongest of all on one particular evening, still vaguely remembered in the locality, of which the auburn-haired poet was the hero. It was not by any means the only evening of which he was the hero. On many nights those passing by his little back garden might hear his high, didactic voice laying down the law to men and particularly to women. The attitude of women in such cases was indeed one of the paradoxes of the place. Most of the women were of the kind vaguely called emancipated, and professed some protest against male supremacy. Yet these new women would always pay to a man the extravagant compliment which no ordinary woman ever pays to him, that of listening while he is talking. And Mr. Lucian Gregory, the red-haired poet, was really (in some sense) a man worth listening to, even if one only laughed at the end of it. He put the old cant of the lawlessness of art and the art of lawlessness with a certain impudent freshness which gave at least a momentary pleasure. He was helped in some degree by the arresting oddity of his appearance, which he worked, as the phrase goes, for all it was worth. His dark red hair parted in the middle was literally like a woman's, and curved into the slow curls of a virgin in a pre-Raphaelite picture. From within this almost saintly oval, however, his face projected suddenly broad and brutal, the chin carried forward with a look of cockney contempt. This combination at once tickled and terrified the nerves of a neurotic population. He seemed like a walking blasphemy, a blend of the angel and the ape.

This particular evening, if it is remembered for nothing else, will be remembered in that place for its strange sunset. It looked like the end of the world. All the heaven seemed covered with a quite vivid and palpable plumage; you could only say that the sky was full of feathers, and of feathers that almost brushed the face. Across the great part of the dome they were grey, with the strangest tints of violet and mauve and an unnatural pink or pale green; but towards the west the whole grew past description, transparent and passionate, and the last red-hot plumes of it covered up the sun like something too good to be seen. The whole was so close about the earth, as to express nothing but a violent secrecy. The very empyrean seemed to be a secret. It expressed that splendid smallness which is the soul of local patriotism. The very sky seemed small.

I say that there are some inhabitants who may remember the evening if only by that oppressive sky. There are others who may remember it because it marked the first appearance in the place of the second poet of Saffron Park. For a long time the red-haired revolutionary had reigned without a rival; it was upon the night of the sunset that his solitude suddenly ended. The new poet, who introduced himself by the name of Gabriel Syme was a very mild-looking mortal, with a fair, pointed beard and faint, yellow hair. But an impression grew that he was less meek than he looked. He signalised his entrance by differing with the established poet, Gregory, upon the whole nature of poetry. He said that he (Syme) was poet of law, a poet of order; nay, he said he was a poet of respectability. So all the Saffron Parkers looked at him as if he had that moment fallen out of that impossible sky.

In fact, Mr. Lucian Gregory, the anarchic poet, connected the two events.

"It may well be," he said, in his sudden lyrical manner, "it may well be on such a night of clouds and cruel colours that there is brought forth upon the earth such a portent as a respectable poet. You say you are a poet of law; I say you are a contradiction in terms. I only wonder there were not comets and earthquakes on the night you appeared in this garden."

The man with the meek blue eyes and the pale, pointed beard endured these thunders with a certain submissive solemnity. The third party of the group, Gregory's sister Rosamond, who had her brother's braids of red hair, but a kindlier face underneath them, laughed with such mixture of admiration and disapproval as she gave commonly to the family oracle.

Gregory resumed in high oratorical good humour.

"An artist is identical with an anarchist," he cried. "You might transpose the words anywhere. An anarchist is an artist. The man who throws a bomb is an artist, because he prefers a great moment to everything. He sees how much more valuable is one burst of blazing light, one peal of perfect thunder, than the mere common bodies of a few shapeless policemen. An artist disregards all governments, abolishes all conventions. The poet delights in disorder only. If it were not so, the most poetical thing in the world would be the Underground Railway."

"So it is," said Mr. Syme.

"Nonsense!" said Gregory, who was very rational when anyone else attempted paradox. "Why do all the clerks and navvies in the railway trains look so sad and tired, so very sad and tired? I will tell you. It is because they know that the train is going right. It is because they know that whatever place they have taken a ticket for that place they will reach. It is because after they have passed Sloane Square they know that the next station must be Victoria, and nothing but Victoria. Oh, their wild rapture! oh, their eyes like stars and their souls again in Eden, if the next station were unaccountably Baker Street!"

"It is you who are unpoetical," replied the poet Syme. "If what you say of clerks is true, they can only be as prosaic as your poetry. The rare, strange thing is to hit the mark; the gross, obvious thing is to miss it. We feel it is epical when man with one wild arrow strikes a distant bird. Is it not also epical when man with one wild engine strikes a distant station? Chaos is dull; because in chaos the train might indeed go anywhere, to Baker Street or to Bagdad. But man is a magician, and his whole magic is in this, that he does say Victoria, and lo! it is Victoria. No, take your books of mere poetry and prose; let me read a time table, with tears of pride. Take your Byron, who commemorates the defeats of man; give me Bradshaw, who commemorates his victories. Give me Bradshaw, I say!"

"Must you go?" inquired Gregory sarcastically.

"I tell you," went on Syme with passion, "that every time a train comes in I feel that it has broken past batteries of besiegers, and that man has won a battle against chaos. You say contemptuously that when one has left Sloane Square one must come to Victoria. I say that one might do a thousand things instead, and that whenever I really come there I have the sense of hairbreadth escape. And when I hear the guard shout out the word 'Victoria,' it is not an unmeaning word. It is to me the cry of a herald announcing conquest. It is to me indeed 'Victoria'; it is the victory of Adam."

Gregory wagged his heavy, red head with a slow and sad smile.

"And even then," he said, "we poets always ask the question, 'And what is Victoria now that you have got there?' You think Victoria is like the New Jerusalem. We know that the New Jerusalem will only be like Victoria. Yes, the poet will be discontented even in the streets of heaven. The poet is always in revolt."

"There again," said Syme irritably, "what is there poetical about being in revolt? You might as well say that it is poetical to be sea-sick. Being sick is a revolt. Both being sick and being rebellious may be the wholesome thing on certain desperate occasions; but I'm hanged if I can see why they are poetical. Revolt in the abstract is—revolting. It's mere vomiting."

The girl winced for a flash at the unpleasant word, but Syme was too hot to heed her.

"It is things going right," he cried, "that is poetical! Our digestions, for instance, going sacredly and silently right, that is the foundation of all poetry. Yes, the most poetical thing, more poetical than the flowers, more poetical than the stars— the most poetical thing in the world is not being sick."

"Really," said Gregory superciliously, "the examples you choose—"

"I beg your pardon," said Syme grimly, "I forgot we had abolished all conventions."

For the first time a red patch appeared on Gregory's forehead.

"You don't expect me," he said, "to revolutionise society on this lawn?"

Syme looked straight into his eyes and smiled sweetly.

"No, I don't," he said; "but I suppose that if you were serious about your anarchism, that is exactly what you would do."

Gregory's big bull's eyes blinked suddenly like those of an angry lion, and one could almost fancy that his red mane rose.

"Don't you think, then," he said in a dangerous voice, "that I am serious about my anarchism?"

"I beg your pardon?" said Syme.

"Am I not serious about my anarchism?" cried Gregory, with knotted fists.

"My dear fellow!" said Syme, and strolled away.

With surprise, but with a curious pleasure, he found Rosamond Gregory still in his company.

"Mr. Syme," she said, "do the people who talk like you and my brother often mean what they say? Do you mean what you say now?"

Syme smiled.

"Do you?" he asked.

"What do you mean?" asked the girl, with grave eyes.

"My dear Miss Gregory," said Syme gently, "there are many kinds of sincerity and insincerity. When you say 'thank you' for the salt, do you mean what you say? No. When you say 'the world is round,' do you mean what you say? No. It is true, but you don't mean it. Now, sometimes a man like your brother really finds a thing he does mean. It may be only a half-truth, quarter-truth, tenth-truth; but then he says more than he means—from sheer force of meaning it."

She was looking at him from under level brows; her face was grave and open, and there had fallen upon it the shadow of that unreasoning responsibility which is at the bottom of the most frivolous woman, the maternal watch which is as old as the world.

"Is he really an anarchist, then?" she asked.

"Only in that sense I speak of," replied Syme; "or if you prefer it, in that nonsense."

She drew her broad brows together and said abruptly—

"He wouldn't really use—bombs or that sort of thing?"

Syme broke into a great laugh, that seemed too large for his slight and somewhat dandified figure.

"Good Lord, no!" he said, "that has to be done anonymously."

And at that the corners of her own mouth broke into a smile, and she thought with a simultaneous pleasure of Gregory's absurdity and of his safety.

Syme strolled with her to a seat in the corner of the garden, and continued to pour out his opinions. For he was a sincere man, and in spite of his superficial airs and graces, at root a humble one. And it is always the humble man who talks too much; the proud man watches himself too closely. He defended respectability with violence and exaggeration. He grew passionate in his praise of tidiness and propriety. All the time there was a smell of lilac all round him. Once he heard very faintly in some distant street a barrel-organ begin to play, and it seemed to him that his heroic words were moving to a tiny tune from under or beyond the world.

He stared and talked at the girl's red hair and amused face for what seemed to be a few minutes; and then, feeling that the groups in such a place should mix, rose to his feet. To his astonishment, he discovered the whole garden empty. Everyone had gone long ago, and he went himself with a rather hurried apology. He left with a sense of champagne in his head, which he could not afterwards explain. In the wild events which were to follow this girl had no part at all; he never saw her again until all his tale was over. And yet, in some indescribable way, she kept recurring like a motive in music through all his mad adventures afterwards, and the glory of her strange hair ran like a red thread through those dark and ill-drawn tapestries of the night. For what followed was so improbable, that it might well have been a dream.

When Syme went out into the starlit street, he found it for the moment empty. Then he realised (in some odd way) that the silence was rather a living silence than a dead one. Directly outside the door stood a street lamp, whose gleam gilded the leaves of the tree that bent out over the fence behind him. About a foot from the lamp-post stood a figure almost as rigid and motionless as the lamp-post itself. The tall hat and long frock coat were black; the face, in an abrupt shadow, was almost as dark. Only a fringe of fiery hair against the light, and also something aggressive in the attitude, proclaimed that it was the poet Gregory. He had something of the look of a masked bravo waiting sword in hand for his foe.

He made a sort of doubtful salute, which Syme somewhat more formally returned.

"I was waiting for you," said Gregory. "Might I have a moment's conversation?"

"Certainly. About what?" asked Syme in a sort of weak wonder.

Gregory struck out with his stick at the lamp-post, and then at the tree. "About this and this," he cried; "about order and anarchy. There is your precious order, that lean, iron lamp, ugly and barren; and there is anarchy, rich, living, reproducing itself—there is anarchy, splendid in green and gold."

"All the same," replied Syme patiently, "just at present you only see the tree by the light of the lamp. I wonder when you would ever see the lamp by the light of the tree." Then after a pause he said, "But may I ask if you have been standing out here in the dark only to resume our little argument?"

"No," cried out Gregory, in a voice that rang down the street, "I did not stand here to resume our argument, but to end it for ever."

The silence fell again, and Syme, though he understood nothing, listened instinctively for something serious. Gregory began in a smooth voice and with a rather bewildering smile.

"Mr. Syme," he said, "this evening you succeeded in doing something rather remarkable. You did something to me that no man born of woman has ever succeeded in doing before."

"Indeed!"

"Now I remember," resumed Gregory reflectively, "one other person succeeded in doing it. The captain of a penny steamer (if I remember correctly) at Southend. You have irritated me."

"I am very sorry," replied Syme with gravity.

"I am afraid my fury and your insult are too shocking to be wiped out even with an apology," said Gregory very calmly. "No duel could wipe it out. If I struck you dead I could not wipe it out. There is only one way by which that insult can be erased, and that way I choose. I am going, at the possible sacrifice of my life and honour, to prove to you that you were wrong in what you said."

"In what I said?"

"You said I was not serious about being an anarchist."

"There are degrees of seriousness," replied Syme. "I have never doubted that you were perfectly sincere in this sense, that you thought what you said well worth saying, that you thought a paradox might wake men up to a neglected truth."

Gregory stared at him steadily and painfully.

"And in no other sense," he asked, "you think me serious? You think me a flaneur who lets fall occasional truths. You do not think that in a deeper, a more deadly sense, I am serious."

Syme struck his stick violently on the stones of the road.

"Serious!" he cried. "Good Lord! is this street serious? Are these damned Chinese lanterns serious? Is the whole caboodle serious? One comes here and talks a pack of bosh, and perhaps some sense as well, but I should think very little of a man who didn't keep something in the background of his life that was more serious than all this talking—something more serious, whether it was religion or only drink."

"Very well," said Gregory, his face darkening, "you shall see something more serious than either drink or religion."

Syme stood waiting with his usual air of mildness until Gregory again opened his lips.

"You spoke just now of having a religion. Is it really true that you have one?"

"Oh," said Syme with a beaming smile, "we are all Catholics now."

"Then may I ask you to swear by whatever gods or saints your religion involves that you will not reveal what I am now going to tell you to any son of Adam, and especially not to the police? Will you swear that! If you will take upon yourself this awful abnegation if you will consent to burden your soul with a vow that you should never make and a knowledge you should never dream about, I will promise you in return—"

"You will promise me in return?" inquired Syme, as the other paused.

"I will promise you a very entertaining evening." Syme suddenly took off his hat.

"Your offer," he said, "is far too idiotic to be declined. You say that a poet is always an anarchist. I disagree; but I hope at least that he is always a sportsman. Permit me, here and now, to swear as a Christian, and promise as a good comrade and a fellow-artist, that I will not report anything of this, whatever it is, to the police. And now, in the name of Colney Hatch, what is it?"

"I think," said Gregory, with placid irrelevancy, "that we will call a cab."

He gave two long whistles, and a hansom came rattling down the road. The two got into it in silence. Gregory gave through the trap the address of an obscure public-house on the Chiswick bank of the river. The cab whisked itself away again, and in it these two fantastics quitted their fantastic town.

CHAPTER II
THE SECRET OF GABRIEL SYME

THE cab pulled up before a particularly dreary and greasy beershop, into which Gregory rapidly conducted his companion. They seated themselves in a close and dim sort of bar-parlour, at a stained wooden table with one wooden leg. The room was so small and dark, that very little could be seen of the attendant who was summoned, beyond a vague and dark impression of something bulky and bearded.

"Will you take a little supper?" asked Gregory politely. "The pate de foie gras is not good here, but I can recommend the game."

Syme received the remark with stolidity, imagining it to be a joke. Accepting the vein of humour, he said, with a well-bred indifference—

"Oh, bring me some lobster mayonnaise."

To his indescribable astonishment, the man only said "Certainly, sir!" and went away apparently to get it.

"What will you drink?" resumed Gregory, with the same careless yet apologetic air. "I shall only have a creme de menthe myself; I have dined. But the champagne can really be trusted. Do let me start you with a half-bottle of Pommery at least?"

"Thank you!" said the motionless Syme. "You are very good."

His further attempts at conversation, somewhat disorganised in themselves, were cut short finally as by a thunderbolt by the actual appearance of the lobster. Syme tasted it, and found it particularly good. Then he suddenly began to eat with great rapidity and appetite.

"Excuse me if I enjoy myself rather obviously!" he said to Gregory, smiling. "I don't often have the luck to have a dream like this. It is new to me for a nightmare to lead to a lobster. It is commonly the other way."

"You are not asleep, I assure you," said Gregory. "You are, on the contrary, close to the most actual and rousing moment of your existence. Ah, here comes your champagne! I admit that there may be a slight disproportion, let us say, between the inner arrangements of this excellent hotel and its simple and unpretentious exterior. But that is all our modesty. We are the most modest men that ever lived on earth."

"And who are we?" asked Syme, emptying his champagne glass.

"It is quite simple," replied Gregory. "We are the serious anarchists, in whom you do not believe."

"Oh!" said Syme shortly. "You do yourselves well in drinks."

"Yes, we are serious about everything," answered Gregory.

Then after a pause he added—

"If in a few moments this table begins to turn round a little, don't put it down to your inroads into the champagne. I don't wish you to do yourself an injustice."

"Well, if I am not drunk, I am mad," replied Syme with perfect calm; "but I trust I can behave like a gentleman in either condition. May I smoke?"

"Certainly!" said Gregory, producing a cigar-case. "Try one of mine."

Syme took the cigar, clipped the end off with a cigar-cutter out of his waistcoat pocket, put it in his mouth, lit it slowly, and let out a long cloud of smoke. It is not a little to his credit that he performed these rites with so much composure, for almost before he had begun them the table at which he sat had begun to revolve, first slowly, and then rapidly, as if at an insane seance.

"You must not mind it," said Gregory; "it's a kind of screw."

"Quite so," said Syme placidly, "a kind of screw. How simple that is!"

The next moment the smoke of his cigar, which had been wavering across the room in snaky twists, went straight up as if from a factory chimney, and the two, with their chairs and table, shot down through the floor as if the earth had swallowed them. They went rattling down a kind of roaring chimney as rapidly as a lift cut loose, and they came with an abrupt bump to the bottom. But when Gregory threw open a pair of doors and let in a red subterranean light, Syme was still smoking with one leg thrown over the other, and had not turned a yellow hair.

Gregory led him down a low, vaulted passage, at the end of which was the red light. It was an enormous crimson lantern, nearly as big as a fireplace, fixed over a small but heavy iron door. In the door there was a sort of hatchway or grating, and on this Gregory struck five times. A heavy voice with a foreign accent asked him who he was. To this he gave the more or less unexpected reply, "Mr. Joseph Chamberlain." The heavy hinges began to move; it was obviously some kind of password.

Inside the doorway the passage gleamed as if it were lined with a network of steel. On a second glance, Syme saw that the glittering pattern was really made up of ranks and ranks of rifles and revolvers, closely packed or interlocked.

"I must ask you to forgive me all these formalities," said Gregory; "we have to be very strict here."

"Oh, don't apologise," said Syme. "I know your passion for law and order," and he stepped into the passage lined with the steel weapons. With his long, fair hair and rather foppish frock-coat, he looked a singularly frail and fanciful figure as he walked down that shining avenue of death.

They passed through several such passages, and came out at last into a queer steel chamber with curved walls, almost spherical in shape, but presenting, with its tiers of benches, something of the appearance of a scientific lecture-theatre. There were no rifles or pistols in this apartment, but round the walls of it were hung more dubious and dreadful shapes, things that looked like the bulbs of iron plants, or the eggs of iron birds. They were bombs, and the very room itself seemed like the inside of a bomb. Syme knocked his cigar ash off against the wall, and went in.

"And now, my dear Mr. Syme," said Gregory, throwing himself in an expansive manner on the bench under the largest bomb, "now we are quite cosy, so let us talk properly. Now no human words can give you any notion of why I brought you here. It was one of those quite arbitrary emotions, like jumping off a cliff or falling in love. Suffice it to say that you were an inexpressibly irritating fellow, and, to do you justice, you are still. I would break twenty oaths of secrecy for the pleasure of taking you down a peg. That way you have of lighting a cigar would make a priest break the seal of confession. Well, you said that you were quite certain I was not a serious anarchist. Does this place strike you as being serious?"

"It does seem to have a moral under all its gaiety," assented Syme; "but may I ask you two questions? You need not fear to give me information, because, as you remember, you very wisely extorted from me a promise not to tell the police, a promise I shall certainly keep. So it is in mere curiosity that I make my queries. First of all, what is it really all about? What is it you object to? You want to abolish Government?"

"To abolish God!" said Gregory, opening the eyes of a fanatic. "We do not only want to upset a few despotisms and police regulations; that sort of anarchism does exist, but it is a mere branch of the Nonconformists. We dig deeper and we blow you higher. We wish to deny all those arbitrary distinctions of vice and virtue, honour and treachery, upon which mere rebels base themselves. The silly sentimentalists of the French Revolution talked of the Rights of Man! We hate Rights as we hate Wrongs. We have abolished Right and Wrong."

"And Right and Left," said Syme with a simple eagerness, "I hope you will abolish them too. They are much more troublesome to me."

"You spoke of a second question," snapped Gregory.

"With pleasure," resumed Syme. "In all your present acts and surroundings there is a scientific attempt at secrecy. I have an aunt who lived over a shop, but this is the first time I have found people living from preference under a public-house. You have a heavy iron door. You cannot pass it without submitting to the humiliation of calling yourself Mr. Chamberlain. You surround yourself with steel instru-instruments which make the place, if I may say so, more impressive than homelike. May I ask why, after taking all this trouble to barricade yourselves in the bowels of the earth, you then parade your whole secret by talking about anarchism to every silly woman in Saffron Park?"

Gregory smiled.

"The answer is simple," he said. "I told you I was a serious anarchist, and you did not believe me. Nor do they believe me. Unless I took them into this infernal room they would not believe me."

Syme smoked thoughtfully, and looked at him with interest. Gregory went on.

"The history of the thing might amuse you," he said. "When first I became one of the New Anarchists I tried all kinds of respectable disguises. I dressed up as a bishop. I read up all about bishops in our anarchist pamphlets, in Superstition the Vampire and Priests of Prey. I certainly understood from them that bishops are strange and terrible old men keeping a cruel secret from mankind. I was misinformed. When on my first appearing in episcopal gaiters in a drawing-room I cried out in a voice of thunder, 'Down! down! presumptuous human reason!' they found out in some way that I was not a bishop at all. I was nabbed at once. Then I made up as a millionaire; but I defended Capital with so much intelligence that a fool could see that I was quite poor. Then I tried being a major. Now I am a humanitarian myself, but I have, I hope, enough intellectual breadth to understand the position of those who, like Nietzsche, admire violence—the proud, mad war of Nature and all that, you know. I threw myself into the major. I drew my sword and waved it constantly. I called out 'Blood!' abstractedly, like a man calling for wine. I often said, 'Let the weak perish; it is the Law.' Well, well, it seems majors don't do this. I was nabbed again. At last I went in despair to the President of the Central Anarchist Council, who is the greatest man in Europe."

"What is his name?" asked Syme.

"You would not know it," answered Gregory. "That is his greatness. Caesar and Napoleon put all their genius into being heard of, and they were heard of. He puts all his genius into not being heard of, and he is not heard of. But you cannot be for five minutes in the room with him without feeling that Caesar and Napoleon would have been children in his hands."

He was silent and even pale for a moment, and then resumed—

"But whenever he gives advice it is always something as startling as an epigram, and yet as practical as the Bank of England. I said to him, 'What disguise will hide me from the world? What can I find more respectable than bishops and majors?' He looked at me with his large but indecipherable face. 'You want a safe disguise, do you? You want a dress which will guarantee you harmless; a dress in which no one would ever look for a bomb?' I nodded. He suddenly lifted his lion's voice. 'Why, then, dress up as an anarchist, you fool!' he roared so that the room shook. 'Nobody will ever expect you to do anything dangerous then.' And he turned his broad back on me without another word. I took his advice, and have never regretted it. I preached blood and murder to those women day and night, and—by God!—they would let me wheel their perambulators."

Syme sat watching him with some respect in his large, blue eyes.

"You took me in," he said. "It is really a smart dodge."

Then after a pause he added—

"What do you call this tremendous President of yours?"

"We generally call him Sunday," replied Gregory with simplicity. "You see, there are seven members of the Central Anarchist Council, and they are named after days of the week. He is called Sunday, by some of his admirers Bloody Sunday. It is curious you should mention the matter, because the very night you have dropped in (if I may so express it) is the night on which our London branch, which assembles in this room, has to elect its own deputy to fill a vacancy in the Council. The gentleman who has for some time past played, with propriety and general applause, the difficult part of Thursday, has died quite suddenly. Consequently, we have called a meeting this very evening to elect a successor."

He got to his feet and strolled across the room with a sort of smiling embarrassment.

"I feel somehow as if you were my mother, Syme," he continued casually. "I feel that I can confide anything to you, as you have promised to tell nobody. In fact, I will confide to you something that I would not say in so many words to the anarchists who will be coming to the room in about ten minutes. We shall, of course, go through a form of election; but I don't mind telling you that it is practically certain what the result will be." He looked down for a moment modestly. "It is almost a settled thing that I am to be Thursday."

"My dear fellow." said Syme heartily, "I congratulate you. A great career!"

Gregory smiled in deprecation, and walked across the room, talking rapidly.

"As a matter of fact, everything is ready for me on this table," he said, "and the ceremony will probably be the shortest possible."

Syme also strolled across to the table, and found lying across it a walking-stick, which turned out on examination to be a sword-stick, a large Colt's revolver, a sandwich case, and a formidable flask of brandy. Over the chair, beside the table, was thrown a heavy-looking cape or cloak.

"I have only to get the form of election finished," continued Gregory with animation, "then I snatch up this cloak and stick, stuff these other things into my pocket, step out of a door in this cavern, which opens on the river, where there is a steam-tug already waiting for me, and then—then—oh, the wild joy of being Thursday!" And he clasped his hands.

Syme, who had sat down once more with his usual insolent languor, got to his feet with an unusual air of hesitation.

"Why is it," he asked vaguely, "that I think you are quite a decent fellow? Why do I positively like you, Gregory?" He paused a moment, and then added with a sort of fresh curiosity, "Is it because you are such an ass?"

There was a thoughtful silence again, and then he cried out—

"Well, damn it all! this is the funniest situation I have ever been in in my life, and I am going to act accordingly. Gregory, I gave you a promise before I came into this place. That promise I would keep under red-hot pincers. Would you give me, for my own safety, a little promise of the same kind?"

"A promise?" asked Gregory, wondering.

"Yes," said Syme very seriously, "a promise. I swore before God that I would not tell your secret to the police. Will you swear by Humanity, or whatever beastly thing you believe in, that you will not tell my secret to the anarchists?"

"Your secret?" asked the staring Gregory. "Have you got a secret?"

"Yes," said Syme, "I have a secret." Then after a pause, "Will you swear?"

Gregory glared at him gravely for a few moments, and then said abruptly—

"You must have bewitched me, but I feel a furious curiosity about you. Yes, I will swear not to tell the anarchists anything you tell me. But look sharp, for they will be here in a couple of minutes."

Syme rose slowly to his feet and thrust his long, white hands into his long, grey trousers' pockets. Almost as he did so there came five knocks on the outer grating, proclaiming the arrival of the first of the conspirators.

"Well," said Syme slowly, "I don't know how to tell you the truth more shortly than by saying that your expedient of dressing up as an aimless poet is not confined to you or your President. We have known the dodge for some time at Scotland Yard."

Gregory tried to spring up straight, but he swayed thrice.

"What do you say?" he asked in an inhuman voice.

"Yes," said Syme simply, "I am a police detective. But I think I hear your friends coming."

From the doorway there came a murmur of "Mr. Joseph Chamberlain." It was repeated twice and thrice, and then thirty times, and the crowd of Joseph Chamberlains (a solemn thought) could be heard trampling down the corridor.

CHAPTER III
THE MAN WHO WAS THURSDAY

BEFORE one of the fresh faces could appear at the doorway, Gregory's stunned surprise had fallen from him. He was beside the table with a bound, and a noise in his throat like a wild beast. He caught up the Colt's revolver and took aim at Syme. Syme did not flinch, but he put up a pale and polite hand.

"Don't be such a silly man," he said, with the effeminate dignity of a curate. "Don't you see it's not necessary? Don't you see that we're both in the same boat? Yes, and jolly sea-sick."

Gregory could not speak, but he could not fire either, and he looked his question.

"Don't you see we've checkmated each other?" cried Syme. "I can't tell the police you are an anarchist. You can't tell the anarchists I'm a policeman. I can only watch you, knowing what you are; you can only watch me, knowing what I am. In short, it's a lonely, intellectual duel, my head against yours. I'm a policeman deprived of the help of the police. You, my poor fellow, are an anarchist deprived of the help of that law and organisation which is so essential to anarchy. The one solitary difference is in your favour. You are not surrounded by inquisitive policemen; I am surrounded by inquisitive anarchists. I cannot betray you, but I might betray myself. Come, come! wait and see me betray myself. I shall do it so nicely."

Gregory put the pistol slowly down, still staring at Syme as if he were a sea-monster.

"I don't believe in immortality," he said at last, "but if, after all this, you were to break your word, God would make a hell only for you, to howl in for ever."

"I shall not break my word," said Syme sternly, "nor will you break yours. Here are your friends."

The mass of the anarchists entered the room heavily, with a slouching and somewhat weary gait; but one little man, with a black beard and glasses—a man somewhat of the type of Mr. Tim Healy—detached himself, and bustled forward with some papers in his hand.

"Comrade Gregory," he said, "I suppose this man is a delegate?"

Gregory, taken by surprise, looked down and muttered the name of Syme; but Syme replied almost pertly—

"I am glad to see that your gate is well enough guarded to make it hard for anyone to be here who was not a delegate."

The brow of the little man with the black beard was, however, still contracted with something like suspicion.

"What branch do you represent?" he asked sharply.

"I should hardly call it a branch," said Syme, laughing; "I should call it at the very least a root."

"What do you mean?"

"The fact is," said Syme serenely, "the truth is I am a Sabbatarian. I have been specially sent here to see that you show a due observance of Sunday."

The little man dropped one of his papers, and a flicker of fear went over all the faces of the group. Evidently the awful President, whose name was Sunday, did sometimes send down such irregular ambassadors to such branch meetings.

"Well, comrade," said the man with the papers after a pause, "I suppose we'd better give you a seat in the meeting?"

"If you ask my advice as a friend," said Syme with severe benevolence, "I think you'd better."

When Gregory heard the dangerous dialogue end, with a sudden safety for his rival, he rose abruptly and paced the floor in painful thought. He was, indeed, in an agony of diplomacy. It was clear that Syme's inspired impudence was likely to bring him out of all merely accidental dilemmas. Little was to be hoped from them. He could not himself betray Syme, partly from honour, but partly also because, if he betrayed him and for some reason failed to destroy him, the Syme who escaped would be a Syme freed from all obligation of secrecy, a Syme who would simply walk to the nearest police station. After all, it was only one night's discussion, and only one detective who would know of it. He would let out as little as possible of their plans that night, and then let Syme go, and chance it.

He strode across to the group of anarchists, which was already distributing itself along the benches.

"I think it is time we began," he said; "the steam-tug is waiting on the river already. I move that Comrade Buttons takes the chair."

This being approved by a show of hands, the little man with the papers slipped into the presidential seat.

"Comrades," he began, as sharp as a pistol-shot, "our meeting tonight is important, though it need not be long. This branch has always had the honour of electing Thursdays for the Central European Council. We have elected many and splendid Thursdays. We all lament the sad decease of the heroic worker who occupied the post until last week. As you know, his services to the cause were considerable. He organised the great dynamite coup of Brighton which, under happier circumstances, ought to have killed everybody on the pier. As you also know, his death was as self-denying as his life, for he died through his faith in a hygienic mixture of chalk and water as a substitute for milk, which beverage he regarded as barbaric, and as involving cruelty to the cow. Cruelty, or anything approaching to cruelty, revolted him always. But it is not to acclaim his virtues that we are met, but for a harder task. It is difficult properly to praise his qualities, but it is more difficult to replace them. Upon you, comrades, it devolves this evening to choose out of the company present the man who shall be Thursday. If any comrade suggests a name I will put it to the vote. If no comrade suggests a name, I can only tell myself that that dear dynamiter, who is gone from us, has carried into the unknowable abysses the last secret of his virtue and his innocence."

There was a stir of almost inaudible applause, such as is sometimes heard in church. Then a large old man, with a long and venerable white beard, perhaps the only real working-man present, rose lumberingly and said—

"I move that Comrade Gregory be elected Thursday," and sat lumberingly down again.

"Does anyone second?" asked the chairman.

A little man with a velvet coat and pointed beard seconded.

"Before I put the matter to the vote," said the chairman, "I will call on Comrade Gregory to make a statement."

Gregory rose amid a great rumble of applause. His face was deadly pale, so that by contrast his queer red hair looked almost scarlet. But he was smiling and altogether at ease. He had made up his mind, and he saw his best policy quite plain in front of him like a white road. His best chance was to make a softened and ambiguous speech, such as would leave on the detective's mind the impression that the anarchist brotherhood was a very mild affair after all. He believed in his own literary power, his capacity for suggesting fine shades and picking perfect words. He thought that with care he could succeed, in spite of all the people around him, in conveying an impression of the institution, subtly and delicately false. Syme had once thought that anarchists, under all their bravado, were only playing the fool. Could he not now, in the hour of peril, make Syme think so again?

"Comrades," began Gregory, in a low but penetrating voice, "it is not necessary for me to tell you what is my policy, for it is your policy also. Our belief has been slandered, it has been disfigured, it has been utterly confused and concealed, but it has never been altered. Those who talk about anarchism and its dangers go everywhere and anywhere to get their information, except to us, except to the fountain head. They learn about anarchists from sixpenny novels; they learn about anarchists from tradesmen's newspapers; they learn about anarchists from Ally Sloper's Half-Holiday and the Sporting Times. They never learn about anarchists from anarchists. We have no chance of denying the mountainous slanders which are heaped upon our heads from one end of Europe to another. The man who has always heard that we are walking plagues has never heard our reply. I know that he will not hear it tonight, though my passion were to rend the roof. For it is deep, deep under the earth that the persecuted are permitted to assemble, as the Christians assembled in the Catacombs. But if, by some incredible accident, there were here tonight a man who all his life had thus immensely misunderstood us, I would put this question to him: 'When those Christians met in those Catacombs, what sort of moral reputation had they in the streets above? What tales were told of their atrocities by one educated Roman to another? Suppose' (I would say to him), 'suppose that we are only repeating that still mysterious paradox of history. Suppose we seem as shocking as the Christians because we are really as harmless as the Christians. Suppose we seem as mad as the Christians because we are really as meek.'"

The applause that had greeted the opening sentences had been gradually growing fainter, and at the last word it stopped suddenly. In the abrupt silence, the man with the velvet jacket said, in a high, squeaky voice—

"I'm not meek!"

"Comrade Witherspoon tells us," resumed Gregory, "that he is not meek. Ah, how little he knows himself! His words are, indeed, extravagant; his appearance is ferocious, and even (to an ordinary taste) unattractive. But only the eye of a friendship as deep and delicate as mine can perceive the deep foundation of solid meekness which lies at the base of him, too deep even for himself to see. I repeat, we are the true early Christians, only that we come too late. We are simple, as they revere simple—look at Comrade Witherspoon. We are modest, as they were modest—look at me. We are merciful—"

"No, no!" called out Mr. Witherspoon with the velvet jacket.

"I say we are merciful," repeated Gregory furiously, "as the early Christians were merciful. Yet this did not prevent their being accused of eating human flesh. We do not eat human flesh—"

"Shame!" cried Witherspoon. "Why not?"

"Comrade Witherspoon," said Gregory, with a feverish gaiety, "is anxious to know why nobody eats him (laughter). In our society, at any rate, which loves him sincerely, which is founded upon love—"

"No, no!" said Witherspoon, "down with love."

"Which is founded upon love," repeated Gregory, grinding his teeth, "there will be no difficulty about the aims which we shall pursue as a body, or which I should pursue were I chosen as the representative of that body. Superbly careless of the slanders that represent us as assassins and enemies of human society, we shall pursue with moral courage and quiet intellectual pressure, the permanent ideals of brotherhood and simplicity."

Gregory resumed his seat and passed his hand across his forehead. The silence was sudden and awkward, but the chairman rose like an automaton, and said in a colourless voice—

"Does anyone oppose the election of Comrade Gregory?"

The assembly seemed vague and sub-consciously disappointed, and Comrade Witherspoon moved restlessly on his seat and muttered in his thick beard. By the sheer rush of routine, however, the motion would have been put and carried. But as the chairman was opening his mouth to put it, Syme sprang to his feet and said in a small and quiet voice—

"Yes, Mr. Chairman, I oppose."

The most effective fact in oratory is an unexpected change in the voice. Mr. Gabriel Syme evidently understood oratory. Having said these first formal words in a moderated tone and with a brief simplicity, he made his next word ring and volley in the vault as if one of the guns had gone off.

"Comrades!" he cried, in a voice that made every man jump out of his boots, "have we come here for this? Do we live underground like rats in order to listen to talk like this? This is talk we might listen to while eating buns at a Sunday School treat. Do we line these walls with weapons and bar that door with death lest anyone should come and hear Comrade Gregory saying to us, 'Be good, and you will be happy,' 'Honesty is the best policy,' and 'Virtue is its own reward'? There was not a word in Comrade Gregory's address to which a curate could not have listened with pleasure (hear, hear). But I am not a curate (loud cheers), and I did not listen to it with pleasure (renewed cheers). The man who is fitted to make a good curate is not fitted to make a resolute, forcible, and efficient Thursday (hear, hear)."

"Comrade Gregory has told us, in only too apologetic a tone, that we are not the enemies of society. But I say that we are the enemies of society, and so much the worse for society. We are the enemies of society, for society is the enemy of humanity, its oldest and its most pitiless enemy (hear, hear). Comrade Gregory has told us (apologetically again) that we are not murderers. There I agree. We are not murderers, we are executioners (cheers)."

Ever since Syme had risen Gregory had sat staring at him, his face idiotic with astonishment. Now in the pause his lips of clay parted, and he said, with an automatic and lifeless distinctness—

"You damnable hypocrite!"

Syme looked straight into those frightful eyes with his own pale blue ones, and said with dignity—

"Comrade Gregory accuses me of hypocrisy. He knows as well as I do that I am keeping all my engagements and doing nothing but my duty. I do not mince words. I do not pretend to. I say that Comrade Gregory is unfit to be Thursday for all his amiable qualities. He is unfit to be Thursday because of his amiable qualities. We do not want the Supreme Council of Anarchy infected with a maudlin mercy (hear, hear). This is no time for ceremonial politeness, neither is it a time for ceremonial modesty. I set myself against Comrade Gregory as I would set myself against all the Governments of Europe, because the anarchist who has given himself to anarchy has forgotten modesty as much as he has forgotten pride (cheers). I am not a man at all. I am a cause (renewed cheers). I set myself against Comrade Gregory as impersonally and as calmly as I should choose one pistol rather than another out of that rack upon the wall; and I say that rather than have Gregory and his milk-and-water methods on the Supreme Council, I would offer myself for election—"

His sentence was drowned in a deafening cataract of applause. The faces, that had grown fiercer and fiercer with approval as his tirade grew more and more uncompromising, were now distorted with grins of anticipation or cloven with delighted cries. At the moment when he announced himself as ready to stand for the post of Thursday, a roar of excitement and assent broke forth, and became uncontrollable, and at the same moment Gregory sprang to his feet, with foam upon his mouth, and shouted against the shouting.

"Stop, you blasted madmen!" he cried, at the top of a voice that tore his throat. "Stop, you—"

But louder than Gregory's shouting and louder than the roar of the room came the voice of Syme, still speaking in a peal of pitiless thunder—

"I do not go to the Council to rebut that slander that calls us murderers; I go to earn it (loud and prolonged cheering). To the priest who says these men are the enemies of religion, to the judge who says these men are the enemies of law, to the fat parliamentarian who says these men are the enemies of order and public decency, to all these I will reply, 'You are false kings, but you are true prophets. I am come to destroy you, and to fulfil your prophecies.'"

The heavy clamour gradually died away, but before it had ceased Witherspoon had jumped to his feet, his hair and beard all on end, and had said—

"I move, as an amendment, that Comrade Syme be appointed to the post."

"Stop all this, I tell you!" cried Gregory, with frantic face and hands. "Stop it, it is all—"

The voice of the chairman clove his speech with a cold accent.

"Does anyone second this amendment?" he said. A tall, tired man, with melancholy eyes and an American chin beard, was observed on the back bench to be slowly rising to his feet. Gregory had been screaming for some time past; now there was a change in his accent, more shocking than any scream. "I end all this!" he said, in a voice as heavy as stone.

"This man cannot be elected. He is a—"

"Yes," said Syme, quite motionless, "what is he?" Gregory's mouth worked twice without sound; then slowly the blood began to crawl back into his dead face. "He is a man quite inexperienced in our work," he said, and sat down abruptly.

Before he had done so, the long, lean man with the American beard was again upon his feet, and was repeating in a high American monotone—

"I beg to second the election of Comrade Syme."

"The amendment will, as usual, be put first," said Mr. Buttons, the chairman, with mechanical rapidity.

"The question is that Comrade Syme—"

Gregory had again sprung to his feet, panting and passionate.

"Comrades," he cried out, "I am not a madman."

"Oh, oh!" said Mr. Witherspoon.

"I am not a madman," reiterated Gregory, with a frightful sincerity which for a moment staggered the room, "but I give you a counsel which you can call mad if you like. No, I will not call it a counsel, for I can give you no reason for it. I will call it a command. Call it a mad command, but act upon it. Strike, but hear me! Kill me, but obey me! Do not elect this man." Truth is so terrible, even in fetters, that for a moment Syme's slender and insane victory swayed like a reed. But you could not have guessed it from Syme's bleak blue eyes. He merely began—

"Comrade Gregory commands—"

Then the spell was snapped, and one anarchist called out to Gregory—

"Who are you? You are not Sunday;" and another anarchist added in a heavier voice, "And you are not Thursday."

"Comrades," cried Gregory, in a voice like that of a martyr who in an ecstacy of pain has passed beyond pain, "it is nothing to me whether you detest me as a tyrant or detest me as a slave. If you will not take my command, accept my degradation. I kneel to you. I throw myself at your feet. I implore you. Do not elect this man."

"Comrade Gregory," said the chairman after a painful pause, "this is really not quite dignified."

For the first time in the proceedings there was for a few seconds a real silence. Then Gregory fell back in his seat, a pale wreck of a man, and the chairman repeated, like a piece of clock-work suddenly started again—

"The question is that Comrade Syme be elected to the post of Thursday on the General Council."

The roar rose like the sea, the hands rose like a forest, and three minutes afterwards Mr. Gabriel Syme, of the Secret Police Service, was elected to the post of Thursday on the General Council of the Anarchists of Europe.

Everyone in the room seemed to feel the tug waiting on the river, the sword-stick and the revolver, waiting on the table. The instant the election was ended and irrevocable, and Syme had received the paper proving his election, they all sprang to their feet, and the fiery groups moved and mixed in the room. Syme found himself, somehow or other, face to face with Gregory, who still regarded him with a stare of stunned hatred. They were silent for many minutes.

"You are a devil!" said Gregory at last.

"And you are a gentleman," said Syme with gravity.

"It was you that entrapped me," began Gregory, shaking from head to foot, "entrapped me into—"

"Talk sense," said Syme shortly. "Into what sort of devils' parliament have you entrapped me, if it comes to that? You made me swear before I made you. Perhaps we are both doing what we think right. But what we think right is so damned different that there can be nothing between us in the way of concession. There is nothing possible between us but honour and death," and he pulled the great cloak about his shoulders and picked up the flask from the table.

"The boat is quite ready," said Mr. Buttons, bustling up. "Be good enough to step this way."

With a gesture that revealed the shop-walker, he led Syme down a short, iron-bound passage, the still agonised Gregory following feverishly at their heels. At the end of the passage was a door, which Buttons opened sharply, showing a sudden blue and silver picture of the moonlit river, that looked like a scene in a theatre. Close to the opening lay a dark, dwarfish steam-launch, like a baby dragon with one red eye.

Almost in the act of stepping on board, Gabriel Syme turned to the gaping Gregory.

"You have kept your word," he said gently, with his face in shadow. "You are a man of honour, and I thank you. You have kept it even down to a small particular. There was one special thing you promised me at the beginning of the affair, and which you have certainly given me by the end of it."

"What do you mean?" cried the chaotic Gregory. "What did I promise you?"

"A very entertaining evening," said Syme, and he made a military salute with the sword-stick as the steamboat slid away.

CHAPTER IV
THE TALE OF A DETECTIVE

GABRIEL SYME was not merely a detective who pretended to be a poet; he was really a poet who had become a detective. Nor was his hatred of anarchy hypocritical. He was one of those who are driven early in life into too conservative an attitude by the bewildering folly of most revolutionists. He had not attained it by any tame tradition. His respectability was spontaneous and sudden, a rebellion against rebellion. He came of a family of cranks, in which all the oldest people had all the newest notions. One of his uncles always walked about without a hat, and another had made an unsuccessful attempt to walk about with a hat and nothing else. His father cultivated art and self-realisation; his mother went in for simplicity and hygiene. Hence the child, during his tenderer years, was wholly unacquainted with any drink between the extremes of absinth and cocoa, of both of which he had a healthy dislike. The more his mother preached a more than Puritan abstinence the more did his father expand into a more than pagan latitude; and by the time the former had come to enforcing vegetarianism, the latter had pretty well reached the point of defending cannibalism.

Being surrounded with every conceivable kind of revolt from infancy, Gabriel had to revolt into something, so he revolted into the only thing left—sanity. But there was just enough in him of the blood of these fanatics to make even his protest for common sense a little too fierce to be sensible. His hatred of modern lawlessness had been crowned also by an accident. It happened that he was walking in a side street at the instant of a dynamite outrage. He had been blind and deaf for a moment, and then seen, the smoke clearing, the broken windows and the bleeding faces. After that he went about as usual—quiet, courteous, rather gentle; but there was a spot on his mind that was not sane. He did not regard anarchists, as most of us do, as a handful of morbid men, combining ignorance with intellectualism. He regarded them as a huge and pitiless peril, like a Chinese invasion.

He poured perpetually into newspapers and their waste-paper baskets a torrent of tales, verses and violent articles, warning men of this deluge of barbaric denial. But he seemed to be getting no nearer his enemy, and, what was worse, no nearer a living. As he paced the Thames embankment, bitterly biting a cheap cigar and brooding on the advance of Anarchy, there was no anarchist with a bomb in his pocket so savage or so solitary as he. Indeed, he always felt that Government stood alone and desperate, with its back to the wall. He was too quixotic to have cared for it otherwise.

He walked on the Embankment once under a dark red sunset. The red river reflected the red sky, and they both reflected his anger. The sky, indeed, was so swarthy, and the light on the river relatively so lurid, that the water almost seemed of fiercer flame than the sunset it mirrored. It looked like a stream of literal fire winding under the vast caverns of a subterranean country.

Syme was shabby in those days. He wore an old-fashioned black chimney-pot hat; he was wrapped in a yet more old-fashioned cloak, black and ragged; and the combination gave him the look of the early villains in Dickens and Bulwer Lytton. Also his yellow beard and hair were more unkempt and leonine than when they appeared long afterwards, cut and pointed, on the lawns of Saffron Park. A long, lean, black cigar, bought in Soho for twopence, stood out from between his tightened teeth, and altogether he looked a very satisfactory specimen of the anarchists upon whom he had vowed a holy war. Perhaps this was why a policeman on the Embankment spoke to him, and said "Good evening."

Syme, at a crisis of his morbid fears for humanity, seemed stung by the mere stolidity of the automatic official, a mere bulk of blue in the twilight.

"A good evening is it?" he said sharply. "You fellows would call the end of the world a good evening. Look at that bloody red sun and that bloody river! I tell you that if that were literally human blood, spilt and shining, you would still be standing here as solid as ever, looking out for some poor harmless tramp whom you could move on. You policemen are cruel to the poor, but I could forgive you even your cruelty if it were not for your calm."

"If we are calm," replied the policeman, "it is the calm of organised resistance."

"Eh?" said Syme, staring.

"The soldier must be calm in the thick of the battle," pursued the policeman. "The composure of an army is the anger of a nation."

"Good God, the Board Schools!" said Syme. "Is this undenominational education?"

"No," said the policeman sadly, "I never had any of those advantages. The Board Schools came after my time. What education I had was very rough and old-fashioned, I am afraid."

"Where did you have it?" asked Syme, wondering.

"Oh, at Harrow," said the policeman

The class sympathies which, false as they are, are the truest things in so many men, broke out of Syme before he could control them.

"But, good Lord, man," he said, "you oughtn't to be a policeman!"

The policeman sighed and shook his head.

"I know," he said solemnly, "I know I am not worthy."

"But why did you join the police?" asked Syme with rude curiosity.

"For much the same reason that you abused the police," replied the other. "I found that there was a special opening in the service for those whose fears for humanity were concerned rather with the aberrations of the scientific intellect than with the normal and excusable, though excessive, outbreaks of the human will. I trust I make myself clear."

"If you mean that you make your opinion clear," said Syme, "I suppose you do. But as for making yourself clear, it is the last thing you do. How comes a man like you to be talking philosophy in a blue helmet on the Thames embankment?"

"You have evidently not heard of the latest development in our police system," replied the other. "I am not surprised at it. We are keeping it rather dark from the educated class, because that class contains most of our enemies. But you seem to be exactly in the right frame of mind. I think you might almost join us."

"Join you in what?" asked Syme.

"I will tell you," said the policeman slowly. "This is the situation: The head of one of our departments, one of the most celebrated detectives in Europe, has long been of opinion that a purely intellectual conspiracy would soon threaten the very existence of civilisation. He is certain that the scientific and artistic worlds are silently bound in a crusade against the Family and the State. He has, therefore, formed a special corps of policemen, policemen who are also philosophers. It is their business to watch the beginnings of this conspiracy, not merely in a criminal but in a controversial sense. I am a democrat myself, and I am fully aware of the value of the ordinary man in matters of ordinary valour or virtue. But it would obviously be undesirable to employ the common policeman in an investigation which is also a heresy hunt."

Syme's eyes were bright with a sympathetic curiosity.

"What do you do, then?" he said.

"The work of the philosophical policeman," replied the man in blue, "is at once bolder and more subtle than that of the ordinary detective. The ordinary detective goes to pot-houses to arrest thieves; we go to artistic tea-parties to detect pessimists. The ordinary detective discovers from a ledger or a diary that a crime has been committed. We discover from a book of sonnets that a crime will be committed. We have to trace the origin of those dreadful thoughts that drive men on at last to intellectual fanaticism and intellectual crime. We were only just in time to prevent the assassination at Hartlepool, and that was entirely due to the fact that our Mr. Wilks (a smart young fellow) thoroughly understood a triolet."

"Do you mean," asked Syme, "that there is really as much connection between crime and the modern intellect as all that?"

"You are not sufficiently democratic," answered the policeman, "but you were right when you said just now that our ordinary treatment of the poor criminal was a pretty brutal business. I tell you I am sometimes sick of my trade when I see how perpetually it means merely a war upon the ignorant and the desperate. But this new movement of ours is a very different affair. We deny the snobbish English assumption that the uneducated are the dangerous criminals. We remember the Roman Em-Emperors. We remember the great poisoning princes of the Renaissance. We say that the dangerous criminal is the educated criminal. We say that the most dangerous criminal now is the entirely lawless modern philosopher. Compared to him, burglars and bigamists are essentially moral men; my heart goes out to them. They accept the essential ideal of man; they merely seek it wrongly. Thieves respect property. They merely wish the property to become their property that they may more perfectly respect it. But philosophers dislike property as property; they wish to destroy the very idea of personal possession. Bigamists respect marriage, or they would not go through the highly ceremonial and even ritualistic formality of biga-my. But philosophers despise marriage as marriage. Murderers respect human life; they merely wish to attain a greater fulness of human life in themselves by the sacrifice of what seems to them to be lesser lives. But philosophers hate life itself, their own as much as other people's."

Syme struck his hands together.

"How true that is," he cried. "I have felt it from my boyhood, but never could state the verbal antithesis. The common criminal is a bad man, but at least he is, as it were, a conditional good man. He says that if only a certain obstacle be removed— say a wealthy uncle—he is then prepared to accept the universe and to praise God. He is a reformer, but not an anarchist. He wishes to cleanse the edifice, but not to destroy it. But the evil philosopher is not trying to alter things, but to annihilate them. Yes, the modern world has retained all those parts of police work which are really oppressive and ignominious, the harrying of the poor, the spying upon the unfortunate. It has given up its more dignified work, the punishment of powerful traitors in the State and powerful heresiarchs in the Church. The moderns say we must not punish heretics. My only doubt is whether we have a right to punish anybody else."

"But this is absurd!" cried the policeman, clasping his hands with an excitement uncommon in persons of his figure and costume, "but it is intolerable! I don't know what you're doing, but you're wasting your life. You must, you shall, join our special army against anarchy. Their armies are on our frontiers. Their bolt is ready to fall. A moment more, and you may lose the glory of working with us, perhaps the glory of dying with the last heroes of the world."

"It is a chance not to be missed, certainly," assented Syme, "but still I do not quite understand. I know as well as anybody that the modern world is full of lawless little men and mad little movements. But, beastly as they are, they generally have the one merit of disagreeing with each other. How can you talk of their leading one army or hurling one bolt. What is this anarchy?"

"Do not confuse it," replied the constable, "with those chance dynamite out-breaks from Russia or from Ireland, which are really the outbreaks of oppressed, if mistaken, men. This is a vast philosophic movement, consisting of an outer and an inner ring. You might even call the outer ring the laity and the inner ring the priesthood. I prefer to call the outer ring the innocent section, the inner ring the supremely guilty section. The outer ring—the main mass of their supporters—are merely anarchists; that is, men who believe that rules and formulas have destroyed human happiness. They believe that all the evil results of human crime are the results of the system that has called it crime. They do not believe that the crime creates the punishment. They believe that the punishment has created the crime. They believe that if a man seduced seven women he would naturally walk away as blameless as the flowers of spring. They believe that if a man picked a pocket he would naturally feel exquisitely good. These I call the innocent section."

"Oh!" said Syme.

"Naturally, therefore, these people talk about 'a happy time coming'; 'the paradise of the future'; 'mankind freed from the bondage of vice and the bondage of virtue,' and so on. And so also the men of the inner circle speak—the sacred priesthood. They also speak to applauding crowds of the happiness of the future, and of mankind freed at last. But in their mouths"—and the policeman lowered his voice—"in their mouths these happy phrases have a horrible meaning. They are under no illusions; they are too intellectual to think that man upon this earth can ever be quite free of original sin and the struggle. And they mean death. When they say that mankind shall be free at last, they mean that mankind shall commit suicide. When they talk of a paradise without right or wrong, they mean the grave.

"They have but two objects, to destroy first humanity and then themselves. That is why they throw bombs instead of firing pistols. The innocent rank and file are disappointed because the bomb has not killed the king; but the high-priesthood are happy because it has killed somebody."

"How can I join you?" asked Syme, with a sort of passion.

"I know for a fact that there is a vacancy at the moment," said the policeman, "as I have the honour to be somewhat in the confidence of the chief of whom I have spoken. You should really come and see him. Or rather, I should not say see him, nobody ever sees him; but you can talk to him if you like."

"Telephone?" inquired Syme, with interest.

"No," said the policeman placidly, "he has a fancy for always sitting in a pitch-dark room. He says it makes his thoughts brighter. Do come along."

Somewhat dazed and considerably excited, Syme allowed himself to be led to a side-door in the long row of buildings of Scotland Yard. Almost before he knew what he was doing, he had been passed through the hands of about four intermediate officials, and was suddenly shown into a room, the abrupt blackness of which startled him like a blaze of light. It was not the ordinary darkness, in which forms can be faintly traced; it was like going suddenly stone-blind.

"Are you the new recruit?" asked a heavy voice.

And in some strange way, though there was not the shadow of a shape in the gloom, Syme knew two things: first, that it came from a man of massive stature; and second, that the man had his back to him.

"Are you the new recruit?" said the invisible chief, who seemed to have heard all about it. "All right. You are engaged."

Syme, quite swept off his feet, made a feeble fight against this irrevocable phrase.

"I really have no experience," he began.

"No one has any experience," said the other, "of the Battle of Armageddon."

"But I am really unfit—"

"You are willing, that is enough," said the unknown.

"Well, really," said Syme, "I don't know any profession of which mere willingness is the final test."

"I do," said the other—"martyrs. I am condemning you to death. Good day."

Thus it was that when Gabriel Syme came out again into the crimson light of evening, in his shabby black hat and shabby, lawless cloak, he came out a member of the New Detective Corps for the frustration of the great conspiracy. Acting under the advice of his friend the policeman (who was professionally inclined to neatness), he trimmed his hair and beard, bought a good hat, clad himself in an exquisite summer suit of light blue-grey, with a pale yellow flower in the button-hole, and, in short, became that elegant and rather insupportable person whom Gregory had first encountered in the little garden of Saffron Park. Before he finally left the police premises his friend provided him with a small blue card, on which was written, "The Last Crusade," and a number, the sign of his official authority. He put this carefully in his upper waistcoat pocket, lit a cigarette, and went forth to track and fight the enemy in all the drawing-rooms of London. Where his adventure ultimately led us we have already seen. At about half-past one on a February night he found himself steaming in a small tug up the silent Thames, armed with swordstick and revolver, the duly elected Thursday of the Central Council of Anarchists.

When Syme stepped out on to the steam-tug he had a singular sensation of stepping out into something entirely new; not merely into the landscape of a new land, but even into the landscape of a new planet. This was mainly due to the insane yet solid decision of that evening, though partly also to an entire change in the weather and the sky since he entered the little tavern some two hours before. Every trace of the passionate plumage of the cloudy sunset had been swept away, and a naked moon stood in a naked sky. The moon was so strong and full that (by a paradox often to be noticed) it seemed like a weaker sun. It gave, not the sense of bright moonshine, but rather of a dead daylight.

Over the whole landscape lay a luminous and unnatural discoloration, as of that disastrous twilight which Milton spoke of as shed by the sun in eclipse; so that Syme fell easily into his first thought, that he was actually on some other and emptier planet, which circled round some sadder star. But the more he felt this glittering desolation in the moonlit land, the more his own chivalric folly glowed in the night like a great fire. Even the common things he carried with him—the food and the brandy and the loaded pistol—took on exactly that concrete and material poetry which a child feels when he takes a gun upon a journey or a bun with him to bed. The sword-stick and the brandy-flask, though in themselves only the tools of morbid conspirators, became the expressions of his own more healthy romance. The sword-stick became almost the sword of chivalry, and the brandy the wine of the stirrup-cup. For even the most dehumanised modern fantasies depend on some older and simpler figure; the adventures may be mad, but the adventurer must be sane. The dragon without St. George would not even be grotesque. So this inhuman land-scape was only imaginative by the presence of a man really human. To Syme's exaggerative mind the bright, bleak houses and terraces by the Thames looked as empty as the mountains of the moon. But even the moon is only poetical because there is a man in the moon.

The tug was worked by two men, and with much toil went comparatively slowly. The clear moon that had lit up Chiswick had gone down by the time that they passed Battersea, and when they came under the enormous bulk of Westmin-ster day had already begun to break. It broke like the splitting of great bars of lead, showing bars of silver; and these had brightened like white fire when the tug, changing its onward course, turned inward to a large landing stage rather beyond Charing Cross.

The great stones of the Embankment seemed equally dark and gigantic as Syme looked up at them. They were big and black against the huge white dawn. They made him feel that he was landing on the colossal steps of some Egyptian pal-ace; and, indeed, the thing suited his mood, for he was, in his own mind, mounting to attack the solid thrones of horrible and heathen kings. He leapt out of the boat on to one slimy step, and stood, a dark and slender figure, amid the enormous masonry. The two men in the tug put her off again and turned up stream. They had never spo-ken a word.

CHAPTER V
THE FEAST OF FEAR

AT first the large stone stair seemed to Syme as deserted as a pyramid; but be-fore he reached the top he had realised that there was a man leaning over the parapet of the Embankment and looking out across the river. As a figure he was quite con-ventional, clad in a silk hat and frock-coat of the more formal type of fashion; he had a red flower in his buttonhole. As Syme drew nearer to him step by step, he did not even move a hair; and Syme could come close enough to notice even in the dim, pale morning light that his face was long, pale and intellectual, and ended in a small triangular tuft of dark beard at the very point of the chin, all else being clean-shaven. This scrap of hair almost seemed a mere oversight; the rest of the face was of the type that is best shaven—clear-cut, ascetic, and in its way noble. Syme drew closer and closer, noting all this, and still the figure did not stir.

At first an instinct had told Syme that this was the man whom he was meant to meet. Then, seeing that the man made no sign, he had concluded that he was not. And now again he had come back to a certainty that the man had something to do with his mad adventure. For the man remained more still than would have been nat-ural if a stranger had come so close. He was as motionless as a wax-work, and got on the nerves somewhat in the same way. Syme looked again and again at the pale, dignified and delicate face, and the face still looked blankly across the river. Then he took out of his pocket the note from Buttons proving his election, and put it before that sad and beautiful face. Then the man smiled, and his smile was a shock, for it was all on one side, going up in the right cheek and down in the left.

There was nothing, rationally speaking, to scare anyone about this. Many people have this nervous trick of a crooked smile, and in many it is even attractive. But in all Syme's circumstances, with the dark dawn and the deadly errand and the loneliness on the great dripping stones, there was something unnerving in it.

There was the silent river and the silent man, a man of even classic face. And there was the last nightmare touch that his smile suddenly went wrong.

The spasm of smile was instantaneous, and the man's face dropped at once into its harmonious melancholy. He spoke without further explanation or inquiry, like a man speaking to an old colleague.

"If we walk up towards Leicester Square," he said, "we shall just be in time for breakfast. Sunday always insists on an early breakfast. Have you had any sleep?"

"No," said Syme.

"Nor have I," answered the man in an ordinary tone. "I shall try to get to bed after breakfast."

He spoke with casual civility, but in an utterly dead voice that contradicted the fanaticism of his face. It seemed almost as if all friendly words were to him lifeless conveniences, and that his only life was hate. After a pause the man spoke again.

"Of course, the Secretary of the branch told you everything that can be told. But the one thing that can never be told is the last notion of the President, for his notions grow like a tropical forest. So in case you don't know, I'd better tell you that he is carrying out his notion of concealing ourselves by not concealing ourselves to the most extraordinary lengths just now. Originally, of course, we met in a cell underground, just as your branch does. Then Sunday made us take a private room at an ordinary restaurant. He said that if you didn't seem to be hiding nobody hunted you out. Well, he is the only man on earth, I know; but sometimes I really think that his huge brain is going a little mad in its old age. For now we flaunt ourselves before the public. We have our breakfast on a balcony—on a balcony, if you please—overlooking Leicester Square."

"And what do the people say?" asked Syme.

"It's quite simple what they say," answered his guide.

"They say we are a lot of jolly gentlemen who pretend they are anarchists."

"It seems to me a very clever idea," said Syme.

"Clever! God blast your impudence! Clever!" cried out the other in a sudden, shrill voice which was as startling and discordant as his crooked smile. "When you've seen Sunday for a split second you'll leave off calling him clever."

With this they emerged out of a narrow street, and saw the early sunlight filling Leicester Square. It will never be known, I suppose, why this square itself should look so alien and in some ways so continental. It will never be known whether it was the foreign look that attracted the foreigners or the foreigners who gave it the foreign look. But on this particular morning the effect seemed singularly bright and clear. Between the open square and the sunlit leaves and the statue and the Saracenic outlines of the Alhambra, it looked the replica of some French or even Spanish public place. And this effect increased in Syme the sensation, which in many shapes he had had through the whole adventure, the eerie sensation of having strayed into a new world. As a fact, he had bought bad cigars round Leicester Square ever since he was a boy. But as he turned that corner, and saw the trees and the Moorish cupolas, he could have sworn that he was turning into an unknown Place de something or other in some foreign town.

At one corner of the square there projected a kind of angle of a prosperous but quiet hotel, the bulk of which belonged to a street behind. In the wall there was one large French window, probably the window of a large coffee-room; and outside this window, almost literally overhanging the square, was a formidably buttressed balcony, big enough to contain a dining-table. In fact, it did contain a dining-table, or more strictly a breakfast-table; and round the breakfast-table, glowing in the sunlight and evident to the street, were a group of noisy and talkative men, all dressed in the insolence of fashion, with white waistcoats and expensive button-holes. Some of their jokes could almost be heard across the square. Then the grave Secretary gave his unnatural smile, and Syme knew that this boisterous breakfast party was the secret conclave of the European Dynamiters.

Then, as Syme continued to stare at them, he saw something that he had not seen before. He had not seen it literally because it was too large to see. At the nearest end of the balcony, blocking up a great part of the perspective, was the back of a great mountain of a man. When Syme had seen him, his first thought was that the weight of him must break down the balcony of stone. His vastness did not lie only in the fact that he was abnormally tall and quite incredibly fat. This man was planned enormously in his original proportions, like a statue carved deliberately as colossal. His head, crowned with white hair, as seen from behind looked bigger than a head ought to be. The ears that stood out from it looked larger than human ears. He was enlarged terribly to scale; and this sense of size was so staggering, that when Syme saw him all the other figures seemed quite suddenly to dwindle and become dwarfish. They were still sitting there as before with their flowers and frock-coats, but now it looked as if the big man was entertaining five children to tea.

As Syme and the guide approached the side door of the hotel, a waiter came out smiling with every tooth in his head.

"The gentlemen are up there, sare," he said. "They do talk and they do laugh at what they talk. They do say they will throw bombs at ze king."

And the waiter hurried away with a napkin over his arm, much pleased with the singular frivolity of the gentlemen upstairs.

The two men mounted the stairs in silence.

Syme had never thought of asking whether the monstrous man who almost filled and broke the balcony was the great President of whom the others stood in awe. He knew it was so, with an unaccountable but instantaneous certainty. Syme, indeed, was one of those men who are open to all the more nameless psychological influences in a degree a little dangerous to mental health. Utterly devoid of fear in physical dangers, he was a great deal too sensitive to the smell of spiritual evil. Twice already that night little unmeaning things had peeped out at him almost pruriently, and given him a sense of drawing nearer and nearer to the head-quarters of hell. And this sense became overpowering as he drew nearer to the great President.

The form it took was a childish and yet hateful fancy. As he walked across the inner room towards the balcony, the large face of Sunday grew larger and larger; and Syme was gripped with a fear that when he was quite close the face would be too big to be possible, and that he would scream aloud. He remembered that as a child he would not look at the mask of Memnon in the British Museum, because it was a face, and so large.

By an effort, braver than that of leaping over a cliff, he went to an empty seat at the breakfast-table and sat down. The men greeted him with good-humoured raillery as if they had always known him. He sobered himself a little by looking at their conventional coats and solid, shining coffee-pot; then he looked again at Sunday. His face was very large, but it was still possible to humanity.

In the presence of the President the whole company looked sufficiently commonplace; nothing about them caught the eye at first, except that by the President's caprice they had been dressed up with a festive respectability, which gave the meal the look of a wedding breakfast. One man indeed stood out at even a superficial glance. He at least was the common or garden Dynamiter. He wore, indeed, the high white collar and satin tie that were the uniform of the occasion; but out of this collar there sprang a head quite unmanageable and quite unmistakable, a bewildering bush of brown hair and beard that almost obscured the eyes like those of a Skye terrier. But the eyes did look out of the tangle, and they were the sad eyes of some Russian serf. The effect of this figure was not terrible like that of the President, but it had every diablerie that can come from the utterly grotesque. If out of that stiff tie and collar there had come abruptly the head of a cat or a dog, it could not have been a more idiotic contrast.

The man's name, it seemed, was Gogol; he was a Pole, and in this circle of days he was called Tuesday. His soul and speech were incurably tragic; he could not force himself to play the prosperous and frivolous part demanded of him by President Sunday. And, indeed, when Syme came in the President, with that daring disregard of public suspicion which was his policy, was actually chaffing Gogol upon his inability to assume conventional graces.

"Our friend Tuesday," said the President in a deep voice at once of quietude and volume, "our friend Tuesday doesn't seem to grasp the idea. He dresses up like a gentleman, but he seems to be too great a soul to behave like one. He insists on the ways of the stage conspirator. Now if a gentleman goes about London in a top hat and a frock-coat, no one need know that he is an anarchist. But if a gentleman puts on a top hat and a frock-coat, and then goes about on his hands and knees—well, he may attract attention. That's what Brother Gogol does. He goes about on his hands and knees with such inexhaustible diplomacy, that by this time he finds it quite difficult to walk upright."

"I am not good at goncealment," said Gogol sulkily, with a thick foreign accent; "I am not ashamed of the cause."

"Yes you are, my boy, and so is the cause of you," said the President good-naturedly. "You hide as much as anybody; but you can't do it, you see, you're such an ass! You try to combine two inconsistent methods. When a householder finds a man under his bed, he will probably pause to note the circumstance. But if he finds a man under his bed in a top hat, you will agree with me, my dear Tuesday, that he is not likely even to forget it. Now when you were found under Admiral Biffin's bed—"

"I am not good at deception," said Tuesday gloomily, flushing.

"Right, my boy, right," said the President with a ponderous heartiness, "you aren't good at anything."

While this stream of conversation continued, Syme was looking more steadily at the men around him. As he did so, he gradually felt all his sense of something spiritually queer return.

He had thought at first that they were all of common stature and costume, with the evident exception of the hairy Gogol. But as he looked at the others, he began to see in each of them exactly what he had seen in the man by the river, a demoniac detail somewhere. That lop-sided laugh, which would suddenly disfigure the fine face of his original guide, was typical of all these types. Each man had something about him, perceived perhaps at the tenth or twentieth glance, which was not normal, and which seemed hardly human. The only metaphor he could think of was this, that they all looked as men of fashion and presence would look, with the additional twist given in a false and curved mirror.

Only the individual examples will express this half-concealed eccentricity. Syme's original cicerone bore the title of Monday; he was the Secretary of the Council, and his twisted smile was regarded with more terror than anything, except the President's horrible, happy laughter. But now that Syme had more space and light to observe him, there were other touches. His fine face was so emaciated, that Syme thought it must be wasted with some disease; yet somehow the very distress of his dark eyes denied this. It was no physical ill that troubled him. His eyes were alive with intellectual torture, as if pure thought was pain.

He was typical of each of the tribe; each man was subtly and differently wrong. Next to him sat Tuesday, the tousle-headed Gogol, a man more obviously mad. Next was Wednesday, a certain Marquis de St. Eustache, a sufficiently characteristic figure. The first few glances found nothing unusual about him, except that he was the only man at table who wore the fashionable clothes as if they were really his own. He had a black French beard cut square and a black English frock-coat cut even squarer. But Syme, sensitive to such things, felt somehow that the man carried a rich atmosphere with him, a rich atmosphere that suffocated. It reminded one irrationally of drowsy odours and of dying lamps in the darker poems of Byron and Poe. With this went a sense of his being clad, not in lighter colours, but in softer materials; his black seemed richer and warmer than the black shades about him, as if it were compounded of profound colour. His black coat looked as if it were only black by being too dense a purple. His black beard looked as if it were only black by being too deep a blue. And in the gloom and thickness of the beard his dark red mouth showed sensual and scornful. Whatever he was he was not a Frenchman; he might be a Jew; he might be something deeper yet in the dark heart of the East. In the bright coloured Persian tiles and pictures showing tyrants hunting, you may see just those almond eyes, those blue-black beards, those cruel, crimson lips.

Then came Syme, and next a very old man, Professor de Worms, who still kept the chair of Friday, though every day it was expected that his death would leave it empty. Save for his intellect, he was in the last dissolution of senile decay. His face was as grey as his long grey beard, his forehead was lifted and fixed finally in a furrow of mild despair. In no other case, not even that of Gogol, did the bridegroom brilliancy of the morning dress express a more painful contrast. For the red flower in his button-hole showed up against a face that was literally discoloured like lead; the whole hideous effect was as if some drunken dandies had put their clothes upon a corpse. When he rose or sat down, which was with long labour and peril, something worse was expressed than mere weakness, something indefinably connected with the horror of the whole scene. It did not express decrepitude merely, but corruption. Another hateful fancy crossed Syme's quivering mind. He could not help thinking that whenever the man moved a leg or arm might fall off.

Right at the end sat the man called Saturday, the simplest and the most baffling of all. He was a short, square man with a dark, square face clean-shaven, a medical practitioner going by the name of Bull. He had that combination of savoir-faire with a sort of well-groomed coarseness which is not uncommon in young doctors. He carried his fine clothes with confidence rather than ease, and he mostly wore a set smile. There was nothing whatever odd about him, except that he wore a pair of dark, almost opaque spectacles. It may have been merely a crescendo of nervous fancy that had gone before, but those black discs were dreadful to Syme; they reminded him of half-remembered ugly tales, of some story about pennies being put on the eyes of the dead. Syme's eye always caught the black glasses and the blind grin. Had the dying Professor worn them, or even the pale Secretary, they would have been appropriate. But on the younger and grosser man they seemed only an enigma. They took away the key of the face. You could not tell what his smile or his gravity meant. Partly from this, and partly because he had a vulgar virility wanting in most of the others it seemed to Syme that he might be the wickedest of all those wicked men. Syme even had the thought that his eyes might be covered up because they were too frightful to see.

CHAPTER VI
THE EXPOSURE

SUCH were the six men who had sworn to destroy the world. Again and again Syme strove to pull together his common sense in their presence. Sometimes he saw for an instant that these notions were subjective, that he was only looking at ordinary men, one of whom was old, another nervous, another short-sighted. The sense of an unnatural symbolism always settled back on him again. Each figure seemed to be, somehow, on the borderland of things, just as their theory was on the borderland of thought. He knew that each one of these men stood at the extreme end, so to speak, of some wild road of reasoning. He could only fancy, as in some old-world fable, that if a man went westward to the end of the world he would find something—say a tree—that was more or less than a tree, a tree possessed by a spirit; and that if he went east to the end of the world he would find something else that was not wholly itself—a tower, perhaps, of which the very shape was wicked. So these figures seemed to stand up, violent and unaccountable, against an ultimate horizon, visions from the verge. The ends of the earth were closing in.

Talk had been going on steadily as he took in the scene; and not the least of the contrasts of that bewildering breakfast-table was the contrast between the easy and unobtrusive tone of talk and its terrible purport. They were deep in the discussion of an actual and immediate plot. The waiter downstairs had spoken quite correctly when he said that they were talking about bombs and kings. Only three days afterwards the Czar was to meet the President of the French Republic in Paris, and over their bacon and eggs upon their sunny balcony these beaming gentlemen had decided how both should die. Even the instrument was chosen; the black-bearded Marquis, it appeared, was to carry the bomb.

Ordinarily speaking, the proximity of this positive and objective crime would have sobered Syme, and cured him of all his merely mystical tremors. He would have thought of nothing but the need of saving at least two human bodies from being ripped in pieces with iron and roaring gas. But the truth was that by this time he had begun to feel a third kind of fear, more piercing and practical than either his moral revulsion or his social responsibility. Very simply, he had no fear to spare for the French President or the Czar; he had begun to fear for himself. Most of the talkers took little heed of him, debating now with their faces closer together, and almost uniformly grave, save when for an instant the smile of the Secretary ran aslant across his face as the jagged lightning runs aslant across the sky. But there was one persistent thing which first troubled Syme and at last terrified him. The President was always looking at him, steadily, and with a great and baffling interest. The enormous man was quite quiet, but his blue eyes stood out of his head. And they were always fixed on Syme.

Syme felt moved to spring up and leap over the balcony. When the President's eyes were on him he felt as if he were made of glass. He had hardly the shred of a doubt that in some silent and extraordinary way Sunday had found out that he was a spy. He looked over the edge of the balcony, and saw a policeman, standing abstractedly just beneath, staring at the bright railings and the sunlit trees.

Then there fell upon him the great temptation that was to torment him for many days. In the presence of these powerful and repulsive men, who were the princes of anarchy, he had almost forgotten the frail and fanciful figure of the poet Gregory, the mere aesthete of anarchism. He even thought of him now with an old kindness, as if they had played together when children. But he remembered that he was still tied to Gregory by a great promise. He had promised never to do the very thing that he now felt himself almost in the act of doing. He had promised not to jump over that balcony and speak to that policeman. He took his cold hand off the cold stone balustrade. His soul swayed in a vertigo of moral indecision. He had only to snap the thread of a rash vow made to a villainous society, and all his life could be as open and sunny as the square beneath him. He had, on the other hand, only to keep his antiquated honour, and be delivered inch by inch into the power of this great enemy of mankind, whose very intellect was a torture-chamber. Whenever he looked down into the square he saw the comfortable policeman, a pillar of common sense and common order. Whenever he looked back at the breakfast-table he saw the President still quietly studying him with big, unbearable eyes.

In all the torrent of his thought there were two thoughts that never crossed his mind. First, it never occurred to him to doubt that the President and his Council could crush him if he continued to stand alone. The place might be public, the project might seem impossible. But Sunday was not the man who would carry himself thus easily without having, somehow or somewhere, set open his iron trap. Either by anonymous poison or sudden street accident, by hypnotism or by fire from hell, Sunday could certainly strike him. If he defied the man he was probably dead, either struck stiff there in his chair or long afterwards as by an innocent ailment. If he called in the police promptly, arrested everyone, told all, and set against them the whole energy of England, he would probably escape; certainly not otherwise. They were a balconyful of gentlemen overlooking a bright and busy square; but he felt no more safe with them than if they had been a boatful of armed pirates overlooking an empty sea.

There was a second thought that never came to him. It never occurred to him to be spiritually won over to the enemy. Many moderns, inured to a weak worship of intellect and force, might have wavered in their allegiance under this oppression of a great personality. They might have called Sunday the super-man. If any such creature be conceivable, he looked, indeed, somewhat like it, with his earth-shaking abstraction, as of a stone statue walking. He might have been called something above man, with his large plans, which were too obvious to be detected, with his large face, which was too frank to be understood. But this was a kind of modern meanness to which Syme could not sink even in his extreme morbidity. Like any man, he was coward enough to fear great force; but he was not quite coward enough to admire it.

The men were eating as they talked, and even in this they were typical. Dr. Bull and the Marquis ate casually and conventionally of the best things on the table—cold pheasant or Strasbourg pie. But the Secretary was a vegetarian, and he spoke earnestly of the projected murder over half a raw tomato and three quarters of a glass of tepid water. The old Professor had such slops as suggested a sickening second childhood. And even in this President Sunday preserved his curious predominance of mere mass. For he ate like twenty men; he ate incredibly, with a frightful freshness of appetite, so that it was like watching a sausage factory. Yet continually, when he had swallowed a dozen crumpets or drunk a quart of coffee, he would be found with his great head on one side staring at Syme.

"I have often wondered," said the Marquis, taking a great bite out of a slice of bread and jam, "whether it wouldn't be better for me to do it with a knife. Most of the best things have been brought off with a knife. And it would be a new emotion to get a knife into a French President and wriggle it round."

"You are wrong," said the Secretary, drawing his black brows together. "The knife was merely the expression of the old personal quarrel with a personal tyrant. Dynamite is not only our best tool, but our best symbol. It is as perfect a symbol of us as is incense of the prayers of the Christians. It expands; it only destroys because it broadens; even so, thought only destroys because it broadens. A man's brain is a bomb," he cried out, loosening suddenly his strange passion and striking his own skull with violence. "My brain feels like a bomb, night and day. It must expand! It must expand! A man's brain must expand, if it breaks up the universe."

"I don't want the universe broken up just yet," drawled the Marquis. "I want to do a lot of beastly things before I die. I thought of one yesterday in bed."

"No, if the only end of the thing is nothing," said Dr. Bull with his sphinx-like smile, "it hardly seems worth doing."

The old Professor was staring at the ceiling with dull eyes.

"Every man knows in his heart," he said, "that nothing is worth doing."

There was a singular silence, and then the Secretary said—

"We are wandering, however, from the point. The only question is how Wednesday is to strike the blow. I take it we should all agree with the original notion of a bomb. As to the actual arrangements, I should suggest that tomorrow morning he should go first of all to—"

The speech was broken off short under a vast shadow. President Sunday had risen to his feet, seeming to fill the sky above them.

"Before we discuss that," he said in a small, quiet voice, "let us go into a private room. I have something very particular to say."

Syme stood up before any of the others. The instant of choice had come at last, the pistol was at his head. On the pavement before he could hear the policeman idly stir and stamp, for the morning, though bright, was cold.

A barrel-organ in the street suddenly sprang with a jerk into a jovial tune. Syme stood up taut, as if it had been a bugle before the battle. He found himself filled with a supernatural courage that came from nowhere. That jingling music seemed full of the vivacity, the vulgarity, and the irrational valour of the poor, who in all those unclean streets were all clinging to the decencies and the charities of Christendom. His youthful prank of being a policeman had faded from his mind; he did not think of himself as the representative of the corps of gentlemen turned into fancy constables, or of the old eccentric who lived in the dark room. But he did feel himself as the ambassador of all these common and kindly people in the street, who every day marched into battle to the music of the barrel-organ. And this high pride in being human had lifted him unaccountably to an infinite height above the monstrous men around him. For an instant, at least, he looked down upon all their sprawling eccentricities from the starry pinnacle of the commonplace. He felt towards them all that unconscious and elementary superiority that a brave man feels over powerful beasts or a wise man over powerful errors. He knew that he had neither the intellectual nor the physical strength of President Sunday; but in that moment he minded it no more than the fact that he had not the muscles of a tiger or a horn on his nose like a rhinoceros. All was swallowed up in an ultimate certainty that the President was wrong and that the barrel-organ was right. There clanged in his mind that unanswerable and terrible truism in the song of Roland—

"Pagens ont tort et Chretiens ont droit."

which in the old nasal French has the clang and groan of great iron. This liberation of his spirit from the load of his weakness went with a quite clear decision to embrace death. If the people of the barrel-organ could keep their old-world obligations, so could he. This very pride in keeping his word was that he was keeping it to miscreants. It was his last triumph over these lunatics to go down into their dark room and die for something that they could not even understand. The barrel-organ seemed to give the marching tune with the energy and the mingled noises of a whole orchestra; and he could hear deep and rolling, under all the trumpets of the pride of life, the drums of the pride of death.

The conspirators were already filing through the open window and into the rooms behind. Syme went last, outwardly calm, but with all his brain and body throbbing with romantic rhythm. The President led them down an irregular side stair, such as might be used by servants, and into a dim, cold, empty room, with a table and benches, like an abandoned boardroom. When they were all in, he closed and locked the door.

The first to speak was Gogol, the irreconcilable, who seemed bursting with inarticulate grievance.

"Zso! Zso!" he cried, with an obscure excitement, his heavy Polish accent becoming almost impenetrable. "You zay you nod 'ide. You zay you show himselves. It is all nuzzinks. Ven you vant talk importance you run yourselves in a dark box!"

The President seemed to take the foreigner's incoherent satire with entire good humour.

"You can't get hold of it yet, Gogol," he said in a fatherly way. "When once they have heard us talking nonsense on that balcony they will not care where we go afterwards. If we had come here first, we should have had the whole staff at the keyhole. You don't seem to know anything about mankind."

"I die for zem," cried the Pole in thick excitement, "and I slay zare oppressors. I care not for these games of gonzealment. I would zmite ze tyrant in ze open square."

"I see, I see," said the President, nodding kindly as he seated himself at the top of a long table. "You die for mankind first, and then you get up and smite their oppressors. So that's all right. And now may I ask you to control your beautiful sentiments, and sit down with the other gentlemen at this table. For the first time this morning something intelligent is going to be said."

Syme, with the perturbed promptitude he had shown since the original summons, sat down first. Gogol sat down last, grumbling in his brown beard about gombromise. No one except Syme seemed to have any notion of the blow that was about to fall. As for him, he had merely the feeling of a man mounting the scaffold with the intention, at any rate, of making a good speech.

"Comrades," said the President, suddenly rising, "we have spun out this farce long enough. I have called you down here to tell you something so simple and shocking that even the waiters upstairs (long inured to our levities) might hear some new seriousness in my voice. Comrades, we were discussing plans and naming places. I propose, before saying anything else, that those plans and places should not be voted by this meeting, but should be left wholly in the control of some one reliable member. I suggest Comrade Saturday, Dr. Bull."

They all stared at him; then they all started in their seats, for the next words, though not loud, had a living and sensational emphasis. Sunday struck the table.

"Not one word more about the plans and places must be said at this meeting. Not one tiny detail more about what we mean to do must be mentioned in this company."

Sunday had spent his life in astonishing his followers; but it seemed as if he had never really astonished them until now. They all moved feverishly in their seats, except Syme. He sat stiff in his, with his hand in his pocket, and on the handle of his loaded revolver. When the attack on him came he would sell his life dear. He would find out at least if the President was mortal.

Sunday went on smoothly—

"You will probably understand that there is only one possible motive for forbidding free speech at this festival of freedom. Strangers overhearing us matters nothing. They assume that we are joking. But what would matter, even unto death, is this, that there should be one actually among us who is not of us, who knows our grave purpose, but does not share it, who—"

The Secretary screamed out suddenly like a woman.

"It can't be!" he cried, leaping. "There can't—"

The President flapped his large flat hand on the table like the fin of some huge fish.

"Yes," he said slowly, "there is a spy in this room. There is a traitor at this table. I will waste no more words. His name—"

Syme half rose from his seat, his finger firm on the trigger.

"His name is Gogol," said the President. "He is that hairy humbug over there who pretends to be a Pole."

Gogol sprang to his feet, a pistol in each hand. With the same flash three men sprang at his throat. Even the Professor made an effort to rise. But Syme saw little of the scene, for he was blinded with a beneficent darkness; he had sunk down into his seat shuddering, in a palsy of passionate relief.

CHAPTER VII

THE UNACCOUNTABLE CONDUCT OF PROFESSOR DE WORMS

"SIT down!" said Sunday in a voice that he used once or twice in his life, a voice that made men drop drawn swords.

The three who had risen fell away from Gogol, and that equivocal person himself resumed his seat.

"Well, my man," said the President briskly, addressing him as one addresses a total stranger, "will you oblige me by putting your hand in your upper waistcoat pocket and showing me what you have there?"

The alleged Pole was a little pale under his tangle of dark hair, but he put two fingers into the pocket with apparent coolness and pulled out a blue strip of card. When Syme saw it lying on the table, he woke up again to the world outside him. For although the card lay at the other extreme of the table, and he could read nothing of the inscription on it, it bore a startling resemblance to the blue card in his own pocket, the card which had been given to him when he joined the anti-anarchist constabulary.

"Pathetic Slav," said the President, "tragic child of Poland, are you prepared in the presence of that card to deny that you are in this company—shall we say de trop?"

"Right oh!" said the late Gogol. It made everyone jump to hear a clear, commercial and somewhat cockney voice coming out of that forest of foreign hair. It was irrational, as if a Chinaman had suddenly spoken with a Scotch accent.

"I gather that you fully understand your position," said Sunday.

"You bet," answered the Pole. "I see it's a fair cop. All I say is, I don't believe any Pole could have imitated my accent like I did his."

"I concede the point," said Sunday. "I believe your own accent to be inimitable, though I shall practise it in my bath. Do you mind leaving your beard with your card?"

"Not a bit," answered Gogol; and with one finger he ripped off the whole of his shaggy head-covering, emerging with thin red hair and a pale, pert face. "It was hot," he added.

"I will do you the justice to say," said Sunday, not without a sort of brutal admiration, "that you seem to have kept pretty cool under it. Now listen to me. I like you. The consequence is that it would annoy me for just about two and a half minutes if I heard that you had died in torments. Well, if you ever tell the police or any human soul about us, I shall have that two and a half minutes of discomfort. On your discomfort I will not dwell. Good day. Mind the step."

The red-haired detective who had masqueraded as Gogol rose to his feet without a word, and walked out of the room with an air of perfect nonchalance. Yet the astonished Syme was able to realise that this ease was suddenly assumed; for there was a slight stumble outside the door, which showed that the departing detective had not minded the step.

"Time is flying," said the President in his gayest manner, after glancing at his watch, which like everything about him seemed bigger than it ought to be. "I must go off at once; I have to take the chair at a Humanitarian meeting."

The Secretary turned to him with working eyebrows.

"Would it not be better," he said a little sharply, "to discuss further the details of our project, now that the spy has left us?"

"No, I think not," said the President with a yawn like an unobtrusive earthquake. "Leave it as it is. Let Saturday settle it. I must be off. Breakfast here next Sunday."

But the late loud scenes had whipped up the almost naked nerves of the Secretary. He was one of those men who are conscientious even in crime.

"I must protest, President, that the thing is irregular," he said. "It is a fundamental rule of our society that all plans shall be debated in full council. Of course, I fully appreciate your forethought when in the actual presence of a traitor—"

"Secretary," said the President seriously, "if you'd take your head home and boil it for a turnip it might be useful. I can't say. But it might."

The Secretary reared back in a kind of equine anger.

"I really fail to understand—" he began in high offense.

"That's it, that's it," said the President, nodding a great many times. "That's where you fail right enough. You fail to understand. Why, you dancing donkey," he roared, rising, "you didn't want to be overheard by a spy, didn't you? How do you know you aren't overheard now?"

And with these words he shouldered his way out of the room, shaking with incomprehensible scorn.

Four of the men left behind gaped after him without any apparent glimmering of his meaning. Syme alone had even a glimmering, and such as it was it froze him to the bone. If the last words of the President meant anything, they meant that he had not after all passed unsuspected. They meant that while Sunday could not denounce him like Gogol, he still could not trust him like the others.

The other four got to their feet grumbling more or less, and betook themselves elsewhere to find lunch, for it was already well past midday. The Professor went last, very slowly and painfully. Syme sat long after the rest had gone, revolving his strange position. He had escaped a thunderbolt, but he was still under a cloud. At last he rose and made his way out of the hotel into Leicester Square. The bright, cold day had grown increasingly colder, and when he came out into the street he was surprised by a few flakes of snow. While he still carried the sword-stick and the rest of Gregory's portable luggage, he had thrown the cloak down and left it somewhere, perhaps on the steam-tug, perhaps on the balcony. Hoping, therefore, that the snow-shower might be slight, he stepped back out of the street for a moment and stood up under the doorway of a small and greasy hair-dresser's shop, the front window of which was empty, except for a sickly wax lady in evening dress.

Snow, however, began to thicken and fall fast; and Syme, having found one glance at the wax lady quite sufficient to depress his spirits, stared out instead into the white and empty street. He was considerably astonished to see, standing quite still outside the shop and staring into the window, a man. His top hat was loaded with snow like the hat of Father Christmas, the white drift was rising round his boots and ankles; but it seemed as if nothing could tear him away from the contemplation of the colourless wax doll in dirty evening dress. That any human being should stand in such weather looking into such a shop was a matter of sufficient wonder to Syme; but his idle wonder turned suddenly into a personal shock; for he realised that the man standing there was the paralytic old Professor de Worms. It scarcely seemed the place for a person of his years and infirmities.

Syme was ready to believe anything about the perversions of this dehumanized brotherhood; but even he could not believe that the Professor had fallen in love with that particular wax lady. He could only suppose that the man's malady (whatever it was) involved some momentary fits of rigidity or trance. He was not inclined, however, to feel in this case any very compassionate concern. On the contrary, he rather congratulated himself that the Professor's stroke and his elaborate and limping walk would make it easy to escape from him and leave him miles behind. For Syme thirsted first and last to get clear of the whole poisonous atmosphere, if only for an hour. Then he could collect his thoughts, formulate his policy, and decide finally whether he should or should not keep faith with Gregory.

He strolled away through the dancing snow, turned up two or three streets, down through two or three others, and entered a small Soho restaurant for lunch. He partook reflectively of four small and quaint courses, drank half a bottle of red wine, and ended up over black coffee and a black cigar, still thinking. He had taken his seat in the upper room of the restaurant, which was full of the chink of knives and the chatter of foreigners. He remembered that in old days he had imagined that all these harmless and kindly aliens were anarchists. He shuddered, remembering the real thing. But even the shudder had the delightful shame of escape. The wine, the common food, the familiar place, the faces of natural and talkative men, made him almost feel as if the Council of the Seven Days had been a bad dream; and although he knew it was nevertheless an objective reality, it was at least a distant one. Tall houses and populous streets lay between him and his last sight of the shameful seven; he was free in free London, and drinking wine among the free. With a somewhat easier action, he took his hat and stick and strolled down the stair into the shop below.

When he entered that lower room he stood stricken and rooted to the spot. At a small table, close up to the blank window and the white street of snow, sat the old anarchist Professor over a glass of milk, with his lifted livid face and pendent eyelids. For an instant Syme stood as rigid as the stick he leant upon. Then with a gesture as of blind hurry, he brushed past the Professor, dashing open the door and slamming it behind him, and stood outside in the snow.

"Can that old corpse be following me?" he asked himself, biting his yellow moustache. "I stopped too long up in that room, so that even such leaden feet could catch me up. One comfort is, with a little brisk walking I can put a man like that as far away as Timbuctoo. Or am I too fanciful? Was he really following me? Surely Sunday would not be such a fool as to send a lame man?"

He set off at a smart pace, twisting and whirling his stick, in the direction of Covent Garden. As he crossed the great market the snow increased, growing blinding and bewildering as the afternoon began to darken. The snow-flakes tormented him like a swarm of silver bees. Getting into his eyes and beard, they added their unremitting futility to his already irritated nerves; and by the time that he had come at a swinging pace to the beginning of Fleet Street, he lost patience, and finding a Sunday teashop, turned into it to take shelter. He ordered another cup of black coffee as an excuse. Scarcely had he done so, when Professor de Worms hobbled heavily into the shop, sat down with difficulty and ordered a glass of milk.

Syme's walking-stick had fallen from his hand with a great clang, which confessed the concealed steel. But the Professor did not look round. Syme, who was commonly a cool character, was literally gaping as a rustic gapes at a conjuring trick. He had seen no cab following; he had heard no wheels outside the shop; to all mortal appearances the man had come on foot. But the old man could only walk like a snail, and Syme had walked like the wind. He started up and snatched his stick, half crazy with the contradiction in mere arithmetic, and swung out of the swinging doors, leaving his coffee untasted. An omnibus going to the Bank went rattling by with an unusual rapidity. He had a violent run of a hundred yards to reach it; but he managed to spring, swaying upon the splash-board and, pausing for an instant to pant, he climbed on to the top. When he had been seated for about half a minute, he heard behind him a sort of heavy and asthmatic breathing.

Turning sharply, he saw rising gradually higher and higher up the omnibus steps a top hat soiled and dripping with snow, and under the shadow of its brim the short-sighted face and shaky shoulders of Professor de Worms. He let himself into a seat with characteristic care, and wrapped himself up to the chin in the mackintosh rug.

Every movement of the old man's tottering figure and vague hands, every uncertain gesture and panic-stricken pause, seemed to put it beyond question that he was helpless, that he was in the last imbecility of the body. He moved by inches, he let himself down with little gasps of caution. And yet, unless the philosophical entities called time and space have no vestige even of a practical existence, it appeared quite unquestionable that he had run after the omnibus.

Syme sprang erect upon the rocking car, and after staring wildly at the wintry sky, that grew gloomier every moment, he ran down the steps. He had repressed an elemental impulse to leap over the side.

Too bewildered to look back or to reason, he rushed into one of the little courts at the side of Fleet Street as a rabbit rushes into a hole. He had a vague idea, if this incomprehensible old Jack-in-the-box was really pursuing him, that in that labyrinth of little streets he could soon throw him off the scent. He dived in and out of those crooked lanes, which were more like cracks than thoroughfares; and by the time that he had completed about twenty alternate angles and described an unthinkable polygon, he paused to listen for any sound of pursuit. There was none; there could not in any case have been much, for the little streets were thick with the soundless snow. Somewhere behind Red Lion Court, however, he noticed a place where some energetic citizen had cleared away the snow for a space of about twenty yards, leaving the wet, glistening cobble-stones. He thought little of this as he passed it, only plunging into yet another arm of the maze. But when a few hundred yards farther on he stood still again to listen, his heart stood still also, for he heard from that space of rugged stones the clinking crutch and labouring feet of the infernal cripple.

The sky above was loaded with the clouds of snow, leaving London in a darkness and oppression premature for that hour of the evening. On each side of Syme the walls of the alley were blind and featureless; there was no little window or any kind of eve. He felt a new impulse to break out of this hive of houses, and to get once more into the open and lamp-lit street. Yet he rambled and dodged for a long time before he struck the main thoroughfare. When he did so, he struck it much farther up than he had fancied. He came out into what seemed the vast and void of Ludgate Circus, and saw St. Paul's Cathedral sitting in the sky.

At first he was startled to find these great roads so empty, as if a pestilence had swept through the city. Then he told himself that some degree of emptiness was natural; first because the snow-storm was even dangerously deep, and secondly because it was Sunday. And at the very word Sunday he bit his lip; the word was henceforth for hire like some indecent pun. Under the white fog of snow high up in the heaven the whole atmosphere of the city was turned to a very queer kind of green twilight, as of men under the sea. The sealed and sullen sunset behind the dark dome of St. Paul's had in it smoky and sinister colours—colours of sickly green, dead red or decaying bronze, that were just bright enough to emphasise the solid whiteness of the snow. But right up against these dreary colours rose the black bulk of the cathedral; and upon the top of the cathedral was a random splash and great stain of snow, still clinging as to an Alpine peak. It had fallen accidentally, but just so fallen as to half drape the dome from its very topmost point, and to pick out in perfect silver the great orb and the cross. When Syme saw it he suddenly straightened himself, and made with his sword-stick an involuntary salute.

He knew that that evil figure, his shadow, was creeping quickly or slowly behind him, and he did not care.

It seemed a symbol of human faith and valour that while the skies were darkening that high place of the earth was bright. The devils might have captured heaven, but they had not yet captured the cross. He had a new impulse to tear out the secret of this dancing, jumping and pursuing paralytic; and at the entrance of the court as it opened upon the Circus he turned, stick in hand, to face his pursuer.

Professor de Worms came slowly round the corner of the irregular alley behind him, his unnatural form outlined against a lonely gas-lamp, irresistibly recalling that very imaginative figure in the nursery rhymes, "the crooked man who went a crooked mile." He really looked as if he had been twisted out of shape by the tortuous streets he had been threading. He came nearer and nearer, the lamplight shining on his lifted spectacles, his lifted, patient face. Syme waited for him as St. George waited for the dragon, as a man waits for a final explanation or for death. And the old Professor came right up to him and passed him like a total stranger, without even a blink of his mournful eyelids.

There was something in this silent and unexpected innocence that left Syme in a final fury. The man's colourless face and manner seemed to assert that the whole following had been an accident. Syme was galvanised with an energy that was something between bitterness and a burst of boyish derision. He made a wild gesture as if to knock the old man's hat off, called out something like "Catch me if you can," and went racing away across the white, open Circus. Concealment was impossible now; and looking back over his shoulder, he could see the black figure of the old gentleman coming after him with long, swinging strides like a man winning a mile race. But the head upon that bounding body was still pale, grave and professional, like the head of a lecturer upon the body of a harlequin.

This outrageous chase sped across Ludgate Circus, up Ludgate Hill, round St. Paul's Cathedral, along Cheapside, Syme remembering all the nightmares he had ever known. Then Syme broke away towards the river, and ended almost down by the docks. He saw the yellow panes of a low, lighted public-house, flung himself into it and ordered beer. It was a foul tavern, sprinkled with foreign sailors, a place where opium might be smoked or knives drawn.

A moment later Professor de Worms entered the place, sat down carefully, and asked for a glass of milk.

CHAPTER VIII
THE PROFESSOR EXPLAINS

WHEN Gabriel Syme found himself finally established in a chair, and opposite to him, fixed and final also, the lifted eyebrows and leaden eyelids of the Professor, his fears fully returned. This incomprehensible man from the fierce council, after all, had certainly pursued him. If the man had one character as a paralytic and another character as a pursuer, the antithesis might make him more interesting, but scarcely more soothing. It would be a very small comfort that he could not find the Professor out, if by some serious accident the Professor should find him out. He emptied a whole pewter pot of ale before the professor had touched his milk.

One possibility, however, kept him hopeful and yet helpless. It was just possible that this escapade signified something other than even a slight suspicion of him. Perhaps it was some regular form or sign. Perhaps the foolish scamper was some sort of friendly signal that he ought to have understood. Perhaps it was a ritual. Perhaps the new Thursday was always chased along Cheapside, as the new Lord Mayor is always escorted along it. He was just selecting a tentative inquiry, when the old Professor opposite suddenly and simply cut him short. Before Syme could ask the first diplomatic question, the old anarchist had asked suddenly, without any sort of preparation—

"Are you a policeman?"

Whatever else Syme had expected, he had never expected anything so brutal and actual as this. Even his great presence of mind could only manage a reply with an air of rather blundering jocularity.

"A policeman?" he said, laughing vaguely. "Whatever made you think of a policeman in connection with me?"

"The process was simple enough," answered the Professor patiently. "I thought you looked like a policeman. I think so now."

"Did I take a policeman's hat by mistake out of the restaurant?" asked Syme, smiling wildly. "Have I by any chance got a number stuck on to me somewhere? Have my boots got that watchful look? Why must I be a policeman? Do, do let me be a postman."

The old Professor shook his head with a gravity that gave no hope, but Syme ran on with a feverish irony.

"But perhaps I misunderstood the delicacies of your German philosophy. Perhaps policeman is a relative term. In an evolutionary sense, sir, the ape fades so gradually into the policeman, that I myself can never detect the shade. The monkey is only the policeman that may be. Perhaps a maiden lady on Clapham Common is only the policeman that might have been. I don't mind being the policeman that might have been. I don't mind being anything in German thought."

"Are you in the police service?" said the old man, ignoring all Syme's improvised and desperate raillery. "Are you a detective?"

Syme's heart turned to stone, but his face never changed.

"Your suggestion is ridiculous," he began. "Why on earth—"

The old man struck his palsied hand passionately on the rickety table, nearly breaking it.

"Did you hear me ask a plain question, you pattering spy?" he shrieked in a high, crazy voice. "Are you, or are you not, a police detective?"

"No!" answered Syme, like a man standing on the hangman's drop.

"You swear it," said the old man, leaning across to him, his dead face becoming as it were loathsomely alive. "You swear it! You swear it! If you swear falsely, will you be damned? Will you be sure that the devil dances at your funeral? Will you see that the nightmare sits on your grave? Will there really be no mistake? You are an anarchist, you are a dynamiter! Above all, you are not in any sense a detective? You are not in the British police?"

He leant his angular elbow far across the table, and put up his large loose hand like a flap to his ear.

"I am not in the British police," said Syme with insane calm.

Professor de Worms fell back in his chair with a curious air of kindly collapse.

"That's a pity," he said, "because I am."

Syme sprang up straight, sending back the bench behind him with a crash.

"Because you are what?" he said thickly. "You are what?"

"I am a policeman," said the Professor with his first broad smile, and beaming through his spectacles. "But as you think policeman only a relative term, of course I have nothing to do with you. I am in the British police force; but as you tell me you are not in the British police force, I can only say that I met you in a dynamiters' club. I suppose I ought to arrest you." And with these words he laid on the table before Syme an exact facsimile of the blue card which Syme had in his own waistcoat pocket, the symbol of his power from the police.

Syme had for a flash the sensation that the cosmos had turned exactly upside down, that all trees were growing downwards and that all stars were under his feet. Then came slowly the opposite conviction. For the last twenty-four hours the cosmos had really been upside down, but now the capsized universe had come right side up again. This devil from whom he had been fleeing all day was only an elder brother of his own house, who on the other side of the table lay back and laughed at him. He did not for the moment ask any questions of detail; he only knew the happy and silly fact that this shadow, which had pursued him with an intolerable oppression of peril, was only the shadow of a friend trying to catch him up. He knew simultaneously that he was a fool and a free man. For with any recovery from morbidity there must go a certain healthy humiliation. There comes a certain point in such conditions when only three things are possible: first a perpetuation of Satanic pride, secondly tears, and third laughter. Syme's egotism held hard to the first course for a few seconds, and then suddenly adopted the third. Taking his own blue police ticket from his own waist coat pocket, he tossed it on to the table; then he flung his head back until his spike of yellow beard almost pointed at the ceiling, and shouted with a barbaric laughter.

Even in that close den, perpetually filled with the din of knives, plates, cans, clamorous voices, sudden struggles and stampedes, there was something Homeric in Syme's mirth which made many half-drunken men look round.

"What yer laughing at, guv'nor?" asked one wondering labourer from the docks.

"At myself," answered Syme, and went off again into the agony of his ecstatic reaction.

"Pull yourself together," said the Professor, "or you'll get hysterical. Have some more beer. I'll join you."

"You haven't drunk your milk," said Syme.

"My milk!" said the other, in tones of withering and unfathomable contempt, "my milk! Do you think I'd look at the beastly stuff when I'm out of sight of the bloody anarchists? We're all Christians in this room, though perhaps," he added, glancing around at the reeling crowd, "not strict ones. Finish my milk? Great blazes! yes, I'll finish it right enough!" and he knocked the tumbler off the table, making a crash of glass and a splash of silver fluid.

Syme was staring at him with a happy curiosity.

"I understand now," he cried; "of course, you're not an old man at all."

"I can't take my face off here," replied Professor de Worms. "It's rather an elaborate make-up. As to whether I'm an old man, that's not for me to say. I was thirty-eight last birthday."

"Yes, but I mean," said Syme impatiently, "there's nothing the matter with you."

"Yes," answered the other dispassionately. "I am subject to colds."

Syme's laughter at all this had about it a wild weakness of relief. He laughed at the idea of the paralytic Professor being really a young actor dressed up as if for the foot-lights. But he felt that he would have laughed as loudly if a pepperpot had fallen over.

The false Professor drank and wiped his false beard.

"Did you know," he asked, "that that man Gogol was one of us?"

"I? No, I didn't know it," answered Syme in some surprise. "But didn't you?"

"I knew no more than the dead," replied the man who called himself de Worms. "I thought the President was talking about me, and I rattled in my boots."

"And I thought he was talking about me," said Syme, with his rather reckless laughter. "I had my hand on my revolver all the time."

"So had I," said the Professor grimly; "so had Gogol evidently."

Syme struck the table with an exclamation.

"Why, there were three of us there!" he cried. "Three out of seven is a fighting number. If we had only known that we were three!"

The face of Professor de Worms darkened, and he did not look up.

"We were three," he said. "If we had been three hundred we could still have done nothing."

"Not if we were three hundred against four?" asked Syme, jeering rather boisterously.

"No," said the Professor with sobriety, "not if we were three hundred against Sunday."

And the mere name struck Syme cold and serious; his laughter had died in his heart before it could die on his lips. The face of the unforgettable President sprang into his mind as startling as a coloured photograph, and he remarked this difference between Sunday and all his satellites, that their faces, however fierce or sinister, became gradually blurred by memory like other human faces, whereas Sunday's seemed almost to grow more actual during absence, as if a man's painted portrait should slowly come alive.

They were both silent for a measure of moments, and then Syme's speech came with a rush, like the sudden foaming of champagne.

"Professor," he cried, "it is intolerable. Are you afraid of this man?"

The Professor lifted his heavy lids, and gazed at Syme with large, wide-open, blue eyes of an almost ethereal honesty.

"Yes, I am," he said mildly. "So are you."

Syme was dumb for an instant. Then he rose to his feet erect, like an insulted man, and thrust the chair away from him.

"Yes," he said in a voice indescribable, "you are right. I am afraid of him. Therefore I swear by God that I will seek out this man whom I fear until I find him, and strike him on the mouth. If heaven were his throne and the earth his footstool, I swear that I would pull him down."

"How?" asked the staring Professor. "Why?"

"Because I am afraid of him," said Syme; "and no man should leave in the universe anything of which he is afraid."

De Worms blinked at him with a sort of blind wonder. He made an effort to speak, but Syme went on in a low voice, but with an undercurrent of inhuman exaltation—

"Who would condescend to strike down the mere things that he does not fear? Who would debase himself to be merely brave, like any common prizefighter? Who would stoop to be fearless—like a tree? Fight the thing that you fear. You remember the old tale of the English clergyman who gave the last rites to the brigand of Sicily, and how on his death-bed the great robber said, 'I can give you no money, but I can give you advice for a lifetime: your thumb on the blade, and strike upwards.' So I say to you, strike upwards, if you strike at the stars."

The other looked at the ceiling, one of the tricks of his pose.

"Sunday is a fixed star," he said.

"You shall see him a falling star," said Syme, and put on his hat.

The decision of his gesture drew the Professor vaguely to his feet.

"Have you any idea," he asked, with a sort of benevolent bewilderment, "exactly where you are going?"

"Yes," replied Syme shortly, "I am going to prevent this bomb being thrown in Paris."

"Have you any conception how?" inquired the other.

"No," said Syme with equal decision.

"You remember, of course," resumed the soi-disant de Worms, pulling his beard and looking out of the window, "that when we broke up rather hurriedly the whole arrangements for the atrocity were left in the private hands of the Marquis and Dr. Bull. The Marquis is by this time probably crossing the Channel. But where he will go and what he will do it is doubtful whether even the President knows; certainly we don't know. The only man who does know is Dr. Bull."

"Confound it!" cried Syme. "And we don't know where he is."

"Yes," said the other in his curious, absent-minded way, "I know where he is myself."

"Will you tell me?" asked Syme with eager eyes.

"I will take you there," said the Professor, and took down his own hat from a peg.

Syme stood looking at him with a sort of rigid excitement.

"What do you mean?" he asked sharply. "Will you join me? Will you take the risk?"

"Young man," said the Professor pleasantly, "I am amused to observe that you think I am a coward. As to that I will say only one word, and that shall be entirely in the manner of your own philosophical rhetoric. You think that it is possible to pull down the President. I know that it is impossible, and I am going to try it," and opening the tavern door, which let in a blast of bitter air, they went out together into the dark streets by the docks.

Most of the snow was melted or trampled to mud, but here and there a clot of it still showed grey rather than white in the gloom. The small streets were sloppy and full of pools, which reflected the flaming lamps irregularly, and by accident, like fragments of some other and fallen world. Syme felt almost dazed as he stepped through this growing confusion of lights and shadows; but his companion walked on with a certain briskness, towards where, at the end of the street, an inch or two of the lamplit river looked like a bar of flame.

"Where are you going?" Syme inquired.

"Just now," answered the Professor, "I am going just round the corner to see whether Dr. Bull has gone to bed. He is hygienic, and retires early."

"Dr. Bull!" exclaimed Syme. "Does he live round the corner?"

"No," answered his friend. "As a matter of fact he lives some way off, on the other side of the river, but we can tell from here whether he has gone to bed."

Turning the corner as he spoke, and facing the dim river, flecked with flame, he pointed with his stick to the other bank. On the Surrey side at this point there ran out into the Thames, seeming almost to overhang it, a bulk and cluster of those tall tenements, dotted with lighted windows, and rising like factory chimneys to an almost insane height. Their special poise and position made one block of buildings especially look like a Tower of Babel with a hundred eyes. Syme had never seen any of the sky-scraping buildings in America, so he could only think of the buildings in a dream.

Even as he stared, the highest light in this innumerably lighted turret abruptly went out, as if this black Argus had winked at him with one of his innumerable eyes.

Professor de Worms swung round on his heel, and struck his stick against his boot.

"We are too late," he said, "the hygienic Doctor has gone to bed."

"What do you mean?" asked Syme. "Does he live over there, then?"

"Yes," said de Worms, "behind that particular window which you can't see. Come along and get some dinner. We must call on him tomorrow morning."

Without further parley, he led the way through several by-ways until they came out into the flare and clamour of the East India Dock Road. The Professor, who seemed to know his way about the neighbourhood, proceeded to a place where the line of lighted shops fell back into a sort of abrupt twilight and quiet, in which an old white inn, all out of repair, stood back some twenty feet from the road.

"You can find good English inns left by accident everywhere, like fossils," explained the Professor. "I once found a decent place in the West End."

"I suppose," said Syme, smiling, "that this is the corresponding decent place in the East End?"

"It is," said the Professor reverently, and went in.

In that place they dined and slept, both very thoroughly. The beans and bacon, which these unaccountable people cooked well, the astonishing emergence of Burgundy from their cellars, crowned Syme's sense of a new comradeship and comfort. Through all this ordeal his root horror had been isolation, and there are no words to express the abyss between isolation and having one ally. It may be conceded to the mathematicians that four is twice two. But two is not twice one; two is two thousand times one. That is why, in spite of a hundred disadvantages, the world will always return to monogamy.

Syme was able to pour out for the first time the whole of his outrageous tale, from the time when Gregory had taken him to the little tavern by the river. He did it idly and amply, in a luxuriant monologue, as a man speaks with very old friends. On his side, also, the man who had impersonated Professor de Worms was not less communicative. His own story was almost as silly as Syme's.

"That's a good get-up of yours," said Syme, draining a glass of Macon; "a lot better than old Gogol's. Even at the start I thought he was a bit too hairy."

"A difference of artistic theory," replied the Professor pensively. "Gogol was an idealist. He made up as the abstract or platonic ideal of an anarchist. But I am a realist. I am a portrait painter. But, indeed, to say that I am a portrait painter is an inadequate expression. I am a portrait."

"I don't understand you," said Syme.

"I am a portrait," repeated the Professor. "I am a portrait of the celebrated Professor de Worms, who is, I believe, in Naples."

"You mean you are made up like him," said Syme. "But doesn't he know that you are taking his nose in vain?"

"He knows it right enough," replied his friend cheerfully.

"Then why doesn't he denounce you?"

"I have denounced him," answered the Professor.

"Do explain yourself," said Syme.

"With pleasure, if you don't mind hearing my story," replied the eminent foreign philosopher. "I am by profession an actor, and my name is Wilks. When I was on the stage I mixed with all sorts of Bohemian and blackguard company. Sometimes I touched the edge of the turf, sometimes the riff-raff of the arts, and occasionally the political refugee. In some den of exiled dreamers I was introduced to the great German Nihilist philosopher, Professor de Worms. I did not gather much about him beyond his appearance, which was very disgusting, and which I studied carefully. I understood that he had proved that the destructive principle in the universe was God; hence he insisted on the need for a furious and incessant energy, rending all things in pieces. Energy, he said, was the All. He was lame, shortsighted, and partially paralytic. When I met him I was in a frivolous mood, and I disliked him so much that I resolved to imitate him. If I had been a draughtsman I would have drawn a caricature. I was only an actor, I could only act a caricature. I made myself up into what was meant for a wild exaggeration of the old Professor's dirty old self. When I went into the room full of his supporters I expected to be received with a roar of laughter, or (if they were too far gone) with a roar of indignation at the insult. I cannot describe the surprise I felt when my entrance was received with a respectful silence, followed (when I had first opened my lips) with a murmur of admiration. The curse of the perfect artist had fallen upon me. I had been too subtle, I had been too true. They thought I really was the great Nihilist Professor. I was a healthy-minded young man at the time, and I confess that it was a blow. Before I could fully recover, however, two or three of these admirers ran up to me radiating indignation, and told me that a public insult had been put upon me in the next room. I inquired its nature. It seemed that an impertinent fellow had dressed himself up as a preposterous parody of myself. I had drunk more champagne than was good for me, and in a flash of folly I decided to see the situation through. Consequently it was to meet the glare of the company and my own lifted eyebrows and freezing eyes that the real Professor came into the room.

"I need hardly say there was a collision. The pessimists all round me looked anxiously from one Professor to the other Professor to see which was really the more feeble. But I won. An old man in poor health, like my rival, could not be expected to be so impressively feeble as a young actor in the prime of life. You see, he really had paralysis, and working within this definite limitation, he couldn't be so jolly paralytic as I was. Then he tried to blast my claims intellectually. I countered that by a very simple dodge. Whenever he said something that nobody but he could understand, I replied with something which I could not even understand myself. 'I don't fancy,' he said, 'that you could have worked out the principle that evolution is only negation, since there inheres in it the introduction of lacuna, which are an essential of differentiation.' I replied quite scornfully, 'You read all that up in Pinckwerts; the notion that involution functioned eugenically was exposed long ago by Glumpe.' It is unnecessary for me to say that there never were such people as Pinckwerts and Glumpe. But the people all round (rather to my surprise) seemed to remember them quite well, and the Professor, finding that the learned and mysterious method left him rather at the mercy of an enemy slightly deficient in scruples, fell back upon a more popular form of wit. 'I see,' he sneered, 'you prevail like the false pig in Aesop.' 'And you fail,' I answered, smiling, 'like the hedgehog in Montaigne.' Need I say that there is no hedgehog in Montaigne? 'Your claptrap comes off,' he said; 'so would your beard.' I had no intelligent answer to this, which was quite true and rather witty. But I laughed heartily, answered, 'Like the Pantheist's boots,' at random, and turned on my heel with all the honours of victory. The real

Professor was thrown out, but not with violence, though one man tried very patiently to pull off his nose. He is now, I believe, received everywhere in Europe as a delightful impostor. His apparent earnestness and anger, you see, make him all the more entertaining."

"Well," said Syme, "I can understand your putting on his dirty old beard for a night's practical joke, but I don't understand your never taking it off again."

"That is the rest of the story," said the impersonator. "When I myself left the company, followed by reverent applause, I went limping down the dark street, hoping that I should soon be far enough away to be able to walk like a human being. To my astonishment, as I was turning the corner, I felt a touch on the shoulder, and turning, found myself under the shadow of an enormous policeman. He told me I was wanted. I struck a sort of paralytic attitude, and cried in a high German accent, 'Yes, I am wanted—by the oppressed of the world. You are arresting me on the charge of being the great anarchist, Professor de Worms.' The policeman impassively consulted a paper in his hand, 'No, sir,' he said civilly, 'at least, not exactly, sir. I am arresting you on the charge of not being the celebrated anarchist, Professor de Worms.' This charge, if it was criminal at all, was certainly the lighter of the two, and I went along with the man, doubtful, but not greatly dismayed. I was shown into a number of rooms, and eventually into the presence of a police officer, who explained that a serious campaign had been opened against the centres of anarchy, and that this, my successful masquerade, might be of considerable value to the public safety. He offered me a good salary and this little blue card. Though our conversation was short, he struck me as a man of very massive common sense and humour; but I cannot tell you much about him personally, because—"

Syme laid down his knife and fork.

"I know," he said, "because you talked to him in a dark room."

Professor de Worms nodded and drained his glass.

CHAPTER IX
THE MAN IN SPECTACLES

"BURGUNDY is a jolly thing," said the Professor sadly, as he set his glass down.

"You don't look as if it were," said Syme; "you drink it as if it were medicine."

"You must excuse my manner," said the Professor dismally, "my position is rather a curious one. Inside I am really bursting with boyish merriment; but I acted the paralytic Professor so well, that now I can't leave off. So that when I am among friends, and have no need at all to disguise myself, I still can't help speaking slow and wrinkling my forehead—just as if it were my forehead. I can be quite happy, you understand, but only in a paralytic sort of way. The most buoyant exclamations leap up in my heart, but they come out of my mouth quite different. You should hear me say, 'Buck up, old cock!' It would bring tears to your eyes."

"It does," said Syme; "but I cannot help thinking that apart from all that you are really a bit worried."

The Professor started a little and looked at him steadily.

"You are a very clever fellow," he said, "it is a pleasure to work with you. Yes, I have rather a heavy cloud in my head. There is a great problem to face," and he sank his bald brow in his two hands.

Then he said in a low voice—

"Can you play the piano?"

"Yes," said Syme in simple wonder, "I'm supposed to have a good touch."

Then, as the other did not speak, he added—

"I trust the great cloud is lifted."

After a long silence, the Professor said out of the cavernous shadow of his hands—

"It would have done just as well if you could work a typewriter."

"Thank you," said Syme, "you flatter me."

"Listen to me," said the other, "and remember whom we have to see tomorrow. You and I are going tomorrow to attempt something which is very much more dangerous than trying to steal the Crown Jewels out of the Tower. We are trying to steal a secret from a very sharp, very strong, and very wicked man. I believe there is no man, except the President, of course, who is so seriously startling and formidable as that little grinning fellow in goggles. He has not perhaps the white-hot enthusiasm unto death, the mad martyrdom for anarchy, which marks the Secretary. But then that very fanaticism in the Secretary has a human pathos, and is almost a redeeming trait. But the little Doctor has a brutal sanity that is more shocking than the Secretary's disease. Don't you notice his detestable virility and vitality. He bounces like an india-rubber ball. Depend on it, Sunday was not asleep (I wonder if he ever sleeps?) when he locked up all the plans of this outrage in the round, black head of Dr. Bull."

"And you think," said Syme, "that this unique monster will be soothed if I play the piano to him?"

"Don't be an ass," said his mentor. "I mentioned the piano because it gives one quick and independent fingers. Syme, if we are to go through this interview and come out sane or alive, we must have some code of signals between us that this brute will not see. I have made a rough alphabetical cypher corresponding to the five fingers—like this, see," and he rippled with his fingers on the wooden table— "B A D, bad, a word we may frequently require."

Syme poured himself out another glass of wine, and began to study the scheme. He was abnormally quick with his brains at puzzles, and with his hands at conjuring, and it did not take him long to learn how he might convey simple messages by what would seem to be idle taps upon a table or knee. But wine and companionship had always the effect of inspiring him to a farcical ingenuity, and the Professor soon found himself struggling with the too vast energy of the new language, as it passed through the heated brain of Syme.

"We must have several word-signs," said Syme seriously—"words that we are likely to want, fine shades of meaning. My favourite word is 'coeval'. What's yours?"

316

"Do stop playing the goat," said the Professor plaintively. "You don't know how serious this is."

"'Lush' too," said Syme, shaking his head sagaciously, "we must have 'lush'—word applied to grass, don't you know?"

"Do you imagine," asked the Professor furiously, "that we are going to talk to Dr. Bull about grass?"

"There are several ways in which the subject could be approached," said Syme reflectively, "and the word introduced without appearing forced. We might say, 'Dr. Bull, as a revolutionist, you remember that a tyrant once advised us to eat grass; and indeed many of us, looking on the fresh lush grass of summer...'"

"Do you understand," said the other, "that this is a tragedy?"

"Perfectly," replied Syme; "always be comic in a tragedy. What the deuce else can you do? I wish this language of yours had a wider scope. I suppose we could not extend it from the fingers to the toes? That would involve pulling off our boots and socks during the conversation, which however unobtrusively performed—"

"Syme," said his friend with a stern simplicity, "go to bed!"

Syme, however, sat up in bed for a considerable time mastering the new code. He was awakened next morning while the east was still sealed with darkness, and found his grey-bearded ally standing like a ghost beside his bed.

Syme sat up in bed blinking; then slowly collected his thoughts, threw off the bed-clothes, and stood up. It seemed to him in some curious way that all the safety and sociability of the night before fell with the bedclothes off him, and he stood up in an air of cold danger. He still felt an entire trust and loyalty towards his companion; but it was the trust between two men going to the scaffold.

"Well," said Syme with a forced cheerfulness as he pulled on his trousers, "I dreamt of that alphabet of yours. Did it take you long to make it up?"

The Professor made no answer, but gazed in front of him with eyes the colour of a wintry sea; so Syme repeated his question.

"I say, did it take you long to invent all this? I'm considered good at these things, and it was a good hour's grind. Did you learn it all on the spot?"

The Professor was silent; his eyes were wide open, and he wore a fixed but very small smile.

"How long did it take you?"

The Professor did not move.

"Confound you, can't you answer?" called out Syme, in a sudden anger that had something like fear underneath. Whether or no the Professor could answer, he did not.

Syme stood staring back at the stiff face like parchment and the blank, blue eyes. His first thought was that the Professor had gone mad, but his second thought was more frightful. After all, what did he know about this queer creature whom he had heedlessly accepted as a friend? What did he know, except that the man had been at the anarchist breakfast and had told him a ridiculous tale? How improbable it was that there should be another friend there beside Gogol! Was this man's silence a sensational way of declaring war? Was this adamantine stare after all only the awful sneer of some threefold traitor, who had turned for the last time? He stood and strained his ears in this heartless silence. He almost fancied he could hear dynamiters come to capture him shifting softly in the corridor outside.

Then his eye strayed downwards, and he burst out laughing. Though the Professor himself stood there as voiceless as a statue, his five dumb fingers were dancing alive upon the dead table. Syme watched the twinkling movements of the talking hand, and read clearly the message—

"I will only talk like this. We must get used to it."

He rapped out the answer with the impatience of relief—

"All right. Let's get out to breakfast."

They took their hats and sticks in silence; but as Syme took his sword-stick, he held it hard.

They paused for a few minutes only to stuff down coffee and coarse thick sandwiches at a coffee stall, and then made their way across the river, which under the grey and growing light looked as desolate as Acheron. They reached the bottom of the huge block of buildings which they had seen from across the river, and began in silence to mount the naked and numberless stone steps, only pausing now and then to make short remarks on the rail of the banisters. At about every other flight they passed a window; each window showed them a pale and tragic dawn lifting itself laboriously over London. From each the innumerable roofs of slate looked like the leaden surges of a grey, troubled sea after rain. Syme was increasingly conscious that his new adventure had somehow a quality of cold sanity worse than the wild adventures of the past. Last night, for instance, the tall tenements had seemed to him like a tower in a dream. As he now went up the weary and perpetual steps, he was daunted and bewildered by their almost infinite series. But it was not the hot horror of a dream or of anything that might be exaggeration or delusion. Their infinity was more like the empty infinity of arithmetic, something unthinkable, yet necessary to thought. Or it was like the stunning statements of astronomy about the distance of the fixed stars. He was ascending the house of reason, a thing more hideous than unreason itself.

By the time they reached Dr. Bull's landing, a last window showed them a harsh, white dawn edged with banks of a kind of coarse red, more like red clay than red cloud. And when they entered Dr. Bull's bare garret it was full of light.

Syme had been haunted by a half historic memory in connection with these empty rooms and that austere daybreak. The moment he saw the garret and Dr. Bull sitting writing at a table, he remembered what the memory was—the French Revolution. There should have been the black outline of a guillotine against that heavy red and white of the morning. Dr. Bull was in his white shirt and black breeches only; his cropped, dark head might well have just come out of its wig; he might have been Marat or a more slipshod Robespierre.

Yet when he was seen properly, the French fancy fell away. The Jacobins were idealists; there was about this man a murderous materialism. His position gave him a somewhat new appearance. The strong, white light of morning coming from one side creating sharp shadows, made him seem both more pale and more angular than he had looked at the breakfast on the balcony. Thus the two black glasses that encased his eyes might really have been black cavities in his skull, making him look like a death's-head. And, indeed, if ever Death himself sat writing at a wooden table, it might have been he.

He looked up and smiled brightly enough as the men came in, and rose with the resilient rapidity of which the Professor had spoken. He set chairs for both of them, and going to a peg behind the door, proceeded to put on a coat and waistcoat of rough, dark tweed; he buttoned it up neatly, and came back to sit down at his table.

The quiet good humour of his manner left his two opponents helpless. It was with some momentary difficulty that the Professor broke silence and began, "I'm sorry to disturb you so early, comrade," said he, with a careful resumption of the slow de Worms manner. "You have no doubt made all the arrangements for the Paris affair?" Then he added with infinite slowness, "We have information which renders intolerable anything in the nature of a moment's delay."

Dr. Bull smiled again, but continued to gaze on them without speaking. The Professor resumed, a pause before each weary word—

"Please do not think me excessively abrupt; but I advise you to alter those plans, or if it is too late for that, to follow your agent with all the support you can get for him. Comrade Syme and I have had an experience which it would take more time to recount than we can afford, if we are to act on it. I will, however, relate the occurrence in detail, even at the risk of losing time, if you really feel that it is essential to the understanding of the problem we have to discuss."

He was spinning out his sentences, making them intolerably long and lingering, in the hope of maddening the practical little Doctor into an explosion of impatience which might show his hand. But the little Doctor continued only to stare and smile, and the monologue was uphill work. Syme began to feel a new sickness and despair. The Doctor's smile and silence were not at all like the cataleptic stare and horrible silence which he had confronted in the Professor half an hour before. About the Professor's makeup and all his antics there was always something merely grotesque, like a gollywog. Syme remembered those wild woes of yesterday as one remembers being afraid of Bogy in childhood. But here was daylight; here was a healthy, square-shouldered man in tweeds, not odd save for the accident of his ugly spectacles, not glaring or grinning at all, but smiling steadily and not saying a word. The whole had a sense of unbearable reality. Under the increasing sunlight the colours of the Doctor's complexion, the pattern of his tweeds, grew and expanded outrageously, as such things grow too important in a realistic novel. But his smile was quite slight, the pose of his head polite; the only uncanny thing was his silence.

"As I say," resumed the Professor, like a man toiling through heavy sand, "the incident that has occurred to us and has led us to ask for information about the Marquis, is one which you may think it better to have narrated; but as it came in the way of Comrade Syme rather than me—"

His words he seemed to be dragging out like words in an anthem; but Syme, who was watching, saw his long fingers rattle quickly on the edge of the crazy table. He read the message, "You must go on. This devil has sucked me dry!"

Syme plunged into the breach with that bravado of improvisation which always came to him when he was alarmed.

"Yes, the thing really happened to me," he said hastily. "I had the good fortune to fall into conversation with a detective who took me, thanks to my hat, for a re-spectable person. Wishing to clinch my reputation for respectability, I took him and made him very drunk at the Savoy. Under this influence he became friendly, and told me in so many words that within a day or two they hope to arrest the Marquis in France.

"So unless you or I can get on his track—"

The Doctor was still smiling in the most friendly way, and his protected eyes were still impenetrable. The Professor signalled to Syme that he would resume his explanation, and he began again with the same elaborate calm.

"Syme immediately brought this information to me, and we came here together to see what use you would be inclined to make of it. It seems to me unquestionably urgent that—"

All this time Syme had been staring at the Doctor almost as steadily as the Doctor stared at the Professor, but quite without the smile. The nerves of both com-rades-in-arms were near snapping under that strain of motionless amiability, when Syme suddenly leant forward and idly tapped the edge of the table. His message to his ally ran, "I have an intuition."

The Professor, with scarcely a pause in his monologue, signalled back, "Then sit on it."

Syme telegraphed, "It is quite extraordinary."

The other answered, "Extraordinary rot!"

Syme said, "I am a poet."

The other retorted, "You are a dead man."

Syme had gone quite red up to his yellow hair, and his eyes were burning fe-verishly. As he said he had an intuition, and it had risen to a sort of lightheaded certainty. Resuming his symbolic taps, he signalled to his friend, "You scarcely realise how poetic my intuition is. It has that sudden quality we sometimes feel in the coming of spring."

He then studied the answer on his friend's fingers. The answer was, "Go to hell!"

The Professor then resumed his merely verbal monologue addressed to the Doctor.

"Perhaps I should rather say," said Syme on his fingers, "that it resembles that sudden smell of the sea which may be found in the heart of lush woods."

His companion disdained to reply.

"Or yet again," tapped Syme, "it is positive, as is the passionate red hair of a beautiful woman."

The Professor was continuing his speech, but in the middle of it Syme decided to act. He leant across the table, and said in a voice that could not be neglected—

"Dr. Bull!"

The Doctor's sleek and smiling head did not move, but they could have sworn that under his dark glasses his eyes darted towards Syme.

"Dr. Bull," said Syme, in a voice peculiarly precise and courteous, "would you do me a small favour? Would you be so kind as to take off your spectacles?"

The Professor swung round on his seat, and stared at Syme with a sort of frozen fury of astonishment. Syme, like a man who has thrown his life and fortune on the table, leaned forward with a fiery face. The Doctor did not move.

For a few seconds there was a silence in which one could hear a pin drop, split once by the single hoot of a distant steamer on the Thames. Then Dr. Bull rose slowly, still smiling, and took off his spectacles.

Syme sprang to his feet, stepping backwards a little, like a chemical lecturer from a successful explosion. His eyes were like stars, and for an instant he could only point without speaking.

The Professor had also started to his feet, forgetful of his supposed paralysis. He leant on the back of the chair and stared doubtfully at Dr. Bull, as if the Doctor had been turned into a toad before his eyes. And indeed it was almost as great a transformation scene.

The two detectives saw sitting in the chair before them a very boyish-looking young man, with very frank and happy hazel eyes, an open expression, cockney clothes like those of a city clerk, and an unquestionable breath about him of being very good and rather commonplace. The smile was still there, but it might have been the first smile of a baby.

"I knew I was a poet," cried Syme in a sort of ecstasy. "I knew my intuition was as infallible as the Pope. It was the spectacles that did it! It was all the spectacles. Given those beastly black eyes, and all the rest of him his health and his jolly looks, made him a live devil among dead ones."

"It certainly does make a queer difference," said the Professor shakily. "But as regards the project of Dr. Bull—"

"Project be damned!" roared Syme, beside himself. "Look at him! Look at his face, look at his collar, look at his blessed boots! You don't suppose, do you, that that thing's an anarchist?"

"Syme!" cried the other in an apprehensive agony.

"Why, by God," said Syme, "I'll take the risk of that myself! Dr. Bull, I am a police officer. There's my card," and he flung down the blue card upon the table.

The Professor still feared that all was lost; but he was loyal. He pulled out his own official card and put it beside his friend's. Then the third man burst out laughing, and for the first time that morning they heard his voice.

"I'm awfully glad you chaps have come so early," he said, with a sort of schoolboy flippancy, "for we can all start for France together. Yes, I'm in the force right enough," and he flicked a blue card towards them lightly as a matter of form.

Clapping a brisk bowler on his head and resuming his goblin glasses, the Doctor moved so quickly towards the door, that the others instinctively followed him. Syme seemed a little distrait, and as he passed under the doorway he suddenly struck his stick on the stone passage so that it rang.

"But Lord God Almighty," he cried out, "if this is all right, there were more damned detectives than there were damned dynamiters at the damned Council!"

"We might have fought easily," said Bull; "we were four against three."

The Professor was descending the stairs, but his voice came up from below.

"No," said the voice, "we were not four against three—we were not so lucky. We were four against One."

The others went down the stairs in silence.

The young man called Bull, with an innocent courtesy characteristic of him, insisted on going last until they reached the street; but there his own robust rapidity asserted itself unconsciously, and he walked quickly on ahead towards a railway inquiry office, talking to the others over his shoulder.

"It is jolly to get some pals," he said. "I've been half dead with the jumps, being quite alone. I nearly flung my arms round Gogol and embraced him, which would have been imprudent. I hope you won't despise me for having been in a blue funk."

"All the blue devils in blue hell," said Syme, "contributed to my blue funk! But the worst devil was you and your infernal goggles."

The young man laughed delightedly.

"Wasn't it a rag?" he said. "Such a simple idea—not my own. I haven't got the brains. You see, I wanted to go into the detective service, especially the anti-dynamite business. But for that purpose they wanted someone to dress up as a dynamiter; and they all swore by blazes that I could never look like a dynamiter. They said my very walk was respectable, and that seen from behind I looked like the British Constitution. They said I looked too healthy and too optimistic, and too reliable and benevolent; they called me all sorts of names at Scotland Yard. They said that if I had been a criminal, I might have made my fortune by looking so like an honest man; but as I had the misfortune to be an honest man, there was not even the remotest chance of my assisting them by ever looking like a criminal. But at last I was brought before some old josser who was high up in the force, and who seemed to have no end of a head on his shoulders. And there the others all talked hopelessly. One asked whether a bushy beard would hide my nice smile; another said that if they blacked my face I might look like a negro anarchist; but this old chap chipped in with a most extraordinary remark. 'A pair of smoked spectacles will do it,' he said positively. 'Look at him now; he looks like an angelic office boy. Put him on a pair of smoked spectacles, and children will scream at the sight of him.' And so it was, by George! When once my eyes were covered, all the rest, smile and big shoulders and short hair, made me look a perfect little devil. As I say, it was simple enough when it was done, like miracles; but that wasn't the really miraculous part of it. There was one really staggering thing about the business, and my head still turns at it."

"What was that?" asked Syme.

"I'll tell you," answered the man in spectacles. "This big pot in the police who sized me up so that he knew how the goggles would go with my hair and socks—by God, he never saw me at all!"

Syme's eyes suddenly flashed on him.

"How was that?" he asked. "I thought you talked to him."

"So I did," said Bull brightly; "but we talked in a pitch-dark room like a coal-cellar. There, you would never have guessed that."

"I could not have conceived it," said Syme gravely.

"It is indeed a new idea," said the Professor.

Their new ally was in practical matters a whirlwind. At the inquiry office he asked with businesslike brevity about the trains for Dover. Having got his information, he bundled the company into a cab, and put them and himself inside a railrailway carriage before they had properly realised the breathless process. They were already on the Calais boat before conversation flowed freely.

"I had already arranged," he explained, "to go to France for my lunch; but I am delighted to have someone to lunch with me. You see, I had to send that beast, the Marquis, over with his bomb, because the President had his eye on me, though God knows how. I'll tell you the story some day. It was perfectly choking. Whenever I tried to slip out of it I saw the President somewhere, smiling out of the bow-window of a club, or taking off his hat to me from the top of an omnibus. I tell you, you can say what you like, that fellow sold himself to the devil; he can be in six places at once."

"So you sent the Marquis off, I understand," asked the Professor. "Was it long ago? Shall we be in time to catch him?"

"Yes," answered the new guide, "I've timed it all. He'll still be at Calais when we arrive."

"But when we do catch him at Calais," said the Professor, "what are we going to do?"

At this question the countenance of Dr. Bull fell for the first time. He reflected a little, and then said—

"Theoretically, I suppose, we ought to call the police."

"Not I," said Syme. "Theoretically I ought to drown myself first. I promised a poor fellow, who was a real modern pessimist, on my word of honour not to tell the police. I'm no hand at casuistry, but I can't break my word to a modern pessimist. It's like breaking one's word to a child."

"I'm in the same boat," said the Professor. "I tried to tell the police and I couldn't, because of some silly oath I took. You see, when I was an actor I was a sort of all-round beast. Perjury or treason is the only crime I haven't committed. If I did that I shouldn't know the difference between right and wrong."

"I've been through all that," said Dr. Bull, "and I've made up my mind. I gave my promise to the Secretary—you know him, man who smiles upside down. My friends, that man is the most utterly unhappy man that was ever human. It may be his digestion, or his conscience, or his nerves, or his philosophy of the universe, but he's damned, he's in hell! Well, I can't turn on a man like that, and hunt him down. It's like whipping a leper. I may be mad, but that's how I feel; and there's jolly well the end of it."

"I don't think you're mad," said Syme. "I knew you would decide like that when first you—"

"Eh?" said Dr. Bull.

"When first you took off your spectacles."

Dr. Bull smiled a little, and strolled across the deck to look at the sunlit sea. Then he strolled back again, kicking his heels carelessly, and a companionable silence fell between the three men.

"Well," said Syme, "it seems that we have all the same kind of morality or immorality, so we had better face the fact that comes of it."

"Yes," assented the Professor, "you're quite right; and we must hurry up, for I can see the Grey Nose standing out from France."

"The fact that comes of it," said Syme seriously, "is this, that we three are alone on this planet. Gogol has gone, God knows where; perhaps the President has smashed him like a fly. On the Council we are three men against three, like the Romans who held the bridge. But we are worse off than that, first because they can appeal to their organization and we cannot appeal to ours, and second because—"

"Because one of those other three men," said the Professor, "is not a man."

Syme nodded and was silent for a second or two, then he said—

"My idea is this. We must do something to keep the Marquis in Calais till tomorrow midday. I have turned over twenty schemes in my head. We cannot denounce him as a dynamiter; that is agreed. We cannot get him detained on some trivial charge, for we should have to appear; he knows us, and he would smell a rat. We cannot pretend to keep him on anarchist business; he might swallow much in that way, but not the notion of stopping in Calais while the Czar went safely through Paris. We might try to kidnap him, and lock him up ourselves; but he is a well-known man here. He has a whole bodyguard of friends; he is very strong and brave, and the event is doubtful. The only thing I can see to do is actually to take advantage of the very things that are in the Marquis's favour. I am going to profit by the fact that he is a highly respected nobleman. I am going to profit by the fact that he has many friends and moves in the best society."

"What the devil are you talking about?" asked the Professor.

"The Symes are first mentioned in the fourteenth century," said Syme; "but there is a tradition that one of them rode behind Bruce at Bannockburn. Since 1350 the tree is quite clear."

"He's gone off his head," said the little Doctor, staring.

"Our bearings," continued Syme calmly, "are 'argent a chevron gules charged with three cross crosslets of the field.' The motto varies."

The Professor seized Syme roughly by the waistcoat.

"We are just inshore," he said. "Are you seasick or joking in the wrong place?"

"My remarks are almost painfully practical," answered Syme, in an unhurried manner. "The house of St. Eustache also is very ancient. The Marquis cannot deny that he is a gentleman. He cannot deny that I am a gentleman. And in order to put the matter of my social position quite beyond a doubt, I propose at the earliest opportunity to knock his hat off. But here we are in the harbour."

They went on shore under the strong sun in a sort of daze. Syme, who had now taken the lead as Bull had taken it in London, led them along a kind of marine parade until he came to some cafes, embowered in a bulk of greenery and overlooking the sea. As he went before them his step was slightly swaggering, and he swung his stick like a sword. He was making apparently for the extreme end of the line of cafes, but he stopped abruptly. With a sharp gesture he motioned them to silence, but he pointed with one gloved finger to a cafe table under a bank of flowering foliage at which sat the Marquis de St. Eustache, his teeth shining in his thick, black beard, and his bold, brown face shadowed by a light yellow straw hat and outlined against the violet sea.

CHAPTER X
THE DUEL

SYME sat down at a cafe table with his companions, his blue eyes sparkling like the bright sea below, and ordered a bottle of Saumur with a pleased impatience. He was for some reason in a condition of curious hilarity. His spirits were already unnaturally high; they rose as the Saumur sank, and in half an hour his talk was a torrent of nonsense. He professed to be making out a plan of the conversation which was going to ensue between himself and the deadly Marquis. He jotted it down wildly with a pencil. It was arranged like a printed catechism, with questions and answers, and was delivered with an extraordinary rapidity of utterance.

"I shall approach. Before taking off his hat, I shall take off my own. I shall say, 'The Marquis de Saint Eustache, I believe.' He will say, 'The celebrated Mr. Syme, I presume.' He will say in the most exquisite French, 'How are you?' I shall reply in the most exquisite Cockney, 'Oh, just the Syme—'"

"Oh, shut it," said the man in spectacles. "Pull yourself together, and chuck away that bit of paper. What are you really going to do?"

"But it was a lovely catechism," said Syme pathetically. "Do let me read it you. It has only forty-three questions and answers, and some of the Marquis's answers are wonderfully witty. I like to be just to my enemy."

"But what's the good of it all?" asked Dr. Bull in exasperation.

"It leads up to my challenge, don't you see," said Syme, beaming. "When the Marquis has given the thirty-ninth reply, which runs—"

"Has it by any chance occurred to you," asked the Professor, with a ponderous simplicity, "that the Marquis may not say all the forty-three things you have put down for him? In that case, I understand, your own epigrams may appear somewhat more forced."

Syme struck the table with a radiant face.

"Why, how true that is," he said, "and I never thought of it. Sir, you have an intellect beyond the common. You will make a name."

"Oh, you're as drunk as an owl!" said the Doctor.

"It only remains," continued Syme quite unperturbed, "to adopt some other method of breaking the ice (if I may so express it) between myself and the man I wish to kill. And since the course of a dialogue cannot be predicted by one of its parties alone (as you have pointed out with such recondite acumen), the only thing to be done, I suppose, is for the one party, as far as possible, to do all the dialogue by himself. And so I will, by George!" And he stood up suddenly, his yellow hair blowing in the slight sea breeze.

A band was playing in a cafe chantant hidden somewhere among the trees, and a woman had just stopped singing. On Syme's heated head the bray of the brass band seemed like the jar and jingle of that barrel-organ in Leicester Square, to the tune of which he had once stood up to die. He looked across to the little table where the Marquis sat. The man had two companions now, solemn Frenchmen in frock-coats and silk hats, one of them with the red rosette of the Legion of Honour, evidently people of a solid social position. Besides these black, cylindrical costumes, the Marquis, in his loose straw hat and light spring clothes, looked Bohemian and even barbaric; but he looked the Marquis. Indeed, one might say that he looked the king, with his animal elegance, his scornful eyes, and his proud head lifted against the purple sea. But he was no Christian king, at any rate; he was, rather, some swarthy despot, half Greek, half Asiatic, who in the days when slavery seemed natural looked down on the Mediterranean, on his galley and his groaning slaves. Just so, Syme thought, would the brown-gold face of such a tyrant have shown against the dark green olives and the burning blue.

"Are you going to address the meeting?" asked the Professor peevishly, seeing that Syme still stood up without moving.

Syme drained his last glass of sparkling wine.

"I am," he said, pointing across to the Marquis and his companions, "that meeting. That meeting displeases me. I am going to pull that meeting's great ugly, mahogany-coloured nose."

He stepped across swiftly, if not quite steadily. The Marquis, seeing him, arched his black Assyrian eyebrows in surprise, but smiled politely.

"You are Mr. Syme, I think," he said.

Syme bowed.

"And you are the Marquis de Saint Eustache," he said gracefully. "Permit me to pull your nose."

He leant over to do so, but the Marquis started backwards, upsetting his chair, and the two men in top hats held Syme back by the shoulders.

"This man has insulted me!" said Syme, with gestures of explanation.

"Insulted you?" cried the gentleman with the red rosette, "when?"

"Oh, just now," said Syme recklessly. "He insulted my mother."

"Insulted your mother!" exclaimed the gentleman incredulously.

"Well, anyhow," said Syme, conceding a point, "my aunt."

"But how can the Marquis have insulted your aunt just now?" said the second gentleman with some legitimate wonder. "He has been sitting here all the time."

"Ah, it was what he said!" said Syme darkly.

"I said nothing at all," said the Marquis, "except something about the band. I only said that I liked Wagner played well."

"It was an allusion to my family," said Syme firmly. "My aunt played Wagner badly. It was a painful subject. We are always being insulted about it."

"This seems most extraordinary," said the gentleman who was decore, looking doubtfully at the Marquis.

"Oh, I assure you," said Syme earnestly, "the whole of your conversation was simply packed with sinister allusions to my aunt's weaknesses."

"This is nonsense!" said the second gentleman. "I for one have said nothing for half an hour except that I liked the singing of that girl with black hair."

"Well, there you are again!" said Syme indignantly. "My aunt's was red."

"It seems to me," said the other, "that you are simply seeking a pretext to insult the Marquis."

"By George!" said Syme, facing round and looking at him, "what a clever chap you are!"

The Marquis started up with eyes flaming like a tiger's.

"Seeking a quarrel with me!" he cried. "Seeking a fight with me! By God! there was never a man who had to seek long. These gentlemen will perhaps act for me. There are still four hours of daylight. Let us fight this evening."

Syme bowed with a quite beautiful graciousness.

"Marquis," he said, "your action is worthy of your fame and blood. Permit me to consult for a moment with the gentlemen in whose hands I shall place myself."

In three long strides he rejoined his companions, and they, who had seen his champagne-inspired attack and listened to his idiotic explanations, were quite startled at the look of him. For now that he came back to them he was quite sober, a little pale, and he spoke in a low voice of passionate practicality.

"I have done it," he said hoarsely. "I have fixed a fight on the beast. But look here, and listen carefully. There is no time for talk. You are my seconds, and everything must come from you. Now you must insist, and insist absolutely, on the duel coming off after seven tomorrow, so as to give me the chance of preventing him from catching the 7.45 for Paris. If he misses that he misses his crime. He can't refuse to meet you on such a small point of time and place. But this is what he will do. He will choose a field somewhere near a wayside station, where he can pick up the train. He is a very good swordsman, and he will trust to killing me in time to catch it. But I can fence well too, and I think I can keep him in play, at any rate, until the train is lost. Then perhaps he may kill me to console his feelings. You understand? Very well then, let me introduce you to some charming friends of mine," and leading them quickly across the parade, he presented them to the Marquis's seconds by two very aristocratic names of which they had not previously heard.

Syme was subject to spasms of singular common sense, not otherwise a part of his character. They were (as he said of his impulse about the spectacles) poetic intuitions, and they sometimes rose to the exaltation of prophecy.

He had correctly calculated in this case the policy of his opponent. When the Marquis was informed by his seconds that Syme could only fight in the morning, he must fully have realised that an obstacle had suddenly arisen between him and his bomb-throwing business in the capital. Naturally he could not explain this objection to his friends, so he chose the course which Syme had predicted. He induced his seconds to settle on a small meadow not far from the railway, and he trusted to the fatality of the first engagement.

When he came down very coolly to the field of honour, no one could have guessed that he had any anxiety about a journey; his hands were in his pockets, his straw hat on the back of his head, his handsome face brazen in the sun. But it might have struck a stranger as odd that there appeared in his train, not only his seconds carrying the sword-case, but two of his servants carrying a portmanteau and a luncheon basket.

Early as was the hour, the sun soaked everything in warmth, and Syme was vaguely surprised to see so many spring flowers burning gold and silver in the tall grass in which the whole company stood almost knee-deep.

With the exception of the Marquis, all the men were in sombre and solemn morning-dress, with hats like black chimney-pots; the little Doctor especially, with the addition of his black spectacles, looked like an undertaker in a farce. Syme could not help feeling a comic contrast between this funereal church parade of apparel and the rich and glistening meadow, growing wild flowers everywhere. But, indeed, this comic contrast between the yellow blossoms and the black hats was but a symbol of the tragic contrast between the yellow blossoms and the black business. On his right was a little wood; far away to his left lay the long curve of the railway line, which he was, so to speak, guarding from the Marquis, whose goal and escape it was. In front of him, behind the black group of his opponents, he could see, like a tinted cloud, a small almond bush in flower against the faint line of the sea.

The member of the Legion of Honour, whose name it seemed was Colonel Ducroix, approached the Professor and Dr. Bull with great politeness, and suggested that the play should terminate with the first considerable hurt.

Dr. Bull, however, having been carefully coached by Syme upon this point of policy, insisted, with great dignity and in very bad French, that it should continue until one of the combatants was disabled. Syme had made up his mind that he could avoid disabling the Marquis and prevent the Marquis from disabling him for at least twenty minutes. In twenty minutes the Paris train would have gone by.

"To a man of the well-known skill and valour of Monsieur de St. Eustache," said the Professor solemnly, "it must be a matter of indifference which method is adopted, and our principal has strong reasons for demanding the longer encounter, reasons the delicacy of which prevent me from being explicit, but for the just and honourable nature of which I can—"

"Peste!" broke from the Marquis behind, whose face had suddenly darkened, "let us stop talking and begin," and he slashed off the head of a tall flower with his stick.

Syme understood his rude impatience and instinctively looked over his shoulder to see whether the train was coming in sight. But there was no smoke on the horizon.

Colonel Ducroix knelt down and unlocked the case, taking out a pair of twin swords, which took the sunlight and turned to two streaks of white fire. He offered one to the Marquis, who snatched it without ceremony, and another to Syme, who took it, bent it, and poised it with as much delay as was consistent with dignity.

Then the Colonel took out another pair of blades, and taking one himself and giving another to Dr. Bull, proceeded to place the men.

Both combatants had thrown off their coats and waistcoats, and stood sword in hand. The seconds stood on each side of the line of fight with drawn swords also, but still sombre in their dark frock-coats and hats. The principals saluted. The Colonel said quietly, "Engage!" and the two blades touched and tingled.

When the jar of the joined iron ran up Syme's arm, all the fantastic fears that have been the subject of this story fell from him like dreams from a man waking up in bed. He remembered them clearly and in order as mere delusions of the nerves—how the fear of the Professor had been the fear of the tyrannic accidents of nightmare, and how the fear of the Doctor had been the fear of the airless vacuum of science. The first was the old fear that any miracle might happen, the second the more hopeless modern fear that no miracle can ever happen. But he saw that these fears were fancies, for he found himself in the presence of the great fact of the fear of death, with its coarse and pitiless common sense. He felt like a man who had dreamed all night of falling over precipices, and had woke up on the morning when he was to be hanged. For as soon as he had seen the sunlight run down the channel of his foe's foreshortened blade, and as soon as he had felt the two tongues of steel touch, vibrating like two living things, he knew that his enemy was a terrible fighter, and that probably his last hour had come.

He felt a strange and vivid value in all the earth around him, in the grass under his feet; he felt the love of life in all living things. He could almost fancy that he heard the grass growing; he could almost fancy that even as he stood fresh flowers were springing up and breaking into blossom in the meadow—flowers blood red and burning gold and blue, fulfilling the whole pageant of the spring. And whenever his eyes strayed for a flash from the calm, staring, hypnotic eyes of the Marquis, they saw the little tuft of almond tree against the sky-line. He had the feeling that if by some miracle he escaped he would be ready to sit for ever before that almond tree, desiring nothing else in the world.

But while earth and sky and everything had the living beauty of a thing lost, the other half of his head was as clear as glass, and he was parrying his enemy's point with a kind of clockwork skill of which he had hardly supposed himself capable. Once his enemy's point ran along his wrist, leaving a slight streak of blood, but it either was not noticed or was tacitly ignored. Every now and then he riposted, and once or twice he could almost fancy that he felt his point go home, but as there was no blood on blade or shirt he supposed he was mistaken. Then came an interruption and a change.

At the risk of losing all, the Marquis, interrupting his quiet stare, flashed one glance over his shoulder at the line of railway on his right. Then he turned on Syme a face transfigured to that of a fiend, and began to fight as if with twenty weapons. The attack came so fast and furious, that the one shining sword seemed a shower of shining arrows. Syme had no chance to look at the railway; but also he had no need. He could guess the reason of the Marquis's sudden madness of battle—the Paris train was in sight.

But the Marquis's morbid energy over-reached itself. Twice Syme, parrying, knocked his opponent's point far out of the fighting circle; and the third time his riposte was so rapid, that there was no doubt about the hit this time. Syme's sword actually bent under the weight of the Marquis's body, which it had pierced.

Syme was as certain that he had stuck his blade into his enemy as a gardener that he has stuck his spade into the ground. Yet the Marquis sprang back from the stroke without a stagger, and Syme stood staring at his own sword-point like an idiot. There was no blood on it at all.

There was an instant of rigid silence, and then Syme in his turn fell furiously on the other, filled with a flaming curiosity. The Marquis was probably, in a general sense, a better fencer than he, as he had surmised at the beginning, but at the moment the Marquis seemed distraught and at a disadvantage. He fought wildly and even weakly, and he constantly looked away at the railway line, almost as if he feared the train more than the pointed steel. Syme, on the other hand, fought fiercely but still carefully, in an intellectual fury, eager to solve the riddle of his own bloodless sword. For this purpose, he aimed less at the Marquis's body, and more at his throat and head. A minute and a half afterwards he felt his point enter the man's neck below the jaw. It came out clean. Half mad, he thrust again, and made what should have been a bloody scar on the Marquis's cheek. But there was no scar.

For one moment the heaven of Syme again grew black with supernatural terrors. Surely the man had a charmed life. But this new spiritual dread was a more awful thing than had been the mere spiritual topsy-turvydom symbolised by the paralytic who pursued him. The Professor was only a goblin; this man was a devil—perhaps he was the Devil! Anyhow, this was certain, that three times had a human sword been driven into him and made no mark. When Syme had that thought he drew himself up, and all that was good in him sang high up in the air as a high wind sings in the trees. He thought of all the human things in his story—of the Chinese lanterns in Saffron Park, of the girl's red hair in the garden, of the honest, beer-swilling sailors down by the dock, of his loyal companions standing by. Perhaps he had been chosen as a champion of all these fresh and kindly things to cross swords with the enemy of all creation. "After all," he said to himself, "I am more than a devil; I am a man. I can do the one thing which Satan himself cannot do—I can die," and as the word went through his head, he heard a faint and far-off hoot, which would soon be the roar of the Paris train.

He fell to fighting again with a supernatural levity, like a Mohammedan panting for Paradise. As the train came nearer and nearer he fancied he could see people putting up the floral arches in Paris; he joined in the growing noise and the glory of the great Republic whose gate he was guarding against Hell. His thoughts rose higher and higher with the rising roar of the train, which ended, as if proudly, in a long and piercing whistle. The train stopped.

Suddenly, to the astonishment of everyone the Marquis sprang back quite out of sword reach and threw down his sword. The leap was wonderful, and not the less wonderful because Syme had plunged his sword a moment before into the man's thigh.

"Stop!" said the Marquis in a voice that compelled a momentary obedience. "I want to say something."

"What is the matter?" asked Colonel Ducroix, staring. "Has there been foul play?"

"There has been foul play somewhere," said Dr. Bull, who was a little pale. "Our principal has wounded the Marquis four times at least, and he is none the worse."

The Marquis put up his hand with a curious air of ghastly patience.

"Please let me speak," he said. "It is rather important. Mr. Syme," he continued, turning to his opponent, "we are fighting today, if I remember right, because you expressed a wish (which I thought irrational) to pull my nose. Would you oblige me by pulling my nose now as quickly as possible? I have to catch a train."

"I protest that this is most irregular," said Dr. Bull indignantly.

"It is certainly somewhat opposed to precedent," said Colonel Ducroix, looking wistfully at his principal. "There is, I think, one case on record (Captain Bellegarde and the Baron Zumpt) in which the weapons were changed in the middle of the encounter at the request of one of the combatants. But one can hardly call one's nose a weapon."

"Will you or will you not pull my nose?" said the Marquis in exasperation. "Come, come, Mr. Syme! You wanted to do it, do it! You can have no conception of how important it is to me. Don't be so selfish! Pull my nose at once, when I ask you!" and he bent slightly forward with a fascinating smile. The Paris train, panting and groaning, had grated into a little station behind the neighbouring hill.

Syme had the feeling he had more than once had in these adventures—the sense that a horrible and sublime wave lifted to heaven was just toppling over. Walking in a world he half understood, he took two paces forward and seized the Roman nose of this remarkable nobleman. He pulled it hard, and it came off in his hand.

He stood for some seconds with a foolish solemnity, with the pasteboard proboscis still between his fingers, looking at it, while the sun and the clouds and the wooded hills looked down upon this imbecile scene.

The Marquis broke the silence in a loud and cheerful voice.

"If anyone has any use for my left eyebrow," he said, "he can have it. Colonel Ducroix, do accept my left eyebrow! It's the kind of thing that might come in useful any day," and he gravely tore off one of his swarthy Assyrian brows, bringing about half his brown forehead with it, and politely offered it to the Colonel, who stood crimson and speechless with rage.

"If I had known," he spluttered, "that I was acting for a poltroon who pads himself to fight—"

"Oh, I know, I know!" said the Marquis, recklessly throwing various parts of himself right and left about the field. "You are making a mistake; but it can't be explained just now. I tell you the train has come into the station!"

"Yes," said Dr. Bull fiercely, "and the train shall go out of the station. It shall go out without you. We know well enough for what devil's work—"

The mysterious Marquis lifted his hands with a desperate gesture. He was a strange scarecrow standing there in the sun with half his old face peeled off, and half another face glaring and grinning from underneath.

"Will you drive me mad?" he cried. "The train—"

"You shall not go by the train," said Syme firmly, and grasped his sword.

The wild figure turned towards Syme, and seemed to be gathering itself for a sublime effort before speaking.

"You great fat, blasted, blear-eyed, blundering, thundering, brainless, Godfor-saken, doddering, damned fool!" he said without taking breath. "You great silly, pink-faced, towheaded turnip! You—"

"You shall not go by this train," repeated Syme.

"And why the infernal blazes," roared the other, "should I want to go by the train?"

"We know all," said the Professor sternly. "You are going to Paris to throw a bomb!"

"Going to Jericho to throw a Jabberwock!" cried the other, tearing his hair, which came off easily.

"Have you all got softening of the brain, that you don't realise what I am? Did you really think I wanted to catch that train? Twenty Paris trains might go by for me. Damn Paris trains!"

"Then what did you care about?" began the Professor.

"What did I care about? I didn't care about catching the train; I cared about whether the train caught me, and now, by God! it has caught me."

"I regret to inform you," said Syme with restraint, "that your remarks convey no impression to my mind. Perhaps if you were to remove the remains of your orig-inal forehead and some portion of what was once your chin, your meaning would become clearer. Mental lucidity fulfils itself in many ways. What do you mean by saying that the train has caught you? It may be my literary fancy, but somehow I feel that it ought to mean something."

"It means everything," said the other, "and the end of everything. Sunday has us now in the hollow of his hand."

"Us!" repeated the Professor, as if stupefied. "What do you mean by 'us'?"

"The police, of course!" said the Marquis, and tore off his scalp and half his face.

The head which emerged was the blonde, well brushed, smooth-haired head which is common in the English constabulary, but the face was terribly pale.

"I am Inspector Ratcliffe," he said, with a sort of haste that verged on harsh-ness. "My name is pretty well known to the police, and I can see well enough that you belong to them. But if there is any doubt about my position, I have a card," and he began to pull a blue card from his pocket.

The Professor gave a tired gesture.

"Oh, don't show it us," he said wearily; "we've got enough of them to equip a paper-chase."

The little man named Bull, had, like many men who seem to be of a mere vi-vacious vulgarity, sudden movements of good taste. Here he certainly saved the situation. In the midst of this staggering transformation scene he stepped forward with all the gravity and responsibility of a second, and addressed the two seconds of the Marquis.

"Gentlemen," he said, "we all owe you a serious apology; but I assure you that you have not been made the victims of such a low joke as you imagine, or indeed of anything undignified in a man of honour. You have not wasted your time; you have helped to save the world. We are not buffoons, but very desperate men at war with a vast conspiracy. A secret society of anarchists is hunting us like hares; not such unfortunate madmen as may here or there throw a bomb through starvation or German philosophy, but a rich and powerful and fanatical church, a church of eastern pessimism, which holds it holy to destroy mankind like vermin. How hard they hunt us you can gather from the fact that we are driven to such disguises as those for which I apologise, and to such pranks as this one by which you suffer."

The younger second of the Marquis, a short man with a black moustache, bowed politely, and said—

"Of course, I accept the apology; but you will in your turn forgive me if I decline to follow you further into your difficulties, and permit myself to say good morning! The sight of an acquaintance and distinguished fellow-townsman coming to pieces in the open air is unusual, and, upon the whole, sufficient for one day. Colonel Ducroix, I would in no way influence your actions, but if you feel with me that our present society is a little abnormal, I am now going to walk back to the town."

Colonel Ducroix moved mechanically, but then tugged abruptly at his white moustache and broke out—

"No, by George! I won't. If these gentlemen are really in a mess with a lot of low wreckers like that, I'll see them through it. I have fought for France, and it is hard if I can't fight for civilization."

Dr. Bull took off his hat and waved it, cheering as at a public meeting.

"Don't make too much noise," said Inspector Ratcliffe, "Sunday may hear you."

"Sunday!" cried Bull, and dropped his hat.

"Yes," retorted Ratcliffe, "he may be with them."

"With whom?" asked Syme.

"With the people out of that train," said the other.

"What you say seems utterly wild," began Syme. "Why, as a matter of fact— But, my God," he cried out suddenly, like a man who sees an explosion a long way off, "by God! if this is true the whole bally lot of us on the Anarchist Council were against anarchy! Every born man was a detective except the President and his personal secretary. What can it mean?"

"Mean!" said the new policeman with incredible violence. "It means that we are struck dead! Don't you know Sunday? Don't you know that his jokes are always so big and simple that one has never thought of them? Can you think of anything more like Sunday than this, that he should put all his powerful enemies on the Supreme Council, and then take care that it was not supreme? I tell you he has bought every trust, he has captured every cable, he has control of every railway line— especially of that railway line!" and he pointed a shaking finger towards the small wayside station. "The whole movement was controlled by him; half the world was ready to rise for him. But there were just five people, perhaps, who would have resisted him... and the old devil put them on the Supreme Council, to waste their time in watching each other. Idiots that we are, he planned the whole of our idiocies! Sunday knew that the Professor would chase Syme through London, and that Syme would fight me in France. And he was combining great masses of capital, and seizing great lines of telegraphy, while we five idiots were running after each other like a lot of confounded babies playing blind man's buff."

"Well?" asked Syme with a sort of steadiness.

"Well," replied the other with sudden serenity, "he has found us playing blind man's buff today in a field of great rustic beauty and extreme solitude. He has probably captured the world; it only remains to him to capture this field and all the fools in it. And since you really want to know what was my objection to the arrival of that train, I will tell you. My objection was that Sunday or his Secretary has just this moment got out of it."

Syme uttered an involuntary cry, and they all turned their eyes towards the far-off station. It was quite true that a considerable bulk of people seemed to be moving in their direction. But they were too distant to be distinguished in any way.

"It was a habit of the late Marquis de St. Eustache," said the new policeman, producing a leather case, "always to carry a pair of opera glasses. Either the President or the Secretary is coming after us with that mob. They have caught us in a nice quiet place where we are under no temptations to break our oaths by calling the police. Dr. Bull, I have a suspicion that you will see better through these than through your own highly decorative spectacles."

He handed the field-glasses to the Doctor, who immediately took off his spectacles and put the apparatus to his eyes

"It cannot be as bad as you say," said the Professor, somewhat shaken. "There are a good number of them certainly, but they may easily be ordinary tourists."

"Do ordinary tourists," asked Bull, with the fieldglasses to his eyes, "wear black masks half-way down the face?"

Syme almost tore the glasses out of his hand, and looked through them. Most men in the advancing mob really looked ordinary enough; but it was quite true that two or three of the leaders in front wore black half-masks almost down to their mouths. This disguise is very complete, especially at such a distance, and Syme found it impossible to conclude anything from the clean-shaven jaws and chins of the men talking in the front. But presently as they talked they all smiled and one of them smiled on one side.

CHAPTER XI
THE CRIMINALS CHASE THE POLICE

SYME put the field-glasses from his eyes with an almost ghastly relief.

"The President is not with them, anyhow," he said, and wiped his forehead.

"But surely they are right away on the horizon," said the bewildered Colonel, blinking and but half recovered from Bull's hasty though polite explanation. "Could you possibly know your President among all those people?"

"Could I know a white elephant among all those people!" answered Syme somewhat irritably. "As you very truly say, they are on the horizon; but if he were walking with them... by God! I believe this ground would shake."

After an instant's pause the new man called Ratcliffe said with gloomy decision—

"Of course the President isn't with them. I wish to Gemini he were. Much more likely the President is riding in triumph through Paris, or sitting on the ruins of St. Paul's Cathedral."

"This is absurd!" said Syme. "Something may have happened in our absence; but he cannot have carried the world with a rush like that. It is quite true," he added, frowning dubiously at the distant fields that lay towards the little station, "it is certainly true that there seems to be a crowd coming this way; but they are not all the army that you make out."

"Oh, they," said the new detective contemptuously; "no they are not a very valuable force. But let me tell you frankly that they are precisely calculated to our value—we are not much, my boy, in Sunday's universe. He has got hold of all the cables and telegraphs himself. But to kill the Supreme Council he regards as a trivial matter, like a post card; it may be left to his private secretary," and he spat on the grass.

Then he turned to the others and said somewhat austerely—

"There is a great deal to be said for death; but if anyone has any preference for the other alternative, I strongly advise him to walk after me."

With these words, he turned his broad back and strode with silent energy towards the wood. The others gave one glance over their shoulders, and saw that the dark cloud of men had detached itself from the station and was moving with a mysterious discipline across the plain. They saw already, even with the naked eye, black blots on the foremost faces, which marked the masks they wore. They turned and followed their leader, who had already struck the wood, and disappeared among the twinkling trees.

The sun on the grass was dry and hot. So in plunging into the wood they had a cool shock of shadow, as of divers who plunge into a dim pool. The inside of the wood was full of shattered sunlight and shaken shadows. They made a sort of shuddering veil, almost recalling the dizziness of a cinematograph. Even the solid figures walking with him Syme could hardly see for the patterns of sun and shade that danced upon them. Now a man's head was lit as with a light of Rembrandt, leaving all else obliterated; now again he had strong and staring white hands with the face of a negro. The ex-Marquis had pulled the old straw hat over his eyes, and the black shade of the brim cut his face so squarely in two that it seemed to be wearing one of the black half-masks of their pursuers. The fancy tinted Syme's overwhelming sense of wonder. Was he wearing a mask? Was anyone wearing a mask? Was anyone anything? This wood of witchery, in which men's faces turned black and white by turns, in which their figures first swelled into sunlight and then faded into formless night, this mere chaos of chiaroscuro (after the clear daylight outside), seemed to Syme a perfect symbol of the world in which he had been moving for three days, this world where men took off their beards and their spectacles and their noses, and turned into other people. That tragic self-confidence which he had felt when he believed that the Marquis was a devil had strangely disappeared now that he knew that the Marquis was a friend. He felt almost inclined to ask after all these bewilderments what was a friend and what an enemy. Was there anything that was apart from what it seemed? The Marquis had taken off his nose and turned out to be a detective. Might he not just as well take off his head and turn out to be a hobgoblin? Was not everything, after all, like this bewildering woodland, this dance of dark and light? Everything only a glimpse, the glimpse always unforeseen, and always forgotten. For Gabriel Syme had found in the heart of that sun-splashed wood what many modern painters had found there. He had found the thing which the modern people call Impressionism, which is another name for that final scepticism which can find no floor to the universe.

As a man in an evil dream strains himself to scream and wake, Syme strove with a sudden effort to fling off this last and worst of his fancies. With two impatient strides he overtook the man in the Marquis's straw hat, the man whom he had come to address as Ratcliffe. In a voice exaggeratively loud and cheerful, he broke the bottomless silence and made conversation.

"May I ask," he said, "where on earth we are all going to?"

So genuine had been the doubts of his soul, that he was quite glad to hear his companion speak in an easy, human voice.

"We must get down through the town of Lancy to the sea," he said. "I think that part of the country is least likely to be with them."

"What can you mean by all this?" cried Syme. "They can't be running the real world in that way. Surely not many working men are anarchists, and surely if they were, mere mobs could not beat modern armies and police."

"Mere mobs!" repeated his new friend with a snort of scorn. "So you talk about mobs and the working classes as if they were the question. You've got that eternal idiotic idea that if anarchy came it would come from the poor. Why should it? The poor have been rebels, but they have never been anarchists; they have more interest than anyone else in there being some decent government. The poor man really has a stake in the country. The rich man hasn't; he can go away to New Guinea in a yacht. The poor have sometimes objected to being governed badly; the rich have always objected to being governed at all. Aristocrats were always anarchists, as you can see from the barons' wars."

"As a lecture on English history for the little ones," said Syme, "this is all very nice; but I have not yet grasped its application."

"Its application is," said his informant, "that most of old Sunday's right-hand men are South African and American millionaires. That is why he has got hold of all the communications; and that is why the last four champions of the anti-anarchist police force are running through a wood like rabbits."

"Millionaires I can understand," said Syme thoughtfully, "they are nearly all mad. But getting hold of a few wicked old gentlemen with hobbies is one thing; getting hold of great Christian nations is another. I would bet the nose off my face (forgive the allusion) that Sunday would stand perfectly helpless before the task of converting any ordinary healthy person anywhere."

"Well," said the other, "it rather depends what sort of person you mean."

"Well, for instance," said Syme, "he could never convert that person," and he pointed straight in front of him.

They had come to an open space of sunlight, which seemed to express to Syme the final return of his own good sense; and in the middle of this forest clearing was a figure that might well stand for that common sense in an almost awful actuality. Burnt by the sun and stained with perspiration, and grave with the bottomless gravity of small necessary toils, a heavy French peasant was cutting wood with a hatchet. His cart stood a few yards off, already half full of timber; and the horse that cropped the grass was, like his master, valorous but not desperate; like his master, he was even prosperous, but yet was almost sad. The man was a Norman, taller than the average of the French and very angular; and his swarthy figure stood dark against a square of sunlight, almost like some allegoric figure of labour frescoed on a ground of gold.

"Mr. Syme is saying," called out Ratcliffe to the French Colonel, "that this man, at least, will never be an anarchist."

"Mr. Syme is right enough there," answered Colonel Ducroix, laughing, "if only for the reason that he has plenty of property to defend. But I forgot that in your country you are not used to peasants being wealthy."

"He looks poor," said Dr. Bull doubtfully.

"Quite so," said the Colonel; "that is why he is rich."

"I have an idea," called out Dr. Bull suddenly; "how much would he take to give us a lift in his cart? Those dogs are all on foot, and we could soon leave them behind."

"Oh, give him anything!" said Syme eagerly. "I have piles of money on me."

"That will never do," said the Colonel; "he will never have any respect for you unless you drive a bargain."

"Oh, if he haggles!" began Bull impatiently.

"He haggles because he is a free man," said the other. "You do not understand; he would not see the meaning of generosity. He is not being tipped."

And even while they seemed to hear the heavy feet of their strange pursuers behind them, they had to stand and stamp while the French Colonel talked to the French wood-cutter with all the leisurely badinage and bickering of market-day. At the end of the four minutes, however, they saw that the Colonel was right, for the wood-cutter entered into their plans, not with the vague servility of a tout too-well paid, but with the seriousness of a solicitor who had been paid the proper fee. He told them that the best thing they could do was to make their way down to the little inn on the hills above Lancy, where the innkeeper, an old soldier who had become devout in his latter years, would be certain to sympathise with them, and even to take risks in their support. The whole company, therefore, piled themselves on top of the stacks of wood, and went rocking in the rude cart down the other and steeper side of the woodland. Heavy and ramshackle as was the vehicle, it was driven quickly enough, and they soon had the exhilarating impression of distancing altogether those, whoever they were, who were hunting them. For, after all, the riddle as to where the anarchists had got all these followers was still unsolved. One man's presence had sufficed for them; they had fled at the first sight of the deformed smile of the Secretary. Syme every now and then looked back over his shoulder at the army on their track.

As the wood grew first thinner and then smaller with distance, he could see the sunlit slopes beyond it and above it; and across these was still moving the square black mob like one monstrous beetle. In the very strong sunlight and with his own very strong eyes, which were almost telescopic, Syme could see this mass of men quite plainly. He could see them as separate human figures; but he was increasingly surprised by the way in which they moved as one man. They seemed to be dressed in dark clothes and plain hats, like any common crowd out of the streets; but they did not spread and sprawl and trail by various lines to the attack, as would be natural in an ordinary mob. They moved with a sort of dreadful and wicked woodenness, like a staring army of automatons.

Syme pointed this out to Ratcliffe.

"Yes," replied the policeman, "that's discipline. That's Sunday. He is perhaps five hundred miles off, but the fear of him is on all of them, like the finger of God. Yes, they are walking regularly; and you bet your boots that they are talking regularly, yes, and thinking regularly. But the one important thing for us is that they are disappearing regularly."

Syme nodded. It was true that the black patch of the pursuing men was growing smaller and smaller as the peasant belaboured his horse.

The level of the sunlit landscape, though flat as a whole, fell away on the farther side of the wood in billows of heavy slope towards the sea, in a way not unlike the lower slopes of the Sussex downs. The only difference was that in Sussex the road would have been broken and angular like a little brook, but here the white French road fell sheer in front of them like a waterfall. Down this direct descent the cart clattered at a considerable angle, and in a few minutes, the road growing yet steeper, they saw below them the little harbour of Lancy and a great blue arc of the sea. The travelling cloud of their enemies had wholly disappeared from the horizon.

The horse and cart took a sharp turn round a clump of elms, and the horse's nose nearly struck the face of an old gentleman who was sitting on the benches outside the little cafe of "Le Soleil d'Or." The peasant grunted an apology, and got down from his seat. The others also descended one by one, and spoke to the old gentleman with fragmentary phrases of courtesy, for it was quite evident from his expansive manner that he was the owner of the little tavern.

He was a white-haired, apple-faced old boy, with sleepy eyes and a grey moustache; stout, sedentary, and very innocent, of a type that may often be found in France, but is still commoner in Catholic Germany. Everything about him, his pipe, his pot of beer, his flowers, and his beehive, suggested an ancestral peace; only when his visitors looked up as they entered the inn-parlour, they saw the sword upon the wall.

The Colonel, who greeted the innkeeper as an old friend, passed rapidly into the inn-parlour, and sat down ordering some ritual refreshment. The military decision of his action interested Syme, who sat next to him, and he took the opportunity when the old innkeeper had gone out of satisfying his curiosity.

"May I ask you, Colonel," he said in a low voice, "why we have come here?"

Colonel Ducroix smiled behind his bristly white moustache.

"For two reasons, sir," he said; "and I will give first, not the most important, but the most utilitarian. We came here because this is the only place within twenty miles in which we can get horses."

"Horses!" repeated Syme, looking up quickly.

"Yes," replied the other; "if you people are really to distance your enemies it is horses or nothing for you, unless of course you have bicycles and motor-cars in your pocket."

"And where do you advise us to make for?" asked Syme doubtfully.

"Beyond question," replied the Colonel, "you had better make all haste to the police station beyond the town. My friend, whom I seconded under somewhat deceptive circumstances, seems to me to exaggerate very much the possibilities of a general rising; but even he would hardly maintain, I suppose, that you were not safe with the gendarmes."

Syme nodded gravely; then he said abruptly—

"And your other reason for coming here?"

"My other reason for coming here," said Ducroix soberly, "is that it is just as well to see a good man or two when one is possibly near to death."

Syme looked up at the wall, and saw a crudely-painted and pathetic religious picture. Then he said—

"You are right," and then almost immediately afterwards, "Has anyone seen about the horses?"

"Yes," answered Ducroix, "you may be quite certain that I gave orders the moment I came in. Those enemies of yours gave no impression of hurry, but they were really moving wonderfully fast, like a well-trained army. I had no idea that the anarchists had so much discipline. You have not a moment to waste."

Almost as he spoke, the old innkeeper with the blue eyes and white hair came ambling into the room, and announced that six horses were saddled outside.

By Ducroix's advice the five others equipped themselves with some portable form of food and wine, and keeping their duelling swords as the only weapons available, they clattered away down the steep, white road. The two servants, who had carried the Marquis's luggage when he was a marquis, were left behind to drink at the cafe by common consent, and not at all against their own inclination.

By this time the afternoon sun was slanting westward, and by its rays Syme could see the sturdy figure of the old innkeeper growing smaller and smaller, but still standing and looking after them quite silently, the sunshine in his silver hair. Syme had a fixed, superstitious fancy, left in his mind by the chance phrase of the Colonel, that this was indeed, perhaps, the last honest stranger whom he should ever see upon the earth.

He was still looking at this dwindling figure, which stood as a mere grey blot touched with a white flame against the great green wall of the steep down behind him. And as he stared over the top of the down behind the innkeeper, there appeared an army of black-clad and marching men. They seemed to hang above the good man and his house like a black cloud of locusts. The horses had been saddled none too soon.

CHAPTER XII
THE EARTH IN ANARCHY

URGING the horses to a gallop, without respect to the rather rugged descent of the road, the horsemen soon regained their advantage over the men on the march, and at last the bulk of the first buildings of Lancy cut off the sight of their pursuers. Nevertheless, the ride had been a long one, and by the time they reached the real town the west was warming with the colour and quality of sunset. The Colonel suggested that, before making finally for the police station, they should make the effort, in passing, to attach to themselves one more individual who might be useful.

"Four out of the five rich men in this town," he said, "are common swindlers. I suppose the proportion is pretty equal all over the world. The fifth is a friend of mine, and a very fine fellow; and what is even more important from our point of view, he owns a motor-car."

"I am afraid," said the Professor in his mirthful way, looking back along the white road on which the black, crawling patch might appear at any moment, "I am afraid we have hardly time for afternoon calls."

"Doctor Renard's house is only three minutes off," said the Colonel.

"Our danger," said Dr. Bull, "is not two minutes off."

"Yes," said Syme, "if we ride on fast we must leave them behind, for they are on foot."

"He has a motor-car," said the Colonel.

"But we may not get it," said Bull.

"Yes, he is quite on your side."

"But he might be out."

"Hold your tongue," said Syme suddenly. "What is that noise?"

For a second they all sat as still as equestrian statues, and for a second—for two or three or four seconds—heaven and earth seemed equally still. Then all their ears, in an agony of attention, heard along the road that indescribable thrill and throb that means only one thing—horses!

The Colonel's face had an instantaneous change, as if lightning had struck it, and yet left it scatheless.

"They have done us," he said, with brief military irony. "Prepare to receive cavalry!"

"Where can they have got the horses?" asked Syme, as he mechanically urged his steed to a canter.

The Colonel was silent for a little, then he said in a strained voice—

"I was speaking with strict accuracy when I said that the 'Soleil d'Or' was the only place where one can get horses within twenty miles."

"No!" said Syme violently, "I don't believe he'd do it. Not with all that white hair."

"He may have been forced," said the Colonel gently. "They must be at least a hundred strong, for which reason we are all going to see my friend Renard, who has a motor-car."

With these words he swung his horse suddenly round a street corner, and went down the street with such thundering speed, that the others, though already well at the gallop, had difficulty in following the flying tail of his horse.

Dr. Renard inhabited a high and comfortable house at the top of a steep street, so that when the riders alighted at his door they could once more see the solid green ridge of the hill, with the white road across it, standing up above all the roofs of the town. They breathed again to see that the road as yet was clear, and they rang the bell.

Dr. Renard was a beaming, brown-bearded man, a good example of that silent but very busy professional class which France has preserved even more perfectly than England. When the matter was explained to him he pooh-poohed the panic of the ex-Marquis altogether; he said, with the solid French scepticism, that there was no conceivable probability of a general anarchist rising. "Anarchy," he said, shrugging his shoulders, "it is childishness!"

"Et ca," cried out the Colonel suddenly, pointing over the other's shoulder, "and that is childishness, isn't it?"

They all looked round, and saw a curve of black cavalry come sweeping over the top of the hill with all the energy of Attila. Swiftly as they rode, however, the whole rank still kept well together, and they could see the black vizards of the first line as level as a line of uniforms. But although the main black square was the same, though travelling faster, there was now one sensational difference which they could see clearly upon the slope of the hill, as if upon a slanted map. The bulk of the riders were in one block; but one rider flew far ahead of the column, and with frantic movements of hand and heel urged his horse faster and faster, so that one might have fancied that he was not the pursuer but the pursued. But even at that great distance they could see something so fanatical, so unquestionable in his figure, that they knew it was the Secretary himself. "I am sorry to cut short a cultured discussion," said the Colonel, "but can you lend me your motor-car now, in two minutes?"

"I have a suspicion that you are all mad," said Dr. Renard, smiling sociably; "but God forbid that madness should in any way interrupt friendship. Let us go round to the garage."

Dr. Renard was a mild man with monstrous wealth; his rooms were like the Musee de Cluny, and he had three motor-cars. These, however, he seemed to use very sparingly, having the simple tastes of the French middle class, and when his impatient friends came to examine them, it took them some time to assure themselves that one of them even could be made to work. This with some difficulty they brought round into the street before the Doctor's house. When they came out of the dim garage they were startled to find that twilight had already fallen with the abruptness of night in the tropics. Either they had been longer in the place than they imagined, or some unusual canopy of cloud had gathered over the town. They looked down the steep streets, and seemed to see a slight mist coming up from the sea.

"It is now or never," said Dr. Bull. "I hear horses."

"No," corrected the Professor, "a horse."

And as they listened, it was evident that the noise, rapidly coming nearer on the rattling stones, was not the noise of the whole cavalcade but that of the one horseman, who had left it far behind—the insane Secretary.

Syme's family, like most of those who end in the simple life, had once owned a motor, and he knew all about them. He had leapt at once into the chauffeur's seat, and with flushed face was wrenching and tugging at the disused machinery. He bent his strength upon one handle, and then said quite quietly—

"I am afraid it's no go."

As he spoke, there swept round the corner a man rigid on his rushing horse, with the rush and rigidity of an arrow. He had a smile that thrust out his chin as if it were dislocated. He swept alongside of the stationary car, into which its company had crowded, and laid his hand on the front. It was the Secretary, and his mouth went quite straight in the solemnity of triumph.

Syme was leaning hard upon the steering wheel, and there was no sound but the rumble of the other pursuers riding into the town. Then there came quite suddenly a scream of scraping iron, and the car leapt forward. It plucked the Secretary clean out of his saddle, as a knife is whipped out of its sheath, trailed him kicking terribly for twenty yards, and left him flung flat upon the road far in front of his frightened horse. As the car took the corner of the street with a splendid curve, they could just see the other anarchists filling the street and raising their fallen leader.

"I can't understand why it has grown so dark," said the Professor at last in a low voice.

"Going to be a storm, I think," said Dr. Bull. "I say, it's a pity we haven't got a light on this car, if only to see by."

"We have," said the Colonel, and from the floor of the car he fished up a heavy, old-fashioned, carved iron lantern with a light inside it. It was obviously an antique, and it would seem as if its original use had been in some way semi-religious, for there was a rude moulding of a cross upon one of its sides.

"Where on earth did you get that?" asked the Professor.

"I got it where I got the car," answered the Colonel, chuckling, "from my best friend. While our friend here was fighting with the steering wheel, I ran up the front steps of the house and spoke to Renard, who was standing in his own porch, you will remember. 'I suppose,' I said, 'there's no time to get a lamp.' He looked up, blinking amiably at the beautiful arched ceiling of his own front hall. From this was suspended, by chains of exquisite ironwork, this lantern, one of the hundred treasures of his treasure house. By sheer force he tore the lamp out of his own ceiling, shattering the painted panels, and bringing down two blue vases with his violence. Then he handed me the iron lantern, and I put it in the car. Was I not right when I said that Dr. Renard was worth knowing?"

"You were," said Syme seriously, and hung the heavy lantern over the front. There was a certain allegory of their whole position in the contrast between the modern automobile and its strange ecclesiastical lamp. Hitherto they had passed through the quietest part of the town, meeting at most one or two pedestrians, who could give them no hint of the peace or the hostility of the place. Now, however, the windows in the houses began one by one to be lit up, giving a greater sense of habitation and humanity. Dr. Bull turned to the new detective who had led their flight, and permitted himself one of his natural and friendly smiles.

"These lights make one feel more cheerful."

Inspector Ratcliffe drew his brows together.

"There is only one set of lights that make me more cheerful," he said, "and they are those lights of the police station which I can see beyond the town. Please God we may be there in ten minutes."

Then all Bull's boiling good sense and optimism broke suddenly out of him.

"Oh, this is all raving nonsense!" he cried. "If you really think that ordinary people in ordinary houses are anarchists, you must be madder than an anarchist yourself. If we turned and fought these fellows, the whole town would fight for us."

"No," said the other with an immovable simplicity, "the whole town would fight for them. We shall see."

While they were speaking the Professor had leant forward with sudden excitement.

"What is that noise?" he said.

"Oh, the horses behind us, I suppose," said the Colonel. "I thought we had got clear of them."

"The horses behind us! No," said the Professor, "it is not horses, and it is not behind us."

Almost as he spoke, across the end of the street before them two shining and rattling shapes shot past. They were gone almost in a flash, but everyone could see that they were motor-cars, and the Professor stood up with a pale face and swore that they were the other two motor-cars from Dr. Renard's garage.

"I tell you they were his," he repeated, with wild eyes, "and they were full of men in masks!"

"Absurd!" said the Colonel angrily. "Dr. Renard would never give them his cars."

"He may have been forced," said Ratcliffe quietly. "The whole town is on their side."

"You still believe that," asked the Colonel incredulously.

"You will all believe it soon," said the other with a hopeless calm.

There was a puzzled pause for some little time, and then the Colonel began again abruptly—

"No, I can't believe it. The thing is nonsense. The plain people of a peaceable French town—"

He was cut short by a bang and a blaze of light, which seemed close to his eyes. As the car sped on it left a floating patch of white smoke behind it, and Syme had heard a shot shriek past his ear.

"My God!" said the Colonel, "someone has shot at us."

"It need not interrupt conversation," said the gloomy Ratcliffe. "Pray resume your remarks, Colonel. You were talking, I think, about the plain people of a peaceable French town."

The staring Colonel was long past minding satire. He rolled his eyes all round the street.

"It is extraordinary," he said, "most extraordinary."

"A fastidious person," said Syme, "might even call it unpleasant. However, I suppose those lights out in the field beyond this street are the Gendarmerie. We shall soon get there."

"No," said Inspector Ratcliffe, "we shall never get there."

He had been standing up and looking keenly ahead of him. Now he sat down and smoothed his sleek hair with a weary gesture.

"What do you mean?" asked Bull sharply.

"I mean that we shall never get there," said the pessimist placidly. "They have two rows of armed men across the road already; I can see them from here. The town is in arms, as I said it was. I can only wallow in the exquisite comfort of my own exactitude."

And Ratcliffe sat down comfortably in the car and lit a cigarette, but the others rose excitedly and stared down the road. Syme had slowed down the car as their plans became doubtful, and he brought it finally to a standstill just at the corner of a side street that ran down very steeply to the sea.

The town was mostly in shadow, but the sun had not sunk; wherever its level light could break through, it painted everything a burning gold. Up this side street the last sunset light shone as sharp and narrow as the shaft of artificial light at the theatre. It struck the car of the five friends, and lit it like a burning chariot. But the rest of the street, especially the two ends of it, was in the deepest twilight, and for some seconds they could see nothing. Then Syme, whose eyes were the keenest, broke into a little bitter whistle, and said,

"It is quite true. There is a crowd or an army or some such thing across the end of that street."

"Well, if there is," said Bull impatiently, "it must be something else—a sham fight or the mayor's birthday or something. I cannot and will not believe that plain, jolly people in a place like this walk about with dynamite in their pockets. Get on a bit, Syme, and let us look at them."

The car crawled about a hundred yards farther, and then they were all startled by Dr. Bull breaking into a high crow of laughter.

"Why, you silly mugs!" he cried, "what did I tell you. That crowd's as law-abiding as a cow, and if it weren't, it's on our side."

"How do you know?" asked the professor, staring.

"You blind bat," cried Bull, "don't you see who is leading them?"

They peered again, and then the Colonel, with a catch in his voice, cried out—"Why, it's Renard!"

There was, indeed, a rank of dim figures running across the road, and they could not be clearly seen; but far enough in front to catch the accident of the evening light was stalking up and down the unmistakable Dr. Renard, in a white hat, stroking his long brown beard, and holding a revolver in his left hand.

"What a fool I've been!" exclaimed the Colonel. "Of course, the dear old boy has turned out to help us."

Dr. Bull was bubbling over with laughter, swinging the sword in his hand as carelessly as a cane. He jumped out of the car and ran across the intervening space, calling out—

"Dr. Renard! Dr. Renard!"

An instant after Syme thought his own eyes had gone mad in his head. For the philanthropic Dr. Renard had deliberately raised his revolver and fired twice at Bull, so that the shots rang down the road.

Almost at the same second as the puff of white cloud went up from this atrocious explosion a long puff of white cloud went up also from the cigarette of the cynical Ratcliffe. Like all the rest he turned a little pale, but he smiled. Dr. Bull, at whom the bullets had been fired, just missing his scalp, stood quite still in the middle of the road without a sign of fear, and then turned very slowly and crawled back to the car, and climbed in with two holes through his hat.

"Well," said the cigarette smoker slowly, "what do you think now?"

"I think," said Dr. Bull with precision, "that I am lying in bed at No. 217 Peabody Buildings, and that I shall soon wake up with a jump; or, if that's not it, I think that I am sitting in a small cushioned cell in Hanwell, and that the doctor can't make much of my case. But if you want to know what I don't think, I'll tell you. I don't think what you think. I don't think, and I never shall think, that the mass of ordinary men are a pack of dirty modern thinkers. No, sir, I'm a democrat, and I still don't believe that Sunday could convert one average navvy or counter-jumper. No, I may be mad, but humanity isn't."

Syme turned his bright blue eyes on Bull with an earnestness which he did not commonly make clear.

"You are a very fine fellow," he said. "You can believe in a sanity which is not merely your sanity. And you're right enough about humanity, about peasants and people like that jolly old innkeeper. But you're not right about Renard. I suspected him from the first. He's rationalistic, and, what's worse, he's rich. When duty and religion are really destroyed, it will be by the rich."

"They are really destroyed now," said the man with a cigarette, and rose with his hands in his pockets. "The devils are coming on!"

The men in the motor-car looked anxiously in the direction of his dreamy gaze, and they saw that the whole regiment at the end of the road was advancing upon them, Dr. Renard marching furiously in front, his beard flying in the breeze.

The Colonel sprang out of the car with an intolerant exclamation.

"Gentlemen," he cried, "the thing is incredible. It must be a practical joke. If you knew Renard as I do—it's like calling Queen Victoria a dynamiter. If you had got the man's character into your head—"

"Dr. Bull," said Syme sardonically, "has at least got it into his hat."

"I tell you it can't be!" cried the Colonel, stamping.

"Renard shall explain it. He shall explain it to me," and he strode forward.

"Don't be in such a hurry," drawled the smoker. "He will very soon explain it to all of us."

But the impatient Colonel was already out of earshot, advancing towards the advancing enemy. The excited Dr. Renard lifted his pistol again, but perceiving his opponent, hesitated, and the Colonel came face to face with him with frantic gestures of remonstrance.

"It is no good," said Syme. "He will never get anything out of that old heathen. I vote we drive bang through the thick of them, bang as the bullets went through Bull's hat. We may all be killed, but we must kill a tidy number of them."

"I won't 'ave it," said Dr. Bull, growing more vulgar in the sincerity of his virtue. "The poor chaps may be making a mistake. Give the Colonel a chance."

"Shall we go back, then?" asked the Professor.

"No," said Ratcliffe in a cold voice, "the street behind us is held too. In fact, I seem to see there another friend of yours, Syme."

Syme spun round smartly, and stared backwards at the track which they had travelled. He saw an irregular body of horsemen gathering and galloping towards them in the gloom. He saw above the foremost saddle the silver gleam of a sword, and then as it grew nearer the silver gleam of an old man's hair. The next moment, with shattering violence, he had swung the motor round and sent it dashing down the steep side street to the sea, like a man that desired only to die.

"What the devil is up?" cried the Professor, seizing his arm.

"The morning star has fallen!" said Syme, as his own car went down the darkness like a falling star.

The others did not understand his words, but when they looked back at the street above they saw the hostile cavalry coming round the corner and down the slopes after them; and foremost of all rode the good innkeeper, flushed with the fiery innocence of the evening light.

"The world is insane!" said the Professor, and buried his face in his hands.

"No," said Dr. Bull in adamantine humility, "it is I."

"What are we going to do?" asked the Professor.

"At this moment," said Syme, with a scientific detachment, "I think we are going to smash into a lamppost."

The next instant the automobile had come with a catastrophic jar against an iron object. The instant after that four men had crawled out from under a chaos of metal, and a tall lean lamp-post that had stood up straight on the edge of the marine parade stood out, bent and twisted, like the branch of a broken tree.

"Well, we smashed something," said the Professor, with a faint smile. "That's some comfort."

"You're becoming an anarchist," said Syme, dusting his clothes with his instinct of daintiness.

"Everyone is," said Ratcliffe.

As they spoke, the white-haired horseman and his followers came thundering from above, and almost at the same moment a dark string of men ran shouting along the sea-front. Syme snatched a sword, and took it in his teeth; he stuck two others under his arm-pits, took a fourth in his left hand and the lantern in his right, and leapt off the high parade on to the beach below.

The others leapt after him, with a common acceptance of such decisive action, leaving the debris and the gathering mob above them.

"We have one more chance," said Syme, taking the steel out of his mouth. "Whatever all this pandemonium means, I suppose the police station will help us. We can't get there, for they hold the way. But there's a pier or breakwater runs out into the sea just here, which we could defend longer than anything else, like Horatius and his bridge. We must defend it till the Gendarmerie turn out. Keep after me."

They followed him as he went crunching down the beach, and in a second or two their boots broke not on the sea gravel, but on broad, flat stones. They marched down a long, low jetty, running out in one arm into the dim, boiling sea, and when they came to the end of it they felt that they had come to the end of their story. They turned and faced the town.

That town was transfigured with uproar. All along the high parade from which they had just descended was a dark and roaring stream of humanity, with tossing arms and fiery faces, groping and glaring towards them. The long dark line was dotted with torches and lanterns; but even where no flame lit up a furious face, they could see in the farthest figure, in the most shadowy gesture, an organised hate. It was clear that they were the accursed of all men, and they knew not why.

Two or three men, looking little and black like monkeys, leapt over the edge as they had done and dropped on to the beach. These came ploughing down the deep sand, shouting horribly, and strove to wade into the sea at random. The example was followed, and the whole black mass of men began to run and drip over the edge like black treacle.

Foremost among the men on the beach Syme saw the peasant who had driven their cart. He splashed into the surf on a huge cart-horse, and shook his axe at them.

"The peasant!" cried Syme. "They have not risen since the Middle Ages."

"Even if the police do come now," said the Professor mournfully, "they can do nothing with this mob."

"Nonsense!" said Bull desperately; "there must be some people left in the town who are human."

"No," said the hopeless Inspector, "the human being will soon be extinct. We are the last of mankind."

"It may be," said the Professor absently. Then he added in his dreamy voice, "What is all that at the end of the 'Dunciad'?

> *'Nor public flame; nor private, dares to shine;*
> *Nor human light is left, nor glimpse divine!*
> *Lo! thy dread Empire, Chaos, is restored;*
> *Light dies before thine uncreating word:*
> *Thy hand, great Anarch, lets the curtain fall;*
> *And universal darkness buries all.'"*

"Stop!" cried Bull suddenly, "the gendarmes are out."

The low lights of the police station were indeed blotted and broken with hurrying figures, and they heard through the darkness the clash and jingle of a disciplined cavalry.

"They are charging the mob!" cried Bull in ecstacy or alarm.

"No," said Syme, "they are formed along the parade."

"They have unslung their carbines," cried Bull dancing with excitement.

"Yes," said Ratcliffe, "and they are going to fire on us."

As he spoke there came a long crackle of musketry, and bullets seemed to hop like hailstones on the stones in front of them.

"The gendarmes have joined them!" cried the Professor, and struck his forehead.

"I am in the padded cell," said Bull solidly.

There was a long silence, and then Ratcliffe said, looking out over the swollen sea, all a sort of grey purple—

"What does it matter who is mad or who is sane? We shall all be dead soon."

Syme turned to him and said—

"You are quite hopeless, then?"

Mr. Ratcliffe kept a stony silence; then at last he said quietly—

"No; oddly enough I am not quite hopeless. There is one insane little hope that I cannot get out of my mind. The power of this whole planet is against us, yet I cannot help wondering whether this one silly little hope is hopeless yet."

"In what or whom is your hope?" asked Syme with curiosity.

"In a man I never saw," said the other, looking at the leaden sea.

"I know what you mean," said Syme in a low voice, "the man in the dark room. But Sunday must have killed him by now."

"Perhaps," said the other steadily; "but if so, he was the only man whom Sunday found it hard to kill."

"I heard what you said," said the Professor, with his back turned. "I also am holding hard on to the thing I never saw."

All of a sudden Syme, who was standing as if blind with introspective thought, swung round and cried out, like a man waking from sleep—

"Where is the Colonel? I thought he was with us!"

"The Colonel! Yes," cried Bull, "where on earth is the Colonel?"

"He went to speak to Renard," said the Professor.

"We cannot leave him among all those beasts," cried Syme. "Let us die like gentlemen if—"

"Do not pity the Colonel," said Ratcliffe, with a pale sneer. "He is extremely comfortable. He is—"

"No! no! no!" cried Syme in a kind of frenzy, "not the Colonel too! I will never believe it!"

"Will you believe your eyes?" asked the other, and pointed to the beach.

Many of their pursuers had waded into the water shaking their fists, but the sea was rough, and they could not reach the pier. Two or three figures, however, stood on the beginning of the stone footway, and seemed to be cautiously advancing down it. The glare of a chance lantern lit up the faces of the two foremost. One face wore a black half-mask, and under it the mouth was twisting about in such a madness of nerves that the black tuft of beard wriggled round and round like a restless, living thing. The other was the red face and white moustache of Colonel Ducroix. They were in earnest consultation.

"Yes, he is gone too," said the Professor, and sat down on a stone. "Everything's gone. I'm gone! I can't trust my own bodily machinery. I feel as if my own hand might fly up and strike me."

"When my hand flies up," said Syme, "it will strike somebody else," and he strode along the pier towards the Colonel, the sword in one hand and the lantern in the other.

As if to destroy the last hope or doubt, the Colonel, who saw him coming, pointed his revolver at him and fired. The shot missed Syme, but struck his sword, breaking it short at the hilt. Syme rushed on, and swung the iron lantern above his head.

"Judas before Herod!" he said, and struck the Colonel down upon the stones. Then he turned to the Secretary, whose frightful mouth was almost foaming now, and held the lamp high with so rigid and arresting a gesture, that the man was, as it were, frozen for a moment, and forced to hear.

"Do you see this lantern?" cried Syme in a terrible voice. "Do you see the cross carved on it, and the flame inside? You did not make it. You did not light it. Better men than you, men who could believe and obey, twisted the entrails of iron and preserved the legend of fire. There is not a street you walk on, there is not a thread you wear, that was not made as this lantern was, by denying your philosophy of dirt and rats. You can make nothing. You can only destroy. You will destroy mankind; you will destroy the world. Let that suffice you. Yet this one old Christian lantern you shall not destroy. It shall go where your empire of apes will never have the wit to find it."

He struck the Secretary once with the lantern so that he staggered; and then, whirling it twice round his head, sent it flying far out to sea, where it flared like a roaring rocket and fell.

"Swords!" shouted Syme, turning his flaming face to the three behind him. "Let us charge these dogs, for our time has come to die."

His three companions came after him sword in hand. Syme's sword was broken, but he rent a bludgeon from the fist of a fisherman, flinging him down. In a moment they would have flung themselves upon the face of the mob and perished, when an interruption came. The Secretary, ever since Syme's speech, had stood with his hand to his stricken head as if dazed; now he suddenly pulled off his black mask.

The pale face thus peeled in the lamplight revealed not so much rage as astonishment. He put up his hand with an anxious authority.

"There is some mistake," he said. "Mr. Syme, I hardly think you understand your position. I arrest you in the name of the law."

"Of the law?" said Syme, and dropped his stick.

"Certainly!" said the Secretary. "I am a detective from Scotland Yard," and he took a small blue card from his pocket.

"And what do you suppose we are?" asked the Professor, and threw up his arms.

"You," said the Secretary stiffly, "are, as I know for a fact, members of the Supreme Anarchist Council. Disguised as one of you, I—"

Dr. Bull tossed his sword into the sea.

"There never was any Supreme Anarchist Council," he said. "We were all a lot of silly policemen looking at each other. And all these nice people who have been peppering us with shot thought we were the dynamiters. I knew I couldn't be wrong about the mob," he said, beaming over the enormous multitude, which stretched away to the distance on both sides. "Vulgar people are never mad. I'm vulgar myself, and I know. I am now going on shore to stand a drink to everybody here."

CHAPTER XIII
THE PURSUIT OF THE PRESIDENT

NEXT morning five bewildered but hilarious people took the boat for Dover. The poor old Colonel might have had some cause to complain, having been first forced to fight for two factions that didn't exist, and then knocked down with an iron lantern. But he was a magnanimous old gentleman, and being much relieved that neither party had anything to do with dynamite, he saw them off on the pier with great geniality.

The five reconciled detectives had a hundred details to explain to each other. The Secretary had to tell Syme how they had come to wear masks originally in order to approach the supposed enemy as fellow-conspirators.

Syme had to explain how they had fled with such swiftness through a civilised country. But above all these matters of detail which could be explained, rose the central mountain of the matter that they could not explain. What did it all mean? If they were all harmless officers, what was Sunday? If he had not seized the world, what on earth had he been up to? Inspector Ratcliffe was still gloomy about this.

"I can't make head or tail of old Sunday's little game any more than you can," he said. "But whatever else Sunday is, he isn't a blameless citizen. Damn it! do you remember his face?"

"I grant you," answered Syme, "that I have never been able to forget it."

"Well," said the Secretary, "I suppose we can find out soon, for tomorrow we have our next general meeting. You will excuse me," he said, with a rather ghastly smile, "for being well acquainted with my secretarial duties."

"I suppose you are right," said the Professor reflectively. "I suppose we might find it out from him; but I confess that I should feel a bit afraid of asking Sunday who he really is."

"Why," asked the Secretary, "for fear of bombs?"

"No," said the Professor, "for fear he might tell me."

"Let us have some drinks," said Dr. Bull, after a silence.

Throughout their whole journey by boat and train they were highly convivial, but they instinctively kept together. Dr. Bull, who had always been the optimist of the party, endeavoured to persuade the other four that the whole company could take the same hansom cab from Victoria; but this was over-ruled, and they went in a four-wheeler, with Dr. Bull on the box, singing. They finished their journey at an hotel in Piccadilly Circus, so as to be close to the early breakfast next morning in Leicester Square. Yet even then the adventures of the day were not entirely over.

Dr. Bull, discontented with the general proposal to go to bed, had strolled out of the hotel at about eleven to see and taste some of the beauties of London. Twenty minutes afterwards, however, he came back and made quite a clamour in the hall. Syme, who tried at first to soothe him, was forced at last to listen to his communication with quite new attention.

"I tell you I've seen him!" said Dr. Bull, with thick emphasis.

"Whom?" asked Syme quickly. "Not the President?"

"Not so bad as that," said Dr. Bull, with unnecessary laughter, "not so bad as that. I've got him here."

"Got whom here?" asked Syme impatiently.

"Hairy man," said the other lucidly, "man that used to be hairy man—Gogol. Here he is," and he pulled forward by a reluctant elbow the identical young man who five days before had marched out of the Council with thin red hair and a pale face, the first of all the sham anarchists who had been exposed.

"Why do you worry with me?" he cried. "You have expelled me as a spy."

"We are all spies!" whispered Syme.

"We're all spies!" shouted Dr. Bull. "Come and have a drink."

Next morning the battalion of the reunited six marched stolidly towards the hotel in Leicester Square.

"This is more cheerful," said Dr. Bull; "we are six men going to ask one man what he means."

"I think it is a bit queerer than that," said Syme. "I think it is six men going to ask one man what they mean."

They turned in silence into the Square, and though the hotel was in the opposite corner, they saw at once the little balcony and a figure that looked too big for it. He was sitting alone with bent head, poring over a newspaper. But all his councillors, who had come to vote him down, crossed that Square as if they were watched out of heaven by a hundred eyes.

They had disputed much upon their policy, about whether they should leave the unmasked Gogol without and begin diplomatically, or whether they should bring him in and blow up the gunpowder at once. The influence of Syme and Bull prevailed for the latter course, though the Secretary to the last asked them why they attacked Sunday so rashly.

"My reason is quite simple," said Syme. "I attack him rashly because I am afraid of him."

They followed Syme up the dark stair in silence, and they all came out simultaneously into the broad sunlight of the morning and the broad sunlight of Sunday's smile.

"Delightful!" he said. "So pleased to see you all. What an exquisite day it is. Is the Czar dead?"

The Secretary, who happened to be foremost, drew himself together for a dignified outburst.

"No, sir," he said sternly "there has been no massacre. I bring you news of no such disgusting spectacles."

"Disgusting spectacles?" repeated the President, with a bright, inquiring smile. "You mean Dr. Bull's spectacles?"

The Secretary choked for a moment, and the President went on with a sort of smooth appeal—

"Of course, we all have our opinions and even our eyes, but really to call them disgusting before the man himself—"

Dr. Bull tore off his spectacles and broke them on the table.

"My spectacles are blackguardly," he said, "but I'm not. Look at my face."

"I dare say it's the sort of face that grows on one," said the President, "in fact, it grows on you; and who am I to quarrel with the wild fruits upon the Tree of Life? I dare say it will grow on me some day."

"We have no time for tomfoolery," said the Secretary, breaking in savagely. "We have come to know what all this means. Who are you? What are you? Why did you get us all here? Do you know who and what we are? Are you a half-witted man playing the conspirator, or are you a clever man playing the fool? Answer me, I tell you."

"Candidates," murmured Sunday, "are only required to answer eight out of the seventeen questions on the paper. As far as I can make out, you want me to tell you what I am, and what you are, and what this table is, and what this Council is, and what this world is for all I know. Well, I will go so far as to rend the veil of one mystery. If you want to know what you are, you are a set of highly well-intentioned young jackasses."

"And you," said Syme, leaning forward, "what are you?"

"I? What am I?" roared the President, and he rose slowly to an incredible height, like some enormous wave about to arch above them and break. "You want to know what I am, do you? Bull, you are a man of science. Grub in the roots of those trees and find out the truth about them. Syme, you are a poet. Stare at those morning clouds. But I tell you this, that you will have found out the truth of the last tree and the top-most cloud before the truth about me. You will understand the sea, and I shall be still a riddle; you shall know what the stars are, and not know what I am. Since the beginning of the world all men have hunted me like a wolf—kings and sages, and poets and lawgivers, all the churches, and all the philosophies. But I have never been caught yet, and the skies will fall in the time I turn to bay. I have given them a good run for their money, and I will now."

Before one of them could move, the monstrous man had swung himself like some huge ourang-outang over the balustrade of the balcony. Yet before he dropped he pulled himself up again as on a horizontal bar, and thrusting his great chin over the edge of the balcony, said solemnly—

"There's one thing I'll tell you though about who I am. I am the man in the dark room, who made you all policemen."

With that he fell from the balcony, bouncing on the stones below like a great ball of india-rubber, and went bounding off towards the corner of the Alhambra, where he hailed a hansom-cab and sprang inside it. The six detectives had been standing thunderstruck and livid in the light of his last assertion; but when he disappeared into the cab, Syme's practical senses returned to him, and leaping over the balcony so recklessly as almost to break his legs, he called another cab.

He and Bull sprang into the cab together, the Professor and the Inspector into another, while the Secretary and the late Gogol scrambled into a third just in time to pursue the flying Syme, who was pursuing the flying President. Sunday led them a wild chase towards the north-west, his cabman, evidently under the influence of more than common inducements, urging the horse at breakneck speed. But Syme was in no mood for delicacies, and he stood up in his own cab shouting, "Stop thief!" until crowds ran along beside his cab, and policemen began to stop and ask questions. All this had its influence upon the President's cabman, who began to look dubious, and to slow down to a trot. He opened the trap to talk reasonably to his fare, and in so doing let the long whip droop over the front of the cab. Sunday leant forward, seized it, and jerked it violently out of the man's hand. Then standing up in front of the cab himself, he lashed the horse and roared aloud, so that they went down the streets like a flying storm. Through street after street and square after square went whirling this preposterous vehicle, in which the fare was urging the horse and the driver trying desperately to stop it. The other three cabs came after it (if the phrase be permissible of a cab) like panting hounds. Shops and streets shot by like rattling arrows.

At the highest ecstacy of speed, Sunday turned round on the splashboard where he stood, and sticking his great grinning head out of the cab, with white hair whistling in the wind, he made a horrible face at his pursuers, like some colossal urchin. Then raising his right hand swiftly, he flung a ball of paper in Syme's face and vanished. Syme caught the thing while instinctively warding it off, and discovered that it consisted of two crumpled papers. One was addressed to himself, and the other to Dr. Bull, with a very long, and it is to be feared partly ironical, string of letters after his name. Dr. Bull's address was, at any rate, considerably longer than his communication, for the communication consisted entirely of the words:—

"What about Martin Tupper now?"

"What does the old maniac mean?" asked Bull, staring at the words. "What does yours say, Syme?"

Syme's message was, at any rate, longer, and ran as follows:—

"No one would regret anything in the nature of an interference by the Archdeacon more than I. I trust it will not come to that. But, for the last time, where are your goloshes? The thing is too bad, especially after what uncle said."

The President's cabman seemed to be regaining some control over his horse, and the pursuers gained a little as they swept round into the Edgware Road. And here there occurred what seemed to the allies a providential stoppage. Traffic of every kind was swerving to right or left or stopping, for down the long road was coming the unmistakable roar announcing the fire-engine, which in a few seconds went by like a brazen thunderbolt. But quick as it went by, Sunday had bounded out of his cab, sprung at the fire-engine, caught it, slung himself on to it, and was seen as he disappeared in the noisy distance talking to the astonished fireman with explanatory gestures.

"After him!" howled Syme. "He can't go astray now. There's no mistaking a fire-engine."

The three cabmen, who had been stunned for a moment, whipped up their horses and slightly decreased the distance between themselves and their disappearing prey. The President acknowledged this proximity by coming to the back of the car, bowing repeatedly, kissing his hand, and finally flinging a neatly-folded note into the bosom of Inspector Ratcliffe. When that gentleman opened it, not without impatience, he found it contained the words:—

"Fly at once. The truth about your trouser-stretchers is known.
—A FRIEND."

The fire-engine had struck still farther to the north, into a region that they did not recognise; and as it ran by a line of high railings shadowed with trees, the six friends were startled, but somewhat relieved, to see the President leap from the fire-engine, though whether through another whim or the increasing protest of his entertainers they could not see. Before the three cabs, however, could reach up to the spot, he had gone up the high railings like a huge grey cat, tossed himself over, and vanished in a darkness of leaves.

Syme with a furious gesture stopped his cab, jumped out, and sprang also to the escalade. When he had one leg over the fence and his friends were following, he turned a face on them which shone quite pale in the shadow.

"What place can this be?" he asked. "Can it be the old devil's house? I've heard he has a house in North London."

"All the better," said the Secretary grimly, planting a foot in a foothold, "we shall find him at home."

"No, but it isn't that," said Syme, knitting his brows. "I hear the most horrible noises, like devils laughing and sneezing and blowing their devilish noses!"

"His dogs barking, of course," said the Secretary.

"Why not say his black-beetles barking!" said Syme furiously, "snails barking! geraniums barking! Did you ever hear a dog bark like that?"

He held up his hand, and there came out of the thicket a long growling roar that seemed to get under the skin and freeze the flesh—a low thrilling roar that made a throbbing in the air all about them.

"The dogs of Sunday would be no ordinary dogs," said Gogol, and shuddered.

Syme had jumped down on the other side, but he still stood listening impatiently.

"Well, listen to that," he said, "is that a dog—anybody's dog?"

There broke upon their ear a hoarse screaming as of things protesting and clamouring in sudden pain; and then, far off like an echo, what sounded like a long nasal trumpet.

"Well, his house ought to be hell!" said the Secretary; "and if it is hell, I'm going in!" and he sprang over the tall railings almost with one swing.

The others followed. They broke through a tangle of plants and shrubs, and came out on an open path. Nothing was in sight, but Dr. Bull suddenly struck his hands together.

"Why, you asses," he cried, "it's the Zoo!"

As they were looking round wildly for any trace of their wild quarry, a keeper in uniform came running along the path with a man in plain clothes.

"Has it come this way?" gasped the keeper.

"Has what?" asked Syme.

"The elephant!" cried the keeper. "An elephant has gone mad and run away!"

"He has run away with an old gentleman," said the other stranger breathlessly, "a poor old gentleman with white hair!"

"What sort of old gentleman?" asked Syme, with great curiosity.

"A very large and fat old gentleman in light grey clothes," said the keeper eagerly.

"Well," said Syme, "if he's that particular kind of old gentleman, if you're quite sure that he's a large and fat old gentleman in grey clothes, you may take my word for it that the elephant has not run away with him. He has run away with the elephant. The elephant is not made by God that could run away with him if he did not consent to the elopement. And, by thunder, there he is!"

There was no doubt about it this time. Clean across the space of grass, about two hundred yards away, with a crowd screaming and scampering vainly at his heels, went a huge grey elephant at an awful stride, with his trunk thrown out as rigid as a ship's bowsprit, and trumpeting like the trumpet of doom. On the back of the bellowing and plunging animal sat President Sunday with all the placidity of a sultan, but goading the animal to a furious speed with some sharp object in his hand.

"Stop him!" screamed the populace. "He'll be out of the gate!"

"Stop a landslide!" said the keeper. "He is out of the gate!"

And even as he spoke, a final crash and roar of terror announced that the great grey elephant had broken out of the gates of the Zoological Gardens, and was careening down Albany Street like a new and swift sort of omnibus.

"Great Lord!" cried Bull, "I never knew an elephant could go so fast. Well, it must be hansom-cabs again if we are to keep him in sight."

As they raced along to the gate out of which the elephant had vanished, Syme felt a glaring panorama of the strange animals in the cages which they passed. Afterwards he thought it queer that he should have seen them so clearly. He remembered especially seeing pelicans, with their preposterous, pendant throats. He wondered why the pelican was the symbol of charity, except it was that it wanted a good deal of charity to admire a pelican. He remembered a hornbill, which was simply a huge yellow beak with a small bird tied on behind it. The whole gave him a sensation, the vividness of which he could not explain, that Nature was always making quite mysterious jokes. Sunday had told them that they would understand him when they had understood the stars. He wondered whether even the archangels understood the hornbill.

The six unhappy detectives flung themselves into cabs and followed the elephant sharing the terror which he spread through the long stretch of the streets. This time Sunday did not turn round, but offered them the solid stretch of his unconscious back, which maddened them, if possible, more than his previous mockeries. Just before they came to Baker Street, however, he was seen to throw something far up into the air, as a boy does a ball meaning to catch it again. But at their rate of racing it fell far behind, just by the cab containing Gogol; and in faint hope of a clue or for some impulse unexplainable, he stopped his cab so as to pick it up. It was addressed to himself, and was quite a bulky parcel. On examination, however, its bulk was found to consist of thirty-three pieces of paper of no value wrapped one round the other. When the last covering was torn away it reduced itself to a small slip of paper, on which was written:—

"The word, I fancy, should be 'pink'."

The man once known as Gogol said nothing, but the movements of his hands and feet were like those of a man urging a horse to renewed efforts.

Through street after street, through district after district, went the prodigy of the flying elephant, calling crowds to every window, and driving the traffic left and right. And still through all this insane publicity the three cabs toiled after it, until they came to be regarded as part of a procession, and perhaps the advertisement of a circus. They went at such a rate that distances were shortened beyond belief, and Syme saw the Albert Hall in Kensington when he thought that he was still in Paddington. The animal's pace was even more fast and free through the empty, aristocratic streets of South Kensington, and he finally headed towards that part of the sky-line where the enormous Wheel of Earl's Court stood up in the sky. The wheel grew larger and larger, till it filled heaven like the wheel of stars.

The beast outstripped the cabs. They lost him round several corners, and when they came to one of the gates of the Earl's Court Exhibition they found themselves finally blocked. In front of them was an enormous crowd; in the midst of it was an enormous elephant, heaving and shuddering as such shapeless creatures do. But the President had disappeared.

"Where has he gone to?" asked Syme, slipping to the ground.

"Gentleman rushed into the Exhibition, sir!" said an official in a dazed manner. Then he added in an injured voice: "Funny gentleman, sir. Asked me to hold his horse, and gave me this."

He held out with distaste a piece of folded paper, addressed: "To the Secretary of the Central Anarchist Council."

The Secretary, raging, rent it open, and found written inside it:—

"When the herring runs a mile,
Let the Secretary smile;
When the herring tries to fly,
Let the Secretary die.
Rustic Proverb."

"Why the eternal crikey," began the Secretary, "did you let the man in? Do people commonly come to your Exhibition riding on mad elephants? Do—"

"Look!" shouted Syme suddenly. "Look over there!"

"Look at what?" asked the Secretary savagely.

"Look at the captive balloon!" said Syme, and pointed in a frenzy.

"Why the blazes should I look at a captive balloon?" demanded the Secretary. "What is there queer about a captive balloon?"

"Nothing," said Syme, "except that it isn't captive!"

They all turned their eyes to where the balloon swung and swelled above the Exhibition on a string, like a child's balloon. A second afterwards the string came in two just under the car, and the balloon, broken loose, floated away with the freedom of a soap bubble.

"Ten thousand devils!" shrieked the Secretary. "He's got into it!" and he shook his fists at the sky.

The balloon, borne by some chance wind, came right above them, and they could see the great white head of the President peering over the side and looking benevolently down on them.

"God bless my soul!" said the Professor with the elderly manner that he could never disconnect from his bleached beard and parchment face. "God bless my soul! I seemed to fancy that something fell on the top of my hat!"

He put up a trembling hand and took from that shelf a piece of twisted paper, which he opened absently only to find it inscribed with a true lover's knot and, the words:—

"Your beauty has not left me indifferent.—From LITTLE SNOWDROP."

There was a short silence, and then Syme said, biting his beard—

"I'm not beaten yet. The blasted thing must come down somewhere. Let's follow it!"

CHAPTER XIV
THE SIX PHILOSOPHERS

ACROSS green fields, and breaking through blooming hedges, toiled six draggled detectives, about five miles out of London. The optimist of the party had at first proposed that they should follow the balloon across South England in hansom-cabs. But he was ultimately convinced of the persistent refusal of the balloon to follow the roads, and the still more persistent refusal of the cabmen to follow the balloon. Consequently the tireless though exasperated travellers broke through black thickets and ploughed through ploughed fields till each was turned into a figure too outrageous to be mistaken for a tramp. Those green hills of Surrey saw the final collapse and tragedy of the admirable light grey suit in which Syme had set out from Saffron Park. His silk hat was broken over his nose by a swinging bough, his coat-tails were torn to the shoulder by arresting thorns, the clay of England was splashed up to his collar; but he still carried his yellow beard forward with a silent and furious determination, and his eyes were still fixed on that floating ball of gas, which in the full flush of sunset seemed coloured like a sunset cloud.

"After all," he said, "it is very beautiful!"

"It is singularly and strangely beautiful!" said the Professor. "I wish the beastly gas-bag would burst!"

"No," said Dr. Bull, "I hope it won't. It might hurt the old boy."

"Hurt him!" said the vindictive Professor, "hurt him! Not as much as I'd hurt him if I could get up with him. Little Snowdrop!"

"I don't want him hurt, somehow," said Dr. Bull.

"What!" cried the Secretary bitterly. "Do you believe all that tale about his being our man in the dark room? Sunday would say he was anybody."

"I don't know whether I believe it or not," said Dr. Bull. "But it isn't that that I mean. I can't wish old Sunday's balloon to burst because—"

"Well," said Syme impatiently, "because?"

"Well, because he's so jolly like a balloon himself," said Dr. Bull desperately. "I don't understand a word of all that idea of his being the same man who gave us all our blue cards. It seems to make everything nonsense. But I don't care who knows it, I always had a sympathy for old Sunday himself, wicked as he was. Just as if he was a great bouncing baby. How can I explain what my queer sympathy was? It didn't prevent my fighting him like hell! Shall I make it clear if I say that I liked him because he was so fat?"

"You will not," said the Secretary.

"I've got it now," cried Bull, "it was because he was so fat and so light. Just like a balloon. We always think of fat people as heavy, but he could have danced against a sylph. I see now what I mean. Moderate strength is shown in violence, supreme strength is shown in levity. It was like the old speculations—what would happen if an elephant could leap up in the sky like a grasshopper?"

"Our elephant," said Syme, looking upwards, "has leapt into the sky like a grasshopper."

"And somehow," concluded Bull, "that's why I can't help liking old Sunday. No, it's not an admiration of force, or any silly thing like that. There is a kind of gaiety in the thing, as if he were bursting with some good news. Haven't you sometimes felt it on a spring day? You know Nature plays tricks, but somehow that day proves they are good-natured tricks. I never read the Bible myself, but that part they laugh at is literal truth, 'Why leap ye, ye high hills?' The hills do leap—at least, they try to.... Why do I like Sunday?... how can I tell you?... because he's such a Bounder."

There was a long silence, and then the Secretary said in a curious, strained voice—

"You do not know Sunday at all. Perhaps it is because you are better than I, and do not know hell. I was a fierce fellow, and a trifle morbid from the first. The man who sits in darkness, and who chose us all, chose me because I had all the crazy look of a conspirator—because my smile went crooked, and my eyes were gloomy, even when I smiled. But there must have been something in me that answered to the nerves in all these anarchic men. For when I first saw Sunday he expressed to me, not your airy vitality, but something both gross and sad in the Nature of Things. I found him smoking in a twilight room, a room with brown blind down, infinitely more depressing than the genial darkness in which our master lives.

358

He sat there on a bench, a huge heap of a man, dark and out of shape. He listened to all my words without speaking or even stirring. I poured out my most passionate appeals, and asked my most eloquent questions. Then, after a long silence, the Thing began to shake, and I thought it was shaken by some secret malady. It shook like a loathsome and living jelly. It reminded me of everything I had ever read about the base bodies that are the origin of life—the deep sea lumps and protoplasm. It seemed like the final form of matter, the most shapeless and the most shameful. I could only tell myself, from its shudderings, that it was something at least that such a monster could be miserable. And then it broke upon me that the bestial mountain was shaking with a lonely laughter, and the laughter was at me. Do you ask me to forgive him that? It is no small thing to be laughed at by something at once lower and stronger than oneself."

"Surely you fellows are exaggerating wildly," cut in the clear voice of Inspector Ratcliffe. "President Sunday is a terrible fellow for one's intellect, but he is not such a Barnum's freak physically as you make out. He received me in an ordinary office, in a grey check coat, in broad daylight. He talked to me in an ordinary way. But I'll tell you what is a trifle creepy about Sunday. His room is neat, his clothes are neat, everything seems in order; but he's absent-minded. Sometimes his great bright eyes go quite blind. For hours he forgets that you are there. Now absent-mindedness is just a bit too awful in a bad man. We think of a wicked man as vigilant. We can't think of a wicked man who is honestly and sincerely dreamy, because we daren't think of a wicked man alone with himself. An absentminded man means a good-natured man. It means a man who, if he happens to see you, will apologise. But how will you bear an absentminded man who, if he happens to see you, will kill you? That is what tries the nerves, abstraction combined with cruelty. Men have felt it sometimes when they went through wild forests, and felt that the animals there were at once innocent and pitiless. They might ignore or slay. How would you like to pass ten mortal hours in a parlour with an absent-minded tiger?"

"And what do you think of Sunday, Gogol?" asked Syme.

"I don't think of Sunday on principle," said Gogol simply, "any more than I stare at the sun at noonday."

"Well, that is a point of view," said Syme thoughtfully. "What do you say, Professor?"

The Professor was walking with bent head and trailing stick, and he did not answer at all.

"Wake up, Professor!" said Syme genially. "Tell us what you think of Sunday."

The Professor spoke at last very slowly.

"I think something," he said, "that I cannot say clearly. Or, rather, I think something that I cannot even think clearly. But it is something like this. My early life, as you know, was a bit too large and loose.

"Well, when I saw Sunday's face I thought it was too large—everybody does, but I also thought it was too loose. The face was so big, that one couldn't focus it or make it a face at all. The eye was so far away from the nose, that it wasn't an eye.

The mouth was so much by itself, that one had to think of it by itself. The whole thing is too hard to explain."

He paused for a little, still trailing his stick, and then went on—

"But put it this way. Walking up a road at night, I have seen a lamp and a lighted window and a cloud make together a most complete and unmistakable face. If anyone in heaven has that face I shall know him again. Yet when I walked a little farther I found that there was no face, that the window was ten yards away, the lamp ten hundred yards, the cloud beyond the world. Well, Sunday's face escaped me; it ran away to right and left, as such chance pictures run away. And so his face has made me, somehow, doubt whether there are any faces. I don't know whether your face, Bull, is a face or a combination in perspective. Perhaps one black disc of your beastly glasses is quite close and another fifty miles away. Oh, the doubts of a materialist are not worth a dump. Sunday has taught me the last and the worst doubts, the doubts of a spiritualist. I am a Buddhist, I suppose; and Buddhism is not a creed, it is a doubt. My poor dear Bull, I do not believe that you really have a face. I have not faith enough to believe in matter."

Syme's eyes were still fixed upon the errant orb, which, reddened in the evening light, looked like some rosier and more innocent world.

"Have you noticed an odd thing," he said, "about all your descriptions? Each man of you finds Sunday quite different, yet each man of you can only find one thing to compare him to—the universe itself. Bull finds him like the earth in spring, Gogol like the sun at noonday. The Secretary is reminded of the shapeless protoplasm, and the Inspector of the carelessness of virgin forests. The Professor says he is like a changing landscape. This is queer, but it is queerer still that I also have had my odd notion about the President, and I also find that I think of Sunday as I think of the whole world."

"Get on a little faster, Syme," said Bull; "never mind the balloon."

"When I first saw Sunday," said Syme slowly, "I only saw his back; and when I saw his back, I knew he was the worst man in the world. His neck and shoulders were brutal, like those of some apish god. His head had a stoop that was hardly human, like the stoop of an ox. In fact, I had at once the revolting fancy that this was not a man at all, but a beast dressed up in men's clothes."

"Get on," said Dr. Bull.

"And then the queer thing happened. I had seen his back from the street, as he sat in the balcony. Then I entered the hotel, and coming round the other side of him, saw his face in the sunlight. His face frightened me, as it did everyone; but not because it was brutal, not because it was evil. On the contrary, it frightened me because it was so beautiful, because it was so good."

"Syme," exclaimed the Secretary, "are you ill?"

"It was like the face of some ancient archangel, judging justly after heroic wars. There was laughter in the eyes, and in the mouth honour and sorrow. There was the same white hair, the same great, grey-clad shoulders that I had seen from behind. But when I saw him from behind I was certain he was an animal, and when I saw him in front I knew he was a god."

"Pan," said the Professor dreamily, "was a god and an animal."

360

"Then, and again and always," went on Syme like a man talking to himself, "that has been for me the mystery of Sunday, and it is also the mystery of the world. When I see the horrible back, I am sure the noble face is but a mask. When I see the face but for an instant, I know the back is only a jest. Bad is so bad, that we cannot but think good an accident; good is so good, that we feel certain that evil could be explained. But the whole came to a kind of crest yesterday when I raced Sunday for the cab, and was just behind him all the way."

"Had you time for thinking then?" asked Ratcliffe.

"Time," replied Syme, "for one outrageous thought. I was suddenly possessed with the idea that the blind, blank back of his head really was his face—an awful, eyeless face staring at me! And I fancied that the figure running in front of me was really a figure running backwards, and dancing as he ran."

"Horrible!" said Dr. Bull, and shuddered.

"Horrible is not the word," said Syme. "It was exactly the worst instant of my life. And yet ten minutes afterwards, when he put his head out of the cab and made a grimace like a gargoyle, I knew that he was only like a father playing hide-and-seek with his children."

"It is a long game," said the Secretary, and frowned at his broken boots.

"Listen to me," cried Syme with extraordinary emphasis. "Shall I tell you the secret of the whole world? It is that we have only known the back of the world. We see everything from behind, and it looks brutal. That is not a tree, but the back of a tree. That is not a cloud, but the back of a cloud. Cannot you see that everything is stooping and hiding a face? If we could only get round in front—"

"Look!" cried out Bull clamorously, "the balloon is coming down!"

There was no need to cry out to Syme, who had never taken his eyes off it. He saw the great luminous globe suddenly stagger in the sky, right itself, and then sink slowly behind the trees like a setting sun.

The man called Gogol, who had hardly spoken through all their weary travels, suddenly threw up his hands like a lost spirit.

"He is dead!" he cried. "And now I know he was my friend—my friend in the dark!"

"Dead!" snorted the Secretary. "You will not find him dead easily. If he has been tipped out of the car, we shall find him rolling as a colt rolls in a field, kicking his legs for fun."

"Clashing his hoofs," said the Professor. "The colts do, and so did Pan."

"Pan again!" said Dr. Bull irritably. "You seem to think Pan is everything."

"So he is," said the Professor, "in Greek. He means everything."

"Don't forget," said the Secretary, looking down, "that he also means Panic."

Syme had stood without hearing any of the exclamations.

"It fell over there," he said shortly. "Let us follow it!"

Then he added with an indescribable gesture—

"Oh, if he has cheated us all by getting killed! It would be like one of his larks."

He strode off towards the distant trees with a new energy, his rags and ribbons fluttering in the wind. The others followed him in a more footsore and dubious manner. And almost at the same moment all six men realised that they were not alone in the little field.

Across the square of turf a tall man was advancing towards them, leaning on a strange long staff like a sceptre. He was clad in a fine but old-fashioned suit with knee-breeches; its colour was that shade between blue, violet and grey which can be seen in certain shadows of the woodland. His hair was whitish grey, and at the first glance, taken along with his knee-breeches, looked as if it was powdered. His advance was very quiet; but for the silver frost upon his head, he might have been one to the shadows of the wood.

"Gentlemen," he said, "my master has a carriage waiting for you in the road just by."

"Who is your master?" asked Syme, standing quite still.

"I was told you knew his name," said the man respectfully.

There was a silence, and then the Secretary said—

"Where is this carriage?"

"It has been waiting only a few moments," said the stranger. "My master has only just come home."

Syme looked left and right upon the patch of green field in which he found himself. The hedges were ordinary hedges, the trees seemed ordinary trees; yet he felt like a man entrapped in fairyland.

He looked the mysterious ambassador up and down, but he could discover nothing except that the man's coat was the exact colour of the purple shadows, and that the man's face was the exact colour of the red and brown and golden sky.

"Show us the place," Syme said briefly, and without a word the man in the violet coat turned his back and walked towards a gap in the hedge, which let in suddenly the light of a white road.

As the six wanderers broke out upon this thoroughfare, they saw the white road blocked by what looked like a long row of carriages, such a row of carriages as might close the approach to some house in Park Lane. Along the side of these carriages stood a rank of splendid servants, all dressed in the grey-blue uniform, and all having a certain quality of stateliness and freedom which would not commonly belong to the servants of a gentleman, but rather to the officials and ambassadors of a great king. There were no less than six carriages waiting, one for each of the tattered and miserable band. All the attendants (as if in court-dress) wore swords, and as each man crawled into his carriage they drew them, and saluted with a sudden blaze of steel.

"What can it all mean?" asked Bull of Syme as they separated. "Is this another joke of Sunday's?"

"I don't know," said Syme as he sank wearily back in the cushions of his carriage; "but if it is, it's one of the jokes you talk about. It's a good-natured one."

The six adventurers had passed through many adventures, but not one had carried them so utterly off their feet as this last adventure of comfort. They had all become inured to things going roughly; but things suddenly going smoothly swamped them. They could not even feebly imagine what the carriages were; it was enough for them to know that they were carriages, and carriages with cushions.

They could not conceive who the old man was who had led them; but it was quite enough that he had certainly led them to the carriages.

Syme drove through a drifting darkness of trees in utter abandonment. It was typical of him that while he had carried his bearded chin forward fiercely so long as anything could be done, when the whole business was taken out of his hands he fell back on the cushions in a frank collapse.

Very gradually and very vaguely he realised into what rich roads the carriage was carrying him. He saw that they passed the stone gates of what might have been a park, that they began gradually to climb a hill which, while wooded on both sides, was somewhat more orderly than a forest. Then there began to grow upon him, as upon a man slowly waking from a healthy sleep, a pleasure in everything. He felt that the hedges were what hedges should be, living walls; that a hedge is like a human army, disciplined, but all the more alive. He saw high elms behind the hedges, and vaguely thought how happy boys would be climbing there. Then his carriage took a turn of the path, and he saw suddenly and quietly, like a long, low, sunset cloud, a long, low house, mellow in the mild light of sunset. All the six friends compared notes afterwards and quarrelled; but they all agreed that in some unaccountable way the place reminded them of their boyhood. It was either this elm-top or that crooked path, it was either this scrap of orchard or that shape of a window; but each man of them declared that he could remember this place before he could remember his mother.

When the carriages eventually rolled up to a large, low, cavernous gateway, another man in the same uniform, but wearing a silver star on the grey breast of his coat, came out to meet them. This impressive person said to the bewildered Syme—

"Refreshments are provided for you in your room."

Syme, under the influence of the same mesmeric sleep of amazement, went up the large oaken stairs after the respectful attendant. He entered a splendid suite of apartments that seemed to be designed specially for him. He walked up to a long mirror with the ordinary instinct of his class, to pull his tie straight or to smooth his hair; and there he saw the frightful figure that he was—blood running down his face from where the bough had struck him, his hair standing out like yellow rags of rank grass, his clothes torn into long, wavering tatters. At once the whole enigma sprang up, simply as the question of how he had got there, and how he was to get out again. Exactly at the same moment a man in blue, who had been appointed as his valet, said very solemnly—

"I have put out your clothes, sir."

"Clothes!" said Syme sardonically. "I have no clothes except these," and he lifted two long strips of his frock-coat in fascinating festoons, and made a movement as if to twirl like a ballet girl.

"My master asks me to say," said the attendant, "that there is a fancy dress ball tonight, and that he desires you to put on the costume that I have laid out. Meanwhile, sir, there is a bottle of Burgundy and some cold pheasant, which he hopes you will not refuse, as it is some hours before supper."

"Cold pheasant is a good thing," said Syme reflectively, "and Burgundy is a spanking good thing. But really I do not want either of them so much as I want to know what the devil all this means, and what sort of costume you have got laid out for me. Where is it?"

The servant lifted off a kind of ottoman a long peacock-blue drapery, rather of the nature of a domino, on the front of which was emblazoned a large golden sun, and which was splashed here and there with flaming stars and crescents.

"You're to be dressed as Thursday, sir," said the valet somewhat affably.

"Dressed as Thursday!" said Syme in meditation. "It doesn't sound a warm costume."

"Oh, yes, sir," said the other eagerly, "the Thursday costume is quite warm, sir. It fastens up to the chin."

"Well, I don't understand anything," said Syme, sighing. "I have been used so long to uncomfortable adventures that comfortable adventures knock me out. Still, I may be allowed to ask why I should be particularly like Thursday in a green frock spotted all over with the sun and moon. Those orbs, I think, shine on other days. I once saw the moon on Tuesday, I remember."

"Beg pardon, sir," said the valet, "Bible also provided for you," and with a respectful and rigid finger he pointed out a passage in the first chapter of Genesis. Syme read it wondering. It was that in which the fourth day of the week is associated with the creation of the sun and moon. Here, however, they reckoned from a Christian Sunday.

"This is getting wilder and wilder," said Syme, as he sat down in a chair. "Who are these people who provide cold pheasant and Burgundy, and green clothes and Bibles? Do they provide everything?"

"Yes, sir, everything," said the attendant gravely. "Shall I help you on with your costume?"

"Oh, hitch the bally thing on!" said Syme impatiently.

But though he affected to despise the mummery, he felt a curious freedom and naturalness in his movements as the blue and gold garment fell about him; and when he found that he had to wear a sword, it stirred a boyish dream. As he passed out of the room he flung the folds across his shoulder with a gesture, his sword stood out at an angle, and he had all the swagger of a troubadour. For these disguises did not disguise, but reveal.

CHAPTER XV
THE ACCUSER

AS Syme strode along the corridor he saw the Secretary standing at the top of a great flight of stairs. The man had never looked so noble. He was draped in a long robe of starless black, down the centre of which fell a band or broad stripe of pure white, like a single shaft of light. The whole looked like some very severe ecclesiastical vestment. There was no need for Syme to search his memory or the Bible in order to remember that the first day of creation marked the mere creation of light out of darkness. The vestment itself would alone have suggested the symbol; and Syme felt also how perfectly this pattern of pure white and black expressed the soul of the pale and austere Secretary, with his inhuman veracity and his cold frenzy, which made him so easily make war on the anarchists, and yet so easily pass for one of them. Syme was scarcely surprised to notice that, amid all the ease and hospitality of their new surroundings, this man's eyes were still stern. No smell of ale or or-orchards could make the Secretary cease to ask a reasonable question.

If Syme had been able to see himself, he would have realised that he, too, seemed to be for the first time himself and no one else. For if the Secretary stood for that philosopher who loves the original and formless light, Syme was a type of the poet who seeks always to make the light in special shapes, to split it up into sun and star. The philosopher may sometimes love the infinite; the poet always loves the finite. For him the great moment is not the creation of light, but the creation of the sun and moon.

As they descended the broad stairs together they overtook Ratcliffe, who was clad in spring green like a huntsman, and the pattern upon whose garment was a green tangle of trees. For he stood for that third day on which the earth and green things were made, and his square, sensible face, with its not unfriendly cynicism, seemed appropriate enough to it.

They were led out of another broad and low gateway into a very large old English garden, full of torches and bonfires, by the broken light of which a vast carnival of people were dancing in motley dress. Syme seemed to see every shape in Nature imitated in some crazy costume. There was a man dressed as a windmill with enormous sails, a man dressed as an elephant, a man dressed as a balloon; the two last, together, seemed to keep the thread of their farcical adventures. Syme even saw, with a queer thrill, one dancer dressed like an enormous hornbill, with a beak twice as big as himself—the queer bird which had fixed itself on his fancy like a living question while he was rushing down the long road at the Zoological Gardens. There were a thousand other such objects, however. There was a dancing lamp-post, a dancing apple tree, a dancing ship. One would have thought that the untamable tune of some mad musician had set all the common objects of field and street dancing an eternal jig. And long afterwards, when Syme was middle-aged and at rest, he could never see one of those particular objects—a lamppost, or an apple tree, or a windmill—without thinking that it was a strayed reveller from that revel of masquerade.

On one side of this lawn, alive with dancers, was a sort of green bank, like the terrace in such old-fashioned gardens.

Along this, in a kind of crescent, stood seven great chairs, the thrones of the seven days. Gogol and Dr. Bull were already in their seats; the Professor was just mounting to his. Gogol, or Tuesday, had his simplicity well symbolised by a dress designed upon the division of the waters, a dress that separated upon his forehead and fell to his feet, grey and silver, like a sheet of rain. The Professor, whose day was that on which the birds and fishes—the ruder forms of life—were created, had a dress of dim purple, over which sprawled goggle-eyed fishes and outrageous tropical birds, the union in him of unfathomable fancy and of doubt. Dr. Bull, the last day of Creation, wore a coat covered with heraldic animals in red and gold, and on his crest a man rampant. He lay back in his chair with a broad smile, the picture of an optimist in his element.

One by one the wanderers ascended the bank and sat in their strange seats. As each of them sat down a roar of enthusiasm rose from the carnival, such as that with which crowds receive kings. Cups were clashed and torches shaken, and feathered hats flung in the air. The men for whom these thrones were reserved were men crowned with some extraordinary laurels. But the central chair was empty.

Syme was on the left hand of it and the Secretary on the right. The Secretary looked across the empty throne at Syme, and said, compressing his lips—

"We do not know yet that he is not dead in a field."

Almost as Syme heard the words, he saw on the sea of human faces in front of him a frightful and beautiful alteration, as if heaven had opened behind his head. But Sunday had only passed silently along the front like a shadow, and had sat in the central seat. He was draped plainly, in a pure and terrible white, and his hair was like a silver flame on his forehead.

For a long time—it seemed for hours—that huge masquerade of mankind swayed and stamped in front of them to marching and exultant music. Every couple dancing seemed a separate romance; it might be a fairy dancing with a pillar-box, or a peasant girl dancing with the moon; but in each case it was, somehow, as absurd as Alice in Wonderland, yet as grave and kind as a love story. At last, however, the thick crowd began to thin itself. Couples strolled away into the garden-walks, or began to drift towards that end of the building where stood smoking, in huge pots like fish-kettles, some hot and scented mixtures of old ale or wine. Above all these, upon a sort of black framework on the roof of the house, roared in its iron basket a gigantic bonfire, which lit up the land for miles. It flung the homely effect of fire-light over the face of vast forests of grey or brown, and it seemed to fill with warmth even the emptiness of upper night. Yet this also, after a time, was allowed to grow fainter; the dim groups gathered more and more round the great cauldrons, or passed, laughing and clattering, into the inner passages of that ancient house. Soon there were only some ten loiterers in the garden; soon only four. Finally the last stray merry-maker ran into the house whooping to his companions. The fire faded, and the slow, strong stars came out. And the seven strange men were left alone, like seven stone statues on their chairs of stone. Not one of them had spoken a word.

They seemed in no haste to do so, but heard in silence the hum of insects and the distant song of one bird. Then Sunday spoke, but so dreamily that he might have been continuing a conversation rather than beginning one.

"We will eat and drink later," he said. "Let us remain together a little, we who have loved each other so sadly, and have fought so long. I seem to remember only centuries of heroic war, in which you were always heroes—epic on epic, iliad on iliad, and you always brothers in arms. Whether it was but recently (for time is nothing), or at the beginning of the world, I sent you out to war. I sat in the darkness, where there is not any created thing, and to you I was only a voice commanding valour and an unnatural virtue. You heard the voice in the dark, and you never heard it again. The sun in heaven denied it, the earth and sky denied it, all human wisdom denied it. And when I met you in the daylight I denied it myself."

Syme stirred sharply in his seat, but otherwise there was silence, and the incomprehensible went on.

"But you were men. You did not forget your secret honour, though the whole cosmos turned an engine of torture to tear it out of you. I knew how near you were to hell. I know how you, Thursday, crossed swords with King Satan, and how you, Wednesday, named me in the hour without hope."

There was complete silence in the starlit garden, and then the black-browed Secretary, implacable, turned in his chair towards Sunday, and said in a harsh voice—

"Who and what are you?"

"I am the Sabbath," said the other without moving. "I am the peace of God."

The Secretary started up, and stood crushing his costly robe in his hand.

"I know what you mean," he cried, "and it is exactly that that I cannot forgive you. I know you are contentment, optimism, what do they call the thing, an ultimate reconciliation. Well, I am not reconciled. If you were the man in the dark room, why were you also Sunday, an offense to the sunlight? If you were from the first our father and our friend, why were you also our greatest enemy? We wept, we fled in terror; the iron entered into our souls—and you are the peace of God! Oh, I can forgive God His anger, though it destroyed nations; but I cannot forgive Him His peace."

Sunday answered not a word, but very slowly he turned his face of stone upon Syme as if asking a question.

"No," said Syme, "I do not feel fierce like that. I am grateful to you, not only for wine and hospitality here, but for many a fine scamper and free fight. But I should like to know. My soul and heart are as happy and quiet here as this old garden, but my reason is still crying out. I should like to know."

Sunday looked at Ratcliffe, whose clear voice said—

"It seems so silly that you should have been on both sides and fought yourself."

Bull said—

"I understand nothing, but I am happy. In fact, I am going to sleep."

"I am not happy," said the Professor with his head in his hands, "because I do not understand. You let me stray a little too near to hell."

And then Gogol said, with the absolute simplicity of a child—

"I wish I knew why I was hurt so much."

Still Sunday said nothing, but only sat with his mighty chin upon his hand, and gazed at the distance. Then at last he said—

"I have heard your complaints in order. And here, I think, comes another to complain, and we will hear him also."

The falling fire in the great cresset threw a last long gleam, like a bar of burning gold, across the dim grass. Against this fiery band was outlined in utter black the advancing legs of a black-clad figure. He seemed to have a fine close suit with knee-breeches such as that which was worn by the servants of the house, only that it was not blue, but of this absolute sable. He had, like the servants, a kind of sword by his side. It was only when he had come quite close to the crescent of the seven and flung up his face to look at them, that Syme saw, with thunder-struck clearness, that the face was the broad, almost ape-like face of his old friend Gregory, with its rank red hair and its insulting smile.

"Gregory!" gasped Syme, half-rising from his seat. "Why, this is the real anarchist!"

"Yes," said Gregory, with a great and dangerous restraint, "I am the real anarchist."

"'Now there was a day,'" murmured Bull, who seemed really to have fallen asleep, "'when the sons of God came to present themselves before the Lord, and Satan came also among them.'"

"You are right," said Gregory, and gazed all round. "I am a destroyer. I would destroy the world if I could."

A sense of a pathos far under the earth stirred up in Syme, and he spoke brokenly and without sequence.

"Oh, most unhappy man," he cried, "try to be happy! You have red hair like your sister."

"My red hair, like red flames, shall burn up the world," said Gregory. "I thought I hated everything more than common men can hate anything; but I find that I do not hate everything so much as I hate you!"

"I never hated you," said Syme very sadly.

Then out of this unintelligible creature the last thunders broke.

"You!" he cried. "You never hated because you never lived. I know what you are all of you, from first to last—you are the people in power! You are the police—the great fat, smiling men in blue and buttons! You are the Law, and you have never been broken. But is there a free soul alive that does not long to break you, only because you have never been broken? We in revolt talk all kind of nonsense doubtless about this crime or that crime of the Government. It is all folly! The only crime of the Government is that it governs. The unpardonable sin of the supreme power is that it is supreme. I do not curse you for being cruel. I do not curse you (though I might) for being kind. I curse you for being safe! You sit in your chairs of stone, and have never come down from them. You are the seven angels of heaven, and you have had no troubles. Oh, I could forgive you everything, you that rule all mankind, if I could feel for once that you had suffered for one hour a real agony such as I—"

Syme sprang to his feet, shaking from head to foot.

"I see everything," he cried, "everything that there is. Why does each thing on the earth war against each other thing? Why does each small thing in the world have to fight against the world itself? Why does a fly have to fight the whole universe? Why does a dandelion have to fight the whole universe? For the same reason that I had to be alone in the dreadful Council of the Days. So that each thing that obeys law may have the glory and isolation of the anarchist. So that each man fighting for order may be as brave and good a man as the dynamiter. So that the real lie of Satan may be flung back in the face of this blasphemer, so that by tears and torture we may earn the right to say to this man, 'You lie!' No agonies can be too great to buy the right to say to this accuser, 'We also have suffered.'

"It is not true that we have never been broken. We have been broken upon the wheel. It is not true that we have never descended from these thrones. We have descended into hell. We were complaining of unforgettable miseries even at the very moment when this man entered insolently to accuse us of happiness. I repel the slander; we have not been happy. I can answer for every one of the great guards of Law whom he has accused. At least—"

He had turned his eyes so as to see suddenly the great face of Sunday, which wore a strange smile.

"Have you," he cried in a dreadful voice, "have you ever suffered?"

As he gazed, the great face grew to an awful size, grew larger than the colossal mask of Memnon, which had made him scream as a child. It grew larger and larger, filling the whole sky; then everything went black. Only in the blackness before it entirely destroyed his brain he seemed to hear a distant voice saying a commonplace text that he had heard somewhere, "Can ye drink of the cup that I drink of?"

When men in books awake from a vision, they commonly find themselves in some place in which they might have fallen asleep; they yawn in a chair, or lift themselves with bruised limbs from a field. Syme's experience was something much more psychologically strange if there was indeed anything unreal, in the earthly sense, about the things he had gone through. For while he could always remember afterwards that he had swooned before the face of Sunday, he could not remember having ever come to at all. He could only remember that gradually and naturally he knew that he was and had been walking along a country lane with an easy and conversational companion. That companion had been a part of his recent drama; it was the red-haired poet Gregory. They were walking like old friends, and were in the middle of a conversation about some triviality. But Syme could only feel an unnatural buoyancy in his body and a crystal simplicity in his mind that seemed to be superior to everything that he said or did. He felt he was in possession of some impossible good news, which made every other thing a triviality, but an adorable triviality.

Dawn was breaking over everything in colours at once clear and timid; as if Nature made a first attempt at yellow and a first attempt at rose. A breeze blew so clean and sweet, that one could not think that it blew from the sky; it blew rather through some hole in the sky. Syme felt a simple surprise when he saw rising all round him on both sides of the road the red, irregular buildings of Saffron Park. He had no idea that he had walked so near London. He walked by instinct along one white road, on which early birds hopped and sang, and found himself outside a fenced garden. There he saw the sister of Gregory, the girl with the gold-red hair, cutting lilac before breakfast, with the great unconscious gravity of a girl.

The End

The Man Who Knew Too Much by G. K. Chesterton

I: THE FACE IN THE TARGET

Harold March, the rising reviewer and social critic, was walking vigorously across a great tableland of moors and commons, the horizon of which was fringed with the far-off woods of the famous estate of Torwood Park. He was a good-looking young man in tweeds, with very pale curly hair and pale clear eyes. Walking in wind and sun in the very landscape of liberty, he was still young enough to remember his politics and not merely try to forget them. For his errand at Torwood Park was a political one; it was the place of appointment named by no less a person than the Chancellor of the Exchequer, Sir Howard Horne, then introducing his so-called Socialist budget, and prepared to expound it in an interview with so promising a penman. Harold March was the sort of man who knows everything about politics, and nothing about politicians. He also knew a great deal about art, letters, philosophy, and general culture; about almost everything, indeed, except the world he was living in.

Abruptly, in the middle of those sunny and windy flats, he came upon a sort of cleft almost narrow enough to be called a crack in the land. It was just large enough to be the water-course for a small stream which vanished at intervals under green tunnels of undergrowth, as if in a dwarfish forest. Indeed, he had an odd feeling as if he were a giant looking over the valley of the pygmies. When he dropped into the hollow, however, the impression was lost; the rocky banks, though hardly above the height of a cottage, hung over and had the profile of a precipice. As he began to wander down the course of the stream, in idle but romantic curiosity, and saw the water shining in short strips between the great gray boulders and bushes as soft as great green mosses, he fell into quite an opposite vein of fantasy. It was rather as if the earth had opened and swallowed him into a sort of underworld of dreams. And when he became conscious of a human figure dark against the silver stream, sitting on a large boulder and looking rather like a large bird, it was perhaps with some of the premonitions proper to a man who meets the strangest friendship of his life.

The man was apparently fishing; or at least was fixed in a fisherman's attitude with more than a fisherman's immobility. March was able to examine the man almost as if he had been a statue for some minutes before the statue spoke. He was a tall, fair man, cadaverous, and a little lackadaisical, with heavy eyelids and a high-bridged nose. When his face was shaded with his wide white hat, his light mustache and lithe figure gave him a look of youth. But the Panama lay on the moss beside him; and the spectator could see that his brow was prematurely bald; and this, combined with a certain hollowness about the eyes, had an air of headwork and even headache. But the most curious thing about him, realized after a short scrutiny, was that, though he looked like a fisherman, he was not fishing.

He was holding, instead of a rod, something that might have been a landing-net which some fishermen use, but which was much more like the ordinary toy net which children carry, and which they generally use indifferently for shrimps or butterflies. He was dipping this into the water at intervals, gravely regarding its harvest of weed or mud, and emptying it out again.

"No, I haven't caught anything," he remarked, calmly, as if answering an unspoken query. "When I do I have to throw it back again; especially the big fish. But some of the little beasts interest me when I get 'em."

"A scientific interest, I suppose?" observed March.

"Of a rather amateurish sort, I fear," answered the strange fisherman. "I have a sort of hobby about what they call 'phenomena of phosphorescence.' But it would be rather awkward to go about in society carrying stinking fish."

"I suppose it would," said March, with a smile.

"Rather odd to enter a drawing-room carrying a large luminous cod," continued the stranger, in his listless way. "How quaint it would be if one could carry it about like a lantern, or have little sprats for candles. Some of the seabeasts would really be very pretty like lampshades; the blue sea-snail that glitters all over like starlight; and some of the red starfish really shine like red stars. But, naturally, I'm not looking for them here."

March thought of asking him what he was looking for; but, feeling unequal to a technical discussion at least as deep as the deep-sea fishes, he returned to more ordinary topics.

"Delightful sort of hole this is," he said. "This little dell and river here. It's like those places Stevenson talks about, where something ought to happen."

"I know," answered the other. "I think it's because the place itself, so to speak, seems to happen and not merely to exist. Perhaps that's what old Picasso and some of the Cubists are trying to express by angles and jagged lines. Look at that wall like low cliffs that juts forward just at right angles to the slope of turf sweeping up to it. That's like a silent collision. It's like a breaker and the back-wash of a wave."

March looked at the low-browed crag overhanging the green slope and nodded. He was interested in a man who turned so easily from the technicalities of science to those of art; and asked him if he admired the new angular artists.

"As I feel it, the Cubists are not Cubist enough," replied the stranger. "I mean they're not thick enough. By making things mathematical they make them thin. Take the living lines out of that landscape, simplify it to a right angle, and you flatten it out to a mere diagram on paper. Diagrams have their own beauty; but it is of just the other sort. They stand for the unalterable things; the calm, eternal, mathematical sort of truths; what somebody calls the 'white radiance of—"

He stopped, and before the next word came something had happened almost too quickly and completely to be realized. From behind the overhanging rock came a noise and rush like that of a railway train; and a great motor car appeared. It topped the crest of cliff, black against the sun, like a battle-chariot rushing to destruction in some wild epic. March automatically put out his hand in one futile gesture, as if to catch a falling tea-cup in a drawing-room.

For the fraction of a flash it seemed to leave the ledge of rock like a flying ship; then the very sky seemed to turn over like a wheel, and it lay a ruin amid the tall grasses below, a line of gray smoke going up slowly from it into the silent air. A little lower the figure of a man with gray hair lay tumbled down the steep green slope, his limbs lying all at random, and his face turned away.

The eccentric fisherman dropped his net and walked swiftly toward the spot, his new acquaintance following him. As they drew near there seemed a sort of monstrous irony in the fact that the dead machine was still throbbing and thundering as busily as a factory, while the man lay so still.

He was unquestionably dead. The blood flowed in the grass from a hopelessly fatal fracture at the back of the skull; but the face, which was turned to the sun, was uninjured and strangely arresting in itself. It was one of those cases of a strange face so unmistakable as to feel familiar. We feel, somehow, that we ought to recognize it, even though we do not. It was of the broad, square sort with great jaws, almost like that of a highly intellectual ape; the wide mouth shut so tight as to be traced by a mere line; the nose short with the sort of nostrils that seem to gape with an appetite for the air. The oddest thing about the face was that one of the eyebrows was cocked up at a much sharper angle than the other. March thought he had never seen a face so naturally alive as that dead one. And its ugly energy seemed all the stranger for its halo of hoary hair. Some papers lay half fallen out of the pocket, and from among them March extracted a card-case. He read the name on the card aloud.

"Sir Humphrey Turnbull. I'm sure I've heard that name somewhere."

His companion only gave a sort of a little sigh and was silent for a moment, as if ruminating, then he merely said, "The poor fellow is quite gone," and added some scientific terms in which his auditor once more found himself out of his depth.

"As things are," continued the same curiously well-informed person, "it will be more legal for us to leave the body as it is until the police are informed. In fact, I think it will be well if nobody except the police is informed. Don't be surprised if I seem to be keeping it dark from some of our neighbors round here." Then, as if prompted to regularize his rather abrupt confidence, he said: "I've come down to see my cousin at Torwood; my name is Horne Fisher. Might be a pun on my pottering about here, mightn't it?"

"Is Sir Howard Horne your cousin?" asked March. "I'm going to Torwood Park to see him myself; only about his public work, of course, and the wonderful stand he is making for his principles. I think this Budget is the greatest thing in English history. If it fails, it will be the most heroic failure in English history. Are you an admirer of your great kinsman, Mr. Fisher?"

"Rather," said Mr. Fisher. "He's the best shot I know."

Then, as if sincerely repentant of his nonchalance, he added, with a sort of enthusiasm:

"No, but really, he's a beautiful shot."

As if fired by his own words, he took a sort of leap at the ledges of the rock above him, and scaled them with a sudden agility in startling contrast to his general lassitude. He had stood for some seconds on the headland above, with his aquiline profile under the Panama hat relieved against the sky and peering over the countryside before his companion had collected himself sufficiently to scramble up after him.

The level above was a stretch of common turf on which the tracks of the fated car were plowed plainly enough; but the brink of it was broken as with rocky teeth; broken boulders of all shapes and sizes lay near the edge; it was almost incredible that any one could have deliberately driven into such a death trap, especially in broad daylight.

"I can't make head or tail of it," said March. "Was he blind? Or blind drunk?"

"Neither, by the look of him," replied the other.

"Then it was suicide."

"It doesn't seem a cozy way of doing it," remarked the man called Fisher. "Besides, I don't fancy poor old Puggy would commit suicide, somehow."

"Poor old who?" inquired the wondering journalist. "Did you know this unfortunate man?"

"Nobody knew him exactly," replied Fisher, with some vagueness. "But one knew him, of course. He'd been a terror in his time, in Parliament and the courts, and so on; especially in that row about the aliens who were deported as undesirables, when he wanted one of 'em hanged for murder. He was so sick about it that he retired from the bench. Since then he mostly motored about by himself; but he was coming to Torwood, too, for the week-end; and I don't see why he should deliberately break his neck almost at the very door. I believe Hoggs—I mean my cousin Howard—was coming down specially to meet him."

"Torwood Park doesn't belong to your cousin?" inquired March.

"No; it used to belong to the Winthrops, you know," replied the other. "Now a new man's got it; a man from Montreal named Jenkins. Hoggs comes for the shooting; I told you he was a lovely shot."

This repeated eulogy on the great social statesman affected Harold March as if somebody had defined Napoleon as a distinguished player of nap. But he had another half-formed impression struggling in this flood of unfamiliar things, and he brought it to the surface before it could vanish.

"Jenkins," he repeated. "Surely you don't mean Jefferson Jenkins, the social reformer? I mean the man who's fighting for the new cottage-estate scheme. It would be as interesting to meet him as any Cabinet Minister in the world, if you'll excuse my saying so."

"Yes; Hoggs told him it would have to be cottages," said Fisher. "He said the breed of cattle had improved too often, and people were beginning to laugh. And, of course, you must hang a peerage on to something; though the poor chap hasn't got it yet. Hullo, here's somebody else."

They had started walking in the tracks of the car, leaving it behind them in the hollow, still humming horribly like a huge insect that had killed a man. The tracks took them to the corner of the road, one arm of which went on in the same line toward the distant gates of the park. It was clear that the car had been driven down the long straight road, and then, instead of turning with the road to the left, had gone straight on over the turf to its doom. But it was not this discovery that had riveted Fisher's eye, but something even more solid. At the angle of the white road a dark and solitary figure was standing almost as still as a finger post. It was that of a big man in rough shooting-clothes, bareheaded, and with tousled curly hair that gave him a rather wild look. On a nearer approach this first more fantastic impression faded; in a full light the figure took on more conventional colors, as of an ordinary gentleman who happened to have come out without a hat and without very studiously brushing his hair. But the massive stature remained, and something deep and even cavernous about the setting of the eyes redeemed his animal good looks from the commonplace. But March had no time to study the man more closely, for, much to his astonishment, his guide merely observed, "Hullo, Jack!" and walked past him as if he had indeed been a signpost, and without attempting to inform him of the catastrophe beyond the rocks. It was relatively a small thing, but it was only the first in a string of singular antics on which his new and eccentric friend was leading him.

The man they had passed looked after them in rather a suspicious fashion, but Fisher continued serenely on his way along the straight road that ran past the gates of the great estate.

"That's John Burke, the traveler," he condescended to explain. "I expect you've heard of him; shoots big game and all that. Sorry I couldn't stop to introduce you, but I dare say you'll meet him later on."

"I know his book, of course," said March, with renewed interest. "That is certainly a fine piece of description, about their being only conscious of the closeness of the elephant when the colossal head blocked out the moon."

"Yes, young Halkett writes jolly well, I think. What? Didn't you know Halkett wrote Burke's book for him? Burke can't use anything except a gun; and you can't write with that. Oh, he's genuine enough in his way, you know, as brave as a lion, or a good deal braver by all accounts."

"You seem to know all about him," observed March, with a rather bewildered laugh, "and about a good many other people."

Fisher's bald brow became abruptly corrugated, and a curious expression came into his eyes.

"I know too much," he said. "That's what's the matter with me. That's what's the matter with all of us, and the whole show; we know too much. Too much about one another; too much about ourselves. That's why I'm really interested, just now, about one thing that I don't know."

"And that is?" inquired the other.

"Why that poor fellow is dead."

They had walked along the straight road for nearly a mile, conversing at intervals in this fashion; and March had a singular sense of the whole world being turned inside out. Mr. Horne Fisher did not especially abuse his friends and relatives in fashionable society; of some of them he spoke with affection. But they seemed to be an entirely new set of men and women, who happened to have the same nerves as the men and women mentioned most often in the newspapers. Yet no fury of revolt could have seemed to him more utterly revolutionary than this cold familiarity. It was like daylight on the other side of stage scenery.

They reached the great lodge gates of the park, and, to March's surprise, passed them and continued along the interminable white, straight road. But he was himself too early for his appointment with Sir Howard, and was not disinclined to see the end of his new friend's experiment, whatever it might be. They had long left the moorland behind them, and half the white road was gray in the great shadow of the Torwood pine forests, themselves like gray bars shuttered against the sunshine and within, amid that clear noon, manufacturing their own midnight. Soon, however, rifts began to appear in them like gleams of colored windows; the trees thinned and fell away as the road went forward, showing the wild, irregular copses in which, as Fisher said, the house-party had been blazing away all day. And about two hundred yards farther on they came to the first turn of the road.

At the corner stood a sort of decayed inn with the dingy sign of The Grapes. The signboard was dark and indecipherable by now, and hung black against the sky and the gray moorland beyond, about as inviting as a gallows. March remarked that it looked like a tavern for vinegar instead of wine.

"A good phrase," said Fisher, "and so it would be if you were silly enough to drink wine in it. But the beer is very good, and so is the brandy."

March followed him to the bar parlor with some wonder, and his dim sense of repugnance was not dismissed by the first sight of the innkeeper, who was widely different from the genial innkeepers of romance, a bony man, very silent behind a black mustache, but with black, restless eyes. Taciturn as he was, the investigator succeeded at last in extracting a scrap of information from him, by dint of ordering beer and talking to him persistently and minutely on the subject of motor cars. He evidently regarded the innkeeper as in some singular way an authority on motor cars; as being deep in the secrets of the mechanism, management, and mismanagement of motor cars; holding the man all the time with a glittering eye like the Ancient Mariner. Out of all this rather mysterious conversation there did emerge at last a sort of admission that one particular motor car, of a given description, had stopped before the inn about an hour before, and that an elderly man had alighted, requiring some mechanical assistance. Asked if the visitor required any other assistance, the innkeeper said shortly that the old gentleman had filled his flask and taken a packet of sandwiches. And with these words the somewhat inhospitable host had walked hastily out of the bar, and they heard him banging doors in the dark interior.

Fisher's weary eye wandered round the dusty and dreary inn parlor and rested dreamily on a glass case containing a stuffed bird, with a gun hung on hooks above it, which seemed to be its only ornament.

"Puggy was a humorist," he observed, "at least in his own rather grim style. But it seems rather too grim a joke for a man to buy a packet of sandwiches when he is just going to commit suicide."

"If you come to that," answered March, "it isn't very usual for a man to buy a packet of sandwiches when he's just outside the door of a grand house he's going to stop at."

"No . . . no," repeated Fisher, almost mechanically; and then suddenly cocked his eye at his interlocutor with a much livelier expression.

"By Jove! that's an idea. You're perfectly right. And that suggests a very queer idea, doesn't it?"

There was a silence, and then March started with irrational nervousness as the door of the inn was flung open and another man walked rapidly to the counter. He had struck it with a coin and called out for brandy before he saw the other two guests, who were sitting at a bare wooden table under the window. When he turned about with a rather wild stare, March had yet another unexpected emotion, for his guide hailed the man as Hoggs and introduced him as Sir Howard Horne.

He looked rather older than his boyish portraits in the illustrated papers, as is the way of politicians; his flat, fair hair was touched with gray, but his face was almost comically round, with a Roman nose which, when combined with his quick, bright eyes, raised a vague reminiscence of a parrot. He had a cap rather at the back of his head and a gun under his arm. Harold March had imagined many things about his meeting with the great political reformer, but he had never pictured him with a gun under his arm, drinking brandy in a public house.

"So you're stopping at Jink's, too," said Fisher. "Everybody seems to be at Jink's."

"Yes," replied the Chancellor of the Exchequer. "Jolly good shooting. At least all of it that isn't Jink's shooting. I never knew a chap with such good shooting that was such a bad shot. Mind you, he's a jolly good fellow and all that; I don't say a word against him. But he never learned to hold a gun when he was packing pork or whatever he did. They say he shot the cockade off his own servant's hat; just like him to have cockades, of course. He shot the weathercock off his own ridiculous gilded summerhouse. It's the only cock he'll ever kill, I should think. Are you coming up there now?"

Fisher said, rather vaguely, that he was following soon, when he had fixed something up; and the Chancellor of the Exchequer left the inn. March fancied he had been a little upset or impatient when he called for the brandy; but he had talked himself back into a satisfactory state, if the talk had not been quite what his literary visitor had expected. Fisher, a few minutes afterward, slowly led the way out of the tavern and stood in the middle of the road, looking down in the direction from which they had traveled. Then he walked back about two hundred yards in that direction and stood still again.

"I should think this is about the place," he said.

"What place?" asked his companion.

"The place where the poor fellow was killed," said Fisher, sadly.

"What do you mean?" demanded March.

"He was smashed up on the rocks a mile and a half from here."

"No, he wasn't," replied Fisher. "He didn't fall on the rocks at all. Didn't you notice that he only fell on the slope of soft grass underneath? But I saw that he had a bullet in him already."

Then after a pause he added:

"He was alive at the inn, but he was dead long before he came to the rocks. So he was shot as he drove his car down this strip of straight road, and I should think somewhere about here. After that, of course, the car went straight on with nobody to stop or turn it. It's really a very cunning dodge in its way; for the body would be found far away, and most people would say, as you do, that it was an accident to a motorist. The murderer must have been a clever brute."

"But wouldn't the shot be heard at the inn or somewhere?" asked March.

"It would be heard. But it would not be noticed. That," continued the investigator, "is where he was clever again. Shooting was going on all over the place all day; very likely he timed his shot so as to drown it in a number of others. Certainly he was a first-class criminal. And he was something else as well."

"What do you mean?" asked his companion, with a creepy premonition of something coming, he knew not why.

"He was a first-class shot," said Fisher. He had turned his back abruptly and was walking down a narrow, grassy lane, little more than a cart track, which lay opposite the inn and marked the end of the great estate and the beginning of the open moors. March plodded after him with the same idle perseverance, and found him staring through a gap in giant weeds and thorns at the flat face of a painted paling. From behind the paling rose the great gray columns of a row of poplars, which filled the heavens above them with dark-green shadow and shook faintly in a wind which had sunk slowly into a breeze. The afternoon was already deepening into evening, and the titanic shadows of the poplars lengthened over a third of the landscape.

"Are you a first-class criminal?" asked Fisher, in a friendly tone. "I'm afraid I'm not. But I think I can manage to be a sort of fourth-rate burglar."

And before his companion could reply he had managed to swing himself up and over the fence; March followed without much bodily effort, but with considerable mental disturbance. The poplars grew so close against the fence that they had some difficulty in slipping past them, and beyond the poplars they could see only a high hedge of laurel, green and lustrous in the level sun. Something in this limitation by a series of living walls made him feel as if he were really entering a shattered house instead of an open field. It was as if he came in by a disused door or window and found the way blocked by furniture. When they had circumvented the laurel hedge, they came out on a sort of terrace of turf, which fell by one green step to an oblong lawn like a bowling green. Beyond this was the only building in sight, a low conservatory, which seemed far away from anywhere, like a glass cottage standing in its own fields in fairyland. Fisher knew that lonely look of the outlying parts of a great house well enough. He realized that it is more of a satire on aristocracy than if it were choked with weeds and littered with ruins. For it is not neglected and yet it is deserted; at any rate, it is disused. It is regularly swept and garnished for a master who never comes.

Looking over the lawn, however, he saw one object which he had not apparently expected. It was a sort of tripod supporting a large disk like the round top of a table tipped sideways, and it was not until they had dropped on to the lawn and walked across to look at it that March realized that it was a target. It was worn and weatherstained; the gay colors of its concentric rings were faded; possibly it had been set up in those far-off Victorian days when there was a fashion of archery. March had one of his vague visions of ladies in cloudy crinolines and gentlemen in outlandish hats and whiskers revisiting that lost garden like ghosts.

Fisher, who was peering more closely at the target, startled him by an exclamation.

"Hullo!" he said. "Somebody has been peppering this thing with shot, after all, and quite lately, too. Why, I believe old Jink's been trying to improve his bad shooting here."

"Yes, and it looks as if it still wanted improving," answered March, laughing. "Not one of these shots is anywhere near the bull's-eye; they seem just scattered about in the wildest way."

"In the wildest way," repeated Fisher, still peering intently at the target. He seemed merely to assent, but March fancied his eye was shining under its sleepy lid and that he straightened his stooping figure with a strange effort.

"Excuse me a moment," he said, feeling in his pockets. "I think I've got some of my chemicals; and after that we'll go up to the house." And he stooped again over the target, putting something with his finger over each of the shot-holes, so far as March could see merely a dull-gray smear. Then they went through the gathering twilight up the long green avenues to the great house.

Here again, however, the eccentric investigator did not enter by the front door. He walked round the house until he found a window open, and, leaping into it, introduced his friend to what appeared to be the gun-room. Rows of the regular instruments for bringing down birds stood against the walls; but across a table in the window lay one or two weapons of a heavier and more formidable pattern.

"Hullo! these are Burke's big-game rifles," said Fisher. "I never knew he kept them here." He lifted one of them, examined it briefly, and put it down again, frowning heavily. Almost as he did so a strange young man came hurriedly into the room. He was dark and sturdy, with a bumpy forehead and a bulldog jaw, and he spoke with a curt apology.

"I left Major Burke's guns here," he said, "and he wants them packed up. He's going away to-night."

And he carried off the two rifles without casting a glance at the stranger; through the open window they could see his short, dark figure walking away across the glimmering garden. Fisher got out of the window again and stood looking after him.

"That's Halkett, whom I told you about," he said. "I knew he was a sort of secretary and had to do with Burke's papers; but I never knew he had anything to do with his guns. But he's just the sort of silent, sensible little devil who might be very good at anything; the sort of man you know for years before you find he's a chess champion."

He had begun to walk in the direction of the disappearing secretary, and they soon came within sight of the rest of the house-party talking and laughing on the lawn. They could see the tall figure and loose mane of the lion-hunter dominating the little group.

"By the way," observed Fisher, "when we were talking about Burke and Halkett, I said that a man couldn't very well write with a gun. Well, I'm not so sure now. Did you ever hear of an artist so clever that he could draw with a gun? There's a wonderful chap loose about here."

Sir Howard hailed Fisher and his friend the journalist with almost boisterous amiability. The latter was presented to Major Burke and Mr. Halkett and also (by way of a parenthesis) to his host, Mr. Jenkins, a commonplace little man in loud tweeds, whom everybody else seemed to treat with a sort of affection, as if he were a baby.

The irrepressible Chancellor of the Exchequer was still talking about the birds he had brought down, the birds that Burke and Halkett had brought down, and the birds that Jenkins, their host, had failed to bring down. It seemed to be a sort of sociable monomania.

"You and your big game," he ejaculated, aggressively, to Burke. "Why, anybody could shoot big game. You want to be a shot to shoot small game."

"Quite so," interposed Horne Fisher. "Now if only a hippopotamus could fly up in the air out of that bush, or you preserved flying elephants on the estate, why, then—"

"Why even Jink might hit that sort of bird," cried Sir Howard, hilariously slapping his host on the back. "Even he might hit a haystack or a hippopotamus."

"Look here, you fellows," said Fisher. "I want you to come along with me for a minute and shoot at something else. Not a hippopotamus. Another kind of queer animal I've found on the estate. It's an animal with three legs and one eye, and it's all the colors of the rainbow."

"What the deuce are you talking about?" asked Burke.

"You come along and see," replied Fisher, cheerfully.

Such people seldom reject anything nonsensical, for they are always seeking for something new. They gravely rearmed themselves from the gun-room and trooped along at the tail of their guide, Sir Howard only pausing, in a sort of ecstasy, to point out the celebrated gilt summerhouse on which the gilt weathercock still stood crooked. It was dusk turning to dark by the time they reached the remote green by the poplars and accepted the new and aimless game of shooting at the old mark.

The last light seemed to fade from the lawn, and the poplars against the sunset were like great plumes upon a purple hearse, when the futile procession finally curved round, and came out in front of the target. Sir Howard again slapped his host on the shoulder, shoving him playfully forward to take the first shot. The shoulder and arm he touched seemed unnaturally stiff and angular. Mr. Jenkins was holding his gun in an attitude more awkward than any that his satiric friends had seen or expected.

At the same instant a horrible scream seemed to come from nowhere. It was so unnatural and so unsuited to the scene that it might have been made by some inhuman thing flying on wings above them or eavesdropping in the dark woods beyond. But Fisher knew that it had started and stopped on the pale lips of Jefferson Jenkins, of Montreal, and no one at that moment catching sight of Jefferson Jenkins's face would have complained that it was commonplace. The next moment a torrent of guttural but good-humored oaths came from Major Burke as he and the two other men saw what was in front of them. The target stood up in the dim grass like a dark goblin grinning at them, and it was literally grinning. It had two eyes like stars, and in similar livid points of light were picked out the two upturned and open nostrils and the two ends of the wide and tight mouth. A few white dots above each eye indicated the hoary eyebrows; and one of them ran upward almost erect. It was a brilliant caricature done in bright dotted lines and March knew of whom. It shone in the shadowy grass, smeared with sea fire as if one of the submarine monsters had crawled into the twilight garden; but it had the head of a dead man.

"It's only luminous paint," said Burke. "Old Fisher's been having a joke with that phosphorescent stuff of his."

"Seems to be meant for old Puggy'" observed Sir Howard. "Hits him off very well."

With that they all laughed, except Jenkins. When they had all done, he made a noise like the first effort of an animal to laugh, and Horne Fisher suddenly strode across to him and said:

"Mr. Jenkins, I must speak to you at once in private."

It was by the little watercourse in the moors, on the slope under the hanging rock, that March met his new friend Fisher, by appointment, shortly after the ugly and almost grotesque scene that had broken up the group in the garden.

"It was a monkey-trick of mine," observed Fisher, gloomily, "putting phosphorus on the target; but the only chance to make him jump was to give him the horrors suddenly. And when he saw the face he'd shot at shining on the target he practiced on, all lit up with an infernal light, he did jump. Quite enough for my own intellectual satisfaction."

"I'm afraid I don't quite understand even now," said March, "exactly what he did or why he did it."

"You ought to," replied Fisher, with his rather dreary smile, "for you gave me the first suggestion yourself. Oh yes, you did; and it was a very shrewd one. You said a man wouldn't take sandwiches with him to dine at a great house. It was quite true; and the inference was that, though he was going there, he didn't mean to dine there. Or, at any rate, that he might not be dining there. It occurred to me at once that he probably expected the visit to be unpleasant, or the reception doubtful, or something that would prevent his accepting hospitality. Then it struck me that Turnbull was a terror to certain shady characters in the past, and that he had come down to identify and denounce one of them. The chances at the start pointed to the host—that is, Jenkins. I'm morally certain now that Jenkins was the undesirable alien Turnbull wanted to convict in another shooting-affair, but you see the shooting gentleman had another shot in his locker."

"But you said he would have to be a very good shot," protested March.

"Jenkins is a very good shot," said Fisher. "A very good shot who can pretend to be a very bad shot. Shall I tell you the second hint I hit on, after yours, to make me think it was Jenkins? It was my cousin's account of his bad shooting. He'd shot a cockade off a hat and a weathercock off a building. Now, in fact, a man must shoot very well indeed to shoot so badly as that. He must shoot very neatly to hit the cockade and not the head, or even the hat. If the shots had really gone at random, the chances are a thousand to one that they would not have hit such prominent and picturesque objects. They were chosen because they were prominent and picturesque objects. They make a story to go the round of society. He keeps the crooked weathercock in the summerhouse to perpetuate the story of a legend. And then he lay in wait with his evil eye and wicked gun, safely ambushed behind the legend of his own incompetence.

"But there is more than that. There is the summerhouse itself. I mean there is the whole thing. There's all that Jenkins gets chaffed about, the gilding and the gaudy colors and all the vulgarity that's supposed to stamp him as an upstart. Now, as a matter of fact, upstarts generally don't do this. God knows there's enough of 'em in society; and one knows 'em well enough. And this is the very last thing they do. They're generally only too keen to know the right thing and do it; and they instantly put themselves body and soul into the hands of art decorators and art experts, who do the whole thing for them. There's hardly another millionaire alive who has the moral courage to have a gilt monogram on a chair like that one in the gun-room. For that matter, there's the name as well as the monogram. Names like Tompkins and Jenkins and Jinks are funny without being vulgar; I mean they are vulgar without being common. If you prefer it, they are commonplace without being common. They are just the names to be chosen to look ordinary, but they're really rather extraordinary. Do you know many people called Tompkins? It's a good deal rarer than Talbot. It's pretty much the same with the comic clothes of the parvenu. Jenkins dresses like a character in Punch. But that's because he is a character in Punch. I mean he's a fictitious character. He's a fabulous animal. He doesn't exist.

"Have you ever considered what it must be like to be a man who doesn't exist? I mean to be a man with a fictitious character that he has to keep up at the expense not merely of personal talents: To be a new kind of hypocrite hiding a talent in a new kind of napkin. This man has chosen his hypocrisy very ingeniously; it was really a new one. A subtle villain has dressed up as a dashing gentleman and a worthy business man and a philanthropist and a saint; but the loud checks of a comical little cad were really rather a new disguise. But the disguise must be very irksome to a man who can really do things. This is a dexterous little cosmopolitan guttersnipe who can do scores of things, not only shoot, but draw and paint, and probably play the fiddle. Now a man like that may find the hiding of his talents useful; but he could never help wanting to use them where they were useless. If he can draw, he will draw absent-mindedly on blotting paper. I suspect this rascal has often drawn poor old Puggy's face on blotting paper. Probably he began doing it in blots as he afterward did it in dots, or rather shots. It was the same sort of thing; he found a disused target in a deserted yard and couldn't resist indulging in a little secret shooting, like secret drinking. You thought the shots all scattered and irregular, and so they were; but not accidental. No two distances were alike; but the different points were exactly where he wanted to put them. There's nothing needs such mathematical precision as a wild caricature. I've dabbled a little in drawing myself, and I assure you that to put one dot where you want it is a marvel with a pen close to a piece of paper. It was a miracle to do it across a garden with a gun. But a man who can work those miracles will always itch to work them, if it's only in the dark."

After a pause March observed, thoughtfully, "But he couldn't have brought him down like a bird with one of those little guns."

"No; that was why I went into the gun-room," replied Fisher. "He did it with one of Burke's rifles, and Burke thought he knew the sound of it. That's why he rushed out without a hat, looking so wild. He saw nothing but a car passing quickly, which he followed for a little way, and then concluded he'd made a mistake."

There was another silence, during which Fisher sat on a great stone as motionless as on their first meeting, and watched the gray and silver river eddying past under the bushes. Then March said, abruptly, "Of course he knows the truth now."

"Nobody knows the truth but you and I," answered Fisher, with a certain softening in his voice. "And I don't think you and I will ever quarrel."

"What do you mean?" asked March, in an altered accent. "What have you done about it?"

Horne Fisher continued to gaze steadily at the eddying stream. At last he said, "The police have proved it was a motor accident."

"But you know it was not."

"I told you that I know too much," replied Fisher, with his eye on the river. "I know that, and I know a great many other things. I know the atmosphere and the way the whole thing works. I know this fellow has succeeded in making himself something incurably commonplace and comic. I know you can't get up a persecution of old Toole or Little Tich. If I were to tell Hoggs or Halkett that old Jink was an assassin, they would almost die of laughter before my eyes. Oh, I don't say their laughter's quite innocent, though it's genuine in its way. They want old Jink, and they couldn't do without him. I don't say I'm quite innocent. I like Hoggs; I don't want him to be down and out; and he'd be done for if Jink can't pay for his coronet. They were devilish near the line at the last election. But the only real objection to it is that it's impossible. Nobody would believe it; it's not in the picture. The crooked weathercock would always turn it into a joke."

"Don't you think this is infamous?" asked March, quietly.

"I think a good many things," replied the other. "If you people ever happen to blow the whole tangle of society to hell with dynamite, I don't know that the human race will be much the worse. But don't be too hard on me merely because I know what society is. That's why I moon away my time over things like stinking fish."

There was a pause as he settled himself down again by the stream; and then he added:

"I told you before I had to throw back the big fish."

II: THE VANISHING PRINCE

This tale begins among a tangle of tales round a name that is at once recent and legendary. The name is that of Michael O'Neill, popularly called Prince Michael, partly because he claimed descent from ancient Fenian princes, and partly because he was credited with a plan to make himself prince president of Ireland, as the last Napoleon did of France. He was undoubtedly a gentleman of honorable pedigree and of many accomplishments, but two of his accomplishments emerged from all the rest. He had a talent for appearing when he was not wanted and a talent for disappearing when he was wanted, especially when he was wanted by the police. It may be added that his disappearances were more dangerous than his appearances. In the latter he seldom went beyond the sensational—pasting up seditious placards, tearing down official placards, making flamboyant speeches, or unfurling forbidden flags. But in order to effect the former he would sometimes fight for his freedom with startling energy, from which men were sometimes lucky to escape with a broken head instead of a broken neck. His most famous feats of escape, however, were due to dexterity and not to violence. On a cloudless summer morning he had come down a country road white with dust, and, pausing outside a farmhouse, had told the farmer's daughter, with elegant indifference, that the local police were in pursuit of him. The girl's name was Bridget Royce, a somber and even sullen type of beauty, and she looked at him darkly, as if in doubt, and said, "Do you want me to hide you?" Upon which he only laughed, leaped lightly over the stone wall, and strode toward the farm, merely throwing over his shoulder the remark, "Thank you, I have generally been quite capable of hiding myself." In which proceeding he acted with a tragic ignorance of the nature of women; and there fell on his path in that sunshine a shadow of doom.

While he disappeared through the farmhouse the girl remained for a few moments looking up the road, and two perspiring policemen came plowing up to the door where she stood. Though still angry, she was still silent, and a quarter of an hour later the officers had searched the house and were already inspecting the kitchen garden and cornfield behind it. In the ugly reaction of her mood she might have been tempted even to point out the fugitive, but for a small difficulty that she had no more notion than the policemen had of where he could possibly have gone. The kitchen garden was inclosed by a very low wall, and the cornfield beyond lay aslant like a square patch on a great green hill on which he could still have been seen even as a dot in the distance. Everything stood solid in its familiar place; the apple tree was too small to support or hide a climber; the only shed stood open and obviously empty; there was no sound save the droning of summer flies and the occasional flutter of a bird unfamiliar enough to be surprised by the scarecrow in the field; there was scarcely a shadow save a few blue lines that fell from the thin tree; every detail was picked out by the brilliant day light as if in a microscope. The girl described the scene later, with all the passionate realism of her race, and, whether or no the policemen had a similar eye for the picturesque, they had at least an eye for the facts of the case, and were compelled to give up the chase and retire from the scene. Bridget Royce remained as if in a trance, staring at the sunlit garden in which a man had just vanished like a fairy. She was still in a sinister mood, and the miracle took in her mind a character of unfriendliness and fear, as if the fairy were decidedly a bad fairy. The sun upon the glittering garden depressed her more than the darkness, but she continued to stare at it. Then the world itself went half-witted and she screamed. The scarecrow moved in the sun light. It had stood with its back to her in a battered old black hat and a tattered garment, and with all its tatters flying, it strode away across the hill.

She did not analyze the audacious trick by which the man had turned to his advantage the subtle effects of the expected and the obvious; she was still under the cloud of more individual complexities, and she noticed most of all that the vanishing scarecrow did not even turn to look at the farm. And the fates that were running so adverse to his fantastic career of freedom ruled that his next adventure, though it had the same success in another quarter, should increase the danger in this quarter. Among the many similar adventures related of him in this manner it is also said that some days afterward another girl, named Mary Cregan, found him concealed on the farm where she worked; and if the story is true, she must also have had the shock of an uncanny experience, for when she was busy at some lonely task in the yard she heard a voice speaking out of the well, and found that the eccentric had managed to drop himself into the bucket which was some little way below, the well only partly full of water. In this case, however, he had to appeal to the woman to wind up the rope. And men say it was when this news was told to the other woman that her soul walked over the border line of treason.

Such, at least, were the stories told of him in the countryside, and there were many more—as that he had stood insolently in a splendid green dressing gown on the steps of a great hotel, and then led the police a chase through a long suite of grand apartments, and finally through his own bedroom on to a balcony that overhung the river. The moment the pursuers stepped on to the balcony it broke under them, and they dropped pell-mell into the eddying waters, while Michael, who had thrown off his gown and dived, was able to swim away. It was said that he had carefully cut away the props so that they would not support anything so heavy as a policeman. But here again he was immediately fortunate, yet ultimately unfortunate, for it is said that one of the men was drowned, leaving a family feud which made a little rift in his popularity. These stories can now be told in some detail, not because they are the most marvelous of his many adventures, but because these alone were not covered with silence by the loyalty of the peasantry. These alone found their way into official reports, and it is these which three of the chief officials of the country were reading and discussing when the more remarkable part of this story begins.

Night was far advanced and the lights shone in the cottage that served for a temporary police station near the coast. On one side of it were the last houses of the straggling village, and on the other nothing but a waste moorland stretching away toward the sea, the line of which was broken by no landmark except a solitary tower of the prehistoric pattern still found in Ireland, standing up as slender as a column, but pointed like a pyramid. At a wooden table in front of the window, which normally looked out on this landscape, sat two men in plain clothes, but with something of a military bearing, for indeed they were the two chiefs of the detective service of that district. The senior of the two, both in age and rank, was a sturdy man with a short white beard, and frosty eyebrows fixed in a frown which suggested rather worry than severity.

His name was Morton, and he was a Liverpool man long pickled in the Irish quarrels, and doing his duty among them in a sour fashion not altogether unsympathetic. He had spoken a few sentences to his companion, Nolan, a tall, dark man with a cadaverous equine Irish face, when he seemed to remember something and touched a bell which rang in another room. The subordinate he had summoned immediately appeared with a sheaf of papers in his hand.

"Sit down, Wilson," he said. "Those are the depositions, I suppose."

"Yes," replied the third officer. "I think I've got all there is to be got out of them, so I sent the people away."

"Did Mary Cregan give evidence?" asked Morton, with a frown that looked a little heavier than usual.

"No, but her master did," answered the man called Wilson, who had flat, red hair and a plain, pale face, not without sharpness. "I think he's hanging round the girl himself and is out against a rival. There's always some reason of that sort when we are told the truth about anything. And you bet the other girl told right enough."

"Well, let's hope they'll be some sort of use," remarked Nolan, in a somewhat hopeless manner, gazing out into the darkness.

"Anything is to the good," said Morton, "that lets us know anything about him."

"Do we know anything about him?" asked the melancholy Irishman.

"We know one thing about him," said Wilson, "and it's the one thing that nobody ever knew before. We know where he is."

"Are you sure?" inquired Morton, looking at him sharply.

"Quite sure," replied his assistant. "At this very minute he is in that tower over there by the shore. If you go near enough you'll see the candle burning in the window."

As he spoke the noise of a horn sounded on the road outside, and a moment after they heard the throbbing of a motor car brought to a standstill before the door. Morton instantly sprang to his feet.

"Thank the Lord that's the car from Dublin," he said. "I can't do anything without special authority, not if he were sitting on the top of the tower and putting out his tongue at us. But the chief can do what he thinks best."

He hurried out to the entrance and was soon exchanging greetings with a big handsome man in a fur coat, who brought into the dingy little station the indescribable glow of the great cities and the luxuries of the great world.

For this was Sir Walter Carey, an official of such eminence in Dublin Castle that nothing short of the case of Prince Michael would have brought him on such a journey in the middle of the night. But the case of Prince Michael, as it happened, was complicated by legalism as well as lawlessness. On the last occasion he had escaped by a forensic quibble and not, as usual, by a private escapade; and it was a question whether at the moment he was amenable to the law or not. It might be necessary to stretch a point, but a man like Sir Walter could probably stretch it as far as he liked.

Whether he intended to do so was a question to be considered. Despite the almost aggressive touch of luxury in the fur coat, it soon became apparent that Sir Walter's large leonine head was for use as well as ornament, and he considered the matter soberly and sanely enough. Five chairs were set round the plain deal table, for who should Sir Walter bring with him but his young relative and secretary, Horne Fisher. Sir Walter listened with grave attention, and his secretary with polite boredom, to the string of episodes by which the police had traced the flying rebel from the steps of the hotel to the solitary tower beside the sea. There at least he was cornered between the moors and the breakers; and the scout sent by Wilson reported him as writing under a solitary candle, perhaps composing another of his tremendous proclamations. Indeed, it would have been typical of him to choose it as the place in which finally to turn to bay. He had some remote claim on it, as on a family castle; and those who knew him thought him capable of imitating the primitive Irish chieftains who fell fighting against the sea.

"I saw some queer-looking people leaving as I came in," said Sir Walter Carey. "I suppose they were your witnesses. But why do they turn up here at this time of night?"

Morton smiled grimly. "They come here by night because they would be dead men if they came here by day. They are criminals committing a crime that is more horrible here than theft or murder."

"What crime do you mean?" asked the other, with some curiosity.

"They are helping the law," said Morton.

There was a silence, and Sir Walter considered the papers before him with an abstracted eye. At last he spoke.

"Quite so; but look here, if the local feeling is as lively as that there are a good many points to consider. I believe the new Act will enable me to collar him now if I think it best. But is it best? A serious rising would do us no good in Parliament, and the government has enemies in England as well as Ireland. It won't do if I have done what looks a little like sharp practice, and then only raised a revolution."

"It's all the other way," said the man called Wilson, rather quickly. "There won't be half so much of a revolution if you arrest him as there will if you leave him loose for three days longer. But, anyhow, there can't be anything nowadays that the proper police can't manage."

"Mr. Wilson is a Londoner," said the Irish detective, with a smile.

"Yes, I'm a cockney, all right," replied Wilson, "and I think I'm all the better for that. Especially at this job, oddly enough."

Sir Walter seemed slightly amused at the pertinacity of the third officer, and perhaps even more amused at the slight accent with which he spoke, which rendered rather needless his boast about his origin.

"Do you mean to say," he asked, "that you know more about the business here because you have come from London?"

"Sounds funny, I know, but I do believe it," answered Wilson. "I believe these affairs want fresh methods. But most of all I believe they want a fresh eye."

The superior officers laughed, and the redhaired man went on with a slight touch of temper:

"Well, look at the facts. See how the fellow got away every time, and you'll understand what I mean. Why was he able to stand in the place of the scarecrow, hidden by nothing but an old hat? Because it was a village policeman who knew the scarecrow was there, was expecting it, and therefore took no notice of it. Now I never expect a scarecrow. I've never seen one in the street, and I stare at one when I see it in the field. It's a new thing to me and worth noticing. And it was just the same when he hid in the well. You are ready to find a well in a place like that; you look for a well, and so you don't see it. I don't look for it, and therefore I do look at it."

"It is certainly an idea," said Sir Walter, smiling, "but what about the balcony? Balconies are occasionally seen in London."

"But not rivers right under them, as if it was in Venice," replied Wilson.

"It is certainly a new idea," repeated Sir Walter, with something like respect. He had all the love of the luxurious classes for new ideas. But he also had a critical faculty, and was inclined to think, after due reflection, that it was a true idea as well.

Growing dawn had already turned the window panes from black to gray when Sir Walter got abruptly to his feet. The others rose also, taking this for a signal that the arrest was to be undertaken. But their leader stood for a moment in deep thought, as if conscious that he had come to a parting of the ways.

Suddenly the silence was pierced by a long, wailing cry from the dark moors outside. The silence that followed it seemed more startling than the shriek itself, and it lasted until Nolan said, heavily:

"'Tis the banshee. Somebody is marked for the grave."

His long, large-featured face was as pale as a moon, and it was easy to remember that he was the only Irishman in the room.

"Well, I know that banshee," said Wilson, cheerfully, "ignorant as you think I am of these things. I talked to that banshee myself an hour ago, and I sent that banshee up to the tower and told her to sing out like that if she could get a glimpse of our friend writing his proclamation."

"Do you mean that girl Bridget Royce?" asked Morton, drawing his frosty brows together. "Has she turned king's evidence to that extent?"

"Yes," answered Wilson. "I know very little of these local things, you tell me, but I reckon an angry woman is much the same in all countries."

Nolan, however, seemed still moody and unlike himself. "It's an ugly noise and an ugly business altogether," he said. "If it's really the end of Prince Michael it may well be the end of other things as well. When the spirit is on him he would escape by a ladder of dead men, and wade through that sea if it were made of blood."

"Is that the real reason of your pious alarms?" asked Wilson, with a slight sneer.

The Irishman's pale face blackened with a new passion.

"I have faced as many murderers in County Clare as you ever fought with in Clapham Junction, Mr. Cockney," he said.

"Hush, please," said Morton, sharply. "Wilson, you have no kind of right to imply doubt of your superior's conduct. I hope you will prove yourself as courageous and trustworthy as he has always been."

The pale face of the red-haired man seemed a shade paler, but he was silent and composed, and Sir Walter went up to Nolan with marked courtesy, saying, "Shall we go outside now, and get this business done?"

Dawn had lifted, leaving a wide chasm of white between a great gray cloud and the great gray moorland, beyond which the tower was outlined against the daybreak and the sea.

Something in its plain and primitive shape vaguely suggested the dawn in the first days of the earth, in some prehistoric time when even the colors were hardly created, when there was only blank daylight between cloud and clay. These dead hues were relieved only by one spot of gold—the spark of the candle alight in the window of the lonely tower, and burning on into the broadening daylight. As the group of detectives, followed by a cordon of policemen, spread out into a crescent to cut off all escape, the light in the tower flashed as if it were moved for a moment, and then went out. They knew the man inside had realized the daylight and blown out his candle.

"There are other windows, aren't there?" asked Morton, "and a door, of course, somewhere round the corner? Only a round tower has no corners."

"Another example of my small suggestion," observed Wilson, quietly. "That queer tower was the first thing I saw when I came to these parts; and I can tell you a little more about it—or, at any rate, the outside of it. There are four windows altogether, one a little way from this one, but just out of sight. Those are both on the ground floor, and so is the third on the other side, making a sort of triangle. But the fourth is just above the third, and I suppose it looks on an upper floor."

"It's only a sort of loft, reached by a ladder, said Nolan. "I've played in the place when I was a child. It's no more than an empty shell." And his sad face grew sadder, thinking perhaps of the tragedy of his country and the part that he played in it.

"The man must have got a table and chair, at any rate," said Wilson, "but no doubt he could have got those from some cottage. If I might make a suggestion, sir, I think we ought to approach all the five entrances at once, so to speak. One of us should go to the door and one to each window; Macbride here has a ladder for the upper window."

Mr. Horne Fisher languidly turned to his distinguished relative and spoke for the first time.

"I am rather a convert to the cockney school of psychology," he said in an almost inaudible voice.

The others seemed to feel the same influence in different ways, for the group began to break up in the manner indicated. Morton moved toward the window immediately in front of them, where the hidden outlaw had just snuffed the candle; Nolan, a little farther westward to the next window; while Wilson, followed by Macbride with the ladder, went round to the two windows at the back. Sir Walter Carey himself, followed by his secretary, began to walk round toward the only door, to demand admittance in a more regular fashion.

"He will be armed, of course," remarked Sir Walter, casually.

"By all accounts," replied Horne Fisher, "he can do more with a candlestick than most men with a pistol. But he is pretty sure to have the pistol, too."

Even as he spoke the question was answered with a tongue of thunder. Morton had just placed himself in front of the nearest window, his broad shoulders blocking the aperture. For an instant it was lit from within as with red fire, followed by a thundering throng of echoes. The square shoulders seemed to alter in shape, and the sturdy figure collapsed among the tall, rank grasses at the foot of the tower. A puff of smoke floated from the window like a little cloud. The two men behind rushed to the spot and raised him, but he was dead.

Sir Walter straightened himself and called out something that was lost in another noise of firing; it was possible that the police were already avenging their comrade from the other side. Fisher had already raced round to the next window, and a new cry of astonishment from him brought his patron to the same spot. Nolan, the Irish policeman, had also fallen, sprawling all his great length in the grass, and it was red with his blood. He was still alive when they reached him, but there was death on his face, and he was only able to make a final gesture telling them that all was over; and, with a broken word and a heroic effort, motioning them on to where his other comrades were besieging the back of the tower. Stunned by these rapid and repeated shocks, the two men could only vaguely obey the gesture, and, finding their way to the other windows at the back, they discovered a scene equally startling, if less final and tragic. The other two officers were not dead or mortally wounded, but Macbride lay with a broken leg and his ladder on top of him, evidently thrown down from the top window of the tower; while Wilson lay on his face, quite still as if stunned, with his red head among the gray and silver of the sea holly. In him, however, the impotence was but momentary, for he began to move and rise as the others came round the tower.

"My God! it's like an explosion!" cried Sir Walter; and indeed it was the only word for this unearthly energy, by which one man had been able to deal death or destruction on three sides of the same small triangle at the same instant.

Wilson had already scrambled to his feet and with splendid energy flew again at the window, revolver in hand. He fired twice into the opening and then disappeared in his own smoke; but the thud of his feet and the shock of a falling chair told them that the intrepid Londoner had managed at last to leap into the room. Then followed a curious silence; and Sir Walter, walking to the window through the thinning smoke, looked into the hollow shell of the ancient tower. Except for Wilson, staring around him, there was nobody there.

The inside of the tower was a single empty room, with nothing but a plain wooden chair and a table on which were pens, ink and paper, and the candlestick. Halfway up the high wall there was a rude timber platform under the upper window, a small loft which was more like a large shelf. It was reached only by a ladder, and it seemed to be as bare as the bare walls. Wilson completed his survey of the place and then went and stared at the things on the table. Then he silently pointed with his lean forefinger at the open page of the large notebook. The writer had suddenly stopped writing, even in the middle of a word.

"I said it was like an explosion," said Sir Walter Carey at last. "And really the man himself seems to have suddenly exploded. But he has blown himself up somehow without touching the tower. He's burst more like a bubble than a bomb."

"He has touched more valuable things than the tower," said Wilson, gloomily.

There was a long silence, and then Sir Walter said, seriously: "Well, Mr. Wilson, I am not a detective, and these unhappy happenings have left you in charge of that branch of the business. We all lament the cause of this, but I should like to say that I myself have the strongest confidence in your capacity for carrying on the work. What do you think we should do next?"

Wilson seemed to rouse himself from his depression and acknowledged the speaker's words with a warmer civility than he had hitherto shown to anybody. He called in a few of the police to assist in routing out the interior, leaving the rest to spread themselves in a search party outside.

"I think," he said, "the first thing is to make quite sure about the inside of this place, as it was hardly physically possible for him to have got outside. I suppose poor Nolan would have brought in his banshee and said it was supernaturally possible. But I've got no use for disembodied spirits when I'm dealing with facts. And the facts before me are an empty tower with a ladder, a chair, and a table."

"The spiritualists," said Sir Walter, with a smile, "would say that spirits could find a great deal of use for a table."

"I dare say they could if the spirits were on the table—in a bottle," replied Wilson, with a curl of his pale lip. "The people round here, when they're all sodden up with Irish whisky, may believe in such things. I think they want a little education in this country."

Horne Fisher's heavy eyelids fluttered in a faint attempt to rise, as if he were tempted to a lazy protest against the contemptuous tone of the investigator.

"The Irish believe far too much in spirits to believe in spiritualism," he murmured. "They know too much about 'em. If you want a simple and childlike faith in any spirit that comes along you can get it in your favorite London."

"I don't want to get it anywhere," said Wilson, shortly. "I say I'm dealing with much simpler things than your simple faith, with a table and a chair and a ladder. Now what I want to say about them at the start is this. They are all three made roughly enough of plain wood. But the table and the chair are fairly new and comparatively clean. The ladder is covered with dust and there is a cobweb under the top rung of it. That means that he borrowed the first two quite recently from some cottage, as we supposed, but the ladder has been a long time in this rotten old dustbin. Probably it was part of the original furniture, an heirloom in this magnificent palace of the Irish kings."

Again Fisher looked at him under his eyelids, but seemed too sleepy to speak, and Wilson went on with his argument.

"Now it's quite clear that something very odd has just happened in this place. The chances are ten to one, it seems to me, that it had something specially to do with this place. Probably he came here because he could do it only here; it doesn't seem very inviting otherwise. But the man knew it of old; they say it belonged to his family, so that altogether, I think, everything points to something in the construction of the tower itself."

"Your reasoning seems to me excellent," said Sir Walter, who was listening attentively. "But what could it be?"

"You see now what I mean about the ladder," went on the detective; "it's the only old piece of furniture here and the first thing that caught that cockney eye of mine. But there is something else. That loft up there is a sort of lumber room without any lumber. So far as I can see, it's as empty as everything else; and, as things are, I don't see the use of the ladder leading to it. It seems to me, as I can't find anything unusual down here, that it might pay us to look up there."

He got briskly off the table on which he was sitting (for the only chair was allotted to Sir Walter) and ran rapidly up the ladder to the platform above. He was soon followed by the others, Mr. Fisher going last, however, with an appearance of considerable nonchalance.

At this stage, however, they were destined to disappointment; Wilson nosed in every corner like a terrier and examined the roof almost in the posture of a fly, but half an hour afterward they had to confess that they were still without a clew. Sir Walter's private secretary seemed more and more threatened with inappropriate slumber, and, having been the last to climb up the ladder, seemed now to lack the energy even to climb down again.

"Come along, Fisher," called out Sir Walter from below, when the others had regained the floor. "We must consider whether we'll pull the whole place to pieces to see what it's made of."

"I'm coming in a minute," said the voice from the ledge above their heads, a voice somewhat suggestive of an articulate yawn.

"What are you waiting for?" asked Sir Walter, impatiently. "Can you see anything there?"

"Well, yes, in a way," replied the voice, vaguely. "In fact, I see it quite plain now."

"What is it?" asked Wilson, sharply, from the table on which he sat kicking his heels restlessly.

"Well, it's a man," said Horne Fisher.

Wilson bounded off the table as if he had been kicked off it. "What do you mean?" he cried. "How can you possibly see a man?"

"I can see him through the window," replied the secretary, mildly. "I see him coming across the moor. He's making a bee line across the open country toward this tower. He evidently means to pay us a visit. And, considering who it seems to be, perhaps it would be more polite if we were all at the door to receive him." And in a leisurely manner the secretary came down the ladder.

"Who it seems to be!" repeated Sir Walter in astonishment.

"Well, I think it's the man you call Prince Michael," observed Mr. Fisher, airily. "In fact, I'm sure it is. I've seen the police portraits of him."

There was a dead silence, and Sir Walter's usually steady brain seemed to go round like a windmill.

"But, hang it all!" he said at last, "even supposing his own explosion could have thrown him half a mile away, without passing through any of the windows, and left him alive enough for a country walk—even then, why the devil should he walk in this direction? The murderer does not generally revisit the scene of his crime so rapidly as all that."

"He doesn't know yet that it is the scene of his crime," answered Horne Fisher.

"What on earth do you mean? You credit him with rather singular absence of mind."

"Well, the truth is, it isn't the scene of his crime," said Fisher, and went and looked out of the window.

There was another silence, and then Sir Walter said, quietly: "What sort of notion have you really got in your head, Fisher? Have you developed a new theory about how this fellow escaped out of the ring round him?"

"He never escaped at all," answered the man at the window, without turning round. "He never escaped out of the ring because he was never inside the ring. He was not in this tower at all, at least not when we were surrounding it."

He turned and leaned back against the window, but, in spite of his usual listless manner, they almost fancied that the face in shadow was a little pale.

"I began to guess something of the sort when we were some way from the tower," he said. "Did you notice that sort of flash or flicker the candle gave before it was extinguished? I was almost certain it was only the last leap the flame gives when a candle burns itself out. And then I came into this room and I saw that."

He pointed at the table and Sir Walter caught his breath with a sort of curse at his own blindness. For the candle in the candlestick had obviously burned itself away to nothing and left him, mentally, at least, very completely in the dark.

"Then there is a sort of mathematical question," went on Fisher, leaning back in his limp way and looking up at the bare walls, as if tracing imaginary diagrams there. "It's not so easy for a man in the third angle to face the other two at the same moment, especially if they are at the base of an isosceles. I am sorry if it sounds like a lecture on geometry, but—"

"I'm afraid we have no time for it," said Wilson, coldly. "If this man is really coming back, I must give my orders at once."

"I think I'll go on with it, though," observed Fisher, staring at the roof with insolent serenity.

"I must ask you, Mr. Fisher, to let me conduct my inquiry on my own lines," said Wilson, firmly. "I am the officer in charge now."

"Yes," remarked Horne Fisher, softly, but with an accent that somehow chilled the hearer. "Yes. But why?"

Sir Walter was staring, for he had never seen his rather lackadaisical young friend look like that before. Fisher was looking at Wilson with lifted lids, and the eyes under them seemed to have shed or shifted a film, as do the eyes of an eagle.

"Why are you the officer in charge now?" he asked. "Why can you conduct the inquiry on your own lines now? How did it come about, I wonder, that the elder officers are not here to interfere with anything you do?"

Nobody spoke, and nobody can say how soon anyone would have collected his wits to speak when a noise came from without. It was the heavy and hollow sound of a blow upon the door of the tower, and to their shaken spirits it sounded strangely like the hammer of doom.

The wooden door of the tower moved on its rusty hinges under the hand that struck it and Prince Michael came into the room. Nobody had the smallest doubt about his identity. His light clothes, though frayed with his adventures, were of fine and almost foppish cut, and he wore a pointed beard, or imperial, perhaps as a further reminiscence of Louis Napoleon; but he was a much taller and more graceful man that his prototype. Before anyone could speak he had silenced everyone for an instant with a slight but splendid gesture of hospitality.

"Gentlemen," he said, "this is a poor place now, but you are heartily welcome."

Wilson was the first to recover, and he took a stride toward the newcomer.

"Michael O'Neill, I arrest you in the king's name for the murder of Francis Morton and James Nolan. It is my duty to warn you—"

"No, no, Mr. Wilson," cried Fisher, suddenly. "You shall not commit a third murder."

Sir Walter Carey rose from his chair, which fell over with a crash behind him. "What does all this mean?" he called out in an authoritative manner.

"It means," said Fisher, "that this man, Hooker Wilson, as soon as he had put his head in at that window, killed his two comrades who had put their heads in at the other windows, by firing across the empty room. That is what it means. And if you want to know, count how many times he is supposed to have fired and then count the charges left in his revolver."

Wilson, who was still sitting on the table, abruptly put a hand out for the weapon that lay beside him. But the next movement was the most unexpected of all, for the prince standing in the doorway passed suddenly from the dignity of a statue to the swiftness of an acrobat and rent the revolver out of the detective's hand.

"You dog!" he cried. "So you are the type of English truth, as I am of Irish tragedy—you who come to kill me, wading through the blood of your brethren. If they had fallen in a feud on the hillside, it would be called murder, and yet your sin might be forgiven you. But I, who am innocent, I was to be slain with ceremony. There would be long speeches and patient judges listening to my vain plea of innocence, noting down my despair and disregarding it. Yes, that is what I call assassination. But killing may be no murder; there is one shot left in this little gun, and I know where it should go."

Wilson turned quickly on the table, and even as he turned he twisted in agony, for Michael shot him through the body where he sat, so that he tumbled off the table like lumber.

The police rushed to lift him; Sir Walter stood speechless; and then, with a strange and weary gesture, Horne Fisher spoke.

"You are indeed a type of the Irish tragedy," he said. "You were entirely in the right, and you have put yourself in the wrong."

The prince's face was like marble for a space then there dawned in his eyes a light not unlike that of despair. He laughed suddenly and flung the smoking pistol on the ground.

"I am indeed in the wrong," he said. "I have committed a crime that may justly bring a curse on me and my children."

Horne Fisher did not seem entirely satisfied with this very sudden repentance; he kept his eyes on the man and only said, in a low voice, "What crime do you mean?"

"I have helped English justice," replied Prince Michael. "I have avenged your king's officers; I have done the work of his hangman. For that truly I deserve to be hanged."

And he turned to the police with a gesture that did not so much surrender to them, but rather command them to arrest him.

This was the story that Horne Fisher told to Harold March, the journalist, many years after, in a little, but luxurious, restaurant near Piccadilly. He had invited March to dinner some time after the affair he called "The Face in the Target," and the conversation had naturally turned on that mystery and afterward on earlier memories of Fisher's life and the way in which he was led to study such problems as those of Prince Michael. Horne Fisher was fifteen years older; his thin hair had faded to frontal baldness, and his long, thin hands dropped less with affectation and more with fatigue. And he told the story of the Irish adventure of his youth, because it recorded the first occasion on which he had ever come in contact with crime, or discovered how darkly and how terribly crime can be entangled with law.

"Hooker Wilson was the first criminal I ever knew, and he was a policeman," explained Fisher, twirling his wine glass. "And all my life has been a mixed-up business of the sort. He was a man of very real talent, and perhaps genius, and well worth studying, both as a detective and a criminal. His white face and red hair were typical of him, for he was one of those who are cold and yet on fire for fame; and he could control anger, but not ambition. He swallowed the snubs of his superiors in that first quarrel, though he boiled with resentment; but when he suddenly saw the two heads dark against the dawn and framed in the two windows, he could not miss the chance, not only of revenge, but of the removal of the two obstacles to his promotion. He was a dead shot and counted on silencing both, though proof against him would have been hard in any case. But, as a matter of fact, he had a narrow escape, in the case of Nolan, who lived just long enough to say, 'Wilson' and point. We thought he was summoning help for his comrade, but he was really denouncing his murderer. After that it was easy to throw down the ladder above him (for a man up a ladder cannot see clearly what is below and behind) and to throw himself on the ground as another victim of the catastrophe.

"But there was mixed up with his murderous ambition a real belief, not only in his own talents, but in his own theories. He did believe in what he called a fresh eye, and he did want scope for fresh methods. There was something in his view, but it failed where such things commonly fail, because the fresh eye cannot see the unseen. It is true about the ladder and the scarecrow, but not about the life and the soul; and he made a bad mistake about what a man like Michael would do when he heard a woman scream. All Michael's very vanity and vainglory made him rush out at once; he would have walked into Dublin Castle for a lady's glove. Call it his pose or what you will, but he would have done it. What happened when he met her is another story, and one we may never know, but from tales I've heard since, they must have been reconciled. Wilson was wrong there; but there was something, for all that, in his notion that the newcomer sees most, and that the man on the spot may know too much to know anything. He was right about some things. He was right about me."

"About you?" asked Harold March in some wonder.

"I am the man who knows too much to know anything, or, at any rate, to do anything," said Horne Fisher. "I don't mean especially about Ireland. I mean about England. I mean about the whole way we are governed, and perhaps the only way we can be governed. You asked me just now what became of the survivors of that tragedy. Well, Wilson recovered and we managed to persuade him to retire. But we had to pension that damnable murderer more magnificently than any hero who ever fought for England. I managed to save Michael from the worst, but we had to send that perfectly innocent man to penal servitude for a crime we know he never committed, and it was only afterward that we could connive in a sneakish way at his escape. And Sir Walter Carey is Prime Minister of this country, which he would probably never have been if the truth had been told of such a horrible scandal in his department. It might have done for us altogether in Ireland; it would certainly have done for him. And he is my father's old friend, and has always smothered me with kindness. I am too tangled up with the whole thing, you see, and I was certainly never born to set it right. You look distressed, not to say shocked, and I'm not at all offended at it. Let us change the subject by all means, if you like. What do you think of this Burgundy? It's rather a discovery of mine, like the restaurant itself."

And he proceeded to talk learnedly and luxuriantly on all the wines of the world; on which subject, also, some moralists would consider that he knew too much.

III: THE SOUL OF THE SCHOOLBOY

A large map of London would be needed to display the wild and zigzag course of one day's journey undertaken by an uncle and his nephew; or, to speak more truly, of a nephew and his uncle. For the nephew, a schoolboy on a holiday, was in theory the god in the car, or in the cab, tram, tube, and so on, while his uncle was at most a priest dancing before him and offering sacrifices. To put it more soberly, the schoolboy had something of the stolid air of a young duke doing the grand tour, while his elderly relative was reduced to the position of a courier, who nevertheless had to pay for everything like a patron. The schoolboy was officially known as Summers Minor, and in a more social manner as Stinks, the only public tribute to his career as an amateur photographer and electrician. The uncle was the Rev. Thomas Twyford, a lean and lively old gentleman with a red, eager face and white hair. He was in the ordinary way a country clergyman, but he was one of those who achieve the paradox of being famous in an obscure way, because they are famous in an obscure world. In a small circle of ecclesiastical archaeologists, who were the only people who could even understand one another's discoveries, he occupied a recognized and respectable place. And a critic might have found even in that day's journey at least as much of the uncle's hobby as of the nephew's holiday.

His original purpose had been wholly paternal and festive. But, like many other intelligent people, he was not above the weakness of playing with a toy to amuse himself, on the theory that it would amuse a child. His toys were crowns and miters and croziers and swords of state; and he had lingered over them, telling himself that the boy ought to see all the sights of London. And at the end of the day, after a tremendous tea, he rather gave the game away by winding up with a visit in which hardly any human boy could be conceived as taking an interest—an underground chamber supposed to have been a chapel, recently excavated on the north bank of the Thames, and containing literally nothing whatever but one old silver coin. But the coin, to those who knew, was more solitary and splendid than the Koh-i-noor. It was Roman, and was said to bear the head of St. Paul; and round it raged the most vital controversies about the ancient British Church. It could hardly be denied, however, that the controversies left Summers Minor comparatively cold.

Indeed, the things that interested Summers Minor, and the things that did not interest him, had mystified and amused his uncle for several hours. He exhibited the English schoolboy's startling ignorance and startling knowledge—knowledge of some special classification in which he can generally correct and confound his elders. He considered himself entitled, at Hampton Court on a holiday, to forget the very names of Cardinal Wolsey or William of Orange; but he could hardly be dragged from some details about the arrangement of the electric bells in the neighboring hotel. He was solidly dazed by Westminster Abbey, which is not so unnatural since that church became the lumber room of the larger and less successful statuary of the eighteenth century. But he had a magic and minute knowledge of the Westminster omnibuses, and indeed of the whole omnibus system of London, the colors and numbers of which he knew as a herald knows heraldry. He would cry out against a momentary confusion between a light-green Paddington and a dark-green Bayswater vehicle, as his uncle would at the identification of a Greek ikon and a Roman image.

"Do you collect omnibuses like stamps?" asked his uncle. "They must need a rather large album. Or do you keep them in your locker?"

"I keep them in my head," replied the nephew, with legitimate firmness.

"It does you credit, I admit," replied the clergyman. "I suppose it were vain to ask for what purpose you have learned that out of a thousand things. There hardly seems to be a career in it, unless you could be permanently on the pavement to prevent old ladies getting into the wrong bus. Well, we must get out of this one, for this is our place. I want to show you what they call St. Paul's Penny."

"Is it like St. Paul's Cathedral?" asked the youth with resignation, as they alighted.

At the entrance their eyes were arrested by a singular figure evidently hovering there with a similar anxiety to enter. It was that of a dark, thin man in a long black robe rather like a cassock; but the black cap on his head was of too strange a shape to be a biretta. It suggested, rather, some archaic headdress of Persia or Babylon. He had a curious black beard appearing only at the corners of his chin, and his large eyes were oddly set in his face like the flat decorative eyes painted in old Egyptian profiles. Before they had gathered more than a general impression of him, he had dived into the doorway that was their own destination.

Nothing could be seen above ground of the sunken sanctuary except a strong wooden hut, of the sort recently run up for many military and official purposes, the wooden floor of which was indeed a mere platform over the excavated cavity below. A soldier stood as a sentry outside, and a superior soldier, an Anglo-Indian officer of distinction, sat writing at the desk inside. Indeed, the sightseers soon found that this particular sight was surrounded with the most extraordinary precautions. I have compared the silver coin to the Koh-i-noor, and in one sense it was even conventionally comparable, since by a historical accident it was at one time almost counted among the Crown jewels, or at least the Crown relics, until one of the royal princes publicly restored it to the shrine to which it was supposed to belong. Other causes combined to concentrate official vigilance upon it; there had been a scare about spies carrying explosives in small objects, and one of those experimental orders which pass like waves over bureaucracy had decreed first that all visitors should change their clothes for a sort of official sackcloth, and then (when this method caused some murmurs) that they should at least turn out their pockets. Colonel Morris, the officer in charge, was a short, active man with a grim and leathery face, but a lively and humorous eye—a contradiction borne out by his conduct, for he at once derided the safeguards and yet insisted on them.

"I don't care a button myself for Paul's Penny, or such things," he admitted in answer to some antiquarian openings from the clergyman who was slightly acquainted with him, "but I wear the King's coat, you know, and it's a serious thing when the King's uncle leaves a thing here with his own hands under my charge. But as for saints and relics and things, I fear I'm a bit of a Voltairian; what you would call a skeptic."

"I'm not sure it's even skeptical to believe in the royal family and not in the 'Holy' Family," replied Mr. Twyford. "But, of course, I can easily empty my pockets, to show I don't carry a bomb."

The little heap of the parson's possessions which he left on the table consisted chiefly of papers, over and above a pipe and a tobacco pouch and some Roman and Saxon coins. The rest were catalogues of old books, and pamphlets, like one entitled "The Use of Sarum," one glance at which was sufficient both for the colonel and the schoolboy. They could not see the use of Sarum at all. The contents of the boy's pockets naturally made a larger heap, and included marbles, a ball of string, an electric torch, a magnet, a small catapult, and, of course, a large pocketknife, almost to be described as a small tool box, a complex apparatus on which he seemed disposed to linger, pointing out that it included a pair of nippers, a tool for punching holes in wood, and, above all, an instrument for taking stones out of a horse's hoof. The comparative absence of any horse he appeared to regard as irrelevant, as if it were a mere appendage easily supplied. But when the turn came of the gentleman in the black gown, he did not turn out his pockets, but merely spread out his hands.

"I have no possessions," he said.

"I'm afraid I must ask you to empty your pockets and make sure," observed the colonel, gruffly.

"I have no pockets," said the stranger.

Mr. Twyford was looking at the long black gown with a learned eye.

"Are you a monk?" he asked, in a puzzled fashion.

"I am a magus," replied the stranger. "You have heard of the magi, perhaps? I am a magician."

"Oh, I say!" exclaimed Summers Minor, with prominent eyes.

"But I was once a monk," went on the other. "I am what you would call an escaped monk. Yes, I have escaped into eternity. But the monks held one truth at least, that the highest life should be without possessions. I have no pocket money and no pockets, and all the stars are my trinkets."

"They are out of reach, anyhow," observed Colonel Morris, in a tone which suggested that it was well for them. "I've known a good many magicians myself in India—mango plant and all. But the Indian ones are all frauds, I'll swear. In fact, I had a good deal of fun showing them up. More fun than I have over this dreary job, anyhow. But here comes Mr. Symon, who will show you over the old cellar downstairs."

Mr. Symon, the official guardian and guide, was a young man, prematurely gray, with a grave mouth which contrasted curiously with a very small, dark mustache with waxed points, that seemed somehow, separate from it, as if a black fly had settled on his face. He spoke with the accent of Oxford and the permanent official, but in as dead a fashion as the most indifferent hired guide. They descended a dark stone staircase, at the floor of which Symon pressed a button and a door opened on a dark room, or, rather, a room which had an instant before been dark. For almost as the heavy iron door swung open an almost blinding blaze of electric lights filled the whole interior. The fitful enthusiasm of Stinks at once caught fire, and he eagerly asked if the lights and the door worked together.

"Yes, it's all one system," replied Symon. "It was all fitted up for the day His Royal Highness deposited the thing here. You see, it's locked up behind a glass case exactly as he left it."

A glance showed that the arrangements for guarding the treasure were indeed as strong as they were simple. A single pane of glass cut off one corner of the room, in an iron framework let into the rock walls and the wooden roof above; there was now no possibility of reopening the case without elaborate labor, except by breaking the glass, which would probably arouse the night watchman who was always within a few feet of it, even if he had fallen asleep. A close examination would have showed many more ingenious safeguards; but the eye of the Rev. Thomas Twyford, at least, was already riveted on what interested him much more—the dull silver disk which shone in the white light against a plain background of black velvet.

"St. Paul's Penny, said to commemorate the visit of St. Paul to Britain, was probably preserved in this chapel until the eighth century," Symon was saying in his clear but colorless voice. "In the ninth century it is supposed to have been carried away by the barbarians, and it reappears, after the conversion of the northern Goths, in the possession of the royal family of Gothland. His Royal Highness, the Duke of Gothland, retained it always in his own private custody, and when he decided to exhibit it to the public, placed it here with his own hand. It was immediately sealed up in such a manner—"

Unluckily at this point Summers Minor, whose attention had somewhat strayed from the religious wars of the ninth century, caught sight of a short length of wire appearing in a broken patch in the wall. He precipitated himself at it, calling out, "I say, does that connect?"

It was evident that it did connect, for no sooner had the boy given it a twitch than the whole room went black, as if they had all been struck blind, and an instant afterward they heard the dull crash of the closing door.

"Well, you've done it now," said Symon, in his tranquil fashion. Then after a pause he added, "I suppose they'll miss us sooner or later, and no doubt they can get it open; but it may take some little time."

There was a silence, and then the unconquerable Stinks observed:

"Rotten that I had to leave my electric torch."

"I think," said his uncle, with restraint, "that we are sufficiently convinced of your interest in electricity."

Then after a pause he remarked, more amiably: "I suppose if I regretted any of my own impedimenta, it would be the pipe. Though, as a matter of fact, it's not much fun smoking in the dark. Everything seems different in the dark."

"Everything is different in the dark," said a third voice, that of the man who called himself a magician. It was a very musical voice, and rather in contrast with his sinister and swarthy visage, which was now invisible. "Perhaps you don't know how terrible a truth that is. All you see are pictures made by the sun, faces and furniture and flowers and trees. The things themselves may be quite strange to you. Something else may be standing now where you saw a table or a chair. The face of your friend may be quite different in the dark."

A short, indescribable noise broke the stillness. Twyford started for a second, and then said, sharply:

"Really, I don't think it's a suitable occasion for trying to frighten a child."

"Who's a child?" cried the indignant Summers, with a voice that had a crow, but also something of a crack in it. "And who's a funk, either? Not me."

"I will be silent, then," said the other voice out of the darkness.

"But silence also makes and unmakes."

The required silence remained unbroken for a long time until at last the clergyman said to Symon in a low voice:

"I suppose it's all right about air?"

"Oh, yes," replied the other aloud; "there's a fireplace and a chimney in the office just by the door."

A bound and the noise of a falling chair told them that the irrepressible rising generation had once more thrown itself across the room. They heard the ejaculation: "A chimney! Why, I'll be—" and the rest was lost in muffled, but exultant, cries.

The uncle called repeatedly and vainly, groped his way at last to the opening, and, peering up it, caught a glimpse of a disk of daylight, which seemed to suggest that the fugitive had vanished in safety. Making his way back to the group by the glass case, he fell over the fallen chair and took a moment to collect himself again. He had opened his mouth to speak to Symon, when he stopped, and suddenly found himself blinking in the full shock of the white light, and looking over the other man's shoulder, he saw that the door was standing open.

"So they've got at us at last," he observed to Symon.

The man in the black robe was leaning against the wall some yards away, with a smile carved on his face.

"Here comes Colonel Morris," went on Twyford, still speaking to Symon. "One of us will have to tell him how the light went out. Will you?"

But Symon still said nothing. He was standing as still as a statue, and looking steadily at the black velvet behind the glass screen. He was looking at the black velvet because there was nothing else to look at. St. Paul's Penny was gone.

Colonel Morris entered the room with two new visitors; presumably two new sightseers delayed by the accident. The foremost was a tall, fair, rather languid-looking man with a bald brow and a high-bridged nose; his companion was a younger man with light, curly hair and frank, and even innocent, eyes. Symon scarcely seemed to hear the newcomers; it seemed almost as if he had not realized that the return of the light revealed his brooding attitude. Then he started in a guilty fashion, and when he saw the elder of the two strangers, his pale face seemed to turn a shade paler.

"Why it's Horne Fisher!" and then after a pause he said in a low voice, "I'm in the devil of a hole, Fisher."

"There does seem a bit of a mystery to be cleared up," observed the gentleman so addressed.

"It will never be cleared up," said the pale Symon. "If anybody could clear it up, you could. But nobody could."

"I rather think I could," said another voice from outside the group, and they turned in surprise to realize that the man in the black robe had spoken again.

"You!" said the colonel, sharply. "And how do you propose to play the detective?"

"I do not propose to play the detective," answered the other, in a clear voice like a bell. "I propose to play the magician. One of the magicians you show up in India, Colonel."

No one spoke for a moment, and then Horne Fisher surprised everybody by saying, "Well, let's go upstairs, and this gentleman can have a try."

He stopped Symon, who had an automatic finger on the button, saying:

"No, leave all the lights on. It's a sort of safeguard."

"The thing can't be taken away now," said Symon, bitterly.

"It can be put back," replied Fisher.

Twyford had already run upstairs for news of his vanishing nephew, and he received news of him in a way that at once puzzled and reassured him. On the floor above lay one of those large paper darts which boys throw at each other when the schoolmaster is out of the room. It had evidently been thrown in at the window, and on being unfolded displayed a scrawl of bad handwriting which ran: "Dear Uncle; I am all right. Meet you at the hotel later on," and then the signature.

Insensibly comforted by this, the clergyman found his thoughts reverting voluntarily to his favorite relic, which came a good second in his sympathies to his favorite nephew, and before he knew where he was he found himself encircled by the group discussing its loss, and more or less carried away on the current of their excitement. But an undercurrent of query continued to run in his mind, as to what had really happened to the boy, and what was the boy's exact definition of being all right.

Meanwhile Horne Fisher had considerably puzzled everybody with his new tone and attitude. He had talked to the colonel about the military and mechanical arrangements, and displayed a remarkable knowledge both of the details of discipline and the technicalities of electricity. He had talked to the clergyman, and shown an equally surprising knowledge of the religious and historical interests involved in the relic. He had talked to the man who called himself a magician, and not only surprised but scandalized the company by an equally sympathetic familiarity with the most fantastic forms of Oriental occultism and psychic experiment. And in this last and least respectable line of inquiry he was evidently prepared to go farthest; he openly encouraged the magician, and was plainly prepared to follow the wildest ways of investigation in which that magus might lead him.

"How would you begin now?" he inquired, with an anxious politeness that reduced the colonel to a congestion of rage.

"It is all a question of a force; of establishing communications for a force," replied that adept, affably, ignoring some military mutterings about the police force. "It is what you in the West used to call animal magnetism, but it is much more than that. I had better not say how much more. As to setting about it, the usual method is to throw some susceptible person into a trance, which serves as a sort of bridge or cord of communication, by which the force beyond can give him, as it were, an electric shock, and awaken his higher senses. It opens the sleeping eye of the mind."

"I'm suspectible," said Fisher, either with simplicity or with a baffling irony. "Why not open my mind's eye for me? My friend Harold March here will tell you I sometimes see things, even in the dark."

"Nobody sees anything except in the dark," said the magician.

Heavy clouds of sunset were closing round the wooden hut, enormous clouds, of which only the corners could be seen in the little window, like purple horns and tails, almost as if some huge monsters were prowling round the place. But the purple was already deepening to dark gray; it would soon be night.

"Do not light the lamp," said the magus with quiet authority, arresting a movement in that direction. "I told you before that things happen only in the dark."

How such a topsy-turvy scene ever came to be tolerated in the colonel's office, of all places, was afterward a puzzle in the memory of many, including the colonel. They recalled it like a sort of nightmare, like something they could not control. Perhaps there was really a magnetism about the mesmerist; perhaps there was even more magnetism about the man mesmerized. Anyhow, the man was being mesmerized, for Horne Fisher had collapsed into a chair with his long limbs loose and sprawling and his eyes staring at vacancy; and the other man was mesmerizing him, making sweeping movements with his darkly draped arms as if with black wings. The colonel had passed the point of explosion, and he dimly realized that eccentric aristocrats are allowed their fling. He comforted himself with the knowledge that he had already sent for the police, who would break up any such masquerade, and with lighting a cigar, the red end of which, in the gathering darkness, glowed with protest.

"Yes, I see pockets," the man in the trance was saying. "I see many pockets, but they are all empty. No; I see one pocket that is not empty."

There was a faint stir in the stillness, and the magician said, "Can you see what is in the pocket?"

"Yes," answered the other; "there are two bright things. I think they are two bits of steel. One of the pieces of steel is bent or crooked."

"Have they been used in the removal of the relic from downstairs?"

"Yes."

There was another pause and the inquirer added, "Do you see anything of the relic itself?"

"I see something shining on the floor, like the shadow or the ghost of it. It is over there in the corner beyond the desk."

There was a movement of men turning and then a sudden stillness, as of their stiffening, for over in the corner on the wooden floor there was really a round spot of pale light. It was the only spot of light in the room. The cigar had gone out.

"It points the way," came the voice of the oracle. "The spirits are pointing the way to penitence, and urging the thief to restitution. I can see nothing more." His voice trailed off into a silence that lasted solidly for many minutes, like the long silence below when the theft had been committed. Then it was broken by the ring of metal on the floor, and the sound of something spinning and falling like a tossed halfpenny.

"Light the lamp!" cried Fisher in a loud and even jovial voice, leaping to his feet with far less languor than usual. "I must be going now, but I should like to see it before I go. Why, I came on purpose to see it."

The lamp was lit, and he did see it, for St. Paul's Penny was lying on the floor at his feet.

"Oh, as for that," explained Fisher, when he was entertaining March and Twyford at lunch about a month later, "I merely wanted to play with the magician at his own game."

"I thought you meant to catch him in his own trap," said Twyford. "I can't make head or tail of anything yet, but to my mind he was always the suspect. I don't think he was necessarily a thief in the vulgar sense. The police always seem to think that silver is stolen for the sake of silver, but a thing like that might well be stolen out of some religious mania. A runaway monk turned mystic might well want it for some mystical purpose."

"No," replied Fisher, "the runaway monk is not a thief. At any rate he is not the thief. And he's not altogether a liar, either. He said one true thing at least that night."

"And what was that?" inquired March.

"He said it was all magnetism. As a matter of fact, it was done by means of a magnet." Then, seeing they still looked puzzled, he added, "It was that toy magnet belonging to your nephew, Mr. Twyford."

"But I don't understand," objected March. "If it was done with the schoolboy's magnet, I suppose it was done by the schoolboy."

"Well," replied Fisher, reflectively, "it rather depends which schoolboy."

"What on earth do you mean?"

"The soul of a schoolboy is a curious thing," Fisher continued, in a meditative manner. "It can survive a great many things besides climbing out of a chimney. A man can grow gray in great campaigns, and still have the soul of a schoolboy. A man can return with a great reputation from India and be put in charge of a great public treasure, and still have the soul of a schoolboy, waiting to be awakened by an accident. And it is ten times more so when to the schoolboy you add the skeptic, who is generally a sort of stunted schoolboy. You said just now that things might be done by religious mania. Have you ever heard of irreligious mania? I assure you it exists very violently, especially in men who like showing up magicians in India. But here the skeptic had the temptation of showing up a much more tremendous sham nearer home."

A light came into Harold March's eyes as he suddenly saw, as if afar off, the wider implication of the suggestion. But Twyford was still wrestling with one problem at a time.

"Do you really mean," he said, "that Colonel Morris took the relic?"

"He was the only person who could use the magnet," replied Fisher. "In fact, your obliging nephew left him a number of things he could use. He had a ball of string, and an instrument for making a hole in the wooden floor—I made a little play with that hole in the floor in my trance, by the way; with the lights left below, it shone like a new shilling." Twyford suddenly bounded on his chair. "But in that case," he cried, in a new and altered voice, "why then of course— You said a piece of steel—?"

"I said there were two pieces of steel," said Fisher. "The bent piece of steel was the boy's magnet. The other was the relic in the glass case."

"But that is silver," answered the archaeologist, in a voice now almost unrecognizable.

"Oh," replied Fisher, soothingly, "I dare say it was painted with silver a little."

There was a heavy silence, and at last Harold March said, "But where is the real relic?"

"Where it has been for five years," replied Horne Fisher, "in the possession of a mad millionaire named Vandam, in Nebraska. There was a playful little photograph about him in a society paper the other day, mentioning his delusion, and saying he was always being taken in about relics."

Harold March frowned at the tablecloth; then, after an interval, he said: "I think I understand your notion of how the thing was actually done; according to that, Morris just made a hole and fished it up with a magnet at the end of a string. Such a monkey trick looks like mere madness, but I suppose he was mad, partly with the boredom of watching over what he felt was a fraud, though he couldn't prove it. Then came a chance to prove it, to himself at least, and he had what he called 'fun' with it. Yes, I think I see a lot of details now. But it's just the whole thing that knocks me. How did it all come to be like that?"

Fisher was looking at him with level lids and an immovable manner.

"Every precaution was taken," he said. "The Duke carried the relic on his own person, and locked it up in the case with his own hands."

March was silent; but Twyford stammered. "I don't understand you. You give me the creeps. Why don't you speak plainer?"

"If I spoke plainer you would understand me less," said Horne Fisher.

"All the same I should try," said March, still without lifting his head.

"Oh, very well," replied Fisher, with a sigh; "the plain truth is, of course, that it's a bad business. Everybody knows it's a bad business who knows anything about it. But it's always happening, and in one way one can hardly blame them. They get stuck on to a foreign princess that's as stiff as a Dutch doll, and they have their fling. In this case it was a pretty big fling."

The face of the Rev. Thomas Twyford certainly suggested that he was a little out of his depth in the seas of truth, but as the other went on speaking vaguely the old gentleman's features sharpened and set.

"If it were some decent morganatic affair I wouldn't say; but he must have been a fool to throw away thousands on a woman like that. At the end it was sheer blackmail; but it's something that the old ass didn't get it out of the taxpayers. He could only get it out of the Yank, and there you are."

The Rev. Thomas Twyford had risen to his feet.

"Well, I'm glad my nephew had nothing to do with it," he said. "And if that's what the world is like, I hope he will never have anything to do with it."

"I hope not," answered Horne Fisher. "No one knows so well as I do that one can have far too much to do with it."

For Summers Minor had indeed nothing to do with it; and it is part of his higher significance that he has really nothing to do with the story, or with any such stories. The boy went like a bullet through the tangle of this tale of crooked politics and crazy mockery and came out on the other side, pursuing his own unspoiled purposes. From the top of the chimney he climbed he had caught sight of a new omnibus, whose color and name he had never known, as a naturalist might see a new bird or a botanist a new flower. And he had been sufficiently enraptured in rushing after it, and riding away upon that fairy ship.

IV: THE BOTTOMLESS WELL

In an oasis, or green island, in the red and yellow seas of sand that stretch beyond Europe toward the sunrise, there can be found a rather fantastic contrast, which is none the less typical of such a place, since international treaties have made it an outpost of the British occupation. The site is famous among archaeologists for something that is hardly a monument, but merely a hole in the ground. But it is a round shaft, like that of a well, and probably a part of some great irrigation works of remote and disputed date, perhaps more ancient than anything in that ancient land. There is a green fringe of palm and prickly pear round the black mouth of the well; but nothing of the upper masonry remains except two bulky and battered stones standing like the pillars of a gateway of nowhere, in which some of the more transcendental archaeologists, in certain moods at moonrise or sunset, think they can trace the faint lines of figures or features of more than Babylonian monstrosity;

while the more rationalistic archaeologists, in the more rational hours of daylight, see nothing but two shapeless rocks. It may have been noticed, however, that all Englishmen are not archaeologists. Many of those assembled in such a place for official and military purposes have hobbies other than archaeology. And it is a solemn fact that the English in this Eastern exile have contrived to make a small golf links out of the green scrub and sand; with a comfortable clubhouse at one end of it and this primeval monument at the other. They did not actually use this archaic abyss as a bunker, because it was by tradition unfathomable, and even for practical purposes unfathomed. Any sporting projectile sent into it might be counted most literally as a lost ball. But they often sauntered round it in their interludes of talking and smoking cigarettes, and one of them had just come down from the clubhouse to find another gazing somewhat moodily into the well.

Both the Englishmen wore light clothes and white pith helmets and puggrees, but there, for the most part, their resemblance ended. And they both almost simultaneously said the same word, but they said it on two totally different notes of the voice.

"Have you heard the news?" asked the man from the club. "Splendid."

"Splendid," replied the man by the well. But the first man pronounced the word as a young man might say it about a woman, and the second as an old man might say it about the weather, not without sincerity, but certainly without fervor.

And in this the tone of the two men was sufficiently typical of them. The first, who was a certain Captain Boyle, was of a bold and boyish type, dark, and with a sort of native heat in his face that did not belong to the atmosphere of the East, but rather to the ardors and ambitions of the West. The other was an older man and certainly an older resident, a civilian official—Horne Fisher; and his drooping eyelids and drooping light mustache expressed all the paradox of the Englishman in the East. He was much too hot to be anything but cool.

Neither of them thought it necessary to mention what it was that was splendid. That would indeed have been superfluous conversation about something that everybody knew. The striking victory over a menacing combination of Turks and Arabs in the north, won by troops under the command of Lord Hastings, the veteran of so many striking victories, was already spread by the newspapers all over the Empire, let alone to this small garrison so near to the battlefield.

"Now, no other nation in the world could have done a thing like that," cried Captain Boyle, emphatically.

Horne Fisher was still looking silently into the well; a moment later he answered: "We certainly have the art of unmaking mistakes. That's where the poor old Prussians went wrong. They could only make mistakes and stick to them. There is really a certain talent in unmaking a mistake."

"What do you mean," asked Boyle, "what mistakes?"

"Well, everybody knows it looked like biting off more than he could chew," replied Horne Fisher. It was a peculiarity of Mr. Fisher that he always said that everybody knew things which about one person in two million was ever allowed to hear of. "And it was certainly jolly lucky that Travers turned up so well in the nick of time. Odd how often the right thing's been done for us by the second in command, even when a great man was first in command. Like Colborne at Waterloo."

"It ought to add a whole province to the Empire," observed the other.

"Well, I suppose the Zimmernes would have insisted on it as far as the canal," observed Fisher, thoughtfully, "though everybody knows adding provinces doesn't always pay much nowadays."

Captain Boyle frowned in a slightly puzzled fashion. Being cloudily conscious of never having heard of the Zimmernes in his life, he could only remark, stolidly:

"Well, one can't be a Little Englander."

Horne Fisher smiled, and he had a pleasant smile.

"Every man out here is a Little Englander," he said. "He wishes he were back in Little England."

"I don't know what you're talking about, I'm afraid," said the younger man, rather suspiciously. "One would think you didn't really admire Hastings or—or—anything."

"I admire him no end," replied Fisher. "He's by far the best man for this post; he understands the Moslems and can do anything with them. That's why I'm all against pushing Travers against him, merely because of this last affair."

"I really don't understand what you're driving at," said the other, frankly.

"Perhaps it isn't worth understanding," answered Fisher, lightly, "and, anyhow, we needn't talk politics. Do you know the Arab legend about that well?"

"I'm afraid I don't know much about Arab legends," said Boyle, rather stiffly.

"That's rather a mistake," replied Fisher, "especially from your point of view. Lord Hastings himself is an Arab legend. That is perhaps the very greatest thing he really is. If his reputation went it would weaken us all over Asia and Africa. Well, the story about that hole in the ground, that goes down nobody knows where, has always fascinated me, rather. It's Mohammedan in form now, but I shouldn't wonder if the tale is a long way older than Mohammed. It's all about somebody they call the Sultan Aladdin, not our friend of the lamp, of course, but rather like him in having to do with genii or giants or something of that sort. They say he commanded the giants to build him a sort of pagoda, rising higher and higher above all the stars. The Utmost for the Highest, as the people said when they built the Tower of Babel. But the builders of the Tower of Babel were quite modest and domestic people, like mice, compared with old Aladdin. They only wanted a tower that would reach heaven—a mere trifle. He wanted a tower that would pass heaven and rise above it, and go on rising for ever and ever. And Allah cast him down to earth with a thunderbolt, which sank into the earth, boring a hole deeper and deeper, till it made a well that was without a bottom as the tower was to have been without a top. And down that inverted tower of darkness the soul of the proud Sultan is falling forever and ever."

"What a queer chap you are," said Boyle. "You talk as if a fellow could believe those fables."

"Perhaps I believe the moral and not the fable," answered Fisher. "But here comes Lady Hastings. You know her, I think."

The clubhouse on the golf links was used, of course, for many other purposes besides that of golf. It was the only social center of the garrison beside the strictly military headquarters; it had a billiard room and a bar, and even an excellent reference library for those officers who were so perverse as to take their profession seriously. Among these was the great general himself, whose head of silver and face of bronze, like that of a brazen eagle, were often to be found bent over the charts and folios of the library. The great Lord Hastings believed in science and study, as in other severe ideals of life, and had given much paternal advice on the point to young Boyle, whose appearances in that place of research were rather more intermittent. It was from one of these snatches of study that the young man had just come out through the glass doors of the library on to the golf links. But, above all, the club was so appointed as to serve the social conveniences of ladies at least as much as gentlemen, and Lady Hastings was able to play the queen in such a society almost as much as in her own ballroom. She was eminently calculated and, as some said, eminently inclined to play such a part. She was much younger than her husband, an attractive and sometimes dangerously attractive lady; and Mr. Horne Fisher looked after her a little sardonically as she swept away with the young soldier. Then his rather dreary eye strayed to the green and prickly growths round the well, growths of that curious cactus formation in which one thick leaf grows directly out of the other without stalk or twig. It gave his fanciful mind a sinister feeling of a blind growth without shape or purpose. A flower or shrub in the West grows to the blossom which is its crown, and is content. But this was as if hands could grow out of hands or legs grow out of legs in a nightmare. "Always adding a province to the Empire," he said, with a smile, and then added, more sadly, "but I doubt if I was right, after all!"

A strong but genial voice broke in on his meditations and he looked up and smiled, seeing the face of an old friend. The voice was, indeed, rather more genial than the face, which was at the first glance decidedly grim. It was a typically legal face, with angular jaws and heavy, grizzled eyebrows; and it belonged to an eminently legal character, though he was now attached in a semimilitary capacity to the police of that wild district. Cuthbert Grayne was perhaps more of a criminologist than either a lawyer or a policeman, but in his more barbarous surroundings he had proved successful in turning himself into a practical combination of all three. The discovery of a whole series of strange Oriental crimes stood to his credit. But as few people were acquainted with, or attracted to, such a hobby or branch of knowledge, his intellectual life was somewhat solitary. Among the few exceptions was Horne Fisher, who had a curious capacity for talking to almost anybody about almost anything.

"Studying botany, or is it archaeology?" inquired Grayne. "I shall never come to the end of your interests, Fisher. I should say that what you don't know isn't worth knowing."

"You are wrong," replied Fisher, with a very unusual abruptness, and even bitterness. "It's what I do know that isn't worth knowing. All the seamy side of things, all the secret reasons and rotten motives and bribery and blackmail they call politics.

I needn't be so proud of having been down all these sewers that I should brag about it to the little boys in the street."

"What do you mean? What's the matter with you?" asked his friend. "I never knew you taken like this before."

"I'm ashamed of myself," replied Fisher. "I've just been throwing cold water on the enthusiasms of a boy."

"Even that explanation is hardly exhaustive," observed the criminal expert.

"Damned newspaper nonsense the enthusiasms were, of course," continued Fisher, "but I ought to know that at that age illusions can be ideals. And they're better than the reality, anyhow. But there is one very ugly responsibility about jolting a young man out of the rut of the most rotten ideal."

"And what may that be?" inquired his friend.

"It's very apt to set him off with the same energy in a much worse direction," answered Fisher; "a pretty endless sort of direction, a bottomless pit as deep as the bottomless well."

Fisher did not see his friend until a fortnight later, when he found himself in the garden at the back of the clubhouse on the opposite side from the links, a garden heavily colored and scented with sweet semitropical plants in the glow of a desert sunset. Two other men were with him, the third being the now celebrated second in command, familiar to everybody as Tom Travers, a lean, dark man, who looked older than his years, with a furrow in his brow and something morose about the very shape of his black mustache. They had just been served with black coffee by the Arab now officiating as the temporary servant of the club, though he was a figure already familiar, and even famous, as the old servant of the general. He went by the name of Said, and was notable among other Semites for that unnatural length of his yellow face and height of his narrow forehead which is sometimes seen among them, and gave an irrational impression of something sinister, in spite of his agreeable smile.

"I never feel as if I could quite trust that fellow," said Grayne, when the man had gone away. "It's very unjust, I take it, for he was certainly devoted to Hastings, and saved his life, they say. But Arabs are often like that, loyal to one man. I can't help feeling he might cut anybody else's throat, and even do it treacherously."

"Well," said Travers, with a rather sour smile, "so long as he leaves Hastings alone the world won't mind much."

There was a rather embarrassing silence, full of memories of the great battle, and then Horne Fisher said, quietly:

"The newspapers aren't the world, Tom. Don't you worry about them. Everybody in your world knows the truth well enough."

"I think we'd better not talk about the general just now," remarked Grayne, "for he's just coming out of the club."

"He's not coming here," said Fisher. "He's only seeing his wife to the car."

As he spoke, indeed, the lady came out on the steps of the club, followed by her husband, who then went swiftly in front of her to open the garden gate. As he did so she turned back and spoke for a moment to a solitary man still sitting in a cane chair in the shadow of the doorway, the only man left in the deserted club save for the three that lingered in the garden. Fisher peered for a moment into the shadow, and saw that it was Captain Boyle.

The next moment, rather to their surprise, the general reappeared and, remounting the steps, spoke a word or two to Boyle in his turn. Then he signaled to Said, who hurried up with two cups of coffee, and the two men re-entered the club, each carrying his cup in his hand. The next moment a gleam of white light in the growing darkness showed that the electric lamps had been turned on in the library beyond.

"Coffee and scientific researches," said Travers, grimly. "All the luxuries of learning and theoretical research. Well, I must be going, for I have my work to do as well." And he got up rather stiffly, saluted his companions, and strode away into the dusk.

"I only hope Boyle is sticking to scientific researches," said Horne Fisher. "I'm not very comfortable about him myself. But let's talk about something else."

They talked about something else longer than they probably imagined, until the tropical night had come and a splendid moon painted the whole scene with silver; but before it was bright enough to see by Fisher had already noted that the lights in the library had been abruptly extinguished. He waited for the two men to come out by the garden entrance, but nobody came.

"They must have gone for a stroll on the links," he said.

"Very possibly," replied Grayne. "It's going to be a beautiful night."

A moment or two after he had spoken they heard a voice hailing them out of the shadow of the clubhouse, and were astonished to perceive Travers hurrying toward them, calling out as he came:

"I shall want your help, you fellows," he cried. "There's something pretty bad out on the links."

They found themselves plunging through the club smoking room and the library beyond, in complete darkness, mental as well as material. But Horne Fisher, in spite of his affectation of indifference, was a person of a curious and almost transcendental sensibility to atmospheres, and he already felt the presence of something more than an accident. He collided with a piece of furniture in the library, and almost shuddered with the shock, for the thing moved as he could never have fancied a piece of furniture moving. It seemed to move like a living thing, yielding and yet striking back. The next moment Grayne had turned on the lights, and he saw he had only stumbled against one of the revolving bookstands that had swung round and struck him; but his involuntary recoil had revealed to him his own subconscious sense of something mysterious and monstrous. There were several of these revolving bookcases standing here and there about the library; on one of them stood the two cups of coffee, and on another a large open book. It was Budge's book on Egyptian hieroglyphics, with colored plates of strange birds and gods, and even as he rushed past, he was conscious of something odd about the fact that this, and not any work of military science, should be open in that place at that moment. He was even conscious of the gap in the well-lined bookshelf from which it had been taken, and it seemed almost to gape at him in an ugly fashion, like a gap in the teeth of some sinister face.

A run brought them in a few minutes to the other side of the ground in front of the bottomless well, and a few yards from it, in a moonlight almost as broad as daylight, they saw what they had come to see.

The great Lord Hastings lay prone on his face, in a posture in which there was a touch of something strange and stiff, with one elbow erect above his body, the arm being doubled, and his big, bony hand clutching the rank and ragged grass. A few feet away was Boyle, almost as motionless, but supported on his hands and knees, and staring at the body. It might have been no more than shock and accident; but there was something ungainly and unnatural about the quadrupedal posture and the gaping face. It was as if his reason had fled from him. Behind, there was nothing but the clear blue southern sky, and the beginning of the desert, except for the two great broken stones in front of the well. And it was in such a light and atmosphere that men could fancy they traced in them enormous and evil faces, looking down.

Horne Fisher stooped and touched the strong hand that was still clutching the grass, and it was as cold as a stone. He knelt by the body and was busy for a moment applying other tests; then he rose again, and said, with a sort of confident despair:

"Lord Hastings is dead."

There was a stony silence, and then Travers remarked, gruffly: "This is your department, Grayne; I will leave you to question Captain Boyle. I can make no sense of what he says."

Boyle had pulled himself together and risen to his feet, but his face still wore an awful expression, making it like a new mask or the face of another man.

"I was looking at the well," he said, "and when I turned he had fallen down."

Grayne's face was very dark. "As you say, this is my affair," he said. "I must first ask you to help me carry him to the library and let me examine things thoroughly."

When they had deposited the body in the library, Grayne turned to Fisher and said, in a voice that had recovered its fullness and confidence, "I am going to lock myself in and make a thorough examination first. I look to you to keep in touch with the others and make a preliminary examination of Boyle. I will talk to him later. And just telephone to headquarters for a policeman, and let him come here at once and stand by till I want him."

Without more words the great criminal investigator went into the lighted library, shutting the door behind him, and Fisher, without replying, turned and began to talk quietly to Travers. "It is curious," he said, "that the thing should happen just in front of that place."

"It would certainly be very curious," replied Travers, "if the place played any part in it."

"I think," replied Fisher, "that the part it didn't play is more curious still."

And with these apparently meaningless words he turned to the shaken Boyle and, taking his arm, began to walk him up and down in the moonlight, talking in low tones.

Dawn had begun to break abrupt and white when Cuthbert Grayne turned out the lights in the library and came out on to the links. Fisher was lounging about alone, in his listless fashion; but the police messenger for whom he had sent was standing at attention in the background.

"I sent Boyle off with Travers," observed Fisher, carelessly; "he'll look after him, and he'd better have some sleep, anyhow."

"Did you get anything out of him?" asked Grayne. "Did he tell you what he and Hastings were doing?"

"Yes," answered Fisher, "he gave me a pretty clear account, after all. He said that after Lady Hastings went off in the car the general asked him to take coffee with him in the library and look up a point about local antiquities. He himself was beginning to look for Budge's book in one of the revolving bookstands when the general found it in one of the bookshelves on the wall. After looking at some of the plates they went out, it would seem, rather abruptly, on to the links, and walked toward the old well; and while Boyle was looking into it he heard a thud behind him, and turned round to find the general lying as we found him. He himself dropped on his knees to examine the body, and then was paralyzed with a sort of terror and could not come nearer to it or touch it. But I think very little of that; people caught in a real shock of surprise are sometimes found in the queerest postures."

Grayne wore a grim smile of attention, and said, after a short silence:

"Well, he hasn't told you many lies. It's really a creditably clear and consistent account of what happened, with everything of importance left out."

"Have you discovered anything in there?" asked Fisher.

"I have discovered everything," answered Grayne.

Fisher maintained a somewhat gloomy silence, as the other resumed his explanation in quiet and assured tones.

"You were quite right, Fisher, when you said that young fellow was in danger of going down dark ways toward the pit. Whether or no, as you fancied, the jolt you gave to his view of the general had anything to do with it, he has not been treating the general well for some time. It's an unpleasant business, and I don't want to dwell on it; but it's pretty plain that his wife was not treating him well, either. I don't know how far it went, but it went as far as concealment, anyhow; for when Lady Hastings spoke to Boyle it was to tell him she had hidden a note in the Budge book in the library. The general overheard, or came somehow to know, and he went straight to the book and found it. He confronted Boyle with it, and they had a scene, of course. And Boyle was confronted with something else; he was confronted with an awful alternative, in which the life of one old man meant ruin and his death meant triumph and even happiness."

"Well," observed Fisher, at last, "I don't blame him for not telling you the woman's part of the story. But how do you know about the letter?"

"I found it on the general's body," answered Grayne, "but I found worse things than that. The body had stiffened in the way rather peculiar to poisons of a certain Asiatic sort. Then I examined the coffee cups, and I knew enough chemistry to find poison in the dregs of one of them. Now, the General went straight to the bookcase, leaving his cup of coffee on the bookstand in the middle of the room. While his back was turned, and Boyle was pretending to examine the bookstand, he was left alone with the coffee cup. The poison takes about ten minutes to act, and ten minutes' walk would bring them to the bottomless well."

"Yes," remarked Fisher, "and what about the bottomless well?"

"What has the bottomless well got to do with it?" asked his friend.

"It has nothing to do with it," replied Fisher. "That is what I find utterly confounding and incredible."

"And why should that particular hole in the ground have anything to do with it?"

"It is a particular hole in your case," said Fisher. "But I won't insist on that just now. By the way, there is another thing I ought to tell you. I said I sent Boyle away in charge of Travers. It would be just as true to say I sent Travers in charge of Boyle."

"You don't mean to say you suspect Tom Travers?" cried the other.

"He was a deal bitterer against the general than Boyle ever was," observed Horne Fisher, with a curious indifference.

"Man, you're not saying what you mean," cried Grayne. "I tell you I found the poison in one of the coffee cups."

"There was always Said, of course," added Fisher, "either for hatred or hire. We agreed he was capable of almost anything."

"And we agreed he was incapable of hurting his master," retorted Grayne.

"Well, well," said Fisher, amiably, "I dare say you are right; but I should just like to have a look at the library and the coffee cups."

He passed inside, while Grayne turned to the policeman in attendance and handed him a scribbled note, to be telegraphed from headquarters. The man saluted and hurried off; and Grayne, following his friend into the library, found him beside the bookstand in the middle of the room, on which were the empty cups.

"This is where Boyle looked for Budge, or pretended to look for him, according to your account," he said.

As Fisher spoke he bent down in a half-crouching attitude, to look at the volumes in the low, revolving shelf, for the whole bookstand was not much higher than an ordinary table. The next moment he sprang up as if he had been stung.

"Oh, my God!" he cried.

Very few people, if any, had ever seen Mr. Horne Fisher behave as he behaved just then. He flashed a glance at the door, saw that the open window was nearer, went out of it with a flying leap, as if over a hurdle, and went racing across the turf, in the track of the disappearing policeman. Grayne, who stood staring after him, soon saw his tall, loose figure, returning, restored to all its normal limpness and air of leisure. He was fanning himself slowly with a piece of paper, the telegram he had so violently intercepted.

"Lucky I stopped that," he observed. "We must keep this affair as quiet as death. Hastings must die of apoplexy or heart disease."

"What on earth is the trouble?" demanded the other investigator.

"The trouble is," said Fisher, "that in a few days we should have had a very agreeable alternative—of hanging an innocent man or knocking the British Empire to hell."

"Do you mean to say," asked Grayne, "that this infernal crime is not to be punished?"

Fisher looked at him steadily.

"It is already punished," he said.

After a moment's pause he went on. "You reconstructed the crime with admirable skill, old chap, and nearly all you said was true. Two men with two coffee cups did go into the library and did put their cups on the bookstand and did go together to the well, and one of them was a murderer and had put poison in the other's cup. But it was not done while Boyle was looking at the revolving bookcase. He did look at it, though, searching for the Budge book with the note in it, but I fancy that Hastings had already moved it to the shelves on the wall. It was part of that grim game that he should find it first.

"Now, how does a man search a revolving bookcase? He does not generally hop all round it in a squatting attitude, like a frog. He simply gives it a touch and makes it revolve."

He was frowning at the floor as he spoke, and there was a light under his heavy lids that was not often seen there. The mysticism that was buried deep under all the cynicism of his experience was awake and moving in the depths. His voice took unexpected turns and inflections, almost as if two men were speaking.

"That was what Boyle did; he barely touched the thing, and it went round as easily as the world goes round. Yes, very much as the world goes round, for the hand that turned it was not his. God, who turns the wheel of all the stars, touched that wheel and brought it full circle, that His dreadful justice might return."

"I am beginning," said Grayne, slowly, "to have some hazy and horrible idea of what you mean."

"It is very simple," said Fisher, "when Boyle straightened himself from his stooping posture, something had happened which he had not noticed, which his enemy had not noticed, which nobody had noticed. The two coffee cups had exactly changed places."

The rocky face of Grayne seemed to have sustained a shock in silence; not a line of it altered, but his voice when it came was unexpectedly weakened.

"I see what you mean," he said, "and, as you say, the less said about it the better. It was not the lover who tried to get rid of the husband, but—the other thing. And a tale like that about a man like that would ruin us here. Had you any guess of this at the start?"

"The bottomless well, as I told you," answered Fisher, quietly; "that was what stumped me from the start. Not because it had anything to do with it, because it had nothing to do with it."

He paused a moment, as if choosing an approach, and then went on: "When a man knows his enemy will be dead in ten minutes, and takes him to the edge of an unfathomable pit, he means to throw his body into it. What else should he do? A born fool would have the sense to do it, and Boyle is not a born fool. Well, why did not Boyle do it? The more I thought of it the more I suspected there was some mistake in the murder, so to speak. Somebody had taken somebody there to throw him in, and yet he was not thrown in. I had already an ugly, unformed idea of some substitution or reversal of parts; then I stooped to turn the bookstand myself, by accident, and I instantly knew everything, for I saw the two cups revolve once more, like moons in the sky."

After a pause, Cuthbert Grayne said, "And what are we to say to the newspapers?"

"My friend, Harold March, is coming along from Cairo to-day," said Fisher. "He is a very brilliant and successful journalist. But for all that he's a thoroughly honorable man, so you must not tell him the truth."

Half an hour later Fisher was again walking to and fro in front of the clubhouse, with Captain Boyle, the latter by this time with a very buffeted and bewildered air; perhaps a sadder and a wiser man.

"What about me, then?" he was saying. "Am I cleared? Am I not going to be cleared?"

"I believe and hope," answered Fisher, "that you are not going to be suspected. But you are certainly not going to be cleared. There must be no suspicion against him, and therefore no suspicion against you. Any suspicion against him, let alone such a story against him, would knock us endways from Malta to Mandalay. He was a hero as well as a holy terror among the Moslems. Indeed, you might almost call him a Moslem hero in the English service. Of course he got on with them partly because of his own little dose of Eastern blood; he got it from his mother, the dancer from Damascus; everybody knows that."

"Oh," repeated Boyle, mechanically, staring at him with round eyes, "everybody knows that."

"I dare say there was a touch of it in his jealousy and ferocious vengeance," went on Fisher. "But, for all that, the crime would ruin us among the Arabs, all the more because it was something like a crime against hospitality. It's been hateful for you and it's pretty horrid for me. But there are some things that damned well can't be done, and while I'm alive that's one of them."

"What do you mean?" asked Boyle, glancing at him curiously. "Why should you, of all people, be so passionate about it?"

Horne Fisher looked at the young man with a baffling expression.

"I suppose," he said, "it's because I'm a Little Englander."

"I can never make out what you mean by that sort of thing," answered Boyle, doubtfully.

"Do you think England is so little as all that?" said Fisher, with a warmth in his cold voice, "that it can't hold a man across a few thousand miles. You lectured me with a lot of ideal patriotism, my young friend; but it's practical patriotism now for you and me, and with no lies to help it. You talked as if everything always went right with us all over the world, in a triumphant crescendo culminating in Hastings. I tell you everything has gone wrong with us here, except Hastings. He was the one name we had left to conjure with, and that mustn't go as well, no, by God! It's bad enough that a gang of infernal Jews should plant us here, where there's no earthly English interest to serve, and all hell beating up against us, simply because Nosey Zimmern has lent money to half the Cabinet. It's bad enough that an old pawnbroker from Bagdad should make us fight his battles; we can't fight with our right hand cut off. Our one score was Hastings and his victory, which was really somebody else's victory. Tom Travers has to suffer, and so have you."

Then, after a moment's silence, he pointed toward the bottomless well and said, in a quieter tone:

"I told you that I didn't believe in the philosophy of the Tower of Aladdin. I don't believe in the Empire growing until it reaches the sky; I don't believe in the Union Jack going up and up eternally like the Tower. But if you think I am going to let the Union Jack go down and down eternally, like the bottomless well, down into the blackness of the bottomless pit, down in defeat and derision, amid the jeers of the very Jews who have sucked us dry—no I won't, and that's flat; not if the Chancellor were blackmailed by twenty millionaires with their gutter rags, not if the Prime Minister married twenty Yankee Jewesses, not if Woodville and Carstairs had shares in twenty swindling mines. If the thing is really tottering, God help it, it mustn't be we who tip it over."

Boyle was regarding him with a bewilderment that was almost fear, and had even a touch of distaste.

"Somehow," he said, "there seems to be something rather horrid about the things you know."

"There is," replied Horne Fisher. "I am not at all pleased with my small stock of knowledge and reflection. But as it is partly responsible for your not being hanged, I don't know that you need complain of it."

And, as if a little ashamed of his first boast, he turned and strolled away toward the bottomless well.

V: THE FAD OF THE FISHERMAN

A thing can sometimes be too extraordinary to be remembered. If it is clean out of the course of things, and has apparently no causes and no consequences, subsequent events do not recall it, and it remains only a subconscious thing, to be stirred by some accident long after. It drifts apart like a forgotten dream; and it was in the hour of many dreams, at daybreak and very soon after the end of dark, that such a strange sight was given to a man sculling a boat down a river in the West country. The man was awake; indeed, he considered himself rather wide awake, being the political journalist, Harold March, on his way to interview various political celebrities in their country seats. But the thing he saw was so inconsequent that it might have been imaginary. It simply slipped past his mind and was lost in later and utterly different events; nor did he even recover the memory till he had long afterward discovered the meaning.

Pale mists of morning lay on the fields and the rushes along one margin of the river; along the other side ran a wall of tawny brick almost overhanging the water. He had shipped his oars and was drifting for a moment with the stream, when he turned his head and saw that the monotony of the long brick wall was broken by a bridge; rather an elegant eighteenth-century sort of bridge with little columns of white stone turning gray. There had been floods and the river still stood very high, with dwarfish trees waist deep in it, and rather a narrow arc of white dawn gleamed under the curve of the bridge.

As his own boat went under the dark archway he saw another boat coming toward him, rowed by a man as solitary as himself. His posture prevented much being seen of him, but as he neared the bridge he stood up in the boat and turned round. He was already so close to the dark entry, however, that his whole figure was black against the morning light, and March could see nothing of his face except the end of two long whiskers or mustaches that gave something sinister to the silhouette, like horns in the wrong place. Even these details March would never have noticed but for what happened in the same instant. As the man came under the low bridge he made a leap at it and hung, with his legs dangling, letting the boat float away from under him. March had a momentary vision of two black kicking legs; then of one black kicking leg; and then of nothing except the eddying stream and the long perspective of the wall. But whenever he thought of it again, long afterward, when he understood the story in which it figured, it was always fixed in that one fantastic shape—as if those wild legs were a grotesque graven ornament of the bridge itself, in the manner of a gargoyle. At the moment he merely passed, staring, down the stream. He could see no flying figure on the bridge, so it must have already fled; but he was half conscious of some faint significance in the fact that among the trees round the bridgehead opposite the wall he saw a lamp-post; and, beside the lamp-post, the broad blue back of an unconscious policeman.

Even before reaching the shrine of his political pilgrimage he had many other things to think of besides the odd incident of the bridge; for the management of a boat by a solitary man was not always easy even on such a solitary stream. And indeed it was only by an unforeseen accident that he was solitary. The boat had been purchased and the whole expedition planned in conjunction with a friend, who had at the last moment been forced to alter all his arrangements. Harold March was to have traveled with his friend Horne Fisher on that inland voyage to Willowood Place, where the Prime Minister was a guest at the moment. More and more people were hearing of Harold March, for his striking political articles were opening to him the doors of larger and larger salons; but he had never met the Prime Minister yet. Scarcely anybody among the general public had ever heard of Horne Fisher; but he had known the Prime Minister all his life. For these reasons, had the two taken the projected journey together, March might have been slightly disposed to hasten it and Fisher vaguely content to lengthen it out. For Fisher was one of those people who are born knowing the Prime Minister. The knowledge seemed to have no very exhilarant effect, and in his case bore some resemblance to being born tired. But he was distinctly annoyed to receive, just as he was doing a little light packing of fishing tackle and cigars for the journey, a telegram from Willowood asking him to come down at once by train, as the Prime Minister had to leave that night. Fisher knew that his friend the journalist could not possibly start till the next day, and he liked his friend the journalist, and had looked forward to a few days on the river. He did not particularly like or dislike the Prime Minister, but he intensely disliked the alternative of a few hours in the train. Nevertheless, he accepted Prime Ministers as he accepted railway trains—as part of a system which he, at least, was not the revolutionist sent on earth to destroy. So he telephoned to March, asking him, with many apologetic curses and faint damns, to take the boat down the river as arranged, that they might meet at Willowood by the time settled; then he went outside and hailed a taxicab to take him to the railway station. There he paused at the bookstall to add to his light luggage a number of cheap murder stories, which he read with great pleasure, and without any premonition that he was about to walk into as strange a story in real life.

A little before sunset he arrived, with his light suitcase in hand, before the gate of the long riverside gardens of Willowood Place, one of the smaller seats of Sir Isaac Hook, the master of much shipping and many newspapers. He entered by the gate giving on the road, at the opposite side to the river, but there was a mixed quality in all that watery landscape which perpetually reminded a traveler that the river was near. White gleams of water would shine suddenly like swords or spears in the green thickets. And even in the garden itself, divided into courts and curtained with hedges and high garden trees, there hung everywhere in the air the music of water. The first of the green courts which he entered appeared to be a somewhat neglected croquet lawn, in which was a solitary young man playing croquet against himself. Yet he was not an enthusiast for the game, or even for the garden; and his sallow but well-featured face looked rather sullen than otherwise. He was only one of those young men who cannot support the burden of consciousness unless they are doing something, and whose conceptions of doing something are limited to a game of some kind. He was dark and well dressed in a light holiday fashion, and Fisher recognized him at once as a young man named James Bullen, called, for some unknown reason, Bunker. He was the nephew of Sir Isaac; but, what was much more important at the moment, he was also the private secretary of the Prime Minister.

"Hullo, Bunker!" observed Horne Fisher. "You're the sort of man I wanted to see. Has your chief come down yet?"

"He's only staying for dinner," replied Bullen, with his eye on the yellow ball. "He's got a great speech to-morrow at Birmingham and he's going straight through to-night. He's motoring himself there; driving the car, I mean. It's the one thing he's really proud of."

"You mean you're staying here with your uncle, like a good boy?" replied Fisher. "But what will the Chief do at Birmingham without the epigrams whispered to him by his brilliant secretary?"

"Don't you start ragging me," said the young man called Bunker. "I'm only too glad not to go trailing after him. He doesn't know a thing about maps or money or hotels or anything, and I have to dance about like a courier. As for my uncle, as I'm supposed to come into the estate, it's only decent to be here sometimes."

"Very proper," replied the other. "Well, I shall see you later on," and, crossing the lawn, he passed out through a gap in the hedge.

He was walking across the lawn toward the landing stage on the river, and still felt all around him, under the dome of golden evening, an Old World savor and reverberation in that riverhaunted garden. The next square of turf which he crossed seemed at first sight quite deserted, till he saw in the twilight of trees in one corner of it a hammock and in the hammock a man, reading a newspaper and swinging one leg over the edge of the net.

Him also he hailed by name, and the man slipped to the ground and strolled forward. It seemed fated that he should feel something of the past in the accidents of that place, for the figure might well have been an early-Victorian ghost revisiting the ghosts of the croquet hoops and mallets. It was the figure of an elderly man with long whiskers that looked almost fantastic, and a quaint and careful cut of collar and cravat. Having been a fashionable dandy forty years ago, he had managed to pre-serve the dandyism while ignoring the fashions. A white top-hat lay beside the Morning Post in the hammock behind him. This was the Duke of Westmoreland, the relic of a family really some centuries old; and the antiquity was not heraldry but history. Nobody knew better than Fisher how rare such noblemen are in fact, and how numerous in fiction. But whether the duke owed the general respect he enjoyed to the genuineness of his pedigree or to the fact that he owned a vast amount of very valuable property was a point about which Mr. Fisher's opinion might have been more interesting to discover.

"You were looking so comfortable," said Fisher, "that I thought you must be one of the servants. I'm looking for somebody to take this bag of mine; I haven't brought a man down, as I came away in a hurry."

"Nor have I, for that matter," replied the duke, with some pride. "I never do. If there's one animal alive I loathe it's a valet. I learned to dress myself at an early age and was supposed to do it decently. I may be in my second childhood, but I've not go so far as being dressed like a child."

"The Prime Minister hasn't brought a valet; he's brought a secretary instead," observed Fisher. "Devilish inferior job. Didn't I hear that Harker was down here?"

"He's over there on the landing stage," replied the duke, indifferently, and re-sumed the study of the Morning Post.

Fisher made his way beyond the last green wall of the garden on to a sort of towing path looking on the river and a wooden island opposite. There, indeed, he saw a lean, dark figure with a stoop almost like that of a vulture, a posture well known in the law courts as that of Sir John Harker, the Attorney-General. His face was lined with headwork, for alone among the three idlers in the garden he was a man who had made his own way; and round his bald brow and hollow temples clung dull red hair, quite flat, like plates of copper.

"I haven't seen my host yet," said Horne Fisher, in a slightly more serious tone than he had used to the others, "but I suppose I shall meet him at dinner."

"You can see him now; but you can't meet him," answered Harker.

He nodded his head toward one end of the island opposite, and, looking steadi-ly in the same direction, the other guest could see the dome of a bald head and the top of a fishing rod, both equally motionless, rising out of the tall undergrowth against the background of the stream beyond. The fisherman seemed to be seated against the stump of a tree and facing toward the other bank, so that his face could not be seen, but the shape of his head was unmistakable.

"He doesn't like to be disturbed when he's fishing," continued Harker. "It's a sort of fad of his to eat nothing but fish, and he's very proud of catching his own. Of course he's all for simplicity, like so many of these millionaires. He likes to come in saying he's worked for his daily bread like a laborer."

"Does he explain how he blows all the glass and stuffs all the upholstery," asked Fisher, "and makes all the silver forks, and grows all the grapes and peaches, and designs all the patterns on the carpets? I've always heard he was a busy man."

"I don't think he mentioned it," answered the lawyer. "What is the meaning of this social satire?"

"Well, I am a trifle tired," said Fisher, "of the Simple Life and the Strenuous Life as lived by our little set. We're all really dependent in nearly everything, and we all make a fuss about being independent in something. The Prime Minister prides himself on doing without a chauffeur, but he can't do without a factotum and Jack-of-all-trades; and poor old Bunker has to play the part of a universal genius, which God knows he was never meant for. The duke prides himself on doing without a valet, but, for all that, he must give a lot of people an infernal lot of trouble to collect such extraordinary old clothes as he wears. He must have them looked up in the British Museum or excavated out of the tombs. That white hat alone must require a sort of expedition fitted out to find it, like the North Pole. And here we have old Hook pretending to produce his own fish when he couldn't produce his own fish knives or fish forks to eat it with. He may be simple about simple things like food, but you bet he's luxurious about luxurious things, especially little things. I don't include you; you've worked too hard to enjoy playing at work."

"I sometimes think," said Harker, "that you conceal a horrid secret of being useful sometimes. Haven't you come down here to see Number One before he goes on to Birmingham?"

Horne Fisher answered, in a lower voice: "Yes; and I hope to be lucky enough to catch him before dinner. He's got to see Sir Isaac about something just afterward."

"Hullo!" exclaimed Harker. "Sir Isaac's finished his fishing. I know he prides himself on getting up at sunrise and going in at sunset."

The old man on the island had indeed risen to his feet, facing round and showing a bush of gray beard with rather small, sunken features, but fierce eyebrows and keen, choleric eyes. Carefully carrying his fishing tackle, he was already making his way back to the mainland across a bridge of flat stepping-stones a little way down the shallow stream; then he veered round, coming toward his guests and civilly saluting them. There were several fish in his basket and he was in a good temper.

"Yes," he said, acknowledging Fisher's polite expression of surprise, "I get up before anybody else in the house, I think. The early bird catches the worm."

"Unfortunately," said Harker, "it is the early fish that catches the worm."

"But the early man catches the fish," replied the old man, gruffly.

"But from what I hear, Sir Isaac, you are the late man, too," interposed Fisher. "You must do with very little sleep."

"I never had much time for sleeping," answered Hook, "and I shall have to be the late man to-night, anyhow. The Prime Minister wants to have a talk, he tells me, and, all things considered, I think we'd better be dressing for dinner."

Dinner passed off that evening without a word of politics and little enough but ceremonial trifles. The Prime Minister, Lord Merivale, who was a long, slim man with curly gray hair, was gravely complimentary to his host about his success as a fisherman and the skill and patience he displayed; the conversation flowed like the shallow stream through the stepping-stones.

"It wants patience to wait for them, no doubt," said Sir Isaac, "and skill to play them, but I'm generally pretty lucky at it."

"Does a big fish ever break the line and get away?" inquired the politician, with respectful interest.

"Not the sort of line I use," answered Hook, with satisfaction. "I rather specialize in tackle, as a matter of fact. If he were strong enough to do that, he'd be strong enough to pull me into the river."

"A great loss to the community," said the Prime Minister, bowing.

Fisher had listened to all these futilities with inward impatience, waiting for his own opportunity, and when the host rose he sprang to his feet with an alertness he rarely showed. He managed to catch Lord Merivale before Sir Isaac bore him off for the final interview. He had only a few words to say, but he wanted to get them said.

He said, in a low voice as he opened the door for the Premier, "I have seen Montmirail; he says that unless we protest immediately on behalf of Denmark, Sweden will certainly seize the ports."

Lord Merivale nodded. "I'm just going to hear what Hook has to say about it," he said.

"I imagine," said Fisher, with a faint smile, "that there is very little doubt what he will say about it."

Merivale did not answer, but lounged gracefully toward the library, whither his host had already preceded him. The rest drifted toward the billiard room, Fisher merely remarking to the lawyer: "They won't be long. We know they're practically in agreement."

"Hook entirely supports the Prime Minister," assented Harker.

"Or the Prime Minister entirely supports Hook," said Horne Fisher, and began idly to knock the balls about on the billiard table.

Horne Fisher came down next morning in a late and leisurely fashion, as was his reprehensible habit; he had evidently no appetite for catching worms. But the other guests seemed to have felt a similar indifference, and they helped themselves to breakfast from the sideboard at intervals during the hours verging upon lunch. So that it was not many hours later when the first sensation of that strange day came upon them. It came in the form of a young man with light hair and a candid expression, who came sculling down the river and disembarked at the landing stage. It was, in fact, no other than Mr. Harold March, whose journey had begun far away up the river in the earliest hours of that day. He arrived late in the afternoon, having stopped for tea in a large riverside town, and he had a pink evening paper sticking out of his pocket. He fell on the riverside garden like a quiet and well-behaved thunderbolt, but he was a thunderbolt without knowing it.

The first exchange of salutations and introductions was commonplace enough, and consisted, indeed, of the inevitable repetition of excuses for the eccentric seclusion of the host. He had gone fishing again, of course, and must not be disturbed till the appointed hour, though he sat within a stone's throw of where they stood.

"You see it's his only hobby," observed Harker, apologetically, "and, after all, it's his own house; and he's very hospitable in other ways."

"I'm rather afraid," said Fisher, in a lower voice, "that it's becoming more of a mania than a hobby. I know how it is when a man of that age begins to collect things, if it's only collecting those rotten little river fish. You remember Talbot's uncle with his toothpicks, and poor old Buzzy and the waste of cigar ashes. Hook has done a lot of big things in his time—the great deal in the Swedish timber trade and the Peace Conference at Chicago—but I doubt whether he cares now for any of those big things as he cares for those little fish."

"Oh, come, come," protested the Attorney-General. "You'll make Mr. March think he has come to call on a lunatic. Believe me, Hook only does it for fun, like any other sport, only he's of the kind that takes his fun sadly. But I bet if there were big news about timber or shipping, he would drop his fun and his fish all right."

"Well, I wonder," said Horne Fisher, looking sleepily at the island in the river.

"By the way, is there any news of anything?" asked Harker of Harold March. "I see you've got an evening paper; one of those enterprising evening papers that come out in the morning."

"The beginning of Lord Merivale's Birmingham speech," replied March, handing him the paper. "It's only a paragraph, but it seems to me rather good."

Harker took the paper, flapped and refolded it, and looked at the "Stop Press" news. It was, as March had said, only a paragraph. But it was a paragraph that had a peculiar effect on Sir John Harker. His lowering brows lifted with a flicker and his eyes blinked, and for a moment his leathery jaw was loosened. He looked in some odd fashion like a very old man. Then, hardening his voice and handing the paper to Fisher without a tremor, he simply said:

"Well, here's a chance for the bet. You've got your big news to disturb the old man's fishing."

Horne Fisher was looking at the paper, and over his more languid and less expressive features a change also seemed to pass. Even that little paragraph had two or three large headlines, and his eye encountered, "Sensational Warning to Sweden," and, "We Shall Protest."

"What the devil—" he said, and his words softened first to a whisper and then a whistle.

"We must tell old Hook at once, or he'll never forgive us," said Harker. "He'll probably want to see Number One instantly, though it may be too late now. I'm going across to him at once. I bet I'll make him forget his fish, anyhow." And, turning his back, he made his way hurriedly along the riverside to the causeway of flat stones.

March was staring at Fisher, in amazement at the effect his pink paper had produced.

"What does it all mean?" he cried. "I always supposed we should protest in defense of the Danish ports, for their sakes and our own. What is all this botheration about Sir Isaac and the rest of you? Do you think it bad news?"

"Bad news!" repeated Fisher, with a sort of soft emphasis beyond expression.

"Is it as bad as all that?" asked his friend, at last.

"As bad as all that?" repeated Fisher. "Why of course it's as good as it can be. It's great news. It's glorious news! That's where the devil of it comes in, to knock us all silly. It's admirable. It's inestimable. It is also quite incredible."

He gazed again at the gray and green colors of the island and the river, and his rather dreary eye traveled slowly round to the hedges and the lawns.

"I felt this garden was a sort of dream," he said, "and I suppose I must be dreaming. But there is grass growing and water moving; and something impossible has happened."

Even as he spoke the dark figure with a stoop like a vulture appeared in the gap of the hedge just above him.

"You have won your bet," said Harker, in a harsh and almost croaking voice. "The old fool cares for nothing but fishing. He cursed me and told me he would talk no politics."

"I thought it might be so," said Fisher, modestly. "What are you going to do next?"

"I shall use the old idiot's telephone, anyhow," replied the lawyer. "I must find out exactly what has happened. I've got to speak for the Government myself tomorrow." And he hurried away toward the house.

In the silence that followed, a very bewildering silence so far as March was concerned, they saw the quaint figure of the Duke of Westmoreland, with his white hat and whiskers, approaching them across the garden. Fisher instantly stepped toward him with the pink paper in his hand, and, with a few words, pointed out the apocalyptic paragraph. The duke, who had been walking slowly, stood quite still, and for some seconds he looked like a tailor's dummy standing and staring outside some antiquated shop. Then March heard his voice, and it was high and almost hysterical:

"But he must see it; he must be made to understand. It cannot have been put to him properly." Then, with a certain recovery of fullness and even pomposity in the voice, "I shall go and tell him myself."

Among the queer incidents of that afternoon, March always remembered something almost comical about the clear picture of the old gentleman in his wonderful white hat carefully stepping from stone to stone across the river, like a figure crossing the traffic in Piccadilly. Then he disappeared behind the trees of the island, and March and Fisher turned to meet the Attorney-General, who was coming out of the house with a visage of grim assurance.

"Everybody is saying," he said, "that the Prime Minister has made the greatest speech of his life. Peroration and loud and prolonged cheers. Corrupt financiers and heroic peasants. We will not desert Denmark again."

Fisher nodded and turned away toward the towing path, where he saw the duke returning with a rather dazed expression. In answer to questions he said, in a husky and confidential voice:

"I really think our poor friend cannot be himself. He refused to listen; he—ah—suggested that I might frighten the fish."

A keen ear might have detected a murmur from Mr. Fisher on the subject of a white hat, but Sir John Harker struck it more decisively:

"Fisher was quite right. I didn't believe it myself, but it's quite clear that the old fellow is fixed on this fishing notion by now. If the house caught fire behind him he would hardly move till sunset."

Fisher had continued his stroll toward the higher embanked ground of the towing path, and he now swept a long and searching gaze, not toward the island, but toward the distant wooded heights that were the walls of the valley. An evening sky as clear as that of the previous day was settling down all over the dim landscape, but toward the west it was now red rather than gold; there was scarcely any sound but the monotonous music of the river. Then came the sound of a half-stifled exclamation from Horne Fisher, and Harold March looked up at him in wonder.

"You spoke of bad news," said Fisher. "Well, there is really bad news now. I am afraid this is a bad business."

"What bad news do you mean?" asked his friend, conscious of something strange and sinister in his voice.

"The sun has set," answered Fisher.

He went on with the air of one conscious of having said something fatal. "We must get somebody to go across whom he will really listen to. He may be mad, but there's method in his madness. There nearly always is method in madness. It's what drives men mad, being methodical. And he never goes on sitting there after sunset, with the whole place getting dark. Where's his nephew? I believe he's really fond of his nephew."

"Look!" cried March, abruptly. "Why, he's been across already. There he is coming back."

And, looking up the river once more, they saw, dark against the sunset reflections, the figure of James Bullen stepping hastily and rather clumsily from stone to stone. Once he slipped on a stone with a slight splash. When he rejoined the group on the bank his olive face was unnaturally pale.

The other four men had already gathered on the same spot and almost simultaneously were calling out to him, "What does he say now?"

"Nothing. He says—nothing."

Fisher looked at the young man steadily for a moment; then he started from his immobility and, making a motion to March to follow him, himself strode down to the river crossing. In a few moments they were on the little beaten track that ran round the wooded island, to the other side of it where the fisherman sat. Then they stood and looked at him, without a word.

Sir Isaac Hook was still sitting propped up against the stump of the tree, and that for the best of reasons. A length of his own infallible fishing line was twisted and tightened twice round his throat and then twice round the wooden prop behind him. The leading investigator ran forward and touched the fisherman's hand, and it was as cold as a fish.

"The sun has set," said Horne Fisher, in the same terrible tones, "and he will never see it rise again."

Ten minutes afterward the five men, shaken by such a shock, were again together in the garden, looking at one another with white but watchful faces. The lawyer seemed the most alert of the group; he was articulate if somewhat abrupt.

"We must leave the body as it is and telephone for the police," he said. "I think my own authority will stretch to examining the servants and the poor fellow's papers, to see if there is anything that concerns them. Of course, none of you gentlemen must leave this place."

Perhaps there was something in his rapid and rigorous legality that suggested the closing of a net or trap. Anyhow, young Bullen suddenly broke down, or perhaps blew up, for his voice was like an explosion in the silent garden.

"I never touched him," he cried. "I swear I had nothing to do with it!"

"Who said you had?" demanded Harker, with a hard eye. "Why do you cry out before you're hurt?"

"Because you all look at me like that," cried the young man, angrily. "Do you think I don't know you're always talking about my damned debts and expectations?"

Rather to March's surprise, Fisher had drawn away from this first collision, leading the duke with him to another part of the garden. When he was out of earshot of the others he said, with a curious simplicity of manner:

"Westmoreland, I am going straight to the point."

"Well?" said the other, staring at him stolidly.

"You have a motive for killing him," said Fisher.

The duke continued to stare, but he seemed unable to speak.

"I hope you had a motive for killing him," continued Fisher, mildly. "You see, it's rather a curious situation. If you have a motive for murdering, you probably didn't murder. But if you hadn't any motive, why, then perhaps, you did."

"What on earth are you talking about?" demanded the duke, violently.

"It's quite simple," said Fisher. "When you went across he was either alive or dead. If he was alive, it might be you who killed him, or why should you have held your tongue about his death? But if he was dead, and you had a reason for killing him, you might have held your tongue for fear of being accused." Then after a silence he added, abstractedly: "Cyprus is a beautiful place, I believe. Romantic scenery and romantic people. Very intoxicating for a young man."

The duke suddenly clenched his hands and said, thickly, "Well, I had a motive."

"Then you're all right," said Fisher, holding out his hand with an air of huge relief. "I was pretty sure you wouldn't really do it; you had a fright when you saw it done, as was only natural. Like a bad dream come true, wasn't it?"

While this curious conversation was passing, Harker had gone into the house, disregarding the demonstrations of the sulky nephew, and came back presently with a new air of animation and a sheaf of papers in his hand.

"I've telephoned for the police," he said, stopping to speak to Fisher, "but I think I've done most of their work for them. I believe I've found out the truth. There's a paper here—" He stopped, for Fisher was looking at him with a singular expression; and it was Fisher who spoke next:

"Are there any papers that are not there, I wonder? I mean that are not there now?" After a pause he added: "Let us have the cards on the table. When you went through his papers in such a hurry, Harker, weren't you looking for something to— to make sure it shouldn't be found?"

Harker did not turn a red hair on his hard head, but he looked at the other out of the corners of his eyes.

"And I suppose," went on Fisher, smoothly, "that is why you, too, told us lies about having found Hook alive. You knew there was something to show that you might have killed him, and you didn't dare tell us he was killed. But, believe me, it's much better to be honest now."

Harker's haggard face suddenly lit up as if with infernal flames.

"Honest," he cried, "it's not so damned fine of you fellows to be honest. You're all born with silver spoons in your mouths, and then you swagger about with ever-lasting virtue because you haven't got other people's spoons in your pockets. But I was born in a Pimlico lodging house and I had to make my spoon, and there'd be plenty to say I only spoiled a horn or an honest man. And if a struggling man stag-gers a bit over the line in his youth, in the lower parts of the law which are pretty dingy, anyhow, there's always some old vampire to hang on to him all his life for it."

"Guatemalan Golcondas, wasn't it?" said Fisher, sympathetically.

Harker suddenly shuddered. Then he said, "I believe you must know every-thing, like God Almighty."

"I know too much," said Horne Fisher, "and all the wrong things."

The other three men were drawing nearer to them, but before they came too near, Harker said, in a voice that had recovered all its firmness:

"Yes, I did destroy a paper, but I really did find a paper, too; and I believe that it clears us all."

"Very well," said Fisher, in a louder and more cheerful tone; "let us all have the benefit of it."

"On the very top of Sir Isaac's papers," explained Harker, "there was a threat-ening letter from a man named Hugo. It threatens to kill our unfortunate friend very much in the way that he was actually killed. It is a wild letter, full of taunts; you can see it for yourselves; but it makes a particular point of poor Hook's habit of fishing from the island. Above all, the man professes to be writing from a boat. And, since we alone went across to him," and he smiled in a rather ugly fashion, "the crime must have been committed by a man passing in a boat."

"Why, dear me!" cried the duke, with something almost amounting to anima-tion. "Why, I remember the man called Hugo quite well! He was a sort of body servant and bodyguard of Sir Isaac. You see, Sir Isaac was in some fear of assault. He was—he was not very popular with several people. Hugo was discharged after some row or other; but I remember him well. He was a great big Hungarian fellow with great mustaches that stood out on each side of his face."

A door opened in the darkness of Harold March's memory, or, rather, oblivion, and showed a shining landscape, like that of a lost dream. It was rather a waterscape than a landscape, a thing of flooded meadows and low trees and the dark archway of a bridge. And for one instant he saw again the man with mustaches like dark horns leap up on to the bridge and disappear.

"Good heavens!" he cried. "Why, I met the murderer this morning!"

Horne Fisher and Harold March had their day on the river, after all, for the little group broke up when the police arrived. They declared that the coincidence of March's evidence had cleared the whole company, and clinched the case against the flying Hugo. Whether that Hungarian fugitive would ever be caught appeared to Horne Fisher to be highly doubtful; nor can it be pretended that he displayed any very demoniac detective energy in the matter as he leaned back in the boat cushions, smoking, and watching the swaying reeds slide past.

"It was a very good notion to hop up on to the bridge," he said. "An empty boat means very little; he hasn't been seen to land on either bank, and he's walked off the bridge without walking on to it, so to speak. He's got twenty-four hours' start; his mustaches will disappear, and then he will disappear. I think there is every hope of his escape."

"Hope?" repeated March, and stopped sculling for an instant.

"Yes, hope," repeated the other. "To begin with, I'm not going to be exactly consumed with Corsican revenge because somebody has killed Hook. Perhaps you may guess by this time what Hook was. A damned blood-sucking blackmailer was that simple, strenuous, self-made captain of industry. He had secrets against nearly everybody; one against poor old Westmoreland about an early marriage in Cyprus that might have put the duchess in a queer position; and one against Harker about some flutter with his client's money when he was a young solicitor. That's why they went to pieces when they found him murdered, of course. They felt as if they'd done it in a dream. But I admit I have another reason for not wanting our Hungarian friend actually hanged for the murder."

"And what is that?" asked his friend.

"Only that he didn't commit the murder," answered Fisher.

Harold March laid down the oars and let the boat drift for a moment.

"Do you know, I was half expecting something like that," he said. "It was quite irrational, but it was hanging about in the atmosphere, like thunder in the air."

"On the contrary, it's finding Hugo guilty that's irrational," replied Fisher. "Don't you see that they're condemning him for the very reason for which they acquit everybody else? Harker and Westmoreland were silent because they found him murdered, and knew there were papers that made them look like the murderers. Well, so did Hugo find him murdered, and so did Hugo know there was a paper that would make him look like the murderer. He had written it himself the day before."

"But in that case," said March, frowning, "at what sort of unearthly hour in the morning was the murder really committed? It was barely daylight when I met him at the bridge, and that's some way above the island."

"The answer is very simple," replied Fisher. "The crime was not committed in the morning. The crime was not committed on the island."

March stared at the shining water without replying, but Fisher resumed like one who had been asked a question:

"Every intelligent murder involves taking advantage of some one uncommon feature in a common situation. The feature here was the fancy of old Hook for being the first man up every morning, his fixed routine as an angler, and his annoyance at being disturbed. The murderer strangled him in his own house after dinner on the night before, carried his corpse, with all his fishing tackle, across the stream in the dead of night, tied him to the tree, and left him there under the stars. It was a dead man who sat fishing there all day. Then the murderer went back to the house, or, rather, to the garage, and went off in his motor car. The murderer drove his own motor car."

Fisher glanced at his friend's face and went on. "You look horrified, and the thing is horrible. But other things are horrible, too. If some obscure man had been hag-ridden by a blackmailer and had his family life ruined, you wouldn't think the murder of his persecutor the most inexcusable of murders. Is it any worse when a whole great nation is set free as well as a family? By this warning to Sweden we shall probably prevent war and not precipitate it, and save many thousand lives rather more valuable than the life of that viper. Oh, I'm not talking sophistry or seriously justifying the thing, but the slavery that held him and his country was a thousand times less justifiable. If I'd really been sharp I should have guessed it from his smooth, deadly smiling at dinner that night. Do you remember that silly talk about how old Isaac could always play his fish? In a pretty hellish sense he was a fisher of men."

Harold March took the oars and began to row again.

"I remember," he said, "and about how a big fish might break the line and get away."

VI: THE HOLE IN THE WALL

Two men, the one an architect and the other an archaeologist, met on the steps of the great house at Prior's Park; and their host, Lord Bulmer, in his breezy way, thought it natural to introduce them. It must be confessed that he was hazy as well as breezy, and had no very clear connection in his mind, beyond the sense that an architect and an archaeologist begin with the same series of letters. The world must remain in a reverent doubt as to whether he would, on the same principles, have presented a diplomatist to a dipsomaniac or a ratiocinator to a rat catcher. He was a big, fair, bull-necked young man, abounding in outward gestures, unconsciously flapping his gloves and flourishing his stick.

"You two ought to have something to talk about," he said, cheerfully. "Old buildings and all that sort of thing; this is rather an old building, by the way, though I say it who shouldn't. I must ask you to excuse me a moment; I've got to go and see about the cards for this Christmas romp my sister's arranging. We hope to see you all there, of course. Juliet wants it to be a fancy-dress affair—abbots and crusaders and all that. My ancestors, I suppose, after all."

"I trust the abbot was not an ancestor," said the archaeological gentleman, with a smile.

"Only a sort of great-uncle, I imagine," answered the other, laughing; then his rather rambling eye rolled round the ordered landscape in front of the house; an artificial sheet of water ornamented with an antiquated nymph in the center and surrounded by a park of tall trees now gray and black and frosty, for it was in the depth of a severe winter.

"It's getting jolly cold," his lordship continued. "My sister hopes we shall have some skating as well as dancing."

"If the crusaders come in full armor," said the other, "you must be careful not to drown your ancestors."

"Oh, there's no fear of that," answered Bulmer; "this precious lake of ours is not two feet deep anywhere." And with one of his flourishing gestures he stuck his stick into the water to demonstrate its shallowness. They could see the short end bent in the water, so that he seemed for a moment to lean his large weight on a breaking staff.

"The worst you can expect is to see an abbot sit down rather suddenly," he added, turning away. "Well, au revoir; I'll let you know about it later."

The archaeologist and the architect were left on the great stone steps smiling at each other; but whatever their common interests, they presented a considerable personal contrast, and the fanciful might even have found some contradiction in each considered individually. The former, a Mr. James Haddow, came from a drowsy den in the Inns of Court, full of leather and parchment, for the law was his profession and history only his hobby; he was indeed, among other things, the solicitor and agent of the Prior's Park estate. But he himself was far from drowsy and seemed remarkably wide awake, with shrewd and prominent blue eyes, and red hair brushed as neatly as his very neat costume. The latter, whose name was Leonard Crane, came straight from a crude and almost cockney office of builders and house agents in the neighboring suburb, sunning itself at the end of a new row of jerry-built houses with plans in very bright colors and notices in very large letters. But a serious observer, at a second glance, might have seen in his eyes something of that shining sleep that is called vision; and his yellow hair, while not affectedly long, was unaffectedly untidy. It was a manifest if melancholy truth that the architect was an artist. But the artistic temperament was far from explaining him; there was something else about him that was not definable, but which some even felt to be dangerous. Despite his dreaminess, he would sometimes surprise his friends with arts and even sports apart from his ordinary life, like memories of some previous existence. On this occasion, nevertheless, he hastened to disclaim any authority on the other man's hobby.

428

"I mustn't appear on false pretences," he said, with a smile. "I hardly even know what an archaeologist is, except that a rather rusty remnant of Greek suggests that he is a man who studies old things."

"Yes," replied Haddow, grimly. "An archaeologist is a man who studies old things and finds they are new."

Crane looked at him steadily for a moment and then smiled again.

"Dare one suggest," he said, "that some of the things we have been talking about are among the old things that turn out not to be old?"

His companion also was silent for a moment, and the smile on his rugged face was fainter as he replied, quietly:

"The wall round the park is really old. The one gate in it is Gothic, and I cannot find any trace of destruction or restoration. But the house and the estate generally—well the romantic ideas read into these things are often rather recent romances, things almost like fashionable novels. For instance, the very name of this place, Prior's Park, makes everybody think of it as a moonlit mediaeval abbey; I dare say the spiritualists by this time have discovered the ghost of a monk there. But, according to the only authoritative study of the matter I can find, the place was simply called Prior's as any rural place is called Podger's. It was the house of a Mr. Prior, a farmhouse, probably, that stood here at some time or other and was a local landmark. Oh, there are a great many examples of the same thing, here and everywhere else. This suburb of ours used to be a village, and because some of the people slurred the name and pronounced it Holliwell, many a minor poet indulged in fancies about a Holy Well, with spells and fairies and all the rest of it, filling the suburban drawing-rooms with the Celtic twilight. Whereas anyone acquainted with the facts knows that 'Hollinwall' simply means 'the hole in the wall,' and probably referred to some quite trivial accident. That's what I mean when I say that we don't so much find old things as we find new ones."

Crane seemed to have grown somewhat inattentive to the little lecture on antiquities and novelties, and the cause of his restlessness was soon apparent, and indeed approaching. Lord Bulmer's sister, Juliet Bray, was coming slowly across the lawn, accompanied by one gentleman and followed by two others. The young architect was in the illogical condition of mind in which he preferred three to one.

The man walking with the lady was no other than the eminent Prince Borodino, who was at least as famous as a distinguished diplomatist ought to be, in the interests of what is called secret diplomacy. He had been paying a round of visits at various English country houses, and exactly what he was doing for diplomacy at Prior's Park was as much a secret as any diplomatist could desire. The obvious thing to say of his appearance was that he would have been extremely handsome if he had not been entirely bald. But, indeed, that would itself be a rather bald way of putting it. Fantastic as it sounds, it would fit the case better to say that people would have been surprised to see hair growing on him; as surprised as if they had found hair growing on the bust of a Roman emperor. His tall figure was buttoned up in a tight-waisted fashion that rather accentuated his potential bulk, and he wore a red flower in his buttonhole. Of the two men walking behind one was also bald, but in a more partial and also a more premature fashion, for his drooping mustache was still yellow, and if his eyes were somewhat heavy it was with languor and not with age. It was Horne Fisher, and he was talking as easily and idly about everything as he always did. His companion was a more striking, and even more sinister, figure, and he had the added importance of being Lord Bulmer's oldest and most intimate friend. He was generally known with a severe simplicity as Mr. Brain; but it was understood that he had been a judge and police official in India, and that he had enemies, who had represented his measures against crime as themselves almost criminal. He was a brown skeleton of a man with dark, deep, sunken eyes and a black mustache that hid the meaning of his mouth. Though he had the look of one wasted by some tropical disease, his movements were much more alert than those of his lounging companion.

"It's all settled," announced the lady, with great animation, when they came within hailing distance. "You've all got to put on masquerade things and very likely skates as well, though the prince says they don't go with it; but we don't care about that. It's freezing already, and we don't often get such a chance in England."

"Even in India we don't exactly skate all the year round," observed Mr. Brain.

"And even Italy is not primarily associated with ice," said the Italian.

"Italy is primarily associated with ices," remarked Mr. Horne Fisher. "I mean with ice cream men. Most people in this country imagine that Italy is entirely populated with ice cream men and organ grinders. There certainly are a lot of them; perhaps they're an invading army in disguise."

"How do you know they are not the secret emissaries of our diplomacy?" asked the prince, with a slightly scornful smile. "An army of organ grinders might pick up hints, and their monkeys might pick up all sort of things."

"The organs are organized in fact," said the flippant Mr. Fisher.

"Well, I've known it pretty cold before now in Italy and even in India, up on the Himalayan slopes. The ice on our own little round pond will be quite cozy by comparison."

Juliet Bray was an attractive lady with dark hair and eyebrows and dancing eyes, and there was a geniality and even generosity in her rather imperious ways. In most matters she could command her brother, though that nobleman, like many other men of vague ideas, was not without a touch of the bully when he was at bay. She could certainly command her guests, even to the extent of decking out the most respectable and reluctant of them with her mediaeval masquerade. And it really seemed as if she could command the elements also, like a witch. For the weather steadily hardened and sharpened; that night the ice of the lake, glimmering in the moonlight, was like a marble floor, and they had begun to dance and skate on it before it was dark.

Prior's Park, or, more properly, the surrounding district of Holinwall, was a country seat that had become a suburb; having once had only a dependent village at its doors, it now found outside all its doors the signals of the expansion of London. Mr. Haddow, who was engaged in historical researches both in the library and the locality, could find little assistance in the latter. He had already realized, from the documents, that Prior's Park had originally been something like Prior's Farm, named after some local figure, but the new social conditions were all against his tracing the story by its traditions. Had any of the real rustics remained, he would probably have found some lingering legend of Mr. Prior, however remote he might be. But the new nomadic population of clerks and artisans, constantly shifting their homes from one suburb to another, or their children from one school to another, could have no corporate continuity. They had all that forgetfulness of history that goes everywhere with the extension of education.

Nevertheless, when he came out of the library next morning and saw the wintry trees standing round the frozen pond like a black forest, he felt he might well have been far in the depths of the country. The old wall running round the park kept that inclosure itself still entirely rural and romantic, and one could easily imagine that the depths of that dark forest faded away indefinitely into distant vales and hills. The gray and black and silver of the wintry wood were all the more severe or somber as a contrast to the colored carnival groups that already stood on and around the frozen pool. For the house party had already flung themselves impatiently into fancy dress, and the lawyer, with his neat black suit and red hair, was the only modern figure among them.

"Aren't you going to dress up?" asked Juliet, indignantly shaking at him a horned and towering blue headdress of the fourteenth century which framed her face very becomingly, fantastic as it was. "Everybody here has to be in the Middle Ages. Even Mr. Brain has put on a sort of brown dressing gown and says he's a monk; and Mr. Fisher got hold of some old potato sacks in the kitchen and sewed them together; he's supposed to be a monk, too. As to the prince, he's perfectly glorious, in great crimson robes as a cardinal. He looks as if he could poison everybody. You simply must be something."

"I will be something later in the day," he replied. "At present I am nothing but an antiquary and an attorney. I have to see your brother presently, about some legal business and also some local investigations he asked me to make. I must look a little like a steward when I give an account of my stewardship."

"Oh, but my brother has dressed up!" cried the girl. "Very much so. No end, if I may say so. Why he's bearing down on you now in all his glory."

The noble lord was indeed marching toward them in a magnificent sixteenth-century costume of purple and gold, with a gold-hilted sword and a plumed cap, and manners to match. Indeed, there was something more than his usual expansiveness of bodily action in his appearance at that moment. It almost seemed, so to speak, that the plumes on his hat had gone to his head. He flapped his great, gold-lined cloak like the wings of a fairy king in a pantomime; he even drew his sword with a flourish and waved it about as he did his walking stick. In the light of after events there seemed to be something monstrous and ominous about that exuberance, something of the spirit that is called fey. At the time it merely crossed a few people's minds that he might possibly be drunk.

As he strode toward his sister the first figure he passed was that of Leonard Crane, clad in Lincoln green, with the horn and baldrick and sword appropriate to Robin Hood; for he was standing nearest to the lady, where, indeed, he might have been found during a disproportionate part of the time. He had displayed one of his buried talents in the matter of skating, and now that the skating was over seemed disposed to prolong the partnership. The boisterous Bulmer playfully made a pass at him with his drawn sword, going forward with the lunge in the proper fencing fashion, and making a somewhat too familiar Shakespearean quotation about a rodent and a Venetian coin.

Probably in Crane also there was a subdued excitement just then; anyhow, in one flash he had drawn his own sword and parried; and then suddenly, to the surprise of everyone, Bulmer's weapon seemed to spring out of his hand into the air and rolled away on the ringing ice.

"Well, I never!" said the lady, as if with justifiable indignation. "You never told me you could fence, too."

Bulmer put up his sword with an air rather bewildered than annoyed, which increased the impression of something irresponsible in his mood at the moment; then he turned rather abruptly to his lawyer, saying:

"We can settle up about the estate after dinner; I've missed nearly all the skating as it is, and I doubt if the ice will hold till to-morrow night. I think I shall get up early and have a spin by myself."

"You won't be disturbed with my company," said Horne Fisher, in his weary fashion. "If I have to begin the day with ice, in the American fashion, I prefer it in smaller quantities. But no early hours for me in December. The early bird catches the cold."

"Oh, I shan't die of catching a cold," answered Bulmer, and laughed.

A considerable group of the skating party had consisted of the guests staying at the house, and the rest had tailed off in twos and threes some time before most of the guests began to retire for the night. Neighbors, always invited to Prior's Park on such occasions, went back to their own houses in motors or on foot; the legal and archeological gentleman had returned to the Inns of Court by a late train, to get a paper called for during his consultation with his client; and most of the other guests were drifting and lingering at various stages on their way up to bed. Horne Fisher, as if to deprive himself of any excuse for his refusal of early rising, had been the first to retire to his room; but, sleepy as he looked, he could not sleep. He had picked up from a table the book of antiquarian topography, in which Haddow had found his first hints about the origin of the local name, and, being a man with a quiet and quaint capacity for being interested in anything, he began to read it steadily, making notes now and then of details on which his previous reading left him with a certain doubt about his present conclusions. His room was the one nearest to the lake in the center of the woods, and was therefore the quietest, and none of the last echoes of the evening's festivity could reach him. He had followed carefully the argument which established the derivation from Mr. Prior's farm and the hole in the wall, and disposed of any fashionable fancy about monks and magic wells, when he began to be conscious of a noise audible in the frozen silence of the night. It was not a particularly loud noise, but it seemed to consist of a series of thuds or heavy blows, such as might be struck on a wooden door by a man seeking to enter. They were followed by something like a faint creak or crack, as if the obstacle had either been opened or had given way. He opened his own bedroom door and listened, but as he heard talk and laughter all over the lower floors, he had no reason to fear that a summons would be neglected or the house left without protection. He went to his open window, looking out over the frozen pond and the moonlit statue in the middle of their circle of darkling woods, and listened again. But silence had returned to that silent place, and, after straining his ears for a considerable time, he could hear nothing but the solitary hoot of a distant departing train. Then he reminded himself how many nameless noises can be heard by the wakeful during the most ordinary night, and shrugging his shoulders, went wearily to bed.

He awoke suddenly and sat up in bed with his ears filled, as with thunder, with the throbbing echoes of a rending cry. He remained rigid for a moment, and then sprang out of bed, throwing on the loose gown of sacking he had worn all day. He went first to the window, which was open, but covered with a thick curtain, so that his room was still completely dark; but when he tossed the curtain aside and put his head out, he saw that a gray and silver daybreak had already appeared behind the black woods that surrounded the little lake, and that was all that he did see. Though the sound had certainly come in through the open window from this direction, the whole scene was still and empty under the morning light as under the moonlight. Then the long, rather lackadaisical hand he had laid on a window sill gripped it tighter, as if to master a tremor, and his peering blue eyes grew bleak with fear. It may seem that his emotion was exaggerated and needless, considering the effort of common sense by which he had conquered his nervousness about the noise on the previous night. But that had been a very different sort of noise. It might have been made by half a hundred things, from the chopping of wood to the breaking of bottles. There was only one thing in nature from which could come the sound that echoed through the dark house at daybreak. It was the awful articulate voice of man; and it was something worse, for he knew what man.

He knew also that it had been a shout for help. It seemed to him that he had heard the very word; but the word, short as it was, had been swallowed up, as if the man had been stifled or snatched away even as he spoke. Only the mocking reverberations of it remained even in his memory, but he had no doubt of the original voice. He had no doubt that the great bull's voice of Francis Bray, Baron Bulmer, had been heard for the last time between the darkness and the lifting dawn.

How long he stood there he never knew, but he was startled into life by the first living thing that he saw stirring in that half-frozen landscape. Along the path beside the lake, and immediately under his window, a figure was walking slowly and softly, but with great composure—a stately figure in robes of a splendid scarlet; it was the Italian prince, still in his cardinal's costume. Most of the company had indeed lived in their costumes for the last day or two, and Fisher himself had assumed his frock of sacking as a convenient dressing gown; but there seemed, nevertheless, something unusually finished and formal, in the way of an early bird, about this magnificent red cockatoo. It was as if the early bird had been up all night.

"What is the matter?" he called, sharply, leaning out of the window, and the Italian turned up his great yellow face like a mask of brass.

"We had better discuss it downstairs," said Prince Borodino.

Fisher ran downstairs, and encountered the great, red-robed figure entering the doorway and blocking the entrance with his bulk.

"Did you hear that cry?" demanded Fisher.

"I heard a noise and I came out," answered the diplomatist, and his face was too dark in the shadow for its expression to be read.

"It was Bulmer's voice," insisted Fisher. "I'll swear it was Bulmer's voice."

"Did you know him well?" asked the other.

The question seemed irrelevant, though it was not illogical, and Fisher could only answer in a random fashion that he knew Lord Bulmer only slightly.

"Nobody seems to have known him well," continued the Italian, in level tones. "Nobody except that man Brain. Brain is rather older than Bulmer, but I fancy they shared a good many secrets."

Fisher moved abruptly, as if waking from a momentary trance, and said, in a new and more vigorous voice, "But look here, hadn't we better get outside and see if anything has happened."

"The ice seems to be thawing," said the other, almost with indifference.

When they emerged from the house, dark stains and stars in the gray field of ice did indeed indicate that the frost was breaking up, as their host had prophesied the day before, and the very memory of yesterday brought back the mystery of today.

"He knew there would be a thaw," observed the prince. "He went out skating quite early on purpose. Did he call out because he landed in the water, do you think?"

Fisher looked puzzled. "Bulmer was the last man to bellow like that because he got his boots wet. And that's all he could do here; the water would hardly come up to the calf of a man of his size. You can see the flat weeds on the floor of the lake, as if it were through a thin pane of glass. No, if Bulmer had only broken the ice he wouldn't have said much at the moment, though possibly a good deal afterward. We should have found him stamping and damning up and down this path, and calling for clean boots."

"Let us hope we shall find him as happily employed," remarked the diplomatist. "In that case the voice must have come out of the wood."

"I'll swear it didn't come out of the house," said Fisher; and the two disappeared together into the twilight of wintry trees.

The plantation stood dark against the fiery colors of sunrise, a black fringe having that feathery appearance which makes trees when they are bare the very reverse of rugged. Hours and hours afterward, when the same dense, but delicate, margin was dark against the greenish colors opposite the sunset, the search thus begun at sunrise had not come to an end. By successive stages, and to slowly gathering groups of the company, it became apparent that the most extraordinary of all gaps had appeared in the party; the guests could find no trace of their host anywhere. The servants reported that his bed had been slept in and his skates and his fancy costume were gone, as if he had risen early for the purpose he had himself avowed. But from the top of the house to the bottom, from the walls round the park to the pond in the center, there was no trace of Lord Bulmer, dead or alive. Horne Fisher realized that a chilling premonition had already prevented him from expecting to find the man alive. But his bald brow was wrinkled over an entirely new and unnatural problem, in not finding the man at all.

He considered the possibility of Bulmer having gone off of his own accord, for some reason; but after fully weighing it he finally dismissed it. It was inconsistent with the unmistakable voice heard at daybreak, and with many other practical obstacles. There was only one gateway in the ancient and lofty wall round the small park; the lodge keeper kept it locked till late in the morning, and the lodge keeper had seen no one pass. Fisher was fairly sure that he had before him a mathematical problem in an inclosed space. His instinct had been from the first so attuned to the tragedy that it would have been almost a relief to him to find the corpse. He would have been grieved, but not horrified, to come on the nobleman's body dangling from one of his own trees as from a gibbet, or floating in his own pool like a pallid weed. What horrified him was to find nothing.

He soon become conscious that he was not alone even in his most individual and isolated experiments. He often found a figure following him like his shadow, in silent and almost secret clearings in the plantation or outlying nooks and corners of the old wall. The dark-mustached mouth was as mute as the deep eyes were mobile, darting incessantly hither and thither, but it was clear that Brain of the Indian police had taken up the trail like an old hunter after a tiger. Seeing that he was the only personal friend of the vanished man, this seemed natural enough, and Fisher resolved to deal frankly with him.

"This silence is rather a social strain," he said. "May I break the ice by talking about the weather?—which, by the way, has already broken the ice. I know that breaking the ice might be a rather melancholy metaphor in this case."

"I don't think so," replied Brain, shortly. "I don't fancy the ice had much to do with it. I don't see how it could."

"What would you propose doing?" asked Fisher.

"Well, we've sent for the authorities, of course, but I hope to find something out before they come," replied the Anglo-Indian. "I can't say I have much hope from police methods in this country. Too much red tape, habeas corpus and that sort of thing. What we want is to see that nobody bolts; the nearest we could get to it would be to collect the company and count them, so to speak. Nobody's left lately, except that lawyer who was poking about for antiquities."

"Oh, he's out of it; he left last night," answered the other. "Eight hours after Bulmer's chauffeur saw his lawyer off by the train I heard Bulmer's own voice as plain as I hear yours now."

"I suppose you don't believe in spirits?" said the man from India. After a pause he added: "There's somebody else I should like to find, before we go after a fellow with an alibi in the Inner Temple. What's become of that fellow in green—the architect dressed up as a forester? I haven't seem him about."

Mr. Brain managed to secure his assembly of all the distracted company before the arrival of the police. But when he first began to comment once more on the young architect's delay in putting in an appearance, he found himself in the presence of a minor mystery, and a psychological development of an entirely unexpected kind.

Juliet Bray had confronted the catastrophe of her brother's disappearance with a somber stoicism in which there was, perhaps, more paralysis than pain; but when the other question came to the surface she was both agitated and angry.

"We don't want to jump to any conclusions about anybody," Brain was saying in his staccato style. "But we should like to know a little more about Mr. Crane. Nobody seems to know much about him, or where he comes from. And it seems a sort of coincidence that yesterday he actually crossed swords with poor Bulmer, and could have stuck him, too, since he showed himself the better swordsman. Of course, that may be an accident and couldn't possibly be called a case against anybody; but then we haven't the means to make a real case against anybody. Till the police come we are only a pack of very amateur sleuthhounds."

"And I think you're a pack of snobs," said Juliet. "Because Mr. Crane is a genius who's made his own way, you try to suggest he's a murderer without daring to say so. Because he wore a toy sword and happened to know how to use it, you want us to believe he used it like a bloodthirsty maniac for no reason in the world. And because he could have hit my brother and didn't, you deduce that he did. That's the sort of way you argue. And as for his having disappeared, you're wrong in that as you are in everything else, for here he comes."

And, indeed, the green figure of the fictitious Robin Hood slowly detached itself from the gray background of the trees, and came toward them as she spoke.

He approached the group slowly, but with composure; but he was decidedly pale, and the eyes of Brain and Fisher had already taken in one detail of the green-clad figure more clearly than all the rest. The horn still swung from his baldrick, but the sword was gone.

Rather to the surprise of the company, Brain did not follow up the question thus suggested; but, while retaining an air of leading the inquiry, had also an appearance of changing the subject.

"Now we're all assembled," he observed, quietly, "there is a question I want to ask to begin with. Did anybody here actually see Lord Bulmer this morning?"

Leonard Crane turned his pale face round the circle of faces till he came to Juliet's; then he compressed his lips a little and said:

"Yes, I saw him."

"Was he alive and well?" asked Brain, quickly. "How was he dressed?"

"He appeared exceedingly well," replied Crane, with a curious intonation. "He was dressed as he was yesterday, in that purple costume copied from the portrait of his ancestor in the sixteenth century. He had his skates in his hand."

"And his sword at his side, I suppose," added the questioner. "Where is your own sword, Mr. Crane?"

"I threw it away."

In the singular silence that ensued, the train of thought in many minds became involuntarily a series of colored pictures.

They had grown used to their fanciful garments looking more gay and gorgeous against the dark gray and streaky silver of the forest, so that the moving figures glowed like stained-glass saints walking. The effect had been more fitting because so many of them had idly parodied pontifical or monastic dress. But the most arresting attitude that remained in their memories had been anything but merely monastic; that of the moment when the figure in bright green and the other in vivid violet had for a moment made a silver cross of their crossing swords. Even when it was a jest it had been something of a drama; and it was a strange and sinister thought that in the gray daybreak the same figures in the same posture might have been repeated as a tragedy.

"Did you quarrel with him?" asked Brain, suddenly.

"Yes," replied the immovable man in green. "Or he quarreled with me."

"Why did he quarrel with you?" asked the investigator; and Leonard Crane made no reply.

Horne Fisher, curiously enough, had only given half his attention to this crucial cross-examination. His heavy-lidded eyes had languidly followed the figure of Prince Borodino, who at this stage had strolled away toward the fringe of the wood; and, after a pause, as of meditation, had disappeared into the darkness of the trees.

He was recalled from his irrelevance by the voice of Juliet Bray, which rang out with an altogether new note of decision:

"If that is the difficulty, it had best be cleared up. I am engaged to Mr. Crane, and when we told my brother he did not approve of it; that is all."

Neither Brain nor Fisher exhibited any surprise, but the former added, quietly:

"Except, I suppose, that he and your brother went off into the wood to discuss it, where Mr. Crane mislaid his sword, not to mention his companion."

"And may I ask," inquired Crane, with a certain flicker of mockery passing over his pallid features, "what I am supposed to have done with either of them? Let us adopt the cheerful thesis that I am a murderer; it has yet to be shown that I am a magician. If I ran your unfortunate friend through the body, what did I do with the body? Did I have it carried away by seven flying dragons, or was it merely a trifling matter of turning it into a milk-white hind?"

"It is no occasion for sneering," said the Anglo-Indian judge, with abrupt authority. "It doesn't make it look better for you that you can joke about the loss."

Fisher's dreamy, and even dreary, eye was still on the edge of the wood behind, and he became conscious of masses of dark red, like a stormy sunset cloud, glowing through the gray network of the thin trees, and the prince in his cardinal's robes reemerged on to the pathway. Brain had had half a notion that the prince might have gone to look for the lost rapier. But when he reappeared he was carrying in his hand, not a sword, but an ax.

The incongruity between the masquerade and the mystery had created a curious psychological atmosphere. At first they had all felt horribly ashamed at being caught in the foolish disguises of a festival, by an event that had only too much the character of a funeral. Many of them would have already gone back and dressed in clothes that were more funereal or at least more formal. But somehow at the moment this seemed like a second masquerade, more artificial and frivolous than the first. And as they reconciled themselves to their ridiculous trappings, a curious sensation had come over some of them, notably over the more sensitive, like Crane and Fisher and Juliet, but in some degree over everybody except the practical Mr. Brain. It was almost as if they were the ghosts of their own ancestors haunting that dark wood and dismal lake, and playing some old part that they only half remembered. The movements of those colored figures seemed to mean something that had been settled long before, like a silent heraldry. Acts, attitudes, external objects, were accepted as an allegory even without the key; and they knew when a crisis had come, when they did not know what it was. And somehow they knew subconsciously that the whole tale had taken a new and terrible turn, when they saw the prince stand in the gap of the gaunt trees, in his robes of angry crimson and with his lowering face of bronze, bearing in his hand a new shape of death. They could not have named a reason, but the two swords seemed indeed to have become toy swords and the whole tale of them broken and tossed away like a toy. Borodino looked like the Old World headsman, clad in terrible red, and carrying the ax for the execution of the criminal. And the criminal was not Crane.

Mr. Brain of the Indian police was glaring at the new object, and it was a moment or two before he spoke, harshly and almost hoarsely.

"What are you doing with that?" he asked. "Seems to be a woodman's chopper."

"A natural association of ideas," observed Horne Fisher. "If you meet a cat in a wood you think it's a wildcat, though it may have just strolled from the drawing-room sofa. As a matter of fact, I happen to know that is not the woodman's chopper. It's the kitchen chopper, or meat ax, or something like that, that somebody has thrown away in the wood. I saw it in the kitchen myself when I was getting the potato sacks with which I reconstructed a mediaeval hermit."

"All the same, it is not without interest," remarked the prince, holding out the instrument to Fisher, who took it and examined it carefully. "A butcher's cleaver that has done butcher's work."

"It was certainly the instrument of the crime," assented Fisher, in a low voice.

Brain was staring at the dull blue gleam of the ax head with fierce and fascinated eyes. "I don't understand you," he said. "There is no—there are no marks on it."

"It has shed no blood," answered Fisher, "but for all that it has committed a crime. This is as near as the criminal came to the crime when he committed it."

"What do you mean?"

"He was not there when he did it," explained Fisher. "It's a poor sort of murderer who can't murder people when he isn't there."

"You seem to be talking merely for the sake of mystification," said Brain. "If you have any practical advice to give you might as well make it intelligible."

"The only practical advice I can suggest," said Fisher, thoughtfully, "is a little research into local topography and nomenclature. They say there used to be a Mr. Prior, who had a farm in this neighborhood. I think some details about the domestic life of the late Mr. Prior would throw a light on this terrible business."

"And you have nothing more immediate than your topography to offer," said Brain, with a sneer, "to help me avenge my friend?"

"Well," said Fisher, "I should find out the truth about the Hole in the Wall."

That night, at the close of a stormy twilight and under a strong west wind that followed the breaking of the frost, Leonard Crane was wending his way in a wild rotatory walk round and round the high, continuous wall that inclosed the little wood. He was driven by a desperate idea of solving for himself the riddle that had clouded his reputation and already even threatened his liberty. The police authorities, now in charge of the inquiry, had not arrested him, but he knew well enough that if he tried to move far afield he would be instantly arrested. Horne Fisher's fragmentary hints, though he had refused to expand them as yet, had stirred the artistic temperament of the architect to a sort of wild analysis, and he was resolved to read the hieroglyph upside down and every way until it made sense. If it was something connected with a hole in the wall he would find the hole in the wall; but, as a matter of fact, he was unable to find the faintest crack in the wall. His professional knowledge told him that the masonry was all of one workmanship and one date, and, except for the regular entrance, which threw no light on the mystery, he found nothing suggesting any sort of hiding place or means of escape. Walking a narrow path between the winding wall and the wild eastward bend and sweep of the gray and feathery trees, seeing shifting gleams of a lost sunset winking almost like lightning as the clouds of tempest scudded across the sky and mingling with the first faint blue light from a slowly strengthened moon behind him, he began to feel his head going round as his heels were going round and round the blind recurrent barrier. He had thoughts on the border of thought; fancies about a fourth dimension which was itself a hole to hide anything, of seeing everything from a new angle out of a new window in the senses; or of some mystical light and transparency, like the new rays of chemistry, in which he could see Bulmer's body, horrible and glaring, floating in a lurid halo over the woods and the wall. He was haunted also with the hint, which somehow seemed to be equally horrifying, that it all had something to do with Mr. Prior. There seemed even to be something creepy in the fact that he was always respectfully referred to as Mr. Prior, and that it was in the domestic life of the dead farmer that he had been bidden to seek the seed of these dreadful things. As a matter of fact, he had found that no local inquiries had revealed anything at all about the Prior family.

The moonlight had broadened and brightened, the wind had driven off the clouds and itself died fitfully away, when he came round again to the artificial lake in front of the house. For some reason it looked a very artificial lake; indeed, the whole scene was like a classical landscape with a touch of Watteau; the Palladian facade of the house pale in the moon, and the same silver touching the very pagan and naked marble nymph in the middle of the pond. Rather to his surprise, he found another figure there beside the statue, sitting almost equally motionless; and the same silver pencil traced the wrinkled brow and patient face of Horne Fisher, still dressed as a hermit and apparently practicing something of the solitude of a hermit. Nevertheless, he looked up at Leonard Crane and smiled, almost as if he had expected him.

"Look here," said Crane, planting himself in front of him, "can you tell me anything about this business?"

"I shall soon have to tell everybody everything about it," replied Fisher, "but I've no objection to telling you something first. But, to begin with, will you tell me something? What really happened when you met Bulmer this morning? You did throw away your sword, but you didn't kill him."

"I didn't kill him because I threw away my sword," said the other. "I did it on purpose—or I'm not sure what might have happened."

After a pause he went on, quietly: "The late Lord Bulmer was a very breezy gentleman, extremely breezy. He was very genial with his inferiors, and would have his lawyer and his architect staying in his house for all sorts of holidays and amusements. But there was another side to him, which they found out when they tried to be his equals. When I told him that his sister and I were engaged, something happened which I simply can't and won't describe. It seemed to me like some monstrous upheaval of madness. But I suppose the truth is painfully simple. There is such a thing as the coarseness of a gentleman. And it is the most horrible thing in humanity."

"I know," said Fisher. "The Renaissance nobles of the Tudor time were like that."

"It is odd that you should say that," Crane went on. "For while we were talking there came on me a curious feeling that we were repeating some scene of the past, and that I was really some outlaw, found in the woods like Robin Hood, and that he had really stepped in all his plumes and purple out of the picture frame of the ancestral portrait. Anyhow, he was the man in possession, and he neither feared God nor regarded man. I defied him, of course, and walked away. I might really have killed him if I had not walked away."

"Yes," said Fisher, nodding, "his ancestor was in possession and he was in possession, and this is the end of the story. It all fits in."

"Fits in with what?" cried his companion, with sudden impatience. "I can't make head or tail of it. You tell me to look for the secret in the hole in the wall, but I can't find any hole in the wall."

"There isn't any," said Fisher. "That's the secret." After reflecting a moment, he added: "Unless you call it a hole in the wall of the world. Look here; I'll tell you if you like, but I'm afraid it involves an introduction. You've got to understand one of the tricks of the modern mind, a tendency that most people obey without noticing it. In the village or suburb outside there's an inn with the sign of St. George and the Dragon. Now suppose I went about telling everybody that this was only a corruption of King George and the Dragoon. Scores of people would believe it, without any inquiry, from a vague feeling that it's probable because it's prosaic. It turns something romantic and legendary into something recent and ordinary. And that somehow makes it sound rational, though it is unsupported by reason. Of course some people would have the sense to remember having seen St. George in old Italian pictures and French romances, but a good many wouldn't think about it at all. They would just swallow the skepticism because it was skepticism. Modern intelligence won't accept anything on authority. But it will accept anything without authority. That's exactly what has happened here.

"When some critic or other chose to say that Prior's Park was not a priory, but was named after some quite modern man named Prior, nobody really tested the theory at all. It never occurred to anybody repeating the story to ask if there was any Mr. Prior, if anybody had ever seen him or heard of him. As a matter of fact, it was a priory, and shared the fate of most priories—that is, the Tudor gentleman with the plumes simply stole it by brute force and turned it into his own private house; he did worse things, as you shall hear. But the point here is that this is how the trick works, and the trick works in the same way in the other part of the tale. The name of this district is printed Holinwall in all the best maps produced by the scholars; and they allude lightly, not without a smile, to the fact that it was pronounced Holiwell by the most ignorant and old-fashioned of the poor. But it is spelled wrong and pronounced right."

"Do you mean to say," asked Crane, quickly, "that there really was a well?"

"There is a well," said Fisher, "and the truth lies at the bottom of it."

As he spoke he stretched out his hand and pointed toward the sheet of water in front of him.

"The well is under that water somewhere," he said, "and this is not the first tragedy connected with it. The founder of this house did something which his fellow ruffians very seldom did; something that had to be hushed up even in the anarchy of the pillage of the monasteries. The well was connected with the miracles of some saint, and the last prior that guarded it was something like a saint himself; certainly he was something very like a martyr. He defied the new owner and dared him to pollute the place, till the noble, in a fury, stabbed him and flung his body into the well, whither, after four hundred years, it has been followed by an heir of the usurper, clad in the same purple and walking the world with the same pride."

"But how did it happen," demanded Crane, "that for the first time Bulmer fell in at that particular spot?"

"Because the ice was only loosened at that particular spot, by the only man who knew it," answered Horne Fisher. "It was cracked deliberately, with the kitchen chopper, at that special place; and I myself heard the hammering and did not understand it. The place had been covered with an artificial lake, if only because the whole truth had to be covered with an artificial legend. But don't you see that it is exactly what those pagan nobles would have done, to desecrate it with a sort of heathen goddess, as the Roman Emperor built a temple to Venus on the Holy Sepulchre. But the truth could still be traced out, by any scholarly man determined to trace it. And this man was determined to trace it."

"What man?" asked the other, with a shadow of the answer in his mind.

"The only man who has an alibi," replied Fisher. "James Haddow, the antiquarian lawyer, left the night before the fatality, but he left that black star of death on the ice. He left abruptly, having previously proposed to stay; probably, I think, after an ugly scene with Bulmer, at their legal interview. As you know yourself, Bulmer could make a man feel pretty murderous, and I rather fancy the lawyer had himself irregularities to confess, and was in danger of exposure by his client. But it's my reading of human nature that a man will cheat in his trade, but not in his hobby. Haddow may have been a dishonest lawyer, but he couldn't help being an honest antiquary. When he got on the track of the truth about the Holy Well he had to follow it up; he was not to be bamboozled with newspaper anecdotes about Mr. Prior and a hole in the wall; he found out everything, even to the exact location of the well, and he was rewarded, if being a successful assassin can be regarded as a reward."

"And how did you get on the track of all this hidden history?" asked the young architect.

A cloud came across the brow of Horne Fisher. "I knew only too much about it already," he said, "and, after all, it's shameful for me to be speaking lightly of poor Bulmer, who has paid his penalty; but the rest of us haven't. I dare say every cigar I smoke and every liqueur I drink comes directly or indirectly from the harrying of the holy places and the persecution of the poor. After all, it needs very little poking about in the past to find that hole in the wall, that great breach in the defenses of English history. It lies just under the surface of a thin sheet of sham information and instruction, just as the black and blood-stained well lies just under that floor of shallow water and flat weeds. Oh, the ice is thin, but it bears; it is strong enough to support us when we dress up as monks and dance on it, in mockery of the dear, quaint old Middle Ages. They told me I must put on fancy dress; so I did put on fancy dress, according to my own taste and fancy. I put on the only costume I think fit for a man who has inherited the position of a gentleman, and yet has not entirely lost the feelings of one."

In answer to a look of inquiry, he rose with a sweeping and downward gesture.

"Sackcloth," he said; "and I would wear the ashes as well if they would stay on my bald head."

VII: THE TEMPLE OF SILENCE

Harold March and the few who cultivated the friendship of Horne Fisher, especially if they saw something of him in his own social setting, were conscious of a certain solitude in his very sociability. They seemed to be always meeting his relations and never meeting his family. Perhaps it would be truer to say that they saw much of his family and nothing of his home. His cousins and connections ramified like a labyrinth all over the governing class of Great Britain, and he seemed to be on good, or at least on good-humored, terms with most of them. For Horne Fisher was remarkable for a curious impersonal information and interest touching all sorts of topics, so that one could sometimes fancy that his culture, like his colorless, fair mustache and pale, drooping features, had the neutral nature of a chameleon. Anyhow, he could always get on with viceroys and Cabinet Ministers and all the great men responsible for great departments, and talk to each of them on his own subject, on the branch of study with which he was most seriously concerned. Thus he could converse with the Minister for War about silkworms, with the Minister of Education about detective stories, with the Minister of Labor about Limoges enamel, and with the Minister of Missions and Moral Progress (if that be his correct title) about the pantomime boys of the last four decades. And as the first was his first cousin, the second his second cousin, the third his brother-in-law, and the fourth his uncle by marriage, this conversational versatility certainly served in one sense to create a happy family. But March never seemed to get a glimpse of that domestic interior to which men of the middle classes are accustomed in their friendships, and which is indeed the foundation of friendship and love and everything else in any sane and stable society. He wondered whether Horne Fisher was both an orphan and an only child.

It was, therefore, with something like a start that he found that Fisher had a brother, much more prosperous and powerful than himself, though hardly, March thought, so entertaining. Sir Henry Harland Fisher, with half the alphabet after his name, was something at the Foreign Office far more tremendous than the Foreign Secretary. Apparently, it ran in the family, after all; for it seemed there was another brother, Ashton Fisher, in India, rather more tremendous than the Viceroy. Sir Henry Fisher was a heavier, but handsomer edition of his brother, with a brow equally bald, but much more smooth. He was very courteous, but a shade patronizing, not only to March, but even, as March fancied, to Horne Fisher as well. The latter gentleman, who had many intuitions about the half-formed thoughts of others, glanced at the topic himself as they came away from the great house in Berkeley Square.

"Why, don't you know," he observed quietly, "that I am the fool of the family?"

"It must be a clever family," said Harold March, with a smile.

"Very gracefully expressed," replied Fisher; "that is the best of having a literary training. Well, perhaps it is an exaggeration to say I am the fool of the family. It's enough to say I am the failure of the family."

"It seems queer to me that you should fail especially," remarked the journalist. "As they say in the examinations, what did you fail in?"

"Politics," replied his friend. "I stood for Parliament when I was quite a young man and got in by an enormous majority, with loud cheers and chairing round the town. Since then, of course, I've been rather under a cloud."

"I'm afraid I don't quite understand the 'of course,'" answered March, laughing.

"That part of it isn't worth understanding," said Fisher. "But as a matter of fact, old chap, the other part of it was rather odd and interesting. Quite a detective story in its way, as well as the first lesson I had in what modern politics are made of. If you like, I'll tell you all about it." And the following, recast in a less allusive and conversational manner, is the story that he told.

Nobody privileged of late years to meet Sir Henry Harland Fisher would believe that he had ever been called Harry. But, indeed, he had been boyish enough when a boy, and that serenity which shone on him through life, and which now took the form of gravity, had once taken the form of gayety. His friends would have said that he was all the more ripe in his maturity for having been young in his youth. His enemies would have said that he was still light minded, but no longer light hearted. But in any case, the whole of the story Horne Fisher had to tell arose out of the accident which had made young Harry Fisher private secretary to Lord Saltoun. Hence his later connection with the Foreign Office, which had, indeed, come to him as a sort of legacy from his lordship when that great man was the power behind the throne. This is not the place to say much about Saltoun, little as was known of him and much as there was worth knowing. England has had at least three or four such secret statesmen. An aristocratic polity produces every now and then an aristocrat who is also an accident, a man of intellectual independence and insight, a Napoleon born in the purple. His vast work was mostly invisible, and very little could be got out of him in private life except a crusty and rather cynical sense of humor. But it was certainly the accident of his presence at a family dinner of the Fishers, and the unexpected opinion he expressed, which turned what might have been a dinner-table joke into a sort of small sensational novel.

Save for Lord Saltoun, it was a family party of Fishers, for the only other distinguished stranger had just departed after dinner, leaving the rest to their coffee and cigars. This had been a figure of some interest—a young Cambridge man named Eric Hughes who was the rising hope of the party of Reform, to which the Fisher family, along with their friend Saltoun, had long been at least formally attached. The personality of Hughes was substantially summed up in the fact that he talked eloquently and earnestly through the whole dinner, but left immediately after to be in time for an appointment. All his actions had something at once ambitious and conscientious; he drank no wine, but was slightly intoxicated with words. And his face and phrases were on the front page of all the newspapers just then, because he was contesting the safe seat of Sir Francis Verner in the great by-election in the west. Everybody was talking about the powerful speech against squirarchy which he had just delivered; even in the Fisher circle everybody talked about it except Horne Fisher himself who sat in a corner, lowering over the fire.

"We jolly well have to thank him for putting some new life into the old party," Ashton Fisher was saying. "This campaign against the old squires just hits the degree of democracy there is in this county. This act for extending county council control is practically his bill; so you may say he's in the government even before he's in the House."

"One's easier than the other," said Harry, carelessly. "I bet the squire's a bigger pot than the county council in that county. Verner is pretty well rooted; all these rural places are what you call reactionary. Damning aristocrats won't alter it."

"He damns them rather well," observed Ashton. "We never had a better meeting than the one in Barkington, which generally goes Constitutional. And when he said, 'Sir Francis may boast of blue blood; let us show we have red blood,' and went on to talk about manhood and liberty, the room simply rose at him."

"Speaks very well," said Lord Saltoun, gruffly, making his only contribution to the conversation so far.

Then the almost equally silent Horne Fisher suddenly spoke, without taking his brooding eyes off the fire.

"What I can't understand," he said, "is why nobody is ever slanged for the real reason."

"Hullo!" remarked Harry, humorously, "you beginning to take notice?"

"Well, take Verner," continued Horne Fisher. "If we want to attack Verner, why not attack him? Why compliment him on being a romantic reactionary aristocrat? Who is Verner? Where does he come from? His name sounds old, but I never heard of it before, as the man said of the Crucifixion. Why talk about his blue blood? His blood may be gamboge yellow with green spots, for all anybody knows. All we know is that the old squire, Hawker, somehow ran through his money (and his second wife's, I suppose, for she was rich enough), and sold the estate to a man named Verner. What did he make his money in? Oil? Army contracts?"

"I don't know," said Saltoun, looking at him thoughtfully.

"First thing I ever knew you didn't know," cried the exuberant Harry.

"And there's more, besides," went on Horne Fisher, who seemed to have suddenly found his tongue. "If we want country people to vote for us, why don't we get somebody with some notion about the country? We don't talk to people in Threadneedle Street about nothing but turnips and pigsties. Why do we talk to people in Somerset about nothing but slums and socialism? Why don't we give the squire's land to the squire's tenants, instead of dragging in the county council?"

"Three acres and a cow," cried Harry, emitting what the Parliamentary reports call an ironical cheer.

"Yes," replied his brother, stubbornly. "Don't you think agricultural laborers would rather have three acres and a cow than three acres of printed forms and a committee? Why doesn't somebody start a yeoman party in politics, appealing to the old traditions of the small landowner? And why don't they attack men like Verner for what they are, which is something about as old and traditional as an American oil trust?"

"You'd better lead the yeoman party yourself," laughed Harry.

"Don't you think it would be a joke, Lord Saltoun, to see my brother and his merry men, with their bows and bills, marching down to Somerset all in Lincoln green instead of Lincoln and Bennet hats?"

"No," answered Old Saltoun, "I don't think it would be a joke. I think it would be an exceedingly serious and sensible idea."

"Well, I'm jiggered!" cried Harry Fisher, staring at him. "I said just now it was the first fact you didn't know, and I should say this is the first joke you didn't see."

"I've seen a good many things in my time," said the old man, in his rather sour fashion. "I've told a good many lies in my time, too, and perhaps I've got rather sick of them. But there are lies and lies, for all that. Gentlemen used to lie just as schoolboys lie, because they hung together and partly to help one another out. But I'm damned if I can see why we should lie for these cosmopolitan cads who only help themselves. They're not backing us up any more; they're simply crowding us out. If a man like your brother likes to go into Parliament as a yeoman or a gentleman or a Jacobite or an Ancient Briton, I should say it would be a jolly good thing."

In the rather startled silence that followed Horne Fisher sprang to his feet and all his dreary manner dropped off him.

"I'm ready to do it to-morrow," he cried. "I suppose none of you fellows would back me up."

Then Harry Fisher showed the finer side of his impetuosity. He made a sudden movement as if to shake hands.

"You're a sport," he said, "and I'll back you up, if nobody else will. But we can all back you up, can't we? I see what Lord Saltoun means, and, of course, he's right. He's always right."

"So I will go down to Somerset," said Horne Fisher.

"Yes, it is on the way to Westminster," said Lord Saltoun, with a smile.

And so it happened that Horne Fisher arrived some days later at the little station of a rather remote market town in the west, accompanied by a light suitcase and a lively brother. It must not be supposed, however, that the brother's cheerful tone consisted entirely of chaff. He supported the new candidate with hope as well as hilarity; and at the back of his boisterous partnership there was an increasing sympathy and encouragement. Harry Fisher had always had an affection for his more quiet and eccentric brother, and was now coming more and more to have a respect for him. As the campaign proceeded the respect increased to ardent admiration. For Harry was still young, and could feel the sort of enthusiasm for his captain in electioneering that a schoolboy can feel for his captain in cricket.

Nor was the admiration undeserved. As the new three-cornered contest developed it became apparent to others besides his devoted kinsman that there was more in Horne Fisher than had ever met the eye. It was clear that his outbreak by the family fireside had been but the culmination of a long course of brooding and studying on the question. The talent he retained through life for studying his subject, and even somebody else's subject, had long been concentrated on this idea of championing a new peasantry against a new plutocracy. He spoke to a crowd with eloquence and replied to an individual with humor, two political arts that seemed to come to him naturally. He certainly knew much more about rural problems than either Hughes, the Reform candidate, or Verner, the Constitutional candidate. And he probed those problems with a human curiosity, and went below the surface in a way that neither of them dreamed of doing. He soon became the voice of popular feelings that are never found in the popular press. New angles of criticism, arguments that had never before been uttered by an educated voice, tests and comparisons that had been made only in dialect by men drinking in the little local public houses, crafts half forgotten that had come down by sign of hand and tongue from remote ages when their fathers were free—all this created a curious and double excitement. It startled the well informed by being a new and fantastic idea they had never encountered. It startled the ignorant by being an old and familiar idea they never thought to have seen revived. Men saw things in a new light, and knew not even whether it was the sunset or the dawn.

Practical grievances were there to make the movement formidable. As Fisher went to and fro among the cottages and country inns, it was borne in on him without difficulty that Sir Francis Verner was a very bad landlord. Nor was the story of his acquisition of the land any more ancient and dignified than he had supposed; the story was well known in the county and in most respects was obvious enough. Hawker, the old squire, had been a loose, unsatisfactory sort of person, had been on bad terms with his first wife (who died, as some said, of neglect), and had then married a flashy South American Jewess with a fortune. But he must have worked his way through this fortune also with marvelous rapidity, for he had been compelled to

446

sell the estate to Verner and had gone to live in South America, possibly on his wife's estates. But Fisher noticed that the laxity of the old squire was far less hated than the efficiency of the new squire. Verner's history seemed to be full of smart bargains and financial flutters that left other people short of money and temper. But though he heard a great deal about Verner, there was one thing that continually eluded him; something that nobody knew, that even Saltoun had not known. He could not find out how Verner had originally made his money.

"He must have kept it specially dark," said Horne Fisher to himself. "It must be something he's really ashamed of. Hang it all! what is a man ashamed of nowadays?"

And as he pondered on the possibilities they grew darker and more distorted in his mind; he thought vaguely of things remote and repulsive, strange forms of slavery or sorcery, and then of ugly things yet more unnatural but nearer home. The figure of Verner seemed to be blackened and transfigured in his imagination, and to stand against varied backgrounds and strange skies.

As he strode up a village street, brooding thus, his eyes encountered a complete contrast in the face of his other rival, the Reform candidate. Eric Hughes, with his blown blond hair and eager undergraduate face, was just getting into his motor car and saying a few final words to his agent, a sturdy, grizzled man named Gryce. Eric Hughes waved his hand in a friendly fashion; but Gryce eyed him with some hostility. Eric Hughes was a young man with genuine political enthusiasms, but he knew that political opponents are people with whom one may have to dine any day. But Mr. Gryce was a grim little local Radical, a champion of the chapel, and one of those happy people whose work is also their hobby. He turned his back as the motor car drove away, and walked briskly up the sunlit high street of the little town, whistling, with political papers sticking out of his pocket.

Fisher looked pensively after the resolute figure for a moment, and then, as if by an impulse, began to follow it. Through the busy market place, amid the baskets and barrows of market day, under the painted wooden sign of the Green Dragon, up a dark side entry, under an arch, and through a tangle of crooked cobbled streets the two threaded their way, the square, strutting figure in front and the lean, lounging figure behind him, like his shadow in the sunshine. At length they came to a brown brick house with a brass plate, on which was Mr. Gryce's name, and that individual turned and beheld his pursuer with a stare.

"Could I have a word with you, sir?" asked Horne Fisher, politely. The agent stared still more, but assented civilly, and led the other into an office littered with leaflets and hung all round with highly colored posters which linked the name of Hughes with all the higher interests of humanity.

"Mr. Horne Fisher, I believe," said Mr. Gryce. "Much honored by the call, of course. Can't pretend to congratulate you on entering the contest, I'm afraid; you won't expect that. Here we've been keeping the old flag flying for freedom and reform, and you come in and break the battle line."

For Mr. Elijah Gryce abounded in military metaphors and in denunciations of militarism. He was a square-jawed, blunt-featured man with a pugnacious cock of the eyebrow. He had been pickled in the politics of that countryside from boyhood, he knew everybody's secrets, and electioneering was the romance of his life.

"I suppose you think I'm devoured with ambition," said Horne Fisher, in his rather listless voice, "aiming at a dictatorship and all that. Well, I think I can clear myself of the charge of mere selfish ambition. I only want certain things done. I don't want to do them. I very seldom want to do anything. And I've come here to say that I'm quite willing to retire from the contest if you can convince me that we really want to do the same thing."

The agent of the Reform party looked at him with an odd and slightly puzzled expression, and before he could reply, Fisher went on in the same level tones:

"You'd hardly believe it, but I keep a conscience concealed about me; and I am in doubt about several things. For instance, we both want to turn Verner out of Parliament, but what weapon are we to use? I've heard a lot of gossip against him, but is it right to act on mere gossip? Just as I want to be fair to you, so I want to be fair to him. If some of the things I've heard are true he ought to be turned out of Parliament and every other club in London. But I don't want to turn him out of Parliament if they aren't true."

At this point the light of battle sprang into Mr. Gryce's eyes and he became voluble, not to say violent. He, at any rate, had no doubt that the stories were true; he could testify, to his own knowledge, that they were true. Verner was not only a hard landlord, but a mean landlord, a robber as well as a rackrenter; any gentleman would be justified in hounding him out. He had cheated old Wilkins out of his free-hold by a trick fit for a pickpocket; he had driven old Mother Biddle to the workhouse; he had stretched the law against Long Adam, the poacher, till all the magistrates were ashamed of him.

"So if you'll serve under the old banner," concluded Mr. Gryce, more genially, "and turn out a swindling tyrant like that, I'm sure you'll never regret it."

"And if that is the truth," said Horne Fisher, "are you going to tell it?"

"What do you mean? Tell the truth?" demanded Gryce.

"I mean you are going to tell the truth as you have just told it," replied Fisher. "You are going to placard this town with the wickedness done to old Wilkins. You are going to fill the newspapers with the infamous story of Mrs. Biddle. You are going to denounce Verner from a public platform, naming him for what he did and naming the poacher he did it to. And you're going to find out by what trade this man made the money with which he bought the estate; and when you know the truth, as I said before, of course you are going to tell it. Upon those terms I come under the old flag, as you call it, and haul down my little pennon."

The agent was eying him with a curious expression, surly but not entirely unsympathetic. "Well," he said, slowly, "you have to do these things in a regular way, you know, or people don't understand. I've had a lot of experience, and I'm afraid what you say wouldn't do. People understand slanging squires in a general way, but those personalities aren't considered fair play. Looks like hitting below the belt."

"Old Wilkins hasn't got a belt, I suppose," replied Horne Fisher. "Verner can hit him anyhow, and nobody must say a word. It's evidently very important to have a belt. But apparently you have to be rather high up in society to have one. Possibly," he added, thoughtfully—"possibly the explanation of the phrase 'a belted earl,' the meaning of which has always escaped me."

"I mean those personalities won't do," returned Gryce, frowning at the table.

"And Mother Biddle and Long Adam, the poacher, are not personalities," said Fisher, "and suppose we mustn't ask how Verner made all the money that enabled him to become—a personality."

Gryce was still looking at him under lowering brows, but the singular light in his eyes had brightened. At last he said, in another and much quieter voice:

"Look here, sir. I like you, if you don't mind my saying so. I think you are really on the side of the people and I'm sure you're a brave man. A lot braver than you know, perhaps. We daren't touch what you propose with a barge pole; and so far from wanting you in the old party, we'd rather you ran your own risk by yourself. But because I like you and respect your pluck, I'll do you a good turn before we part. I don't want you to waste time barking up the wrong tree. You talk about how the new squire got the money to buy, and the ruin of the old squire, and all the rest of it. Well, I'll give you a hint about that, a hint about something precious few people know."

"I am very grateful," said Fisher, gravely. "What is it?"

"It's in two words," said the other. "The new squire was quite poor when he bought. The old squire was quite rich when he sold."

Horne Fisher looked at him thoughtfully as he turned away abruptly and busied himself with the papers on his desk. Then Fisher uttered a short phrase of thanks and farewell, and went out into the street, still very thoughtful.

His reflection seemed to end in resolution, and, falling into a more rapid stride, he passed out of the little town along a road leading toward the gate of the great park, the country seat of Sir Francis Verner. A glitter of sunlight made the early winter more like a late autumn, and the dark woods were touched here and there with red and golden leaves, like the last rays of a lost sunset. From a higher part of the road he had seen the long, classical facade of the great house with its many windows, almost immediately beneath him, but when the road ran down under the wall of the estate, topped with towering trees behind, he realized that it was half a mile round to the lodge gates. After walking for a few minutes along the lane, however, he came to a place where the wall had cracked and was in process of repair. As it was, there was a great gap in the gray masonry that looked at first as black as a cavern and only showed at a second glance the twilight of the twinkling trees. There was something fascinating about that unexpected gate, like the opening of a fairy tale.

Horne Fisher had in him something of the aristocrat, which is very near to the anarchist. It was characteristic of him that he turned into this dark and irregular entry as casually as into his own front door, merely thinking that it would be a short cut to the house. He made his way through the dim wood for some distance and with some difficulty, until there began to shine through the trees a level light, in lines of silver, which he did not at first understand. The next moment he had come out into the daylight at the top of a steep bank, at the bottom of which a path ran round the rim of a large ornamental lake. The sheet of water which he had seen shimmering through the trees was of considerable extent, but was walled in on every side with woods which were not only dark, but decidedly dismal. At one end of the path was a classical statue of some nameless nymph, and at the other end it was flanked by two classical urns; but the marble was weather-stained and streaked with green and gray. A hundred other signs, smaller but more significant, told him that he had come on some outlying corner of the grounds neglected and seldom visited. In the middle of the lake was what appeared to be an island, and on the island what appeared to be meant for a classical temple, not open like a temple of the winds, but with a blank wall between its Doric pillars. We may say it only seemed like an island, because a second glance revealed a low causeway of flat stones running up to it from the shore and turning it into a peninsula. And certainly it only seemed like a temple, for nobody knew better than Horne Fisher that no god had ever dwelt in that shrine.

"That's what makes all this classical landscape gardening so desolate," he said to himself. "More desolate than Stonehenge or the Pyramids. We don't believe in Egyptian mythology, but the Egyptians did; and I suppose even the Druids believed in Druidism. But the eighteenth-century gentleman who built these temples didn't believe in Venus or Mercury any more than we do; that's why the reflection of those pale pillars in the lake is truly only the shadow of a shade. They were men of the age of Reason; they, who filled their gardens with these stone nymphs, had less hope than any men in all history of really meeting a nymph in the forest."

His monologue stopped abruptly with a sharp noise like a thundercrack that rolled in dreary echoes round the dismal mere. He knew at once what it was—somebody had fired off a gun. But as to the meaning of it he was momentarily staggered, and strange thoughts thronged into his mind. The next moment he laughed; for he saw lying a little way along the path below him the dead bird that the shot had brought down.

At the same moment, however, he saw something else, which interested him more. A ring of dense trees ran round the back of the island temple, framing the facade of it in dark foliage, and he could have sworn he saw a stir as of something moving among the leaves. The next moment his suspicion was confirmed, for a rather ragged figure came from under the shadow of the temple and began to move along the causeway that led to the bank. Even at that distance the figure was conspicuous by its great height and Fisher could see that the man carried a gun under his arm. There came back into his memory at once the name Long Adam, the poacher.

With a rapid sense of strategy he sometimes showed, Fisher sprang from the bank and raced round the lake to the head of the little pier of stones. If once a man reached the mainland he could easily vanish into the woods. But when Fisher began to advance along the stones toward the island, the man was cornered in a blind alley and could only back toward the temple. Putting his broad shoulders against it, he stood as if at bay; he was a comparatively young man, with fine lines in his lean face and figure and a mop of ragged red hair. The look in his eyes might well have been disquieting to anyone left alone with him on an island in the middle of a lake.

"Good morning," said Horne Fisher, pleasantly. "I thought at first you were a murderer. But it seems unlikely, somehow, that the partridge rushed between us and died for love of me, like the heroines in the romances; so I suppose you are a poacher."

"I suppose you would call me a poacher," answered the man; and his voice was something of a surprise coming from such a scarecrow; it had that hard fastidiousness to be found in those who have made a fight for their own refinement among rough surroundings. "I consider I have a perfect right to shoot game in this place. But I am well aware that people of your sort take me for a thief, and I suppose you will try to land me in jail."

"There are preliminary difficulties," replied Fisher. "To begin with, the mistake is flattering, but I am not a gamekeeper. Still less am I three gamekeepers, who would be, I imagine, about your fighting weight. But I confess I have another reason for not wanting to jail you."

"And what is that?" asked the other.

"Only that I quite agree with you," answered Fisher. "I don't exactly say you have a right to poach, but I never could see that it was as wrong as being a thief. It seems to me against the whole normal notion of property that a man should own something because it flies across his garden. He might as well own the wind, or think he could write his name on a morning cloud. Besides, if we want poor people to respect property we must give them some property to respect. You ought to have land of your own; and I'm going to give you some if I can."

"Going to give me some land!" repeated Long Adam.

"I apologize for addressing you as if you were a public meeting," said Fisher, "but I am an entirely new kind of public man who says the same thing in public and in private. I've said this to a hundred huge meetings throughout the country, and I say it to you on this queer little island in this dismal pond. I would cut up a big estate like this into small estates for everybody, even for poachers. I would do in England as they did in Ireland—buy the big men out, if possible; get them out, anyhow. A man like you ought to have a little place of his own. I don't say you could keep pheasants, but you might keep chickens."

The man stiffened suddenly and he seemed at once to blanch and flame at the promise as if it were a threat.

"Chickens!" he repeated, with a passion of contempt.

"Why do you object?" asked the placid candidate. "Because keeping hens is rather a mild amusement for a poacher? What about poaching eggs?"

"Because I am not a poacher," cried Adam, in a rending voice that rang round the hollow shrines and urns like the echoes of his gun. "Because the partridge lying dead over there is my partridge. Because the land you are standing on is my land. Because my own land was only taken from me by a crime, and a worse crime than poaching. This has been a single estate for hundreds and hundreds of years, and if you or any meddlesome mountebank comes here and talks of cutting it up like a cake, if I ever hear a word more of you and your leveling lies—"

"You seem to be a rather turbulent public," observed Horne Fisher, "but do go on. What will happen if I try to divide this estate decently among decent people?"

The poacher had recovered a grim composure as he replied. "There will be no partridge to rush in between."

With that he turned his back, evidently resolved to say no more, and walked past the temple to the extreme end of the islet, where he stood staring into the water. Fisher followed him, but, when his repeated questions evoked no answer, turned back toward the shore. In doing so he took a second and closer look at the artificial temple, and noted some curious things about it. Most of these theatrical things were as thin as theatrical scenery, and he expected the classic shrine to be a shallow thing, a mere shell or mask. But there was some substantial bulk of it behind, buried in the trees, which had a gray, labyrinthian look, like serpents of stone, and lifted a load of leafy towers to the sky. But what arrested Fisher's eye was that in this bulk of gray-white stone behind there was a single door with great, rusty bolts outside; the bolts, however, were not shot across so as to secure it. Then he walked round the small building, and found no other opening except one small grating like a ventilator, high up in the wall. He retraced his steps thoughtfully along the causeway to the banks of the lake, and sat down on the stone steps between the two sculptured funeral urns. Then he lit a cigarette and smoked it in ruminant manner; eventually he took out a notebook and wrote down various phrases, numbering and renumbering them till they stood in the following order: "(1) Squire Hawker disliked his first wife. (2) He married his second wife for her money. (3) Long Adam says the estate is really his. (4) Long Adam hangs round the island temple, which looks like a prison. (5) Squire Hawker was not poor when he gave up the estate. (6) Verner was poor when he got the estate."

He gazed at these notes with a gravity which gradually turned to a hard smile, threw away his cigarette, and resumed his search for a short cut to the great house. He soon picked up the path which, winding among clipped hedges and flower beds, brought him in front of its long Palladian facade. It had the usual appearance of being, not a private house, but a sort of public building sent into exile in the provinces.

He first found himself in the presence of the butler, who really looked much older than the building, for the architecture was dated as Georgian; but the man's face, under a highly unnatural brown wig, was wrinkled with what might have been centuries. Only his prominent eyes were alive and alert, as if with protest. Fisher glanced at him, and then stopped and said:

"Excuse me. Weren't you with the late squire, Mr. Hawker?"

"Yes, sir," said the man, gravely. "Usher is my name. What can I do for you?"

"Only take me into Sir Francis Verner," replied the visitor.

Sir Francis Verner was sitting in an easy chair beside a small table in a large room hung with tapestries. On the table were a small flask and glass, with the green glimmer of a liqueur and a cup of black coffee. He was clad in a quiet gray suit with a moderately harmonious purple tie; but Fisher saw something about the turn of his fair mustache and the lie of his flat hair—it suddenly revealed that his name was Franz Werner.

"You are Mr. Horne Fisher," he said. "Won't you sit down?"

"No, thank you," replied Fisher. "I fear this is not a friendly occasion, and I shall remain standing. Possibly you know that I am already standing—standing for Parliament, in fact—"

"I am aware we are political opponents," replied Verner, raising his eyebrows. "But I think it would be better if we fought in a sporting spirit; in a spirit of English fair play."

"Much better," assented Fisher. "It would be much better if you were English and very much better if you had ever played fair. But what I've come to say can be said very shortly. I don't quite know how we stand with the law about that old Hawker story, but my chief object is to prevent England being entirely ruled by people like you. So whatever the law would say, I will say no more if you will retire from the election at once."

"You are evidently a lunatic," said Verner.

"My psychology may be a little abnormal," replied Horne Fisher, in a rather hazy manner. "I am subject to dreams, especially day-dreams. Sometimes what is happening to me grows vivid in a curious double way, as if it had happened before. Have you ever had that mystical feeling that things have happened before?"

"I hope you are a harmless lunatic," said Verner.

But Fisher was still staring in an absent fashion at the golden gigantic figures and traceries of brown and red in the tapestries on the walls; then he looked again at Verner and resumed: "I have a feeling that this interview has happened before, here in this tapestried room, and we are two ghosts revisiting a haunted chamber. But it was Squire Hawker who sat where you sit and it was you who stood where I stand." He paused a moment and then added, with simplicity, "I suppose I am a blackmailer, too."

"If you are," said Sir Francis, "I promise you you shall go to jail." But his face had a shade on it that looked like the reflection of the green wine gleaming on the table. Horne Fisher regarded him steadily and answered, quietly enough:

"Blackmailers do not always go to jail. Sometimes they go to Parliament. But, though Parliament is rotten enough already, you shall not go there if I can help it. I am not so criminal as you were in bargaining with crime. You made a squire give up his country seat. I only ask you to give up your Parliamentary seat."

Sir Francis Verner sprang to his feet and looked about for one of the bell ropes of the old-fashioned, curtained room.

"Where is Usher?" he cried, with a livid face.

"And who is Usher?" said Fisher, softly. "I wonder how much Usher knows of the truth."

Verner's hand fell from the bell rope and, after standing for a moment with rolling eyes, he strode abruptly from the room. Fisher went but by the other door, by which he had entered, and, seeing no sign of Usher, let himself out and betook himself again toward the town.

That night he put an electric torch in his pocket and set out alone in the darkness to add the last links to his argument. There was much that he did not know yet; but he thought he knew where he could find the knowledge. The night closed dark and stormy and the black gap in the wall looked blacker than ever; the wood seemed to have grown thicker and darker in a day. If the deserted lake with its black woods and gray urns and images looked desolate even by daylight, under the night and the growing storm it seemed still more like the pool of Acheron in the land of lost souls. As he stepped carefully along the jetty stones he seemed to be traveling farther and farther into the abyss of night, and to have left behind him the last points from which it would be possible to signal to the land of the living. The lake seemed to have grown larger than a sea, but a sea of black and slimy waters that slept with abominable serenity, as if they had washed out the world. There was so much of this nightmare sense of extension and expansion that he was strangely surprised to come to his desert island so soon. But he knew it for a place of inhuman silence and solitude; and he felt as if he had been walking for years.

Nerving himself to a more normal mood, he paused under one of the dark dragon trees that branched out above him, and, taking out his torch, turned in the direction of the door at the back of the temple. It was unbolted as before, and the thought stirred faintly in him that it was slightly open, though only by a crack. The more he thought of it, however, the more certain he grew that this was but one of the common illusions of light coming from a different angle. He studied in a more scientific spirit the details of the door, with its rusty bolts and hinges, when he became conscious of something very near him—indeed, nearly above his head. Something was dangling from the tree that was not a broken branch. For some seconds he stood as still as a stone, and as cold. What he saw above him were the legs of a man hanging, presumably a dead man hanged. But the next moment he knew better. The man was literally alive and kicking; and an instant after he had dropped to the ground and turned on the intruder. Simultaneously three or four other trees seemed to come to life in the same fashion. Five or six other figures had fallen on their feet from these unnatural nests. It was as if the place were an island of monkeys. But a moment after they had made a stampede toward him, and when they laid their hands on him he knew that they were men.

With the electric torch in his hand he struck the foremost of them so furiously in the face that the man stumbled and rolled over on the slimy grass; but the torch was broken and extinguished, leaving everything in a denser obscurity. He flung another man flat against the temple wall, so that he slid to the ground; but a third and fourth carried Fisher off his feet and began to bear him, struggling, toward the doorway. Even in the bewilderment of the battle he was conscious that the door was standing open. Somebody was summoning the roughs from inside.

The moment they were within they hurled him upon a sort of bench or bed with violence, but no damage; for the settee, or whatever it was, seemed to be comfortably cushioned for his reception. Their violence had in it a great element of haste, and before he could rise they had all rushed for the door to escape. Whatever bandits they were that infested this desert island, they were obviously uneasy about their job and very anxious to be quit of it. He had the flying fancy that regular criminals would hardly be in such a panic. The next moment the great door crashed to and he could hear the bolts shriek as they shot into their place, and the feet of the retreating men scampering and stumbling along the causeway. But rapidly as it happened, it did not happen before Fisher had done something that he wanted to do.

Unable to rise from his sprawling attitude in that flash of time, he had shot out one of his long legs and hooked it round the ankle of the last man disappearing through the door. The man swayed and toppled over inside the prison chamber, and the door closed between him and his fleeing companions. Clearly they were in too much haste to realize that they had left one of their company behind.

The man sprang to his feet again and hammered and kicked furiously at the door. Fisher's sense of humor began to recover from the struggle and he sat up on his sofa with something of his native nonchalance. But as he listened to the captive captor beating on the door of the prison, a new and curious reflection came to him.

The natural course for a man thus wishing to attract his friends' attention would be to call out, to shout as well as kick. This man was making as much noise as he could with his feet and hands, but not a sound came from his throat. Why couldn't he speak? At first he thought the man might be gagged, which was manifestly absurd. Then his fancy fell back on the ugly idea that the man was dumb. He hardly knew why it was so ugly an idea, but it affected his imagination in a dark and disproportionate fashion. There seemed to be something creepy about the idea of being left in a dark room with a deaf mute. It was almost as if such a defect were a deformity. It was almost as if it went with other and worse deformities. It was as if the shape he could not trace in the darkness were some shape that should not see the sun.

Then he had a flash of sanity and also of insight. The explanation was very simple, but rather interesting. Obviously the man did not use his voice because he did not wish his voice to be recognized. He hoped to escape from that dark place before Fisher found out who he was. And who was he? One thing at least was clear. He was one or other of the four or five men with whom Fisher had already talked in these parts, and in the development of that strange story.

"Now I wonder who you are," he said, aloud, with all his old lazy urbanity. "I suppose it's no use trying to throttle you in order to find out; it would be displeasing to pass the night with a corpse. Besides I might be the corpse. I've got no matches and I've smashed my torch, so I can only speculate. Who could you be, now? Let us think."

The man thus genially addressed had desisted from drumming on the door and retreated sullenly into a corner as Fisher continued to address him in a flowing monologue.

"Probably you are the poacher who says he isn't a poacher. He says he's a landed proprietor; but he will permit me to inform him that, whatever he is, he's a fool. What hope can there ever be of a free peasantry in England if the peasants themselves are such snobs as to want to be gentlemen? How can we make a democracy with no democrats? As it is, you want to be a landlord and so you consent to be a criminal. And in that, you know, you are rather like somebody else. And, now I think of it, perhaps you are somebody else."

There was a silence broken by breathing from the corner and the murmur of the rising storm, that came in through the small grating above the man's head. Horne Fisher continued:

"Are you only a servant, perhaps, that rather sinister old servant who was butler to Hawker and Verner? If so, you are certainly the only link between the two periods. But if so, why do you degrade yourself to serve this dirty foreigner, when you at least saw the last of a genuine national gentry? People like you are generally at least patriotic. Doesn't England mean anything to you, Mr. Usher? All of which eloquence is possibly wasted, as perhaps you are not Mr. Usher.

"More likely you are Verner himself; and it's no good wasting eloquence to make you ashamed of yourself. Nor is it any good to curse you for corrupting England; nor are you the right person to curse. It is the English who deserve to be cursed, and are cursed, because they allowed such vermin to crawl into the high places of their heroes and their kings. I won't dwell on the idea that you're Verner, or the throttling might begin, after all. Is there anyone else you could be? Surely you're not some servant of the other rival organization. I can't believe you're Gryce, the agent; and yet Gryce had a spark of the fanatic in his eye, too; and men will do extraordinary things in these paltry feuds of politics. Or if not the servant, is it the . . . No, I can't believe it . . . not the red blood of manhood and liberty . . . not the democratic ideal . . ."

He sprang up in excitement, and at the same moment a growl of thunder came through the grating beyond. The storm had broken, and with it a new light broke on his mind. There was something else that might happen in a moment.

"Do you know what that means?" he cried. "It means that God himself may hold a candle to show me your infernal face."

Then next moment came a crash of thunder; but before the thunder a white light had filled the whole room for a single split second.

Fisher had seen two things in front of him. One was the black-and-white pattern of the iron grating against the sky; the other was the face in the corner. It was the face of his brother.

Nothing came from Horne Fisher's lips except a Christian name, which was followed by a silence more dreadful than the dark. At last the other figure stirred and sprang up, and the voice of Harry Fisher was heard for the first time in that horrible room.

"You've seen me, I suppose," he said, "and we may as well have a light now. You could have turned it on at any time, if you'd found the switch."

He pressed a button in the wall and all the details of that room sprang into something stronger than daylight. Indeed, the details were so unexpected that for a moment they turned the captive's rocking mind from the last personal revelation. The room, so far from being a dungeon cell, was more like a drawing-room, even a lady's drawing-room, except for some boxes of cigars and bottles of wine that were stacked with books and magazines on a side table. A second glance showed him that the more masculine fittings were quite recent, and that the more feminine background was quite old. His eye caught a strip of faded tapestry, which startled him into speech, to the momentary oblivion of bigger matters.

"This place was furnished from the great house," he said.

"Yes," replied the other, "and I think you know why."

"I think I do," said Horne Fisher, "and before I go on to more extraordinary things I will, say what I think. Squire Hawker played both the bigamist and the bandit. His first wife was not dead when he married the Jewess; she was imprisoned on this island. She bore him a child here, who now haunts his birthplace under the name of Long Adam. A bankruptcy company promoter named Werner discovered the secret and blackmailed the squire into surrendering the estate. That's all quite clear and very easy. And now let me go on to something more difficult. And that is for you to explain what the devil you are doing kidnaping your born brother."

After a pause Henry Fisher answered:

"I suppose you didn't expect to see me," he said. "But, after all, what could you expect?'"

"I'm afraid I don't follow," said Horne Fisher.

"I mean what else could you expect, after making such a muck of it?" said his brother, sulkily. "We all thought you were so clever. How could we know you were going to be—well, really, such a rotten failure?"

"This is rather curious," said the candidate, frowning. "Without vanity, I was not under the impression that my candidature was a failure. All the big meetings were successful and crowds of people have promised me votes."

"I should jolly well think they had," said Henry, grimly. "You've made a landslide with your confounded acres and a cow, and Verner can hardly get a vote anywhere. Oh, it's too rotten for anything!"

"What on earth do you mean?"

"Why, you lunatic," cried Henry, in tones of ringing sincerity, "you don't suppose you were meant to win the seat, did you? Oh, it's too childish! I tell you Verner's got to get in. Of course he's got to get in. He's to have the Exchequer next session, and there's the Egyptian loan and Lord knows what else. We only wanted you to split the Reform vote because accidents might happen after Hughes had made a score at Barkington."

"I see," said Fisher, "and you, I think, are a pillar and ornament of the Reform party. As you say, I am not clever."

The appeal to party loyalty fell on deaf ears; for the pillar of Reform was brooding on other things. At last he said, in a more troubled voice:

"I didn't want you to catch me; I knew it would be a shock. But I tell you what, you never would have caught me if I hadn't come here myself, to see they didn't ill treat you and to make sure everything was as comfortable as it could be." There was even a sort of break in his voice as he added, "I got those cigars because I knew you liked them."

Emotions are queer things, and the idiocy of this concession suddenly softened Horne Fisher like an unfathomable pathos.

"Never mind, old chap," he said; "we'll say no more about it. I'll admit that you're really as kind-hearted and affectionate a scoundrel and hypocrite as ever sold himself to ruin his country. There, I can't say handsomer than that. Thank you for the cigars, old man. I'll have one if you don't mind."

By the time that Horne Fisher had ended his telling of this story to Harold March they had come out into one of the public parks and taken a seat on a rise of ground overlooking wide green spaces under a blue and empty sky; and there was something incongruous in the words with which the narration ended.

"I have been in that room ever since," said Horne Fisher. "I am in it now. I won the election, but I never went to the House. My life has been a life in that little room on that lonely island. Plenty of books and cigars and luxuries, plenty of knowledge and interest and information, but never a voice out of that tomb to reach the world outside. I shall probably die there." And he smiled as he looked across the vast green park to the gray horizon.

VIII: THE VENGEANCE OF THE STATUE

It was on the sunny veranda of a seaside hotel, overlooking a pattern of flower beds and a strip of blue sea, that Horne Fisher and Harold March had their final explanation, which might be called an explosion.

Harold March had come to the little table and sat down at it with a subdued excitement smoldering in his somewhat cloudy and dreamy blue eyes. In the newspapers which he tossed from him on to the table there was enough to explain some if not all of his emotion. Public affairs in every department had reached a crisis. The government which had stood so long that men were used to it, as they are used to a hereditary despotism, had begun to be accused of blunders and even of financial abuses. Some said that the experiment of attempting to establish a peasantry in the west of England, on the lines of an early fancy of Horne Fisher's, had resulted in nothing but dangerous quarrels with more industrial neighbors. There had been particular complaints of the ill treatment of harmless foreigners, chiefly Asiatics, who happened to be employed in the new scientific works constructed on the coast. Indeed, the new Power which had arisen in Siberia, backed by Japan and other powerful allies, was inclined to take the matter up in the interests of its exiled subjects; and there had been wild talk about ambassadors and ultimatums. But something much more serious, in its personal interest for March himself, seemed to fill his meeting with his friend with a mixture of embarrassment and indignation.

Perhaps it increased his annoyance that there was a certain unusual liveliness about the usually languid figure of Fisher. The ordinary image of him in March's mind was that of a pallid and bald-browed gentleman, who seemed to be prematurely old as well as prematurely bald. He was remembered as a man who expressed the opinions of a pessimist in the language of a lounger. Even now March could not be certain whether the change was merely a sort of masquerade of sunshine, or that effect of clear colors and clean-cut outlines that is always visible on the parade of a marine resort, relieved against the blue dado of the sea. But Fisher had a flower in his buttonhole, and his friend could have sworn he carried his cane with something almost like the swagger of a fighter. With such clouds gathering over England, the pessimist seemed to be the only man who carried his own sunshine.

"Look here," said Harold March, abruptly, "you've been no end of a friend to me, and I never was so proud of a friendship before; but there's something I must get off my chest. The more I found out, the less I understood how you could stand it. And I tell you I'm going to stand it no longer."

Horne Fisher gazed across at him gravely and attentively, but rather as if he were a long way off.

"You know I always liked you," said Fisher, quietly, "but I also respect you, which is not always the same thing. You may possibly guess that I like a good many people I don't respect. Perhaps it is my tragedy, perhaps it is my fault. But you are very different, and I promise you this: that I will never try to keep you as somebody to be liked, at the price of your not being respected."

"I know you are magnanimous," said March after a silence, "and yet you tolerate and perpetuate everything that is mean." Then after another silence he added: "Do you remember when we first met, when you were fishing in that brook in the affair of the target? And do you remember you said that, after all, it might do no harm if I could blow the whole tangle of this society to hell with dynamite."

"Yes, and what of that?" asked Fisher.

"Only that I'm going to blow it to hell with dynamite," said Harold March, "and I think it right to give you fair warning. For a long time I didn't believe things were as bad as you said they were. But I never felt as if I could have bottled up what you knew, supposing you really knew it. Well, the long and the short of it is that I've got a conscience; and now, at last, I've also got a chance. I've been put in charge of a big independent paper, with a free hand, and we're going to open a cannonade on corruption."

"That will be—Attwood, I suppose," said Fisher, reflectively. "Timber merchant. Knows a lot about China."

"He knows a lot about England," said March, doggedly, "and now I know it, too, we're not going to hush it up any longer. The people of this country have a right to know how they're ruled—or, rather, ruined. The Chancellor is in the pocket of the money lenders and has to do as he is told; otherwise he's bankrupt, and a bad sort of bankruptcy, too, with nothing but cards and actresses behind it. The Prime Minister was in the petrol-contract business; and deep in it, too. The Foreign Minister is a wreck of drink and drugs. When you say that plainly about a man who may send thousands of Englishmen to die for nothing, you're called personal. If a poor engine driver gets drunk and sends thirty or forty people to death, nobody complains of the exposure being personal. The engine driver is not a person."

"I quite agree with you," said Fisher, calmly. "You are perfectly right."

"If you agree with us, why the devil don't you act with us?" demanded his friend. "If you think it's right, why don't you do what's right? It's awful to think of a man of your abilities simply blocking the road to reform."

"We have often talked about that," replied Fisher, with the same composure. "The Prime Minister is my father's friend. The Foreign Minister married my sister. The Chancellor of the Exchequer is my first cousin. I mention the genealogy in some detail just now for a particular reason. The truth is I have a curious kind of cheerfulness at the moment. It isn't altogether the sun and the sea, sir. I am enjoying an emotion that is entirely new to me; a happy sensation I never remember having had before."

"What the devil do you mean?"

"I am feeling proud of my family," said Horne Fisher.

Harold March stared at him with round blue eyes, and seemed too much mystified even to ask a question. Fisher leaned back in his chair in his lazy fashion, and smiled as he continued.

"Look here, my dear fellow. Let me ask a question in turn. You imply that I have always known these things about my unfortunate kinsmen. So I have. Do you suppose that Attwood hasn't always known them? Do you suppose he hasn't always known you as an honest man who would say these things when he got a chance? Why does Attwood unmuzzle you like a dog at this moment, after all these years? I know why he does; I know a good many things, far too many things. And therefore, as I have the honor to remark, I am proud of my family at last."

"But why?" repeated March, rather feebly.

"I am proud of the Chancellor because he gambled and the Foreign Minister because he drank and the Prime Minister because he took a commission on a contract," said Fisher, firmly. "I am proud of them because they did these things, and can be denounced for them, and know they can be denounced for them, and are standing firm for all that. I take off my hat to them because they are defying blackmail, and refusing to smash their country to save themselves. I salute them as if they were going to die on the battlefield."

After a pause he continued: "And it will be a battlefield, too, and not a metaphorical one. We have yielded to foreign financiers so long that now it is war or ruin, Even the people, even the country people, are beginning to suspect that they are being ruined. That is the meaning of the regrettable incidents in the newspapers."

"The meaning of the outrages on Orientals?" asked March.

"The meaning of the outrages on Orientals," replied Fisher, "is that the financiers have introduced Chinese labor into this country with the deliberate intention of reducing workmen and peasants to starvation. Our unhappy politicians have made concession after concession; and now they are asking concessions which amount to our ordering a massacre of our own poor. If we do not fight now we shall never fight again. They will have put England in an economic position of starving in a week. But we are going to fight now; I shouldn't wonder if there were an ultimatum in a week and an invasion in a fortnight. All the past corruption and cowardice is hampering us, of course; the West country is pretty stormy and doubtful even in a military sense; and the Irish regiments there, that are supposed to support us by the new treaty, are pretty well in mutiny; for, of course, this infernal coolie capitalism is being pushed in Ireland, too. But it's to stop now; and if the government message of reassurance gets through to them in time, they may turn up after all by the time the enemy lands. For my poor old gang is going to stand to its guns at last. Of course it's only natural that when they have been whitewashed for half a century as paragons, their sins should come back on them at the very moment when they are behaving like men for the first time in their lives. Well, I tell you, March, I know them inside out; and I know they are behaving like heroes. Every man of them ought to have a statue, and on the pedestal words like those of the noblest ruffian of the Revolution: 'Que mon nom soit fletri; que la France soit libre.'"

"Good God!" cried March, "shall we never get to the bottom of your mines and countermines?"

After a silence Fisher answered in a lower voice, looking his friend in the eyes.

"Did you think there was nothing but evil at the bottom of them?" he asked, gently. "Did you think I had found nothing but filth in the deep seas into which fate has thrown me? Believe me, you never know the best about men till you know the worst about them. It does not dispose of their strange human souls to know that they were exhibited to the world as impossibly impeccable wax works, who never looked after a woman or knew the meaning of a bribe. Even in a palace, life can be lived well; and even in a Parliament, life can be lived with occasional efforts to live it well. I tell you it is as true of these rich fools and rascals as it is true of every poor footpad and pickpocket; that only God knows how good they have tried to be. God alone knows what the conscience can survive, or how a man who has lost his honor will still try to save his soul."

There was another silence, and March sat staring at the table and Fisher at the sea. Then Fisher suddenly sprang to his feet and caught up his hat and stick with all his new alertness and even pugnacity.

"Look here, old fellow," he cried, "let us make a bargain. Before you open your campaign for Attwood come down and stay with us for one week, to hear what we're really doing. I mean with the Faithful Few, formerly known as the Old Gang, occasionally to be described as the Low Lot. There are really only five of us that are quite fixed, and organizing the national defense; and we're living like a garrison in a sort of broken-down hotel in Kent. Come and see what we're really doing and what there is to be done, and do us justice. And after that, with unalterable love and affection for you, publish and be damned."

Thus it came about that in the last week before war, when events moved most rapidly, Harold March found himself one of a sort of small house party of the people he was proposing to denounce. They were living simply enough, for people with their tastes, in an old brown-brick inn faced with ivy and surrounded by rather dismal gardens. At the back of the building the garden ran up very steeply to a road along the ridge above; and a zigzag path scaled the slope in sharp angles, turning to and fro amid evergreens so somber that they might rather be called everblack. Here and there up the slope were statues having all the cold monstrosity of such minor ornaments of the eighteenth century; and a whole row of them ran as on a terrace along the last bank at the bottom, opposite the back door. This detail fixed itself first in March's mind merely because it figured in the first conversation he had with one of the cabinet ministers.

The cabinet ministers were rather older than he had expected to find them. The Prime Minister no longer looked like a boy, though he still looked a little like a baby. But it was one of those old and venerable babies, and the baby had soft gray hair. Everything about him was soft, to his speech and his way of walking; but over and above that his chief function seemed to be sleep. People left alone with him got so used to his eyes being closed that they were almost startled when they realized in the stillness that the eyes were wide open, and even watching. One thing at least would always make the old gentleman open his eyes. The one thing he really cared for in this world was his hobby of armored weapons, especially Eastern weapons, and he would talk for hours about Damascus blades and Arab swordmanship. Lord James Herries, the Chancellor of the Exchequer, was a short, dark, sturdy man with a very sallow face and a very sullen manner, which contrasted with the gorgeous flower in his buttonhole and his festive trick of being always slightly overdressed. It was something of a euphemism to call him a well-known man about town. There was perhaps more mystery in the question of how a man who lived for pleasure seemed to get so little pleasure out of it. Sir David Archer, the Foreign Secretary, was the only one of them who was a self-made man, and the only one of them who looked like an aristocrat. He was tall and thin and very handsome, with a grizzled beard; his gray hair was very curly, and even rose in front in two rebellious ringlets that seemed to the fanciful to tremble like the antennae of some giant insect, or to stir sympathetically with the restless tufted eyebrows over his rather haggard eyes. For the Foreign Secretary made no secret of his somewhat nervous condition, whatever might be the cause of it.

"Do you know that mood when one could scream because a mat is crooked?" he said to March, as they walked up and down in the back garden below the line of dingy statues. "Women get into it when they've worked too hard; and I've been working pretty hard lately, of course. It drives me mad when Herries will wear his hat a little crooked—habit of looking like a gay dog. Sometime I swear I'll knock it off. That statue of Britannia over there isn't quite straight; it sticks forward a bit as if the lady were going to topple over. The damned thing is that it doesn't topple over and be done with it. See, it's clamped with an iron prop. Don't be surprised if I get up in the middle of the night to hike it down."

They paced the path for a few moments in silence and then he continued. "It's odd those little things seem specially big when there are bigger things to worry about. We'd better go in and do some work."

Horne Fisher evidently allowed for all the neurotic possibilities of Archer and the dissipated habits of Herries; and whatever his faith in their present firmness, did not unduly tax their time and attention, even in the case of the Prime Minister. He had got the consent of the latter finally to the committing of the important documents, with the orders to the Western armies, to the care of a less conspicuous and more solid person—an uncle of his named Horne Hewitt, a rather colorless country squire who had been a good soldier, and was the military adviser of the committee. He was charged with expediting the government pledge, along with the concerted military plans, to the half-mutinous command in the west; and the still more urgent task of seeing that it did not fall into the hands of the enemy, who might appear at any moment from the east. Over and above this military official, the only other person present was a police official, a certain Doctor Prince, originally a police surgeon and now a distinguished detective, sent to be a bodyguard to the group. He was a square-faced man with big spectacles and a grimace that expressed the intention of keeping his mouth shut. Nobody else shared their captivity except the hotel proprietor, a crusty Kentish man with a crab-apple face, one or two of his servants, and another servant privately attached to Lord James Herries. He was a young Scotchman named Campbell, who looked much more distinguished than his bilious-looking master, having chestnut hair and a long saturnine face with large but fine features. He was probably the one really efficient person in the house.

After about four days of the informal council, March had come to feel a sort of grotesque sublimity about these dubious figures, defiant in the twilight of danger, as if they were hunchbacks and cripples left alone to defend a town. All were working hard; and he himself looked up from writing a page of memoranda in a private room to see Horne Fisher standing in the doorway, accoutered as if for travel. He fancied that Fisher looked a little pale; and after a moment that gentleman shut the door behind him and said, quietly:

"Well, the worst has happened. Or nearly the worst."

"The enemy has landed," cried March, and sprang erect out of his chair.

"Oh, I knew the enemy would land," said Fisher, with composure. "Yes, he's landed; but that's not the worst that could happen. The worst is that there's a leak of some sort, even from this fortress of ours. It's been a bit of a shock to me, I can tell you; though I suppose it's illogical. After all, I was full of admiration at finding three honest men in politics. I ought not to be full of astonishment if I find only two."

He ruminated a moment and then said, in such a fashion that March could hardly tell if he were changing the subject or no:

"It's hard at first to believe that a fellow like Herries, who had pickled himself in vice like vinegar, can have any scruple left. But about that I've noticed a curious thing. Patriotism is not the first virtue. Patriotism rots into Prussianism when you pretend it is the first virtue. But patriotism is sometimes the last virtue. A man will swindle or seduce who will not sell his country. But who knows?"

"But what is to be done?" cried March, indignantly.

"My uncle has the papers safe enough," replied Fisher, "and is sending them west to-night; but somebody is trying to get at them from outside, I fear with the assistance of somebody inside. All I can do at present is to try to head off the man outside; and I must get away now and do it. I shall be back in about twenty-four hours. While I'm away I want you to keep an eye on these people and find out what you can. Au revoir." He vanished down the stairs; and from the window March could see him mount a motor cycle and trail away toward the neighboring town.

On the following morning, March was sitting in the window seat of the old inn parlor, which was oak-paneled and ordinarily rather dark; but on that occasion it was full of the white light of a curiously clear morning—the moon had shone brilliantly for the last two or three nights. He was himself somewhat in shadow in the corner of the window seat; and Lord James Herries, coming in hastily from the garden behind, did not see him. Lord James clutched the back of a chair, as if to steady himself, and, sitting down abruptly at the table, littered with the last meal, poured himself out a tumbler of brandy and drank it. He sat with his back to March, but his yellow face appeared in a round mirror beyond and the tinge of it was like that of some horrible malady. As March moved he started violently and faced round.

"My God!" he cried, "have you seen what's outside?"

"Outside?" repeated the other, glancing over his shoulder at the garden.

"Oh, go and look for yourself," cried Herries in a sort of fury. "Hewitt's murdered and his papers stolen, that's all."

He turned his back again and sat down with a thud; his square shoulders were shaking. Harold March darted out of the doorway into the back garden with its steep slope of statues.

The first thing he saw was Doctor Prince, the detective, peering through his spectacles at something on the ground; the second was the thing he was peering at. Even after the sensational news he had heard inside, the sight was something of a sensation.

The monstrous stone image of Britannia was lying prone and face downward on the garden path; and there stuck out at random from underneath it, like the legs of a smashed fly, an arm clad in a white shirt sleeve and a leg clad in a khaki trouser, and hair of the unmistakable sandy gray that belonged to Horne Fisher's unfortunate uncle. There were pools of blood and the limbs were quite stiff in death.

"Couldn't this have been an accident?" said March, finding words at last.

"Look for yourself, I say," repeated the harsh voice of Herries, who had followed him with restless movements out of the door. "The papers are gone, I tell you. The fellow tore the coat off the corpse and cut the papers out of the inner pocket. There's the coat over there on the bank, with the great slash in it."

"But wait a minute," said the detective, Prince, quietly. "In that case there seems to be something of a mystery. A murderer might somehow have managed to throw the statue down on him, as he seems to have done. But I bet he couldn't easily have lifted it up again. I've tried; and I'm sure it would want three men at least. Yet we must suppose, on that theory, that the murderer first knocked him down as he walked past, using the statue as a stone club, then lifted it up again, took him out and deprived him of his coat, then put him back again in the posture of death and neatly replaced the statue. I tell you it's physically impossible. And how else could he have unclothed a man covered with that stone monument? It's worse than the conjurer's trick, when a man shuffles a coat off with his wrists tied."

"Could he have thrown down the statue after he'd stripped the corpse?" asked March.

"And why?" asked Prince, sharply. "If he'd killed his man and got his papers, he'd be away like the wind. He wouldn't potter about in a garden excavating the pedestals of statues. Besides—Hullo, who's that up there?"

High on the ridge above them, drawn in dark thin lines against the sky, was a figure looking so long and lean as to be almost spidery. The dark silhouette of the head showed two small tufts like horns; and they could almost have sworn that the horns moved.

"Archer!" shouted Herries, with sudden passion, and called to him with curses to come down. The figure drew back at the first cry, with an agitated movement so abrupt as almost to be called an antic. The next moment the man seemed to reconsider and collect himself, and began to come down the zigzag garden path, but with obvious reluctance, his feet falling in slower and slower rhythm. Through March's mind were throbbing the phrases that this man himself had used, about going mad in the middle of the night and wrecking the stone figure. Just so, he could fancy, the maniac who had done such a thing might climb the crest of the hill, in that feverish dancing fashion, and look down on the wreck he had made. But the wreck he had made here was not only a wreck of stone.

When the man emerged at last on to the garden path, with the full light on his face and figure, he was walking slowly indeed, but easily, and with no appearance of fear.

"This is a terrible thing," he said. "I saw it from above; I was taking a stroll along the ridge."

"Do you mean that you saw the murder?" demanded March, "or the accident? I mean did you see the statue fall?"

"No," said Archer, "I mean I saw the statue fallen."

Prince seemed to be paying but little attention; his eye was riveted on an object lying on the path a yard or two from the corpse. It seemed to be a rusty iron bar bent crooked at one end.

"One thing I don't understand," he said, "is all this blood. The poor fellow's skull isn't smashed; most likely his neck is broken; but blood seems to have spouted as if all his arteries were severed. I was wondering if some other instrument . . . that iron thing, for instance; but I don't see that even that is sharp enough. I suppose nobody knows what it is."

"I know what it is," said Archer in his deep but somewhat shaky voice. "I've seen it in my nightmares. It was the iron clamp or prop on the pedestal, stuck on to keep the wretched image upright when it began to wobble, I suppose. Anyhow, it was always stuck in the stonework there; and I suppose it came out when the thing collapsed."

Doctor Prince nodded, but he continued to look down at the pools of blood and the bar of iron.

"I'm certain there's something more underneath all this," he said at last. "Perhaps something more underneath the statue. I have a huge sort of hunch that there is. We are four men now and between us we can lift that great tombstone there."

They all bent their strength to the business; there was a silence save for heavy breathing; and then, after an instant of the tottering and staggering of eight legs, the great carven column of rock was rolled away, and the body lying in its shirt and trousers was fully revealed. The spectacles of Doctor Prince seemed almost to enlarge with a restrained radiance like great eyes; for other things were revealed also. One was that the unfortunate Hewitt had a deep gash across the jugular, which the triumphant doctor instantly identified as having been made with a sharp steel edge like a razor. The other was that immediately under the bank lay littered three shining scraps of steel, each nearly a foot long, one pointed and another fitted into a gorgeously jeweled hilt or handle. It was evidently a sort of long Oriental knife, long enough to be called a sword, but with a curious wavy edge; and there was a touch or two of blood on the point.

"I should have expected more blood, hardly on the point," observed Doctor Prince, thoughtfully, "but this is certainly the instrument. The slash was certainly made with a weapon shaped like this, and probably the slashing of the pocket as well. I suppose the brute threw in the statue, by way of giving him a public funeral."

March did not answer; he was mesmerized by the strange stones that glittered on the strange sword hilt; and their possible significance was broadening upon him like a dreadful dawn. It was a curious Asiatic weapon. He knew what name was connected in his memory with curious Asiatic weapons. Lord James spoke his secret thought for him, and yet it startled him like an irrelevance.

"Where is the Prime Minister?" Herries had cried, suddenly, and somehow like the bark of a dog at some discovery.

Doctor Prince turned on him his goggles and his grim face; and it was grimmer than ever.

"I cannot find him anywhere," he said. "I looked for him at once, as soon as I found the papers were gone. That servant of yours, Campbell, made a most efficient search, but there are no traces."

There was a long silence, at the end of which Herries uttered another cry, but upon an entirely new note.

"Well, you needn't look for him any longer," he said, "for here he comes, along with your friend Fisher. They look as if they'd been for a little walking tour."

The two figures approaching up the path were indeed those of Fisher, splashed with the mire of travel and carrying a scratch like that of a bramble across one side of his bald forehead, and of the great and gray-haired statesman who looked like a baby and was interested in Eastern swords and swordmanship. But beyond this bodily recognition, March could make neither head nor tail of their presence or demeanor, which seemed to give a final touch of nonsense to the whole nightmare. The more closely he watched them, as they stood listening to the revelations of the detective, the more puzzled he was by their attitude—Fisher seemed grieved by the death of his uncle, but hardly shocked at it; the older man seemed almost openly thinking about something else, and neither had anything to suggest about a further pursuit of the fugitive spy and murderer, in spite of the prodigious importance of the documents he had stolen. When the detective had gone off to busy himself with that department of the business, to telephone and write his report, when Herries had gone back, probably to the brandy bottle, and the Prime Minister had blandly sauntered away toward a comfortable armchair in another part of the garden, Horne Fisher spoke directly to Harold March.

"My friend," he said, "I want you to come with me at once; there is no one else I can trust so much as that. The journey will take us most of the day, and the chief business cannot be done till nightfall. So we can talk things over thoroughly on the way. But I want you to be with me; for I rather think it is my hour."

March and Fisher both had motor bicycles; and the first half of their day's journey consisted in coasting eastward amid the unconversational noise of those uncomfortable engines. But when they came out beyond Canterbury into the flats of eastern Kent, Fisher stopped at a pleasant little public house beside a sleepy stream; and they sat down to eat and to drink and to speak almost for the first time. It was a brilliant afternoon, birds were singing in the wood behind, and the sun shone full on their ale bench and table; but the face of Fisher in the strong sunlight had a gravity never seen on it before.

"Before we go any farther," he said, "there is something you ought to know. You and I have seen some mysterious things and got to the bottom of them before now; and it's only right that you should get to the bottom of this one. But in dealing with the death of my uncle I must begin at the other end from where our old detective yarns began. I will give you the steps of deduction presently, if you want to listen to them; but I did not reach the truth of this by steps of deduction. I will first of all tell you the truth itself, because I knew the truth from the first. The other cases I approached from the outside, but in this case I was inside. I myself was the very core and center of everything."

Something in the speaker's pendent eyelids and grave gray eyes suddenly shook March to his foundations; and he cried, distractedly, "I don't understand!" as men do when they fear that they do understand. There was no sound for a space but the happy chatter of the birds, and then Horne Fisher said, calmly:

"It was I who killed my uncle. If you particularly want more, it was I who stole the state papers from him."

"Fisher!" cried his friend in a strangled voice.

"Let me tell you the whole thing before we part," continued the other, "and let me put it, for the sake of clearness, as we used to put our old problems. Now there are two things that are puzzling people about that problem, aren't there? The first is how the murderer managed to slip off the dead man's coat, when he was already pinned to the ground with that stone incubus. The other, which is much smaller and less puzzling, is the fact of the sword that cut his throat being slightly stained at the point, instead of a good deal more stained at the edge. Well, I can dispose of the first question easily. Horne Hewitt took off his own coat before he was killed. I might say he took off his coat to be killed."

"Do you call that an explanation?" exclaimed March. "The words seem more meaningless, than the facts."

"Well, let us go on to the other facts," continued Fisher, equably.

"The reason that particular sword is not stained at the edge with Hewitt's blood is that it was not used to kill Hewitt."

"But the doctor," protested March, "declared distinctly that the wound was made by that particular sword."

"I beg your pardon," replied Fisher. "He did not declare that it was made by that particular sword. He declared it was made by a sword of that particular pattern."

"But it was quite a queer and exceptional pattern," argued March; "surely it is far too fantastic a coincidence to imagine—"

"It was a fantastic coincidence," reflected Horne Fisher. "It's extraordinary what coincidences do sometimes occur. By the oddest chance in the world, by one chance in a million, it so happened that another sword of exactly the same shape was in the same garden at the same time. It may be partly explained, by the fact that I brought them both into the garden myself . . . come, my dear fellow; surely you can see now what it means. Put those two things together; there were two duplicate swords and he took off his coat for himself. It may assist your speculations to recall the fact that I am not exactly an assassin."

"A duel!" exclaimed March, recovering himself. "Of course I ought to have thought of that. But who was the spy who stole the papers?"

"My uncle was the spy who stole the papers," replied Fisher, "or who tried to steal the papers when I stopped him—in the only way I could. The papers, that should have gone west to reassure our friends and give them the plans for repelling the invasion, would in a few hours have been in the hands of the invader. What could I do? To have denounced one of our friends at this moment would have been to play into the hands of your friend Attwood, and all the party of panic and slavery. Besides, it may be that a man over forty has a subconscious desire to die as he has lived, and that I wanted, in a sense, to carry my secrets to the grave. Perhaps a hobby hardens with age; and my hobby has been silence. Perhaps I feel that I have killed my mother's brother, but I have saved my mother's name. Anyhow, I chose a time when I knew you were all asleep, and he was walking alone in the garden. I saw all the stone statues standing in the moonlight; and I myself was like one of those stone statues walking. In a voice that was not my own, I told him of his treason and demanded the papers; and when he refused, I forced him to take one of the two swords. The swords were among some specimens sent down here for the Prime Minister's inspection; he is a collector, you know; they were the only equal weapons I could find. To cut an ugly tale short, we fought there on the path in front of the Britannia statue; he was a man of great strength, but I had somewhat the advantage in skill. His sword grazed my forehead almost at the moment when mine sank into the joint in his neck. He fell against the statue, like Caesar against Pompey's, hanging on to the iron rail; his sword was already broken. When I saw the blood from that deadly wound, everything else went from me; I dropped my sword and ran as if to lift him up. As I bent toward him something happened too quick for me to follow. I do not know whether the iron bar was rotted with rust and came away in his hand, or whether he rent it out of the rock with his apelike strength; but the thing was in his hand, and with his dying energies he swung it over my head, as I knelt there unarmed beside him. I looked up wildly to avoid the blow, and saw above us the great bulk of Britannia leaning outward like the figurehead of a ship. The next instant I saw it was leaning an inch or two more than usual, and all the skies with their outstanding stars seemed to be leaning with it. For the third second it was as if the skies fell; and in the fourth I was standing in the quiet garden, looking down on that flat ruin of stone and bone at which you were looking to-day. He had plucked out the last prop that held up the British goddess, and she had fallen and crushed the traitor in her fall. I turned and darted for the coat which I knew to contain the package, ripped it up with my sword, and raced away up the garden path to where my motor bike was waiting on the road above. I had every reason for haste; but I fled without looking back at the statue and the body; and I think the thing I fled from was the sight of that appalling allegory.

"Then I did the rest of what I had to do. All through the night and into the daybreak and the daylight I went humming through the villages and markets of South England like a traveling bullet, till I came to the headquarters in the West where the trouble was. I was just in time. I was able to placard the place, so to speak, with the news that the government had not betrayed them, and that they would find supports if they would push eastward against the enemy. There's no time to tell you all that happened; but I tell you it was the day of my life. A triumph like a torchlight procession, with torchlights that might have been firebrands. The mutinies simmered down; the men of Somerset and the western counties came pouring into the market places; the men who died with Arthur and stood firm with Alfred. The Irish regiments rallied to them, after a scene like a riot, and marched eastward out of the town singing Fenian songs. There was all that is not understood, about the dark laughter of that people, in the delight with which, even when marching with the English to the defense of England, they shouted at the top of their voices, 'High upon the gallows tree stood the noble-hearted three . . . With England's cruel cord about them cast.' However, the chorus was 'God save Ireland,' and we could all have sung that just then, in one sense or another.

"But there was another side to my mission. I carried the plans of the defense; and to a great extent, luckily, the plans of the invasion also. I won't worry you with strategics; but we knew where the enemy had pushed forward the great battery that covered all his movements; and though our friends from the West could hardly arrive in time to intercept the main movement, they might get within long artillery range of the battery and shell it, if they only knew exactly where it was. They could hardly tell that unless somebody round about here sent up some sort of signal. But, somehow, I rather fancy that somebody will."

With that he got up from the table, and they remounted their machines and went eastward into the advancing twilight of evening. The levels of the landscape were repeated in flat strips of floating cloud and the last colors of day clung to the circle of the horizon. Receding farther and farther behind them was the semicircle of the last hills; and it was quite suddenly that they saw afar off the dim line of the sea. It was not a strip of bright blue as they had seen it from the sunny veranda, but of a sinister and smoky violet, a tint that seemed ominous and dark. Here Horne Fisher dismounted once more.

"We must walk the rest of the way," he said, "and the last bit of all I must walk alone."

He bent down and began to unstrap something from his bicycle. It was something that had puzzled his companion all the way in spite of what held him to more interesting riddles; it appeared to be several lengths of pole strapped together and wrapped up in paper. Fisher took it under his arm and began to pick his way across the turf. The ground was growing more tumbled and irregular and he was walking toward a mass of thickets and small woods; night grew darker every moment. "We must not talk any more," said Fisher. "I shall whisper to you when you are to halt. Don't try to follow me then, for it will only spoil the show; one man can barely crawl safely to the spot, and two would certainly be caught."

"I would follow you anywhere," replied March, "but I would halt, too, if that is better."

"I know you would," said his friend in a low voice. "Perhaps you're the only man I ever quite trusted in this world."

469

A few paces farther on they came to the end of a great ridge or mound looking monstrous against the dim sky; and Fisher stopped with a gesture. He caught his companion's hand and wrung it with a violent tenderness, and then darted forward into the darkness. March could faintly see his figure crawling along under the shadow of the ridge, then he lost sight of it, and then he saw it again standing on another mound two hundred yards away. Beside him stood a singular erection made apparently of two rods. He bent over it and there was the flare of a light; all March's schoolboy memories woke in him, and he knew what it was. It was the stand of a rocket. The confused, incongruous memories still possessed him up to the very moment of a fierce but familiar sound; and an instant after the rocket left its perch and went up into endless space like a starry arrow aimed at the stars. March thought suddenly of the signs of the last days and knew he was looking at the apocalyptic meteor of something like a Day of judgment.

Far up in the infinite heavens the rocket drooped and sprang into scarlet stars. For a moment the whole landscape out to the sea and back to the crescent of the wooded hills was like a lake of ruby light, of a red strangely rich and glorious, as if the world were steeped in wine rather than blood, or the earth were an earthly paradise, over which paused forever the sanguine moment of morning.

"God save England!" cried Fisher, with a tongue like the peal of a trumpet. "And now it is for God to save."

As darkness sank again over land and sea, there came another sound; far away in the passes of the hills behind them the guns spoke like the baying of great hounds. Something that was not a rocket, that came not hissing but screaming, went over Harold March's head and expanded beyond the mound into light and deafening din, staggering the brain with unbearable brutalities of noise. Another came, and then another, and the world was full of uproar and volcanic vapor and chaotic light. The artillery of the West country and the Irish had located the great enemy battery, and were pounding it to pieces.

In the mad excitement of that moment March peered through the storm, looking again for the long lean figure that stood beside the stand of the rocket. Then another flash lit up the whole ridge. The figure was not there.

Before the fires of the rocket had faded from the sky, long before the first gun had sounded from the distant hills, a splutter of rifle fire had flashed and flickered all around from the hidden trenches of the enemy. Something lay in the shadow at the foot of the ridge, as stiff as the stick of the fallen rocket; and the man who knew too much knew what is worth knowing.

The End

CPSIA information can be obtained
at www.ICGtesting.com
Printed in the USA
LVOW13s1721101116

512465LV00010B/992/P